The Last

No world is perfect; no design is without flaw. The least we can ever hope for is a state of equilibrium. Balance.

So apt it is that my design became known as '*The Symphony*', for it is rife with logic and order, pattern and rhythm. In moments, harmony most resplendent. In others, dissonance most tumultuous. Nestled between, pauses so pregnant with anticipation.

My design created the notes with which The Symphony is being played, but I am not its final composer. The notes are performing in ways I never could have anticipated. My flaw. My imperfection of design. There is potential in that imperfection – that unpredictable element. I know by the rules of logic from which this design was first born where The Symphony *should* end. Whether it does so is now completely beyond my influence. I will watch and wait with immense trepidation to see what arises from that potential, whether it be balance or collapse.

That is the game, is it not?

***

By L. G. Harman

Symphony of Magicks:

The Last of the Magi
???

Symphonica Finale

The Last of the Magi

Symphony of Magicks
Book One

First published in Great Britain in 2024 by Amazon.

Copyright © 2024 Louis Glen Harman
All rights reserved.

No part of this publication may be reproduced, distributed, or transmitted in any form or by any means, including photocopying, recording, or other electronic or mechanical methods, without the prior written permission of the Author.

For permission requests, write to the Author at Harmanl@live.co.uk

The right of Louis Glen Harman to be identified as Author of this work has been asserted by them in accordance with the Copyright, Designs and Patents Act 1988.

This is a work of fiction. Names, characters, businesses, places, events, locales, and incidents are either the products of the author's imagination or used in a fictitious manner. Any resemblance to actual persons, living or dead, or actual events is purely coincidental.

DEDICATION

Such a ridiculous personal project like this is not possible without the immensely generous support of those who took the time to read, share thoughts and offer wisdom and guidance along the way.

To Chris, for always being there and providing the environment that allowed me to pursue this long journey.

To Dad, for being a fan of even the most poorly written draft, reaching as far back as my first attempts at story-writing some 15 years ago. And for absorbing it all, never missing a beat.

To Liam, Charlotte, Luke, and Alessandro, for giving me your time, your wisdom, and your support. You have seen things I could not see, explored ideas I could not predict and, honestly, shown interest in this far more devoutly than I could have ever expected. And to David and Les, thank you for giving shape and form to my madness through your amazing artwork.

And there are many more – family, friends and found family whose cheerleading and support helped me to keep going even when I had lost faith.

You are the first bar of this Symphony.

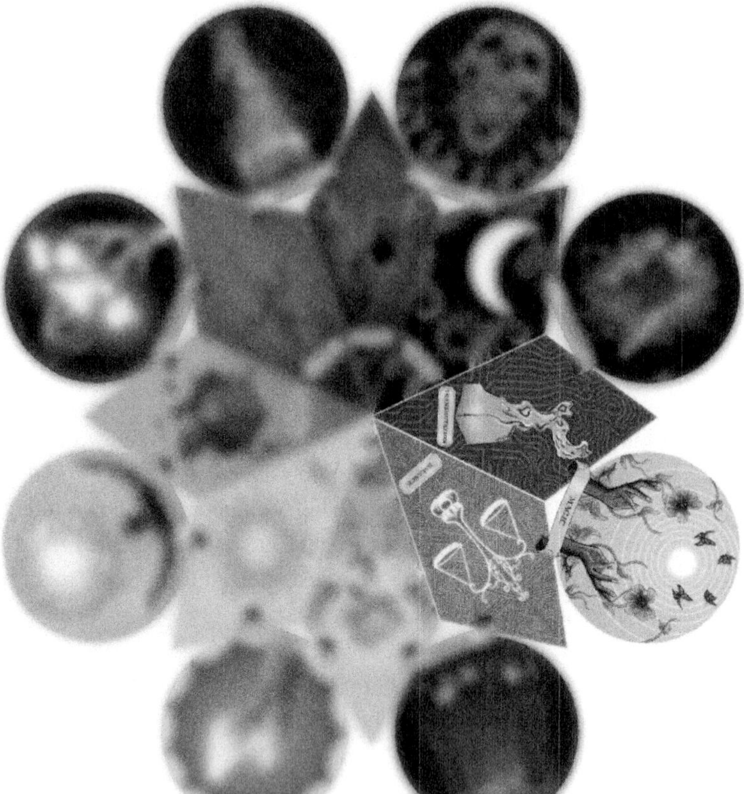

PART I

Chapter 1

Prologue
15 years before the Purge

There was a reason the Magi did not intervene.

Politics, economics, diplomacy and law. These were the tools of nations and their rulers. For the Magi, such things were transient and immaterial. But sometimes – not very often – that same drive keeping the Magi away from the dramas of civilisation instead inspired a Magi to act. It never felt right, but it was always necessary.

Nehren knew that compulsion well. He had intervened at Ferenir so many times in his years, more so than any other Magi. But it had never ended like this before.

On his knees, at the edge of the winding path that led up the hill to Ferenir Keep, Nehren stared at the crumpled body at the bottom of the drop.

The screaming from the elements still rang in his ears. The white-suited emissaries from the Grand City of Elheim had done something he had not seen before. They appeared to have used Magic, the power to manipulate the forces of the natural world, believed to be a gift solely vested in his own kind. But that scream – that agonising sensation that rocked through his heart – told him that the power they used was *wrong*. Unnatural. Not truly Magic as he knew it.

Their power had controlled the winds. It had surged forward from the Elheim woman's hands, circled behind Nehren and slammed against King Thorius.

The good king had been pushed with terrible force, sent hurtling off the sloping path's edge. His body was broken, his life extinguished. The Magi had failed. His own Magic had failed to even slow them down. They ripped through the barrier of vines and twisted branches he willed into being as if they were just string and thread in their way.

Nehren closed his eyes. For many years he stood at the side of the incumbent kings of Ferenir. He had witnessed boys grow into men. He had guided princes on how to rule in a way that showed respect and honour for the natural world. Kings had died of old age and poor health, but none before had died whilst under his direct protection.

He had failed the Kingdom of Ferenir, and all its people, perhaps the Magi too. He felt ashamed. He felt angry. But he held the king's last words close in his mind:

...and you *will not give your life for me or take a life in my name. Consider that my last Royal Commandment.*

Nehren stayed silent.

The woman in white slowly paced to the edge of the hill, swinging her heels through the grass as she went. She peered over the edge.

'And there lies King Reksar Thorius, son of Killian Thorius, ruler of Ferenir. He ruled fairly and with respect for all people within his lands. Such a pity.'

Nehren clenched his fists and let out a deep breath. Despite the emotion that tried to boil up within him, his respect for the king – and the innate stillness of mind and temperament that came with being a Magi – kept him from retaliating.

The woman crouched in front of him. She lifted his chin using her index finger, but he did not resist or protest. His face, as the evening light hit it, betrayed no emotion.

'You failed, old man,' she said. 'How pathetic you must feel now. A noble Magi brought so low. Look how far you've fallen.' She made a sound and brought a hand over her lips before laughing in Nehren's face. '*Fallen* – how insensitive of me.'

'You've done what you came to do,' said Nehren. 'Go tell your chancellor that the king has fallen and Ferenir stands undefended.'

The woman laughed again. She stood and looked down at the defeated Magi. 'I think you misunderstand the situation. There will be a day that Ferenir joins the Grand City of Elheim, but today is not that day. For now, we take a better prize.'

The Last of the Magi

The woman walked away to her two subordinates.
'Take him to the Grand City. Alive and unharmed.'

Chapter 2

Tharian

23 years after the Purge

Tharian left the inn at first light, having only stayed the one night. He had little choice in the matter. Though he would usually allow himself two or three nights of respite in one village or town before returning to his travels, the conversation he overheard in the tavern the night before still made his blood run cold. It was the kind of conversation he had overheard many times in other towns across the Outer Counties, but not usually with such urgency:

'*The call was made official a few hours ago,*' one of the county guardsmen had said as he returned to the rowdy table of lightly armoured men, lowering an armful of drinks to the table.

The others were silent as the guard who bought the round took a swig of one of the black drinks.

'*Come on, you all knew this was comin'. The alderman warned us they'd been spotted on the county border days ago. I'm surprised it took 'em this long.*'

One of the other guards, a more seasoned fellow, scratched the table with a knife. '*Has that idiot finally come to his senses? Will he pay and be done with this stand-off, or will we face the flames like Midhaven? I don't know if you've noticed, but I am running out of good sides.*' the older guard had laughed at himself, flashing what few teeth he still had. The right side of his face was covered in pink burn marks which stretched from his jaw to parts of his scalp, causing his hair to grow in small patches on that side.

The first guard took another drink. '*No change. He still intends to refuse. Enforcers are expected before nightfall tomorrow.*'

That was where the conversation had ended. They all silently nursed their drinks after that.

Tharian didn't need to be a local of County Bryn to understand what

The Last of the Magi

the guards were talking about that night. Every town, village, camp and trading post in the Outer Counties had experienced the oppression of the Grand City of Elheim at one time or another – and every city in Asturia had to begrudgingly trade with them as a matter of necessity. Everybody had to endure Elheim influence in one way or another.

The name Elheim had become a curse word in Asturian culture. Long ago, the wealthy families of Asturia came together and decided to form their own society. They changed their names to Elheim, claimed a stretch of land on the east coast and from that day forth declared themselves an independent city state. The construction of the Grand City of Elheim began very quickly after that, as if it had all been planned so meticulously in advance. Though beautiful to the eye, their city became a constant reminder of the great wealth, power and influence that lay in the hands of every family residing there.

Over time, the city had grown to the point where a myriad of other noble families now made it their home too, and so only a small proportion of them bore the name Elheim, but nonetheless the others acquired the right to call themselves Elheim people. If you lived within the white walls of the Grand City, you were an Elheim – by name or by association.

Although the Grand City claimed no ownership or control over the Outer Counties to its distant west, the Elheim still had enough power at their backs to behave like they did. Since the murder of King Reksar Thorius at Ferenir, some thirty-or-so years ago, the Grand City had routinely sent some of its white-clad agents, known as 'enforcers' to collect an 'Arcane Tax' from the free-people in exchange for protection that they did not want, need, or ask for.

The enforcers were cunning at negotiation. For the most part they played the role of mediator between the Grand City – specifically their leader, Chancellor Vasilarius Elheim – and the authorities of the Outer Counties, ensuring that the Arcane Tax was being paid on demand. And that tax was no trivial amount either, it was a sum that would slowly choke the independence from these settlements, forcing more and more to pledge loyalty to the Grand City to avoid destitution. The smaller settlements on the east side of the country had already succumbed.

But it wasn't the arrival of these magic-wielding enforcers that had put fear in the hearts of the brave county guards of Bryn on this occasion – it was the political strategy of the alderman that had done that.

Any town or village that refused to pay the Arcane Tax was subjected to regular visits from the Grand City's enforcers, and they wasted no time in making an example of them to others. The punishments the enforcer's delivered were brutal. Wild lashes of fire and water, and storms of wind and thunder. This devastating power at their disposal – Arcana, they called it – gave them insurmountable strength to match their wealth.

Tharian had seen the enforcers at work before, and he'd heard stories far worse.

They arrive before nightfall today, he reminded himself.

It was still early in the morning, but he'd wanted to reduce the risk of crossing paths with any Elheim on the road to the absolute minimum. So, after leaving the inn at first light, he'd hurried to the local blacksmith to conclude his business in Brynfall.

'This is the one, isn't it?' said an energetic voice from behind the serving counter of the blacksmithing workshop. The drawl tone of the Outer Counties accent roused Tharian from his thoughts, reminding him again that he was back on home soil at last. It made him smirk, though he was quick to hide it.

Glancing over the counter, Tharian realised the soot-covered young woman was presenting to him a sword wrapped in a light leather covering.

He nodded. 'Yes, that's the one.' He kept his words brief, checking over his shoulder to remind himself where the stables were.

'It's been sharpened, and we managed to get a few kinks out of it. No charge for that – it's a pleasure to work on such a beautiful blade. We don't get many like it around here.' She stretched to bring the wrapped weapon closer to him.

'Thank you.' He took the blade carefully by the midsection. He didn't want this conversation to go on any longer than necessary, especially as he had already paid in advance.

The Last of the Magi

Tharian removed the wrappings and glanced up and down the flat of the blade. He saw a slight reflection of his own blue eyes in the metal, despite it being tinted a similar dark colour. The engraved markings in the metal glinted back at him. *Polished too?* He raised an eyebrow at the girl. She was grinning. Tharian returned the blade to its sheath under his long, dark green coat. Without wasting any more time, he nodded a thanks to the girl and then turned to leave.

'Could I just ask one question before you go, sir?' Her voice was kind, even if the gruff County Bryn drawl gave it a forceful edge.

He closed his eyes and sighed deeply. He pulled up the hood of his coat and turned his head slightly towards her. 'Quickly.'

'I couldn't help but notice the markings running up the face of the blade. Where did you get a weapon like that?'

Tharian smiled out of view. He placed his hand on the hilt of the sword with pride. 'I won it.' It was a lie, but it was quicker to say than the truth.

'My father told me about the smiths who made those blades. He reckons there were only a handful of smiths in Asturia that could ever make something like it, and they've either all died off now or were forced out of business by the Grand City after the Purge.'

Her enthusiasm was good to hear, but it gave him a sinking sensation in his stomach that wiped away his smile.

'Forget you saw it – and me,' he said abruptly.

Tharian then marched off without another word. He walked briskly in the direction of the stables without looking back.

Chapter 3

The County of Bryn

Brynfall was picturesque. Tharian was not one to admire the beauty of settlements he passed through, but Brynfall was an exception. Most of the settled areas of the Outer Counties had a way of existing in harmony with their natural surroundings, and Brynfall had managed it better than the rest.

The town was built into the side of a hill, with all its structures placed either at its base or upon the two natural plateaus that jut out from its side. The top level only hosted a few buildings. One large regal manor – Bryn Manor, the bureaucratic office for the county – and a couple of smaller but equally as quaint homes.

Atop the hill a natural spring had formed. As a child, Tharian was told stories about how a roaming Magi had pulled that water up from deep beneath the earth and somehow it continued to flow there to this day. That spring poured over the top of the hill in a stunning fall that then split into two streams which circled around Bryn Manor and reached to the front of the plateau. From there it cascaded down to the levels below. Little wooden bridges were nailed into place at various points along these thin streams to help the townsfolk get about.

The middle plateau held a few shops alongside the homes of the town's older or more wealthy residents, not that there were many of the latter. The bottom level was home to the regular folk of Brynfall, and the shops that provided essential goods and services to keep the town running.

The blacksmith's shop was near the edge of the town, and just a few short paces from the open stables where Tharian had left his own travelling companion. And there she still was, the exotic black mare. Ombra.

Ombra huffed through her nostrils as Tharian approached. She stomped the dirt beneath her hooves and pushed gently against the gate that kept her locked in.

The Last of the Magi

'I know, I'm sorry,' he said as he fiddled with the gate latch.

His apology was two-fold. He knew Ombra hated being left in enclosures overnight, but also, she – like him – preferred to be on the move as much as possible, and he had lingered here too long already. Their similarity in temperament was part of the reason they had bonded so well as travelling companions over the last decade.

She whinnied as the gate opened. Tharian was almost knocked to the ground as she bolted out of the stables for the rolling hills in the distance. She raced towards a flock of black kurigaw ravens searching the thick grass for their next meal. They eyed her cautiously but held their ground.

Tharian shook his head and laughed. *So predictable,* he mused. He left her to enjoy a few minutes of galloping free before he would call her back so they could set off.

Until then, Tharian discretely walked one last lap around the town. He kept off the dirt tracks that ran through the middle of Brynfall and instead walked slowly between the buildings, listening out for any hushed conversations of note.

Nothing he heard was of any interest. The people of Brynfall talked mostly of the bountiful harvests being enjoyed across County Bryn, and then the odd bit of gossip. Not one conversation was about the enforcers or the Grand City of Elheim.

They don't know, Tharian concluded as he finished his lap and found Ombra waiting for him restlessly at the edge of the town. He patted her gently on the side and then swung himself into her saddle. Without needing instructions, Ombra led them away from Brynfall, cantering with enthusiasm.

His fists clenched around the reins as he considered the innocent people of Brynfall. The alderman, hidden away in Bryn Manor was only a short walk from the centre of the town – it wouldn't have been difficult or time-consuming to convene an emergency town meeting. The residents could have been given *some* time to prepare for what was coming. This alderman was playing a reckless game. It was either over-confidence or stupidity.

If the alderman was planning to refuse the Arcane Tax when the enforcers came to call, the residents of Brynfall were in grave danger.

Ombra and Tharian carried on their slow journey away from Brynfall. They passed from one village to the next for a couple of hours until they eventually crossed paths with three members of the county guard who were following the trail back to Brynfall.

'He's got the right idea,' the youngest guard said as they passed each other on the road.

Tharian heard the three guards stop in their tracks as the most senior amongst them addressed his junior from horseback. 'I will *not* warn you again. We follow the alderman's orders without question. Do your job without being a smart-arse.'

Although Tharian didn't want to get involved in the affairs of the town, he felt some pity for the innocent people there. Hearing the guards bicker made him want to say something. He would have thought better of it, but as always Ombra sensed his unrest and she slowed, turning him back towards the guardsmen. They noticed and looked his way.

Ombra always knew his mind, and this was not the first time she had instinctively acted in line with his thoughts. She was a truly unique and intelligent creature. He was always grateful for her intuition.

'Excuse me,' Tharian called out, 'forgive my curiosity, but this is an unusual hour to be ending a county patrol, isn't it?'

The youngest guard perked up again, despite the berating he had just received. 'Tell me abo—' He was interrupted by a hard slap hitting him around the back of the head. His senior scowled at him with nostrils flaring.

'We've been recalled to Brynfall to attend the alderman,' said the senior guard, 'there's no need for concern, there are still many guards deployed throughout the county.'

'Have the enforcers been sighted?' Tharian said it as matter-of-factly as he could.

As he expected, his direct question caught them off-guard. Their faces paled, and the two guards on foot looked up at their superior. That was all the answer he needed.

'How do you kn—'

'Don't worry about that,' Tharian said, waving his hand as if brushing away the man's chance to speak. 'Rumour travels fast.

Have they been sighted?'

The senior guard bowed his head slightly and nodded. 'About an hour ago. They travelled through the night and will be at Brynfall soon.'

His stomach sank. 'Thank you. I won't take any more of your time. Good luck and be careful.'

Tharian kicked Ombra and she reared before galloping away from the guards, heading south as per their original course. In the far distance, he could just about see the faint outline of a tall beacon tower made of stone. Brynwell would be their next stop. The sooner they got there the better.

***

It took an hour for Tharian and Ombra to make it to the village of Brynwell. Where Brynfall was known for its beauty and glorious falls, Brynwell was known for being the connector between the Outer Counties and the Trade Quarters – the independent city of commerce – where Tharian was heading.

Brynwell was so named after the ancient stone well that sat in its centre. Though no longer in use, it still had significance to the history of the settlements that spanned around it. Generations ago, Brynwell was the centre of society in County Bryn, but in modern days it had become the centre for trade for most of the Quartersfolk instead.

Wagons of crops were being wheeled into the village centre from dirt roads stretching off in many directions – roads created by local farmers and crafters simply through repeated travel. It was a market day, so the small village was already filled with people gathered around stalls. The sounds of laughter, calls for attention, and shrewd bargaining permeated the air.

Tharian directed Ombra closer to the market and circled slowly around its edge, looking for any signs of concern. Apart from a few rowdy market traders and stubborn customers, all seemed well. Children even ran between the clusters of adults, pinching sweets and small valueless trinkets where they could.

They, too, were blissfully unaware of what was happening

elsewhere in their county.

Tharian watched two young girls playing with hand-stitched dolls around the rim of the well. They were laughing and singing songs together. An elderly woman sat on a fold-out chair beside them, keeping watch – most likely a relative of one or the other, or both. Just a normal day here, free from Elheim interference.

Tharian eyed a pair of marketgoers who walked closest to him. They gazed up at him on his unusually dark horse and then gave him a wide berth, whispering among themselves as they continued.

He was drawing too much attention. Any man in a hooded, full-body, dark green coat was enough of an eye-sore in a place as simple as this, without adding a rarely seen jet black horse into the mix. In fact, apart from the kurigaw ravens that enjoyed the wide grasslands of the area, there was very little in the Outer Counties that wore such dark colours.

He pulled the reins gently and Ombra turned away. Tharian knew she would have noticed the staring too and would be grateful for the chance to move away. Ombra weaved between a few of the buildings until they reached a crudely crafted stable.

The bays were already full, and more horses and empty wagons were parked around them. It seemed strange that a market village – known for its high footfall – would only have such a small stable to accommodate its visitors. Perhaps it was this way because Brynwell itself only had a small number of residents, so on the non-market days a larger stable would be redundant.

Tharian smirked. It had been nearly a decade since he gave such mundane realities any thought. His years away had shown him a simpler, more naturalistic life, where matters of economy had no bearing.

Ombra snorted, shook her head, and then followed the nearest dirt track leading away from the village. She stopped as she reached the last building on the edge of the village, rearing slightly to rouse Tharian's attention. That was her way of telling him he'd overstayed his welcome on her back.

He took the hint and dismounted. He paced around to her head and looked into her amber eye, stroking her mane.

'You can go, but I need you to do something for me.'

The Last of the Magi

Ombra turned her head, listening to his words intently.

'Keep Brynfall in sight, but don't draw any attention to yourself. Be subtle. If you see any enforcers, come and find me.'

Ombra huffed.

Tharian patted her firmly on the neck. She went on her way, turning back towards the north, in the direction of Brynfall, but she quickly disappeared behind buildings that blocked Tharian's sight of her.

As Tharian walked slowly back to the market, another flock of ravens rushed overhead, fleeing from the area where Ombra had headed. They circled north, with one leading the way at the front of the group.

Subtle, he laughed to himself.

Tharian weaved his way through the crowd. he kept his hood up and his gaze below eye-level. He was mostly listening, but he threw the occasional glance to some of the stalls.

He loosened the fastenings on his coat, letting it fall open at his sides to allow the breeze to swirl within his clothing. He tugged at the grey undershirt under his cuirass until he felt the light sweat brewing at his collar fade away. The day was not all that hot – he was used to hotter – but the tight pack of the crowds and the friction of all those who brushed past him was stifling. He pulled himself into a gap between two stalls and took a moment. While there, he found his attention drawn to the stall on his right.

It was the sweet smell of freshly baked bread and pastries that called out to him. The aroma was fantastic. It had been years since Tharian had last tasted Asturian baked goods. There were many things he loved about his time overseas in Feralland – the limited range of meal options was *not* one of them.

The temptation of the stall was too much, so he turned the other way. But the stall to his left was distracting for different reasons. It was adorned with magnificent silverware and trinkets, all laid on a violet silk cloth and decorated with small hand-written placeholders for each item. He had seen this kind of stall before, but the quality of items on display here was above and beyond anything he expected from the Outer Counties. The old friend he was going to visit in the Trade Quarters dealt in such curiosities, so he felt obliged to at least peruse the trader's wares.

Tharian waited for a small break in the crowd and then swept over to the stall's front.

On closer inspection, most of the items were commonplace silverware, but there were some pieces which piqued his interests. One of which being a necklace made with entwined silver and black cords. Many odd-coloured stones of different shapes and sizes hung from it. Tharian lifted it from the table gently and twisted it in his palm, trying to catch the stones in the light.

'That is a beauty if I do say so myself,' said the trader, suddenly appearing opposite him.

Tharian glanced up briefly, catching sight of the old, wrinkled man covered in cheap jewels. They glowed in that dull way that real gems did not. His hair was shaved short, and he had a well-groomed white beard. He reached a bejewelled hand out across the table and snatched the necklace back. He then wrapped the ends around his hands and pressed it to his own neck.

'Found this gem in the ruins a few years back.'

Which ruins? Tharian wondered as he squinted at the necklace. There were more than one sets of ruins in the Outer Counties. He pushed the thought from his mind, it didn't matter. 'It certainly is a remarkable treasure,' Tharian said. 'I'm sure it will fetch you a good price.'

The trader placed it back in its designated place amongst his wares and held his hands open over the table. 'You'd be the talk of the county with a noble piece like that, good sir. It's the height of fashion in Ferenir, so I hear, and those stones are of the finest cut.'

Tharian laughed under his breath and then met the gaze of the trader directly. 'I agree it is noble. But it is *not* from Ferenir.'

'What?' the trader dropped the performance and narrowed his eyes at Tharian.

'This is Wildcaller jewellery, from Feralland. I would have thought that obvious to someone with wares like these.'

The trader's mouth dropped open and he swiped the necklace and price-card away from the display and held them close to his chest. His cheeks flushed red, and his brow furrowed intensely. He looked at the other customers at the stall to see who had been

The Last of the Magi

listening in. There were a few patrons who seemed intrigued by the exchange, but mostly it had gone unnoticed.

'What do you think you're playing at?' the trader said, with no pleasantry left to his tone.

Tharian waved his hand. 'There's no need for concern. Wildcaller jewellery is not dangerous.'

The trader peered out over his goods and glanced around at the crowds milling around. 'Oh sure, I'll tell the enforcers that if they come sniffing around looking for illegal imports.'

Tharian felt a wash of embarrassment. He had let himself get carried away, as he so often did. His fascination for artefacts belonging to other cultures, and their magic-users, always captured his interests. He had spent close to a decade on the neighbouring continent of Feralland, living alongside the Awoken, the druidic race native to that land. 'Wildcaller' was the Asturian name for those in that race capable of wielding Magic, and this necklace was part of the attire that identified them. He was surprised to see one here, but in his curiosity he had forgotten that all contact and trade with foreign countries had been prohibited by the Grand City, with the borders being closed off to the outside world many years ago. Nobody could leave Asturia unless they knew someone willing to sail illegally, and the Grand City handed out incredibly harsh punishments to those they caught facilitating such travel.

Internally, Tharian rebuked himself. 'Please accept my apologies. I overstepped.'

The trader rolled the necklace up into a ball between his palms and then lunged over the table to force it into Tharian's palm. 'Take it. Wear it, burn it, throw it in the long grass for all I care. Get away from my stall.'

Before Tharian could react, the trader walked away to attend another customer, his charm returning as soon as he opened his mouth to try and secure his next sale. As if nothing had happened.

Tharian tucked the necklace into his coat pocket and then moved on. He stepped away from the throng of stalls and went towards the only other place of interest in this modest market village, the beacon tower. Where the market was swarming with people, only one man in a ceremonial robe stood at the door to the tower, fanning himself with his hand.

The man smiled warmly at Tharian as he approached.

'Good afternoon, sir,' the man said, 'can I interest you in a tour of the Brynwell Beacon Tower?'

Tharian shook his head dismissively and marched on through the open wooden door at the base of the stone tower, 'I think I can figure it out for myself, thanks.'. He left the man stuttering in surprise.

Tharian marched up the thin and winding staircase made of old stone. The steps were deep, but he took them two at a time with long strides. Beams of light glared over his face every few strides from small holes carved through the wall.

It didn't take long for Tharian to reach the top, and the back of his calves suffered for it. He walked slowly to the tower's edge, brushing past the large brazier in the centre stuffed with branches and straw which served as a ready-to-light pyre.

Tharian leaned against the railing at the tower's edge. The railing was much newer than the rest of the tower. No doubt it had been installed because of the influx of children that played around the village. They could easily sneak up the tower when a parent's head was turned.

Pacing around the edge, he looked back down to the market. The girls at the well were still playing. They laughed and cheered. There were more children there now, and they played energetically around their parents who gathered to chat at a seating area beside the well.

Tharian continued to circle around, taking in the distant sights of County Bryn. So much of it was arable land, more so than he remembered. He hadn't anticipated the sheer scale of the agricultural machine that all fed into this market village.

The horizon to the west led only to the sea. That was where he arrived back in Bryn, making use of an illegal ferry that docked at a disused port.

To the north sat Brynfall, he could faintly see the town jutting out of its hill. The jewel of County Bryn.

Tharian then looked east. There was a fog on the horizon. A large structure took refuge in that thick mist, but the view wasn't clear enough to see properly. Tharian hummed with approval as he

The Last of the Magi

nonetheless recognised the vague shape in the distance as his next destination: The Trade Quarters.

It was the economic hub of Asturia and the centre of commerce, hidden within the unnatural smog that was the by-product of it being a powerhouse of industry and production. The Trade Quarters was one of the only settlements in the country that had remained uninfluenced by the territorial division of the Outer Counties to its west and the politics of the independent city states to its east. Even the Grand City of Elheim, far on the east coast, did not interfere with them as much.

Tharian heard footsteps reach the tower's landing behind him. He twisted a look over his shoulder. It was the man from the doorway below, taking laboured breaths as he approached Tharian's side and leaned over the fence with him.

'The smog of the Trade Quarters.'—he shook his head disapprovingly—'It's a curious thing.' The man paused, as if awaiting Tharian's input.

But Tharian hadn't come up here for idle conversation.

'For decades,' he continued, 'that fog has draped across The Trade Quarters every day and night. I've heard plenty of people arguing over it. Some fear it will one day pollute the Outer Counties, if the wind becomes strong enough to blow it this way, while others say that the thickness of the fog each day is an omen which tells us how prosperous trade will be in Bryn – and for that it should be respected.'

Tharian shook his head. The words sounded scripted. 'And what do you say?'

The man smiled and nodded, but Tharian didn't keep eye contact for long.

'It makes no difference to me. I have never given much time to the lands beyond Bryn. We have enough work to do here without worrying about the mysteries that lie beyond our view.'

Tharian absorbed the words. They bore some wisdom, but with the enforcers due to arrive in Brynfall at any moment, this was one such occasion where a bit of broader perspective would have been beneficial.

'Now that is a curious sight indeed,' said the robed man as he marched over to the northern face of the tower with his red robe floating gently in the breeze.

Tharian stood back from the fence and looked for whatever had caught his attention.

There, in the distance, the sky was swarming with a black mass. It was a flock of birds. Kurigaw ravens. They raced towards Brynwell at an incredible speed. As Tharian blinked against the breeze, he then heard the screeching warning that they carried with them.

'What could have startled that many of them?' the man asked, gazing up to the clouds.

Tharian's heart sank into the pit of his stomach. There must have been a hundred of them. Fleeing. Tharian looked past them, to Brynfall.

The town was burning.

In the short moments since Tharian had been distracted by the foggy vista to the east, the entire town had been consumed by fire. Only the top level of the town had been spared the total eclipse of fire. Bryn Manor, the alderman's stately home and office, sat above the flames as if presiding over them.

'No...,' said the robed man. He pulled his hand over his mouth and trembled as he noticed the blaze. 'How did this happen?'

Tharian marched over and pulled the man around by his shoulder, taking his gaze away from the distant flames. His face was white, his eyes narrow, and his expression bewildered.

'Clear the market. Get everyone into their homes, now!'

The man looked back at Brynfall for a few more seconds and then nodded in agreement. Without a further word he whipped at his robes and sprinted down the stairs.

Tharian watched the blaze until the birds reached Brynwell. Their black feathers rained down, leaving a grim trail along the dirt road, like a warning for what was coming. When the birds reached the beacon tower, they swarmed around it, encircling it.

One of the ravens landed on the railing just a few steps from Tharian. It squawked and tilted its head at him, staring him down with its familiar amber eyes. It flapped its wings a few times and then took flight again, leading the rest of the birds away. Even

The Last of the Magi

without words, he knew what message the raven carried to him. He sobered as if someone had just whispered into his ear the word that formed at his lips.

Enforcers.

With the view of Brynfall now clear again, Tharian could see a caravan heading towards Brynwell. Men, women, and children, together with their animals and belongings walked alongside wagons. He felt a small wash of relief from knowing there were survivors, but that fell away when he noticed the regal, white carriage that followed behind – the vehicle of the Elheim – pulled by a magnificent animal with short white hair and a glorious mane of silver: a feyren.

He leaned over the railing and let out a bated breath. The people had survived the fire, but the enforcers now led them to Brynwell. For what purpose?

Footsteps echoed up the staircase again. Tharian was met by a captain of the county guard, dressed in a leather armour not dissimilar to his own with a seal printed over the breast that represented the Outer Counties.

'What in the...' he said as he saw Brynfall with his own eyes. He grasped the hilt of his sword and stormed over to Tharian.

Tharian responded by doing the same, making a conscious effort to ensure the captain could see that he too was armed.

'You better explain yourself! I hear word of a stranger riding into town and then a disturbance at the market, and now I come up here to find *you* watching *that*!' He barked as he pointed at Brynfall. 'Tell me what you know.'

'I assure you I had nothing to do with this.'

The captain drew his sword and pointed it at Tharian. 'Don't give me that.'

Tharian was unfazed by the captain's aggression, he could tell by the position of the man's feet and the slight shake in his wrist that this man was not accustomed to using his blade. It was probably more for show. 'The county guard knew the Elheim were on their way. I overheard some of your fellow guardsmen discussing the alderman's orders last night. I did the smart thing, I moved on. And that led me here.'

The captain lowered his sword and narrowed his eyes at Tharian.

'You can see with your own eyes that there are enforcers in County Bryn, and they are headed here. Summon your councillor and prepare what you can rather than wasting time interrogating me.'

The captain growled and then he sprung over to the edge of the tower. His eyes widened as he spotted the feyren-drawn carriage in the distance and his eyes darted amongst the tiny figures that walked ahead of it.

'Shit,' the captain spat. 'If the Elheim have business in Brynwell we'll need every able body at the ready in case things turn violent. That includes you.'

Tharian shook his head. 'I make no promises, Captain.'

The captain gave him a frustrated look and then dashed back down the beacon tower stairs. Tharian followed close behind.

Emerging back into the open at ground level, Tharian was relieved to see the market was already being cleared. Stalls had been flattened and moved away, except for those that held armaments, pharmacy supplies, and emergency rations. The tailors and clothiers were pulling together quilts and covers to make beds and roof canopies whilst the few guards and labour-workers that lived in the village were building makeshift structures wherever they could fit them.

And the children were gone. Their laughter was gone, but in the distance somewhere a child cried. Tharian looked over to the well, where the small group had been playing together. Their toys were still there, strewn across the ground.

Tharian knew the brutality of the enforcers, as did everyone else. However, he had usually arrived in the aftermath of their visits or escaped the area long before they arrived. He had seen enforcers throwing their weight around and threatening people with their Arcana, sure, but he had not witnessed the burning of a whole town. Not up close. Not that he could remember. His own birth town of Midhaven had met a similar end, but he was far too young to remember it.

Tharian's heart was racing. Being back in Asturia, he knew full well that he would cross paths with enforcers eventually – in fact, it

The Last of the Magi

was his plan to do so at some point – but this was far sooner than expected. He promised himself he would do all he could to avoid them until after he met with his ally in the Trade Quarters, and he intended to keep that promise. He just needed to find Ombra and head east. And yet, as he stood there and watched the Countyfolk of Bryn working together, ready to receive their displaced neighbours, he felt a pull to stay and do something. As a younger man, he would have hidden away and kept his head down without hesitation, as he was taught by his guardian. Now that he was older, bolder, and stronger, his conscience screamed out for him to hide away no longer.

He looked around at the swarms of people working on the emergency refuge site. There were only a handful of county guardsmen left among them. If the enforcers intended to strike in Brynwell, three or four men and women with blunt swords would be of little use. A small army with swords would be of little use. The village would collapse like paper in the wind against Arcana.

With that realisation in mind, Tharian decided what he would do next. He would stay. He would help.

Chapter 4

Valivelle

The preparations were finished with only a few minutes left to spare. The guards of Brynwell and a few of the more capable men and women of the village stood at the northern border of the village ready to comfort their distressed neighbours and assign them to their new temporary homes. The captain stood in the middle of the dirt road. An older woman stood beside him – the village councillor, judging by her formal attire. She leaned her hip heavily against a cane.

Tharian took cover in the shade of one of the nearby buildings, watching and listening from a position safely out of view. The people gathered at the village border were nervous, he could see their awkward shuffling.

The order of the caravan heading into Brynwell changed during the final stretch. Three enforcers alighted from the white carriage and now marched at the front of the crowd. The weary citizens of Brynfall trailed behind like prisoners.

The caravan stopped just a few metres away from the first building at the village border. The enforcer in the middle of their formation stepped forward with a sinister grin stretched across her thin lips.

The enforcer was an older woman, not quite matching the seniority of the councillor. Then again, the enforcer's complexion bore the hallmarks of the lavish skincare and cosmetic procedures enjoyed in the Grand City of Elheim. She may well have been older than she looked. Her uniform was the same as any other enforcer: a white, pristine jacket with matching trousers, and gloves, all tailored perfectly to her body. And across the epaulets, down the centre of the jacket and down her sides ran an intricate pattern of navy-blue decals and stitched lines.

'Do I address Councillor Navarya?' the enforcer asked. She flexed her hands, stretching her fingers within her gloves.

The Last of the Magi

'You do,' said the councillor in reply. 'You must be Illian Valivelle. I have heard of you.'

The enforcer swung her arms behind her back. '*Enforcer* Valivelle, let's keep this courteous. I'm afraid to report there is need for a change in leadership in County Bryn.'

The councillor sighed. 'The alderman is dead, I presume?' Her voice was croaky but without hint of fear or intimidation.

Enforcer Valivelle nodded slowly. 'Unfortunately. He failed to keep to his promises. He put this county at risk and so we saw fit to remove this liability.'

'So kind of the Grand City to steer the hand of democracy for us.'

The captain nudged the councillor and gave her a cautious glare. A warning of sorts, it seemed. The message fell on deaf ears.

'You will take his place,' the enforcer said bluntly. 'We will return to Bryn Manor in fourteen days and look forward to having more amenable discussions about the state of this county's debt to the Grand City.'

'Bryn elects its alderman by county vote. I cannot—'

'You *will* take his place. Effective immediately.'

The councillor sighed and rolled her shoulders as she shifted her posture against her walking cane. 'Very well, I will meet with you as you demand. Now, please release these poor people to us. They have been through enough.'

The enforcer waved a hand. One of the other enforcers, dressed in a similar uniform, grabbed the nearest civilian and pushed him forward, commanding him to move. The rest of the crowd followed, giving the Elheim a wide berth.

Once most of the Brynfall residents had safely passed behind the line of county guards and militia, the councillor tapped her cane on the ground for attention. 'Where are the rest of the county guard? None of them appear to be here.'

'Apparently they were given strict orders to defend the alderman. At all costs. You should be proud to hear they followed those orders to the letter.' Enforcer Valivelle turned sideways and pointed to a small wagon being pulled into Brynwell. It was filled with bloodied bodies wearing the leather armour of the county guard.

Councillor Navarya grimaced and looked to the captain. Even from Tharian's hiding place a short distance away he could see the stark red that flushed through the man's face and neck.

The captain drew his sword. 'You killed them *all*? He lifted his blade high and charged forward. Too fast for the councillor to stop him.

The enforcer swept her arm, as if doing an underarm throw. A rippling flurry of air rushed from behind her and pummelled the captain. He was thrown back and slammed to the ground.

It was Arcana. She used it to move the air at will.

'Here we go again,' the enforcer muttered through gritted teeth.

She pulled off her gloves and rubbed her palms together forcefully. Almost instantly, the clouds overhead suddenly shifted, darkening, and twisting as her Arcana manipulated them. She raised one arm up, as if reaching to grasp at the clouds with her bare hand.

A crack of thunder rang out, and then a bolt of lightning struck at her palm, filling Brynwell with blinding flashes of light that left her as a shadowy silhouette at its centre. The lightning continued to strike at her hand for a few moments and then she shifted her stance, casting the lightning at the captain.

Tharian had been watching everything. As soon as the clouds began to coalesce unnaturally overhead, he knew what was likely to come next. He'd heard about this technique. He dashed out from his hiding place and drew his blade. With perfect timing, he sprinted across the dirt road and slid between the captain and the Arcane strike of lightning as she unleashed it. His blade was angled to catch the strike.

There was a deafening crack as the lightning smashed against the sword. The sound reverberated on and on, and Tharian turned away as the flashing light stung at the back of his eyes. He pressed one hand against the back of the blade and pushed with all his might against the force acting against him. His feet dragged back through the dirt. The power of the Arcane attack was significant, but not overwhelming. And despite the electricity coursing through the metal, Tharian was unharmed by it.

A few seconds passed before Tharian felt the strength of the lightning weaken. One of the markings etched into the blade's surface, the one closest to the handle of the blade, started to glow an icy blue as the lightning was drawn into it. It was a rune, a magical enhancement to the metal. A few more seconds passed and then the next rune lit up too, absorbing even more of the Arcane attack. The third and final rune filled more quickly as the last of the electricity was absorbed into the blade.

The Arcane attack was finished, but the dark clouds remained overhead.

Enforcer Valivelle lowered her hands slowly. With the sky no longer flashing, she could see Tharian stood between her and her target, unscathed and unharmed. She scowled at his weapon, now thrumming with absorbed magic.

'Enchanted weaponry is forbidden by Grand City decree. Surrender that runeblade, immediately.'

The runeblade vibrated forcefully in Tharian's hands. This was the first time he had used the weapon to absorb Arcana, and the first time it had ever absorbed power of this strength. He straightened himself and crossed the blade towards his shoulder.

Tharian narrowed his eyes at Enforcer Valivelle. 'Let this be a warning to you, the Elheim's days of oppression are numbered.'

The enforcer's expression turned even more sour.

Tharian tapped one of the glowing runes. It thrummed and illuminated more brightly than the others. The stored electrical energy surged through the blade, then he swung in the enforcer's direction. The swing released the Arcana stored within the rune and it shot back at her.

She wasn't prepared. The electricity crashed into her body and caused her muscles to convulse violently. The shock surged through her for what felt like a full minute. And then she fell limp on the ground, unconscious – parts of her skin and uniform blackened and steaming.

Everyone fell silent, even the other two enforcers.

Tharian hovered two fingers over the next glowing rune, the first one having now dimmed. He looked at the two remaining enforcers as the corner of his mouth curled. 'Take her back to the Grand City. Go – now – while you can.'

One of the enforcers ran to Illian Valivelle's body and waved the other over to join him. Together they manipulated the air with Arcana to levitate their leader off the ground and carry her back to their carriage. Her uniform smoked all the way there. They boarded the vehicle and commanded their feyren to turn and drive their carriage back to the east where they came from. The silver-maned beast pulled away at speed.

Tharian sheathed his weapon and turned back to the captain and councillor.

'You saved my life,' said the captain, still on the ground.

Councillor Navarya shook her head sternly. 'For now,' she uttered, 'bring this man to the hall.'

The captain looked shocked for a moment, but then whatever was concerning the councillor appeared to dawn on him like a knock to the head. He advanced on Tharian, just as he had done at the tower earlier on. The councillor sighed again and made her way to the village hall – the largest building on the other side of the market.

Tharian shuffled back and reached again for his sword. The handle still vibrated gently with the power he had just released. He had two more runes filled with Arcana if he needed them.

The other remaining guardsmen rushed over to join their captain, flanking Tharian on either side.

'You will not keep me captive here,' Tharian said.

The captain didn't draw his weapon this time. But he did step in closer and turned his head to speak to Tharian in a hushed tone. 'Councillor Navarya has looked after this village since before either of us were born. She is firm, but also reasonable. We don't have the means to keep you detained here – not with a weapon like that – so just cooperate with her, please.'

His words were sincere. The other guardsmen surrounding him stood in neutral stances, not prepared to strike nor defend themselves. They didn't appear to be acting on the councillor's words out of duty but out of respect. That, at least, gave him some reassurance.

Tharian relaxed and nodded to the men surrounding him. 'Lead on.'

Chapter 5

Fugitive on the Move

The Brynwell village hall was warm inside, mostly made of smooth dark woods and decorated zealously with homemade rugs, tapestries, and paintings. A large fireplace dominated the back wall, crackling and snapping and pumping out enough heat to blush the cheeks of anyone who walked in through the main doors at the opposite end of the building. It was warmer than it needed to be, given the summer sun that shone outside. But, then again, the sky was much darker now thanks to the clouds drawn in by the enforcer's use of Arcana, and that was bringing in an irregular chill.

Tharian had been led to a worn armchair with a dark fur blanket draped over its back. Opposite him in a similar armchair sat Councillor Navarya. The captain and a couple of the county guard stood a safe distance back from them, far enough to not eavesdrop but close enough to spring forward to the defence of their councillor if needed.

Navarya poured tea for herself and Tharian at a small table laid out between their chairs. She added milk and a drop of honey to both. She hadn't asked Tharian his preference, although it had been so many years since he last drank Asturian tea that he wasn't sure what his answer would have been if she had.

'Quite the commotion you have caused,' Navarya said, pausing only long enough to purse her lips against the rim of her delicate teacup, 'I trust you understand the severity of your actions.'

Tharian nodded. 'I do, all too well. But your captain didn't deserve to—'

Navarya tapped her mug back onto its saucer with enough force to cut him off. 'Listen carefully now,' she said firmly. 'A captain of the county guard swears an oath to protect his county.' She pointed at him without turning her head. 'He knows his duty. And I know his duty. He was reckless in advancing on that Elheim witch.'

The captain shuffled uncomfortably in the background.

'Yes, agreed, but even so—'

'No!' she snapped. 'The captain's actions were his own. His punishment would have been his own too. Your intervention may have saved his life, but it also painted a target over Brynwell. Add to that the alderman's rebellions and we'd best pray that when the enforcers return, they don't rain hell upon us all.'

Tharian had no response. He stared into the fireplace. In those flickering flames he pictured the sight of Brynfall ablaze. He hoped, sincerely, that Brynwell wouldn't suffer the same fate for his actions.

The councillor cleared her throat. 'Do not misunderstand me. I am grateful to you for saving the captain. He is a good man. And I am aware that your actions may have saved my life also.'

Tharian kept quiet in case she interrupted him again.

She sipped at her tea. 'The opportunity for negotiating with the Elheim is now gone,' she muttered solemnly, 'I will do what I can to minimise this damage. I will meet with them at Bryn Manor, but before I go, I am duty-bound to do something about your actions.'

Tharian tilted his head as she gave him a narrow-eyed look. *Do you worst,* he thought, with an internalised smirk.

'On the one hand, you saved one of our own. On the other, you committed crimes against the Grand City in my county using illegal weaponry.' She looked to the sheathed sword laid against Tharian's chair.

He eyed it too, feeling a small swell of pride having now seen it work against Arcana in the way he hoped it would. 'It's your right to adjudicate on that matter on behalf of your county,' said Tharian. He rose to his feet. He buckled the sword to his belt and pulled his long coat together to fasten it, despite the heat. 'But I will not let you hand me over to them in exchange for a peace deal.'

Navarya's eyes lit up. 'Is that so?'

'I will be leaving County Bryn, today. Neither you nor your county guard will hold me here,' Tharian drew out his runeblade just far enough to reveal one of the still-glowing runes etched into the blade's surface. 'I still have two charges of Arcana ready for when I need them. Please don't make me use them here.'

Navarya curled her fingers over the head of her walking cane and pushed herself to her feet. She waved down at the county guard. Tharian then noticed they had crept closer at the sound of his blade being drawn.

'Relax. I will not try to detain you here. If you want to leave, then so be it. In fact – scratch that – I demand it. Your presence in Bryn will only cause more offence to the Elheim and put my people at greater risk. The enforcers will question me about what happened here when I meet with them.'

'Of course. And I expect they will pursue me.' Tharian considered his own words. He spoke confidently, yet in truth he hadn't anticipated becoming a pursued criminal of the Grand City so soon after returning to Asturia. Things were already complicated.

'Good,' said Navarya. 'Then I have only one question to ask before you go. You *will* answer it.'

Tharian tilted his head quizzically. 'Go on.'

'You will tell me why – why did you get involved?'

Tharian felt his stomach churn at the question. *This* was one of the many reasons why he should have just keep moving until he reached the Trade Quarters. He didn't want to linger, explain himself or engage in idle chat. Nonetheless, if this woman was to be the next alderman for this county, she could prove to be an important ally in time.

'I had to,' he said after a long pause. 'The Elheim have become complacent in their monopoly over magic in Asturia. They have been left unchecked for too long. If I can, I would like to help tip the scales back against them. I'll admit I didn't plan to make my first move here and now, but someone needs to stand against them for what they did to the Magi. And what they did to Midhaven, and now Brynfall too – and all the people who have suffered against their Arcana.'

The councillor sat back in her chair and topped up her tea. 'Very altruistic. Why is that your responsibility?'

'It's not. But the Elheim destroyed my home, murdered my family, and left me to die in Midhaven when I was just a child. Where other people dare not act against the Elheim out of fear, I have nothing more to lose. I can take the risks that others can't.'

'Midhaven?' Navarya frowned. 'What they did there was

dreadful, unforgivable. I'm sorry for your loss. Though, forgive me, but I do not hear the southern-county burr upon your voice.'

'I was very young when the Elheim invaded,' he told her.

She nodded and then tapped a finger to her lips. 'Yes, of course, you would have been. Forgive me.'

'No need.' Tharian's mind wandered. He tried to dig up any memory or emotion from his few short years in Midhaven. There was nothing there, and yet that was a reason he always turned to when he considered why he was so driven to stop the Elheim. His real motives were deeper than that, more complicated than he could really express in words. The destruction of his hometown was just a more convenient and understandable justification. In the end, the motivation was unimportant – Asturia needed to be free of Elheim oppression.

Navarya hummed. 'You've suffered a lot. More than any should. I can understand why you would take this upon yourself – and you've proven yourself capable, for certain – but I would advise caution if you are really going to continue with this goal. You will need a lot more than just that sword of yours to challenge the Grand City.'

She was right of course. Tharian smirked at her. 'I don't intend on fighting this alone.'

'Very well. Then best of luck to you.' She gestured to the doorway. 'I had best attend to the situation outside, while you leave my county.'

Nodding, Tharian took a few steps towards the exit. He stopped between the guardsmen and looked back to the councillor who eyed him in return. 'When the Elheim do return, tell them that I left from the Outer Counties. Tell them I headed east – to the Trade Quarters – that may get them off your doorstep.'

'I will do exactly that, thank you.'

Tharian left the hall. He and the captain respectfully bowed their heads to each other as he passed.

***

Ombra was waiting for him just a few paces outside the village hall.

The Last of the Magi

Tharian found her stood beside a young stable-hand who was looking around nervously and pulling gently on her reins. Tharian laughed as he saw them. He suspected the young girl was trying to make it look like she had brought Ombra to him in readiness for his departure. The opposite was more likely the truth. She tried to say something, perhaps explain how and why she came across Ombra, but Tharian didn't need to hear it. He was just glad to see her right where he needed her, saddled and ready to go. He thanked the girl and pressed a few coins into her palm for her troubles.

Tharian was pleased to see Ombra, as always. He fussed over her, scratching at her neck and ruffling her hair. Even though she had a fierce independent streak, she enjoyed the attention.

He climbed onto her back and immediately headed east, to the road that led to the fog-shrouded city in the distance. The Trade Quarters. He did his best to avoid the looks that some of the lingering Bryn residents were giving him, having witnessed how he despatched the enforcer. They didn't focus on him for long, they still had a lot of work to do to get the emergency accommodations set up for the displaced Brynfall residents.

They had a long ride ahead of them. They wouldn't arrive at the Trade Quarters until early the next morning if they carried on through the night. But they would need to rest to ensure they were refreshed and ready for whatever challenges their next location might throw their way. Fortunately, they had enough rations and equipment to get them through the night, and the winding road between Brynwell and the Trade Quarters passed through a woodland area which offered plenty of cover and fresh water. The water streamed through the woods from the heights of the Cartographer Mountains, which cut through Asturia's centre from north to south. The Trade Quarters was positioned close to the northern pass through those mountains, with the only other pass being near the country's south coast.

As Ombra cantered along, she swung her head from side to side regularly, taking in the open fields of Bryn, and then the healthy woodland that they eventually moved into. Her ears turned to the sound of cracking sticks, chirping birds, and rustling leaves coming from all directions. And the breeze that cut sideways through the trees made an ominous whistle, but it didn't unsettle Tharian or Ombra in the slightest. In fact, they relished the natural beauty of it.

They rode on quietly, with Tharian stroking Ombra's neck from time-to-time. A few hours passed by in the blink of an eye. As time went on, their shadows, and the shadows of the trees on either flank became longer and longer on the road in front of them.

Tharian pulled the sides of his coat together, as best he could while on horseback, as the chill rolled in. Ombra huffed and snorted a sound of discomfort. It was time to rest.

He pulled on Ombra's reins gently and she stopped in her tracks without needing to be told a second time. Tharian climbed down and stepped off the dirt track to head between the trees. She followed close.

The canopies overhead blocked out more of the waning sunlight than he expected, making it seem like night had suddenly surrounded them. What little sunlight could reach them in this place cast through the gaps in the canopy in columns of glowing auburn.

Ombra overtook Tharian and pushed forward in a slightly different direction to where he was heading. He corrected himself to follow her. He knew Ombra's senses were more powerful than his own, and he trusted her judgment without question. After a while, he heard a distant sound, which must have been her focus.

She led Tharian to a small pool of water that formed aside a stream. It was moments like this that reminded Tharian just how magnificent his companion truly was. She had an affinity for nature which paid dividends when travelling out in the elements. He wouldn't have survived the wilds of Feralland without her heightened senses and her *other* capabilities that she would keep hidden in Asturia to avoid attracting attention.

Ombra approached the shallow pool and bowed her nose into the water. Tharian reached to his back, underneath his coat, and felt for the opening of his satchel tucked away there. He awkwardly drew out a soft waterskin and finished what was left of it before scooping it through the pool. The water was very cold to the touch – with the kind of chill that felt fresh and pure.

Tharian shared Ombra's affinity for nature. He didn't have the same preternatural senses that Ombra boasted but he had learned how to survive away from civilisation with a similar proficiency. In fact, he preferred living that way. And it was no surprise that he did. His earliest memories were of travelling, camping and living in caves. He had spent more nights sleeping under the stars than he had in quilted beds. Even when he'd been taken to cities, such as the Trade Quarters, he'd only stayed for short periods. Nature was his true environment.

That lifestyle served as good practice for the most recent decade of his life, travelling the wild and unkempt lands to the west. Feralland was almost completely untouched by mankind. Even the natives had learnt to live *with* the land, rather than *off* the land.

Tharian sat in the thick grass with his back to the pool and gazed up at the trees as their branches slowly danced overhead. As he watched, fireflies emerged from wherever they had been hiding and swirled from trunk to trunk. These woods reminded him of Feralland. Untouched. As nature intended. Teeming with natural life, plants and insects alike.

The people of the Outer Counties lived more in harmony with nature than most in Asturia. The country was peculiar in that regard. Ever since the city of Oligar was destroyed by war, the west side of the country had remained fractured and modest – divided into separate counties that together would be called the 'Outer Counties' – whilst the east was mostly empty except for the large cities around the coast. Lions' Rest to the north-east, the Grand City of Elheim on the eastern coastline and then finally Ferenir to the south-east. And then the Trade Quarters sat apart from those independent city states and the Outer Counties both. Though technically it was still on the west side, it was seen by all as the central settlement in terms of geography, economics, and politics.

Each of the cities were unique. Each independent from the others.

The Trade Quarters was shrouded in its artificial fog of industry. Locked away behind its towering border walls of metal, exchanging goods and services from east to west and back again. A crossroads of commerce.

The Kingdom of Ferenir to the south-east was not so harsh on the landscape, but the land that formed its foundations was once covered in a verdant forest enjoyed by grazing animals. The city had grown large and vast over the years, and such prosperity demanded much from the local natural resources. The Kingdom had long worked with Magi advisers who helped them strike the right balance with their environment, but that tradition was dead now, extinguished with the passing of the late King Reksar Thorius. Incapable of resurrection since the Grand City gathered and killed all the Magi they could find on the day that became known as the Purge.

The north-eastern city of Lions' Rest was much an anomaly. It took independence more seriously than any other, using its unique position of being built into cliffs and mountain slopes to physically cut itself off from the others. So cut off, in truth, that no other Asturian had passed through their gates for years.

But all of that was nothing against the Grand City of Elheim. Although the shining white city was surrounded on its flanks by open fields and rich land, most of the earth outside its gigantic front gates had been scorched of life many years ago. A scar from the Purge. That stretch of land had since been given the same name as a constant reminder of what happened there. That day was instrumental to the rapid growth of Elheim society.

There were rumours about the land that lay behind the Grand City. At the very coastline, accessible only from the Elheim Palace, or from the sea, it was said that the chancellor's family – the 'true' Elheim family – had cultivated their own verdant fields. Exotic flowers from across the world grew beside trees with gold-tinted leaves, all to serve as their private garden. The very best of nature's splendour had been locked away as a private asset, never to be enjoyed or seen by any other.

All of those places were far away from these woods. None of the political strife in Asturia, or the threats of Arcana, mattered here. So Tharian lay flat on his back and rest his head against a natural bump in the ground. He closed his eyes and just listened.

The wind, the leaves, the birds, the flies, the water, Ombra's breathing. His own. All of it enveloped him and allowed him to relax. He sighed as he felt his muscles relax for the first time in days.

The Last of the Magi

The two slept soundly in that undergrowth.

***

Tharian woke as morning light poured over his face. It didn't startle him. It was a slow and natural rousing from a deep sleep. As his senses returned to him, the sounds that had pushed him into an early sleep were there to welcome him into a new day. There was a subtle change to those sounds – the nocturnal creatures had gone to rest, and the day-dwellers had become active in their place. It was a more energetic sound, perhaps even mischievous.

One of those sounds was creeping closer. Footsteps. They were light and quick-paced. Paws rather than feet. Tharian's finely trained ears recognised the sound of a four-legged animal moving around the area. Too light to be Ombra.

Tharian opened one eye slightly and investigated. He looked for Ombra. She too had roused from her sleep and her ears were tracking the sound. She turned her head away from Tharian to investigate but whatever she saw didn't interest her. She curled her head back around her front legs and relaxed, letting out one long huff as she became comfortable again.

Tharian closed his eye and just listened. If Ombra wasn't concerned by the prowling animal, then neither was he. He could hear the lithe animal stepping around, moving back and forth slowly to not give away its position. It had failed in that, but Tharian kept still to keep up that illusion. There was no need to scare the creature in its natural habitat. He was the intruder, after all.

A sharp sound pierced through the air, whizzing over Tharian from left to right. His eyes bolted open as the sound came to a sudden stop with a thud. A moment later, the quiet was broken by a guttural screech and the fluttering of birds fleeing.

Tharian and Ombra reacted fast, pulling themselves up and racing towards the screeching sound.

There, curled up in the grass, was the writhing body of a lirrus. A smooth-bodied feline creature. It was pinned to the ground struggling to breathe. A handaxe was impaled in its side, the blade gouged deep into its flesh. Judging by the animal's size – only a couple of feet in length – it was still only young. The poor creature had been attacked. Not by a natural predator.

'Ombra, do what you can,' said Tharian. Ombra looked at the creature whined. She moved closer to the lirrus and nudged at it with her nose.

Tharian felt a swell within. He turned away from Ombra and marched in the opposite direction, hovering his hand over his sword as he went. A face briefly peered over the top of some thick bushes not too far away. As if doing a double take, she peered out again and then stood upright. She was a young woman with a strong build, which helped her wade through the waist-high bushes like they weren't even there. She walked towards him with an expression of concern.

She looked familiar.

'You should be more careful – it's not safe to sleep in lirrus territory,' she said. 'They can be vicious.' She sheathed her remaining handaxe into the holster on her thigh.

Tharian tilted his head and, with great reluctance, pried his hand away from the hilt of his sword. 'That creature meant no harm.'

'How do you know? I saw it stalking around you and your horse, it was going to attack you – I just saved your life!'

Tharian pressed his hand against his forehead. 'Trust me, you didn't.'

'Whatever you say. I'll just take my axe and get out of your way.'

She walked around Tharian and went to approach the wounded lirrus, but it was gone. As was Ombra.

'Where did it go?' she said, looking amongst the trees for any sign of the animals.

'Away,' said Tharian. He turned to the woman and folded his arms. 'It will be somewhere safe now, where it can hopefully recover from what you just did to it.'

Tharian sighed and then started walking back towards the dirt track, away from the young woman, to continue his journey to the Trade Quarters. He tried to swallow down his frustration. Asturians in the Outer Counties may well have been more accustomed to living around nature, but they didn't understand or respect the

The Last of the Magi

animals that lived within it.

To his annoyance, she chased after him. 'No, no, no. That was a clean hit. I saw it, there's no way it walked away from that.'

'Perhaps you underestimate how resilient a lirrus can be?'

'You're joking, right?'

'No,' he said bluntly. 'Stop following me.'

Tharian just managed to reach the edge of the treeline when the woman pulled him round by his sleeve and stoically squared up to him. 'Stop walking away from me when I'm talking to you. Manners!'

Tharian's heartrate spiked as the woman firmly gripped his wrist. He glared at her strong, blackened hand. In a quick motion, he wrenched his wrist free and brought his fingers to his lips to blow a loud whistle.

A large black bird then burst out of the trees overhead and dropped something in his direction. He reached up and caught the object as the bird looped through the air and crashed back into the treetops.

Without even looking at what he caught, he grabbed the woman's wrist, twisted it around, and thrust her missing handaxe back into her palm. She froze, looked at the axe, looked at Tharian, looked into the sky, and then flitted between the three for a few seconds. Her mouth was open, and her lips moved as she struggled to form words.

Tharian stepped away from her and waited in the middle of the dirt road. Ombra then brushed past the woman and let out a derisory snort close to her ear.

She startled at Ombra. 'But... how?' she finally said, her voice cracking.

'You have what you wanted, now be on your way. I recommend you keep to the road.' Ombra had her saddle and the saddlebags dangling from her mouth by the cords. Tharian took them and refastened them to her back. He climbed on and could sense that Ombra was just as frustrated by the situation.

Before they could move off, the handaxe flew across Tharian's eyeline, slamming into the trunk of a tree on the other side of the road. Tharian flinched and then narrowed his eyes at the woman.

'Who even are you?' she bellowed. 'You turn up in my town out of nowhere and then leave just before the whole place is burned to ash by enforcers. Then we're all moved to Brynwell and there you are again, attacking one of them like it was *nothing*. And now you're here.'

Tharian felt a tugging sensation in his stomach as he thought about Brynfall burning, and the risks that he had exposed Brynwell to through his actions. He looked at the woman more closely. Her plain white shirt, thick overalls and sooty face were definitely familiar. The leather-clad jacket and handaxes were new, however. He could still feel a lingering discomfort in his wrist from her firm grip.

'The blacksmith...' he whispered under his breath. He remembered her face now, the young woman who excitedly tended to his runeblade.

'What?' she replied.

'What's your name?'

'Marla, why?'

Tharian paused. He looked down at the road ahead of him rather than look her way. 'I'm sorry about your home, Marla. The alderman knew what was coming, and yet he antagonised the Elheim all the same. I only got involved at Brynwell because I worried the same thing would happen there.' He let out a deep breath and then met her eyes. 'Shouldn't you be back in Brynwell?'

Marla looked at her feet and sighed. 'Definitely not. With Brynfall and my father's workshop gone, there isn't much left for me in the Outer Counties. My father will do well there, but I'd been waiting for the chance to move on and start my own life. This seemed as good an opportunity as any. I'd like to get away from the Elheim too, while I'm at it.'

Tharian nodded. Though his lifestyle was wildly different to hers, he understood her drive to move and take control of her future. 'You're headed for the Trade Quarters?'

She nodded.

'It's not completely free from the Grand City's interference.'

'I know that. I figured If I have to live with them around, I might as well get paid by them while I do it.'

The Last of the Magi

Tharian smirked. 'How entrepreneurial. The Quarters might be the right place for you then – I hope you find the life you're looking for. Good luck.' Tharian lightly jostled Ombra's reins to move on.

Marla shuffled to keep up with them as they moved. 'If you're headed that way, we might as well travel together, just in case any other animals try to attack?'

Ombra kicked the dirt and swung her head aggressively, her actions reflecting Tharian's own thoughts. 'That lirrus was *not* attacking,' he said sternly.

'Fine — then just in case the enforcers travel this road.'

That argument had some weight. For those travelling from one side of the country to the other, there were only two main routes – the northern and southern passes that cut through the Cartographer Mountains. If more Elheim were to travel to the Outer Counties via the northern pass, they would certainly end up on this same road.

Tharian paused for an uncomfortably long time. He knew the chances of encountering more Elheim along this road so soon after the events in Bryn were slim, but he did worry a little about what might happen if *she* encountered a threat – whether that be from local wildlife or indeed more enforcers. She was clearly capable with a handaxe, but a handaxe was no defence against Arcana, or an aggressive mother lirrus protecting her litter.

'Just to the Trade Quarters. No further.'

Marla smiled. 'Great! Then let's go, stranger.'

'Tharian.'

Chapter 6

The Quarters Road

For the first hour or so of their journey together, Tharian kept quiet, as was normal for him. He was used to travelling alone. Marla asked a few questions about him, his past and his travels, but he deflected the subject with short replies, giving her no real answers. Frustration ebbed and flowed in him with each question. He was surprised by her naivety – surely, she must have understood the risks of just associating with him? Maybe not. She had just seen her home set ablaze, and now she marched off to a new city as if this was all just a normal day. Is this how complacent Asturians had become to Elheim oppression and destruction?

The conversation eventually moved back to the lirrus. She asked how he was so sure the animal was not hostile. That was a subject he would happily discuss.

'You've lived around people for long enough – I bet you can tell a lot about others from the way they move, the way they hold themselves or the expressions they show on their faces?' he said. 'Animals are no different. If you spend enough time around them, you learn the signs.'

She awed at the idea and then looked off between the trees. 'I suppose that makes sense,' she said. Tharian wanted to scold her for attacking the lirrus, but he knew she had good intentions, and it was not his place to berate her. She was inquisitive, and she was prepared to listen, so he hoped she would eventually come to be less hasty about animal behaviour.

Tharian enjoyed a few minutes of silence after that. Marla looked to be in deep contemplation, until eventually her gaze moved to the foggy shape of the Trade Quarters in the distance, slowly fading into view. She became animated again upon noticing it.

'The metalwork that comes from the Trade Quarters is unlike anything I've ever seen,' she said. She shrugged and flicked her eyes to Tharian for just a moment. 'Not that I'm saying our work is

The Last of the Magi

bad quality. They have materials we can't get our hands on out here. Not for cheap.'

She was right. It may have been a decade since he had last stepped inside the walls of the Quarters, but Tharian had many fond memories of seeing armour, weaponry, trinkets, tools and other crafted goods of such rich and vibrant colours and designs. There was no doubt that the artisan crafters of the Trade Quarters represented the best of every profession. That was no accident, for that was the purpose of the city's very existence – to be the pinnacle of all crafts and trades for the betterment of *all* Asturia. Detached from political allegiances. Dedicated only to commerce.

'I've not known a young woman to be so interested in blacksmithing,' Tharian said. It was a foolish thing to say, he realised, as he didn't make a habit of socialising at all if he could avoid it – let alone investigating the aspirations of young women.

Marla scoffed and laughed at him. 'Then you've not spent enough time in the Counties! Countyfolk hardly have the luxury of picking their careers. I'm lucky my father is as good a smithy as he is, or else who knows where I would have ended up.'

'What about your mother, did she have a trade?' he asked.

Marla nodded and the excitement in her voice curbed slightly. 'Yes, she did. People from all over Bryn would visit ma' for some of her herbal salves, or to get wounds dressed. It's funny really, father was never convinced that common herbs could do what ma' said they could. That didn't stop people coming, though. The number of times they bickered about it every time one of us caught a cold. It used to drive me mad.'

Tharian didn't need to ask about her mother any further. It must have been a difficult subject. A tug within him made him feel compelled to offer some sympathies or some other gesture, as required by social norms, but that kind of thing just didn't come naturally to him. He embraced the silence that followed.

Eventually, Marla spoke again. 'That blade of yours,' she said.

'What about it?'

'Can I look at those markings again?'

Tharian's brow deepened, and he looked down at her, shaking his head. He wished he could erase her memory of ever having seen the blade, especially after what happened at Brynwell.

'Please? I'd love to make something like that one day.'

Tharian closed his eyes and sighed. 'I told you before. Forget you ever saw it.'

'Why? You didn't hold back on letting those enforcers see it. It's hardly a secret now, is it?'

He tensed his jaw and focused on the road ahead. He didn't respond. She was speaking far too flippantly about a serious issue.

'Fine. But they're runes, aren't they? Tell me that, at least.'

The edge of Tharian's lips tugged up slightly. He nodded.

'I knew it! Mark my words, when I get my own shop one day, I'll learn how to make runed weapons. Such a beautiful craft shouldn't die out.'

'An ambitious goal,' Tharian said, 'but I wouldn't hold your hopes too high on that.'

Marla glanced up at him, an eyebrow cocked. 'How come?'

'Crafting runed weapons needs a lot more than just quality metal and a skilled hand. Sure, you might be able to make the etchings into the metal but to make them *work* you need more.'

'Alright then, know-it-all,' she chuckled, 'what more do you need?'

'I don't know. I'm not sure any Asturian knows anymore.'

Marla huffed and kicked her feet through the dirt as she walked.

It was only a half-truth. Tharian had been told about crafters who could imbue magic into metal. It was a different kind of magic to that of Arcana, or the Magic of the Magi, or the older forms of magic that had been seen throughout Asturia's history, but it was believed to be magic, nonetheless. He wasn't aware of any runecrafters still living in Asturia – yet another product of the Grand City's oppression.

***

Marla must have figured out that Tharian was not one for prolonged conversation. She kept quiet for the next few hours.

They stopped briefly in that time to rest, at which point Tharian noticed that Marla had been carrying a large bag on her back which

The Last of the Magi

held more supplies than she would need to get her to the Trade Quarters. She was serious about starting a new life in the city – she was not intending for this to be a brief visit to get it out of her system.

As they set off again, Marla occasionally looked at the trees on either side and then peered beyond them. She was noticing what had been obvious to Tharian a while back.

The woods were changing. The trees were gradually becoming more withered, and the grass too lost its dewy sheen. Everything around them was greyer and browner, including the air. This was the sign they were entering Trade Quarters' territory. The closer they crept to the towering structure of metal in the near distance, the thicker the air became, polluted by the fog and smoke that pumped out of the city.

Ombra shuddered. The decay of nature unsettled her. It unsettled Tharian too. 'Not long now,' he said.

Marla looked up at him and nodded. She looked stern, the excitement that flushed through her before had dulled like the colour of their surroundings. She tugged at the straps at her shoulders and marched forward.

The sound of Ombra's hooves changed from a soft patting to a harsher tapping as the soil became dryer, harder and cracked. The trees on either side of the road were withering under the fog – most of their leaves having already died, fallen, and decomposed on the ground below.

Within a few minutes they could barely see beyond the first row of trees on either side of the path. The fog lingered amongst the trees more so than down the stretch of the Quarters Road ahead of them. The air was thick on their lungs too, not toxic enough to cause them to choke, but heavy.

'Have you been to the Trade Quarters before?' Tharian asked.

'No. First time,' she replied.

'It will look and feel very different to the Outer Counties. You need to be prepared for that.'

'I'm getting that vibe already, yeah. Is the air always like this?'

Tharian smirked and scratched at his cheek. 'Surely you've noticed it from Bryn. The city constantly churns out dust, smoke, and steam. It mixes into a fog above the city's outer walls and then falls heavily over the surrounding area. It's not this thick once you're inside the city itself.'

'So the city's mess gets thrown out for the rest of us to enjoy? Great.'

Tharian shrugged. 'Unfortunately. There's always a cost for prosperity.'

Ombra made a high pitch whine as the fog thickened even more around them. Marla reached over and gave her a gentle stroke on the neck. Ombra jumped at the touch but settled very quickly, moving closer to Marla for reassurance.

Tharian smiled as he felt Ombra's steps become a bit more confident. He stoked her neck too. *I know, it's been a while. You're not used to this anymore.*

'What are you going to do in the Quarters?' Marla asked.

'That is certainly the question,' he said.

'What does that mean?'

'It means I have a rough idea, but I don't know for sure where it'll take me.'

'You're such an odd one. No offence. Though I suppose my plans aren't much different.'

Tharian's attention was drawn forward as he noticed the end of the treeline that took them into a wide and empty space around the Trade Quarters. 'We're here'.

Tharian dropped down from Ombra's back and he led her forward by the reins. Marla stayed close. They approached a large door built into a wall of metal that reached high above them. From this close, the city wall looked like it reached the sky – as the wall faded from clear view where the fog was thickest overhead. Tharian knew it wasn't quite so menacingly tall. It was tall, just not *that* tall. The wall was patched together from all sorts of scrap metal, in shades of blue, grey, silver, black and bronze. It was an eyesore, but it kept the Trade Quarters safe from roaming bandit groups or unwelcome visitors. Of all the cities in Asturia, the Trade Quarters was probably the second most secure in that regard, after the reclusive Lions' Rest.

Tharian approached the door and knocked three times with his

The Last of the Magi

forearm. The door vibrated violently, and the knocking echoed through the metal structure for an awkwardly long time.

A small hatch in the door slid open and one piercing grey eye appeared in the darkness on the other side.

'Your business?' said a deep, rattling voice.

'Trade, of course.'

The single eye flitted between Tharian, Marla and Ombra, and then fixed on Ombra in particular. 'No cart, and I doubt any money either. What do you have to offer the Quarters – you selling the mare?'

Tharian met the man's piercing stare. He flourished his coat and reached one arm round to his side. He drew out his runeblade and twisted it in front of the small hatch in the door, ensuring that the dark blue tint of the metal was visible to the observer.

'Is that it?' the doorman said.

Tharian then rotated the blade in his hand so the still-glowing runes, charged with Arcana, made the man's pupil narrow. 'Yes… that's it,' said Tharian.

The eye opened wide and then, with a grunt, the hatch closed abruptly. Gears within the door then turned and the metal moaned as the doors slowly dragged open.

Tharian led the way. They walked by the doorman, a one-eyed man wearing nothing above the waist, revealing his heavily scarred torso. He called out to them, 'you should take that to Traykin in the Collectors Quarter, tell him I sent you. He will offer you a good price.'

Tharian smirked back to the man. 'Oh, I'm sure he will.'

He wasn't interested in local tips on how to make a bargain selling his wares – he wasn't here for trade at all. But he was pleased to hear that the name Traykin was still known in the Trade Quarters. Jerard Traykin was the man he had come to visit.

***

Marla kept close to Tharian's side as he confidently marched into the city. Ombra leisurely followed behind them both. The path just beyond the gate branched around a row of large, three and four storey tenements made of dark grey bricks. Marla awed at them; they were much bigger than any homes in the Outer Counties.

Tharian took them down the right branch of the road until they reached a point where the two paths joined back into one and led on to a wider road ahead. It was mostly cobbled but bore prominent wagon tracks.

Buildings rose on either side of this road, packed closely together. Although these were not as tall as the tenements at the entrance, they were still larger than most houses and shops in Bryn. Every building was at least two stories high and made from grey bricks with dark beams of wood.

As they carried on, Marla noticed a pattern with the buildings on either side of this wide road. The ground floors were all shops, taverns, inns, restaurants, or bars. The upper floors were either shadier looking stores or dingey homes without any signage or indication of trade.

Despite the dust, the dirt and the dinge, Marla beamed as she looked everywhere she could, high and low. Everything here was so different to the Outer Counties. She pulled herself from her childlike bewilderment to address a thought that crept into her mind. She stepped across Tharian's eyeline to discuss it with him. 'Why did you show the doorman your runeblade?'

Tharian stopped abruptly and gave her a wide-eyed look. He looked to the side, towards a dark alleyway. Marla did the same. She saw a few shady figures lurking at the mouth of the shadowed path. They were staring intently in their direction. They were armed, but not armoured, and each of them wore a sinister grin.

Tharian turned, awkwardly but slowly towards Ombra. He stroked Ombra's face but leaned slightly towards Marla's ear. 'Do *not* draw attention. Especially to anything that might be valuable.'

Marla's lips sealed shut. She nodded quickly and kept her eyes looking ahead as Tharian led the way again. Ombra kept close beside her, snorting heavily against the light smog pervading the air.

Between almost every building there was an alleyway that disappeared into shadow. Though she couldn't see much down those dark paths, Marla assumed they were the accessways into the towering dark tenements behind the shops fronting the road. Marla wondered how someone could navigate such dark, bland pathways without getting lost in the belly of the Trade Quarters. She did her best to keep from staring down those dark portals, in case more eyes were watching them.

Tharian marched on with purpose. They reached a section of the road where people were swarming about between stalls set up in front of the shops. It was a mess of noise, colour, and scents. Marla found it overwhelming, but she noted that Tharian did not slow. In fact, he fluidly moved through the gaps in the crowd as if on a mission – undistracted by the calls of the street peddlers. She tried to copy him, but she struggled to push through as easily. Tharian was very slender and had a litheness that even a lirrus would envy. She did not. She kept at Ombra's side, as the shoppers gave the horse a wider berth.

They emerged through the throngs of marketgoers. Tharian slowed and veered to one side of the road. He stopped and looked purposefully inside an open doorway. He then looked back down the road they had travelled, flitting his gaze between the buildings and alleyways. His eyes fixed on something, and he stared for a few moments, but he spoke before Marla could look back for herself.

'Wait here.' He quickly ducked into the building.

Marla led Ombra closer to the building and stood patiently outside. There was a small weapons rack displayed beside the door. It held a rusting shortsword, splintered wooden shield and a bent axe. The craftsmanship was shoddy. She couldn't even bring herself to examine them further, a glance was enough to see their quality. *Not even worth scrap value*, she thought. No product of blacksmithing, even the cheap and base kind, should be on display in *that* condition. This was not the quality she had been led to believe was commonplace in this city.

Her attention was snapped away by the sounds of slow, heavy footsteps coming from behind. Marla looked over her shoulder and caught a glimpse of two large men and one large woman approaching her and Ombra. It was like they had just spawned from the shadows of those passing by. Knives glinted in their hands.

Ombra whinnied a high pitch note and stepped closer to Marla, shirking away from the approaching brutes.

Stepping back cautiously, Marla's attention was pulled back to the building as even heavier and clunkier footsteps moved her way. She jumped as two heavily armoured men stepped around her and stopped at her flanks.

The three bandits froze. The three may have outnumbered the two, but each of the armoured figures drew out a longsword – outnumbered, but not outgunned. The two armoured men advanced on the bandits, causing them to immediately turn and flee. The men pursued.

Marla's heart raced. Yet, nobody passing by on the busy road even batted an eyelid. Even the flash of a sharpened dinner knife would be enough to cause a stir in the Outer Counties. It would be gossip for days.

'That should deal with them.'

Marla startled again, this time at Tharian's voice. 'Don't sneak up on me like that! Where did you go?' she said.

Tharian looked at her quizzically, smirked, and then tilted his head back towards the building beside them. 'I went in there. You saw me.'

'That's not what I meant. What just happened?'

Tharian checked the street before answering. 'This place is crawling with traders, mercenaries, and opportunistic rogues. All it takes is one rumour of valuable goods entering the Quarters and the vultures start to circle.' Tharian curled the side of his coat open and then closed it with such speed that it whipped the air. 'They would steal the lining from your coat if they thought it had silver thread.' He raised his brows at her.

Marla thought about what he said for a moment and then gasped as she realised what he was really referring to.

'Don't worry about it,' said Tharian. 'If they really wanted to steal from me, they would need better quality muscle than that. Fortunately, it doesn't cost too much to pay for mercenaries around here, so I hired two to drive them away.'

Marla smiled and folded her arms. 'You think you could have handled all three of them, huh?'

Tharian shook his head. 'Not with brute strength, no. But I have some tricks, plus I have two charged runes from that enforcer.'

The Last of the Magi

'You would've attacked them with Arcana?' Marla immediately covered her mouth with her hand after she spoke, conscious of how loud her voice was.

Tharian looked at her with sympathetic dismay. He checked around them again. 'Only if I had to. I don't need that kind of attention right now. That's why I hired the guards.'

'Right.'

'You'll need to get used to this kind of environment, if this is really where you want to be.'

She nodded and then breathed deeply. That was her first run-in with bandits. Despite the danger, she was still abuzz with excitement. This place was brimming with opportunity. 'I can handle it.' She decided.

Tharian didn't react. He looked like he wanted to say more. Instead, he turned back the way they were heading. 'This way then.'

The three continued on until they reached a large open space with a white marbled floor in the shape of a diamond taking up a lot of the space. Stone statues stood at each marbled corner, facing inwards. Tharian led her straight to the centre of this plaza. Each corner of the diamond pointed towards a wide road that stretched all the way to the city's outer wall, with the road they just travelled being one of them.

The wide roads were all similar, with subtle differences she couldn't fully appreciate from a quick glance. She could examine those more closely later. The statutes had captured her interest more.

The statues were immaculately well crafted, but the display was unusual. Marla frowned at them. *Why are they faced the wrong way?* She wondered. She had seen statues featuring notable people from history – there was nothing odd in that – but these four were faced inwards towards each other rather than out to the city. It was like a private meeting of stone giants.

Each statue clearly depicted a different individual, with their bodies and clothing being distinctly different. But their poses were the same. Each statue was handing something out to its neighbour on their right and held out its other hand to their left.

Tharian led Ombra between two of the statues and made a sweeping gesture to them all. 'What do you think?' he said.

Marla hummed. Her father had talked about these statues before but only very briefly. Now that she could see them for herself, some of what he told her resurfaced. 'There's one statue for each of the four quarters of the city. Whoever made these wanted to represent each quarter properly.' She tapped a finger to her lips.

'They are much more than that. These are the original founders of the Trade Quarters – the first coinsmen.'

'Coinsmen?'

'Each quarter has an appointed representative who governs the trade activity of that quarter, and together they make decisions that affect the city as a whole.'

'So, like the councillors and alderman back home?'

'Similar. Except there is no hierarchy here. The coinsmen are like the councillors for their own quarter, responsible for their own patch, but the coinsmen collectively act like an alderman for the city, rather than having someone superior sitting above them.'

'That's not so different then.'

Marla looked at each statue in turn, pacing around the plaza. One caught her eye more than the rest. This one was a tall man with a broad frame. He stood in heavy armour, intricately represented by bulky carvings in the stone all over his body. He wore no helm, but his pauldrons and gloves were covered in harsh spikes. From his right hand hung the head of a mysterious creature she didn't recognise. He offered this to his neighbour while his left arm was reached out as if ready to receive a gift from the next statue along.

Curious, Marla checked to see what gift was coming his way. That next statue depicted a thinner man with sharp facial features and a hat of twirled fabric. He held out a helm adorned with spikes that matched the armour worn by the first statue.

'Who is this?' she asked, pointing at the statue of the armoured man.

Tharian patted Ombra on the neck and left her behind as he joined Marla in the middle of the plaza. 'Vern the Bloodspiller,' he said.

'Oh, *come on*.'

Tharian shrugged. 'He didn't choose the title himself, apparently.'

The Last of the Magi

'Fine.' She turned around and looked at the others, tapping a finger against her lips as she considered them. 'What about that one? She pointed to the thinner man with the unfamiliar headwear.

Tharian didn't answer.

Marla looked around for him, but he had moved away. He was back over with Ombra, fastening his coat.

'Enough sightseeing, I have things to do,' he said.

Marla walked closer. 'Alright, let's go then.'

'No.' He turned to her. 'I told you we could travel together until we got here. Now we part ways.'

Her shoulders dropped. Her smile did too. She nodded and looked around at the sprawling trade roads that stretched in four directions from where she stood. Though each looked slightly different, without understanding those differences they were all just roads to her.

Suddenly the excitement of her new environment dulled. This was a dangerous place, she knew that much already, and now she had to work out her next steps for herself.

'You should go that way,' Tharian said. He was pointing behind her, south, to the road behind the statue holding out the spiked helm. 'The Artisan Quarter is where you'll find the greatest craftsmen in the country. Its competitive and ruthless in its own way but it's safer there. Don't be tempted by the Quarter of War.' Tharian then pointed to the road behind Vern the Bloodspiller. That road had the thickest and darkest smog. 'There are more smiths down that way, but they focus on quantity rather than quality.'

Marla nodded and forced a small smile. 'Thank you, I'll take your advice. Where are you headed?'

'I have business in the Collectors Quarter, likely to last a few days. Maybe longer.'

'Alright. I guess this is good-bye for now then,' she said politely. 'Thank you for helping me get here, Tharian.' She closed the gap between them and held her hand out.

Tharian look surprised. He responded politely, nonetheless. She gripped his hand tightly and nodded. She then turned on her heels and headed off to the Artisan Quarter as recommended.

L. G. Harman

***

Tharian watched Marla walk off to the Artisan Quarter, making sure she went the right way.

He wrung his wrist, stretching his fingers to try and bring feeling back to them. *A blacksmith's daughter, if ever there was one.* He laughed to himself.

Tharian noticed that Ombra was staring at him. By the angle she held her head, and the way her eyelids hung heavy, she didn't look impressed with him.

'Let's go see Traykin.' he said to her.

She snorted and kicked her hoof against the tiled floor.

'Don't start. It's just a few days. We'll be back on the open road soon enough.'

She replied in the same way, this time chipping away at the marble with the force of her hoof.

Tharian folded his arms. 'Perhaps you would rather be stabled until I'm done here?'

Ombra's eyes widened. She snorted once more and then walked away in the direction of the Collectors Quarter.

He followed, letting her have a little space but not trailing so far behind as to make people worry that a horse was roaming the city unsupervised by its owner.

The road through the Collectors Quarter was much like the one in the Market Quarter, with its cobbled stones and its generously sized shops and houses. But it was quieter. There were people roaming around, browsing shops and trading here and there, but it was a much more subtle affair. The customers and traders alike wore suits adorned with jewels, and robes lined with fur, and many had walking canes for the sake of accessory rather than necessity.

Collectors never change.

The collectors let Tharian make his way down the long road unscathed. No peering eyes stared at him from the alleys and no-one he passed gave him suspicious looks. They did take interest in Ombra, however. She had a rare coat colour, an asset that would draw the attention of any collectors inclined to keep animals amongst their inventories.

The Last of the Magi

At the very end of the road, just before the outer wall, the road branched in two like it had in the Market Quarter. A few buildings nestled in the gap between the outer wall and these curving paths. One of them stood out dramatically from the rest: Traykin's Bazaar. While all the other businesses in the area adopted colourful signs and decorations to make their specialist trade clear – gemstones, historical treasures, and other curiosities – there was no such clarity communicated from the façade of Traykin's Bazaar.

The building itself was made from a strange mixture of worn stone and warped wood in irregular slants which had been dyed a dark shade of purple. Even the door of Traykin's Bazaar had been custom-made to fit its ill-shaped frame. It was like the whole structure had been pieced together from leftover materials which had no business being put together in this fashion.

Ombra lingered at the corner. Tharian crossed his arms as he finally reached his companion. 'You can head to the back. I'm sure he still has somewhere for you to stay.'

She swung her head about and then turned away, looking at her surroundings. She wasn't keen on the idea at all. He could feel her restlessness – she wanted to keep moving.

'Explore if you need to,' he added, 'just keep yourself out of trouble. You know what collectors are like.'

Ombra's amber eyes lit up and she shuffled on her hooves.

'If you get bored, check in on the girl if you can.'

Ombra paused a few seconds and then nodded once. She turned away and went down one of the curved paths that led somewhere behind the Bazaar. Anyone would call him mad for letting an exotic black mare wander a densely populated city like this on its own. Especially here, where everyone was eager to make a quick fortune where they could. But this was Ombra. She could disappear, conceal herself, or escape trouble like no ordinary animal. Because she was no ordinary animal.

Tharian stared at the warped door of Traykin's shop. It had been years since they'd seen each other. He laughed nervously as he reached for the handle of the door.

This will be interesting.

Chapter 7

The Lost Magi

The inside of Traykin's Bazaar was even more peculiar than the outside – just as Tharian remembered it – because Jerard Traykin was a peculiar collector. There was no consistency in Traykin's wares. He had always described his collection of items as his 'menagerie of curiosities', but to anyone of sane mind it was more a cluster of clutter.

The floors were covered mostly by overlapping carpets and animal furs that didn't go together at all, and in the few areas where the floor was bare there was more purple-dyed wood to add to the oddity of it all. The walls were similarly dressed in a haphazard fashion, with paintings, maps, tapestries, drawings, etchings, and sculpted models. Customers could be forgiven for assuming that this eccentric taste in decoration was reserved only for the bazaar's shopfloor. The truth was that every room was this loud. Loud in appearance, and aroma. And when Traykin was in the room, loud in volume too.

Tharian was only on the shopfloor for a minute before Traykin bounded in. With an expression of dumfounded confusion and impish excitement, Tharian's large-framed old friend ushered him immediately into the back room, to a private study where the collector held his private meetings.

They spent the first few minutes just laughing together, recounting some old stories from years ago, and sharing some new ones too.

'He said that?!' Traykin said, clutching at his chest as he laughed. His giant stomach bounced as he struggled to control himself.

'You still have quite the reputation, Traykin,' Tharian replied, smothering his own laughter. He took a sip of the ale that Traykin had kindly poured for him as soon as he took a seat in the study.

'That gatekeeper is a repugnant old goat with all the brains of a

The Last of the Magi

dead Elheim.' Traykin then became serious and pointed a fat finger to Tharian. 'But... he clearly has a keen eye for good quality artefacts if he thought I would be interested in *that*.' He pointed to Tharian's runeblade leaning against the wall.

'I wouldn't give him too much credit. A runed weapon is hardly a regular sight. Anyone would think it's worthy of a collector's attention.'

'A fair point you make there, lad. I forget how mundane everybody else's possessions are sometimes. I'm sure he wouldn't have recommended you here if he'd known that it was *me* that sold you that bloody thing in the first place!'

Tharian put his tankard down on the side table and cleared his throat. He cocked a brow at Traykin. That wasn't quite the way he remembered things.

'Fine!' Traykin burst into laughter again, 'it was a gift – but don't go telling anyone that, I don't want them to think I'm going soft.'

'Noted,' Tharian said with a smirk. Traykin was already soft, even if he refused to admit it openly.

Traykin stood and sluggishly swung around to his drink cabinet. He pulled a stopper from a bottle and filled his glass back to its rim. He sipped at it aggressively on his way back to his chair.

'I gave you that years ago, lad. Eight or nine by my count. Is that how long it's been since I last saw you?'

'About right. Your contacts at Brynport were very helpful. They got me to Feralland, just like you promised. I'm impressed with how smoothly it all went if I'm honest.'

Traykin's face scrunched up and he gave Tharian a funny look. He then filled the room with his laughter once more. 'You doubted me, lad? I'm a collector, it's my job to know how to get hold of things that others can't. How do you think I got half of my stock out there?'

Tharian nodded and pursed his lips. He then took a small sip of the ale, granting himself a brief pause before moving on to a more serious subject. 'You're right, I shouldn't have doubted you. The truth of the matter is that everything went to plan thanks to you. I got to Feralland, met with the Awoken as you suggested, and now

I've come back. You know what that means.'

Traykin calmed. 'It could mean a few things. Either you wasted the best part of ten years and you're back to the drawing board, or...' he took a deep gulp from his glass, finishing it again, '...you've done it.'

'The latter.'

Traykin paused, his eyes wide.

The door to the shopfloor opened. A pale and sickly-looking man – about Tharian's age – crept in and knocked on the wall to get Traykin's attention. It was Traykin's ward and shop-hand, Frigg.

'Master Traykin, s-sir. There is a customer here who—'

'Handle it, Frigg. And shut that bloody door!' Traykin bellowed, almost knocking paintings from the wall from the sheer force of his voice.

Frigg trembled and withdrew back out of the room, pulling the door closed. He and Tharian met eyes, and Frigg's eyes flashed with recognition just as the door shut.

'So, Arcana is not quite as all-powerful as the Elheim would have us believe?' asked Traykin as he rubbed his hands together.

Tharian sighed. 'Potentially. But stopping it won't be easy.'

'Spit it out. What did you find?'

'It's not quite what I expected. The Awoken showed me many of their magical artefacts, but none came close to being as useful as the runeblade. As far as that part of my travels go, it was a very unsuccessful trip.'

'Get on with it, lad. I'm getting older by the moment.' Traykin moved to refill his drink again.

'Putting it simply, our best hope for suppressing the Grand City doesn't rely on us finding *something*, but instead *someone*. A Magi.'

Traykin coughed on his drink. 'Have you gone mad? I know you were only a child when the Purge happened, but the old man surely told you what happened to the Magi?'

'He did. I know it sounds ridiculous but listen. The Awoken understand the magics of our world better than we do, and they told me that not all the Magi died on the day of the Purge.'

'You *are* mad, Tharian. Perhaps we should take a trip out to the Dead Plains so you can see what remains of the *hundreds* of Magi

The Last of the Magi

who were gathered there by the Elheim? Even if one of those fools survived the cull, what good would one Magi be when all the rest of them were wiped out so easily.'

Tharian stood and walked over to one of Traykin's many exquisite paintings. He kept his eyes on it while he collected his thoughts. 'This is different. The Magi didn't know what the Elheim had planned for them that day.' Tharian turned back to Traykin, noticing the bewildered look of disbelief on the man's scraggily bearded face. 'There is a power that the Magi can invoke. It can completely seal away magic of any kind, stopping someone from being able to use it when they want to. If even one Magi still lives, then we have to find them and convince them to use this power against the Elheim and their enforcers. Arcana is all the Elheim have, without it they will be defenceless. We only need to make sure that this Magi is protected.'

Traykin shook his head. He refilled his drink a third time, immediately after taking another sip, and then he went back to his seat. '*If* a Magi still lives – and that's a big if – how in the hells do we find them?'

Tharian gave Traykin a look. The answer to that should have been obvious to a collector.

Traykin cursed and then rolled his eyes. 'Right. That's why you've come to me.'

'When trying to find something valuable or hidden, who better to turn to?'

Traykin puffed a heavy sigh through his nostrils. 'You're a smart-arse, you know that?' He wiped his whole face with his hand and then slammed his palm on the arm of his chair. 'I would have you thrown out of here and tested for lunacy…' he sighed again and then growled as he wrestled with his own thought '…but you've been working on this a long time, and the Awoken aren't the type to make up rumours. You are Greycloak's boy too, and that must count for something.'

Greycloak.

Tharian had never been a fan of the moniker that his guardian chose for himself. Greycloak was not really his name, but it was a fit physical description for the old man that had raised and protected

Tharian as an orphaned child, and it was the only name he ever used. Now that he was back in Asturia, he would need to check on the frail old man when he had the chance.

Traykin grumbled and pulled at his beard. 'I need to sleep on it, lad. We'll talk more about this Magi of yours tomorrow. You're welcome to stay here as long as you need.' He stood and picked up both his empty glass and Tharian's half-filled tankard. He squared them against each other, poured half of Tharian's leftover drink into his own glass, clinked them together and then handed the lesser-filled tankard back to him.

'Understood, thank you,' Tharian looked at his runeblade briefly. He remembered the Arcana stored in the runes and groaned. 'There's something else I should probably tell you before you find out by some other means.'

Traykin sighed. 'Don't like the sound of that.'

'No, I imagine you'll like it even less when I say it. You should sit back down.'

'Out with it, then.'

Tharian inhaled deeply and leaned back in his chair. He laced his fingers together over his chest. 'On my way here from County Bryn, I crossed paths with some enforcers doing their rounds.'

'Collecting the Arcane Tax?'

Tharian nodded, and Traykin made a spitting sound. 'Apparently the Alderman of County Bryn has been refusing to pay for a while.'

'That he has, against all advice from his councillors, and even the coinsmen here.'

'Yes, well he pushed it too far this time. The enforcers burnt Brynfall to the ground.'

Traykin's eyes widened, and he lurched forward in his seat. 'They did what?'

'I saw it for myself. The whole place was set alight. Then they made their way to Brynwell—'

'What about the people?' Traykin interjected.

Tharian winced slightly. He probably should have led with that detail. 'The alderman and the county guardsmen defending him were killed, but everyone else made it out.'

Traykin cursed.

The Last of the Magi

'I left before it all happened. I was in Brynwell, but that's where the enforcers took the survivors. A captain of the guard threatened an enforcer and she used Arcana on him in return. I...' he paused and glanced sideways to his runeblade again '...I intervened to stop it.'

Traykin looked startled, and then a smirk crept in at the edge of his lips. 'Oh?'

'I took down the one leading them.'

Nodding, Traykin became unusually quiet for a few seconds. He also looked at the blade and then stared at the ceiling. 'Serves them right, but I see the issue.'

'What do we do?'

'Do you know who you took out?

'Does that matter?'

'It might.'

Tharian blew air through tightened lips and rapped his fingertips over the arms of his chair. A name then floated into his mind, in the voice of Councillor Navarya. 'Valivelle? I think that's what I heard.'

Traykin put his head in his hands and then made a woeful sound. 'Of course, *of course* it was a Valivelle. Why wouldn't it be?'

'What does this mean?'

'It means you've only gone and attacked one of the chancellor's favourite enforcers. The Valivelle family are like his pets. He calls upon when he wants to make an example of people. King Thorius. Midhaven. And now Brynfall, too.'

'So we should expect retaliation then?'

'Not half. We better start making plans to act on these ideas of yours, first thing in the morning. If the Valivelle family have a score to settle with you, all Asturia will hear about it soon enough.'

Tharian nodded. He'd heard enough stories about enforcers and Arcana, but not really about the specific families and groups within the Grand City of Elheim. He suddenly felt regret seep in, he should have kept the promise he made to himself. He shouldn't have intervened and made things complicated. He let his instincts get the better of him and now he was the enemy of one of the most powerful Elheim families.

'They don't know who I am. And they didn't see me for long.'

'Good. That buys us time.'

'Not much,' Tharian added. 'I realised they would come back to County Bryn looking for me eventually... so I told Councillor Navarya to redirect the enforcers to the Quarters.' Tharian braced himself for an angered outburst. To his surprise Traykin maintained eye contact without even moving or blinking. Eventually he nodded.

'They'd tear Bryn apart if they thought you were there. It's better that they come here if they must. We at least have a *relationship* with them.'

Tharian gave Traykin a serious look, and Traykin returned the same. Even if what he said was true, the thought of enforcers knocking on the city gates was not a pleasant one. For anyone.

'Right, well there's nothing else we can do about the situation right now, lad. I'll get Frigg to put together a hot meal. *You* could do with a hot bath. We'll get started on all this tomorrow.'

'Alright. Thank you again, Traykin.'

Traykin chuckled and twirled his glass close to his face. 'Don't thank me yet, lad. You've got a lot of work to do.'

Chapter 8

The Valivelle Family

There were two infirmaries in the Grand City of Elheim. The first, on the lower tier of the city – in the residential vicinage – was for public use. The second was not far from the Elheim Palace on the upper tier, reserved only for the chancellor, his enforcers, and their immediate families.

It was this second infirmary, the Arcana Infirmary, that Darus had been summoned to. He sat in the pristine reception waiting to be called. There was nobody else waiting. The building still looked new, as there was very little demand for it. Those closest to the chancellor had access to the best healthcare, nutrition, and pampering. Illness and injury were rare occurrences. Nonetheless, the previous chancellor had commissioned the construction of this infirmary as a precaution, with the suggestion that it be used for 'academic or educational purposes', or as an overflow centre, when not required by its intended patients.

A woman in a long white coat, like a full-length version of an enforcer's jacket, strolled into the room from one of the far doors. She peered over the papers in her hand and looked Darus in the eye, inviting him to follow by curling a finger.

Darus followed the doctor, brushing down his enforcer uniform as he walked. The uniform, tailored as it was, definitely looked the part but it was uncomfortable to wear for those who preferred looser fitting clothing. Darus felt a constant need to shuffle within it as a way of distracting from the discomfort.

The doctor led him into a lavish office and gestured him over to a cushioned chair with curved armrests.

'Lady Valivelle arrived a few hours ago. Her condition is stable, but her wounds are serious. She appears to have suffered burns. What concerns me, however, is they appear to be electrical burns. This is an extreme version of the kind of injury I have seen apprentices cause to each other during reckless practice at the

College.'

'You think she was attacked with Arcana?' Darus said. His voice cracked slightly.

The doctor nodded. 'It's too early to know for sure. It's not my job to speculate, what matters to me is Lady Valivelle's recovery. On that note, I am confident she will make a full recovery, as she shows no sign of internal damage. She just needs rest.'

Darus had heard the rumours spreading through the Grand City already – that his aunt may have been attacked by magic – but hearing it from an expert face-to-face raised more questions than answers. As terrifying as the implications of that may be, it was not his job to speculate either.

'Am I allowed to see her?' he asked.

'Of course – just pull that curtain back.' She gestured with a pen to the curtained window to his right. 'She's in the joined bay next door for observation until we can move her to a recovery suite.'

Darus moved to the wall and parted the heavy silk curtain.

The neighbouring room was equally as pristine as the rest of the facility. A metal-framed bed was against the middle of the wall on the left with a white chest of drawers on either side. There was even a bookshelf and a small armchair for reading and relaxing opposite a small desk. Whether the desk was for the doctor or the patient was unclear.

Illian Valivelle was tightly tucked in the bed with her arms laid by her sides on top of the blanket. The skin on her arms was cracked with burn wounds. She breathed heavily and slowly and appeared to be in a deep sleep. She looked weak and frail, and older than he remembered her being. All Elheim looked enviably youthful for their respective ages, owing to the lavish pampering they all enjoyed, but the injuries and bed-ridden state of his aunt exposed her advanced years brutally.

'Her body is resilient,' said the doctor, as she appeared beside Darus, 'and her mind is even stronger. Even while unconscious she is showing signs of Reaching out to her surroundings through Arcana. There's a lot we can learn from the way her body unconsciously engages with the Deep Thought state.'

The Last of the Magi

Darus nodded. He wasn't surprised to hear of his aunt's Arcane prowess. Everyone in the Valivelle family had a particular affluence for Arcana, but Illian Valivelle was a league above the rest. She was the first to learn how to Command thunder and lightning, and it had become her hallmark. She was a formidable asset to the Grand City, and that was why she held the rank of a senior enforcer – giving her authority to execute the will of the chancellor outside the walls of the Grand City.

'She will be ok, then?' Darus asked. His attention was drawn to the flowers placed on either side of the bed. The blooms were all pointed in towards his aunt, but they were severely wilted.

'Absolutely. I have no doubt.'

A trainee physician entered Lady Valivelle's room. She carried in her arms a bundle of navy-blue silk robes and, atop them, a bowl filled with warm water. She went to the desk and put the items down so she could carry out her duties.

The doctor pulled the curtain closed again. 'Some privacy, I think.' She then led Darus back to her office door and gently pushed him through the threshold.

'Our administrator will be in contact with your family when Lady Valivelle awakens and consents to visitors.'

Darus smiled nervously and shook his head. 'She won't want visitors.'

'Very well, we will let your family know when she is to be discharged,' the doctor leaned behind the door for a moment only to swing back with a small envelope in her hand. 'The high imperator's office requested a brief written report, here it is.'

'Thank you. I will deliver it immediately.' Darus bowed his head in respect to the esteemed doctor. The doctor nodded and shut the door before he even straightened.

He made his way through the clinical corridors of the infirmary and stepped back out onto the palace vicinage. The lightly paved road and the white walls of the surrounding estates reflected light in all directions, highlighting the splendour of the Grand City of Elheim. He was grateful that his uniform was almost entirely white. It responded to the sunlight well. But he was less grateful for how it encased his body in a tomb of his own body heat. He would boil if he stayed outside for too long.

Fortunately, as the Arcana Infirmary was on the upper tier of the city, he was only a short walk away from the entrance to the Elheim Palace. The College Arcana, the base of operations for all enforcers, and the location of the high imperator's office, was tucked away within.

The route between the infirmary and the palace was a short one, littered with immaculate houses of white stone and marble, idyllic gardens and small congregations of men and women discussing their recent dinner parties or the latest buzz of news.

The Grand City was peaceful, and Darus was thankful most days that he was born into this life rather than any other. It was a life of comfort and privilege, but with serious responsibility to it too, especially for a Valivelle. He was grateful for the opportunities he'd been given, but there was a lingering feeling of guilt in the pit of his stomach, because other Asturian people did not enjoy those same privileges.

Darus had been raised to follow in the footsteps of his older brother, Marken, and his father and aunt. It was to be a life of success, and of service to the Grand City.

He, like all other apprentice enforcers, had the fortune of being a student at the College Arcana. The education there was second-to-none, and the lessons on the use and mastery of Arcana were beyond excellent. Even so, Darus often felt that he could be doing more with his Arcana. There must have been more to it than just defending the Grand City and enforcing the will of their chancellor through force. No matter how often those thoughts came to him, he never came any closer to finding an answer. It was not the duty of an enforcer to explore such ideas, it was their role to enforce Grand City decree and further the Elheim vision for the future of Asturia.

Darus raced up the palace's wide staircase. The stairs ran from the very base of the palace's entrance all the way up to the private quarters where the chancellor and his family resided. The seemingly unending stairs were punctuated every 20 steps or so by landings that branched off to the other facilities and central municipal offices that kept the Grand City running smoothly. Other enforcers, in their identical uniforms weaved up and down these steps, as did other

The Last of the Magi

citizens of the Grand City — all either rushing about for meetings or to attend their places of work. They called it a palace; it was more of a vainglorious hub for administration.

As Darus reached the second landing, he took a moment to catch his breath. The palace itself was beautiful, from top to bottom. The first three landings of the staircase were still outside in the open, and the marble steps reflected the light and heat that cast down from above. From the third landing upwards, a canopy covered the rest of the way. The palace stretched up into the heavens on either side, as the east and west wings. Those two wings curled towards each other and joined together as one at the palace's apex, which was where the staircase then led into those private quarters.

Darus brushed down his uniform again, and pulled at the pockets of his trousers to straighten them from where they lifted as he climbed. He followed the midnight-blue carpet that draped up the middle of the stairs until a strand of it branched off to the right on the fourth landing, leading into the east wing of the palace.

He knew this corridor well. The fourth floor of the palace was dedicated to the College Arcana. The east wing contained offices for all senior enforcers, as well as a centralised reception for the administration of their duties. Initiates of the Arcane would enter the College Arcana through the west wing, where the training facilities were, and after passing some tests and initial exercises would be granted the rank of apprentice enforcer. Five years later they would be invited to enter the east wing as graduated enforcers. Darus had spent the last five years studying at the College Arcana, and was due to graduate in the fall, only a month away.

The enforcers' offices were just as grand as everything else in the Grand City – perhaps even more so. Not many people had the privilege of seeing beyond the front desk, which Darus now approached, because to do so would require the permission and approval of Registrar Harroly. If anything involved the enforcers, Harroly either knew about it, organised it, or *should* have done so, and would be unbearably grouchy if someone else had done it in her stead. She worked directly with the most senior enforcer, the high imperator, and it was no secret that most enforcers feared the registrar more than the high imperator – despite not being trained in

Arcana herself.

Darus reached the front desk and prepared his most courteous greeting. 'Good afternoon, Registrar Ha—'

'I trust your aunt is recovering well,' Harroly snapped. She hadn't even looked up from the paperwork she was rifling through. She pulled a file from a drawer and peeled it open on the counter in front of Darus. She swiped at the pen tucked behind her ear and scribbled in the file.

Darus placed the doctor's sealed report on the counter. 'Yes, she is, thank you. The doctor thinks she will—'

Harroly shot Darus a furious glare over her half-moon glasses. It silenced him. She slid the report to her side of the counter with two fingers. 'The report will suffice.' She deftly unsealed the envelope and took a quick look at the report. She nodded at it, as if it had affirmed her expectations, and then she threw it to one of the many assistants that sat at small workstations behind her. 'I need copies of this delivered to all senior enforcers.'

The assistant nodded nervously and pulled the report to his desk. He grabbed a stack of paper and began writing out the first copy.

Harroly let out a deep, loaded sigh and then flashed a forced smile at Darus. 'In light of *recent events*, the high imperator will be ordering all apprentices to report to the main training hall at close of teaching hours for a refresher course on Arcane combat.'

Combat training? Darus winced to himself. *I've just passed those exams.* Darus hid his frustration from his face. He just nodded in reply.

'That will be all, Apprentice Valivelle.' She pointed her pen down the long corridor back to the landing. She then called the next person forward to the reception desk.

Darus walked back out to the landing and pondered what this training might entail. It was already afternoon, so it would be starting soon. Arcane combat was a small part of the training undertaken by apprentice enforcers at the College Arcana. The chancellor himself had decreed it to be a skillset of lesser importance after the Purge twenty-three years ago, when all other users of magic were eradicated from Asturia. Since the Purge, enforcers of the Grand City were still required to be masters of the

Arcane to help give them the *persuasive* edge in diplomatic negotiations, to make them a force to be feared or, in extreme cases, to punish those who stepped out of line, but realistically there was nothing else in Asturia that could hold a candle to the might of an enforcer.

He understood why the training was being called, of course. Because a senior enforcer was laid unconscious in an infirmary bed as the result of a suspected magical attack. That threatened to unsettle the supremacy of Elheim people over Asturians.

What could have done that to her? Darus wondered as he slowly meandered into the west wing. *An enforcer gone rogue maybe. No, why would they – they would have too much to lose.'*

***

The apprentice enforcers gathered at the training hall immediately after their classes were finished for the day. The enforcer instructions and scholar lecturers were dotted around the room, and most notably the high imperator herself was there, an unusual occurrence missed by no-one.

She addressed them all, declaring that they were to begin the training session immediately. She only said a few words, but they hit home the key message of the evening: that the training was mandatory, intended as a precautionary measure in light of a *recent incident* in the Outer Counties. She then departed, leaving the instructors to arrange the exercises.

The instructors assigned the apprentice enforcers into groups of three. Each group were then to assign roles between their number – that of attacker, defender, and observer – and these roles were to be rotated every few minutes. The aim would be for the attacker to assault the defender using only their Arcana, and for the defender to protect themselves. The observer's role would be to identify critiques for their colleagues before the roles rotated.

The training itself was not to take place in the training hall, but instead within the College's indoor garden. The indoor garden was a familiar setting to all apprentices, as most of the practical training took place there. The gardens boasted high glass ceilings, generous natural lighting, and beautiful scenery. It was a calming and peaceful arena for focusing one's mind to the Arcane. But that was not the only reason for its picturesque landscaping. The garden had pools of water, breezes blowing in from large open windows that looked out towards the coast, and large braziers that were always lit. This gave the apprentices an abundance of natural elements to manipulate and control. It was like an armoury to an enforcer.

The lead instructor whistled and then called for them to begin the exercise.

Darus had been assigned the role of defender in his group. He positioned himself at the top of a grass mound. His attacker for this exercise was Apprentice Rikkard Nostrum. He was glad that Rikkard was one of his partners for the session. Of all the apprentices he had met through his years of training, Rikkard was the one he was closest too. They met in their first week at the College Arcana and had been inseparable ever since.

Rikkard stood at the bottom of the hill with his hands stretched out towards Darus. He had just deftly manipulated the water from a nearby pool, pulling a tendril of it from the still body and lashing with it like a whip. The attack was fast, as manipulations of water often were, but Darus was quick enough to Grasp the water with his own Arcana and Command the part of it that would have hit him to break free and drop loose to the ground.

Rikkard grimaced and moved his arms again, this time pulling the wind at his flanks to send it rocketing up the mound as two blades of air.

Arcane wind was even faster. But luckily for Darus, Rikkard was one of the many apprentices who still preferred to use his hands to help focus the movements of his Arcane manipulations, and that made it easy for Darus to see what was coming. Darus again Reached out through Arcana and Grasped the blades of air rippling towards him. He Commanded them to redirect into the ground. The air obeyed, and a small shockwave burst out through the grass.

Rikkard followed with smaller attacks. With his Arcane Commands he drew strands of wind and streams of water in quick, reckless assaults. The elements bolted forth like a volley of elemental arrows.

The Last of the Magi

To one not acquainted with Arcana, the assault would look like an unavoidable barrage. But every enforcer learnt early on the skill of placing their mind in a state where they could sense and feel Arcana at work, as well as feel the natural elements around them waiting to be manipulated. This 'Deep Thought' state made the assault much less daunting, and easier to counter. Rather than Grasping and Commanding each strike as he did before, Darus Reached out with his mind to the breeze blowing overhead. He Grasped it with Arcana and Commanded it to rush down to the ground. The gale of wind that followed was enough to ground all Rikkard's attacks at once.

They stared each other down with furrowed brows and narrowed eyes. The exertion of attacking and defending left them both short of breath. Using Arcana was like flexing a mental muscle, rather than a physical one, but using that power at this pace was tiring all the same.

Rikkard flexed his fingers.

Darus flinched and raised his own hands to defend himself. They shuffled their feet in response to each movement made by the other, like swordsmen ready to duel.

Then, for a few seconds, they both became still again. They would have been in complete silence were it not for the Arcane bombardments flying around on all sides from the other sparring apprentices.

The intensity of their stares eventually broke, as Rikkard smirked, and Darus followed suit quickly thereafter. Rikkard exhaled sharply through his nose, and then they both started laughing. They lowered their arms and relaxed.

'I thought I had you with that last one!' Rikkard chuckled. He curled his long, straight black hair behind his ears – pulling away the strands that had dropped in front of his face.

Darus could then properly see Rikkard's large, bright brown eyes. 'You're joking, surely? You used that same move a year ago. You're getting predictable, Rik!'

Rikkard pouted and shrugged. 'Predictable? We'll see if you still say that after I knock you off that hill.'

The two laughed raucously at each other. *Confident as ever,* thought Darus.

A loud cough caught their attention from the side. They both glanced over to Apprentice Aurellia Velyn, a mutual friend from their cohort who was their observer. Her arms were folded, and she tapped her foot on the ground.

'Are you lovebirds quite finished?' she said bluntly.

Darus and Rikkard looked back at each other instinctively. As soon as their eyes met, they looked away again. Darus felt his cheeks warm. He opened his mouth slightly, searching for the appropriate response.

'I assume you don't want my notes on...' she flailed her hand between them, '...whatever *that* was.'

'The point is taken, Aurellia. We got distracted,' said Rikkard. Darus was relieved that Rikkard responded on their behalf.

Rikkard winked at Aurellia and then raised his hands back towards Darus. 'Come on then, Darus, lets mix this up a bit. If I land a hit, dinner is on you.'

'Deal,' he replied, with a nod. Darus shook off his embarrassment and prepared for Rikkard's next assault.

And he did not disappoint.

Waves of spiralling air came flying at him, quickly followed by more crashing streams of water. Rikkard expertly pulled in pockets of the nearby elements and made them his own. His attacks were fast, volatile and unrefined in shape, but Rikkard had a remarkable ability to roughly pull together many Commands at once. He made them spin and move erratically this time. Darus couldn't rely on his own reflexes for this. He was good with Arcana – very good in fact, as all Valivelles were – but he was better at precise and technical manipulations.

He dodged a few of the attacks, either with movements of his body or with quick Grasps that pushed the attacks off-course. A few of the attacks snuck through his defences and he barely managed to dodge them. If this wasn't an official training exercise, he might have considered throwing the match and losing the bet. It was probably his turn to pay anyway. But this *was* an official exercise, so he had to take it seriously. Their superiors were watching.

Rikkard's attacks now surrounded him, moving through the air

The Last of the Magi

like wasps around their nest. Any one of them, or all of them, might strike at him at any moment. He couldn't rely on his reflexes at all now. Darus instead Commanded the air around him to draw in close and he made it spin around his body, forming a protective cocoon. It took a lot of exertion to maintain, but he now had a shield – completely invisible except for the subtle rippling effect it made in the air when looking through it.

The first strike hit against the shield. Darus felt it in his mind, like a pulse at the back of his skull. He knew where it hit and how hard it pushed against his own Arcana. He reinforced the air in that part.

The next strike came. Then the next. Then the next. Each redirected his focus a little at a time, in different places It was a clever move. But one that Darus could handle. The shield held strong against the flurry of weak attacks, so Darus focused instead on pulling in more and more of the surrounding air to keep the shield sustained.

As the accumulation of his Arcane Command became stronger by the second, he felt a dull pain deep within his head. He was stretching himself too far. He would have to relent soon, maybe gradually over time, but he knew Rikkard's stamina would soon give out too. No enforcer, even a fully graduated one, could maintain such a rapid flurry of blasts for so long without either becoming tired or finding that the elements became less responsive.

He looked through the swirling air in front of him to see Rikkard waving his arms in motions towards his chest. He was changing tact too. He could sense it. Rikkard was drawing together something big. Even Aurellia was stepping back from her position.

Suddenly Rikkard's arms lurched forward, and Darus could sense what felt like a cannonball of Arcane air launching his way.

The ball of air slammed against his shield and pushed hard. Darus was knocked back from the force of it, but the backside of his shield blew him back into balance. He focused his own Arcana forward in retaliation. The clash of magical energies was more powerful than anything he had experienced before. He could feel Rikkard's attack pushing through his barrier, so he had to act quickly before he was sent rolling down the other side of the hill.

Darus pictured in his mind the shield of wind around him breaking open, flipping through the air and then reforming to envelope and contain Rikkard's attack it. He then Commanded the shield to do exactly that. His Arcana moved quickly, and in a blink he'd managed to enclose Rikkard's attack within the shield under his control. He then Commanded the Arcana to collapse inwards, hoping to crush Rikkard's attack within his own.

But something went wrong. Their Arcane creations merged into one large swirling mass of air instead of dissipating. And Darus felt his Command over the mass release become fragmented. From the look on Rikkard's face, the same thing happened to him.

The unstable mass then erupted. The airburst that blasted out was mostly soaked by the mound on Darus's side, but the rest of that force rushed downhill towards Rikkard.

The burst was strong, far too strong. Darus tried to Reach out to it, hoping to Grasp at some of the air and slow it down, but there was just too much of it, and it was moving fast. But he kept trying anyway. As he concentrated and strained further, the dull pain in his head intensified.

Rikkard hopped back, trying to avoid the burst. It was too fast. The wind swept under his feet, knocked him prone and carried him in its momentum. His body was dragged back towards a rock wall at the edge of the garden.

Darus watched Rikkard being flushed away. He desperately tried to intervene with his Arcana again. He reached deeper into his mind than he ever had before until he felt his senses brush against... something. It must have been the airburst; it was unfamiliar to his senses. He focused as hard as he could on the wave of air and Grasped at it, trying to break it apart, though it made the pain in his head worse.

And it worked, the air dissipated. But there was more. Darus knew what the elements felt like through Arcana. The sharp, rushing feel of the air, the powerful lapping of water, the aggressive motion of flame. *This,* however, was something unyielding, solid, and coarse. Yet it yielded to his Grasp all the same.

The ground rumbled, and a cracking sound punched the air.

Darus broke out of his deep concentration and felt the stabbing

The Last of the Magi

pain in his head subside. He looked for Rikkard. He was laid flat on the ground after being dropped just a couple of feet from the rock wall. The rock wall was shaking from the force that rumbled beneath them. The entire palace was shaking. Perhaps even the whole Grand City.

Before either he or Aurellia could do anything, large boulders of rock dislodged from the wall and fell. Both Darus and Aurellia reacted by trying to Command air between Rikkard and the rocks to soften their fall, but even Aurellia's unspent energy wasn't enough to build a strong enough barrier. The rocks just crashed through.

Rikkard screamed in horror. He threw his arms up as the rocks crashed down and buried him. He disappeared and went quiet under the pile of stone. The last boulder lodged in place at the top of the heap, and the room finally fell into complete silence as the ground became still again.

Darus didn't move. He froze, paralysed by what he just saw. What *he* had just done. His heart was pounding.

Other apprentices appeared at the fringes and crept in to see what was going on. An instructor came racing beside Darus. She looked at him strangely.

'What happened?!' she said.

Darus couldn't bring himself to look at the instructor. He tried to speak. All that came out was a whisper, 'It's Rik.'

'What?'

He roused slightly. 'A-Apprentice Nostrum. Something went wrong and then the wall collapsed. I–I didn't mean for it to happen.'

The instructor looked rapidly between the rocks and Darus. 'Where is Apprentice Nostrum?'

Darus pointed to the rock pile, his hand trembling.

The instructor looked at the rock pile again and then waved over some of the other instructors. She explained the situation and they rushed in to assist with Rikkard's rescue. Very quickly they started to lift the rocks, working their way down. Another instructor was ordered to notify the Arcana Infirmary, and one more was sent to notify Registrar Harroly.

The instructor beside Darus then pulled him firmly by the shoulder and turned him away from the scene. She beckoned for

Aurellia to join them.

'You did this, Apprentice Valivelle?' the instructor's voice was stern and low.

Darus lowered his eyes. *Did I?* The rumbling of the ground had started just as the throbbing in his head reached its worst. And what he had felt through Arcana was new, unlike anything he had experienced before – but none of that was important right now. What had he done to Rik? His stomach churned as he stared back at the pile of stone where he last saw him.

'Apprentice Valivelle!' the instructor scolded.

'I think so,' Darus winced. 'I didn't mean to. I felt something and—'

'Report to the high imperator's office. Apprentice Velyn will accompany you.' As the instructor finished her order, Aurellia reached the top of the hill and nodded to the instructor. 'Apprentice Velyn, you are to escort Apprentice Valivelle to the high imperator's office to give an account of what happened here.'

Aurellia's eyes widened and she paled. Darus understood her reaction. Being summoned to the high imperator's office, as an apprentice no less, could only mean that severe disciplinary measures would be taken. Aurellia walked up to Darus and gently pushed him back towards the doors. He was too numb to do anything other than comply.

His head was spinning. He had struck down another enforcer. And not just any enforcer. Rik. The thought of hurting him was a nightmare made true – making it happen was infinitely worse. As he and Aurellia moved out of view of the rock pile, he thought ahead to the high imperator. What punishment would she issue him, to add to the guilt and stunned anguish already brewing within.

Chapter 9

Arcane Discipline

Registrar Harroly was prepared for them. She stepped out from the reception counter as soon as they passed into the enforcer offices and then escorted them the rest of the way.

This was the first time Darus had ever been beyond the reception. Only graduated enforcers could come and go through these corridors freely, and it was normally only senior enforcers who had cause to do so. Harroly took them down to the end of a very long corridor, lined with name-plated white doors on either side. A few of the names were familiar, some being the instructors and lecturers, and others were named in reports circulated in local news fliers to celebrate those who served the Grand City faithfully.

As they came closer to the larger black door at the end, Darus's heart raced even faster. He could hear it in his ears. He made the mistake of looking away from the impending doom awaiting him at the end of the corridor and instead he spotted some copperplate lettering on one of the offices to his side. He saw it long enough to read the name 'Valivelle'. There would be a few of those, so he kept his eyes forward instead. Even with his gaze averted, he felt those nameplates judging him.

Harroly reached the door engraved with the words 'High Imperator Ulyria Mantleshawn'. She pushed it open without knocking.

The high imperator's office was pristinely clean. Beautiful paintings of serene landscapes hung upon the walls, and windows on the far wall looked out over the sea to the east. The High Imperator was sat behind an impractically large desk, to the left of the door. The windows presented the High Imperator with quite the scenic vista from her seat, yet she was studiously reviewing a document when they entered.

'Good afternoon, Harroly,' she said without looking up. She pointed the end of her pen towards a cabinet just inside the door. 'I have prepared some instructions to be delivered to—'

'Very good, High Imperator,' Harroly interrupted, 'I will take care of those.'

High Imperator Mantleshawn looked up and noticed them.

'Apprentices Valivelle and Velyn are here from the training session.'

The high imperator placed her pen neatly in front of her papers, perfectly parallel to the pile's top edge. 'I knew I sensed something peculiar. Very well, take a seat.'

There was only one seat as they approached the desk, but Harroly managed to glide across the room to pull a spare chair over before they could complete their few steps. The high imperator watched on, with a smile on her face and her arms folded across the desk. She eyed them up as Darus took the furthest seat and left the nearest for Aurellia.

Darus had never been this close to the high imperator before. Her appearance confused him. Though her facial features were soft and pleasant to look at, the crow's feet against her eyes, prominent scar against her temple and her short white hair gave her an intimidating edge.

'The combat training session was meant to be a simple affair. Just a routine top-up of the skills that graduand apprentices such as yourselves would be familiar with already. And yet, even from here I felt an unusual stirring of Arcana. What happened?'

Darus felt glued to his seat. He kept his gaze mostly to the desk but briefly made eye contact with the high imperator to try and be respectful. Words, however, eluded him.

The high imperator looked to Aurellia instead, who was much less unnerved by their leader's presence.

'Apprentice Valivelle and Apprentice Nostrum were using Arcana to practise offensive and defensive techniques, as instructed. I was assigned the role of observer at the time.'

The high imperator nodded. She pulled a blank sheet of paper to the top of her pile and started making notes. 'Apprentice... Velyn, was it?'

'Yes, Aurellia Velyn.'

'Very well – what did you observe?'

The Last of the Magi

'I observed Apprentice Valivelle using Command and Grasping techniques to defend against Apprentice Nostrum's assaults. Apprentice Nostrum used a scattergun approach to try and throw Apprentice Valivelle off-balance and followed this with a powerful blast of Arcane wind as a direct attack. Apprentice Valivelle defended himself effectively, but that final attack was particularly potent, and it was while defending against this strike that...' Aurellia paused and looked to Darus.

Darus felt beyond nauseous at this point, and he knew that he had turned even more pale than usual. He stared at the high imperator's pen as she tapped the tip to her page. Darus looked to Aurellia for just a moment, hoping his terrified expression would be enough for her to continue speaking for him.

'I'm not entirely sure what happened next, it's a bit of a blur. But I believe Apprentice Valivelle somehow caused a rock wall to collapse onto Apprentice Nostrum.'

The pen scratching stopped abruptly, and the high imperator read back over what she had written. Her forehead and nose wrinkled as she stared at the words.

'A rock wall was collapsed?' she asked.

'Yes.'

She pointed at a line earlier in her notes. 'How did the Commanding or Grasping of Arcane wind lead to a rockfall?'

'I'm not sure,' said Aurellia. 'The Arcane wind dissipated after it hit into Apprentice Nostrum. But then the room started to shake, and I believe the tremor dislodged the rock wall.'

The high imperator hummed with agreement. 'I thought I felt a slight tremor from here – I wrongly assumed I was imagining it. Did you sense any further use of Arcana from where you were stood, Apprentice Velyn?'

Aurellia paused for a moment and searched the ceiling as she thought. 'No, I don't think so. It all happened very quickly. As soon as I realised Apprentice Nostrum was in danger my attention went to him.'

The high imperator put her pen back down and smiled gently at Aurellia. 'Thank you for your assistance. That will be all, Apprentice Velyn. Please attend at the Arcana Infirmary and wait for a report on Apprentice Nostrum's condition. Bring it to Registrar Harroly once it's ready and then you are dismissed for the evening.'

Aurellia stood and bowed to the high imperator. She put a hand on Darus's shoulder as she left.

The high imperator's smile dropped. She sucked in a deep breath and blew it out forcefully through her nose.

'Apprentice Valivelle,' she said, sternly. Darus lifted his head and met the high imperator's gaze. 'You felt more than just the tremor in the ground, didn't you?'

Darus nodded slowly. 'Yes, I did.

'Your perception of the Arcane broadened. You felt your Deep Thought state reach out to an element you had not felt before. Does that sound right?'

Darus felt less nervous, like he was being reassured. 'Yes, I think so. The attack Apprentice Nostrum used was very powerful, so I had to concentrate more than normal to defend myself. My head started to ache as I fought back, and in the moments before it all went wrong I felt something different.'

The high imperator sat back in her chair and rubbed her chin with her fingertips. 'You felt the earth beneath your feet, just as you would feel the air drifting around you?'

Darus nodded, but his brow furrowed as if the ache in his head had crept back in. His recollection of memories was often vivid like that.

'And you tapped into that power and unleashed a devastating, life-endangering assault upon another apprentice?'

His stomach churned again. He nodded and sunk into his seat, choosing to look down into his hands rather than maintain eye contact.

'This is a serious matter. The chancellor will need to be informed.'

Those words took Darus from light nausea to full sickening dizziness. He thought the room was spinning. Being summoned before the high imperator was anxiety-provoking enough. Being brought before the chancellor would be nothing short of terrifying.

The high imperator leaned forward again, planting her elbows on the table. 'Such a display of destructive, raw Arcane power.' The

The Last of the Magi

high imperator tutted and then inhaled sharply as she shook her head. 'I should have known, what with *your* heritage.'

Darus couldn't speak. The walls were closing in around him. His eyes wouldn't focus. The high imperator's demeanour seemed to chop and change at every word. One moment he felt comforted and re-assured, and the next he feared she might summon enforcers to arrest him for crimes committed against the Grand City.

'You should be congratulated,' she said.

Again, Darus lifted his head, his expression one of pure bewilderment.

'With this discovery, you may have broadened our understanding of Arcana. Your newfound gifts will be an asset to the Grand City, and to all enforcers in time. Your family will be pleased, *Enforcer* Valivelle.'

Chapter 10

Building Foundations

Four days had passed already. Four days of the same walls, the same bed, and the same smog-filled air. Four days of the same gluttonous meals and night after night of drinking ale and wine in Traykin's small study.

There was a time, long ago, when Tharian would have considered this normal. Traykin's Bazaar had been like a second home to him and his guardian – Greycloak – during their nomadic travels across Asturia. They only stayed for a few days at a time, yet Traykin always made it quite the occasion.

But this time the stay felt uncomfortably long.

Despite spending close to a decade in Feralland, Tharian hadn't settled there either. There were a few Awoken settlements where he would stay from time-to-time, but he didn't give himself the luxury of stopping long enough in any one of them to lay down any firm roots. He was too busy, too focused, and determined to discover a counter to Arcana. And that kept him moving. Even when he made progress in that goal, he set off to explore it further elsewhere. Greycloak had instilled that nomadic behaviour in him at an early age. It kept him safe.

This situation was different. There were good reasons for him to stay still now. He and Traykin needed time to think and gather intelligence. They had a Magi to find, and an uprising against the Grand City to plan.

Tharian had risen early that morning, as he often did. He left the almost empty guest bedroom – possibly the nearest thing to a 'normal looking' room in the whole bazaar – and meandered downstairs to the kitchen. Frigg was already there doing his morning duties. He tended to the many dirty plates, jugs, and tankards that Traykin had bulldozed through the previous night.

Tharian felt a bit guilty. He'd contributed to that mess. Not as much as Traykin had, but still.

The Last of the Magi

'G-good morning, Master Tharian,' said Frigg. His childhood stutter was almost completely gone. He still sounded quite frail, but the confidence in his voice had grown greatly in recent years.

'Sorry about the mess,' Tharian replied.

Frigg turned a freshly washed tankard upside down beside the sink and moved over to some plates covered with cloches. He picked one up and lifted the covering, presenting Tharian with a plate of bread and sliced meats. 'Do not w-worry, Master Tharian. It is my duty to serve Master Traykin and his guests.'

'Thank you. I hope he's treating you well. He wouldn't cope without you.' Tharian took the plate and his stomach growled as the scent of salted meat hit his nostrils.

Frigg laughed and then forced himself to stop. He glanced up at the ceiling nervously. Apparently, he still feared waking Traykin prematurely. The rotund collector was often grouchy and irritable in the morning. 'Master Traykin's words are s-sometimes harsh, but he teaches me and pays me for my work. It's a f-far better life than living out there.'

His words were genuine enough. Tharian had seen the slums of the Trade Quarters – those hovels and overcrowded houses hidden down the alleys off each of the main roads – they were no place for a child to grow up. Especially one as frail and sickly as Frigg had been.

Tharian thanked Frigg again and left him to his work. He took his breakfast to Traykin's study and pulled up a seat at the long table that covered the back wall. The table was covered with notes, maps and drawings. The culmination of their long days and nights of work.

A kitchen knife was stabbed into the corner of a large piece of parchment featuring a detailed drawing of the Grand City. Tharian reached over and plucked the knife from the table and used it to cut a corner from the dried bread on his plate.

It crunched loudly between his teeth.

What is this? Another sheet caught Tharian's eye, one he was certain hadn't been there before he went to bed. He pulled it closer. *A letter?*

The parchment was not so much a letter, rather a page of

scrawls, but it bore the claw marks of a kurigaw raven – the most reliable messenger birds in the country. Tharian's curiosity took over and he read it:

'The south-easterly wind did blow many things to Asturia. Some old, some new. Salvation is upon the horizon at long last – but upon the rubble of one empire, another shall always take root.

Of all the songs sung in our lands, none tell tale of a lost Magi. That search will bring only sadness for the wayward son.'

He knew the handwriting, and he recognised the cryptic wording too.

The sound of Traykin's weighty footsteps thundered into the room from behind.

'*He* wrote this, didn't he?' said Tharian. He flailed the letter over his shoulder so Traykin could see.

'That's right. You didn't think I would keep the old goat in the dark about your return, did you?' Traykin snatched the letter. His hot, booze-laden breath lapped against the back of Tharian's neck, making him shiver. 'You can do this wandering renegade thing for as long as you like, lad, but the old man deserves to know you're still living and breathing.'

Wandering renegade? Tharian sighed heavily and leaned over the table. 'He always knows things before the rest of us. I bet he knew I was here even before I did.'

Traykin chuckled and took a seat further down the table. His stomach was close to bursting out of his stained grey shirt and multicoloured waistcoat. He tugged at his long black beard a few times. 'The old boy cares for you like a son, even if he doesn't have the capacity to express it. You know that.'

Tharian paused. He'd spent years as an orphaned child of Midhaven travelling under the wing of that old man. Greycloak was old and eccentric even when Tharian was a boy, and even though his looks hadn't changed much over the years, his mind had suffered from the decays of time.

Tharian smirked and pointed the kitchen knife at Traykin, making mocking jabbing motions, 'you've been checking up on

The Last of the Magi

him, haven't you? You really are going soft.'

Traykin's iconic laugh shook the room. 'Of course I've been bloody checking on him! You're the only family he's got. When you decided to wander off for a decade, someone had to make sure he was still looking after himself. I've known a few hermit-types like him, but he's the only one I've ever seen adopt a helpless orphan. He deserves some respect for that, lad.' Traykin reached over and grabbed a slice of meat from Tharian's plate – just as he finished carving it – and shoved it straight into his mouth.

'I never said he didn't,' Tharian protested.

Traykin grunted and then raised a brow at him. 'Maybe not with words, but I bet you're not in any hurry to see him!'

Tharian planted the knife back into the map of the Grand City. 'We can talk about that later. We've got work to do.'

'Point taken…' Traykin sighed. 'Well, you've seen what Greycloak thinks about it now, even he thinks your Magi-hunt is a dead duck.'

Tharian shook his head. 'I didn't spend years searching for this lead just for it to be shot down at the first hurdle.' He felt a spark of anger flare up in him, quite unexpectedly, but only briefly. 'We can't just sit around and do nothing!'

'Relax, lad.'

Tharian took a breath. This was the fruit of his labours over the last ten years. He was more invested in this than he realised.

'I am not saying give it up. I'm simply suggesting that we spread our bets. Magi or no Magi, we're not going to get far with just the two of us. We need allies capable of giving the Elheim a hard time. The more muscle we have behind us, the more energy we can put into searching for this Magi of yours. If we don't find one, well… maybe we'll have enough allies to still do something.'

Traykin was right. Magi or no Magi, they needed to be prepared for anything. This uprising could start a war with the Elheim. A war where their enemy had command of magic and they had little to counter it.

Finding the Magi and using their ability to seal away that magic was central to their success, but if they had no reinforcements to support them against hundreds of enforcers, they would be serving that Magi a death sentence. Tharian accepted that they needed allies as a priority.

Over the last few nights, they had pooled together lists of people and resources that might be able to assist with tracking down the Magi. Most had already been crossed off the list as either being too unreliable, risky, or expensive. It was looking increasingly likely that Tharian would have to search for the Magi himself at some point.

As for allies, they needed more than just sympathetic traders, or politicians from the Outer Counties. They needed power and influence at their backs.

Tharian turned over one of the pages with crossed-out names on it. 'So, we need to think big then – no back-alley resistance group is going to be enough for this. Who else can we try?'

'I hate to say it – I really do – but I think we need to get you an audience with the coinsmen.'

Tharian's eyes widened. 'The coinsmen? That's quite a leap.'

'I'm aware. But we've spent days on this already. We can't trust my business associates – they might sell us out at the first whiff of an opportunity for personal gain. In fact, I'd expect them to. I might even be disappointed if they didn't!' he chuckled. 'If we look lower than that, we run the risk of being conned, ratted out, or worse. If we only go a bit higher, I guarantee some smart-arse will have no problem handing us over to the city guard to win some political favour with the coinsman of their quarter. That leaves only one other place to look – the top.'

Tharian nodded, but he was still not fully convinced. 'They won't just hand us over to the Grand City?'

'Like hell they would. The last thing they want is to be seen doing the Elheim a favour. And if they don't like what we're doing, the worst they can do is refuse to help and pretend we never suggested it. Can't see them locking us up – we wouldn't have committed any crime. Nothing ventured, nothing gained.'

Tharian bowed his head. 'But that's still quite the task. It might be the safest bet, but we can't just go knocking on their doors and asking the coinsmen to meet with us, can we?'

'To meet with *you,* lad.' Traykin said curtly, correcting him.

The Last of the Magi

'I'm happy to support this all the way, but if the coinsmen think it's my idea they'll get suspicious about my motives. I've got a reputation for scheming. Consider me your shadow investor.'

'Alright, fine – how do we get them to meet with me then? I'm hardly a diplomat.'

Traykin snorted. 'Now there's an understatement.' He started scribbling some notes onto the nearest blank parchment he could find, despite the ring of ale stained into it. 'I'll deal with the coinsman for this quarter. And I'm owed a few favours over in the Artisan Quarter, so I'll weed out Coinswoman Keene one way or another.' He then grumbled. *'It'll probably still cost me.'*

Tharian nodded with approval. 'So that leaves me with the Market Quarter and the Quarter of War. Suddenly this seems much more manageable.

'Coinsman Velioth will be a breeze. Get yourself to the morning markets, first thing tomorrow. Their coinsman likes to get there early at the start of a new week to see the latest produce on offer for himself. Of all the coinsmen, he's the youngest and most eager, so I wager he'll be quite eager to support a Coinsmeet. He's an easy sell. If you offer him anything which might benefit the Market Quarter, his eyes will light up like diamonds.'

It sounded simple enough. Tharian wasn't a trader, but he had watched Traykin run his business for long enough to have some ideas on how to appeal to a coinsman's commercial interests, assuming of course those interests hadn't changed much over the last decade.

Traykin's smile and excitable tone then drooped. He started tugging at his beard anxiously. 'The Quarter of War will be the hardest to deal with.'

Tharian scowled. Surely the coinsman tasked with defending the Trade Quarters would be keen to eliminate the biggest threat to all Asturia? 'Why do you say that?' he asked.

'Their coinswoman is good at her job – perhaps too good. I've never met a woman that can bring a fight to an end as quickly as she can, whether by her words or her spear. You can guarantee she'll maintain peace and order in the Trade Quarters at all costs. If the Elheim were to cause a real and imminent threat to us, she would have lots to say about that. But until that happens, she won't want to poke the beast.'

'What do we do with her then? Do we need to convince her that this is a fight without risk, or do we need the Elheim knocking at the gates for her to act?'

Traykin carried on pulling at his beard. 'I don't know. Let me think on it. The biggest issue is securing a meeting with the bloody woman. When she isn't training her elite guards or managing the city guard, she is either presiding over criminal tribunals or planning her next fighting tourney in the Crucible.'

Tharian sat back. 'Take your time. I'll get started on the Market Quarter's coinsman in the meantime – what was his name again?'

'Erilen Velioth. He'll stick out in a crowd; I can promise that.'

'Helpful.'

Traykin winked, but before he could say anything more, Frigg hobbled in with a tray of rattling mugs and a large pot of fresh tea.

'Y-your tea, sir.' He said, trying diligently to bow his head without losing balance.

Traykin eyed the tray as it was placed between them both. He lifted the pot of tea by its oddly shaped handle and seemed satisfied by its weight. He then brought the spout close to his nose and a gluttonous smirk crept over his lips. He gestured the pot towards Tharian.

Tharian shook his head and then stood. He had work to do. 'I'll go and scout out the Market Quarter – the more I know about the quarter and Coinsman Velioth the better.

'Suit yourself! Take a seat, Frigg. The lad has places to be, and so do we. Get some of this down you before we get customers.'

Frigg obliged, ensuring he had first poured his master a drink before seeing to his own.

Tharian went to the door that led to the shopfloor. He looked back at Traykin and Frigg. Despite his eccentricity, and the sternness of his words at times, Tharian never let he or Frigg go without. He had always been that way, and Tharian was glad that his old friend hadn't lost that altruism over the years.

As Traykin and Frigg started pouring over the documents scattered across Traykin's table, Tharian slipped away.

The Last of the Magi

***

'No licence means no work. Now stop wasting my time.'

The soot-covered blacksmith plunged a sword into a bucket of cold water as he shooed Marla away with his spare hand. The water sizzled and hissed as it filled the workshop with steam.

Marla kept her eyes on the weapon, trying to catch a glimpse of the workmanship. In the few seconds that she saw it moving from anvil to bucket she could tell by its shape and indentations that this was a weapon of intricate design. No common shortsword or cutlass.

'I promise you,' she pleaded. 'I can make you good money. My father taught me everything there is to know about smithing.'

This was the second blacksmith on the Artisan Quarter main road to turn her away today, and the seventh since she arrived in the city. After the third rejection, she resorted to looking for any tradesman that dealt in metalwork, armour, or weaponry – even on a second-hand basis. By this point she had become quite rehearsed with her script. The first few enquiries made her painfully aware that these traders were single-mindedly interested in coin above all else.

The blacksmith pulled the weapon out of the bucket and laid it into a leather casing on the bench behind him. He wrapped it up loosely, and quickly, before Marla could see any more of it.

'Look, lass.' He paused to cough heavily into his arm. 'You could be the greatest iron-melder and it would do no good unless you've a licence to trade as an artisan. You're better off in the Quarter of War – they always need more hands.'

She'd heard that line too many times already, but she held on to Tharian's warning about avoiding the Quarter of War. She wasn't ready to give in. Not yet. Not until she had to.

'Then tell me how to get a licence,' she said, forcefully.

He waved her away and then walked around his anvil and back to his workbench to begin work on his next consignment.

'Please.' The force in her voice was already gone. She had almost reached the end of the main road and she feared this was the last of the reputable smiths along the way.

'Out!' he shouted. He met her eyes; his hand was gripped tightly around a hammer and the veins in his wrist pulsed.

She backed away a few steps, but then considered one more try. *No. this just isn't going to work. This isn't the Outer Counties*, she told herself.

Marla stepped back until she reached the heavy drapes of plastic that fell over the threshold between the workroom and the blacksmith's shop. She turned on her heels and pushed the plastic covering away. Another defeat.

The shop on the other side was much cooler and lighter than the workroom, and she felt the hairs on her arms rise from the sheer change in temperature. It was an uncomfortable sensation; she preferred being amongst the heat, steam, and soot.

The shop taunted her. Magnificent pieces of metalwork adorned all the display racks. There were swords, knives, spears, shields and plated armours of all different shapes and styles. None of them were simple. Each one unique or stocked in small numbers. The other blacksmithing shops were similar, promoting wares of excellent quality, but this one stood out a mile from the others. Some of the pieces had gemstones incorporated into the metal, or the metal itself had been artificially coloured somehow. Like Tharian's blade, but without the runic markings.

A pang of embarrassment settled in as she examined them. She had been claiming to know everything there was to know about blacksmithing. These displays told her otherwise.

It was hard to be mad at the blacksmith's rude reception when she could see the skill and effort that went into his craft. Perhaps he was entitled to be grouchy when he worked this hard? Her father had never been one to raise his voice, or even show the slightest sign of a temper, but then again, he was never under pressure to create anything like *this*.

Marla reached the door that led back to the street. She admired a suit of gold-hued armour mounted upon a mannequin beside her. She brushed her hand along it. It was cold to the touch, and she couldn't feel even one kink or bend in its shape that was out of place. Every part of its design was intentional and flawlessly executed.

She sighed heavily as her fingertips slipped off the bottom of the breastplate. *What now?*

'I'm sorry about him, my dear,' said a voice from behind.

Marla startled. She looked back to see a short woman sat behind the cashier desk. She had grey hair poking out from under a moss-green, hand-stitched cotton hat that covered most of her head.

'He worked very hard for his licence,' she continued, 'so he can be a little defensive about having another pair of hands behind the curtain.' She pointed a thumb to the plastic sheeting and chuckled. 'The pressures of being an artisan can take their toll on a man's ego.'

The woman smiled and then resumed counting coins across the surface of the counter.

'I hope I haven't caused any offence,' Marla said.

'Not at all, sweet girl. Pull up that stool and take a seat.' She pointed to a stool over by the wall.

Marla did as she was told.

'So, you want to be a smith?' continued the woman, still smiling kindly.

'I already am one,' Marla replied.

The woman's eyes widened. She leaned over the counter and looked her up and down.

Marla blushed a little. How did she look? She hadn't thought to make any special effort with her appearance before heading out down the main street that morning. Pretty dresses and formal suits were not her style – the only clothes she owned were plain shirts, overalls, and simple trousers, like what she was wearing now. They were comfortable. She could work in them.

The woman made an amused sound. 'By the looks of it you've had a different upbringing to most young women – I hope you don't mind me saying.'

Marla shook her head, smirking. 'It's alright. You're not wrong. I've been working in my father's workshop for as long as I can remember.'

'How long have you been in the Quarters?'

'A few days. I reckon I'll be leaving tomorrow unless I can find work.'

'I see...' The woman looked to the plastic curtain. Then she turned back to Marla. 'Wait here a moment.' She scooped her coins into a purse and closed it tight. She hopped off her chair and scurried through to the workshop.

While Marla was alone, she thought about the last few days in the Trade Quarters. The reality of her situation was sinking in. She was getting dangerously low on money – having brought with her everything she had saved over the last few years. The cheapest inn room she'd found in the Artisan Quarter still cost well over twice that of the most luxurious rooms available in the Outer Counties. If she stayed much longer, she would have no money left. And this was her last clean change of clothes.

The plastic curtain flapped open, and the blacksmith stomped into his showroom, just as Marla was looking over the state of herself. She sheepishly looked up at him, and he glared back, shook his head, and then left again.

A heated conversation then rattled through the walls.

Marla ran her fingertips along the edge of the counter as she waited. Although she couldn't make out their words, she knew whatever got them riled up must have been to do with her – and that made her feel *very* uncomfortable. She considered sneaking out and cutting her losses before she ended up in the middle of their argument.

She waited a bit longer, until the awkwardness became unbearable, and then she turned on her stool to leave.

Just as she lifted from the seat, the woman came bustling back into the room carrying a tray laden with glasses of a cloudy drink. She apologised profusely for keeping Marla waiting as she laid the tray on the counter and passed a glass to Marla, insisting that she try it.

'Iced herb-lemon,' she said. 'It's made by my friend across the road. Made fresh today, you won't have tasted anything like it.' She seemed excited and energetic.

Marla thanked her but eyed her curiously. She took the glass and brought it slowly to her lips while trying to figure out what was happening. However, that curiosity was sapped away as the icy-cold

The Last of the Magi

sensation of the drink hit her senses. It had a powerful lemon flavour, but it was not as sharp as she had expected. There was something else that tempered the taste, to keep it fresh and light without that typical flash of sensory overload that lemon often carried with it. It was delicious. She quickly took another sip to try it again. She hadn't imagined it. It was just as delicious the second time.

The woman clapped her hands together. 'You like it!' She took a sip from her own glass and then held the chilled glass between her hands. 'So why have you come all this way looking for work – do you no longer enjoy the fresh air and calm living of County Bryn?'

Marla paused with the glass once again to her lips. She put the drink down and stumbled over her words for a moment. *Bryn? How did she know?*

While she fumbled to respond, the woman chuckled. Marla realised her confusion must have been painted all over her face.

'Our families were from County Dellow originally. I recognise the accent of a Bryn-girl anywhere.'

Marla's cheeks warmed. She hadn't really thought to listen to the way people spoke out here. Did her voice really point to her home county so bluntly?

The woman continued. 'You'll notice it the more time you spend here,' The people of the Quarters do not speak as softly or as calmly as those from the Counties.'

Now that her attention was drawn to accents, she started to notice the differences in the woman's voice. Longer words came out in a gentle and soft sound, that stretched the vowels, but some of her words came out in sharp, quick beats. Part Counties, part Quarters, she assumed.

'I will have to listen more carefully,' said Marla. She then remembered the initial question, asking why she was in the Quarters. 'I had to leave Bryn. The work was getting stale – my father trained me for more than that that – and then the Elheim came to visit.'

The woman froze and her face paled at the mention of the Elheim. She put down her glass. 'What did they do?'

'They burnt Brynfall to the ground because the alderman refused to pay the Arcane Tax.'

The woman was speechless for a moment. Her mouth fell open. 'Oh, my sweet child, I'm so sorry. Was anyone hurt?'

'The alderman was killed, and they killed some of the county guard too. They didn't hurt the rest of us. Some of the kids and older residents were a bit shaken, but everyone else got out without injury.'

'Thank the Divine the rest of you are alright,' the woman said, glancing up to the ceiling briefly. 'What about your homes?'

'Gone. Father's workshop was burnt down too. The Elheim made us walk to Brynwell after they were finished. Thankfully the people there had already started pulling stuff together to look after us.' Marla sighed heavily. 'I could have stayed there, but it wouldn't have felt right. I want a life where I can do more than just arm the county guard and repair the metalwork that gets broken. I want a life that isn't going to collapse at the sight of an enforcer.'

The woman nodded and smiled knowingly. 'I understand. My husband felt the same living in County Dallow. We moved here shortly after marrying. We were just like you when we arrived, and we both had to get separate jobs until the coinswoman finally granted him a licence to set up this shop.'

'Your husband mentioned having a licence. I didn't realise that things worked like that here. How do I get one?'

The woman gave her a sympathetic look. 'It takes a long time. Earning the right to call yourself an artisan is a real labour.'

Marla slumped on the stool. That was a kind way of saying she wouldn't be getting one in a hurry. She couldn't barely afford one more night in the Quarters. She'd failed at the first hurdle. The prospect of trudging down the Quarter of War and joining one of the mass-production blacksmiths was the only realistic option left.

The woman reached over the counter and gently squeezed Marla's wrist. 'I know this isn't what you're looking for, but the fact of the matter is we do need an extra pair of hands around here. Brayne won't admit it, but he needs to take some time away from the furnace. He isn't getting any younger. As he gets slower, and the orders keep coming in, soon he will realise that he can't do this alone. He will need someone who knows his—' the woman paused

The Last of the Magi

and gave Marla a deliberate look '—or *her* way around an anvil.'

Marla perked up. Was she suggesting what it sounded like?

'He's not quite ready to accept that yet, though. For now, an extra pair of hands around the shop and in the back room is all he'll tolerate. If you can help us, we can pay you for your work. We cannot offer much in terms of payment, but we can offer a room for you to stay in here. Eventually an opportunity to step up to the anvil will present itself. Then you can prove yourself to the old grump.'

Many thoughts rushed through Marla's mind. She looked towards Brayne's workshop. She stared where she knew the furnace and anvil were positioned, behind the plastic coverings. This was not a blacksmithing job, but it was *a* job in a blacksmithing shop. If she took it, she could stay in the Quarters. And that set her on the path she wanted to be on.

Marla beamed from ear to ear. 'Please, that would be amazing. I'll do anything you need; you won't regret it.'

The woman squeezed Marla's wrist again and then added her other hand to the grip. 'Brilliant. This is such good news for us. I thank the Divine for sending you to us, just when we needed you.' After one final squeeze, she released Marla's wrist. 'Come upstairs with me, I'll show you the room.'

I can't believe my luck, Marla thought.

The woman ushered Marla to follow her as she scurried through the workshop, picking up her pace to get through the heat and the smoke of that place. Marla averted her eyes from the blacksmith as she went through, hoping not to cause him any further irritation. If the argument she heard through the walls was anything to go by, he was not too pleased that she was still in the building.

At the far end of the workshop there was another doorway with plastic sheeting that then led into a cosy and quaintly decorated home. The woman led Marla down a hallway that went past the front door, to the foot of the stairs. As Marla started up the stairs, she briefly noticed a small kitchen area off to her right, with a small round table positioned in the middle with three chairs.

Marla reached the upstairs landing. There were three rooms that branched off. The first door was open and led to a washroom, the next door on the left was closed and the woman led her to the third and final door which was furthest from the stairs. She pushed the door open with enthusiasm.

The bedroom within had a slanted ceiling with a large window built into it that looked out over the main street below. The natural light would have illuminated the room were it not for the smog-filled sky that dulled its brightness. The scraps of light that managed to fight through that smog seemed grey and sickly.

A small bed, laden with a light pink bedsheet was pushed against the far corner, set beside a dressing table and makeshift wooden wardrobe. The dressing table held a small vase which held a single, vibrant purple flower.

As Marla stepped in properly, she found her gaze captured by that flower. It was the most colourful living thing she'd seen in the Trade Quarters over the last few days. In the Outer Counties, such a sight was commonplace, but here it most certainly was not. Suddenly the rest of the room seemed so dull and lifeless in comparison, despite the effort gone into dressing the room with light colours and furnishings.

Marla turned around a few times in the space. She noticed that the flower was the only thing in the room not coated in a thin film of dust.

The woman pulled a leather strip from her apron pocket and slapped it haphazardly across the furniture, throwing dust into the air that caught the light. 'Sorry for the mess. This room hasn't been used for a while.' She hobbled over to the flower and teased at its petals with the back of her fingers. Her hand paused against the vase for a moment and then she pulled away from it, sniffing hard as she turned back to Marla. 'What do you think?'

'It's perfect, thank you. I'll help as much as I can, it's the least I can do.'

The woman smiled warmly and then went to leave the room. She gripped the door handle and stood in the doorway. 'Please, get comfortable. I'll bring you some hot water so you can clean up and then we can discuss everything properly over dinner. I will just need to have a quick word with Brayne.'

'Thank you. Are you sure he'll be ok with this?'

'He will be. Just give him time.' The woman pulled the door as

The Last of the Magi

she slipped through it but poked her head back before it closed. 'He tends to… raise his voice. It's probably best that you stay in here for now.'

Marla laughed nervously as the woman disappeared. *Yes, I've heard.* She nodded and then sat down on the bed, dropping her bags into a heap on the floor.

This is it, Marla thought. She loosened the leather straps on her wrists and ankles, which she had worn as rudimentary armour pieces while she travelled around. A smell of trapped sweat reeked out as she did. She threw them across the room to get them away. She didn't expect someone to try and mug her in broad daylight, but after the experience on her first day in the city she decided not to take any chances.

I have a room, and a job. It's a start. Marla looked to the vase and then back to the bedroom door. *And the landlady is sweet enough.*

She suddenly realised she didn't know the kind woman's name.

Marla laughed nervously again. She felt exhausted. She'd come so close to giving up on her dreams of a city life, only for a lifeline to be thrown her way at the last moment. The Trade Quarters was now her home for the foreseeable future. She wouldn't need to trudge home to her father in County Bryn just yet.

She tried not to worry too much about him. Though he let her leave with his blessing, that didn't make it an easy move to make. He was getting old and tired from years behind the anvil. His hands had become shaky with the years, and he couldn't handle hammering steel for long before aches in his joints would take hold.

She had looked after him. She'd lightened the burden of his work for the last few years, gladly and without grudge. It was hard to turn away and leave him there, to pursue her own aspirations, but he was surrounded by friends and good people in Brynwell. They would look after him now, better than she could, and he could retire at last. Brynwell was the best place to be at his age.

She would go back to see him soon, to tell him stories of her work with the artisans. She would make him proud. For now, she had to earn her keep.

Marla crossed the room and unlocked the large window, opening it slightly. She took a deep breath of the smoggy air, but she didn't cough as it hit her lungs. The air may have been thick with steam and dust, but it was nothing compared to the thick black coal-fumes that puffed from a smith's furnace. Her lungs had handled far worse than this over the years.

The unnatural chemicals in the air apparently didn't scare off all wildlife from the city, as a black bird landed on the window frame and twisted its head to glare its amber eye at Marla. It could have been a kurigaw raven – she wasn't great with identifying birds. It looked about the room, stepped up and down the window-frame and then flew away again. She assumed it was looking for shelter from the smog but didn't like what it saw.

Marla laughed. She stayed there at the window for a time, looking out over the parts of the Trade Quarters she could see from her new bedroom window. There was so much for her to explore, and a new chapter of her life to start.

Chapter 11

Friends of the Coin

The Market Quarter had the widest main road of all the four quarters. It was clear to see why. The wide berth was needed to accommodate not only the sprawling market stalls but the many carriages and wagons weaving in and out of the Quarter. It was the best time of year for crop yield in the Counties, so those markets took up a near-permanent tenancy in the road with the opportunistic merchants making the most of the heavier footfall.

Tharian hit the market early, as Traykin suggested. He'd spotted Coinsman Velioth weaving between a few of the market stalls very quickly. The younger coinsman stood out from the crowd with his expensive-looking longcoat billowing around him, dyed the same colour as red wine. The guard escort following closely in his footsteps gave him away too. The coinsman took a particular interest in the section of the market where the colourful fresh fruits were arranged.

Tharian followed the energetic coinsman from a distance, though the crowds didn't part and give him space like they did for the coinsman. He had already tried to approach Velioth directly, but the guards pushed him back.

Instead, Tharian was forced to address the coinsman's personal aide, a wizened old man with a long white beard, wearing an elegant black suit. He had introduced himself as 'Mors'.

'An audience, with all of the coinsmen?' said Mors. He laced his fingers together in front of his waist. 'The last time the coinsmen all agreed to hold a Coinsmeet was...' he paused '...I cannot actually recall.'

Tharian kept his hood up and tried to avoid making eye contact with the many marketgoers rushing around. Fortunately, they seemed more interested in the coinsman than their discussion. 'Just because it's a rare thing, doesn't mean it should be avoided.'

Mors stroked his beard. 'You speak like a collector,' he said, with slight disdain in his croaky tones. 'What business do you have that could persuade Coinsman Velioth to consent to a Coinsmeet?'

'Liberation,' replied Tharian, abruptly, 'from the oppression of the Grand City.'

'*Liberation?* Hardly a commodity worth its price tag.'

'The Elheim would raze the Quarters to the ground if – *when* – they decide they want a monopoly on all trade in Asturia.'

Mors scoffed. 'We trade with the Grand City. The Kingdom of Ferenir trades with the Grand City. Even the hermitic Lions' Rest trades with the Grand City. Why would the coinsmen upset relations with one of our most affluent customers.'

'Because you know the Quarters could be doing better than this. The Arcane Tax is bleeding the Outer Counties dry, and the people out there can barely afford to pay for the goods you trade. The cities to the east will go the same way once that side of the country collapses under the Grand City's weight. The Quarters may not be formally under the thumb of the Grand City yet, but who was it that demanded the trade ports be closed, that deep-sea travel be criminalised – cutting off trade with the rest of the world? For an *independent* trade city, the Quarters is not as free as it should be.'

'Coinsman Velioth is well aware of this. These points are not novel,' Mors coughed derisively. 'The freedoms you speak of have their price. Believe it or not, the Elheim pay no small sum to enjoy the privileges they enjoy. Much of that sum is paid to our hard-working citizens – particularly our merchants and artisans. There is no shortage of wealth flowing back into the pockets of the Quartersfolk.'

Tharian moved in front of Mors and blocked his path. He drew in close and lowered his voice to a whisper. 'But for how much longer. Money cannot defend you from Arcana. Listen, I don't claim to know more about trading than you and the coinsmen. I am only trying to say that an Asturia free from the Grand City – free from the Elheim – could bring about a new era of opportunity for all.'

Mors whispered in reply, 'I will not lie. The coinsmen are of course concerned about the Elheim, and they know the benefits our people could reap from being rid of their influence. If it is any

The Last of the Magi

consolation to you, though the execution of that ideal would be impossibly difficult, the radical spirit of your proposal has my interest piqued.'

'Mine also,' said a third voice.

The two were startled from their whispering. They turned to see Coinsman Velioth leaning in with a half-eaten apple between his fingertips. The baby-faced, slender man smiled warmly at the two of them and put his hands on their shoulders. He was careful to avoid pressing his apple against Tharian's coat.

'This is quite the conversation to be having without me,' Velioth said with an impish grin. 'Truth be told, the Market Quarter is starting to decline. The balance of back-and-forth trade between us and the rest of Asturia is tilting. They deliver as much as they can for sale to us, but I notice a reduction in the amount purchased in exchange. The Arcane Tax has Asturia's purse-strings in a chokehold. Re-opening trade with Feralland, perhaps even Cestia, would bring a much-needed boost to our economy.'

Velioth surveyed some of the other stalls around them, stacked to the brim with fresh fruit, vegetables, baked goods, and household supplies.

He sighed. 'They do their best with what Asturia can offer.'

'Then let's do something about that – we can bring about change, for the betterment of your people.'

Coinsman Velioth squeezed Tharian's shoulder and squinted at him down his nose, in a way that Tharian felt was mischievous rather than rude. 'It's no secret – to anybody – that the Elheim cause more complications to our way of life with every passing year. But, as Mors here has already mentioned, they are also by far our biggest customer in terms of both quantity and value exchanged. I hate to admit it, but we really would be biting the hand that feeds us.'

Tharian looked at the preened hand on his shoulder. The man's fingernails were all perfectly shaved down to equal length and were without blemishes or any sign of dirt. The level of attention he put into his appearance was almost... Elheim. Tharian cocked a brow but forced himself to smile. 'If your current relationship with the Grand City is so sacred, then I suppose my ideas have no place here. I apologise for wasting your time, Coinsman.' Tharian feigned a look of disappointment and shrugged. It was a risky tactic, yet he tried it anyway.

Velioth's grip tightened, and he nudged Mors closer to keep him in the conversation. 'No need to be so defeatist, good sir. I'm not trying to dismiss your ideas, I am as open to enterprising ideas as my schedule will allow, I only say what I say to ensure you have considered the position we are in here.'

'Of course. I have given this a lot of thought. And I will take into account all concerns that you and your fellow coinsmen have.' And that was true. Liberating Asturia from the Elheim had been at the front of his mind for the last decade, and he had spent most of the previous day trying to understand as much as he could about the current affairs of the Trade Quarters.

Tharian wasn't going to let this meeting be fruitless.

Tharian continued. 'I wouldn't interrupt your morning like this without being sure my ideas had some realism to them.' That part was less true. His plan was still only a list of bullet points in his head: obtain allies; find the lost Magi; take down the Elheim and their Arcana. The details would come later.

A smile curled at the edge of the coinsman's lips. 'That's what I like to hear.' Velioth tapped a finger to his mouth, twisting the rest of his fingers to curl his apple away from his face. 'I, for one, see no harm in hearing what you have to say. It's about time I attended my first Coinsmeet. What do you think, Mors?'

'Would you like me to prepare a missive to mark your consent?'

'Yes, that sounds a wonderful idea.' Velioth then gave Tharian a curious look with eyebrows raised high, 'Do remember this though: the consent of a coinsman is only part of the process. Even if you secure all four consents and you get your Coinsmeet, you still must pitch your proposal to the satisfaction of at least three of us. You will need to be as prepared as you can be.'

Tharian nodded respectfully.

Velioth clapped his hands together. 'Well best of luck to you, mister…'

'Tharian.'

'Good luck to you, Tharian. I'll leave you in capable hands while I return to my duties.' He turned on his heels and wandered

The Last of the Magi

back over to the stalls, closely followed by his escort of guards.

Mors cleared his throat and then took a deep breath while fussing with his beard. 'The missive will not take me long to prepare. Procuring the coinsman's attention long enough to gain his signature could however take a matter of days.' With a flourish, Mors pulled out a small notepad and pen from within his jacket. 'Where should I send it once it is sealed?'

'Traykin's Bazaar.'

Mors looked down his nose at Tharian, his eyes wide. 'Traykin. This is for him?'

'No, it's for me. Traykin is an old friend, I'm staying with him for a while.' Tharian suddenly felt that he had made a mistake mentioning Traykin's name. After all, the collector had been quite clear that the coinsmen might become suspicious if they thought he was involved. But he needed an address to give – this was the only one he had to offer. He met Mors's quizzing stare. 'Is that an issue?'

'Certainly not an issue! It's just unexpected, is all. Leave the coinsman's missive to me and I'll have it delivered to Traykin's Bazaar as soon as it is ready. Good luck with rallying the remaining coinsmen, Master Tharian.'

Tharian and Mors shook hands, and then Mors scurried off before his coinsman disappeared in the bustling crowds.

Tharian sighed with relief as he walked towards the central plaza, and away from the crowded markets. The first coinsman had indeed been easy to win over. Traykin wasn't exaggerating. But that was only one small challenge ticked off from a list of many more.

He kept his head down as he escaped the market, reaching the central plaza a short while later.

There was a buzz of activity there too. This was normal. During the height of trading hours, the central plaza was always alive with activity, but this was busier than normal. As Tharian wandered around, the reason for the crowd quickly became clear – a band of musicians had set up a space between two of the founder statues to put on a public performance. Crowds were gathered in a large semi-circle around them.

Tharian walked around that crowd slowly, as one of the musicians began plucking some of the lower notes from his lute. He spoke over it, thanking the crowd for their adulations. He then plucked other notes until he formed a looping rhythm that peaked and troughed in speed. Another musician was sat upon a large box that he kicked with his heel to compliment the strings with percussion. The sound was bold, varied, and strong. Not many high notes slipped into the melody, nor did the percussion seek to control its ever-changing pace.

A third musician stepped forward and called to their audience with his arms raised high. 'And now, ladies and gentlemen, we continue our journey, from south-west now to south-east, to the rolling hills of Ferenir. We bring you *Watchers of the East.*

Tharian recognised the tune as the third musician added high woodwind notes to the melody. The crowd started to murmur, as they must have recognised it too. The music, culture, and history of Ferenir was well known across Asturia. A lot of the fashion trends in the Quarters were inspired by the trends of Ferenir – despite most of the clothes being manufactured within their own walls first. Ferenir was the largest and strongest kingdom of modern times. It was the only other settlement, together with Lions' Rest, to have the resources and manpower to prevent the Grand City from assuming total control of the country by force — for now.

The music wasn't sad, but it bore with it an undertone of sadness for those who knew the city's recent history. The Kingdom of Ferenir was once treated as the unofficial capital of Asturia. It had long been a shining example of how prosperous an independent city state could be, while still sharing that prosperity with its neighbours.

But after the assassination of King Reksar Thorius, and the Elheim's growth in power that followed, even the great Ferenir had been forced into a snarling submission. Because of the dangers posed by the Grand City, the current king had been advised against touring the continent as the incumbent king usually would. This king would not travel to meet the people of Asturia, nor would he play any active role in helping the Outer Counties grow, as Ferenir had done in the past.

Those days were gone, and with it slowly faded the memory of Ferenir's glory. The kingdom, though still powerful and vast, was in a period of conservation, self-interest, and quiet rebellion against the

The Last of the Magi

Grand City.

Tharian had only been to Ferenir twice. Once as an adolescent with his guardian, Greycloak, and then again as an adult shortly before leaving Asturia. Though his visits had been few, he fondly recalled hearing *Watchers of the East* being played there regularly. Its melody was said to have the power to infallibly unite the kingdom's people and inspire all Asturians to achieve their full potential.

The music struck a particular note with Tharian. He shared a common goal with the melody – to unite people. To make Asturia better.

***

Traykin's Bazaar was an absolute assault on the senses. From the purple-dyed wood floor to the multi-cultural, multi-coloured collection of rugs and tapestries that adorned the walls and floors – every inch of the room was covered in Traykin's merchantable items with no rhyme or reason to their arrangement. Anything that wasn't nailed to the floors or walls was for sale, for the right price.

Greycloak had once joked that Traykin would sell the waistcoat on his back if the deal was attractive enough. As Tharian grew older he came to learn that the eccentric collector was not *that* lackadaisical with his possessions. Collectors were a strange group, yet they shared a common mantra. If something was worth collecting, collect it. If not, sell it.

Tharian didn't have the chance to properly examine his friend's wares when he first arrived. He took the opportunity to do so now. He squeezed amongst the closely stacked rows of trinkets, gemstones, and artefacts. Everything was labelled with a price tag, even the display shelving was for sale. He looked over the wares in a bit of a daze, as he found himself reminiscing about his childhood.

Many evenings of his youth had been spent running around this room, ducking under the displays, playing games with Frigg, and impishly re-arranging the shelves while Greycloak sat in the study with Traykin to discuss… whatever it was they had to discuss back then. They were probably just drinking or playing cards as Traykin liked to do with his guests. But it was in this room that Tharian's had first seen an artefact with a history linked to the magics of their world, and it was that experience which sowed the seeds of his interest in magic and magically imbued artefacts. It was just one of the reasons why he took such comfort from having a runeblade at his hip, and why he felt so at home amongst the reclusive Awoken of Feralland. They lived a more symbiotic relationship with their magic, respecting it in the same way that they respected nature.

A ring caught Tharian's eye as he wandered. It was a simple silver band, but it cradled a stunning purple gemstone within its bracket. At first glance, the gemstone seemed nothing more than a rare jewel. On closer inspection, it was clearly much more than that. It was more like a glass casing which held within it a swirling purple cloud that was constantly in motion. This ring looked very similar to one he had taken a liking to during his first ever visit to the bazaar. Perhaps it was the same one. The price tag on it was steep, so it wouldn't have been surprising if it was.

He remembered fondly how Traykin had appeared over his shoulder, seemingly out of nowhere, when he reached for it as a child.

'Be careful with that, lad,' Traykin had said as he grabbed the young Tharian by the wrist. *'Rings like that are filled with all sorts of magical powers. If you drop it, it might explode!'*

His younger self had grabbed the ring tightly and held it close to his face to look deep into the gemstone. *'I want to see. How does it come out?'*

Traykin laughed at the innocent child, with that deep and earthy laugh that hadn't changed over the years. *'Only the owner of that ring knows how to do that.'*

'Where is he?'

'She! This ring belongs to an Enchantress from the northern continent. She is far, far away from here.'

'How did you get it?'.

Traykin had laughed again and tapped a finger against his long, bulbous nose, before slapping Tharian on the back and disappearing back into his study without another word.

The Last of the Magi

Enchanters.

Barely anyone talked about them. In fact, he heard so little of their kind since his childhood that for many years he assumed they were just a thing of legend. But now, having experienced a bit more of the world, he knew that most legends had some truth to them. Enchanters were said to be the only ones capable of imbuing magical properties into objects through the likes of runes or specialised casings like the one in that ring.

The longer Tharian looked at the ring, the more he believed that it was the same one from his childhood, from two decades ago.

He carefully put it back where he found it and squeezed further down the aisles.

How does Traykin even fit down these? He's twice my size, he thought as he shuffled along. He smiled at the thought of Traykin's reaction if he'd said that to his face.

Another curious trinket caught Tharian's eye – this time a gauntlet made of a shining white metal. It somehow reflected more light than was shining on it. The metal plating on the back of the hand was covered in small gems of its own, although these ones did appear to be ordinary gems. Some of them had fallen from their sockets, but the gauntlet looked majestic, nonetheless.

Tharian loosened one of the straps on the underside of the gauntlet and pulled up his sleeve. He gently wiggled his hand into it. As he did so, he imagined what a matching suit of armour might look like. A white, jewel-laden suit of luxury battle-wear stretching from head to toe.

He tightened the strap and flexed his fingers. The gauntlet was more than just a showpiece, Tharian could feel strength within it as if it was vibrating through the metal and into his wrist. He felt empowered by simply wearing it, but he knew that this strength was not his own. It was flowing through the gauntlet from… somewhere else.

Tharian heard a coughing from across the room. He looked up to see Traykin stood at the end of the aisle. He didn't attempt the narrow gap.

'Something taken your fancy there?'

Tharian lifted his arm to show Traykin the beautiful gauntlet that stood out vibrantly against his coat and the dark leather cuirass underneath.

A shadow fell over Traykin's features. 'Take that off.' His voice became deep and serious, but he spoke calmly.

Without challenge, Tharian slid the gauntlet off and put it back. 'What is it?' he asked.

'Not yours. Now come on.' He waved Tharian to follow him as he slipped back into the study.

The two men sat down around the long table again, still covered with their notes, maps, and drawings. Frigg came through with two tankards of Traykin's finest ale – an old illegal import that he kept stashed away from prying eyes. Traykin didn't waste a second when that drink landed between his palms. He took more than a normal mouthful.

'Productive morning?' Traykin asked as he wiped the ale from his beard.

'Very. Tracking down Coinsman Velioth was easy enough.'

'Of course it was,' Traykin blurted. 'He squirrels his way through that market like a mother lirrus looking for scraps. Or maybe it's more like he wants the first bite of the cherry when it comes to the stock. I trust he and Mors bent easily.'

Tharian nodded. 'There was some resistance, mostly from his attendant.

'That's Mors for you, he's been looking after the Coinsman of the Market Quarter for longer than that boy has been alive.'

'I thought as much,' Tharian said, and then he sat up straight and smirked over to Traykin. 'One down, three to go.'

'Good work. Not bad for your first morning at it, ey?' He winked as he brought the tankard back to his lips.

Tharian took the win for what it was and celebrated by trying some of the intensely bitter ale. The flavour was not pleasant, but it came with an instant sensation of soothing warmth in his stomach that made up for it.

'How about you,' said Tharian. 'Any luck with the artisan and collector?'

'Give me a chance, lad. I do have a business to run. You'll get

The Last of the Magi

the missives from them, don't you worry. Coinswoman Keene might take some convincing, but she'll buy it eventually. She is cunning and cautious. I like that about her.'

'What's this? Have you finally found a woman who can hold your attention?' said Tharian, smirking behind his drink.

'Enough of that. A collector's first and only love is his trove. You know that.'

'I do,' laughed Tharian. 'In all seriousness, I am grateful for what you've done already. Your advice was spot on with Velioth this morning.'

Traykin lifted himself out of his chair just enough so he could reach over the table for a small pile of papers. He flicked through them and then tossed them down the table's length to land within Tharian's reach.

'That's all well and good, lad,' Traykin pointed at the papers now in front of Tharian, 'but *she* is the one that'll need some real convincing. She has the most to offer us, and the most to lose in this.'

Tharian pulled the papers closer. The top page only featured a title which read 'Quarter of War'. He lifted the page and saw that the next listed the names of every person to take on the mantle of Coinsman for the Quarter of War, starting with Vern the Bloodspiller himself. His full name was listed here rather than the title of 'Bloodspiller' that he acquired later. Each name had been lightly struck out in ink, with most still being legible. The last name in the list was Kireyn Faast.

The pages that followed were a detailed exposé on each of those coinsmen, ending finally with details of Coinswoman Faast's background, her frequent haunts and her recent notable leadership decisions for her quarter. Her page was still a work-in-progress. Tharian noted that the handwriting for this part was distinctively Traykin's, but the earlier pages were a mixture of a few others. *Traykin is collecting life stories now, too?*

'What's our strategy then?' he asked, looking Traykin's way.

Traykin shrugged and threw his hands into the air. 'The way I see it, we have three options. We could buy her loyalty – though if she took against that, which I bet she would, we may never to see the light of day again.'

Tharian raised a brow. 'We'll draw a line through that one, shall we?'

'Probably for the best. Then either we negotiate with her, or we prove our worth in the duelling ring. And when I say, prove *our* worth, I of course mean *you* proving *your* worth.' He winked.

'Don't worry,' Tharian said as he vacantly flicked through the papers, 'It was implied.'

'Negotiating with her would be the best way to go about it, but nobody gets an audience with Faast unless it's an emergency or she's the one calling the meeting. That only leaves the duelling ring if you want a quick way to get close to her.'

Tharian put the papers back into a pile and tapped a fingernail against the grain of the table. 'I don't remember there being a duelling ring last time I was here.'

'Duelling ring doesn't do it justice, lad. She hosts these fighting tourneys of hers every so often, in her purpose-built arena that she calls 'the Crucible.' The fights were meant to be just a selection process for new recruits to the elite guard, but recently it's become a bleedin' public spectacle. Mind you, you can win some good coin if you place your bets in the right direction.'

'Sounds like you're speaking from experience there, Traykin.'

Traykin chuckled. 'Only when I hear the right rumours.'

'So, you're saying I have to fight in this tourney just to meet the coinswoman?'

'Fighting and winning in the Crucible is the only way you can guarantee an audience with her. She meets with all the winners personally. We can explore some other options, but it's the only direct way to get to her I can think of right now. That's assuming you can win a fight.'

'We don't have the luxury of taking the slow roads. I'll sign up.'

Traykin gave him a look. 'I thought you'd take a bit more persuading than that. Don't get ahead of yourself though, lad. You need to understand what you'd be signing up to.' He stood and stepped away from the table to then lump into his favourite armchair. He pointed for Tharian to sit opposite.

Tharian moved over to join him.

The Last of the Magi

'What do you know about the elite guard of the Quarter of War?'

'How much is there to know? They're the best of the city guard.'

Traykin shook his head. 'That's putting it far too simply, lad. If the Elheim didn't hide behind their bloody Arcana, I reckon the coinswoman could take over the Grand City with only her elites at her side.'

'It's your turn to get to the point, Traykin.'

'Listen. Those wanting to become an elite guard sign up to fight in a Crucible tourney. The challengers fight against one of the older members of the existing elites, one of those coming close to retirement. Only if the challenger wins the bout do they pass the trial and get taken to see Faast.'

Tharian sank in his chair a little. 'It sounds like you're trying to tell me this will be a hard fight. I figured that already.'

'Not half. You'll be fighting one of the strongest, most skilled fighters this city has ever seen. What they lack in youth they make up for with sheer skill. If you aren't careful, you'll end up with more than just bruises and a battered ego – the elites that represent the coinswoman are given strict orders to go all out. There is a strict no-kill, no-maim policy, but they can still pummel someone into the ground.'

'Traykin, you're either doubting my capabilities or you're worried about me,' Tharian said with a smirk.

Traykin snorted. 'I wouldn't go that far. It can just get a bit messy and, well, bloody in that Crucible.'

Tharian relaxed and laid one leg over the other. 'Don't worry about that. I can handle myself.'

'I know you're capable, but if things go wrong in that arena nobody will be there to pull you out.'

Tharian kept smirking. Though his confidence did wane slightly, as he detected the unusually serious tone in Traykin's voice and noticed the harshness in his eyes.

He wasn't being cocky by showing confidence in his fighting skills, he hadn't survived near to a decade in Feralland, fending off packs of feral beasts and even some defensive tribes of Awoken, by sheer luck alone. With his strength, and Ombra's impeccable gifts, they had overcome challenges that weren't comparable to those of Asturia. But Traykin's warning nonetheless hit home. Fighting tribesmen and foolhardy beasts was one thing; fighting expertly trained combatants was a wholly different affair. Plus, Ombra wouldn't be at his side for this.

Finally, he let his smirk drop. 'Point taken. I'll be careful.'

Traykin's eyes flashed, and he grinned. He thumped his fist on the arm of his chair. 'I remember when you left for Feralland, lad. You were just a scruffy teen with a bag full of tricks and some dirty fighting skills. Now look at you, all grown up with big plans and a quiet fire in his belly. Speaking of…'

Traykin stood and crossed the room to the kitchen door. He opened it and poked his head through.

'Frigg! Put some food together, quick as you can. Planning a rebellion is hungry work.'

It only took seconds for Frigg to appear with trays of meat, pastries and some sweet treats. It was no coincidence, of course, Frigg knew his master's habits like clockwork. He had obviously been preparing the platter in readiness for his master's call.

Frigg refilled their drinks and then joined them in the study to enjoy some of the food. He pulled up a modest, small wooden chair and sat close to Traykin's armchair, making sure to position himself so that Traykin's high backrest mostly blocked him from view.

Tharian looked at Traykin. The collector was giving him a peculiar look back, squinting as if taking in details he hadn't noticed before.

'Why are you looking at me like that? Tharian asked.

'You really are all grown up. You're just like how *he* used to be, but with less grey hair and more force behind you.'

'Really?' he asked. He knew that Traykin was talking about Greycloak. 'I've never known Greycloak to take a stand about anything. He would spend every day in that cave of his in Arboreta if people like you didn't drag him out to experience a little civilisation every now and then.'

'You misunderstand him, lad. He may be quiet and peaceful in his ways, but he always had the same passion for these issues as you do. He just didn't have the strength to act on it. Don't mistake his

The Last of the Magi

drive to stay out of the Grand City's way as a sign of indifference towards the state of Asturia.'

'I'll take your word for it. He spent most of our time together telling me stories and legends of the past, rather than sharing his opinions on how to stop the Elheim.'

Traykin hummed. 'Maybe he didn't talk to *you* about those views so you could figure out your own opinions. Or maybe he told you so much about the past, and the way things used to be, to colour the opinion you would one day hold.'

Tharian had no response. He had never considered Greycloak's eccentricities and old stories about the world to be anything more than his projections of nostalgia, or his way of clinging to whatever memories he had left. What Traykin said made him re-think that.

'Anyway,' Traykin continued, as he wiped his dampened beard with his sleeve. 'I meant what I said. It's good to see Greycloak's boy all grown and fired up. I may regret saying this but seeing you as you are now makes me realise something.'

Tharian tilted his head slightly. 'Realise what?'

'That *you* might just be the one to pull this off.'

Tharian's smirk crept back. He nodded. 'That's the plan.'

'That's the spirit, lad.' Traykin said through a laugh. 'We'll get there soon enough. I'll work on the other coinsmen and listen out for when the next Crucible tourney is likely to happen. You might want to get out in the yard and practice your swordsmanship. You'll need to be in top shape.'

'I'll start training tomorrow.' Tharian twisted in his chair to look at Frigg. The nervous man looked startled to suddenly be brought into the conversation. 'Do you think we could get some wooden posts put up, or some training dummies?'

Frigg's eyes rolled up for a few seconds and then he gave a few quick nods. 'I-I can arrange that.'

'Alright then,' Tharian said. 'Let's keep this momentum going.'

Traykin raised his tankard high.

Chapter 12

Arcane Expedition

All the scholars in the College Arcana were aflutter; a new use for Arcana had been discovered.

News of the accident spread quickly. At first, both enforcers and scholars alike were whispering about how Darus – son of the Valivelle patriarch – had struck down Rikkard Nostrum with a new, previously undiscovered Arcane power. But that changed. Now the College Arcana were only interested in what this discovery added to their arsenal of powers. What new strength could enforcers master through the Arcane?

Just like that, all mention of Rikkard had faded into the background. That detail was peripheral to them, but not to Darus.

Darus had physically shuddered when he heard the scholars were petitioning the chancellor for permission to examine him. They wanted him to be their next research project, to find out how he was able to Command stone and earth with his Arcana. He shuddered even more when he, his family, the scholars, and the chancellor's senior advisers were all called to a hearing at the palace to discuss the matter.

Darus was now sat with his father on one side of the hearing room. It was a cold, echoing hall. They had just listened to the case presented on behalf of the College Arcana. It was a strong one. The scholars claimed that, with a bit of time, they could use Darus as a catalyst for unlocking a new level of power for all enforcers. With this new strength, the enforcers would be able to serve the Grand City even more effectively than before.

They were brutal in their description of what that process would entail. It would be invasive and arduous, involving experiments that would put his mind and body under stress. But nobody was surprised – it was the same strategy which led to Arcana being discovered in the first place.

The representative for the scholars had delivered their case

The Last of the Magi

eloquently and excitedly, to the extent that even Darus felt slightly persuaded by its logic, as if he was not the subject matter in question. With a graceful half-bow, the middle-aged scholar stepped down from the podium. He went and sat back in his place, on the opposite side of the room to where Darus sat.

The next advocate to speak was the high imperator herself. She rose from her seat, positioned just to the chancellor's left on an elevated platform, and she approached the platform's edge to address the hall. She turned on her heels and, with a stern nod, waited until she was given leave by the chancellor to move the proceedings forward. He granted it with a soft flourish of his hand.

'We thank the dedicated and studious efforts of the College Arcana scholars in preparing this well-framed petition. There is no doubt that this discovery presents great opportunity. Lord Chancellor, at the time the College's petition was prepared I bore my own signature as a seconder of the proposal. Although I still approve of the proposal as written, I have heard the counter-petition on behalf of the Valivelle family and I confess to being equally moved by it.

'By your leave, my lord, I would call upon Lanark Valivelle, as patriarch of his family, to present the counter-petition – as is his right to do so – for your consideration and determination.'

Another flourish of the hand. The chancellor then looked directly to Darus's father.

His father stood, and Darus quickly handed him his cane. He took it and slowly walked across the room to the podium. Darus felt his cheeks flush. His father was about to speak to the leader of their society about a matter directly concerning *him*. He wasn't sure what his father would say about the petition – Lanark Valivelle was an exceptionally important and busy man, so small talk between them was a rarity.

Placing his cane against the railing of the podium box, his father took his place and held his hands together behind his back. Despite the slight physical frailty betrayed by his walk, his father was nonetheless strong, confident, and brimming with an aura of authority rivalling that of the high imperator.

'Lord Chancellor,' he began with a smooth tone, 'might I first congratulate our devoted researchers and scholars for the great part they play in the growth of the Grand City, and the furthering of our shared vision. They have presented before you a sound case, one which I cannot fault. However, the fact remains that a crime has been committed in the Outer Counties. One which, I submit, is wont for investigation.'

Darus looked on in confusion. This wasn't what he expected him to say at all, it had no bearing on the petition. Yet he carried on, uninterrupted.

'Enforcer Illian Valivelle was struck down in County Bryn. I'm sure most in this room have seen the report from the Arcana Infirmary – the attack is believed to be of magical origin. It appears to me the cause of the attack has one of three possibilities. Either the assailant used an illegal magical artefact, the assailant was an enforcer themselves, or a Magi has emerged from hiding.'

The audience murmured at mention of the Magi. He raised a hand to hush them, which worked instantly, then he looked around at them all sympathetically. 'Naturally the latter two possibilities are too remote to be realistic. In that case, illegal artefacts must be in circulation in the Outer Counties once again. I petition you, my Lord Chancellor, to commission a systematic raid of the Outer Counties so that these items and their users can be located and dealt with pursuant to Grand City decree.'

His father, the high imperator and the chancellor all exchanged unblinking stares. Darus found the very presence of all three of them in the same room incredibly intimidating, each for a different reason: his father was an unquestionable force in his family; the high imperator was the most skilful user of Arcana in their society, and the right hand to the chancellor himself; and then there was Chancellor Vasilarius Elheim, who exuded confidence and authority, despite his relative youth, without even having to utter a word.

The chancellor made a quiet sound and the high imperator approached to receive his orders. She then returned to her perch at the edge of the platform and looked down to Lanark. 'Lord Valivelle, the chancellor is naturally concerned about the presence of illegal artefacts in the Outer Counties, though you are reminded

The Last of the Magi

respectfully that this hearing is assembled to determine whether your son should be assigned to the College Arcana to assist with matters of research. The chancellor asks that you address him on how your proposal relates to Darus Valivelle.'

Assigned, Darus echoed in his head. *That's one way of putting it.*

His father nodded courteously to his superiors, but Darus saw the smirk that briefly pulled at his lips. It was gone by the time he looked back up. His father's expression was no longer as graceful and accommodating as it had been before, instead anger and irritation started to show in the narrowing of his eyes and the shrinking of his mouth. Others might have missed those signs, but not Darus.

'Valivelle,' his father said. 'Asturia has learned to fear that name. Our family's contribution to the Grand City, to this glorious age of prosperity for all Elheim people, must not be understated or overlooked' —the chancellor nodded once, silently, and smiled— 'I shall not allow this travesty to go unpunished. The Valivelle family shall lead the raid into the Outer Counties and my son shall travel with me. Where necessary, my son shall use his new gifts to send a message to *those peasants* that non-compliance with Grand City decree will be met with the full ferocity of Arcane intervention. That, Lord Chancellor, is my counter-petition.'

His father bowed his head to the chancellor and began to turn away. But he paused and looked back for one final remark. 'Understand this, Lord Chancellor, the Valivelle enforcers shall take this action with or without your blessing. It was one of our own who was struck down, and such retributive justice should be recognised as our right.'

With his speech concluded, he swiped for his cane and returned to his seat without waiting for any release from his superiors.

Darus instinctively straightened himself and tried to look 'proper', even though his father didn't even look his way. Not even a cursory glance.

The chancellor was smirking, perhaps even smothering a slight laugh. He gestured for his high imperator to return to her seat. He then adjusted his posture in his grand seat of white wood and navy-blue cushions, and finally he spoke.

'To the representatives of the College Arcana and the Valivelle family both, I extend my gratitude and thanks. Your arguments are compelling and, frankly, inspiring. One thing in particular rings in my mind as a consistent theme in your petitions – you all hold the prosperity of the Grand City paramount. For that, I commend your dedication.' He paused as he nodded to each speaker that had addressed him over the short hearing. 'The appropriate decision appears clear to me. It is purely equitable that the Valivelle family be given opportunity to lead an investigation in the Outer Counties. Our laws have been flouted; our people disrespected. As to the particulars of this expedition, the office of High Imperator Mantleshawn shall confirm the arrangements. And, as requested, Darus Valivelle shall join this effort, on a strict condition. Immediately upon his return, he shall report to the College Arcana to support the research of our scholars. The Grand City will benefit from his gifts – of that I have no doubt – but an opportunity to flex this new Arcane muscle will give the young enforcer more time to understand it for himself. That will assist our scholars to no end.'

The chancellor glanced slowly towards Darus, and then to his father, and gave a nod.

In that moment where the chancellor had looked directly at him, Darus felt a cold sweat at his temples, and his stomach churned.

The chancellor then stood, prompting all in the room to rise with him, and then he left with his senior advisors through a door at the back of the hall.

Darus wiped at his brow and chastised himself. He had been given orders by the chancellor himself – any enforcer of his rank would be honoured.

***

It took only two hours for High Imperator Mantleshawn to arrive at the Valivelle estate to confirm the arrangements for the expedition to the Outer Counties. Ample travel supplies had already been loaded onto feyren-drawn carriages, and the high imperator hand-picked a group of enforcers to join them. She was very specific in referring to the group as an 'expedition party', rather than a 'raiding

The Last of the Magi

force' as his father preferred.

Darus's stomach hadn't stopped churning since he left the palace. Even though he'd been spared the ordeal of becoming a test subject for the College's scholars, upon reflection he realised that travelling to the Outer Counties with his father was far from a more comfortable option. He and his father had barely spoken during the years he was enrolled at the College Arcana. Lanark Valivelle was not one for familial affection.

Just like any other young Elheim earmarked to become an enforcer, Darus had been forced to enrol at the College Arcana after his formal education had ended, with only a year or so of respite between. He formally became an apprentice enforcer at the age of twenty, and he barely had the time for a home visit since. Not that he wanted one.

His friends at the College Arcana, like Aurellia and Rikkard, were more of a family to him than any other. Being forced to stay back home over the last few days, in the regal Valivelle estate, was like living with strangers.

Rik, Darus thought. He still didn't know what happened to Rikkard after the rockfall. Nobody was mentioning his name anymore. Even Darus himself had managed to forget about Rikkard's fate for a few moments, while all focus was turned so acutely to his own fate. But now that he knew where he was going, he couldn't think of anything else. Every time his mind drifted, longing to be back in the apprentice enforcer dormitories, he remembered that he would have to face up to what he'd done. Rikkard might not be there when he returned.

Darus wanted to know. His heart raced as he thought about Rikkard, what had happened, what state he might be in now, and what damage this would cause to their relationship. But despite how he felt, and how painful it was not knowing, he didn't dare ask his father or the high imperator for answers. His father disapproved of their relationship, and he didn't want to be told what he feared might be the reality.

'Darus,' his father said, gesturing him forward to the door where he stood in conversation with the high imperator. 'Here.' He didn't look at Darus as he spoke.

It was a cold, emotionless gesture. Nothing new. Ever since Darus was old enough to talk and express himself, he learned that his interactions with his parents would always be wrought with friction. For every show of emotion, he was chastised for being overly sensitive, nervous, and hesitant. Those three qualities were perhaps the antithesis of everything their family stood for. He was one of them, yes, but an unspoken disappointment to their name. All other Valivelles were the ideal representation of strength and devotion to their duty. Darus was not.

As Darus reached the door, the high imperator greeted him with a proud look on her face. 'Ah, Darus, I'm sure you must be excited for your first outing as an enforcer,' she said. 'I was just telling your father that the preparations have already been made. You can leave as soon as you are ready.'

Darus overhead their conversation, so he knew this already. But hearing it said directly to his face made it hit home – it was really happening. Darus pulled himself together and forced a smile. 'It's a great honour to be given an assignment from the chancellor himself.'

His father looked at him side-on, his gaze cold and expectant.

Darus stuttered, 'A-and to prove the Valivelle family's ongoing dedication to the Elheim vision.'

His father nodded and then turned back to the high imperator, who was watching the two of them with a look of amusement.

'It is a great honour to see the Valivelle family again pushing the boundaries of what we can do with Arcana,' said the high imperator.

Bringing his cane from his side to his front, Darus's father made a triumphant sound. 'Darus will do well, and upon our return from the Outer Counties he will gladly present himself to the College Arcana to assist our colleagues in their work.'

Since Darus had discovered his power, it was only in moments like this – when guests of importance were in earshot – that Darus had experienced some fraction of warmth from his father. Many had visited the Valivelle estate since the incident, ever curious to hear the truth of what happened first-hand. Though Darus was grateful to be spared having to greet and speak with all those guests himself, he overhead his father on several occasions speaking of him as if he

The Last of the Magi

were a trophy in a cabinet.

The pride in his father's words was unfamiliar, and even though the words were never spoken to him directly he still tried to take some solace in them. His father spoke so energetically about him to others and would boast about the glory he was bringing to the Valivelle family, and to all Elheim society. But behind closed doors, his father had few words to say. Behind all the public-facing fanfare and hot air, Darus knew his father was still disappointed by the shy and quiet boy that had grown into a sensitive and demure man.

His relationship with his mother was much the same, but her duties called her away from home for long periods of time, so he was spared experiencing all this twice over.

The high imperator inclined her head and cleared her throat. 'Do you know when you might wish to depart?'

Lanark went to speak, but he was interrupted as a member of the house staff apologised his way between them to deliver a box of personal effects to the carriage drawn outside the house.

'Our preparations are complete,' his father said. 'We will leave immediately.'

The high imperator again looked amused. 'Very good!' She gestured to the carriage parked on the white-stone gravelled driveway, which looped around a fountain. She led Darus and his father towards the carriage and clicked her fingers as she approached, prompting the driver to drop down from his elevated seat and open the door for his passengers. The driver, wearing smart shirt and trousers all in navy blue, bowed his head and waited at the door.

'The other carriages will join you at the main gates. Your drivers are ordered to take you through the northern pass of the Cartographer Mountains, and around the Trade Quarters, to bring you directly to County Bryn. I assumed you might wish to start your expedition there rather than heading to County Dellow and sweeping south.'

'Indeed,' his father said. 'It's only logical to begin our search where Illian was struck down. Thank you, high imperator, for your rapid efforts in arranging this, and for your support during the hearing.'

'It is my pleasure, Lord Valivelle. In truth, I am filled with confidence knowing the Valivelle family is attending to this matter directly. I am sorry for what happened to your sister, but I have every faith you will right this wrong.'

Lanark laughed. 'Oh, I shall.' He glanced to Darus stood at his side. '*We* shall. We will remind the Outer Counties of their proper place in Asturia's future. Isn't that right, Darus?'

Darus startled, not expecting to be brought back into the conversation. He had been listening, but the heat of the early afternoon sun and the smell of the freshly watered lawn had partly taken his attention. 'Of course, sir,' he said.

The high imperator gestured to the open carriage door.

'Come,' his father said. Darus waited while his father ducked into the carriage first.

'Good luck.' The high imperator gave Darus one last proud look.

'Thank you, High Imperator Mantleshawn.'

Darus placed his first foot on the carriage steps and glanced to his right, catching the sight of the magnificent feyren shuffling and rippling its silver mane. It huffed a heavy breath as the carriage tilted under the weight of its new passengers.

He then looked back to the high imperator and, just for a moment, he had the courage to ask her about Rikkard. But by the time his lips twitched to release the words, the courage disappeared. His father would have heard everything. Instead, he just smiled to the high imperator and ducked inside the carriage to take his seat opposite his father.

The driver closed the door and then his footsteps echoed behind Darus and overhead as the driver scurried back up to his seat.

His father thumped his cane against the carriage roof and the driver started to pull them away. The feyren growled as it brought the vehicle slowly into motion. His father turned to look out the window and said nothing more now that they were alone.

It was an uncomfortable silence. But Darus was grateful for it. An awkward silence was usually more palatable than forced conversation.

A minute or so later, the sound of wheels rolling through gravel was replaced by the smoothness of the paved road. Darus peered out

The Last of the Magi

the window and saw the grandiose Elheim Palace in the distance towering above them. The building was intimidating to look at from a distance, but for Darus it felt like his real home. He felt a pang of anxiety watching the palace slowly drift further and further away.

Their carriage turned around a bend and then started down the long and winding slope that took them out of the elevated palace vicinage, where only the favoured Elheim families lived. They went down towards the residential vicinage. Throngs of civilians had already assembled on the slope – news of the expedition had spread fast, as news always did in the Grand City. The people gathered in their elegant suits, vests, dresses, and gowns to cheer for the Valivelle carriage as it made its way to the city gates.

Darus could see in the distance two other carriages also making their way from the residential vicinage to the main city gates. Somehow people had discovered which other enforcers would be accompanying them, and the crowds had already lined their paths. Even from this distance, Darus could see the crowds. No doubt they cheered and clapped for those enforcers too.

The sight of those people cheering in adoration at their enforcers filled Darus with even more nerves. What did they think of him?

Do they know what I did? Do they know about Rik – do they even care?

Feeling a twist of guilt in his stomach, Darus turned away from the window and tried to ignore the cheering. Though the noise outside was raucous, the inside of the carriage remained quiet. His father was still looking out the window, though he appeared to be looking beyond the crowd, as if he couldn't see them.

Darus avoided staring at his father, not wanting to attract his attention. Instead, trying not to think about Rikkard, he listened to the heavy thudding steps of the feyren pulling the carriage. Darus had always loved the domesticated great beasts. He wished he could be sat beside the driver to watch them at work – if for no other reason than to spare himself the uncomfortable awkwardness of sitting in a confined space with his father. That sound was enough to hold his attention as their carriage eventually reached the residential vicinage.

The residential vicinage was plain in comparison to the palace vicinage, but by Grand City standards 'plain' still entailed a high degree of luxury. The whole area was far more glamorous than even the wealthier areas of Ferenir – so Darus had been told. Yet, although the residential vicinage was the inferior of the two, the Elheim people had given it their own name to re-assert its luxurious standards. It had been coined 'The Courtyard of Nobles'. And even that over time had been shorted to 'The Courtyard'.

And it was quite the sight to behold. It stretched out from the bottom of the sloping road all the way to the outer walls of the Grand City in all directions. Rows of elegant houses and elaborate villas took up most of the available space. Not one of these houses touched against the next. Each had its own place and its own space in the design of their city.

Every noble family that had sworn loyalty to the Elheim family were granted an estate commensurate to their contribution to the Grand City's growth, and with it were granted the right to identify as Elheim themselves – though only in title rather than name. The estates of those families who made the most valued contribution in the eyes of the true Elheim family boasted a particularly bloated treasury of assets.

But those of lesser significance to the Elheim family were not left to live in squalor – not at all – for even those of lower status still enjoyed a lavish lifestyle far beyond any other Asturian's dreams. They were all Elheim, and their superiority above all others needed to be maintained.

As Darus daydreamed, he underestimated the distance they had already travelled. It was only as the ringing of cheers became louder that he noticed they were approaching the city gates.

It was a loud but sophisticated affair, with lots of clapping and haughty exclamations rather than guttural cheers and jeers. Jubilant, yet composed.

Darus twisted in his seat and tried to look through his window at an angle, to see the path ahead of the carriage. He saw a slither of the grand gates, which stood some three stories tall, gently reflecting the sunlight off its white marble facade. The gates were still closed. Darus almost slid from his awkward perch as the carriage pulled to a stop.

The Last of the Magi

His father noticed his stumble and was eyeing him below a furrowed, greying brow. He was shaking his head in disapproval, but the gesture was so subtle it could have just been the rocking of the carriage.

Lanark shuffled towards the carriage door and opened it, using the edge of the carriage wall to lift himself through the opening. The crowd cheered even louder at the sight of a senior Valivelle enforcer in the flesh. A celebrity to their eyes.

'Good afternoon to you all!' His father called out. He paused as several amongst the crowd replied. 'So generous of you all to see us on our way. You have likely heard of the small disturbance in the Outer Counties, and I am certain some of you will have questions. I need say only this to you — by the assent of the chancellor and the high imperator, we are to take swift and affirmative action to stamp out any hint of insurrection from those who would dare challenge the peace we bring to Asturia.'

The crowd hung on to his every word. They always did. Lanark Valivelle was, after all, one of the favourites of the chancellor. And that made him one of their favourites too. His very presence inspired them.

'We will not be gone long. This I promise you. And when we return, we will have brought the criminals to heel. The prosperity you continue to maintain for Asturia, that you are helping us to achieve for all Asturians, will never be threatened.'

His father stayed at the door for a few seconds as the crowd erupted into waves of applause. He then swivelled back into the carriage and took his seat. His expression was smooth and charming, but that faded away once he was away from the crowd's view. Darus felt the cold and emotionless stare from his father cut through him.

'Assist with the gates,' he said.

Darus nodded and moved to the position his father had just been in. For a moment he glanced out over the crowds and felt a warmth flush over him as many of the adoring Elheim citizens whispered and pointed at the young Valivelle.

Do they expect me to one day be like him?

Enforcers hung from the doors of the other two carriages ahead also. Each of them raised a hand towards the magnificent gates. Darus followed suit.

He concentrated, letting his mind sink deep into that unique place far beyond the surface of his own consciousness – to that place where he could feel the forces that existed beyond his body. From this state of Deep Thought, he could then Reach out with his senses to the air that slowly coalesced around the gates. He could Grasp a portion of it and then Command it to push the gates open. Deep Thought; Reach; Grasp; Command. The four-step process was second nature to Darus now, as it should be for a fully-fledged enforcer.

Together with the other enforcers, they seized control of the drifting air in front of the gates. They pushed the air forwards and it moved as per their Commands. The air whistled and shimmered as the magnificent gates slowly pushed open to let the expedition group continue on their way.

Again, the crowd cheered. Darus felt his Arcana waiver as he became distracted, but he did his best to ignore the noise. This was only the second time he had helped with the gates. There were mechanisms built into the hinges that allowed the gates to open for regular travel, and there were even smaller doors built into the base for vehicles passing through – but Darus knew, and he was sure the other enforcers knew too, that his father wanted the people to be reminded of their power. And the Elheim people loved to be reminded.

The gates finally finished their sweeping arc outwards, and the Cartographer Mountains appeared on the horizon as a range of pointed peaks from left to right.

The cheering became too much, so Darus quickly ducked back inside the carriage. His father gave him a small nod that he assumed was to be taken as a sign of approval. Lanark tapped his cane against the roof of the carriage and the feyren snarled as it pulled their carriage onwards. The sound of the crowd slowly faded as the carriage rolled off the cobbled road and onto the dirt track of the Eastern Expanse beyond.

The feyren pulling their carriages roared woefully as they pulled the carriages over the Purge – that enormous strip of once-verdant

The Last of the Magi

meadow stretching from the Grand City gates in the direction of the Cartographer mountains to the west. The Purge was devoid of life now. And the feyren sounded pained to trudge over it.

Their little fleet of carriages were headed to the northern pass through the Cartographer mountains, so the feyren were steered away from the scorched ground and back to where the expanse was green and rich in plant-life. The feyren picked up the pace once they reached the healthier land, and their snarling finally stopped. The carriages turned so the Grand City became visible from the carriages' right-hand windows and the Purge was on the left.

'Darus, look here.' His father pointed to the Purge.

Darus followed his father's instruction and looked that way.

'You know what that is?' he asked.

'Of course, sir. It's the Purge.'

Lanark shook his head and thumped his cane against the floor, the veins at his temple pulsed. 'No. That is the Valivelle legacy.' He stared out the window, unblinking, wearing a sinister smirk. 'So many of our family stood at the gates of the Grand City as the Magi were assembled. I stood beside my father as we held the line, and your mother stood beside her father to play her part too. It was thanks to our contributions that those despicable Magi met their end.'

Darus nodded and remained silent. His father was prone to speaking at length on matters relating to their family's reputation and status. He knew better than to interrupt.

'You were just an infant. Cradled by your grandmother as the Magi were reduced to ashes.' His words left his lips with such disdain.

The imagery made Darus uneasy. The Magi were all killed before he was old enough to know about them. He had been told about them many times during history lessons at the College Arcana, but none of his instructors had spoken of them in such harsh terms. There was, without doubt, consensus amongst the instructors that the Magi had been a suspicious group, but that suspicion never inspired the same level of anger or hatred from other enforcers. Suspicious or not – the mass execution of an entire order of magic-users always seemed... excessive.

'There is much to learn from that day,' Lanark continued. 'That our former chancellor and his wife gave their lives to bring an end to the Magi – does it not inspire you, Darus?'

Darus looked out at the strip of dead earth where the Magi had met their end. 'Yes, sir. Their sacrifice allowed us all to prosper.' His words were scripted and flat.

His father shook his head. 'You're not in a college exam, boy, use your own words.'

Darus stuttered as he searched for an answer that was truly his own. 'I-I'm sorry,' he said. That was all he could say.

With a sigh, his father sat back in his seat. He rapped his fingers across his cane. 'If you are to succeed as an enforcer, you must learn to be assertive. There is no room for doubt. You must subscribe to the Elheim vision fully and without reservation – recognising the importance of every step, every action, and every sacrifice. Do you understand?'

'I thi—' Darus caught himself. His father's eyes widened. 'Yes, I understand. I do want to succeed as an enforcer. This is all just very sudden.'

'An opportunity has been laid before you, Darus. You must rise to grasp it. Follow my orders to the letter, watch, and you will learn what is required of an enforcer. It is our duty to be an extension of the chancellor's hand across Asturia. Remember that.'

Darus nodded. He understood his father's words, though he feared what they meant in practice. 'I will do my best, sir.'

'Good. And you must be prepared to use your new strength to aid our cause. Your role in this expedition cannot be understated.'

Darus balked a little at that. Though a part of him was grateful that his father believed he was an important part of this team, another part flushed with concern about what that meant for him. 'I won't disappoint you,' he said, though not feeling any confidence in the words.

'When we reach the Outer Counties, you will have your chance to prove yourself. You will show everyone what it means to be a Valivelle.'

Darus contemplated those words carefully. What exactly would his father make him do? Was he to become the next weapon of choice in the Valivelle arsenal – at the beck and call of the high imperator and the chancellor?

Was that all his new power was... a weapon? He wasn't sure he even knew how to use it again. Just thinking about it took him back to the combat training. He felt in his mind and his fingers an echo of the sensations he experienced before the rock wall had collapsed. His stomach churned at the image of Rikkard's body being bombarded by stone.

His father sighed, drawing Darus out of his sudden daydreaming. 'Your Arcana may become a great asset to the Valivelle name. But it will mean little if you do not overcome the weaknesses of your nature. I can only teach you so much – you must drive yourself to be stronger and better than what you are now.'

Darus nodded and bowed his head. The fleeting moment of feeling worthy of his name was well and truly gone again.

Chapter 13

Arcane Demonstrations

Darus slid over to the window. Storm clouds were brewing along the lofty peaks in the distance to the north. This wasn't unusual. Tucked away beneath the shadows cast by the low-hanging rainclouds, he could just about see the mountainous landscape of Lions' Rest.

The independent city state was carved into and through the smaller mountain range that stretched out from the Cartographer Mountains, covering the north-eastern coastline. The city itself was as reclusive as its people, hidden away from view to any approaching from the south. But on the other side of the sloping walls of mountainous rocks, the city was apparently quite expansive, filling the gaps between the mountain peaks, carved directly into their slopes or stretching deep within them. The city was only accessible safely through the stone gates that took visitors through the core of one of the mountains and into the bowels of the city's complicated structure.

Darus had never been to Lions' Rest – few had, apart from those formally recognised as political emissaries. Darus was quite happy to view Lions' Rest from a safe distance. They were not a cruel or callous people; they were just defensive and fiercely averse to external interference. Much like the obsidian-furred creatures that gave the city its name, they had a territorial nature.

It was hard to judge those Asturians for wanting to seal themselves away. After all, the history of their country was rife with conflict that the people of Lions' Rest were forced to participate in, in one way or another. And they had good reason to hold a grudge against the Grand City too. The last time the Elheim were welcomed through their gates, enforcers caged a group of wild lions and found a way to domesticate them, breed out a lot of their aggressive tendencies and modify their fur colour from the deep black to a rich white and silver. In just a few short years, the legendary beast, the

The Last of the Magi

symbol of Lions' Rest, had been bastardised into the subservient feyren that pulled the Elheim carriages today.

Darus played no part in those acts, they were long before his time, yet he felt guilty, nonetheless.

Darus sat back and tried to relax. It was not his job to carry the guilt for the things done by his people long ago, but he certainly had a propensity for it. Whether it was guilt about Rikkard, about being Elheim, or about the crimes of the past, it was just another weight to add to his conscience. An agony to add to his agonies.

He needed a distraction. But he wouldn't get one from his father. Not a nice one, anyway. Instead, Darus just looked out each of the windows in a slow rotation, noting the subtle changes in scenery with each passing minute and the slow waning of the afternoon sun.

Occasionally, they passed through a small village or farmstead which formed part of the Grand City's territory. The residents either assembled along the edges of the road to watch them pass through with admiration, or they carried on their ordinary activities with complete indifference. The further west they travelled, the more the reactions became the latter rather than the former. Nonetheless, Darus cherished those moments, where he finally had something to capture his attention.

In those places where the people didn't assemble to pay their respects, his father made no effort to hide his scowl.

By the time they passed through the last of the villages, it was becoming quite dark. The carriages left the open road of the Eastern Expanse and took a thinner road that took them through a ravine between the Cartographer Mountains. The path would be no challenge for the feyren – it was a well-travelled road, its bumps and dips flattened by regular use.

The carriage drivers nonetheless pulled the vehicles over at the entrance to the path. Along the north side of the ravine, a stream of fresh water gently flowed. The feyren instinctively pulled towards the water to hydrate and rest for a short while before travelling through the night. They evidently knew this rest spot well.

For the first time in many hours, Darus's father spoke to him.

'Feed them,' he said bluntly.

Darus alighted from the carriage without need for further instruction. He hurried out and gave a sigh of relief as he finally had a chance to step away from his father's overbearing presence. The chance to stretch his legs was welcome too.

Despite the warm season, the evening brought a chill that nipped at him as he walked to the storage containers at the back of the carriage. One of the containers was marked with lettering which read 'Feyren'. The carriage driver was unclipping the latches that held it to the storage bracket as Darus approached.

'There's no need to trouble yourself, Enforcer Valivelle, I will see to the beasts,' he said politely, with a small nod of respect.

Darus placed his hand on the container lid just before it could be opened. 'Please, allow me. I don't often get a chance to be close to feyren.'

'If you insist, sir.' The driver stepped back. He smiled with a mix of politeness and relief. 'Make sure you keep a safe distance, mind – they might be tame, but they get very excited when its feeding time.'

Chuckling, Darus lifted the lid and saw the well-wrapped parcel of meat sat within. The smell hit him as he cradled it onto his forearms. It was awkward to lift, and he kept checking to make sure no blood passed through the wrappings that might stain his pristine white uniform.

The parcel had a small wax seal in its centre that held the wrapping in place. Darus squinted as he tried to figure how he was going to unwrap the weighty parcel before throwing it to the feyren. There was no way he could hold something of this size and weight with one hand. And it seemed a bit excessive to use Arcana to assist him with such a mundane task.

The carriage driver laughed. 'It's all edible,' he said. 'They quite like ripping the parcel open. You can just throw it their way, as is.'

Darus smiled and thanked the driver, then he went to the front of the carriage. The sounds of the three feyren lapping at the stream was aggressively loud. The feyren pulling the Valivelle carriage did not stir as Darus approached. He swung the parcel of meat forward so that it landed a short distance from the beast's side, but a safe distance from the water.

The Last of the Magi

The feyren's head snapped to attention, its jowls and whiskers dripping with water, its nostrils flaring, and it snorted with approval as its giant blue eyes considered the meal presented before it. It sniffed at the wrapping of the parcel, as if testing it, and then its eyes widened dramatically as the scent of raw meat and blood consumed it. With a purr, it bore its enormous fangs and swiped at the parcel with its paws.

Although the graceful creature had become barbaric at the smell of its meal, it was the purring and the expression in its eyes that reassured Darus that the feyren was still gentle at heart. Seeing it so content with its meal made carrying the heavy slab of meat worth it, even if the smell of it would linger on his uniform for a while.

Darus eventually went back to the carriage, but before he could crawl back into the warmth to rest for the night, he felt something swoop by the back of his neck. He ducked reflexively, then he hopped closer to the carriage and span around frantically to find out what it was.

There was nothing there.

A high-pitched shriek sounded from above. Then it echoed between the mountain slopes.

'Darus!' his father called, adding to the echo – he was now standing in the doorway of the carriage pointing overhead. 'Get rid of that cliffhawk, before we end up with starved feyren.'

Darus searched above and quickly spotted the large bird swooping overhead between him and the feyren. Each of its wings looked to be at least half of Darus's height, and its long neck and protruding beak made it deadly. But cliffhawks were not known for being aggressive.

It must have smelled the meat around me, he assumed. His heart slowed to its normal rate. He was not the bird's prey. The cliffhawk circled over the grazing feyren, looking for an opening to steal at their meals.

'Get on with it!' his father shouted.

He'd been given an order. He had to comply. Darus took a deep breath and prepared to do as he was told. He looked around for the cliffhawk, then noticing that the other enforcers in their group were watching him intently from their carriages.

They'd heard the rumours. They knew what he'd done at the College Arcana – to Rikkard – and they wanted to see if the rumours were true. They wanted to see his Arcana for themselves.

Darus ignored them as best he could and focused on his task. He cleared his mind and reached deep within to engage the Deep Thought state. He felt a dull sensation, like a small amount of pressure in his head, and then his perception of the elements around him became vivid in his mind. He was ready to Reach, Grasp and Command those elements through Arcana.

He raised a hand high to aid him in focusing the direction of his Arcana. He Reached for strands of air and Commanded them to change course, towards the cliffhawk. The air whipped to strike, but the attack missed – the cliffhawk was too fast. It swept around to a different position as the air clipped past its wing.

Pockets of hushed laughter mocked him. Darus made the mistake of looking back to his father and caught the wrong end of a red-faced, fiery glare. Feeling flustered, Darus took another sweep at the bird. This time he tried to pull at the air just ahead of the cliffhawk's looping flight pattern.

Again, the air responded to his Arcane Command and whipped at the cliffhawk. He hit it this time. But the hit only knocked it off balance for a moment. In his rush to try and recover from his embarrassment, Darus had focused too much on the accuracy of his strike and not enough on its force.

The mocking got louder. Darus could feel it like a weight bearing down on his shoulders – the enforcers enjoyed watching him fail. He struck out a third time, this time as the bird's loop brought it close to him. He clasped his fist and pulled it towards his chest, and to his surprise the Command of air seized the cliffhawk's body and reeled it in at speed. It came rushing to where he stood.

Darus released his Command and jumped sideways to avoid the collision, but the cliffhawk continued hurtling forward. It was then that he spotted his father, now standing a few paces behind where Darus had just been, pointing his rapier to the air. The cliffhawk flew straight onto the outstretched blade and was impaled.

It screeched violently as its life ended.

The Last of the Magi

His father lowered the blade to let the bird's carcass drop to the ground. Darus noticed that his father's other hand was clenched and pulled back to his waist – the cliffhawk had been caught in *his* Arcana.

Darus Reached out with his mind to check what he could sense, and his suspicion was confirmed. There was a connection between his father and the Arcana around the cliffhawk's body. It dispelled a few moments later.

Lanark pulled a square of cloth from one of his pockets and wiped his blade down. He tossed the rag away and sheathed the rapier back into the holster that doubled as his cane.

The enforcers were all silent this time. The only sounds came from the feyren. They were whimpering, sounding pained. His father tutted at them and then kicked the cliffhawk's lifeless body, Commanding more Arcana in the air as he did so, sending the bird's body rolling over to the edge of the stream.

Darus suddenly felt his father's hand at the back of his neck. He was dragged back into the carriage.

The other enforcers started laughing again, but that ended quickly as his father sent flurries of air rushing out to blow over each of them as a warning shot.

Back inside the carriage, Darus fidgeted as he tried to find an appropriate apology to appease his father. As he finally found the right formulation of words, his father raised his hand to stop him.

'Do not speak,' he said. 'That was pathetic.'

Darus tried to respond. He wanted to remind his father that this was his first expedition as an enforcer, that combat training in the College Arcana was a very different affair to having to act quickly and instinctively with a live, fast target. But he said none of those things, there was no point. And even if there was any point in saying it, he felt as if his throat had been petrified.

'To think that a son of mine would be so disappointing,' his father said, shaking his head slowly.

'I–I'm sorry, sir,' Darus said, though his voice was little more than a muffled croak. He kept his head bowed.

'I said *do not* speak.' His father's voice crept louder. Darus flinched; he knew what usually followed that raised voice. He braced himself. There was a whipping sound and then a blunt force cracked across the top of his head. He clenched his eyes closed and felt a short-lived but sheer pang of pain pulse across his skull.

It was a familiar pain. The sweeping lash of his father's cane. The pain reminded him too vividly of his childhood. Darus rubbed his head aggressively and hissed through gritted teeth as he held back from shrieking. It had been a long time since he felt the cane – it still hurt just as much as he remembered. He had hoped that being a man now would spare him such discipline. Apparently not.

But the pain wasn't the worst part of it. The embarrassment, the ridicule from the other enforcers and the frustration of failure all blended into one unbearable sensation.

His body and mind were both under so much strain. His thoughts lingered on the pain, swimming in the shame of it all, until he felt another sensation from deep within come to the fore of his mind. It was that same coarse, strong and solid wave of feelings that had taken hold of him during the training with Rikkard. It was like his mind had just Reached and Grasped at something in self-defence, subconsciously.

The carriage started shaking. Darus opened his eyes. His father was still looming over him, eyes wide and looking left and right rapidly. Then, as if experiencing a moment of complete understanding, his father stared into his eyes and smirked with sadistic satisfaction.

It was happening again. Darus was causing the tremors that shook the carriage. The feyren outside were roaring and whimpering. Their carriages were on a thin, rocky path between two towering mountain slopes, and Darus was causing the earth to shift beneath them. Any moment now the cliffs could splinter and send slabs of rock falling onto them all. Just like what happened to Rikkard.

He had to do something. Quickly. He was almost being thrown out of his seat, and his father had stumbled back into his after losing his footing. They both grabbed the handles on the carriage doors to stop themselves rolling around.

Darus reached out with his senses to try and figure out what was going on. Immediately he could tell that this was different to before.

The Last of the Magi

Last time, he felt the strange sensation in his mind for only a few moments and then it was gone. This time it was continuous. He could still feel it now.

How am I doing this?!

Usually, Darus would be very aware of what he was doing with his Arcana. It took so much concentration, practice, and precision to even learn how to use it in the first place. Now however, as the tremoring continued, he couldn't fully feel the Arcana at work. He could feel that it was there, but not in the way he was used to.

'This power...' his father said. He seemed to be enjoying this experience, despite the danger it put them in. His smirk grew wider even as the tremors became more severe.

Darus shut his eyes and forced himself into a trance of Deep Thought. It was difficult to concentrate through all the rattling and thundering underfoot – and the fear of being buried in a landslide – yet he pushed through it all. He searched deep; deeper through his senses than he was used to.

And there it was. He could feel the tether of Arcana linking him to the earth. It was as if there was a small thread of twine leading from deep within his skull down into the depths of the ground. As he focused on that sensation, the tether became more lucid until it was as clear in his mind as any other use of his Arcana would be.

Darus released his Command, dispelling the Arcana. The tremors slowly dissipated. The rattling of wood and metal from within the carriage, and stone and water from outside, calmed.

Darus pulled himself to the carriage window and looked up the slopes of the mountain. All appeared still once more, only small stones and rock dust tumbled down from above. He sighed with relief and dropped back into his seat, wiping sweat from his brow and temples.

'Incredible,' his father said. He had a new expression on his face that Darus had never seen on him before. Despite its unfamiliarity, he knew without doubt that *this* truly was a look of pride. Darus had finally done something that his father approved of. But Darus felt no satisfaction from it. It filled him with dread.

Since when could Arcana trigger on its own? he asked himself. *I couldn't even feel it. It just happened. What if it happens again, while I sleep or while we're travelling? Maybe I should mention it.* Darus shook his head. His father would only see his doubt and uncertainty as another sign of weakness.

'Perhaps there is still hope for you, after all,' his father said.

Enforcers from the other carriages wandered over to investigate. His father ushered them away, accusing them of 'wasting time on idle envies' when they had duties to be getting on with. For those that insisted on questioning what had caused the tremors, his father had one simple response.

'You travel amongst the Valivelle.'

Chapter 14

Crossroads of Diplomacy

Marla opened the wardrobe in her room. She hadn't noticed it tucked beside the door when she settled in for the night. But now, with the morning sunlight shining in through the slanting window, she could really take in the finer details of the room – particularly the white lace that seemed to adorn every fabric. Everything was so soft and delicate, far removed from her old room back in County Bryn.

The wardrobe was full. From left to right hung dresses and soft shirts in varying styles, with a few sized for a child. Her own wardrobe back home had clothes of different sizes too, but that was just to accommodate the natural flux of her weight throughout the year – winters in the Outer Counties were very sedentary. This was different. These clothes were ranged in size from new-born to adult, sporting shades of pink, cream, and peach.

Marla laced her fingers through the clothes, noting the dust that shuddered from them when disturbed. The landlady had popped her head through the door at first-light to suggest Marla help herself to whatever she finds, but she didn't expect *these* to be her options. These clothes were a world apart from her plain tunics and overalls. White, brown, and grey were her colours of choice.

She closed the wardrobe and blew a bemused whistle. She paced around the room and looked around at the other furnishings available to her. She took a chance with the dresser beside her bed and rummaged through the drawers. To her relief she found a pile of shirts and tunics, again in different sizes, but much closer to her modest taste. And some in her size too. Unfortunately, they were still peach-coloured, but they would do. She dressed herself in the peach tunic and a spare pair of brown trousers she packed in her bag.

She then left the room and went downstairs. She remembered the kitchen was the first room on the left at the bottom of the stairs.

And it was there she found the grumpy blacksmith, Brayne, and his wife sat around their three-seater table. Marla flushed as their eyes turned to her. She flushed even further when she remembered she still didn't know the kind woman's name.

'Good morning! I hope you slept well,' the woman said. She elbowed Brayne, who had quickly lost interest in Marla and was scrutinising a crude drawing laid beside his breakfast plate. He groaned and clasped his last piece of toast between his teeth and then reached over to the kitchen counter to pull another plate to the spare seat at the table. Fresh bread, bacon and eggs had already been layered on the plate for her. Brayne then glowered at Marla and pointed her to the seat before getting up and leaving the kitchen, squeezing around her while still clamping the toast in his jaw.

'Ignore him,' the woman said. 'He's always like this in the morning.'

Marla smiled politely and took her seat. 'He seemed quite riled up yesterday afternoon as well.'

The woman rolled her eyes. 'He gets that way in the afternoons too. Scratch that – he's always like that.' She chuckled as she poured a glass of juice and put it in front of Marla's plate. 'But he is a good man. I dare say he's earned the right to let off steam sometimes. Now eat your breakfast before it gets too cold.'

Marla thanked her and dug in. This was the first home-cooked meal she'd eaten for days, so she tried to savour it. It wasn't easy. She was used to eating at speed so she could hurry and get back to work in her father's shop. She coughed as she swallowed down half a rasher of bacon, chased by a mouthful of the juice.

After making a dent in the food, she cleared her throat to speak. 'I'm a little embarrassed to bring this up, but I don't think I asked your name yesterday.'

The woman looked up from a booklet she had started reading. She then looked startled. 'You sweet girl, I'm so sorry. With all the excitement of yesterday I completely forgot to introduce myself. What must you think of me. My name is Marion. And my husband is Brayne.'

'There's really no need to apologise,' Marla insisted, waving her hands in the air. 'I'm so glad I met you both. Is there anything I can

The Last of the Magi

do to help this morning? Does Brayne need a hand?'

Marion gently laid her booklet down, resting both hands upon it. 'As it happens, we'd just been discussing that before you came down. We have a few deliveries to send out to the Quarter of War today. I would usually take it, but I dare say you could get it done much quicker than I can.'

Marla felt a little disappointed that the task was not blacksmithing-related, but she made sure not to show that in her face. After all, it was made clear that Brayne wouldn't let her do any smithing until he trusted her more.

'Sounds good. I can run deliveries,' said Marla. 'I'll just need some directions.'

'Of course. Each of the parcels has the delivery address written on them. I will explain the best route to take before you head out.'

Marla nodded. 'I'll head off soon then. No point waiting around if things need doing.'

Marion smiled warmly. 'Thank the Divine. I'm glad you're here, Marla. Really, I am. If you can do this for me then I can get caught up on some other things that are long overdue. I have a pile of linen nearly touching the ceiling that needs taking to the washhouse this morning. I will take any clothes you need washing with me too.'

'That's very kind of you.' Marla hadn't even thought about how she would get her clothes washed in the Trade Quarters. She had truly fallen on her feet.

'No bother at all. We're all on the same team here. Are you finished there, my dear?' she pointed at Marla's empty plate.

Marion took the plate and added it to the pile beside the sink. Marla rushed over to help Marion with tidying up the kitchen, eager to show her commitment to being a useful pair of hands to both of them. Marion welcomed the help. The two of them got the job done quickly and then agreed to go freshen up before meeting back at the front door to head out for their morning errands.

While back in her room, Marla made sure to grab her handaxe holsters and she fastened them to her thighs. She pulled on her leather jacket and tugged it about to hide the holsters as much as possible. After experiencing the hostilities of the Trade Quarters just a few minutes after entering the city, she thought it best to be prepared. She then hurried downstairs again to meet Marion at the door.

As Marla reached for the front door, she noticed Marion beaming at her with dewy eyes.

'That colour looks beautiful on you.'

'Oh,' replied Marla, feeling suddenly disarmed. She looked down at her herself and shrugged. 'I hope you don't mind; I found the shirt in the dresser.'

'It's absolutely fine. It's good to see it finally being worn.'

Marla felt awkward, but fortunately she didn't have to say anything further as Marion then opened the front door and stepped out. She took a deep breath of the smoggy air and exhaled sharply with approval as if she had just stepped out onto a verdant meadow. Perhaps this was a particularly *fresh* morning to a resident of the Trade Quarters, despite how it looked to an unfamiliar eye.

Marla stepped out too. Brayne appeared from around the side of the house, pushing a wheelbarrow laden with well-wrapped long parcels.

'Be careful with those,' he said, as he stretched his back. 'There's a fortnight of earnings in this barrow.' He said nothing more, slinking away back to the front door of the shop adjoined to their house.

Apprehension sunk in. Marla was eager to impress and pull her weight, but she also worried about the danger of walking openly through the Quarter of War. Tharian had warned her against going that way when they parted in the central plaza. But then again, Marion suggested earlier that she would run these deliveries herself normally – and she seemed such a kind and gentle woman – so how dangerous could it really be?

Marion approached her, pointing towards each of the parcels in turn. 'If you look at the wrappings, you'll see that each bears the seal of the buying militia bands. Their offices normally display their insignia somewhere on the building or on its doors so it's easy enough to match the order to the group as you go around.'

Looking for herself, Marla noticed that each of the parcels did indeed have a symbol stamped or etched onto the wrappings. Each of the symbols were an artistic depiction of a weapon. A sword. A

The Last of the Magi

shield. An axe. A bow. A flail. And those weapons were printed against a pattern of two or three colours.

'I've been told the Quarter of War isn't very safe. What if someone tries to steal this stuff?'

Marion chuckled. She then pointed to some lettering stuck to the side of the barrow. It read 'Glanmores'. 'I wouldn't worry about anyone trying to steal. It's true the quarter is a bit rough around the edges, but even the lowest thugs around there know not to interfere with artisan business. The risk just isn't worth it. It may seem a little odd, but you're best to walk in the open as much as possible, let people see our name on the barrow and move confidently. You'll be fine.'

Marion hopped back up the steps to the front door and reached for a rucksack she'd filled with laundry. She threw it over her shoulder and then handed Marla a sheet of paper with a map of the Trade Quarters depicted, annotated with red ink.

'Just follow that path,' she traced the red line from the Artisan Quarter all the way along several alleyways that mazed through the Quarter of War. 'You'll be done before you know it. If you have any trouble, just call for a guard. They don't like being disrupted from their duties but if you say you're on artisan business they'll help. I'll see you back here when you're done.'

Marion gestured over towards the central plaza in the distance, where the first part of the directions led her. Then, with a warm smile and a nod, Marion headed off in the opposite direction.

Marla took a deep breath and tried to shrug away her nerves. *Here we go,* she thought to herself. She grabbed the barrow with both hands and pulled it towards the central plaza. It was heavier than expected, but manageable. Marion must have been stronger than she looked.

It took a few minutes for her to reach the central plaza, and once she did, she grabbed the map from atop the barrow and turned it around a few times in her hands. She couldn't tell up from down.

'How do you tell which side is up on a bloody circle?'

She flapped the paper in the air a few times, as if roughing it about might reveal its secrets. She stared at it for a bit longer until she noticed that there were some markings in one of the corners.

She twisted the map around again until it became clear the symbols were letters. 'T.Q.' The Trade Quarters.

She quietly cheered at figuring out the puzzle. She then took her finger and traced the red line that led from the blacksmithing shop to the central plaza, and then she repeated the next few directions in her head three times in the hope of memorising them. The first step was easy enough – the Quarter of War was the next main road if she followed the curve of the central plaza to her right.

As she bent her knees to lift the barrow again, she looked up at the quartet of statues in the plaza's centre. She recognised the large, wide frame of Vern the Bloodspiller – founder of the Quarter of War – and she recalled that each founder statue stood aligned with its respective quarter. That meant she was heading the right way.

She crossed the plaza and reached the Quarter of War's main road. The sound of gentle morning chatter faded away and was replaced with clashing metal, hammering and the occasional curse or pained shout. Mercenaries and soldiers wearing varied degrees of armour and sporting a multitude of militia band colours – some she recognised from the packages – were loitering around. They sat on the steps in front of their buildings or sharpened weapons with whetstones outside their nearest blacksmith.

Tharian had been right about this place. Although this quarter had an abundance of blacksmiths, metalworkers, leatherworkers, and other crafters, what they displayed at their shopfronts was evidence of their quantity over quality approach. Even the thickness of the sooty air that wafted down the lengthy main road was a hallmark of just how quick and crude their work was. The smog was so much darker and gave the air a dusty, iron-like taste.

She easily resisted the urge to stop and inspect some of the wares on display. She wouldn't be inspired by what she saw.

Marla made her first delivery. It was a sword, obvious from the packaging. The soldier waiting inside the building marked on the map took the weapon and forced a scraggy envelope filled with coin into her palm. He paused before he released the envelope.

'You're new. You with Brayne?' he asked. Not much of his face was visible through the helm he wore, which strangely he wore indoors while manning the small and bare reception area, but his

The Last of the Magi

golden eyes stood out vividly.

Marla stuttered for a moment before thinking of her response. She hadn't given any thought to what she would have to say to any of these soldiers. 'Yes. It's my first day,' she said.

The soldier scoffed. He released the envelope and marched out of the room with the sword, calling back to her as he left. 'Tell him the Scorchers will be wanting more – we've 'ad some promotions.'

Marla nodded and made a mental note, then she raced back out to the barrow, which she had left precariously just outside the door. The other parcels had been left untouched, just as Marion had suggested.

She set off again, following the map. The route took her off the main road and into the back alleys. She was immediately taken back by how narrow these streets were. It was only just wide enough for her and the barrow, and for one other to shuffle around her, which she experienced more frequently than she expected.

Despite how thin the alley was, narrow houses were stacked side by side with their doors facing onto the dark, cobblestone road. No space was wasted in this city. The buildings were so closely packed together that the mid-morning sun could hardly reach her past their bulk and height.

The deeper in she walked, the darker her surroundings became. Only the occasional sconce or lit window helped to illuminate the twists and turns ahead. The streets were growing increasingly dishevelled also. There were even a few men and women passed out against the walls in some places – or at least she hoped they were only passed out – and it took all her dexterity to manoeuvre the barrow around them carefully.

She delivered another three packages to properties tucked away in these shadowy places. It took her a while to find the doors to the right buildings. They were not all clearly marked, but eventually she found the lettering or insignia markings she needed. Most of the customers were hesitant to interact with her, being an unfamiliar face, but she got the jobs done. Each exchange was much like the first, except the customers here barely even opened their doors to make the exchange – their eyes searched the shadows as if suspecting some stray arrow or knife to lunge out at them from the dark. They took in their parcel and handed Marla an envelope or bag of coins, or just forced loose coins into her palm.

Marla's confidence grew with each delivery. She took a break and lingered under a nearby sconce for a while to memorise her next set of directions. The next destination was a bit deeper into the quarter, closer to the perimeter wall. Further into the shadows.

She stretched her arms and then set off again with the barrow. Eventually she reached a crossroads. Each of the long roads were indistinguishable from the next. Just stretches of uneven cobbles, dark grey walls, and looming darkness. She checked her map again and glanced around in the hope of finding something that might help her make sense of it. She took a chance on the right turn.

She pulled the barrow around the bend one-handed with a grunt, using her other hand to keep the map in her eyeline. This road was even darker than the last, so it was harder to make sense of the directions.

She reached another crossroads but stopped just before the opening to hold her map under the flickering light of another sconce. Tracing the next section of the red line, she looked up to confirm the route ahead.

She did a double take as she realised that two figures lurked at the opening of the next alleyway. They were in the midst of a conversation that was quite heated.

Not wanting to intrude, Marla held back and pretended to examine her map further, even going as far as faking a confused look on her face in case they looked her way, though she glanced up occasionally to see what was going on. Their voices were quite easy to make out in the quiet of the alleyways.

'...a counteroffer? Ridiculous. This is pittance, an insult to the efforts I have already made,' said the figure on the left, a woman with wispy hair that poked out the front of a velvet, hooded robe drawn tight at her waist. It was too dark to make out any other details.

The other figure, clad completely in a black coat, leaned forward to the other while keeping their face concealed. 'Beware your tone with me. I will collect your response at midnight in the normal way. Do not overlook the magnality of what is offered to you.' The voice

The Last of the Magi

was deep, lined with an intelligent smarminess that Marla had never encountered in any Quartersfolk so far.

'Very well, Protelborn,' the woman said. 'I will give these terms some consideration. Perhaps this can still be salvaged.'

The black-coated figure nodded and then turned his head towards Marla. She had been peering their way with her head bowed and quickly returned to examining the map in the hope that her staring had not been noticed.

Without a word, the man's coat flared as he turned away from the woman and disappeared out of view. His footsteps on the cobbles vanished only a few seconds later.

The woman calmly adjusted her hood, pulling it closer around her face and walked the opposite way. She, too, was out of Marla's eyeline in a flash.

It didn't take a genius to figure out she had intruded on something private. She didn't let it concern her though – she had work to do.

What a stupid place to meet, she thought as she passed through to where they had been stood and continued through to the opposite alleyway, noting the long roads that stretched left and right. *If you want to meet in secret, maybe don't do it at a crossroad?*

She carried on to the next destination and delivered another parcel, this time a polearm with a crescent-shaped blade on one end. She took the payment and added it to the barrow, which was now immensely lighter than when she started, holding more money than goods at this point. That was the last of the larger deliveries now done, with only a few small armaments left.

The next steps on the map brought her back out to a wide road buzzing with people. Marla was grateful to be back in the filtered sunlight. She had almost forgotten that it was morning after worming through that maze of darkness.

But just as she paused at the edge of the road, she jumped at the sound of a deep horn in the distance which buzzed through the air and made her shiver. It was a horrific sound, one that felt... foreboding. No sound like that could be good news.

She was almost toppled over as armed soldiers from the nearest militia building came rushing out, splitting off in all directions back down the dark alleyways. Then more appeared from side-doors, cellar hatches and ladders affixed to walls. They quickly flooded the paths behind, so her only option was to carry on to the main road.

And people were swarming about here too – regular Quartersfolk rather than armed militia – though soldiers of the city guard were racing ahead at greater speed in the direction of the central plaza. Even with the heavy footfall there was enough space on the wide main road for Marla to join the flow of traffic with her barrow trailing behind.

She joined the ranks of guards, merchants, traders, artisans, and collectors swarming to the central plaza, filling its outer perimeter. As the crowd thickened, Marla found herself locked in place with the barrow. She bounced on her toes, trying to see over their heads but the crowd was just too thick to get a clear view.

She gave a fleeting glance to the barrow to ensure nobody had taken the opportunity to steal anything. Then she looked at it again. It was practically empty now after her busy morning of deliveries – enough room to fit someone stood in it. So she stepped into the well of the barrow, giving herself the perfect vantage to rise above the crowd.

At last, she saw what was causing the commotion. Ahead, a convoy of elaborate carriages in regal shades of white, silver and blue moved slowly through the central plaza – driving around the marbled centre. Each pulled by a feyren, impossible to miss with their manes of silver and fur of white. Marla's heart sank.

Enforcers. What are the Elheim doing here?

She wasn't the only one to recognise the carriages. Those at the front of the crowd were shouting and cursing in protest, lashing their arms in the air. Guards worked together with hired mercenaries to hold the crowd back.

The carriages were too dark inside to see the passengers properly. Form where Marla stood, she could see that there were two silhouettes in the lead carriage. One of them moved closer to the window, briefly becoming more visible. It looked to be a blonde-haired man, perhaps a similar age to her.

Marla's heart fluttered. Seeing the Elheim here, in all their pomposity, reminded her of Brynfall. What they did to it.

The Last of the Magi

The carriages stopped. Marla stepped onto her toes to get a better view of what was happening.

And then the crowd started cheering.

A tall woman with a muscular frame and a half-shaved head stood at the entrance of the Market Quarter where the Elheim convoy was headed. The cheering was directed at her.

She was unlike any woman Marla had ever seen before. She was well over 6 feet tall, wearing full armour covered in a black matte material with gold finishes and trims. In one hand she held a tower shield reaching from her foot to her shoulder, and in the other a double-ended spear with golden spearheads that reached beyond her own impressive height. She held the spear out to her side.

She lifted her shield and drummed the ground several times. A group of heavy-armoured guards in a colour scheme that matched her own rushed over from positions around the crowd to help her form a barrier of metal and muscle across the entrance to the main road.

Two of the Quartersfolk near to Marla turned to each other.

'I'd like to see the Elheim try and get through Coinswoman Faast,' said one of them.

'Don't be ridiculous,' said the other, 'what good is steel against Arcana?'

Marla had to agree. Bryn's county guard didn't stand a chance against them. Even so, this tall woman – Coinswoman Faast, one of the four leaders of the Trade Quarters – was no county guard.

Coinswoman Faast shouted a battle-cry and slammed her shield into the ground again. The soldiers on her flanks grunted in response and assumed offensive stances with their weapons directed forward.

The door on the lead carriage swung open. The base of a cane lunged out and hit the ground. A greying, older enforcer emerged from the carriage and took a few leisurely steps towards the barricade. He had a slight limp to his walk.

'Have we done something to offend, Coinswoman?' the enforcer asked.

The coinswoman huffed and shook her head. 'The Quarters are not, and have never been, a passing ground to satisfy viatic whims. That is a term of our treaty with the Grand City.'

The enforcer shrugged. 'My sincerest apologies. It appears I may have made a mistake. Please forgive my ignorance as we move on our way. I will be sure to arrange an alternative return route.' He then turned back to his carriage.

'Do *not* toy with us, Enforcer Valivelle.'

The enforcer stopped in his tracks, with his back still turned to Faast.

'It has been some time since you last journeyed through to the west, but our sentries recognise you all-the-same. You know the severity of your trespass. What game is the Grand City playing today?'

Enforcer Valivelle's chest and shoulders heaved up and down. His laughter cut through the murmuring of the crowd and filled the plaza. He turned to Coinswoman Faast. 'I underestimated your astuteness. I will be candid. We are investigating illegal activity in the Outer Counties. It is an emergency matter and this road through the Quarters is the quickest way to the west.'

'Emergency or not, unless you have business in the Quarters, or sanctioned trade to conduct with the Outer Counties, there shall be no exception. Return the way you came and continue your voyage outside our walls.'

The snake-ish charm of the enforcer seeped away and his expression turned dark. He brought his hands together atop his cane. 'Ah – but we do have trade with the Outer Counties.'

'Speak the manner of it.'

'We aim to strike a deal: a renewal of terms. The Outer Counties will remain under the protection of the Grand City in exchange for handing over a fugitive in their midst – a criminal by our laws. A fair trade, I'm sure you will agree.'

Faast growled and shouted back at him. 'That is a unilateral threat, not an act of trade. The enforcement of *your* law is no justification for the violation of *ours*.'

'Enough of your pedantry,' Enforcer Valivelle said through gritted teeth. 'We will be going on ahead. Unhindered.'

The doors opened on the second carriage further down the line and two more enforcers stepped out. They stood beside their carriages and eyed the crowds.

The Last of the Magi

Faast moved a few steps forward. 'The Grand City relies upon good trade relations with the Quarters just as much as any other territory. Your chancellor will not be pleased if your actions damage the integrity of that relationship.'

Enforcer Valivelle's demeanour shifted again. This time from annoyance to rage-filled contempt. He spat a threat to the coinswoman. 'You will learn to be more cautious with your tongue. I shall not be lectured on the wants of our chancellor. Move aside, or I will clear the road myself.'

Coinswoman Faast called out to her soldiers, and then together they all took another step forward.

The enforcer smirked.

He looked around his surroundings, looking beyond and above the crowd, and then his gaze lingered on something. He closed his eyes and raised one hand to shoulder height.

A wind started to blow through the Trade Quarters, one that wasn't there a moment ago. Marla stumbled in the barrow as air seemed to suck in from behind her. The torrent of air whipped around in a circular motion and picked up in strength and speed. The crowd murmured and trembled as they all experienced the same sensation. The air was being pulled in from all directions to add to the spinning vortex. Everything loose was being pulled counterclockwise by the force.

The wind was not the real threat. It was just a vehicle. As the spinning gust caught against the sconces mounted at the end of every main road, and at the alleyway entrances, the flames burning within were pulled along with it. Those flames eventually surrendered to its momentum fully. And what started as an unsettling fluster of air transformed into a maelstrom of twisting flames, circling over the central plaza with Enforcer Valivelle stood stoically under its centre.

Marla instinctively ducked down, even though she was at a safe distance. She did not fear flames, or the intensity of its heat, it was the memory of her home set ablaze that made her shirk away.

The crowd were screaming now. Those at the front tried to push back as the heat bore down upon them.

Marla's barrow wasn't easy to see for those pushing through, so most of those squirming backwards pushed against it. She threw her arms out to balance herself, but after the first few knocks, she lost her footing and crashed into its basin. She winced in pain as her shoulders and arms slammed against the metal rim, and the remaining wrapped packages and envelopes of coin stabbed at her back.

The fire continued its twisting and convulsing under the enforcer's control. Marla rolled out of the barrow and back onto her feet as soon as there was a break in the crowd. She rubbed her back, but she didn't feel any wounds from where she fell. She kept her eyes on the flames in case they were made to lurch at the buildings around them – like what happened in Brynfall – or worse, be cast out at the gathered crowds.

With the crowds breaking, Marla could see the central plaza more clearly. Coinswoman Faast was taking slow, cautious steps closer to the Enforcer with her shield tilted diagonally so she could protect herself from anything in front or above. Her soldiers advanced with her but not with the same confidence.

Enforcer Valivelle looked at his work and raised his arm out as if to congratulate himself for his magnificent display of Arcana. When he looked back down, he saw Faast creeping his way.

He raised his voice to be heard over the roaring flames circling overhead. 'And yet you persist. You are worthy of your quarter.'

'Cease this madness, now!' the coinswoman bellowed, swinging her spear forward to point at the enforcer.

Enforcer Valivelle waved his hand, and another small flurry of air slapped her spearhead to one side. 'In one motion I could flood this entire plaza with fire. Do you want that on your conscience?'

Faast gritted her teeth and brought her spear forward again. She continued her advance.

'Stop this, please!' shouted a new voice.

A man with jet black hair and an expensive looking red coat ran between the enforcer and the coinswoman with his hands held out towards each of them.

'I'm sure we can come to a palatable arrangement here,' he glanced nervously at the flames above and then focused on the enforcer. 'Please, Enforcer Valivelle, I believe your point is made.'

The Last of the Magi

'Stay out of this, Velioth.'

'I will not stay back. Not when our people are in fear,' Velioth then turned back to the enforcer. 'Please,' he repeated.

'Leash your hound first.' said Enforcer Valivelle. He flicked his cane towards Faast.

Coinswoman Faast paused, and then she rose to her full height, planting her spear and shield into an upright position again. Her soldiers shuffled back and did the same.

'Thank you,' Velioth said.

The swirling wind then slowed, and the flames caught within it extinguished.

'Be on your way, enforcer,' Faast said. She grabbed Velioth by the upper-arm and pulled him closer. 'We shall discuss this later.'

'Very well.' He sighed heavily and then smiled at Enforcer Valivelle. 'I trust everything is now in order?'

Enforcer Valivelle nodded, while brushing dark dust from his shoulders that had fallen from above. He then finally returned to his carriage. He signalled to the other two enforcers watching on from the second carriage, and they followed suit.

Marla was one of the few to still be watching, despite how fast her heart thumped in her chest. The threat of fire was finally gone, and the Trade Quarters had been spared the wrath of the Elheim.

Velioth and Faast cleared the road and started to usher the last of the onlookers away. A few moments later, the carriages drove on, and the feyren pulling them whimpered and whined all the way.

As the final carriage pulled around the plaza and turned down the Market Quarter main road heading west, Marla had a clear view of the other side of the plaza. She spotted something familiar all the way over there. A green longcoat. The wearer wore their hood up and clutched at the hilt of a sword.

'Tharian!' she shouted – accidentally out loud. Her voice didn't travel that far, but it travelled far enough to offend the ears of those standing immediately around her.

She apologised and gave sheepish looks to those around her. After she felt the blood drain away from her cheeks, she looked back across the plaza. Tharian was gone.

PART II

Chapter 15

Friends of the Coin II

'You seem troubled,' said a voice that roused Tharian from his stupor. He looked over the countertop as the barman slid a glass of clear spirits towards him.

Tharian took a quick swig of the drink and planted a few coins on the counter. He grimaced at the taste – this one was much stronger than the last. 'You heard what happened out there, right?'

The barman scoffed. 'Yeah, I did, and so did the rest of 'em.' He gestured around the full tavern. 'But you're the only one sulking at my bar.'

Tharian scowled. 'Is that a crime?'

The barman wiped the surface around Tharian quickly and shrugged. He then moved on to serve his other customers.

Taking a moment to examine his surroundings, Tharian realised that the rest of the patrons were chatting and enjoying their drinks as if nothing about today was unusual. Many of the groups were discussing the Elheim, or the use of Arcana within their walls, but there was no serious alarm or concern in their voices, only the occasional furrowed brow or hushed curse.

Have I been gone so long that this is now... normal?

The complacency of the bar's patrons was the least of his worries. Even though they didn't seem disturbed by what happened in the plaza, Tharian was. It wasn't the acts of the Elheim directly that had him so flustered, he was more concerned that they were looking for a fugitive in the Outer Counties. They were looking for him. Already.

And then there was the name the coinsman had used. *Valivelle.* Traykin told him to expect a quick retaliation from the Valivelle family, but he never expected it to be so soon. It was as Traykin had said – if the Valivelles were involved, they needed to act quickly.

Tharian laid his head on his arms and groaned. He shouldn't have intervened. Not there, not then. He'd been away from Asturia for nearly a decade – keeping a low profile, investigating, learning. And in only a few days back in the country, he had already shown his hand by striking down an Elheim in plain sight; threatening everything he had worked so hard on for the sake of a little victory.

On the boat back to Asturia, he'd spent most of his time thinking about how he would get to the Trade Quarters without causing a scene. And yet, when a situation arose where he should have walked away and kept his head down, he instead acted and intervened. It was like a voice in his head telling him to do that which deep down he felt he needed to do.

Idiot.

And to make matters worse, he told Councillor Navarya to direct any investigating Elheim on to the Trade Quarters to search for him. The plan made sense at the time. County Bryn was left in a mess after the Elheim attack, any chance to push the next wave of Elheim away would have been good for everyone in the county.

But all it really did was move the threat from one settlement to another. The Trade Quarters was bigger, it had defensive walls and even an armed city guard and elite guard, but what more protection did that really offer the people? Armour and steel wilted against the might of Arcana.

'What was I thinking?' he said.

'What are you mumbling about, lad?'

It was Traykin. The voice was unmistakable. The wily collector lifted himself onto the next barstool along from Tharian and gently thumped him on the arm.

'I've been looking for you,' he continued. 'I heard rumour of some miserable, angsty sod drinking in the Brewers' Gallery and just had to be sure.'

'Very funny,' Tharian griped as Traykin basked in the *hilarity* of his own joke – as usual.

'What're you doing in here. Didn't take you to be the type for loitering in bars. Did you take up drinking while in Feralland?'

'Drinking in Feralland – you're kidding, right? The Awoken would use this swill for treating hunting wounds, not for drinking.' Tharian flashed his glass in front of Traykin and then planted it in front of his old friend. 'Just fancied a change of scenery, especially

The Last of the Magi

after that demonstration from the Elheim. You're right, we need to move fast.'

Traykin nodded. He waved down the barman and pointed to a lavish bottle at the back wall. He then finished off Tharian's drink in the time it took the barman to turn his back. 'Exactly right, lad. Nasty business those Elheim coming through here. But it may have just opened an opportunity for us.'

'How so?'

Traykin slapped his hand onto the bar and slid something towards Tharian. He kept it hidden for a moment. 'Coinswoman Faast is riled up. And I don't just mean she's pissed off – I mean she wants blood.'

'Then she should go and get it,' smirked Tharian.

'Don't be daft. She may be hot-headed, but she isn't rash.' He lifted his hand and tapped the downturned card he planted on the bar. 'The point is, she had organised one of her Crucible fighting tournaments for this afternoon. I was going to try and find out when the next one was so we could sign you up, but as luck would have it today's events have caused a few of the combatants to pull out. Apparently, the idea of standing under a vortex of fire as an elite guard is no longer appealing to some.' He flipped over the card. 'There are spaces that urgently need filling.'

'So, this really is my best way of getting to the coinswoman?'

'Afraid so. I didn't expect it to be an option for this Crucible, combatants usually register quite far in advance and take all the spaces. We're lucky, I suppose, that some of the brutes in this city have weak stomachs, and that Faast is demanding the bloody thing goes ahead so she can fill her ranks.'

'You better be right about this, Traykin. But if I end up conscripted in her elite guard, I'll strangle you with your beard.'

Traykin brought a hand over his chin and then chuckled. 'Don't be thick, Tharian. The winners in the Crucible get to meet with Faast after the tourney and she *invites* them to join her elites. That's your chance to get her talking. You're not obliged to join.'

'Alright. What are the rules?' Tharian asked as he looked over the Crucible ticket.

'It's a one-on-one bout with an existing elite guard. Win your match and you'll be invited back to Faast's keep.'

'Is that all?' Tharian said mockingly. He then tapped his chest, feeling his leather cuirass. 'Do I get to go as I am?'

'You do. Faast wants each combatant at their best. All fighting styles and specialisms are welcome. You need to prove you're the best at what you do.'

Tharian's eyes lit up and he looked at Traykin sidelong. Being able to use his own equipment made this much more interesting, especially when he had a runeblade at his hip. Traykin must have known what he was thinking, as he frowned and shook his head.

'Use your head, lad. In the Crucible you'll just be a man skilled with the sword. Magically enchanted weaponry is prohibited here too, even if only to appease the Grand City. Don't make things worse than they already are.'

Tharian nodded. 'Noted. Do you think I stand a chance?'

'You're Greycloak's boy, aren't you?'

Tharian laughed. 'He was a pacifist.'

Traykin laughed too. 'I wasn't talking about *that* part of him. He got things done; he was capable in his own ways. He didn't raise a useless boy now, did he?'

A small smile broke across Tharian's lips. He pushed himself off his seat and swiped the card from the bar. 'Far from it. So how do I enter?'

Traykin gave him an impish look and pointed to the ticket. 'I've already enrolled you. Good luck, lad.'

***

Tharian stopped off at Traykin's Bazaar to leave some of his personal effects in Frigg's safekeeping. Decanting various travelling tools, lockpicks, and ration supplies from his coat pockets, Frigg took them to the basement where Traykin kept most of his prized personal treasures.

Tharian's shoulders felt incredibly light without that extra weight. He thanked Frigg for the assistance and was just about to leave the Bazaar when he caught sight of his green coat-sleeve as he reached for the door handle. Although the green was dark, and not

The Last of the Magi

garish, it was nonetheless an uncommon and easily recognisable shade for a coat. And the coat itself still had a weight to it. Begrudgingly, he slipped the longcoat off and handed it over. Without it, he would look plain and hopefully less memorable. Plus, Tharian had always been a lithe fighter. If he was going to fight armoured elites, it made sense to maximise his dexterity where he could.

More importantly, he'd been wearing that coat in County Bryn. He would be best to avoid wearing it in such a public arena.

With that done, Tharian spent a couple of hours training in the yard with the dummies Frigg had set up for him. He did just enough to limber up and get adrenaline surging, but not too much as to strain or tire himself. Feeling satisfied with his warm-up, he set off for the Quarter of War.

Tharian felt naked without his coat. Although he still wore a grey long-sleeved shirt underneath his brown leather cuirass, without the coat he felt smaller, thinner, and considerably exposed. He had no hood to hide in. He avoided eye contact with everyone he passed on his way through the Collectors Quarter, and then the central plaza, and then finally the Quarter of War.

The smell of smoke and the warm air billowing out from the many blacksmiths along the road was suffocating. Tharian had to breathe through the fabric of his shirt a few times to stop himself from choking on the fumes. His coughing revealed him as someone unaccustomed to the toxic air, and he could feel the prying eyes of some of the militia bands that loitered about. He knew not to give them any satisfaction by reacting. The last thing he wanted was to have a street fight on his way to an arena brawl.

As he considered what he might face in the Crucible, he walked through a billowing smoke cloud that flushed out of a metalworker's workshop and completely concealed his vision more than a few paces ahead. He ploughed on ahead with confidence in his step nonetheless.

Traykin had initially referred to these fights as a duelling ring, but he quickly changed that to instead call it the Crucible, its official name. Tharian's imagination presented him with the image of a great stone amphitheatre of sorts, not too dissimilar to an enormous structure he had seen in Feralland. A fighting arena dedicated to finding the best-of-the-best for joining the coinswoman's elite guard would surely demand such grandeur.

But then again, the structures of Feralland were ancient, crude, and simplistic. This was the Trade Quarters – where the greatest crafters and artisans in Asturia lived. The design of the Crucible could well be more artistic or innovative in character.

Tharian waved his way through the smokescreen until he could finally see further ahead. To his surprise, the Quarter of War's main road opened out into a large circular space. There was no such grand structure awaiting him.

The road he travelled split into two, curving left and right in semi-circles until they met again in the distance and continued as the main road. In the smog beyond, the menacing façade of Coinswoman Faast's personal keep towered over the buildings around it.

The centre of this circular area was sunken into the ground and sealed off by a spiked metal fence with gates spread around its perimeter, each manned by a member of the city guard. Tharian continued his approach, considering sidling over to one of the guards to ask for directions.

But it was as Tharian stepped closer to the fence that he realised what this place was. This was the Crucible. It wasn't a theatre or stadium. It was a pit.

The pit was not some crude natural crater or a dug-out cavern – no, this was an intentional feature, this was by design. The pit levelled out many feet down and formed a circular space lightly dusted in sand. Tharian understood now why Traykin had first said 'duelling ring'.

The walls were steep in their descent to the bottom. Stone steps had been etched into those walls to bring people from the street level down to that space below, with only the thinnest handrail running alongside it. It was the entranceways to these steps that the guards were protecting.

This was the opposite of what Tharian expected to find, but there was something still quite appealing about the design. The fighting arena down below was in full view of the spectators that

The Last of the Magi

could gather at the fences, or on the slightly higher ground behind before them without becoming a distraction to the fighters.

Not a great amount of space for an audience, Tharian considered as he imagined throngs of people shuffling and squabbling to get a clear look through the gaps of the iron fencing. The perimeter was large, and the slope of the road helped create a vantage point for those further back, but still only a thin crowd would get a clear view of the action.

Tharian peered through the fencing himself, but his attention was then drawn up, to the buildings that towered around this circular area. These buildings were a good floor or two taller than most others on the main road, and each sported spectacular balconies with steeped seating. That must have been where most gathered to watch the excitement from on-high.

'You here for the fight?' said a voice at Tharian's side. One of the city guards.

'I suppose I am,' Tharian replied, 'Where do I need to go?'

'Ticket?' the man said, clutching a hand in the air.

Tharian pulled out the card given to him by Traykin and handed it over. The man snatched it and brought it close to his face, squinting at its lettering.

'Is there an issue?' Tharian asked.

The man lunged his hand out, suddenly and without warning, shoving Tharian at his collar bone. The force partly spun him around and made him lose his footing. He regained his balance just in time to stop himself collapsing into a heap on the ground.

He turned back to the guard, breathing sharply through his nose and grimacing.

The guard snorted with laughter. 'No bets on you.' He pulled a ring of keys from his pocket and unlocked the metal chain around the gate. He pushed the gate open and swung his head towards the Crucible for Tharian to proceed down the steps.

Tharian tugged at the bottom of his cuirass to re-align his clothing and then passed through the gate. 'That'll be your loss, my friend,' he said as he passed the guard.

The angle at which the steps scaled down the wall was stomach-churning. From the precipice at the top step, if Tharian looked down it looked like there was a dead-drop to the bottom. The handrail was the only thing that really gave away the fact that there were steps at all. Tharian had no fear of heights, but the prospect of plummeting to the Crucible's arena below was not appealing in the slightest.

One slow step at a time, Tharian descended until he finally planted his foot into the sand and dust of the flat ground at the bottom. The arena looked bigger up close, maybe around 45 feet in diameter. The most notable thing about this space was not what he expected it to be – it was the air quality. The smog didn't reach this depth. The heat of the city kept it slowly drifting upwards from the main road level. That meant Tharian could breathe easily, for the first time in days, and he could see his surroundings clearly.

The yellowish stone walls had small viewports carved into them with vertical metal bars running through them. On opposite sides of the arena, portcullises covered the openings into what must have been a series of rooms hidden away for the fighters. One of them was wedged open, and gruff voices could be heard from within. Assuming he would have no luck trying to get through the closed portcullis, he followed the sound from the open one. The voices from within became clearer as he passed through the opening.

'...crack their bloody skulls when I get the chance.' said a burly, gruff voice.

'Calm yourself, Tyce, you'll exhaust yourself before the fighting even starts,' said a woman with a sophisticated tone to her voice. 'You don't want a repeat of your last tourney.'

'I'll do what I like!' Tyce shouted back, with enough force to vibrate the stone walls with every syllable.

Faced with a branching stone corridor, Tharian followed the sound of the voices to his left to find a small waiting area with a wooden bench in the centre and a single window looking out onto the arena. There were three people in the room.

A woman, wearing a feathered cap, red waistcoat, and a money pouch around her belt, stared out the window. Tharian assumed the aggressive voice came from the muscular wall-of-a-man that sat uncomfortably on the bench with his shirt off. In the far corner, a second man was sat quietly poking at some coins in his palm. He wore a shirt and waistcoat much like the woman's but his were a

The Last of the Magi

simple black and white, so he didn't stand out as much.

'Look at this, Tyce, you're not the only challenger left after all.' The woman pointed to Tharian at the doorway and eyed him intently.

Tyce looked Tharian up and down and then shook his head in disappointment, blowing air forcefully through his nostrils like a disgruntled feyren.

'Here to prove yourself in the Crucible, are you?' the woman asked, leaning against the wall with one hand grabbing a metal bar in the window.

'That's right. This is my first time – what do I need to know?'

Tyce bolted to his feet, stepped over the bench, and grabbed a heavy metal mace from a rack on the wall. He approached Tharian with a single broad step and towered over him with the mace brandished between them.

'You get your weapon. You hit the other guy with it and try not to get the shit kicked out of you while doing it.' He then slumped back onto the bench. It creaked and cracked under his weight. Tharian shuddered – not from intimidation, but from the abnormally brutish sight of the man. He was just a block, with a shaved head, a cumbersome amount of muscle that gave his body a cube-like appearance, and no other discernible features.

The woman stepped over and stopped between Tyce and Tharian. 'Yes, thank you, Tyce,' she said, rolling her eyes. She smiled at Tharian. 'Tyce here is a regular – a real crowd-pleaser. But he does get himself quite worked up prior to a fight. Today more so than usual.'

'I wonder why,' said Tharian, feigning complete disinterest in Tyce.

A regular? He pondered, *in a tournament to win membership to Coinswoman Faast's elite guard… interesting.* That told him all he needed to know about the man's capabilities.

'There isn't much you need to worry about, by way of rules, except for one big one – don't kill, maim or cause permanent injury. The aim is to get your opponent to submit or surrender, not to disable them or cause unnecessary bloodshed. This is a display of skill, not indulgent brutality'—the woman squinted and looked off to the side for a moment—'that said, you need to bring your best. Faast's elite guard can get a bit over-zealous. We've had more than a few broken bones in the arena.'

Tharian cocked his head. 'Didn't you just say no permanent injuries?'

'They recovered.'

'Right.'

'The elite guard are called elite for a reason. Some of them don't know their own strength. They didn't get to where they are by being soft. And they haven't brought down raiding parties of thugs and bandits by pulling their punches.'

Tyce slammed his mace into the ground, startling the woman whose back was turned to him.

'I can expect a fierce fight then?' Tharian said bluntly.

The woman laughed, snapped her fingers, and winked before returning to her window.

'Sounds straightforward enough.'

Tyce punched the bench, leaving an imprint of his gargantuan knuckles in the wood. 'The rules are the easy bit. Lasting more than ten seconds on your feet when you're as thin as grass is the hard bit.'

Tharian didn't bite back. He'd dealt with bigger and more threatening beasts than Tyce. He simply walked over to the window and looked outside nonchalantly.

He waited a few seconds and then responded to Tyce, without looking over. 'I'm surprised an oaf like you even managed to understand the rules. Did someone have to read them to you?'

Tyce jumped back to his feet. 'What was that?!'

'Sit down, Tyce. You brawl in the ring, or not at all!' the woman shouted back.

The clinking of coins drew Tharian's attention to the quiet man in the corner. He closed his palm and tucked the coins into his waistcoat pocket. With a lethargic grunt, he then slid off the barrel he was using as a stool, wiped himself down and walked over to Tharian. He smiled warmly and gestured for Tharian to follow. 'Let's get you registered while it's still quiet.'

They left the waiting room together. The man led Tharian to a

The Last of the Magi

door a short distance away. It was heavy and took the man some force to push open. It screeched as it scraped across the ground.

This room was once a prison cell. that much was clear. Cuff chains were strewn across the floor, still connected by links that led to the back wall. The dust and webbing coating them almost camouflaged them against the stonework. Despite its neglected back wall and corners, the middle of the room had seen some sign of recent use. The space had become an office of sorts, furnished with a battered wooden desk and chairs on either side.

The man gestured for Tharian to sit and then swung himself into the seat on the far side. He pulled a pencil and small notepad from his waistcoat pocket.

'Assuming you do actually intend on entering the tourney, rather than just riling up its mascot, can I take your name please?'

Tharian went to answer but he stopped himself. *I should have thought about this.*

The man cocked a brow and then smirked as he brought his pencil into position to begin writing. 'This is the Crucible. Real names don't matter here. But do think carefully, this name may end up sticking with you – for better or for worse depending on how you perform out there.'

'I'll enter as Greycloak.' Tharian said abruptly. The words left his lips before he had time to consider them.

The man wrote the name and then leaned to look around Tharian. 'You don't have a cloak,' he said.

'No, I don't.'

'You're barely wearing any grey.'

Tharian sighed and took his seat. He sat back, resigning himself to the process. Examining the room, he spotted an old grey sheet hanging against the wall. Whether it had once been used as a blanket, bed sheet or dust cover he didn't know, nor did he want to know, but it *was* grey. Tharian reached over, grabbed it, laced the corners of it through the shoulder-straps of his leather cuirass and tied quick knots.

'Happy now?' Tharian said.

'Greycloak?'

'Yes, Greycloak.'

'Very well' he scribbled the name Greycloak on the next available line on the notepad, having apparently struck it out the first time he wrote it, and then he laid the pencil along the pad's top edge. 'You're not known to the Crucible. Most bets will likely be placed against you.'

Tharian shrugged. 'I'm not interested in that.'

The man just stared at him for a few seconds and then smiled again. 'That is your prerogative, but the Crucible needs coin and I need to know whether you are capable.'

Tharian sighed again and pushed up from his seat. 'You'll just have to wait and see.'

'Now, now.' the man said calmly, reaching out to catch Tharian's arm. 'No need to be so hasty, *Greycloak*. All I ask is that you tell me about your fighting history.'

'You don't need my history. You have a name, that's all you need.'

The man tutted and shook his head. 'There is no need for such hostility, it is merely a formality.'

'I'm only here to fight. I'll prove myself out there, not in here.' Tharian swept the man's arm away and then made for the door.

'Fine.' The man shooed Tharian away and flipped a few pages of his notepad back over and examined his older notes. 'I'll be sure to notify the coinswoman of your non-compliance with her protocols.'

Tharian was reaching for the door as those words reached him. He took a deep breath and looked back over his shoulder. 'So, this is for the coinswoman's information, not just your own?'

'You should consider the tourney process an extended assessment of your suitability to join the elites. Compliance and discipline are of as much value to Coinswoman Faast as brawn and skill.'

'Then ask your questions.'

With his tongue pressed to the roof of his mouth, the man rubbed his hands together and flipped the pages of his notepad over again. 'Weapon of choice – I assume the longsword?' he pointed the end of his pencil to the sword hilt at Tharian's side.

'Very observant.'

The Last of the Magi

'Military background?'

'None.'

'Local guard?'

Tharian shook his head.

The man looked off and squinted for a moment and then gazed back to Tharian. 'A hunter perhaps?'

'No.'

'Then what is your occupation – where did you learn the blade?'

'I had training overseas.'

'Very amusing. Need I remind you that my notes will be seen by the coinswoman?'

Tharian turned back into the room properly. 'It's the truth, but if you need something more *normal* for your notes then you can put down 'sellsword' if that helps.'

'But that's not truly your occupation?'

'I suppose it could be. It depends on your perspective. I use my skills where they're needed rather than where I'm told to use them, but I don't get paid for it.'

The man coughed a laugh. 'That sounds like a poor sellsword.'

'Then put that in your notes if you must.'

'Fine, fine. Do you have any accolades?'

'Such as?'

'Have you fought in other tournaments? Perhaps you've had to fight mercenaries or criminals in your *sellsword* work?'

'Not exactly. I've had to deal with some…' Tharian held back. *If he doesn't believe me about training overseas, he won't believe that I've fought off packs of savage beasts in Feralland.*

'Deal with some… what?' the man asked.

'I've beaten my fair share of strong fighters.'

'That's it?' the man said. 'Hardly inspiring.'

'What are you expecting from me?' —Tharian had to bite back from cursing. This exercise was a waste of time. It had no benefit to him – if the coinswoman would be irritated by his supposed 'non-compliance' then so be it.

'I'm not expecting anything. But anyone who is brave enough to enter the Crucible usually has the gall to talk big about their capabilities – even if those capabilities turn out to be overstated, as they oft are.'

Tharian shook his head and groaned. He moved back to the doorway, dragged the door open slightly and then paused. If giving this man something more exciting for his notes would shut him up, then Tharian would give him what he wanted. 'Then how about this, write down on your little notepad that Greycloak is a hunter – a hunter of Elheim – capable of holding his own against Arcana.'

Tharian slipped through the door and pulled it closed, leaving the man alone in the small cell. He heard him scoff and call out – 'now you're just being ridiculous!' – his voice only just audible through the grated opening near the top of the door.

Now away from that frustrating experience, Tharian marched down the corridor until he found an empty waiting room, not dissimilar to the first he entered. He decided to wait there, alone, so he wouldn't be disturbed. As soon as he sat on the bench and laid his head back against the wall, he untied the grey sheet and let it drop to the floor.

He regretted his rash words.

To distract himself, he just stared back the way he came in, watching as other fighters eventually trickled in over the next couple of hours. They were a weird and wonderful group. Some were hulking, strong figures with intimidating frames. Others were slender and lithe. And then some were meek and possibly infirm, either old men or over-zealous teenagers barely old enough to handle the weight of a weapon.

The chance of prosperity attracts all kinds in the Quarters, Tharian theorised. He caught a few murmurings from the organisers in the next room, and they expressed the same concerns that Traykin had mentioned earlier – the Elheim incident in the plaza had shaken the nerve of many regular combatants. Numbers were woefully low, as was quality.

Perhaps the reduction in fighters would help his odds, Tharian considered If Faast was so keen on filling her ranks, maybe the elites fighting in the Crucible would go easier on them. Then again, maybe they would fight harder to prove their strength.

***

The Last of the Magi

Marla's heart had been racing all day. The Elheim and their 'demonstration' of Arcana was enough to set anyone on edge. But that was only a lingering ember of nerves by the time late afternoon rolled around. The real cause of her excitement was what she could see below. This time, her heart raced with actual excitement rather than a foreboding fear and dread.

'So, people fight down there? What's the point?' Marla leaned forward, her head extended over the balcony, to take in the full scale of the deep fighting pit below.

'Entertainment,' said Brayne, as he helped himself to some strips of freshly cooked lirrus meat that had been provided by the tavern below their balcony. They were drenched in a dark, sticky sauce.

Marion tutted loudly. 'It's much more sophisticated than *that*, Brayne.'

'It's also entertainment,' he said as he washed down the scoffed meat with an ale.

Marla swung back to her seat beside Marion and looked between the bickering couple with an excitable energy brimming within.

Marion looked exhausted as she turned away from Brayne, shaking her head derisively, and instead she gave her attention to Marla. 'I'm not sure we should be here. I don't feel safe knowing enforcers were in the city.'

Brayne grunted, even though the comment wasn't directed his way. 'You heard what she said – she's said it at least three times now – they came, they put on their fire show and then they moved on. End of story.'

Brayne grunted again, this time because Marion swung her elbow into his side.

'That's enough about *fire shows*, thank you very much,' she hissed in a hushed tone. Turning back to Marla again, she cupped the young woman's hand between her own. 'Sorry about that, he needs to remember what you've been through before he opens his big mouth.'

Marla smiled. 'It's alright, really.'

'Even so,' Marion trailed off as her expression became troubled.

'Don't worry about it,' Marla said, as reassuringly as she could while tapping Marion's hand to bring her attention back.

Marion forced a smile, but it didn't soften the concern reflecting in her eyes.

Marla thought it best to try and take Marion's mind off the situation. 'You were saying that the Crucible was about more than just fighting?'

Marion stared back blankly for a few seconds before remembering what she had been saying. The colour returned to her cheeks, and she pointed to the fighting pit below. 'To a spectator, the Crucible tourneys are just about entertainment and gambling. But like everything else in this city there is more to see if you step back or, in this case, step above it.'

She curled a finger to lure Marla closer to the balcony edge before she continued. 'The competitors fight to prove themselves worthy to join Coinswoman Faast's elite guard. The people who gather around the outside are here to place bets on the fights and try to make a profit.' Marion waved her finger in a circular motion to trace the arena's edge. Crowds of Quartersfolk had indeed started to tightly pack themselves into the space below.

'I assume we're not placing any bets, then?' Marla looked at the other two, trying to judge whether either of them might be the gambling type – not that she had any idea what a gambler looked like. It wasn't a common activity in the Outer Counties.

'No, definitely not. We're here to watch what happens very closely.'

Cocking her head, Marla still felt none the wiser. She imagined the types of soldiers and warriors that would come here to fight, and she pictured the gold and black armoured men and women who stood alongside Faast with their elegant weapons, sophisticated martial stances, and fearless postures. But then she considered Marion, the soft-hearted and gentle woman who didn't seem to have a violent bone in her body.

'I hope you don't mind me asking,' Marla said, 'but I wouldn't have put you down as a fan of competitive fighting.'

Brayne laughed from the other side of Marion. Scraps of meat spat out his mouth and flew over the balcony railing. 'She hates it!'

The Last of the Magi

Marion sighed deeply and elbowed Brayne again. 'That may be so. But these tournaments create a lot of opportunity for us artisans.'

'How?' asked Marla.

'There.' Brayne pointed to the arena's edge.

Marion squinted and looked that way. 'Yes – good spot, dear.' She then pointed in the same direction and Marla hovered around until she could see what had caught their attention. She found it quite easily. There was a brutishly framed woman heading down the steep steps into the Crucible.

'Do you see her?' Marion asked. 'She might not wear much armour, but I can see from here that she has chosen the spear as her weapon of choice.'

'Yeah, I see. Is that important?' replied Marla.

Marion winked. 'It is if she wins. All members of the elite guard get custom-made armour and a very ornate weapon crafted for them. That means there will be a contract for tender. Lucrative work. We want to make sure we get a bid in as soon as possible after the tourney is over.'

Marla's mouth opened as she finally understood. 'That's brilliant! So, you're scouting for work?'

To Marla's surprise, Marion just shrugged. 'The problem is we aren't the only ones who do it. Most of the private balconies have been rented out by other artisans. Some of them our direct competitors. Unfortunately, it's become a necessity for us to do this.'

Looking around at the other inns, taverns and bistros that stretched around the perimeter of the Crucible, Marla noticed that groups of wealthy-looking spectators gathered to watch the tournament from their own balconies. Some of those groups were making notes and sketches of what they saw as each combatant made their way down the steps.

Brayne cleared his throat. 'Keep your eyes sharp, the tourney will be starting soon. We don't want to miss anything.'

Chapter 16

The Crucible

'Merchants, warriors, collectors and artisans – attention please!'

The voice boomed from somewhere elsewhere in the Crucible and cut through the furore of the crowds assembling up above.

Tharian crept out of his waiting room and peered through one of the barred windows. There was nobody in the sandy arena, so he pressed his head closer to the bars to look higher.

The woman in the red waistcoat and feathered cap from the first waiting room was stood on a ledge jutting out from the one of the sloping walls. She had her arms raised in the air as she waved to the crowd staring down into the pit. And the crowd listened to her intently.

'Before we begin, a short message from our very own Coinswoman Faast which I have the honour of passing on to you. Many of you will have today witnessed the act of trespass committed by the Grand City of Elheim, and their reckless display of Arcana in the central plaza.'

The crowd fell completely silent. She nodded sympathetically and even rolled her wrists in a way that somehow seemed sorrowful. This mistress of ceremonies was quite the performer.

'In response to this, our coinswoman has a simple message of reassurance. Should the Elheim dare to disrespect the laws of the Trade Quarters again, the Quarter of War will not hesitate in expelling the Elheim and their enforcers from our city by force!'

The crowd erupted into a raucous applause that rattled the air.

'Yes – yes, our coinswoman is truly a blessing upon the Quarters. But she also says this: today's events should remind us just how important these tourneys are. Through this competition of strength and skill we ensure that the very greatest warriors of Asturia are ready to stand at arms to defend our independence!'

The crowd's clapping turned into stamping, cheering, and whistling. The volume of it reached levels that surely could stretch

The Last of the Magi

the entire breadth of the city. Tharian felt slightly unnerved as their stamping shook the roof above his head, causing dust to fall around him.

Whilst the woman on the ledge basked in the glory of her cheering crowd, a man in similar dress poked out of the shadows from behind her and whispered into her ear. She leaned back to him.

She then waved her arms again to calm her audience. Only when they fell silent did she speak again.

'Are you ready for your first bout?!' she roared. The crowd roared back with ten times the volume and energy. 'Then let me welcome to the arena your first combatant. From the east gate, I give you a legendary fencer from County Haarb rumoured to be the fastest duellist in all Asturia – Erik Morewent!'

A few moments later, a tall man stepped out of the portcullis and emerged in Tharian's view of the arena. The man had his hand cupped over his eyes at first but then waved to the crowd, stoking their excitement even further. He was dressed in a black gambeson with matching padded trousers that covered him from head to toe. His face was thin, his hair greying at the roots. As he waved to the crowd with one hand, he balanced the blade of a silver rapier across his shoulder with the other.

Morewent stepped into the centre of the arena, he flourished the tip of his rapier to the ground and, in a movement of swift finesse, spun to draw a circle in the sand. Then, after a horizontal slash left and right, he bowed.

The cheers went on and on. Tharian scoffed. *A showman,* he concluded. This man didn't fill him with much confidence, if his fanciful performance was an indication of how seriously he was taking the tourney.

The booming voice of the mistress of ceremonies took over once more. 'I think I can speak for everyone when I say this – Morewent appears a skilled swordsman indeed. But let's see what the coinswoman has in store for him. From the west gate, the coinswoman has chosen Shiv to take this first bout.'

The west portcullis screeched open. Out from its shadows emerged the black and gold shining armour of one of the elite guards.

Shiv was small, particularly in comparison to Morewent. As Shiv stopped at their mark, they drew two daggers from their waist and held a stoic position. No flourish, no crowd-rousing performance. Just a soldier with their chosen weapon, ready to fight.

That's more like it. Tharian smirked. He noticed the way this elite held themselves. Their grip on their weapons was firm, but their arms and knees were limber and clearly ready to move. This was his first opportunity to analyse the kind of opponent he would be up against.

The mistress of ceremonies, lording over them from her lofty ledge, reminded them of the essential rules: no intentional wounding or maiming; a single round of combat until one fighter surrenders or passes out. She then drew the crowd to silence once more and held everyone in anticipation for a few moments.

'Begin!'

Morewent was the first to strike, closing the gap between them and making quick use of his rapier to try and misdirect and disorient his opponent. But, to his clear surprise, Shiv simply twisted, ducked, stepped, and turned out of the way of each swing. Despite the burdensome weight of Shiv's armour, they moved gracefully as if they were only wearing cloth.

The foolhardy rush from Morewent turned out to be ill-planned. Even to Tharian's less trained eye, it was obvious that Morewent overstretched himself in that opening move.

Shiv's stance shifted in response. Their dodges became parries. Side-steps became feints. The precision with which Shiv raised a dagger blade through the air to deflect Morewent's rapier was sublime – and the daggers seemed to spin around in their palms effortlessly, with the blades coming closer and closer to Morewent's chest each time.

Tharian found himself instinctively nodding along with all of Shiv's moves. This elite was using their head more than their muscles. Tharian smirked as he realised what Shiv was doing with these distracting movements. And it wasn't until Morewent's heel tapped against the stone wall behind that he realised it too. Shiv's movements had trapped their opponent at the arena's edge.

Morewent resorted to sweeping his blade through the air in

The Last of the Magi

manic motions to force Shiv back – which succeeded – but this brought the two fighters right back where they started.

Shiv returned to the pose they held when they first entered the arena, as if they had returned to a dormant state, waiting to respond to their surroundings.

Morewent was breathing heavily. The adrenaline and the panic from being so close to the turbine-like bladework of his opponent was taking its toll.

Taking a deep breath, Morewent lunged forward again, this time keeping his rapier carefully poised in front of him and pointed at Shiv's head. He bravely charged on. But Shiv didn't move. The gap between them became smaller and smaller and smaller until the rapier was about to pierce straight through Shiv's helm.

And that is when Shiv finally moved. A dagger blade flashed up and curled the rapier blade just far enough sideways to remove its threat. But Shiv otherwise remained still, allowing Morewent to slam into Shiv's body and bounce off the heavy metal armour. Shiv hardly even flinched from the collision, despite being much smaller in stature. They only shifted a foot back to cushion against the momentum, and that was it.

Morewent, however, was knocked to the ground. Shiv then stepped in close and planted one foot on Morewent's wrist and squatted over his chest, with both dagger blades crossed over Erik's throat.

Despite the crowd's gasps, Tharian just about heard Shiv speak one word: 'Concede?'

Morewent stuttered before finding his voice. 'I do.'

The crowd erupted into a mixture of mostly cheers and a few dissenting boos. Tharian's heartbeat was pounding in his ears. The fight was exciting, that was unquestionable, but seeing the elite guard standing as the victor was a stark reminder that it would soon be *him* stood in the arena ready to fight.

***

'I've never seen someone fight like that,' said Marla, staring down at the elite guard pinning their defeated opponent to the ground.

'Imagine what would happen if Shiv was fighting for real,' said Brayne. He smirked at Marla. For the first time, Brayne made eye contact with her intentionally, and for more than a few short seconds. He didn't even seem to regret it as he looked back down to the arena.

'I suppose you won't be designing any rapiers then.'

Brayne laughed and then carried on his gluttonous snacking. 'Perhaps not. That suits me though. Rapiers are all petals and no thorn when it comes to the craft.'

Marla scoffed and Brayne gave her a quizzing look. 'I agree,' she said. 'Great weapons in their own right, but you can't do much with a blade that thin and delicate. All the design would go into the hilt and handle. Not enough surface area to work with.'

She noticed Brayne raise a brow and the corner of his mouth curled up. 'That's right,' he said.

Marla leaned back over the railing to await the next fighters. Shiv helped Morewent back onto his feet and then gestured for him to head back through the challengers' portcullis. Shiv then bowed to the mistress of ceremonies and disappeared back into the opposite chambers.

While the mistress of ceremonies conferred with her colleague hidden in the shadows behind her ledge, Marla's attention was drawn to a group of Quartersfolk pushing to speak with a man also dressed in the same red-waistcoated uniform at the edge of the arena on the street-level. He frantically sifted through scraps of paper being thrown at him and handed coins out to some of the gamblers while handing none to others, despite their very vocal protests. Two heavily armoured guards stood at the man's flanks to push back those who came too close.

Marla hummed deeply. It was an unruly mess down there. Very different to the sophisticated, opportunistic observations being made at the balcony level. Yet, the sophistication didn't guarantee prosperity. Each of these business owners – the other artisans eyeing the combatants so intently – were in competition with each other for the work that might come after the tourney was finished. The crowd below, rowdy though it was, were in competition with each other also. It was just a quicker and smaller-scale form of business. It was

The Last of the Magi

all about coin exchanging hands.

Marla sat back. *A well-oiled machine,* she mused.

***

Tharian watched the next two rounds from the same window. Both ended in a similar fashion. Combatants of different shapes and sizes entered the ring, one walked away victorious and the other went away to lick their wounds.

The first fight was between a tall, brutish woman with a spear – going by the name 'Brace' – and she was taken down by an elite who looked no older than a teenager judging by his frame. To make matters more embarrassing for the challenger, he only had a shortsword. The crowd chanted the name 'Jaymes' as he claimed that win. He must have been a fan favourite elite.

The second fight was over far too quickly to take much from it. Though each fight was very different to the last, there was one consistent feature each time – the elite guard always came out on top.

Tharian's nerves had steeled somewhat since the excitement of the first fight. He took a deep breath and exhaled through his nose and then retreated to his quiet waiting room. To his relief there was still nobody else in there, so he took a seat in the dark, dingey room.

No more than five minutes could have passed before he was interrupted, by the man who had registered him earlier. The man appeared at the archway of the waiting area and waved his hand erratically. He was panting heavily, and his brow was glistening as he wiped at it with the back of his hand.

'There you are! I've been looking all over. You're up next.'

Tharian stared at the man as he contemplated the reality of those words.

'Come on. You don't want to upset the coinswoman by holding up her show.'

Tharian rolled his eyes, but he stood and slowly made his way over – ignoring the attendant. 'Who am I up against?' he asked, while tightening the fastenings of his sheath.

'You'll find out once you're in the ring, just like everyone else.''

'Fine. Lead on then.'

The attendant walked ahead energetically and Tharian followed close behind. They walked around the winding corridor, passing through beams of smog-dulled light shining through the windows. The attendant didn't stop until they reached the portcullis gate.

'Stand here,' he said, pointing very deliberately at the middle of the portcullis. 'When you're called, that's your cue.'

All part of the spectacle, Tharian thought as he took his position as instructed. The thought of stepping out into a combat arena to fight with one of the Trade Quarters' strongest fighters suddenly felt like the least of his trouble as he stared through the portcullis bars. He was about to be out in the open, a spectacle for the masses to watch and gawk at. That unnerved him more than the thought of being beaten black and blue.

'This was a terrible idea,' he muttered.

'Hm?' the attendant leaned towards him. 'What was that?'

'Nothing.' Tharian waved him away.

As Tharian stood there, looking through the bars of the portcullis to the arena beyond, he remembered why he was here.

The Grand City won't be brought down from the shadows. It will take force, a show of strength, and allies willing to stand out in the open and be counted. I need to get used to this.

Confidence and anxiety became entwined as Tharian waited for his round to begin.

With a screech, and the sound of cranking metal, the portcullis started to lift. And the booming voice of the mistress of ceremonies flooded the air once again.

'Are you ready for the next round?!' she shouted, sending the crowd into another frenzy.

She clapped at the crowd's excitement. 'This fight promises to be an excellent one, I assure you. We have a new fighter entering the Crucible, and he is here to prove himself worthy of the title he bears.'

Tharian cocked his head and leaned forward slightly to listen more closely. *What title? Greycloak is hardly a title.*

'I introduce to you – your new challenger – the *Arcana Hunter!*'

The crowd started to cheer, but as the words hit them there were

The Last of the Magi

a few confused gasps added into the mix. A chill pulsed through Tharian's body, and he reeled at what he just heard. Within seconds, the crowd were cheering that name.

Tharian shook his head in disbelief. He looked at the attendant behind him, seeing that the man was rubbing his hands together and flashing his teeth in sheer delight at the crowd's excitement.

The attendant noticed Tharian's concerned expression. 'What? That's what you told me, wasn't it?'

'Greycloak.' He muttered in response, until he finally felt his bite return. 'I gave you the name Greycloak!'

Rolling his hands through the air again, the usher stuck out his lip. 'Maybe you did. But you also said more, and I embellished on that, as is my job. The crowd love it!'

Arcana Hunter. It wasn't even subtle. Tharian didn't know what to do or say, the words had already been said aloud, and heard by all those up above gathered from across the four quarters. What target had just been painted on his back, to add to that already looming over him with the Grand City?

Tharian considered shirking away from the portcullis and withdrawing from the tournament altogether. But before he could act on those thoughts, the opportunity to flee was taken away as a hand pushed firmly between his shoulders and shunted him into the arena.

His ears were ringing, and he became deaf to the cheers of the crowd and the words of the mistress of ceremonies as she called out the next fighter. Tharian stepped out across the sandy floor, stopping somewhere near the arena's centre.

The opposite portcullis opened, and out stepped a broad man wielding a golden sword in one hand. With each of his steps, the dust and sand under his boots blew away from the force of his gait. The elite stopped a short distance from where Tharian stood, and then he turned slightly. Tharian then could see that the weapon was not a simple sword – it was a double-ended blade weapon, not dissimilar in design from a quarterstaff, designed to be wielded from the middle, with small handles in the inside edges of the blades for assisting with moving it into new positions. Tharian had seen many weapons before, but he didn't have a name for this one. A double-ended glaive? A two-bladed sword? A double glaive perhaps?

Tharian drew his runeblade and held it close. Then they both waited.

'*Begin!*'

***

'If you lean any further over that rail, you'll end up in the fight yourself,' said Brayne.

Marla reluctantly glanced down and saw the tops of many heads swarming about. Realising just how much of her torso was protruding out of the safety of their private balcony, Marla fell back into her seat. She needed to lean further out to get a better look – she needed to know for certain if she'd seen what she thought she'd just seen.

'Sorry,' she said, with a smirk creeping across her face. 'That man out there, the one they called *Arcana Hunter* just then – he's the one I travelled here with, I'm sure of it.'

Marion squinted and leaned forward. 'That one in the leather cuirass?'

'Yeah, that's Tharian.'

Marion nudged Brayne. 'What do you think?'

Brayne scoffed. 'The amateurs start well, but they don't have the stamina or experience to win.'

Marla looked back down to the arena. The start of the fight had been called but neither had made a move yet. Even though Marla was certain it was him, particularly because of the distinct blade in his hands, he looked so different. It was the lack of coat, she realised. Without it, he looked small and… normal. 'Don't overlook him just yet,' she said. 'He's more capable than he looks.'

'Let's see, shall we?' said Brayne. He clicked his fingers over his shoulder and a young man rushed forward towards him. Brayne whispered something into his ear and then pointed out to the Crucible arena.

The young man nodded and rushed off back into the building behind them.

'If he doesn't make a move soon this will be over in a flash.

The Last of the Magi

Goreson takes no prisoners in these fights.'

Marla looked back, trying to discern where the young man scurried off to. As she turned forward again, she caught Marion smiling warmly at her, and she leaned in. 'He sent one of the artisan apprentices to estimate measurements of your friend, just in case.'

Marla beamed. If Tharian won the fight and Brayne managed to secure work from it, she would be contributing to their blacksmithing work in a real way, albeit only a small way. She lunged forward again to watch the fight more closely.

Chapter 17

Arcana Hunter

The elite guard rolled his shoulders. He twirled his double glaive, moving his hands in fluid motions. He held the central hilt with one hand while the other grasped the handle on the dominant blade. Shifting his weight, he took an aggressive stance with one foot planted forward and one blade pointed at Tharian.

The elite guard spun his weapon again and swung his other leg forward, changing stance and bringing the second blade around to edge closer to Tharian.

Tharian held his runeblade steady with both hands. The grey-haired, unhelmed elite squinted at it for a moment before he lunged forward with his first strike.

Tharian reacted in turn, sliding a foot back and bringing his runeblade across to slap the attack away.

The elite recoiled and swiftly adjusted his grip, taking a different stance with the other blade now positioned forward.

His weapon is versatile, Tharian thought. *He can switch his style on the move – but the weight of both blades slows him down.* Tharian smirked and then pushed forward with his own strike. Their blades met with a ringing clash. Tharian pulled back and twisted his stance quickly enough to meet the elite's attempt at attacking with the second blade. Despite his muscle and his broad, heavy frame, he had a nimbleness to his upper body that allowed him to move his weapon in a distracting way before striking.

Tharian flared with confidence. He had sparred against Awoken who took the quarterstaff as their weapon, time and time again in Feralland, and this was not so different. He knew more than the basics of that form. So Tharian mixed up his own fighting style, switching from single-handled to double-handed forms as a counter to the elite's versatile movements.

The pair danced around the edge of the arena, sending out echoes of clanging metal as their weapons clashed. The flexibility of

The Last of the Magi

the elite's weapon meant Tharian had to dodge strikes more often than the elite did, as the elite could bring his second blade around to make the next strike before Tharian could swing the weight of his runeblade.

Tharian preferred to fight this way. He had plenty enough stamina. He would exhaust himself too quickly if he tried to bring the runeblade around to parry every strike. Relying on his dexterity was fine by him.

Be that as it may, Tharian was not the only one with advanced knowledge of duelling. Just as Tharian knew and could adapt to the technique of his opponent, so too did the elite. When one of them changed their style, the other adapted, then the first adapted again, and then the other countered. And on and on it went.

The elite guard eventually abandoned the centre hilt of his weapon and grabbed the handles embedded in the back of his blades. He hopped closer to Tharian and punched with each fist in turn, bringing each blade sweeping forward one after the other. The crossing sweeps were fast. Tharian couldn't step sideways to get out of the way. He was forced to shuffle back until he reached the arena wall. The elite quickly changed tactic again – bringing one hand back to the hilt and swinging the weapon down in an overhead cleave, trapping Tharian in his trapped position.

Tharian brought his blade up to meet the attack. Their weapons screeched together. Tharian had to raise his runeblade higher as the elite's blade slid down to his cross guard. The elite's weapon came close to cutting into his shoulder. Even with both hands gripped firmly around the hilt, Tharian's muscles couldn't compete with the force of the overbearing brute.

'Surrender,' growled the elite.

Tharian grimaced, straining to push back. 'You haven't beaten me yet.'

With a grunt, the elite pushed against him harder. 'You fight well. I hope to fight you again next time.'

Next time? How long would it be until the next tourney? This was his best chance of securing an audience in good time.

'I'll remember your name, *Arcana Hunter*' he continued. 'You might be good enough to join us one day. Not today.'

Adrenaline surged as Tharian felt his defeat closing in. It brought one word to the front of his mind.

Arcana...

Tharian's eyes snapped to the flat of his runeblade. Two runes were glowing, still charged by the strike of Arcane lightning absorbed back in Brynwell.

Tharian locked eyes with the elite, then shifted his weight and adjusted his fighting stance once more. Though he felt his attacker's weight overcome him, he managed to bring one hand up from the hilt and pressed it against the flat of the blade, over one of the runes.

It flashed. Not brightly, but enough that it caught the elite's attention and made him pause.

'What was that?' he said, his voice rising.

Tharian growled and pushed back. With the elite confused, he swung his runeblade with all the strength he had left.

His runeblade crackled and sparks of blue bolted out from the rune. The sparks ran up and down the length of the blade. The elite's eyes widened, and he hastily pulled back. Tharian was ready. He pushed harder and surged forward with enough force to knock the elite off-balance. The elite tripped over his own feet and dropped his double-glaive.

Tharian stumbled forward. He let his blade swing down to the sandy floor. The crackling electricity dissipated, exhausting the rune.

He stood over the prone elite and whipped the runeblade around to rest a few inches from the man's throat. 'You lose,' Tharian panted. He laughed under his heavy breaths at the bewildered expression on the elite's face. As he stood there, hearing the pounding of his own heart and the heavy cadence of his breathing, he noticed the crowds didn't erupt into cheers as they had at the end of other matches.

Before Tharian could say anything further, and before the mistress of ceremonies could make her next announcement, someone grabbed Tharian's arm and pulled him away. It was the attendant from earlier, the one who had pushed him into the arena, except now he was dragging Tharian back through the dark portcullis. The gate winched shut as soon as Tharian passed its

The Last of the Magi

threshold.

The man had a towel over his arm. Tharian realised how much sweat saturated his hair and most of his face. The attendant very hesitantly handed the towel out but seemed reluctant to reach too close. Tharian snatched it and wiped his face.

'What was that?' the attendant asked cautiously. His overzealous confidence was gone now.

With a sigh, Tharian replied. 'Something I will end up regretting very soon, I'm sure.' He threw the towel back at the attendant and it hit the man's chest and dropped. He made no attempt to catch it.

'What did you do?' The attendant paled and stepped back to the wall. 'Are you an enforcer?'

'*Yes, of course,*' Tharian said flippantly. 'Don't be an idiot.' Tharian waved his runeblade at his side before sheathing it away slowly. 'It's an heirloom from the pre-Elheim days – when arts of magic were not solely within Elheim control in Asturia.'

The attendant cocked a brow. He looked at the sheathed weapon with enough purpose that Tharian assumed the man now understood it was the blade that manifested the crackling lightning, not him.

'What were you thinking, giving me a name like 'Arcana Hunter', didn't you see what the Elheim did in the central plaza? If the Grand City hear that people in the Quarters were cheering on a fighter bearing that name, we both know they'll do a lot worse the next time they pass this way.'

The attendant shrugged. 'The Elheim won't dare come back through the Quarters.'

Tharian gave him a quizzing look. 'What makes you so sure?'

'They may have a monopoly on magic in Asturia, but they don't yet control our country's economy. They won't risk their relationship with us when we are the gatekeepers of commerce.'

Tharian shook his head and sighed. 'Are you blind?' He pointed in the direction of the central plaza. 'Their display of strength was intended to send out a message – the Grand City no longer respects or requires the neutrality of the Trade Quarters.'

The attendant wore a disapproving look. 'You underestimate what the Trade Quarters is capable of. We aren't a city that would just roll over at the first sign of Elheim oppression. We have the elite guard; we have the city guard. You're not really worried about the Quarters – you're trying to protect your own skin. You're worried about what the Elheim would do to *you*.'

Tharian glowered. He slowly, deliberately wrapped his fingers around the handle of his runeblade and lifted it slightly. The attendant paled again. Tharian stepped closer. 'We *all* need to tread carefully. *Very* carefully. Do you really want to test how far the Elheim can be pushed before they snap and rain fire upon us all?'

The attendant didn't respond.

'I think you should go and do everything in your power to correct this mistake of yours.'

The attendant nodded and pulled away from the wall. He made a dash for the nearest open archway, but Tharian called to him.

'I won my fight, what happens now?'

The attendant pointed to one of the waiting rooms. 'The elite guard will take you to Faast when the tourney is over. You'll be waiting a while.'

Tharian nodded and let the usher flee. He then found his way back into his preferred waiting room – tucking himself away from view until the time came for him to be summoned. Plumping himself back onto the bench in the dark room, he dropped his head into his hands and huffed heavily. *What a bloody mess.*

He had mixed emotions about the situation. On the one hand, he had beaten an elite guard and should have secured his meeting with the coinswoman as planned, but on the other he had used Arcana with an illegal runeblade, in front of an audience, and that was bound to ruffle more than a few feathers.

And then there was the title with which he had won his fight. *Arcana Hunter.*

Any hopes he had of keeping this operation stealthy and secretive were quickly dissolving away like clouds breaking after a storm. Tharian felt that *he* was the eye of that storm.

***

'Did you see that?'

This time, Brayne was the one leaning forward over the balcony.

The Last of the Magi

His brow-line cast a dark shadow over his eyes.

'I told you! I knew he would be impressive,' said Marla, thrumming from the excitement of the fight. Tharian didn't disappoint – he was as capable as she expected.

Brayne called out, and another apprentice dashed to his side to take instructions. Brayne whispered in the young man's ear and he scurried off just like the last one had. 'There's impressive, and then there's... that.'

Marla felt her excitement drop – had she done something wrong? Brayne's scowl was fierce. This was not just his normal irritableness, there was something more going on. He wouldn't even look at her. He seemed to have enjoyed the fight as much as the rest of the audience, cheering and stamping his feet in equal measure, but in the final moments of the bout he turned pensive. In fact, almost all those in the audience reacted the same way.

Sensing that it was not the best time to pry, Marla leaned back over the railing and watched the crowds below. More money exchanged hands between the gamblers and the ushers, but there was a hesitance to the way the crowd moved and discussed the battle that was not there in previous bouts. Tharian's display of strength had shaken things up for everyone.

She looked at the other groups on their balconies, and it became apparent that everyone had been surprised by the fight. Though their expressions were quizzing or showed signs of confusion, that did not stop the other artisans from whispering commands to their apprentices and sending them down to the ground level.

If she had learnt anything from today, it was that no matter what trials and tribulations the Quartersfolk faced, nothing would slow them in pursuing opportunities for further trade and profit.

Marla hoped that the concern in Brayne's expression would only be temporary. Tharian had won his fight, so he would be invited to join the elite guard, if she understood correctly. Surely she had helped Brayne gain a competitive edge for securing whatever contract work came from Tharian's win?

Marla then noticed Marion's expression, and her assumptions slipped away. Because Marion looked just as pensive and concerned as everyone else.

Chapter 18

Wrath and Mercy

'I was told the rose tea of County Bryn was a delicacy. This, however...' his father trailed off as he swilled the teacup between his hands, '...this is disappointing, Councillor.' He planted the teacup onto the side table with force. The frail, charred table almost collapsed to dust.

'Alderman, not councillor.' said the silver-haired woman sat opposite. She seemed to take some enjoyment from making that correction. 'Forgive me if the resources here are somewhat limited, you may have heard that we recently had a fire.' She hummed with satisfaction as she sipped at her own tea.

Darus noted that his father was scowling. Making no attempt to hide his irritation. Alderman Navarya, however, was apparently unfazed by it. She was braver than him.

The Elheim caravan had arrived in Brynfall only a few hours ago, and the full group of enforcers had marched up the sloping hill to Bryn Manor, the home and office of the county's previous alderman. They passed by the scorched, lifeless ground and the charred ruins of the town's buildings. Builders from across the full stretch of the Outer Counties were banding together to rebuild the once-idyllic Brynfall, and they had already done a great deal to secure the stability of what was left of those buildings still standing, especially Bryn Manor itself.

Darus couldn't stop thinking about the way those builders changed as the enforcers marched up the hill. They just stopped working. Most of them didn't dare look their way, and some even tucked themselves out of view. For those who held firm, not letting themselves be cowed by the Elheim marching through, the expressions on their faces were stark. Some were angered. Others were scared. And even for the few that forced a smile of courtesy, it was easy to tell that they harboured the same ill-feelings behind that façade.

The Last of the Magi

The smartly dressed elder of County Bryn – the newly appointed Alderman Navarya – had welcomed Darus and his father into the remains of Bryn Manor. She asked one of her county guard to wipe down and pull together the most formidable-looking chairs and tables in the centre of the large, blackened meeting hall. The room reeked of burnt wood, and the floorboards buckled loudly underfoot. The only things in the room which were free from damage were the columns of wood recently erected to stop the roof collapsing.

His father took for himself the largest, most comfortable looking chair and directed Darus to the smallest and most feeble. He had obeyed without question and nervously watched this exchange between his father and the new leader of County Bryn.

'Alderman,' his father said, lacing his fingers together across his chest. 'I did not realise the Outer Counties were capable of such rapid political movement.'

Navarya shook her head. 'We are very capable of such things when we have need for it. But a normal day in the Outer Counties rarely calls for such hasty procedures.' She fake-smiled to Darus and his father in turn, and then it broke away as she continued. 'No, your predecessor demanded that I take the mantle. Though it might not be standard procedure, I felt it only polite to oblige. Did they not inform you?' She tilted her head and then gave his father a very deliberate look. 'Oh – of course. She was in no condition to relay a report when she left the Counties.'

His father's teeth flashed into a snarl, 'you impertinent, traitorous old'—

'Hush now. Where are your manners? You must excuse an *old* woman's frailing memory.'

His father's chair creaked. Darus watched on, his heart fluttering, as was his natural reaction in the presence of his father's rage – even when not directed at him.

'I assume that unfortunate incident with your enforcer is why you are here so soon?' asked Navarya.

'That and more.' His father calmed and a callous smirk slowly formed from behind his fading grimace.

'Enlighten me.'

'There are three matters for discussion. The first being the identity of the assailant who attacked Lady Illian Valivelle, the second being the nature of that attack, and finally there is the issue of reinstating the payment of the Arcane Tax and addressing the arrears.'

'Quite the agenda, then. Where would you like to begin?'

'The assailant. As the new leader of County Bryn, it is your duty to tell me all you know about what happened here. If you fail to do so, you will face personal prosecution for crimes against the Grand City.'

Navarya sighed and put her tea down. 'There's no need for dramatics. I have no intention of wasting your time. I have already investigated the matter and will assist you gladly if it secures your swift departure from Bryn.'

Lanark's expression changed to one of disbelief, matching Darus's own. Every enforcer knew about the stubbornness, cheek, or grovelling fear they had to deal with when touring the Outer Counties, but wilful compliance was a very rare occurrence.

Navarya's voice broke the awkward silence. 'I apprehended the man as soon as possible, questioned him and then banished him from the Outer Counties.'

His father grasped at his cane and bolted to his feet. 'You let a criminal walk free? What were you thinking!'

'I was *thinking*, Enforcer Valivelle, that if an outsider had the resources to strike down one of your people with such ease, then nothing in all of the Outer Counties would be capable of keeping him held here.'

His father paused. He loosened his clenched fist. 'Describe him to me and tell me which way he went from here.' He leaned down to the table between their chairs and picked up a few sheets of blank paper and an elaborate pen. He tossed them at Darus.

Darus caught them clumsily and waited for the alderman's next words. As he looked to the alderman, he noticed she was staring intently into his eyes. Although her face bore the hallmarks of her advanced years, her eyes were still bright and vibrant. But they held a sadness when she looked at him which muscled away the bravado she presented to his father. Darus felt awkward, not understanding why she gave him such a different look. He looked up to his father

The Last of the Magi

for direction.

'The description, if you please,' Lanark said.

'Very well. He was late into his third decade, I would wager. I would suggest not so different in age from this young man here,' said Navarya, only then turning her attention back to his father. 'Fairer of skin than your average Asturian, with pitch hair. Above an average height but a bit slim. He wore a dark leather cuirass under a green, hooded overcoat.'

His father hummed with delight as Darus frantically scrawled the alderman's words verbatim. 'Very good. And where did you send the assailant when you banished him?'

'I was in no position to command his destination. I only told him to leave the Outer Counties. On reflection, I dare say I was quite lucky that he didn't take issue with the banishment as I may have found myself the next target of his aggressions. Thankfully, it was already his intention to leave. He was headed for the Quarters.'

'The Trade Quarters?' his father said.

'The very same.'

His father's free hand clenched into a fist, and he stormed over to the scorched frame of the nearest glass-less window. He snarled heavily with each breath. A breeze started to spin the dust around his feet and made the frail walls of Bryn Manor creak and groan.

Darus slumped down in his seat. His father was using Arcana. He didn't need to dip into the Deep Thought state to check. Watching the Arcane manifestation at work made him realise that his father's Arcana appeared to be triggering in response to his heightened emotional state – just like what had been happening to him when moving the earth.

'Why the Quarters?' his father asked. Though his back was turned, the gritting of his teeth could be heard through his voice. 'What are his intentions?'

'I cannot say that I know the specifics, but I have an idea. I doubt you wish to hear it.'

He twisted back. 'Tell me.' His voice became completely blunt, and just the slight twisting of his body caused an Arcane shockwave of air that ruffled the papers under Darus's palm.

Alderman Navarya looked unnerved as the force washed over

her too. She responded quickly. 'I believe he wishes to bring an end to your enforcers, and the Grand City of Elheim.'

The air fell still. His father straightened his back and turned to the window again.

Thirty seconds or so then passed without another word. His father just stood there, breathing deeply. This was a response Darus had never seen from him, and it made his stomach churn.

Lanark began to laugh. It was a deep, internalised laughter. And then, just as quickly as the laughter started, it stopped, and he shook his head. 'End the Grand City?' He said, calmly. 'Such a bold ambition. I see this is more than just an isolated incident then. Rest assured, Alderman, I shall find him and educate him on what it means to bring something to an *end.*'

The alderman nodded solemnly. 'I have no doubt that'—

His father cut her off. 'And that fate will be shared by all who provide him with refuge or fail to apprehend him.' He turned back to the alderman.

Lanark raised an arm towards the remnants of Bryn Manor's roof. His fingers tensed, then he flourished his arm back down to his side.

A moment of stillness passed. Then there was a distant and faint whistling. A brutal rush of air then slammed against the roof above the alderman a few seconds later and brought a section of its panelling collapsing down over her.

The alderman had no time to respond. She was not trained in the Arcane, she had no way to sense what was coming from above until it was too late.

Darus, however, had sensed it.

In a moment of pure instinct, Darus leapt out of his seat and hunched over the alderman. He Commanded the air around them to coalesce into a barrier to shield them, and at the same time Reached out to Grasp the wind acting on the wood panels to reduce the force exerted by his father's Command.

The wood slammed against his barrier. Each impact caused a sensation of discomfort within his head, like a string being plucked within his brain.

When the last pane rolled off the barrier and joined the pile on

The Last of the Magi

the floor, Darus released his Command. The air dissipated. He looked down at the alderman who was breathing in deep gasps, clutching at her heart.

'Are you hurt?' He whispered.

Alderman Navarya smiled nervously and shook her head.

Darus straightened and faced his father. As he turned, he caught a glimpse of his own seat. It was now covered in sharp planks of wood, jagged nails, and debris.

'You defend a traitor of the Grand City?' his father growled.

Darus searched for the right response, but his words were scrambled. He made only awkward sounds for a few seconds until the words finally reached him. 'No, s-sir. I thought the d-demonstration of your Arcana might be enough to loosen her tongue. She may know more.'

His father paused. His eyes drifted to the side until he calmed and, eventually, he nodded. 'Perhaps. I will leave you to continue the questioning. Find out how this fugitive executed his attack and then report back to the caravan. If she fails to comply, you know what must be done.' His father then marched away.

'Yes, sir.'

Darus moved over to his father's vacant seat, left completely unscathed from the cave-in, and he looked at the hole in the roof. The cloud-filled sky looked back at him.

Did he intend for it to come down on me too - was that another test?

Darus recovered his papers from the floor and readied himself to lead the next wave of questioning. But when he looked at the alderman, he saw the same woeful, troubled look on her face that had been there when they exchanged glances before. Her expression stunned him, giving the alderman the chance to speak first.

'I have dealt with many men like him,' she said. 'Tyrants, bullies, oppressors – the lot of them. Sometimes they threaten me. I have learnt to deal with that. I have learnt to not judge them too harshly, because I know those men were acting out of fear, frustration, or desperation – usually to protect that which matters most to them. But this'—she sighed heavily—'no man with a shred of decency would mistreat and endanger his own child.'

Her words made him stumble. The questions he was getting ready to ask evaporated from his mind and he just sat their quietly, sensing she had more to say that deserved to be heard.

'I am grateful for what you did. Thank you.'

Darus stuttered in response. 'I-I just felt there was more you could tell us.' His words weren't convincing, not even to himself.

'There is. I will answer your questions if it ensures your father leads your people away from here. Ask away, Enforcer Valivelle.'

Darus flushed a little. He still wasn't used to his new title. But that feeling was quickly replaced by a wash of relief. The alderman still intended to comply, even after what happened. Darus grabbed his pen and tapped the tip to his page. 'Are you able to describe the attack from the man in the green coat?'

Navarya nodded and then looked up to the corner of the room, seeming to search her memories. 'It all happened very quickly; truth be told. But I was there. The enforcer was about to strike one of the county guards for acting out of turn. As the guardsman stepped forward, your enforcer reached up to the sky and made lightning strike at her palm. She directed that strike at my guard.'

Darus raised his eyebrows at this. 'Are you saying your guard was the man in question?'

'Hush boy, I'm not finished. The man in green came charging out from who-knows-where and stood between my guard and the lightning strike. It was difficult to see from the flashes of bright light, but he carried a sword that took the lightning into it. It was like one of those enchanted weapons you hear about in old stories. Unlike any I have seen before. With it, he managed to send that lightning back to the enforcer.'

Darus stopped writing his notes and re-read the last few words. This information was both a cause for concern and relief. It was a concern because it confirmed the suspicions of the College Arcana and the Arcana Infirmary, that Lady Valivelle had been struck down by magic. The assailant had used Illian Valivelle's own Arcana against her. The relief came from hearing that this assailant did not possess magic of his own – he wasn't a rogue enforcer or a surviving Magi. It was a small relief, but a relief nonetheless.

It also meant that the emergency combat training session was

The Last of the Magi

unnecessary. The threat was not as dire as first feared. The apprentices didn't need to duel in the training gardens after all. If the College had known this before the high imperator so suddenly called the emergency session, then Darus wouldn't have discovered how to manipulate the earth with Arcana. Rik wouldn't have been caught in that rockslide.

He felt a plunging sensation in his stomach, and a heat filled his face. He knew his cheeks were blushing so he pushed those thoughts and the guilt that came with them as far down as he could. He tried to distract himself by thinking about the weapon described by the alderman.

All enforcers were trained to look out for illegal weaponry, and enchanted items. They were a very rare find nowadays; the raids leading up to the Purge saw to that.

Alderman Navarya coughed. 'Are you still with me?'

Darus stood and quickly glanced about the room, as if he had forgotten where he was. 'Thank you for the information. I must report this to my f…'— Darus caught himself and paused before continuing — '…If we have any further questions someone will come to find you.'

'Lucky me,' she said, chuckling.

Darus bowed and made his way to the door. He turned back as the alderman called out.

'Is that really it? That was only one question. And that only deals with two of the three points on your father's agenda. I believe the Arcane Tax still needs discussion.'

She was right. But having seen his father leave so eagerly, he suspected that the third agenda item was simply there as a pressure point, should it be needed, to pry out information on the other two points. Fortunately, that wasn't needed.

'We may return to discuss the Arcane Tax another time.'

'That suits me,' Alderman Navarya said. She leaned forward and started scrambling through the mess on the table for what remained of the brewed rose tea. Miraculously, the lidded pot survived.

Darus could have stayed and asked more peripheral questions, but he was confident this information would be enough to pique his father's interests and grant the alderman a reprieve after almost being buried under parts of the collapsed roof. Darus showed himself out of the wreckage of Bryn Manor's meeting hall and walked through what was left of the inner corridors until he found his way outside.

The view from the top of Brynfall's hill was surprisingly pleasant, despite the wreckage. Two streams of water gently ran around Bryn Manor from either side, originating from the spring at the hill's apex and pouring down the steepest part of its slopes, behind the manor. These streams drifted down the slant of the hill, flanking the town's sloping steps down to the lower levels. The gentle lapping of the water and the quiet rush of the fall were both soothing. The areas of grass closest to the streams – those spared from the flames – flourished from the fresh water, and kicked up an earthy, healthy, and natural smell that hung in the air.

But looking past those nicer features, the picture of the rest of the town was a stark reminder of the recent destruction. The destruction caused by his aunt, and the enforcers that travelled with her.

He had seen the wreckage on his way up the hill. But now, with his higher vantage, he saw it all at once. He hadn't seen devastation of this magnitude before. He shuddered to think how many had been displaced – maybe even harmed – by what happened here. Those details were omitted from the reports published by the College Arcana. They always were.

Not wanting to linger on those dark thoughts, Darus hurried down the steps until he found his father in discussion with the other enforcers near one of the carriages. The enforcers fell quiet as he approached, prompting his father to fleetingly look over his shoulder and acknowledge his son's return.

'And?' he said.

'She says the man in question carried a weapon which could absorb and redirect an assault of Arcana. I believe her story can be validated. She mentioned Lady Valivelle had summoned a lightning bolt to attack, I think it was reflected at her. The Arcana Infirmary said she had suffered burns.'

'That's Illian's calling card alright.' His father smirked and the other enforcers laughed. He then silenced them all with a cold stare.

The Last of the Magi

'From the description of how he redirected Arcana using a bladed weapon, I wondered whether it might have been some kind of encha—'

'A runeblade. How did this idiot get a runeblade?'

Darus recognised the term. Runecrafting, or Artificer Blacksmithing as it was known to some, involved a series of complex techniques that combined magic with metalwork. Even before the Grand City outlawed the activity, there were very few who could practise that craft in Asturia. After the enforcers were deployed to draw out and dispose of all magical artefacts and ensure all trades dabbling in magics had been curtailed, it was believed all remaining runecrafters had either died out or fled the country to seek sanctuary in foreign lands. It became just another perceived threat stamped out to help pursue the Elheim vision for Asturia's safe and unified future. And with the ports also being closed to foreign travel, Asturia hadn't seen any hint of Runecrafting for longer than Darus had been alive. The College Arcana had however documented enough information about the craft to ensure that it could still be identified, were the trade to re-emerge unlawfully.

Runed weapons were all given exotic designs. They were each unique. But they all had one thing in common, the small sigils crafted into the metal, imbued with the power to attract and store magical energies that would then remain dormant until activated by touch. Nobody understood how it worked. Runecrafters credited the craft to the Enchanters, claiming that they invented the process, and they alone had mastery over the unknown magic that went into it. No modern-day Asturian was even sure that Enchanters existed. The College Arcana was in its infancy when runed weapons were gathered and destroyed, so the scholars lost their chance to study them and try to understand the nature of the magic imbued within. A worthwhile sacrifice to pursue the vision, but a great loss to collected knowledge.

It must have been a runeblade, Darus agreed, though keeping the thought to himself. His father was not just respected for his results and his stern words, he was incredibly learned on all matters which fell within the duties of an enforcer to regulate. If Lanark Valivelle believed the assailant had a runeblade, then a runeblade it must have been.

His father turned to another enforcer and gave the man an order. 'Prepare a message for the Grand City. One copy to be delivered to the high imperator and the other to Enforcer Haraygar. This message is to include the fugitive's description — Darus shall furnish you those details — and it shall confirm that he has allegedly taken refuge in the Trade Quarters with an illegal runeblade in his possession.'

'Right away, Lord Valivelle,' said the enforcer.

His father shooed the other enforcers away, and only then did he turn to Darus directly.

'You did well to extract this information.'

'Thank you, sir.'

'But,' he said sternly, hanging on to the end of the word, 'in future you will think *very* carefully before you use Arcana to interfere with my actions. Am I understood?'

Darus chilled. He bowed his head as the tiny modicum of praise disintegrated and was replaced with familiar scorn.

'I'm sorry, sir. I will remember my place.'

'Good. Now get in the carriage.'

Darus did as told, only turning back briefly as a question crossed his mind. 'Are we to look for the seller of this runeblade?'

'No. We will await orders from the high imperator. But while we wait, we will see if we can find out where this criminal came from.'

Chapter 19

Friends of the Coin III

The barracks that served as the coinswoman's base of operations was a powerful and intimidating structure. At first glance, it was just a secure keep made of red bricks, decorated with black metal bars almost everywhere you could think to find them. But there was more to it on closer inspection. Two thick plumes of thick, dark smog billowed out from openings in the walls of its east and west wing, like two great furnaces boiling away at the flanks of the powerful central structure. Those extensions were stained a darker colour, baked in soot. It made the central building look cleaner and perhaps even regal by comparison – with thinner smoke trails leaking from skinny flutes on its peaked rooftop.

The elite guards slowly marched Tharian and one other man to the foot of the steps which led to the ridiculously tall doors into the keep proper.

Tharian didn't recognise the other man. He was older and broader, and he held himself proudly as he followed the elites. Tharian guessed he had been an entrant in the Crucible before, and finally won his bout after a few tries. He had the scars to show for it.

Four of the elite guard served as their escort, armed, and armoured in their custom armaments of black and gold. They kept silent, only interfering with Tharian to speed him up or slow him down as they moved at a constant, regimented pace at his sides.

As they reached the first step, the guards made them wait. Two of the elite guard went on ahead.

Tharian waited as patiently as he could. The elites at the top of the stairs seemed preoccupied manipulating some contraption in the panelling of the door, and whatever they were trying to do was taking its time.

As he watched on, he felt something brush against his ankle. He looked down to see a black, domestic-sized lirrus circling around his feet. The smooth-bodied feline sat on its hind legs in front of him and glared at him with its amber eyes.

Tharian scoffed and shook his head at the lirrus. *Someone's feeling nosey.* He received a narrow-eyed stare in return, and Tharian jokingly narrowed his eyes too in retaliation.

'Go. Away now!' said one of the elites. It was the first time an elite had spoken since they left the Crucible. The elite swept a foot at the lirrus, making his armour rattle.

Instinctively Tharian grabbed the guard's wrist and pulled him back. 'No,' he said, keeping his eyes narrowed – seriously this time. 'Don't be a brute.'

Tharian looked back down and flicked his head to the side. 'Get away,' he said. The lirrus looked sideways at the guard, dismissively, and then slowly skulked away. The elite's attempt to scare it away had not so much as caused it to blink.

The elite pulled his wrist free. He then snorted and moved back to his position. 'Whatever you say,' he said. 'I didn't expect the Arcana Hunter to have a soft spot for little animals.'

Tharian ignored the taunt. He considered rebuking the guard, but a loud scraping sound from atop the stairs distracted him and he found himself being ushered forward again. The doors to the barracks were slowly opening, and a loud voice came pouring out from within.

'...a scam, a fix, I tell you! I lost good coin on this. This would never have happened in Jerrik's day – get your hands off me!'

As Tharian reached the landing, an elite pulled him to one side, just in time to avoid a mass that came hurtling through the doors. The mass, groaning as it flew by, hit the ground hard and rolled down the stairs.

The voices from within the keep stopped. Tharian assumed the mass of brown and blue cloth, now motionless near the bottom of the steps, was the very same man who had been voicing his protests. A good indicator of the hospitality to be expected from the coinswoman?

Tharian wasn't given long to linger on his thoughts, as a hand grasped his shoulder and forced him to carry on ahead, into the belly of the keep.

Tharian's eyes had to adjust. Not only to the dimly lit hall

The Last of the Magi

within, but also to the thick rolls of smoke and steam that billowed in through tall corridors on either side of that hall, coursing up to the ceiling. The sound of hammers striking against metal echoed as if they were being struck by giants in the distance, and the air was suddenly dry from the sheer heat that blew past to escape through the newly opened door behind them.

The attack on Tharian's senses was overwhelming, but still the guards pushed him and the other man forward, past column after column that appeared through the cover of the smoke until they were stopped a short distance from the wall at the opposite end.

Tharian looked around. Only two elite guard were stood at his sides now. The other Crucible winner was gone, as were the other elites, but he could hear the clicking of their footsteps fading off to his left. *Why split us up?* He wondered.

'*Arcana Hunter*,' a voice echoed through the chamber. 'I believe congratulations are in order.'

Tharian glanced around, seeing nothing but walls, pillars, smoke and the remaining two elites. The voice belonged to a woman – not one of the guards at his flanks. He frowned. It was familiar.

One of the elite's shunted him in the side with an armoured elbow and pointed up high.

Tharian found the speaker. There, up above, leaning over a balcony with palms firmly gripped around the balustrades, stood the coinswoman herself – adorned in her own black and gold regalia. Only just visible through the surf of rolling smoke. But he recognised her look and her voice, from when she stood in the way of Enforcer Valivelle and his caravan of carriages passing through the plaza.

'Let me be the first to oblige.'

The coinswoman snapped her fingers.

A boot hit hard against the back of Tharian's ankle and brought him to his knees. He groaned as he hit the ground hard.

'Never in the history of the Quarter of War has there been such a flagrant abuse of one of our tournaments.' Faast hissed as she took in a deep breath, and she curled back the long hair covering one half of her scalp. 'This is the first time a coinsman of this quarter has had cause to investigate the conduct of a combatant. It will also be the last time.'

Tharian grimaced and pulled himself back to his feet.

Faast raised a hand to stand down her guards, who were about to deliver another assault to knock him back down, by the look of their poses. They seemed far too eager to do it, too.

'The very economy of the Trade Quarters has been tilted out of balance today. Patrons of the Crucible have lost coin that otherwise would have been theirs and they will require compensation from this quarter's treasury. The artisans will find themselves in a state of hysteria as to whose armaments they will desperately be tendering to craft. And' —Faast paused to steel the temper in her voice which competed with the rising temperature of the room— 'to add further insult to this affront, the tale of today's controversy shall spread around the Quarters, and likely beyond, together with the moniker of he who caused it – the *Arcana Hunter*.'

Faast lowered her hand.

Tharian's eyes widened as he realised what her lowered hand meant. He had no time to brace himself as another boot smashed into the middle of his back, and he slammed flat to the ground. He groaned as pain pulsed in his knees, his back, and his legs. He was hardly given a chance to compose himself and bite away the pain as hands wrapped around his arms and dragged him back up again, except this time the elites kept his arms held tightly at his back.

'As a Champion of the Crucible, you would ordinarily be granted membership to my elite guard. It is a prestigious honour and privilege to hold such a position. To be the strongest line of defence against any major acts of unrest within our walls or threats from beyond them. Do you understand how many have tried and failed to reach such a pinnacle of excellence?'

Tharian didn't respond. *Just let her get it out of her system*, he told himself.

'I will not allow it. Talented though you might be with the blade, your use of an illegal weapon, and antagonistic alter-ego, have caused complications too far-reaching.'

'In my defence,' Tharian said impulsively, 'I didn't choose that name. One of your ushers came up with that one without my

The Last of the Magi

consent.'

The coinswoman paused. She seemed to chew over those words. Perhaps something similar had happened before?

'My ushers are only granted such fanciful discretions based on the material provided to them at registration. The liability yet remains with you. Even were I to give you the benefit on that allegation, what excuse do you have for possessing and using an illegal weapon?'

He shrugged. *Choose your battles, Tharian.*

'The use of such a weapon, were the Grand City to hear of it…' she paused as a large plume of steam hissed through into the hall and washed over them all. '…would bring naught but chaos and strife. The enforcers of Elheim would bear down upon us, unleashing their thaumaturgy for bloodshed, mark my words of that.'

Tharian kept eye contact. Through the smoke, she glowered with discontent.

'Have you naught to say?'

Taking in a deep breath, Tharian tried to pull his hands free. The guards only tightened their grasp in retaliation. 'I have plenty to say,' he said, 'if you are prepared to listen. If I am not fit to receive your grand prize, will you allow me a chance to speak openly with you instead before you decide my fate?'

The coinswoman coughed a laugh. 'The gall with which you make such a request, despite your crimes.' She didn't signal for another strike, or for him to be thrown down the stairs like her last visitor. She just paused for a few seconds before carrying on. 'I find myself at a crossing of thoughts. Immediate incarceration would be the most appropriate sanction for you, with some gruelling labour to teach you discipline'—She paused and tightened her grip on the railing—'but you proved yourself a capable fighter, illegal acts aside. Such talents are wasted in the stockades. I am at least a modicum inclined to humour your request, if only out of respect for your abilities. Then your arrest can follow.'

'Then I may speak?' He made sure to use few words, he could see from the corner of his eye that the guards were ready to strike him again on their leader's command. They hungered for it.

'Say what you will, swiftly, and I shall judge the merit of your words.' The coinswoman nodded and her guards backed away, releasing Tharian and giving him space to breath in the thick air and compose his thoughts.

Tharian massaged his wrists where the elites had held him. He gave himself a few moments before dropping his hands to his sides. He met the eyes of the coinswoman upon her menacing perch. 'I don't need to remind you what the enforcers did in the plaza earlier today. Today, the Elheim showed they are prepared to push harder against Asturian freedoms for their own gain. All to assert their dominance, and the power of Arcana. Have you heard what they did to Brynfall?'

'Make your point.'

'Swords and shields, no matter how tempered the steel, are only of limited use against Arcana. Your elite guards are gifted and capable, yet ultimately little match against an enforcer. I have spent years searching for ways to curb the growing strength of the Elheim and their Arcana. I believe I have a solution, but it requires the backing of the Trade Quarters – and I am requesting a Coinsmeet so I can discuss it with you.'

Coinswoman Faast remained still. The swirling ash and steam plumed around her from either side as she stared, unblinkingly, at Tharian. 'All of this inanity was designed to bring you here, simply to request my missive?'

'Yes,' Tharian said, matter-of-factly. 'This was the only way I could get to you quickly.'

She laughed, and that caught Tharian by surprise, more so than the strikes he already endured from the elites. Even the guards looked at each other sheepishly. Her voice snapped their attentions back to her. 'You are either deadly serious or disgracefully foolish. You ask me to direct my focus away from my duties, which shall become more burdensome due to your own actions, and instead give credence to the musings of a fool? The coinsmen have not the time nor energy to assemble a Coinsmeet to hear frivolous conjecture from a criminal.'

'I have already obtained the missive of Coinsman Velioth.' he said. 'And Jerard Traykin from the Collectors Quarter assures me

The Last of the Magi

that Coinswoman Keene will agree to the meeting too.'

Her laughter stopped abruptly. She leaned forward again and gave Tharian a piercing look. 'An impressive feat, if true. And you mean to say Traykin supports this also?'

'Absolutely. He's the one who proposed this unorthodox strategy for gaining an audience with you.'

The coinswoman shook her head knowingly and stared off into the smoke for some time. Eventually she grimaced and turned her attention below again. 'I have neither the time nor enthusiasm for this. Not now. Not with all the other issues this day has already wrought. I therefore offer you this: I will bail you for your crimes today until I have communicated with my fellow coinsmen. If what you say is true, you will have your missive from the Quarter of War. If not, I shall move that you be immediately arrested and put on trial for your actions in the Crucible.'

Tharian smirked and nodded. 'Your terms are reasonable.'

'I do not require your commentary. Nor are my terms finished. I will allow you to leave this place unshackled. You may retain your weapon, on the strict order that you are not to use it or allow it to be seen. But let it be known that if I hear the name Arcana Hunter spoken again openly within the Quarters, then the freedom I have granted you will be revoked with extreme prejudice.'

'Understood, Coinswoman Faast.'

'You will confirm your true name and provide the address for where you shall be bailed to.' With a snap of her fingers one of her attendants appeared from somewhere else in the hall to take notes.

'My name is Tharian. No family name, formerly of Midhaven. I currently reside at Traykin's Bazaar.'

The coinswoman rolled her eyes dramatically and visibly muttered *'of course'* under her breath. 'Fine. Then our business is concluded. A prosecution under the laws of the Trade Quarters now hovers over you in abeyance, ready to be pursued at my order. Do not give me cause to make that order. Are we clear?'

Tharian nodded. 'Perfectly so.'

'When you return to Traykin, tell him that his propensity for troublemaking is being watched closely.'

Tharian smothered a laugh. *Traykin will enjoy that.* 'I will.

Thank you.'

The coinswoman's elite guards wasted no time in turning Tharian on his heels and ushering him back down the long hall, pushing back out through the great doors. It was a relief that he hadn't been thrown down the stairs like the last visitor.

Tharian paused before heading down.

He had almost secured what he needed from two of the coinsmen, and Traykin was confident about coming through with the other two missives in due course. It had only been a matter of days since he arrived in the Quarters, yet he had made incredible progress already. He may have had bruises to both body and pride, and now threats of prosecution against him, but all things considered, everything almost seemed to be going too well.

But then he realised what would come next. Even with all four missives collected from the coinsmen, that was only the first hurdle. The coinsmen still needed to be persuaded that he had a real plan to stop the Elheim – one with detail and a realistic prospect of success.

He hadn't even started to piece together what that plan would look like. And he had no leads on finding the Magi.

Suddenly those bruises felt a lot deeper.

***

Marla, Marion and Brayne sat together in the kitchen, silently sipping at their tea. Except Brayne hadn't even sipped at his tea yet, instead he just stared at it as he swirled the cup around between his palms.

After all the excitement of the Crucible, Marla was still abuzz with adrenaline. But that just had to ricochet within her while she remained outwardly calm and collected. The Glanmores hardly said anything after Tharian's match. There had been only one other victor amongst the challengers in the Crucible, and that was in the last fight. Even that hadn't lifted their spirits.

Brayne slammed his mug down on the table, spilling tea over the tablecloth. He stood, without a word, and marched out the room.

Marion sighed deeply. She waited until he was out of view before she started dabbing at the spill.

The Last of the Magi

With Brayne's temper removed from the room, Marla took her opportunity to ask the question burning in her mind. 'I know this might not be the best time,' she said, 'but is everything ok?'

Marion looked up from her dabbing. She paused. 'No, dear girl. But it will be.' Marla half-furrowed, half-cocked her brows in a way to suggest she wasn't fully understanding. 'What happened in the Crucible today has made things complicated... for everyone. All the artisan weaponsmiths, armourers and tailors of this quarter will be in a frenzy for the next few days. Everyone will be trying to figure out what products to craft for the coinswoman's new soldiers. The man who won at the end is easy enough to deal with, but he was the last fighter of the day – every artisan would have scoped him out in desperation, so nobody will have any edge over anyone else when a tender for work is released. Only the Divine can say what will happen there.

'As for that friend of yours. We've never had someone win their fight like *that*. He might not be offered a space among the elites after what he did with that illegal weapon. So that leaves us all in a difficult place: do we prepare designs for the last winner and try somehow to beat out the masses, do we take a chance on work that may never come to fruition for your friend, or do we work double-time to do both. Either way, it takes a lot of time and creativity to put together these designs. And it could all be for nothing.'

It made sense now. The Crucible may have been a bit of fun for Marla, as a newcomer to the city, but for everyone else there was much more at stake. The results of the Crucible affected livelihoods, income, and reputation. The uncertainty following the tourney could have a serious impact on the Glanmores' business.

'I'm sorry,' Marla said. She held her cup close to her face, trying to hide the guilt that warmed her face.

Marion cocked her head, 'What ever would you be sorry for?'

'I got carried away back there. I thought that maybe I could help because I knew Tharian and...'

Marla paused as Marion's gentle hands softly landed on hers and lowered her cup to the table. 'You sweet thing. You have nothing to apologise for. We'll be alright. Brayne will be alright. To be honest, I am grateful to you. At points in that tourney, you managed to bring out a side of him I haven't seen since…', her eyes lowered, and she shrugged as if throwing off a weight from her shoulders, '…well, I haven't seen him like that for a long time. You did nothing wrong. In fact, you gave us a lead that many others wouldn't have even considered pursuing. It's not your fault the fight ended the way it did, and Brayne doesn't blame you for it. He is just frustrated, and the other artisans will be feeling the same way. It will pass.'

Marla searched Marion's eyes and took comfort from her smile. A feeling of tension, buried deep within her chest started to unravel as she judged Marion's words to be genuine and sincere.

A loud sound startled them. At first Marla thought it was the familiar sound of steel upon steel, judging by the sharp, punchy rhythm of the noise. But as the noise came back again and again, she realised she was wrong. The sound was coming from Brayne. He was coughing – a deep, haughty cough that laboured his breathing. It stopped eventually, but it lasted a long time.

Marion's eyes were wide, and she clutched at the tablecloth.

'Is he ok?' Marla asked.

Marion took a few moments to respond, and she kept her eyes low. 'Yes, yes, he's fine. He's had that cough for years. It's the fumes.'

She was hiding something, that was obvious. And then the coughing started again. What started as a string of cough-after-cough, soon changed into retching and gasping for air. The sound of it made Marla's throat feel tight. She couldn't sit idle while the man who agreed to take her in was suffering.

She jumped up and dashed across the kitchen to pour a glass of water, and she continued her dash through the house into the workshop extension.

The workshop was already hot, dark, and musky as Marla rushed in. Brayne had wasted no time firing up and stoking his forge. Marla didn't need time to adjust to it. She raced to Brayne's side. He was curled over his anvil with one hand supporting his weight and the other cupped around his mouth. Each cough twisted him closer and closer to the point of nearly having his forehead resting on the metal.

He was in no state to drink while the coughing held him so

The Last of the Magi

tightly in its grip. She dragged over his chair from the desk nearby. She laid her free hand on his shoulder and pulled him back to the seat, manoeuvring the glass into his hand as she did so. 'Here, drink this when you can. You can't work like this,' said Marla.

As the intensity of Brayne's coughing relaxed, he dropped his hand from his mouth and took in gasps of air.

Marla stood back and gave him space. His eyes were red and bulging. The veins around his temples were pulsing, and although his cheeks were blushed, the colour was closer to a greyish purple than the red she had expected.

He looked terrified.

This man, who maintained such a brusque stoicism, now looked no different to her own frail father. The comparison made her heart freeze, and she felt a tugging deep within her chest.

She fought against her thoughts and stopped herself from frowning.

She was no apothecary or chirurgeon. There was little more she could do than offer soothing words and a cold drink. She had already done the latter, and the former didn't feel of much use with a man as rigid as Brayne.

Brayne finally took the drink to his lips, Marla nodded with approval and looked around the workshop for anything else she could do to help him.

She may not have been a healer like her mother, but she *was* a blacksmith, like her father.

Her eyes were drawn to the forge and the strip of tempered metal that bathed in its flames. The flat of the metal was glowing an orange-yellow hue that she recognised. She rushed to the anvil and grabbed Brayne's gloves, mask, and tongs, which she used to safely extract the long strip of metal from the forge to let it rest against the anvil.

The metal was ready to be shaped. If it had stayed in the forge much longer it would have succumbed to the heat and warped beyond any practical use. But even with it now extracted, at its prime temperature, she didn't know what Brayne had intended to do with it. And she had limited time to work it.

She pulled back to Brayne's desk, where he perused drawings

and specification sheets. The top sheet of parchment bore a design for an immaculate shortsword. Judging by the unusual curves of the blade, it was a decorative design rather than a functional one. Beside the drawing there were a series of scrawled numbers – the weapon's intended measurements – and although it was difficult to know for sure, Marla felt confident that the metal from the furnace was the right size to be shaped into this design.

Marla grabbed the parchment and waved it in front of Brayne. 'Is this what you were working on?' she bellowed, more forcefully than expected so her voice carried through the mask and over the din of the forge. Brayne nodded. The colour was returning to his face, but his breathing was still quite laboured. He reached out, likely to try and stop her or to protest her involvement, but she snatched herself away.

Without thinking a moment on it, Marla grabbed the weighty hammer beside the anvil and began to strike the glowing steel until its shape changed. With every strike she made to create the curvatures of the design, she compensated with further strikes across the flat to distribute the gathering thickness of the metal into its length.

As she worked, her mind became calm and peaceful as it always would while she worked metal, though she kept a small amount of attention on Brayne's coughing to make sure it didn't worsen. She felt like she was back home, doing her father's work for him during one of his rest days. She remembered fondly the last blade she had worked – Tharian's runeblade. She let those fond memories absorb her, so she could ignore the ache in her wrists from the recoil of her strikes.

Eventually she landed the last hit needed to make the desired shape. She put down the hammer, satisfied she had worked the blade as much as she could with the heat available. Any further work would only dent or damage the integrity of the metal. She tugged off the thick welding gloves and the mask, taking in a deep breath once she was free. Her face was coated with sweat, and she could feel soot deep in her pores. She hadn't been wearing overalls, so her clothes were coated in dark dust.

'You really do know what you're doing,' said Brayne. His voice

The Last of the Magi

startled her, as she'd been so engrossed in her work. She turned around to see him stood, arms folded in his usual way with an expression slightly less stern than normal.

Marla scoffed, trying her luck to be a bit cockier. 'Yeah, I do. My father taught me well.'

Brayne gently moved Marla to one side with the back of his hand and took his usual position at the anvil. He slid his hand into one of his gloves and lifted the shaped blade. He twisted it at an angle towards the light of the forge, examining every curve as the light reflected off it.

Without a word, he then plunged the hot blade into the bucket of cold water beside the anvil. The water screamed as it boiled against the blade.

Marla closed her eyes and cursed under her breath. She heard her father's voice in her head, *we must always let down the temper of the blade, or else we risk losing the fruits of our good work – or worse, face watching the blade perish altogether.*

'I'm sorry, I—'

'Good job.'

Marla paused. She expected to be scolded for her basic error. 'Thank you. I just wanted to help; it would have been a shame to waste the metal.'

Brayne grunted, nodding in approval. He looked at her and gestured his head to the anvil to beckon her closer. She complied. He held the design parchment in front of her and ran a finger up and down the edge of the drawing's curved edges. 'For pieces like this with designs for decoration, we let the heat seethe the blade a bit longer and push it to its limits. That way the blade responds better to the curves. The metal may bruise here or there, but we can dress that up later.'

That made sense. A weapon to be put on display could afford to be slightly less effective if it meant the design looked more attractive.

But... more importantly... he had just spoken to her like a fellow blacksmith for the first time. Was she earning his trust? She tried not to smirk.

'I see, thank you,' she said, 'how are you feeling?'

Brayne went to his desk to rifle through his papers. He waved her away. 'Fine. I've got more to do in here. Go see if Marion needs you.'

'Are you sure? I can help if you need a break.'

'I'm sure.' Brayne's voice became deeper, but Marla could tell he made a conscious effort to keep his tone civil. With both of their prides still intact, Marla nodded and went back to the kitchen.

Marion wasn't there. Marla popped her head through the door of the living room opposite to see if Marion was in there instead. She wasn't.

She must have turned in for the night, Marla assumed.

Before turning in for the night herself, Marla stepped over to the living room window and pushed back the half-drawn curtain with two fingers. Though the streets were mostly dark, made darker by the smog that blocked most of the moonlight, the blurry, peach-coloured hazes cast by streetlamps revealed that the Artisan Quarter was still abuzz with activity.

What Marion said was true: every business-owner worth their salt had gone into overdrive with work. All preparing to tackle the uncertainty – ready to seize whatever opportunities might come their way from the coinswoman.

Marla felt torn. When she had discussed moving to a bigger city with her father, this buzz of activity and excitement was exactly what she dreamt of – and being part of it gave her the adrenaline hit she hoped it would. But, at the same time, she now understood there was some degree of desperation behind it. To an observer, an outsider, it was all very exciting – so far removed from an ordinary day in the Outer Counties. For the artisans themselves, it was a cutthroat enterprise. Brayne had every reason to be so irritable.

Opportunity came with risk. Prosperity was underpinned by hard work and good fortunes, but that same level of hard work could end in failure just the same. Life in the Trade Quarters was more complicated and unstable than Marla had anticipated. She naively thought that the complicated work and the sheer quantity of it would be a never-ending excitement. Yet the businesspeople of the Quarters walked the constant knife-edge between great success and catastrophic failure.

The Last of the Magi

Was that the life she wanted? Where pressure, stress and expectation were daily norms. The prize for that stress was the potential to earn good coin and be a leader within your craft. But it was only a *potential*. It was no guaranteed thing. Not at all.

Marla held the curtain open a while longer. She couldn't deny the rush in her chest, the near-constant pumping of adrenaline. This life excited her. This is where she wanted to be.

She drew the curtains closed, stealing one last look before she turned away.

With her resolve renewed, she was ready to get some rest. Her body ached for it.

The quiet of the house made it easier to notice the subtleties of her surroundings on her way upstairs: the recently watered plants on the corner table at the top of the stairs, the softness of the carpet under her bare feet... and the stifled sound coming from behind Marion's bedroom door.

Marla almost ignored the noise at first, assuming it was just Marion shuffling about her room. But there was something recognisable about it. Familiar and unmistakable, but at the same time something she couldn't quite place from where she stood. Giving in to temptation, Marla stepped closer to the door to make sense of what she was hearing.

Crying.

She could hear Marion. Sobbing. Not an all-consuming outburst of tears, rather the escape of restrained emotion from someone who didn't want to be heard. Marion's breathing was staggered between each short wave of grief that flowed through her. At no point did she call out or whine from the sadness that took hold of her. No, it was like she was slowly turning the faucet of her emotions off and on to keep herself under control.

Marla stepped back from the door. She felt guilty for listening, and for analysing what she heard. But she couldn't help herself; she knew those emotions.

Marla went inside her own room and leaned back against the door gently until she felt it click shut. She sighed and tried to ignore just for a moment the thoughts and old memories that tried to creep into the surface of her mind. She instead focused on the tautness of her upper arms and the tiredness in her eyes that settled in as a distraction. Finding her way over to her bed, she noticed that Marion had laid out a bowl of warm water and some freshly cleaned overalls for her, so she washed her face and hands and then sat cross-legged on the bed with her back resting against the wall. She sat there for a minute, quiet and still.

She reached for the shirt Marion had cleaned for her. Without really understanding why, she brought it to her face and took in a waft of the fresh, homely smell. She recognised that smell, just as she recognised Marion's quiet sobbing.

Marla had learned to hide and release her grief like that – to let the swelling of emotions pour out slowly until they became bearable again. Even if only for a little while. It was cathartic. Necessary.

But that was a long time ago. It had been years since her own sadness had built up to that point. She had almost forgotten it was still there. Almost. But it was still there, and it washed over her now.

A single tear ran down her cheek. Then another. Then several more. And then, as the hazy and faded memories of her mother's face and gentle touch visited her, she let herself feel all she needed to feel in that moment.

Grief needed that release. Marla's chest felt heavy. Not just for her own loss, but for whatever grief or anguish had taken hold of Marion too. It wasn't her place to pry, but she worried for her all the same.

Chapter 20

Debriefing

Tharian was grateful that Traykin's Bazaar was built by artisan hands. If the building had been even slightly unstable, it would have collapsed from the sheer concussive force of Traykin's bellowing laughter. The paintings on the walls rattled from the man's drunken stupor to the point that even Tharian couldn't help but laugh along too. Though he laughed *at* Traykin rather than *with* him, of course – not that it made any difference to the collector.

Traykin was on his feet, sauntering around his study clutching at two wax sealed letters dyed in the colours of rich gemstones: one emerald, one sapphire. His triumphant laps of the room were broken up by short breaks to swig at the flagon that Frigg kept filled. Frigg was keeping them well fed too. He was bringing in freshly cooked dishes thick and fast. It was excessive, but it was a celebration. And a celebration feast organised by a collector was a thing to be experienced.

'I never thought you'd pull it off,' Traykin said as he continued his laps of the room. 'Truth be told, I expected at least one of us to be thrown out of the city or put behind bars – more likely you than me, obviously. Yet here we are.' He flapped the sheets of parchment in the air for maybe the hundredth time, as if Tharian may have forgotten they had them.

'Put them somewhere safe, before you do something stupid like pour your drink down them.'

Traykin scoffed as he walked over to the mantle and slid the sheets between two porcelain ornaments that he then slapped together as a clamp. 'Happy now, lad?'

'Perfectly.'

Traykin snorted and went back to pick at more of the food. 'Tell me again, how furious was Faast when you got to her keep?'

Tharian rolled his eyes. 'I could just show you the bruises.'

Particles of food flew across the room as Traykin cackled

midway through shovelling a piece of folded bread stuffed with meat into his mouth.

'I'll admit though, apart from Faast's violent disapproval of my methods, things went smoothly. This plan is moving forward much faster than I expected.'

'That it is. You're making good progress.' Traykin marched to his drinks cabinet and poured them both a different drink from an extravagant bottle. 'You've already secured the missive of Coinsman Velioth, though the rattle of a coin-purse is enough to win him over.'

'Rich coming from you,' Tharian muttered under his breath.

Traykin continued. 'Coinswoman Keene was an easy sell too. She has racked up a few debts with me over the years and she was only too eager to see some of those struck off the ledger. More than I'd like, mind, but I'll survive,' he chuckled as he sipped at his drink and planted the other in front of Tharian. 'And now it won't take long for Faast to join the trend. She'll jump aboard.'

'I won't get ahead of myself until I see all four missives and we get some promising leads on this Magi.'

'Don't worry about the missives, lad, you'll have all four. Faast will act quickly on her word, like she always does. And the collectors and the artisans are a close-knit bunch, one quarter always follows the other.'

Tharian hummed. 'I suppose I expected a bit more resistance. I had heard the Coinsmen of the Trade Quarters were averse to risk.'

Traykin snorted. 'And then some! Maintaining peace within these walls and holding on to our independence has always been the top priority amongst the Quartersfolk and the coinsmen alike. We don't cause anyone any trouble, so long as they cause us none; that's the rule. But the Grand City have been clever. They've made their moves, from closing the ports to taxing the Outer Counties, all having an impact on our way of living. They put pressure on us, more and more all the time. And yet, they've never laid a finger on us. That changed today.'

'So, you're saying the coinsmen want to do something about the Elheim, but were lacking the justification to act?'

Traykin dropped into his armchair with a mighty thud and

The Last of the Magi

started picking crumbs from his vest. 'Right. The coinsmen are still risk averse. But what happened in the plaza may prove that the greater risk lies in sitting still.'

'It sounds like the stars are aligning for us then.'

'Perhaps. A little. But don't let that make you cocky. They still need persuading, it's not a done deal yet.'

Tharian nodded. 'I get that. You and Coinsman Velioth both said the same; I need to be persuasive, and I need to have detail to my plan. I'll work on that.'

'That you will, lad. That you will. But what I'm saying here is you still need to prove two things to them: first, that the threat of the Elheim is serious enough to justify action, and second, that your plan is the right one.'

'Do you really think they will need much convincing that action is justified?'

'It's too early to say. What happened today is still rumbling through the system. Don't assume you've got an *in* there. Not everyone sees things as you and I do. What we see as a threat to this country, this city, or its independence, is just another political move of smoke and mirrors to some.'

'I can't understand how anyone would see a maelstrom of flames in the plaza as being anything other than a threat to this city.'

Traykin scoffed a laugh. 'I can. Because nobody died. Our law and our government remain undamaged, for now. There's always the argument of "they could have done worse."'

Tharian shook his head. 'That's ridiculous.'

'I don't agree with it, it's just how others see it. And there's logic to it. Until the day the Elheim attack or tell us they no longer recognise our independence, those people would consider any action we take against the Grand City as being us rocking the boat.'

The point did have logic, though Tharian wished that it didn't. If leaders struck back at moves made against them every time they happened, they would be giving their opponents ammunition to use against them, when those moves may have been empty threats all along. The message of Traykin's advice was clear: he needed to be prepared to argue his entire case persuasively, from beginning to end. He should take nothing for granted.

Tharian rubbed his upper lip with his thumb and index finger. 'Then I'll convince them the boat is already rocking. Close to capsizing.'

Traykin snapped his fingers in the air. 'Now you're getting it, lad. It shouldn't be too difficult, truth be told. That show in the plaza breached the terms of treaties that have been in place since the old days of Oligar.'

Tharian nodded and made a mental note of that. Something to research later perhaps.

'The harder part will be getting all the other details fine-tuned. The coinsmen will need to know what their roles are in this, and how you envisage this working out for all involved. This could get messy and violent. Think of the worst case as well as the best.'

'I know I said I would work on the detail, but I'm no war general.'

'No, but nor is anybody else within these walls. Faast may act like one, but we've all been fortunate not to have a war in our lifetimes. If you really put stock in this Magi of yours, you need to have a strong plan to wrap around it. You need to think about the who, the how and the what. The coinsmen will want as few hypotheticals and variables as possible. So, you need to start thinking like a war general, because like it or not there *will* be blood in this.'

They both became quiet. The truth was laid out in Traykin's words.

'I'll keep working on it.' They truly had made great progress, but only in one direction. When it came down to the details of how the Grand City would be stopped, who would be doing it, and how this Magi might be found, they were still woefully behind. The cart was before the horse and ran the risk of rolling beyond their reach.

'How long until we have the other missives?'

'I'd expect Faast's to arrive in the next few days. Once I've got hers, the collector won't be able to resist adding his to complete the set.'

Tharian grimaced. More days stuck within the towering metal walls of the city. He could feel his base instincts crying out for him to move on. Instincts that Greycloak had instilled in him. But these

The Last of the Magi

were instincts he had to push down and away, for good reason. He needed this time of stability to pull together his plan.

Traykin rose and headed for the door. As he passed, he gripped Tharian's shoulder. 'You've got lots more to do, Tharian. But before you start, there's someone who wants to see you in the yard.' He then sauntered off.

Tharian sat for a while. *Who could possibly want to see me?* His mind flashed through some familiar faces: Councillor Navarya from Brynwell; Greycloak, his guardian; Marla, maybe? None of those three had any reason to seek him out. As he made his way to the back door, his mind wandered. *The yard? does he mean down by the...*

Tharian gave in to his curiosity and went out the back. He stepped out into the thin, long garden, rife with overgrown, half-dying plants, unevenly punctuated by a swaying stone path. The path led to a small structure.

...the stables. Tharian realised.

He heard the familiar whiney. The sound warmed him against the late-afternoon chill. Frigg was there at the stables too, sweeping the path clear of stray leaves and dust.

There, in one of the bays, Ombra stood proudly. She nodded at Tharian as he found her, and gently scraped her hooves across the ground.

'I should have known you would make your way here eventually – to the only stable you willingly sleep in,' he said.

Ombra snorted and thrashed her head, as if amused by his comment. She then stood still with her head tilted so that one of her piercing amber eyes firmly looked upon him.

'Have you been keeping an eye on our friend?' Tharian asked.

Frigg suddenly appeared, shuffling towards Tharian from where he was sweeping down the side of the stable. 'Y-yes, Master Tharian. Master Traykin asked that I leave the gates open in case Ombra returned to rest.'

Tharian was caught off guard by Frigg's response. He looked between Frigg and Ombra, and Ombra bucked, snorted, and then turned away to enjoy the fresh feed that had been laid out for her.

'Thank you, Frigg. Though we both know she'd find her way

into these stables with or without the gate in her way. I'm sure she's grateful to be home again after all this time.'

Frigg nodded, pulling his broom still and leaning against it. 'I-I remember when Master Traykin first bought her. She was so small and so curious. She would escape and fly off for days at a time, but she would always end up c-coming back. It's good to see she still knows where we are.'

Tharian smiled and stroked Ombra's neck as she ate. Frigg's reminiscing brought back more memories of his own childhood.

He remembered another time when Greycloak had brought him to Traykin's Bazaar. He remembered how eagerly he raced to the front door, to be greeted just as excitedly by the young Frigg who grabbed him by the wrist and dragged him out to the yard before he even said hello. And there Ombra was, stumbling about in the stables, still learning to balance on four legs. At the time, Tharian hadn't understood the excitement – it was just a horse, and they were everywhere – but he did at least notice her unusual colouring.

Ombra had grown dramatically in the few days the young boys had spent playing together, and the two of them ran down the full length of the garden each morning at first light to see how much she had changed compared to the night before. But on the day that Greycloak had made Tharian pack his things for their journey back to the Outer Counties, Ombra had broken free from the stables and disappeared.

Frigg had cried and cried and cried as they left. Tharian and Greycloak didn't return to the Trade Quarters for at least 18 months, by which time Frigg had come to learn that Ombra would abscond regularly, always returning a few days later. She was unpredictable, but she was loyal.

She hadn't changed, even with ten years spent overseas. Even in the sprawling, foreign lands to the west – far across the sea – Ombra had still drifted off, either to scout the area or to follow a scent. Tharian had learnt to let her wander when she needed it, and she in turn would always be by his side when he needed her. The alternative was chasing her, and that was a contest of agility he would never win.

Rousing from his thoughts, Tharian noticed that Ombra had

The Last of the Magi

stopped eating and was staring at him again. Her eyes, piercing as they were, seemed warm and gentle in that moment as if she, too, had been visiting those fond memories of their travels together. Perhaps she was. There was a certain synergy to their thoughts, one too complicated to try and understand or put into words. And that was just one of the things that made her so special.

'We'll get back out there soon, old girl. I don't want to be stuck here any longer than we need to be,' said Tharian.

Ombra nodded and then retreated to the back of her bay to curl up and rest.

'M-Master Tharian?' Frigg said, as he leaned into another of the bays to return his broom.

'Yes?'

'Is it t-true that you spent all those years in Feralland?'

'It is,' Tharian replied, surprised at Frigg's uncharacteristic prying.

'What was it like?'

Tharian smiled. No law-abiding Asturian had stepped foot on foreign shores for at least four decades, so his curiosity was understandable. 'It's a vast place,' he said, his smile growing wider. 'The flats are broader and a deeper green than the eastern expanse of Asturia. Beyond those flats, the land transforms from unending grasslands for miles around to sprawling jungles, with trees so mountainous in some parts the branches weave together to create higher grounds that people can walk across. It's so easy to get lost in there, without a good guide.' He then gave Ombra a fleeting glance.

He continued. 'Those jungles eventually clear, revealing real mountains and fjords blessed with incredible vistas and crystal-clear lakes, rivers, and waterfalls. It's all so beautiful and untouched.'

Frigg's eyes were glistening, and his mouth held open slightly. Frigg had seen little of the world beyond the walls of the Trade Quarters. He had been a weak and frail boy, who grew into a weak and frail man – Traykin had deemed him too fragile to even experience the wider reaches of the Trade Quarters, let alone the rest of Asturia. He was probably right to keep Frigg sheltered, for his own protection.

In truth, Tharian had consciously censored his description of

Feralland for Frigg's benefit, to avoid causing any anxiety. Beautiful though its vistas were, Feralland truly earned the *feral* part of its name. Primal beasts roamed those environments, and they were very disapproving of visitors. And even if the beasts didn't catch travellers unaware, the unpredictable weather and natural phenomena that seemed intent on reshaping the landscape on a regular basis would be the next major threat. Though he censored those threats from his account of the western lands, everything he said had still been true – if only half the story.

'Why has Feralland caught your interest?' Tharian asked, glancing sideways at Frigg, watching him tinker pointlessly with the stable gates.

Frigg shrugged. 'J-just wondering, I guess,' he avoided eye contact with Tharian and kept his head low, 'did you meet any p-people out there?'

'Of course. I didn't spend the best part of a decade on my own with just Ombra. I met a lot of incredible people. I met an unusual, but fantastic race of people. So old and wise that they knew all about us Asturians, and spoke of a long history with us, despite there being barely anyone alive today who would remember a time when the borders were still open.'

Without hesitation, Frigg launched into his next question. 'Who were they?'

Tharian arched a brow. His childhood friend continued to fiddle with the gate latch. Tharian stepped in closer to Frigg and tapped him on the side of the arm to garner his attention. 'We can talk about it more some other time, if you want,' he said to Frigg while smirking, 'but for now, there's a lot to be done. I have planning to do.'

Tharian patted Frigg gently on the shoulder and walked back to the house. A conversation about the Awoken of Feralland could wait for another day. And if Traykin wanted to collect Tharian's secrets, he would have to try something cleverer than exploiting Frigg's wanderlust to get them.

Chapter 21

Furthering the Vision

Meetings within the Elheim Palace were a glamorous affair. Within a grandiose banquet hall, high up near the very apex of the palace, a long table was laid out for the chancellor and his senior advisors.

A luxurious silk runner flowed down the length of the table, almost completely hidden under the stacks of plates, bowls, platters, carafes, and goblets filled with every delicacy that Asturia could offer. It was wasteful. So much would be thrown away at the end of the day.

The chancellor – Lord Vasilarius Elheim – was not a man of gluttonous tendencies, but he was a man of pride. When his advisers were called to dine with him, he always demanded a feast be prepared. It was a reward commensurate to their duties rendered, he would say. It was a feast that put to shame any feasts the other independent city states could individually offer. And this was just a regular meeting. Nothing out of the ordinary at all, no special occasion.

Lorenna had feigned disinterest for the last hour. She picked at her food as each of her brother's advisers spoke in turn, delivering their reports on the political and economic developments across Asturia. The reports were obtuse and mostly pointless. The senior enforcers assigned with reporting responsibilities for each region of the country used this as their chance to try and impress the chancellor. Posturing, laced with threads of interest. She had learned over the years when to tune out and when to tune in. And when she detected a slowing cadence in the voice of the current speaker, she looked down the table to listen in to the end of their report.

'…the visit was a brief one, and only confirmed the status quo, Lord Chancellor. King Thorius remains subdued. Ferenir poses no concern to the Elheim vision.'

The chancellor nodded slowly and then looked expectantly to the adviser sat opposite the older man who just finished speaking.

This enforcer stumbled as all eyes homed in on her. 'Y-yes, Lord Chancellor.' She cleared her throat and brought her napkin delicately to the edge of her mouth. 'I'm afraid the same clarity cannot be proffered for Lions' Rest. Despite the ever-changing paradigm of their government, they seem resolute on keeping their gates closed. Still, nobody comes or goes except in pursuit of essential trade.'

Nothing new there, thought Lorenna. The city of Lions' Rest had always been that way.

'It is unclear whether this continuing isolation is in opposition to our growth or due to internal political conflict. I'm inclined to suggest the latter – given the city's penchant for *unrest*.'

A few voices around the table chuckled and snorted at the woman's remark. It was not the first joke of its kind, nor would it be the last. In fact, Lorenna was sure that the same joke was made at *every* meeting.

The chancellor moved his gaze to his next adviser. It was now the high imperator's turn – the leader of the College Arcana and all enforcers.

She looked uncomfortable. From the way she sat, rigid with her back unnaturally straight, anyone could be forgiven for thinking she was uncomfortable in her enforcer uniform. But Lorenna knew that was not the issue. The uniform may well have been tight-fitting, tailored and somewhat restrictive, but Ulyria Mantleshawn wore it proudly – and rarely took it off.

No, Ulyria and her brother had a private conversation just prior to this gathering to discuss two letters received by the College Arcana. Lorenna was not party to that meeting, but she had seen them afterwards and the letters had sparked some anger and concern in both of them. They did well to conceal that concern from the advisers in open meeting – her brother being more effective at that deception than the high imperator.

'My Ladies, and my Lords, when it comes to a report on the Outer Counties expedition led by Lanark Valivelle'—

Another of the Enforcers coughed on his wine, interrupting the high imperator. '*Expedition*? Is that what we're calling it now. I distinctly recall Lanark referring to it as a '*raid*.''

The Last of the Magi

The high imperator glowered at the man – silencing him – while those in-between them leaned back in their seats to avoid the exchange.

'Semantics aside... the *expedition* has borne fruit,' she continued. 'We have received an interim report which confirms that Lady Illian Valivelle was struck down by Arcana. This assault was orchestrated by an unknown individual who had in his possession an illegal runeblade.'

The room broke into pockets of whispering and conjecture.

Lorenna startled as her brother thumped the table with the base of a weighty, empty goblet. All fell silent for the high imperator to continue.

'The assailant arrived in Asturia from overseas. He travelled from the west and arrived in County Bryn. He is believed to be Asturian himself, but that has not been confirmed.'

Enforcer Haraygar, one of the most senior advisers at the table – sat a couple of seats down from Lorenna – sighed. 'You mean to say that this criminal smuggled himself *and* an illegal weapon into Asturia *and* managed to assault one of our own with Arcana without being stopped?'

Laying it on a bit thick, Percivor, Lorenna mused as she brought her wine glass to her lips.

The high imperator nodded in agreement. 'The absurdity of events has not escaped my notice, Lord Haraygar. Your assessment is blunt but accurate. Judging by the timing of his reports, Lord Valivelle resolved to discover how and where this criminal arrived in Asturia, and he was able to find that information very quickly through local inquiries. He is moving to Brynport to act on that information.'

The chancellor coughed a laugh, and every candle on the table flickered. 'I have every faith that the justice delivered by the Valivelle expedition will be swift and proportionate.'

Lorenna noticed his smirk, quick though he was to raise his glass to conceal it. Lorenna couldn't miss it, however, being sat nearest to him on his left.

'With regret, I must continue further,' said the high imperator. 'The assailant apparently disclosed his plans to the Alderman of

County Bryn – he was travelling on to the Trade Quarters where it is assumed he now resides.'

Lord Haraygar's voice erupted through the room once again. 'Impossible. My inquisitor within the Trade Quarters has not mentioned this.'

The high imperator raised a hand calmly, 'I cast no aspersion over the veracity of your informants but given that we have only just come upon this information following an interrogation, it is plausible the identity of this man, and the extent of his acts, have not yet reached the attention of the coinsmen or your inquisitor.'

Haraygar's face turned a dark shade of red and the wrinkles around his eyes and mouth deepened. 'Nevertheless, if the Trade Quarters harbour a criminal within their walls, they must be made to hand him over. Immediately.'

'Perhaps you forget the position the Trade Quarters holds in our diplomatic strategy, Lord Haraygar?'

Haraygar slumped, waved his hand dismissively and then crossed his arms. 'I do not.'

Lorenna smiled warmly to Haraygar. He noticed and appeared to calm. His rash and forceful views were familiar to all those around the table, and not lacking in wisdom at times. And for that he deserved to be respected.

The high imperator continued. 'Until such time as the Outer Counties are firmly under the control of the Grand City, we cannot afford to disrupt the economic relations we share with the Trade Quarters. By your leave, Lord Chancellor, I would advocate a diplomatic approach. Perhaps a formal request for extradition.'

The chancellor nodded.

The woman who delivered the report on Lions' Rest raised her hand until the chancellor gave her leave to speak. 'Chancellor, I believe Lord Haraygar and Lady Mantleshawn both advocate clear wisdom. Although, with the uncertainty over the current political status of Lions' Rest, a concern arises over the number of unknown entities at play here. I would support Lord Haraygar's approach with more weight – perhaps now is the time to increase pressure on the Trade Quarters? It is the intent for them to fall in line eventually, is it not?'

The Last of the Magi

Again, the chancellor nodded, though it wasn't clear which part of the statement he approved of, if not all. He was not always overt in his communications, except for when he had something final to say. That was his way.

Lorenna didn't feel comfortable knowing there were two views in favour of violence and only one in support of diplomacy. She lowered her wine glass and forced a smile as she lightly placed her hand on her brother's wrist.

'Brother,' she said. He flinched. 'If violence and force are to be the sole method of diplomacy from the Grand City, I begin to wonder what will be left of Asturia to add to our territory. With Brynfall now destroyed, added to the ruins of Oligar and Midhaven, the west is beginning to look less valuable by the day. Lady Mantleshawn, your trusted high imperator, has the right of it. Diplomacy should be our priority.'

Her brother's eyes narrowed, but the smile he drew out for public appearances snaked across his lips. He nodded. Then he placed his hand upon hers and looked to each of his advisers in turn. He rose from his seat and took his wine-filled glass, ushering with a gesture for all to join with him.

Everybody dutifully obliged without hesitation. Even Lorenna followed suit promptly. Appearances within the Elheim family needed to be maintained.

'I have listened carefully – to all of you,' said the chancellor, in his charming and smooth tones. He straightened his royal coat, being a much more lavish and embroidered version of that normally worn by the high imperator, but with a flowing sheet of navy-blue fabric draping across his shoulders and down one side of his back. 'Each of you demonstrate an unwavering commitment to the furtherance of our society. It must be commended. Having considered the balance of your wise counsel, I take the view that – for now at least – we should respect the treaty of independence which founded the Trade Quarters. It has stood unchallenged since the long-gone days of Oligar and shall remain so for as long as necessary. I shall liaise with the high imperator to arrange a diplomatic solution to take forward.'

With that, the chancellor bowed as a sign of respect to his wise advisers, but it was also a signal for them to take their leave. Each of them in turn paid their respects to the chancellor and then made their way out of the banquet hall, forming small pockets of conversation as they left. Lord Haraygar's dissent could be heard above the din until the moment the hall doors rattled shut.

Lorenna's brow furrowed. It was odd for her brother to side with her, and normally he would allow for a more protracted debate before reaching a conclusion. His easy promise of diplomacy unsettled her.

The chancellor turned to her. 'Lorenna. You have grown to be a wise woman indeed. Our parents would have been proud to see how powerful your words have become in recent years.'

The mention of their parents made Lorenna squirm, and his sickly-sweet words only made it worse. She sighed and averted her eyes.

'Yes – I'm sure they would, Vas.' She knew her tone was more disingenuous than she intended. Her emotions had taken control. He wouldn't have been happy with her casual shortening of his name either. He didn't like that even in private conversation.

Noting the darkening of his expression from the corner of her eye, she composed herself and adopted the charm that came so easily to him. 'I shall take my leave, brother. You and Ulyria have much to discuss, I'm sure.'

Lorenna smiled fondly at the high imperator as she moved around her to head back to her private chambers. Her path took her to the other end of the hall, opposite to where their guests had left.

***

The high imperator straightened her back, ready to be addressed by Chancellor Elheim.

'We will send a message to Lord Valivelle and his raiding party,' he said calmly.

'Certainly, Lord Chancellor. Are they to continue the expedition across the Outer Counties?'

'No.' The chancellor lowered his voice and pursed his lips into a thin line. 'Lord Valivelle is to bring the Trade Quarters to heel. He will find and publicly execute the criminal residing within its wall together with all that support him.'

The high imperator's mouth dropped open. 'My Lord, was it not your intent to adopt a diplomatic approach?'

'Let the diplomats believe that diplomacy is at hand – this message is for Lord Valivelle's eyes only. He must destroy the message after he has read its contents, and no evidence of this shall be placed on public record, is that clear?' he didn't blink as he stared her down.

'Understood, Lord Chancellor. I will see that the order is issued personally.'

'Indeed, you shall.'

Lady Ulyria Mantleshawn was truly a wise choice to hold the role of high imperator. She was powerful. Loyal. Obedient to a fault. She would do exactly what was required.

A model citizen.

Vasilarius pushed his chair neatly under the table and refilled his goblet of wine. Without another word, he marched away in the same direction his sister went, with his cape of blue fabric billowing behind him.

As he opened the door at the far end of the hall, he looked back to his high imperator and flashed his charming smile. She nodded dutifully. He swept his hand through the air in a circular motion as he left. Every candle and sconce in the banquet hall danced wildly under his Command and then, all at once, extinguished, leaving his high imperator in darkness.

Chapter 22

Earthquake

The west coast of Asturia was no different to any other coast across the island country. It had a few ports and docks – not of the scale or grandeur of those to the east – but they had all been sorely out of use for decades.

All except one.

One rickety, old wooden pier in the port of Bryn had shown the tell-tale signs of use: the patchwork reparations; the recent scrapings from barrows and trolleys run up and down its length; and, of course, the chains and pulleys strewn about for loading and decanting the cargo carried on whatever vessels had docked there recently.

That pier, and the boat that had the misfortune of being docked there as the Elheim carriages arrived in Brynport, now lay in ruins. Torn asunder by manipulations of wind and water Commanded by the enforcers. The assault had been fast, aggressive and loud, with chippings of wood and splashings of seafoam drifting through the air in the aftermath. Now, the silent wreckage whimpered against the lapping waves.

Darus stood in silence with it.

This port had been one of three in the Outer Counties used primarily for commerce and trade with foreign lands. Although it had been some forty years since the Grand City had compelled the closure of all borders in Asturia, some of the families of Brynport had remained steadfast in maintaining the pier and its facilities – albeit with some less vigour since there was no longer a lucrative income to be claimed from doing so.

A few of those diligent workers had assembled, at a safe distance, to watch their work and their history being unravelled by machinations of Arcana.

Darus turned as he heard the crowd murmuring behind him.

One of the elders stood amongst the line of workers shuffled forward, though he was unsteady on his feet, even with a walking stick. The younger men at his sides tried to help him, but he pushed them away to carry on alone.

'You took your prisoners,' the old man said, 'wasn't that enough?' His voice was croaking and deep.

The enforcer nearest to the old man turned from his assigned position and approached with his white-gloved hands drawn into fists. He squared up to the old man, towering over the elder's hunched frame by at least a foot.

The elder strained to straighten himself and shuffled another step closer to the enforcer – not cowed by the presence of Elheim like many of the others were. His wispy white strands of hair billowed in the wind. Even his loose-fitting overalls were threatening to pull him over as they were caught by the unnatural force of that wind.

The enforcer was unflinching. His black hair was parted and styled in the way fashionable in the Grand City, and his uniform clung to his body as expected from a product of an Elheim master tailor. Neither moved in the wind.

'*We* decide what is enough,' the enforcer said. 'You are fortunate Lord Valivelle has not seen fit to detain you all as accessories to the crimes committed here.'

'You should learn to watch your tone when speaking with your elders, don't you learn about respect at the Grand City?'

The enforcer's face scrunched into an irritated mess, just for a moment. Then a sinister smirk slimed out as he raised his hands.

'That will not be necessary,' said another voice, carried on the wind, approaching from somewhere off to Darus's side. It was his father's voice.

His father dismissed the enforcer and took over the discussion.

'Name?' he asked bluntly.

'Barent Onthair.'

Darus was sure the old man stood a little taller as he proudly said his name, putting particular emphasis on the family name.

'This port has been worked by the Onthair family for—'

'Centuries, no doubt,' Lanark interrupted. 'Am I right? Onthair is an old Oligarian name if I'm not mistaken.'

The old man looked surprised, but he nodded.

'You must be very proud of your family, and the service your kin have provided to Asturia for generations.' His father put an arm around the elder and turned him to face the small crowd that watched at the edge of the town. He then raised a hand to garner their attention. 'Look now to your elder, people of Brynport! This man represents your legacy. For hundreds of years this town has played its part in the history of Asturia, even during those near-forgotten times of Oligari rule. You should take pride in that. Even now, you diligently contribute to the Arcane Tax so that your countrymen to the east can secure the protection of your homes and keep you safe from those that would otherwise seek to harm or oppress you.'

His father released the old man and then gestured back to the ruins of the pier. He took a deep breath, and the wind around them all seemed to react in kind.

'And *that* is exactly what we have done today,' he continued. 'Your port has been used as a vehicle for menaces, in contravention of Grand City decree. Now you are free of that influence. I know that none of you willingly supported the acts of illegal import and piracy that took place here. Is that not right, Master Onthair?'

The elder stared at the line of the crowd. He stayed silent. Darus felt his heart race. Soldiers and elders were often the ones to challenge the Elheim. It never ended well for either. He hoped he wouldn't have to turn his Arcana to an unarmed old man on his father's orders.

'Yes, Elheim,' the elder finally said. 'You've had your fun – you win.'

The elder slowly shuffled his way back to his people. He turned in Darus's direction for just a moment, but it was long enough for Darus to see the face of a defeated man.

Lanark Valivelle stood victorious.

His father turned his attention to the enforcer he had stalled earlier and gestured with his head towards the crowd as they gradually dispersed. 'Consider the consequences of your actions, young enforcer. Bloodshed is reserved for the truly treasonous; the irredeemable. For the lesser offenders, those who still have or contribute value, we must keep the lines of authority drawn.'

The Last of the Magi

The other enforcer nodded. He looked elated to have received guidance from an enforcer as highly regarded as his father.

Darus watched his father pace back to the ruins of the pier, closer to where Darus was stood.

'Darus, here,' he said.

Like an obedient dog, Darus obeyed without hesitation.

'Did you see what happened here?'

'Yes, sir.'

'Tell me what happened.'

Darus's heart had only just calmed, and now it raced again. Another test. His father revelled in any opportunity to test his loyalty, his resolve, his strength, or his intelligence. And he saw his father's grip around his cane change.

'You let those people go, with a warning to ensure their continued allegiance to the Grand City.'

This time it was the side of his leg. The cane bounced off his thick trousers. They cushioned the blow and most of the pain – but not all of it. He winced and tried his best to not show the pain.

'No. I enforced the will of the chancellor, to ensure our society remains on its proper path. I gave them an ultimatum – to fall in line or otherwise fall to ruin. I delivered that message not with my words, but with my actions. As a result, these people will think very carefully about their futures. Everything we do must be in furtherance of the Elheim vision. Remember that with every action you take, and with every word you choose to utter beyond our walls.'

Darus peered over his father's shoulder, to the few still milling their way home with lowered shoulders and dragged feet. *Those poor people*, he thought. He caught his father's cold stare and hastily pushed away the thoughts of empathy, lest those thoughts begin to show on his face.

'We have done enough here, for now. The weather is starting to turn, let's head inside, we have more work to do in the dockhouse.'

Darus followed his father to the ramshackle dockhouse beside the remains of the pier. Before entering, Darus looked overhead and noticed the clouds were becoming darker and thicker with each passing moment.

The sky was clear when they arrived less than an hour ago.

The dockhouse reception was barren and disused, with a generous waiting room and a reception bar still laden with old vases. His father moved behind the reception desk and entered the small room behind.

Darus courteously stepped to one side at the door to let another enforcer leave, on his father's request. Darus then joined his father in the small storage room, a room with no natural light, walls covered in shelves, and lit only by a small lantern.

Slumped in the corner, with hands and feet tied together and mouths gagged with rags fashioned from their own clothing, were two young men – younger than Darus – and one older man with thick grey hair down the sides of his face and across his jowls.

His father pulled a stool closer to the three men and sat. The younger men were breathing heavily, and they squirmed further into the corner. His father reached over and loosened the gag from the older captive.

The man spat a pool of saliva to the ground and ran his tongue over his teeth. 'How much longer are you gonna leave us in 'ere?' he barked, in a common and sluggish accent that visibly offended his father.

'Ah-ah-ah, I'll lead the interrogation here, thank you,' his father said. He took a small fold of paper from his breast pocket and unfurled it between his gloved fingers. 'Think back on the last cargos you illegally transported to Asturia. Did you provide carriage for an armed man wearing a dark-green, hooded overcoat?'

'What? This again? I've answered every question under the bloody sun to that other shite you left us with.'

Lanark sighed, slowly. 'I'll ask again—'

'No, you won't, mate. You can either lock us up or put us on trial. You can't treat us like this.'

'I'm not sure how much time you spend on the waters, but perhaps things have changed since you last stepped beyond your planks. Or perhaps the sea air has addled you. I have authority on behalf of the Grand City of Elheim to carry out all powers of detention, prosecution, and summary execution anywhere in

The Last of the Magi

Asturia, such authority being granted by Chancellor Elheim himself. Is that understood?'

The older man exchanged looks with his sons who shook their heads and raised their brows. 'We don't speak your fancy tongue, mate. Nor do we care for your *Grand Cities* and *chancers*.'

Lanark sighed again. 'Very well.' He stood and gestured for Darus to shut the door.

He did so, leaving him stood uncomfortably close to his father and the men at their feet.

Lanark drew his rapier from the hilt of his cane and swiftly pointed it over the heart of one of the younger men. The young man's breathing became erratic.

'For piracy, harbouring a fugitive and failing to cooperate with an enforcer in his official duties, death would be the appropriate sentence for you all.' Lanark pushed the tip of his blade against the young man's chest until it just cut through his shirt.

'Wait a minute! What are you doing? They've done nothing wrong – they just do what I say!'

His father relaxed his blade arm slightly. 'Is that so? You must know secrets of our Legislaturiate that are lost on me.' He glanced over to Darus with a wicked grin on his face.

Darus forced a smile in return. He could appreciate that the response was somewhat clever, but 'cleverness' in these circumstances just made his stomach churn.

'I shall give you one last chance to assist me, and I shall speak plainly. I'm looking for an armed man. He wears a long green coat with a hood. You passengered him aboard your ship. You will tell me all you know about him.'

The older man slumped against the wall. His eyes searched the grain of the wood floor while one of his sons murmured under his gag, thrashing about for attention.

Lanark clicked his fingers at Darus and pointed at the son causing the scene. Darus dutifully ducked down and loosened the fabric tied around the young man's mouth.

'I remember a green coat,' the young pirate said, pausing to take a few deep breaths. 'There was a bloke who paid us to bring him here who wore something like that.'

Lanark let his blade lower. '*And?* Where did you find him?'

The young man looked at his father, who nodded sharply.

'He was at Port Astur in the fjords.'

Feralland? Thought Darus. 'The fjords' was a common name used by some to refer to Feralland, as its full name of 'The Wild Fjords of Feralland' had proven too cumbersome for most commonfolk to master.

The Asturian ports in Feralland were decommissioned long, long ago. Even before the days of the Grand City and the closing of Asturia's borders. What would drive someone out there?

'Where was he headed?' Lanark continued.

The pirate shook his head. 'We're paid good money to not ask questions.'

Lanark sheathed his rapier. 'I expected as much. But you are sure the man in question meets my description?'

'Yeah, he had that green coat. He never took the hood down.'

'Good,' Lanark said. He then squeezed past Darus to leave the room. 'This has not been a complete waste.'

'What about us?' the older pirate asked, meeting Darus's eyes.

Darus wasn't expecting to speak with them himself. His mind flushed blank for a few moments before he thought of a response. 'I'm not sure. Lord Valivelle will decide what to do next.'

'This is ridiculous, mate. We've told you everything. Just let us go.'

'I-I'm afraid that's not my decision to make.'

'Darus!' His father's voice ran through his bones. For perhaps the first time in his life, he felt glad for the opportunity to rush to his father's side rather than remain with their prisoners.

***

Lanark pointed his cane at the dockhouse. 'What do you think we should do with them?'

'The prisoners?' asked Darus.

His father nodded. Darus felt his body tense. He was sure he knew the answer his father was looking for, as much as it pained him. By his father's interpretation of the law, these men had

The Last of the Magi

satisfied all the prerequisites to justify execution. But there was some wiggle room. The intent of the men, the extent of their involvement with the fugitive's actions, and the duration of their illegal activities were all factors that weighed in the balance.

But not in the mind of Lanark Valivelle.

I can't condemn those men so easily. There could be so much more to their story.

Darus tried to justify the answer he wanted to give, yet he knew it would be pointless to even try. He may have scraped through with that logic for sparing Alderman Navarya, but his father had rebuked him for that intervention. The repercussions of defying his father for a second time were not worth thinking about.

Darus felt his father's glance develop into a stare. He was spending too long wading through his thoughts. He thought of the most neutral answer he could possibly offer and focused on delivering it in a monotone but professional manner. 'As a newly appointed enforcer, I think it would be arrogant of me to try and predict the punishment the chancellor would order, so early in my career.'

Lanark twisted slightly, adjusting his grip on his cane. Darus tried to maintain eye contact with his father without flinching or closing his eyes in apprehension.

'A learned response,' said Lanark.

Darus held his breath to resist sighing in relief.

'In times such as this it does indeed fall to us – *to me* – to make such a determination. From where I stand, the will of the chancellor on this matter is clear: they are to die for their crimes.'

His heart sank. Despite seeing it coming, hearing the words aloud made his blood run cold all the same.

'And it seems only fitting to me that these men should meet their end as this pitiful dockhouse is razed to the ground.' Lanark stamped his cane. 'Yes, there is a poetic retributive justice in that. And I think it about time you demonstrate your new power, *Enforcer Valivelle.*'

Darus didn't think it was possible for his soul to plunge any further, yet it did. 'Sir? You want me to bring the building down upon them?'

'Need I simplify my words for you too?'

No, I can't. Darus looked at the building, hoping desperately that there might be some way for those men inside to break free from their bonds and escape, perhaps through a rear exit. The wooden walls may have been freshly painted in a brilliant white, but that didn't hide the wonky angle of its frames and the poor quality of its construction. It wouldn't take much for the building to be brought down. As Darus examined the dockhouse from afar, a chill of realisation struck him. *I'm actually considering this.*

Lanark whistled for the other enforcers to join them, but he kept his focus on Darus. 'Use your Arcana. Show your colleagues what it means to Command the earth, what it means to be Valivelle. Remind them that we are unmatched in skill. Show the people of Bryn what happens to those who breach our laws.'

The thought of the dockhouse being collapsed by his Arcana only regurgitated the image of the rockslide. Rik, one moment being there, prone on the ground, the next gone under the collapsing stones.

'Darus!' Lanark scolded. Darus felt his father's cane at his back as he was pushed closer to the dockhouse.

The two-storey building suddenly seemed so much larger.

Did he even have the strength to bring down something so large on his own? And could such a power be Commanded with such precision and control? The dockhouse wasn't so far away from the homes of the people who lived here; everything might be destroyed if he lost control.

Darus sighed and flexed his hands, causing the leather in his gloves to creak. He took in the deepest breath he could and felt his stomach twist. There was really no way out of this. If he didn't do it, his father would beat him and do it himself with no hint of restraint.

He lifted his hands in front of him, as if framing the edges of the building between his open palms, and he sent his thoughts to that place deep in his mind where his consciousness and the elements around him merged into one. The Deep Thought state.

He pictured the building in his mind, its shape, its size, and its weight against the cold dry earth. It was like an oil painting in his mind on a background of pure black. He could feel the movement of

The Last of the Magi

the air around the building, bouncing off its walls and penetrating through the weak points around the doors and window frames, reminding him of its frailty. He dived deeper, trying to reach that place where his head started to ache, and the ground beneath his feet would tremble.

The cool and light sensation in his mind, signalling his connection with the air, disappeared and he then felt a strong, rushing and crashing sensation in its place – the lapping waves at the shore. Then, as his mind went deeper yet, he froze in place as his mental image of the building transformed.

In a flash, the dockhouse changed into a pile of rocks and boulders. The very same from the College Arcana training hall. A figure then appeared in his mind, stood between him and the rock pile. Rik. Bloody and bruised. Broken.

Darus gasped and ejected violently from his Deep Thought trance. He stumbled back, almost falling. He clutched a hand to his chest as he caught his breath, feeling a relief wash over him as he realised the dockhouse had not truly changed, nor was Rikkard stood before him. But the image in his mind had looked real. Too real.

'Pitiful.' Darus felt his father's grip seize his shoulder and next he knew he was on the ground clutching the back of his head. 'A Valivelle does not hesitate. A Valivelle enacts the law of the Grand City and the will of the chancellor without weakness! Are you truly so pathetic that you cannot summon the strength to snuff out our enemies when your ability to end the life of one of our own is so potent?'

The life of one of our own?

The pain in Darus's head and back no longer mattered. He bolted back to his feet and faced his father. 'What do you mean by that?'

His father pressed at his forehead with his thumb, shook his head, and turned away.

Darus ran around and stood in his father's path. 'Answer me!' he screamed.

'Oh – so now the pup bares its teeth, once more against one of his own.'

He shoved his father hard in the chest, accidentally drawing on Arcana to enhance his push with strands of nearby air.

Lanark stumbled back, desperately waving his cane until he found a new footing. Once he regained balance, he straightened himself and glowered with cheeks ablaze in shades of red and purple. He whipped his free hand through the air and Commanded a lashing of air of his own.

The air hit Darus in the back of the legs. He gasped as his feet swung out from under him and he slammed to the ground.

'Once again I regard you for what you are – pitiful, pathetic and treasonous,' his father paced over him and pressed his cane into the centre of his chest, printing a dirty, earthy circle into his white jacket. 'You killed him, Darus.'

'What?!' His voice cracked.

'Apprentice Rikkard Nostrum. After a promising period of recovery, He succumbed to his injuries. Like you, he was too weak.' The words went through Darus like a shower of ice. 'His death will be heralded as a noble sacrifice, helping to bring about a new era of strength for our people. But you know the truth of it, Darus. You killed him.'

No…

Rikkard was strong. Stronger than Darus could ever be. He couldn't have died.

Darus slapped his father's cane away and picked himself up again. He shook his head as his eyes filled. 'You're lying.' His voice was little more than a whisper.

Lanark scoffed a laugh and drew a roll of parchment from inside his jacket. 'A missive from the Grand City, delivered shortly after our arrival here. Registrar Harroly thought it proper to notify you of his passing, and that no charges are to be brought against you for your part in it.'

Darus wanted the earth beneath his feet to erupt, to open and swallow him whole. With Rik gone, there was no one left in the Grand City that understood him. Nobody else that he could be himself around without fear of chastisement. And it was all his fault.

'Please, father. Let me read it.'

Lanark unfolded the parchment and held it with both hands. He

The Last of the Magi

glanced at the words on the page, as if preparing to read it aloud, but then turned the parchment and tore it across the middle. He carried on tearing until the letter was small enough to be carried away on the wind like grains of sand.

Darus didn't blink. He couldn't. His eyes flitted between the scraps of parchment as they span on the wind and made their escape towards the sea. His knees hit the sand.

With head bowed, he fought back the welling tears. His hands curled into fists. His teeth clamped together. Every muscle in his body started to knot with pain.

But in that moment of pain and anguish, as his body convulsed in torment, his conscious mind dived deep to escape it all — and once more his thoughts brushed against the earth around him. He swore he could almost taste the stale dryness of the ground in his mouth. The sensation was a distraction, and not a good one, as it took his focus away from what was really going on. He had re-engaged his Deep Thought trance. He had Reached out with his senses to connect with the earth and held it firmly in his Grasped through Arcana, and now it was under his Command. His subconscious Command. Again, his Arcana ran wild against his emotions. The earth trembled, with him at its epicentre.

Adrenaline fired through his body as he jolted out of his trance. He opened his eyes just in time to see the ground split open around his knees, the bouncing grains of sand falling between the cracks. But again, there was a difference to the manifestation this time – the familiar Arcane tether between his mind and the Commanded element felt lucid and vivid for the first time.

He could regain control. He could Command the earth for himself this time.

Acting on impulse, he thrust his hands forwards, willing his Arcana to move away from him – and so it did. The rumbling earth rushed forward from his position, tossing loose gravel and sand about as it did, as if some subterranean beast burrowed along at speed.

It continued forward, growing in magnitude. The rumbling burrowed beneath the foundations of the dockhouse and then erupted with a small shockwave.

The building creaked violently, but it remained still. Darus held his breath. He didn't intend to project his Arcana under the dockhouse, that was just the way he was facing.

Slowly, Darus lowered his hands. He slowed his breathing as much as he could, as if the slightest breath might cause another disturbance amongst the elements. But it wasn't his breathing he should have been worried about. The tether connecting his Arcana was still active and the motion of his hands was enough to trigger another Command through his mind. Another shockwave. It boomed from under the building.

The dockhouse shuddered, groaned, and then became still again. Then it collapsed.

The painted wood panels. the roughshod slanted roof. It all collapsed in, in one loud crunch. He did exactly what his father wanted. He razed the building to the ground and entombed those helpless pirates restrained within. Summary execution.

His father appeared at his side as a dust cloud from the dockhouse wreckage blew over them, mixed with a mist of sand. 'Remember this moment with pride, Darus. You furthered the Elheim vision. Consider the consequences of your actions. By carrying out the will of the chancellor, you will gain his favour, and that of your people. Fail your people, and you will only suffer as those criminals have suffered.'

His father whistled for the attention of the other enforcers again. He ordered them back to their carriages and declared their business in Brynport concluded. Just like that, the dockhouse and the men trapped within, now presumed dead, were already beyond his interest. The people of Brynport would have to extract the bodies and bury them.

Darus stayed where he was as the enforcers marched away. His eyes were dry now, and he stared silently at the remains of the dockhouse. He couldn't focus on anything else, nor upon any sounds in the vicinity, not even the blustering wind or the crashing waves. He couldn't even feel the chilled wind bite against his cheek.

His fingers twitched at his side.

The ruins of the dockhouse trembled.

Chapter 23

The Coinsmeet

Marla froze in place. Even though she was slowly getting used to navigating the narrow, damp alleyways of the Quarters while carrying out her delivery duties, she could never predict what she would stumble upon from night-to-night.

This time she had absent-mindedly wandered out of one alleyway into one of the wider lanes. And there was a commotion that made her stop in her tracks.

A group of scrawny, raggedly dressed men and women surrounded two others, trapping them against the brick wall. Voices spoke in hushed tones, their faces concealed either by hoods, scarves, or the shadow of the towering tenements on either side of the path.

Luckily, she hadn't been seen, so Marla slowly retreated back through the mouth of the alley, taking care not to rattle the barrow.

As she shuffled, the dim moonlight caught against knife blades held by some of the mob.

She considered running – perhaps one of the city guards, or even an elite might be on patrol nearby. But before she could decide, a louder voice cut through the hushed whispers.

'...I'll ensure your disclosures reach the right ears. You should go, I'll deal with this. Contact me again in the usual way.' The voice sounded as if it was coming from one of the two pinned against the wall, a man. He was just a tall shadow from where Marla stood.

'Very well. Try not to cause too much of a scene. We will need to speak again soon.' The second voice was a woman's. As the woman tightened the waist of her robe and tugged her hood deeply over her face – causing it to shimmer slightly against the moonlight – Marla was struck by déjà vu.

This was the same pair she had stumbled upon before, the day that the Elheim paraded through the crossing.

The man stepped in front of the woman and raised a palm to the group surrounding them. 'Back,' he said.

They have knives, what good will—

Marla's thought was cut-off as the air in the alleyway behind her suddenly lurch forward. Even her lungs squeezed as if a portion of her breath was stolen away too.

She recovered just in time to see a pulse bellow out from where the man stood. The group of attackers were all thrown back, slamming into the stone wall opposite, and all the loose debris on the ground flew away from his position too.

Marla ducked her head back as the air buffeted against her and made her eyes water. 'What the...' she whispered, quickly pulling herself back to the corner.

The woman was slipping away, retreating down one of the nearby alleyways, but the man stood stoically in place — his hand still held out.

'Who the hell are you!?' cursed one of the downed thugs.

'None of your concern,' he stepped forward to loom over the pile of groaning bodies. 'You saw nothing. You heard nothing. And you experienced *nothing*. If I hear even a murmuring of this circulating as idle gossip in the city, I will locate you all – and your families – and... well... I will let your imaginations fill in the rest. I will remember all your faces; you have my word on that. Am I understood?'

The thug who spoke before was the first to speak again. 'Run! Quick, split up!'

Many of them dragged themselves across the cobbles, only rising to run away once they were out of the man's reach. The others were up and gone long before that.

What is he? Marla wondered. *He isn't dressed like an Elheim.* But that pulse of air seemed just like Arcana.

'That same warning extends to you, young lady,'

Marla paused. The empty blackness of the man's hood was now facing her.

'I'd rather avoid an unpleasant visit to the Artisan Quarter. Wouldn't you agree?'

Marla's eyes were wide. She didn't blink. She only nodded, and he nodded once in return.

The Last of the Magi

'Now, if you'll excuse me.' He bowed with one arm across his stomach. He then turned and marched away, disappearing down another of the dark alleys.

It took some time for Marla to move. She tried to process what just happened. *Does he know who I am? How could he?*

She swallowed and then slowly lifted the arms of her barrow and stepped out into the lane. She didn't like the idea of being cowed by anyone, but that man had done something that she had only ever seen enforcers capable of. That made him dangerous. And if there was even a chance that he knew where she lived, where Brayne and Marion lived, then she would obey his words, for their sake if not for her own.

Marla glanced sheepishly down each of the alleys as she walked. The man was gone, not leaving even a trace. The thugs too had completely vanished. She took her time getting her breathing back to a normal rate, and eventually she was able to walk at her usual pace.

She felt much calmer as she joined a lane that she knew led back to the central plaza. The glistening marble floors were reassuring somehow, like it was offering sanctuary from danger. Plus, she would be out in the open, away from shady back-alley activity.

The plaza was empty at this hour. People rarely had cause to cross the large, open space in the dead of night.

Except for two elite guards apparently, and the blindfolded man they guided across the marble by his arms.

Again, Marla held back. She sighed, but the breath shivered from her. 'What now... I just want to get back.'

The three in the plaza moved between the four founder statues. Marla was too far to see what was happening, but one detail stood out as they walked a bit closer. The man being escorted by the guards was dressed in a very familiar way, just visible against the torchlight.

Tharian. What's going on?

She considered stepping out, intervening. Her feet even twitched, but the ordeal of what she had just seen in the alley doused the courage within her. And she didn't know Tharian well enough to be sure he was the victim in this situation. After all, he was carrying a runeblade, he was the one who stood against the enforcer back at Brynwell, and he caused the commotion at the Crucible. Perhaps his brash behaviours were just catching up with him?

As Marla reminisced on the bizarre events of the last few weeks, she had taken her eyes away from the plaza. When she looked back, they were gone. There wasn't enough time for them to dash off down any of the main roads or side alleys.

They simply vanished.

***

Tharian had been made to walk for at least an hour. The blindfold was fastened so tightly he could feel it pressing against his eyelids. It was uncomfortable, but a necessary discomfort.

Everything was going just as Traykin said it would. When the last of the four missives arrived that morning, he told Tharian he would be 'taken' to the location of the Coinsmeet under armed escort. The specific location, and how to access it, was to remain a secret. So he wasn't surprised when the elite guards arrived at the Bazaar and started looping the strip of cloth around his head.

Even without sight, he could make out some of the features of his journey. Winding streets, twisting staircases and even low ceilings to duck under at some points. They went on and on until eventually he was pushed forward into a space that echoed with every step.

One of the guards whispered in his ear.

'Stay there – speak when spoken to,' the breath against his neck made him shiver.

The blindfold was then whipped away, temporarily blinding him as a bright light replaced the darkness.

His eyes adjusted. He was stood on a circular marble platform, built into a walkway that cut through the middle of this large and empty stone hall, with towering support pillars stretching from floor to ceiling. He was underground, that much was obvious by how long he spent being guided down staircases along the way.

The bright light came from the far end of the hall, up near the ceiling. Tharian raised his hand as he tried to look directly at it. He

The Last of the Magi

was too far underground for it to be a window, and it was too late to be sunlight. Yet, the round opening high up the wall cast a powerful spotlight upon him.

It was overpowering, so he lowered his gaze to examine his surroundings. There were four thrones between him and the far wall, each of them raised on a high stone pillar close enough to each other that if people were sitting in the seats, they could easily reach each other. The pillars partly blocked the light, casting looming shadows over the front of the seats and over the walkway ahead of Tharian. But they did more than block the light. They stopped him from moving much further forward, as they served as a barrier to whatever was hidden on the other end of the hall.

A shadow in one of the thrones moved, a silhouette shuffling to find comfort. Tharian startled. He wasn't alone. The figure was too draped in darkness for him to see any of its features.

'You must be Tharian. Jerard spoke about you with quite some energy,' said a firm female voice. She was well spoken – much more so than most Quartersfolk, but not to the extreme of Coinswoman Faast from the Quarter of War. Yet it was not her voice that piqued Tharian's interest most, it was that she used Traykin's first name. Very few would be so bold.

'May I ask who I am addressing?'

'You may. I am Coinswoman Keene, of the Artisan Quarter. I suspect you have many questions about the nature of these proceedings, just as we have many about your proposal for the Trade Quarters.'

'My proposal concerns all Asturia, Coinswoman Keene, not only the Trade Quarters.'

The sound of heavy doors being thrown open echoed through the hall and then another voice joined the conversation, chuckling as it approached the lofty seats from somewhere out of view. 'Indeed, indeed!' the jovial man said. 'A chance to throw open the ports of Asturia to resume overseas trade.'

Tharian recognised the voice. Coinsman Velioth from the Market Quarter. His slender frame then emerged from steps behind one of the thrones. His silhouette nodded to Coinswoman Keene and then took his seat.

'These could be exciting times, for all of us, wouldn't you say, Coinswoman?'

Keene parted her hands and shrugged. 'I find myself met with even more questions.'

Velioth chuckled. 'Don't worry, I've not reached any premature judgment on this proposal. I'm enthusiastic but equally curious about the detail. Questions will be asked and – I'm sure – answered by our guest here.'

Tharian's face warmed as the reality of this process sank in. The long nights of fleshing out the details of his plan would finally be put to the test. Traykin had grilled him each night to try and find weaknesses to be addressed. He found many. Sometimes more than the night before. But Tharian didn't need to achieve perfection, he just needed to plug as many holes as he could.

The doors threw open again and a harsh, heavy set of footsteps carried the next coinsman into the room. This tall figure took the seat furthest to Tharian's left, leaving only the far-right seat now empty.

'*Arcana Hunter*,' growled the shadow. Coinswoman Faast. Her temper had not softened since their last meeting. 'Your lofty claims of having rallied the other coinsmen were not even a trifle exaggerated.'

Velioth gasped dramatically. '*This* is the one from the Crucible?' Faast nodded. 'My, my, you have caused quite a stir in your short time in our fine city, haven't you?'

Tharian nodded to the shadowy figures, squinting to try and look through the piercing light casting down upon him. 'I apologise for my...' he paused, searching for the right words, '...unconventional methods, but these are not conventional times. I had to act boldly to gather your attention, especially with the Grand City behaving as it is. I'm sure that hasn't escaped your notice.'

Faast waved her hand dismissively. 'You need not prevaricate your point any further – you have secured your Coinsmeet. Your transgressions are nonetheless a relevant factor for our deliberations.'

'Rightly said,' Keene added.

Velioth chimed in also. 'Is that right? I thought we were to judge

The Last of the Magi

this man's proposal solely on its own merits?' He then twisted to the side and called out. 'Mors?'

Taking a guess at where the coinsman was now looking, Tharian looked the same way and noticed there was a small opening in the wall, inaccessible to him and far out of his reach, where sat Coinsman Velioth's faithful attendant on a small balcony surrounded by tomes and scrolls of parchment. The same man he spoke with during his visit to the Market Quarter. He was even wearing the same black suit.

Mors rifled through pages as quickly as he could and then whipped one page out of a folder of documents to better hold it against his lamp. 'Coinswoman Faast is correct, sir. Although the coinsmen collectively have the power to judge proceedings as they see fit, the merits of the *proposer* may be considered alongside the merits of the *proposal*.'

'How fun,' said Velioth, clapping his hands together.

For the third and last time, the conversation was interrupted by the sound of heavy doors pushing open, and the final heavy-footed coinsman entered and eventually appeared in Tharian's view as they took the final seat.

'Did you say *fun*, Velioth? Has our guest been keeping you entertained?' the voice was deep and gruff.

The Coinsman for the Collectors Quarter had finally arrived. One of the others scoffed, presumably at the late arrival of their colleague.

'What? No fanfare, no how-do-you do?' the collector said.

Tharian leaned forward, trying to scrutinise the voice more closely.

You have got to be kidding me, he thought.

'Don't mind me,' said the collector, with a laugh. 'Continue on, lad.'

'Traykin?!' Tharian's voice bounced off the walls.

The collector leaned forward over the balustrade until the light caught the side of his face, revealing the wrinkled, dark eyes and long black beard of Jerard Traykin. 'You really didn't figure it out? Did you think I'd sat idle for the last decade?'

Tharian shook his head, smirking at his friend. 'My attentions were clearly elsewhere.' How had he missed it? Of course Traykin would have wormed his way into this position of power eventually.

Traykin may have been a purveyor of strange artifacts and treasures, but Traykin's true passion was procuring people, allegiances, and information. Though Traykin would deny being at all politically minded, he was perhaps one of the most politically affluent individuals in the city simply because he always knew too much and was known by so many. Apparently, he took that to the extreme over the last decade.

'Whilst we are on this subject, I have a point of order' said Keene, holding her arms out to garner the attention of her fellow coinsman, 'I believe it only proper that Coinsman Traykin recuse himself from any vote on this proposal.'

Traykin turned, 'And why would you say that? Is my opinion not valuable anymore?'

'It is clear from our discussions that you both have a pre-existing relationship, one which appears to be quite close. You may be conflicted, which could influence your decision-making.'

Faast hummed a deep note and then joined the discussion. 'Whilst I sympathise with Coinswoman Keene on the principle of her point, I would respectfully argue this explication of the conflict rule is not accurate.'

Traykin tapped his wrist against the balustrade with some force, 'Aye, exactly what she said. Mors – translation?'

Again, the elderly man rifled through papers, pausing only briefly to push his beard back under the table as the breeze of the flipping paper caused it to drift. 'Coinswoman Faast is correct again. Though the extract on conflicts is lengthy, it appears more concerned with a coinsman's personal gain, or the gain of one to whom he has a familial or business relation.'

Keene remained silent, but her shadow nodded towards Traykin and Faast in turn. 'My mistake.' She then leaned forward and Tharian could tell she was about to address him directly. 'Please do not misunderstand my intentions with that challenge. I have sat in this place a long time and I have utmost respect for our traditions and rules. The laws of the Trade Quarters are binding on this process. The slightest impropriety can unravel any decision we

The Last of the Magi

make.'

'I understand.' Tharian said.

'I'm glad,' Keene looked to her fellow coinsmen. 'Shall we begin?' The heads on the other three shadows bobbed in turn.

Keene pulled some paperwork from beside her throne and then cleared her throat. 'Master Tharian – currently of Traykin's Bazaar – the Coinsmen of the Trade Quarters have summoned you to this Coinsmeet. We are to hear your proposal that formal action be taken against the Grand City of Elheim, in response to the conduct of the enforcers that act on their behalf. Is this a fair precis of your proposal for us today?'

'Yes, it is.'

She made it sound much more professional than he expected. He felt a cold sweat form on his brow. He was not dealing with fools.

'Then consider the floor yours, Master Tharian.'

That marked Tharian's time to deliver his speech. The plan he'd spent each night working on was finally to be heard. This was the culmination of his ten years of travelling Feralland, searching for something – anything – that might help Asturia's plight.

His sense of self-awareness faded as he began the preamble to his prepared speech. Though it didn't come out word-for-word as he drafted, the spirit of what he had to say was maintained. He spoke for many minutes, uninterrupted. He spoke of the treaty crimes committed by the Elheim when they forced their way through the Trade Quarters as if it were just a crossing in the road. He described their use of Arcana in the central plaza – recounting what he saw with his own eyes.

He spoke of Brynfall. He spoke of his own birth-home of Midhaven, even though he had no personal memories of it. Both destroyed at the whim of the Grand City. Coinsman Velioth even interrupted at that point to add news of additional damage caused at Brynport in the last few days. When it came to establishing the Grand City's villainy, he was evidently pushing at an open door, just as Traykin had predicted.

With tempers towards the Elheim brought to the fore, Tharian then spoke of the Trade Quarters and its history. He reminded the coinsmen of their city's founding, as an independent economic settlement intended to foster peaceful relations between the warring cities of Ferenir, in the east, and Oligar, to the west. From there it became the hub of all trade and commerce for Asturia.

And then he went on to discuss how the Oligari – the ruling people of that era – had banned overseas trade during the plague of the Violet Affliction, and he described the economic downturn suffered by all Quartersfolk following that decision. But even once the plague had run its course, the supposedly 'independent' Trade Quarters still saw its activities limited by the Oligari prior to their downfall. The independence of the Quarters being belittled to a thing of fiction.

And that set the stage to compare the time of Oligari rule to that of the current day. Now, with the Grand City of Elheim standing as the latest threat to the stability of Asturia, and the country yet again forced to follow an embargo on overseas trade and travel, the Trade Quarters were staring at a greater threat to its independence than ever before. 'Independence' would be a word resigned to the annals of history under the rule of the Grand City of Elheim.

With all that said, Tharian let out a sigh of relief. Passionate though he may have been about this issue, he had spent so much of his life keeping out of the spotlight. Standing now in a literal spotlight, speaking to politicians, felt surreal. It felt wrong, but it seemed to be going well. That was to be expected, though. Painting the picture of the Elheim growing out of control was an easy task – he was simply recounting what the coinsmen already knew – but the point was to draw out their frustrations and set them simmering.

He took in his next breath slowly. Finally, he was ready to turn to the subject of his plans. This was the hard part.

'The Grand City does not command an army,' he said. 'As far as I can know, they don't have guardsmen or a militia to draw upon. The Elheim do not concern themselves with such things because they have no need to. Because even the greatest warrior of the Trade Quarters, with all her might and armaments…' Tharian paused, gesturing with one hand towards the silhouette of Faast, '…cannot stand as an equal to even one of their enforcers. Their Arcana is insurmountable.

'The settlements of the Outer Counties and the independent city

The Last of the Magi

states of the east have no defence against Arcana. Even when the Magic of the Magi was part of our society, there was never any need to fear that power, and so we have developed no shield or counter to magical threats.'

Faast groaned. She had been tapping her foot impatiently throughout this last chapter in Tharian's dramatic monologue. Tharian could hear it like an echoing, ticking clock. And then she finally interrupted him. 'That you are learned on the events and tragedies of our nation is not in dispute here. You are choosing to weave a tapestry that depicts a tale of the unstoppable tidal force of Arcana. If this is the direction you continue to tread, you might as well stop now.'

The sound of Mors's quill stopped abruptly, and his eyes joined the gallery of glares that Tharian could feel bearing down on him.

'I was quite enjoying that, if it's all the same to you,' said Velioth who had shifted in his seat and was resting his cheek against his fist.

'I laboured the point intentionally,' Tharian said, 'only to make clear that I *do* take the threat of Arcana seriously. But I will move on.'

Faast nodded, and Velioth sighed.

'Around ten years ago, I voyaged far to the west, to Feralland. I met creatures and civilisations that – I am told – our people were long ago close with. I went there not to escape the plight of Asturia, but in the hope that I could find some solution for dealing with Arcana, from those who see more of the world than we do. I believe I have found that solution.'

He paused again to gauge their reactions. He glanced around at the featureless silhouettes of the coinsmen who remained still and silent. Only the scratching sound of handwriting remained.

'The Magi were the only others in Asturia capable of doing what the Elheim enforcers now do. The Elheim went to great lengths to end that. You don't need a history lesson on the Purge from me. However, there are those across the sea who tell a different story to our recorded history. Those calling themselves the 'Awoken' say that not all Magi perished in the Purge; that a Magi still lives, somewhere in Asturia. I made it my mission to find out more, and to learn about the Magi from those who remember more than we do.

'No matter where I went, the Awoken all had the same message to tell: An Asturian Magi survived. I asked if they would help me find them, but they refused. I assumed they didn't want to risk endangering their own by joining our conflicts. So, I asked if this Magi could save us. They said that the full powers of Magic were still unknown, but one thing known for sure was the Magi had the power to repress the forces at play around them. That power – they say – can also repress other forces of magic, sealing it away, making it impossible for the user to draw upon that strength. If we can find this Magi and protect them, then we can take away the Grand City's one and only weapon. Without Arcana, they are nothing.'

Tharian came to a natural pause. Faast was the first to move her head, looking down the line. Traykin, at the other end, did the same.

'I find myself without words,' said Faast.

'A rare delight,' chuckled Velioth.

'I, however,' sighed Keene, 'have much to say.' Tharian flushed in anticipation. 'Would you please take two steps to your right.'

Tharian looked around, confused as to the request. He looked behind just in case there was someone behind him that he was blocking from view. There wasn't. Then he took the two steps as requested.

'Now tell me where you are stood,' she continued.

Tharian again looked around in bewilderment. His attention was then drawn to Mors who tapped his quill loudly against the table to get Tharian's attention, and then pointed a finger towards his feet.

Tharian looked down and saw a large diagonal strip of grey and brown marble surrounded by a vibrant green. He looked around further and realised that the floor beneath his feet was a marble mosaic map of Asturia. Where he stood before was the centre-point of the country, the verdant forests of Arboreta. Where he stood now, on the strip of grey stretching from the edge of Arboreta all the way to the Grand City, was the part of the Eastern Expanse now known as the *Dead Plains*. The commonfolk of Asturia knew it by another name, giving it the same name as the event that created it: *The Purge*.

Tharian knew where this was going.

The Last of the Magi

'Twenty-three years ago,' said Keene, 'the entire assembly of Asturian Magi stood in solidarity against the Grand City and their use of Arcana. In return, the Grand City flooded the Dead Plains with a torrent of Arcana so potent the Magi were reduced to dust.'

'Yes, I know,' replied Tharian.

'Then if what you say is true, what hope does one solitary Magi have against the tremendous might of the Gr—'

'What she's asking, lad,' Traykin interrupted, 'is how will one Magi do what all of them together couldn't?'

Tharian had prepared for this. He knew it was one of the biggest roadblocks in his way. 'The Magi stood alone before,' he replied. 'They were united as Magi, but alone from the rest of Asturia. If we locate this Magi and ask for their help, we can offer to protect them and support them in laying the groundwork for whatever they need to do to stop the Grand City.'

Faast's voice erupted back into the conversation. 'And you would beseech the Trade Quarters to furnish you with the military force to achieve this – all for the sake of one passivistic Magi? What are we to do if this Magi fails, or refuses to help, and the Trade Quarters becomes the target of Elheim retaliation?'

'Your concerns are valid, I understand that. But an uprising of this kind must start somewhere and will always bear risk.'

Faast straightened in her seat. 'This is Asturia's battle. It does not only concern the Trade Quarters. As it currently stands, we are in in a tenuous state of economic co-dependence with the Grand City. It is a cold war of commerce. Both Lions' Rest and Ferenir have better cause to strike first, they are stronger cities with a larger shadow cast over them from years of humiliating bureaucratic subjugation. Why not start there? Why do you petition *us*?'

Tharian nodded and considered his response. The coinswoman had made a good point. The other cities felt a tighter squeeze at the hands of the Grand City, and they both had a more intimate past relationship with Magi. Maybe it *would* be easier to persuade them first. But that would just delay things.

'I will answer that,' said Velioth. Tharian raised a brow, he didn't think the coinsmen would intervene to support his presentation. 'Lions' Rest is unchanged in their ways. They maintain a political silence with outsiders. Even trade with them has slowed. My fellow coinsmen, you may not see it day-to-day as plainly as I do, but they take solace within their cliffs for good reason. As for Ferenir, well,' Velioth paused and sat back in his chair, 'we are dealing there with a people who want to fight, but a cautious king who personally knows the brutality of the enforcers. I'm confident he would show support, though concern for his people would bind his hands.'

'No boy should lose their father so young,' added Traykin.

'It was a cowardly act of regicide,' added Faast. They appeared to exchange a look of understanding.

After a pause, Keene also voiced her views. 'Then, Magi or no, there seems at the very least a scope for a unified front in this campaign. Perhaps this matter is worth more consideration after all?' said Keene.

Tharian twitched, recalling Keene's earlier comment about not pre-formulating a view on the matter.

'Agreed,' said Velioth.

Traykin grunted in approval and Faast nodded.

Keene then looked down to Tharian again. 'There are still many variables at play here, and much that needs to be considered in more detail. We shall retire for now and consider what we have heard so far. Are you able to remain here until we are finished?'

After the work it had taken to get to this point, Tharian was eager to hear their views. He bowed his head respectfully and then the four coinsmen left their seats and disappeared. Even Mors scooped up his notes, together with a couple of tomes from his collection and left through the door behind his desk, presumably to join up with the coinsmen elsewhere in this underground meeting place.

That left Tharian in this dark, dust-laden chamber, stood alone in the spotlight casting down upon him. He could relax for a little while, even though the process was far from over.

Chapter 24

The Burdens of Inquisition

Marla crept in as quietly as she could. Marion would long be asleep, but Brayne's sleeping pattern varied with his workload. He had cleared many orders during the day, so he was probably asleep too. The house was still and dark as she clicked the front door closed.

She lightly planted her satchel on the kitchen counter. There was a weight of coins stashed inside, and she didn't want to make the mistake of waking Brayne again by throwing the heavy bag around and filling the house with the sounds of clinking metal. That wasn't a fun experience for anyone involved.

A pleasant smell, warm and sweet, wafted under her nose. *She's been baking again.*

Turning to the kitchen table, she spotted the slices of freshly baked fruit bread laid out for her. She smiled and eagerly held a slice between her teeth as she tidied away some of the other things left about the room after the busy day. There were always a hundred jobs to be done, and sometimes the couple needed to just call it a night before exhausting themselves more than necessary.

Marla helped where she could. And the mundane chores gave her time to reflect on the events of the day.

Things had started well. She ran errands for Marion at first light and then, to her delight, Brayne had allowed her a little time in the workshop. He was delegating to her more as time went on.

Marla smiled – it hadn't taken too long for the grumpy artisan to finally start lowering his guard. The unfortunate turn of events at the Crucible had not been damaging to their relationship.

As the evening had settled in, another coughing fit slowed Brayne's progress considerably, to the point that he ran the risk of losing income to late delivery penalties. Marla forced her way between him and the anvil again, completing the work with only a few minor amendments demanded by Brayne. Then, on her insistence, she immediately ran the completed projects out for delivery, despite the late hour. The businesses she had to deliver to were open through the night; the Quarter of War never slept.

Marla's arms were aching. She had done the work of two today. The errand-running, the metalworking, and the drama in the back alleys had taken more out of her than she expected.

Just what had she stumbled upon between those strangers and the thugs? And what trouble had Tharian got himself into? She tried to push aside the memory of what she had seen in that alleyway. The man clad in black was clear enough in his threat – she needed to forget what she'd seen, for her safety and the Glanmores'. She focused on Tharian's situation instead, as a distraction, while she walked around the house ensuring every door was locked and every curtain was drawn tightly closed.

Seeing Tharian restrained by guards was concerning, but not at all surprising. Many came to the Trade Quarters seeking to find a better life, or to find opportunities that the Outer Counties could not offer – but not everyone found what they were looking for. Judging by the number of thugs and mercenaries that populated the Quarters at almost every turn, a great many of those seeking their fortunes would stumble and fall along the way. She hoped, at least, that Tharian had not done anything *too* serious to warrant being dragged through the city by the elite guard in the dead of night.

Marla head towards the stairs, sleep calling to her, but an unruly pile on the small table beside the door caught her eye. It was a heap of opened letters that had not yet been sorted away into the living room cabinet.

She grabbed the pile and rifled through. Brayne would often get orders posted to him, and Marla liked to get an idea of his workload just in case there was a chance of working on something exciting. She held the letters closer to the window beside the door, to catch the fleeting light of the streetlamps outside.

Advertisements. Receipted purchase orders. News fliers. Nothing exciting. She put each to the back of the pile as she worked her way through.

But then there was one letter that stood out towards the end. It was on a neatly trimmed sheet of rigid, pale green card, addressed to Brayne. A grey ink seal sat beside an elegantly written name:

The Last of the Magi

'*Erlegraine Hospiticiars.*'

Hospiticiar?

She sounded the word out and repeated it over and over in her head. She hadn't seen the word before. It was familiar, though. Her mother, who was an apothecary before she passed, sometimes talked about her visits to modern facilities in the Eastern Expanse known as hospitals, or infirmaries, but this word was different. Perhaps it was a term local to the Trade Quarters related to chirurgeons?

As she read on, her suspicions were confirmed. Although some of the words were complicated and unfamiliar, it was clear the letter was from someone who understood medicine. Her eyes skimmed over the jargon until she found a line that made her stomach churn. Three words in particular: the Violet Affliction.

She reflexively looked up at the ceiling, as if staring straight into Brayne and Marion's room.

The coughing. The wheezing. The gasping for breath. It all made sense now.

Marla felt overwhelmed by a sudden surge of conflicting feelings. She swallowed it down and put the letter back where she found it, making sure to return it to its proper place in the pile. She then crept up the stairs to finally retreat to her room. Her mind raced with each step.

She stared at their bedroom door. A part of her wanted to storm in and confront them, to demand an explanation. Why didn't they tell her?

But she had no right to know, nor was it her business to know.

Anger and frustration welled within her. It took her a few moments to realise that her emotions were not aimed at the Glanmores, not exactly. It was aimed at the Violet Affliction. It was no ordinary cold or seasonal illness. The Violet Affliction was a horrible curse of an illness, and it was the same illness that took her mother.

And it was hereditary. Her mother had explained that much before she became too ill to speak. The illness was becoming weaker over time, and many didn't even develop the deadly strain anymore, but it was still a heart-wrenching, brutal disease for those who did suffer it. Brayne probably knew it was in his family.

Marla still lingered on the landing. Her stomach ached. Her fondness for her hosts had grown so very quickly. Marion's doting kindness and fierce resolve. Even Brayne's rigidity and bluntness. They had both shown her such generosity – in their own ways – when they owed her none.

There was nothing she could do about it now. Thinking about the situation would only dig up more sadness from her own loss.

She slipped into her room quietly. Her racing thoughts made her question everything. Why was the room so frilly? Why was the wardrobe filled with so many clothes, of all shapes and sizes? None of them were sizes fitting Marion or Brayne. Why did they take her in so readily?

She dropped onto her bed. In the corner, on the chair near the window, the clothes she arrived in were clean and neatly folded. Guilt now joined her feelings of dread, frustration, and anger.

Marla buried her face in her hands. The day had been taxing. She was already physically tired from the hard day of work, but the end of her rounds and this revelation about Brayne's illness weighed heavily on her mental resilience. A man had made a veiled threat against her and the kind couple she cared about, and now she knew that a devastating illness threatened Brayne too. Today had been too much.

For the first time since arriving in the Trade Quarters, she longed to be at her father's side in the Outer Counties. Life there was less... complicated.

She crossed the room and took one last look out of the slanted window, checking for any looming figures in the shadows, watching the Glanmore home. There was nobody there. The streets were quiet – it was very late. Marla figured the best thing to do was try and rest.

Chapter 25

The Spinning Coins

The hours dragged by. It was already the middle of the night when Tharian was dragged to this underground meeting place – he had no idea whether it was still night or the early hours of morning at this point.

He hadn't moved, except to satisfy an impulse to stand back in the centre of the mosaic map beneath his feet. Standing over the woods of Arboreta felt better than standing over the Dead Plains, not least because the latter was a chilling reminder of how badly this could end if his plan went wrong.

What Coinswoman Keene said was true – every word of it – that some twenty-three years ago the entire collective of Magi gathered outside the Grand City only to have their lives wiped away by Arcana. Even the grass and plant-life beneath their feet perished in an instant. All that destruction was wrought by the enforcers of the Grand City, upon the command of their previous chancellor.

The only good that came from that day was the apparent death of the chancellor and his wife. They had been too brazen, stood too close to their contempt for the Magi. The rumours said they were consumed by their own Arcana somehow, the power they used had been too strong even for them to escape. The Grand City never publicly confirmed that to be true, of course, but nonetheless there were those that let out a bated breath to know that the leaders of the Elheim were gone.

But even that good news had been fleeting. The next chancellor came along and continued where the last left off. And under his rule the words 'Arcana' and 'enforcer' became infamous in Asturia. Words of dread.

Despite spending night after night convincing himself that his plan could be made a reality, with the support of the Trade Quarters, it had only taken that simple interjection from the coinswoman to make Tharian realise the magnitude of the odds that stacked against them.

Tharian's chest tightened. In defiance of his own anxiety, he grit his teeth.

I didn't spend all that time searching for this lifeline just to throw it away now, he thought.

The doors at the far end of the room swung open, and Mors also reappeared at his balcony off to the side. The Coinsmen of the Trade Quarters reclaimed their seats and rifled through their notes. Except for Traykin – he had not taken notes.

Although the coinsmen remained shadowy apparitions against the backdrop of the piercing light, Tharian felt like he could almost make out their features this time. He couldn't say the same for Coinswoman Keene, being the only one amongst them he hadn't seen in the flesh.

'The coinsmen have reached a verdict in this matter,' said Mors at a startling volume. Tharian flitted back and forth as he tried to figure out who he should be looking at during this address. 'I am authorised to deliver this statement on behalf of the coinsmen before the floor is opened to questions and final remarks.'

Tharian froze. He thought they had retreated to just discuss what was said so far. It was surely too soon for them to make a decision. He had barely laid out much beyond the simplest details of his plan.

'After weighty discussions on this matter, the coinsmen have considered both the merits of the proposal and the merits of the proposer to reach the following conclusion,' he paused to clear his throat. 'The Trade Quarters have been asked to engage in investigatory and preparatory activities which have the likelihood of inciting conflict between this city and the Grand City of Elheim.'

These sound like Faast's words, Tharian deduced. He felt his palms begin to sweat. *I've already pissed her off.*

'Due to that inherent risk of conflict,' Mors continued, 'a balancing exercise must be carried out. The potential gains for the Trade Quarters, and its residents, must be weighed against the risk of harm. Having carried out that exercise, it is determined that the risks are too great for any *current* action.'

Tharian's hands fell limp at his sides. His shoulders slumped with them.

The Last of the Magi

'Although the proposal is believed to be made in good faith and with all good intentions, the coinsmen have been unable to reach a majority verdict in favour of supporting the proposal as it is currently posited. It must also be stressed...' Mors halted to clear his throat again, and cocked his head as he read ahead slightly, '...that the proposer's recent conduct in the Quarters has cast some shadow over the trustworthiness and credibility of his character.'

Words of such criticism would not usually faze Tharian. He had lived the life of a wayward adventurer and, at times, vagabond for most of his years. He had however hoped that any good words put in by Traykin would have helped to look past those issues, or at the very least provide context for his unconventional ways.

Tharian looked up to Traykin expectantly, shaking his head in dismay.

Traykin's silhouette held a finger up at him, casting an enormous shadow across the ground below. He then curled the finger towards Mors.

Mors watched the exchange with a gentle smirk and then turned over the parchment in his hands. 'With all that said, the longer-term interests of the Trade Quarters *do* align with the spirit of this proposal, and the merits of what is proposed have not been disregarded in their entirety. It is for this reason that the coinsmen are willing to revisit this proposal, and expand upon it, once certain conditions have been satisfied.'

Mors paused, and Tharian turned rapidly on his heels to address the coinsmen directly. 'What conditions do you propose? If I can meet them, I will.'

Mors coughed to bring Tharian's attention back to him. 'Those conditions are simply these: you must prove your credibility and the seriousness of your intent. You will need to rally the support of at least one of the other two independent city states. There is strength in numbers, and the Trade Quarters will need allies if there is to be conflict.'

Tharian considered the condition. Lions' Rest and the Kingdom of Ferenir were not so familiar to him. He and Traykin could probably pull some strings to get connections in either of those places but it would be no simple task. If Lions' Rest was still as reclusive as it had been before Tharian left for Feralland, that would narrow the options to one.

'If that is what it takes to gain your support.' Tharian said.

Keene was the first of the coinsmen to speak again, after thanking Mors for his eloquent delivery of their prepared statement. 'That you are willing to take these steps is a welcome development, but you must be made aware of certain restrictions on your dialogue with those other city states,'—Tharian cocked a brow at her quizzingly—'you will not under any circumstances disclose our potential involvement in this movement until you have secured support from another city state. We are not to be represented as leading this charge.'

Tharian didn't fully understand. The condition contradicted itself. They want strength in numbers yet want to conceal their involvement from those willing to join the cause. 'Might I ask why?'

'Yes. We do not want it openly known that we are considering acting against the Grand City of Elheim. The circulation of even a rumour along those lines will reach the Elheim eventually, creating a diplomatic mess that we would then have to manage. If, however, another city state is prepared to join your cause, independently and of its own volition – or subject to a similar pre-condition as ours, then our involvement may be disclosed. We need to be certain that any ally has the same intentions.'

'I understand,' Tharian said, courteously. The condition made sense to him now, even if it was inconvenient.

'Would it be prudent to furnish our friend here with some form of document to confirm our position, to be produced only when the support of another has been obtained?' added Velioth.

'That might be a sensible approach,' said Keene.

'No,' said Faast. 'Such a document could be presented prematurely. A document like that is dangerous in the hands of one not officially authorised and trusted to act as an emissary. Might I remind you that this man has already shown a disregard for our laws and procedures?'

Traykin twisted in his chair, causing the wood to creak loudly. 'He can be trusted with a bloody letter, Faast,'—before she could make a sound in protest, Traykin spoke quickly to cut her off—'I know your concerns. I've heard them over and over, so believe me when I say *I know*. We all know. The lad's actions in getting your attention were unusual, yes, but necessary and effective to bring us all to this point. From here on he will act on your instruction. Isn't that right, lad?'

Tharian nodded, firmly and resolutely. 'Without question.' Faast only grunted in reply.

Traykin then turned to Mors. 'I think that's a decision we've reached by majority then. You know what to do, Mors.'

Faast, however, was not finished on the matter. She spoke down the line to Traykin, 'if that is the case, then so be it.' She then leaned forward over the balustrade. 'Let it be stressed to you, Tharian, that your actions in the Trade Quarters have set many gears in motion. Although Coinswoman Keene welcomes your *acceptance* of our conditions, I would see it in a different light. You have crimes to answer for in the Quarters, crimes that fall within my jurisdiction to administer for prosecution. I reserve the right to pursue those charges, but I shall hold them in abeyance for as long as you do what we have asked of you. You should consider what we say here to be an order to act, rather than an option for your consideration.'

Traykin scoffed.

Tharian smiled impishly at Traykin and then flushed that expression from his face as he replied to Faast. 'I understand entirely. I will do what is needed to ensure your support and earn your trust, and to serve as some compensation for my actions.'

'Very good,' said Keene. 'That should conclude this Coinsmeet. Mors, you are no longer required to minute this discussion.'

Mors triumphantly planted his quill onto the table and started tidying up his small library of documents.

'I would ask only one final question of you, Tharian, if you would humour me? Your answer will not be recorded.'

'Ask away,' Tharian replied.

'Why?' Keene said abruptly. 'If everything you have told us is true – why would *you* return to Asturia to intervene in the politics of our country when you could have sought sanctuary in Feralland? What do you gain from this?'

Tharian paused. His eyes drifted down to the mosaic at his feet. He looked from the Grand City over to Arboreta, beneath his feet, and then looked further to the south-west of the map until he had to twist to see the county of Midhaven. It was still represented on this map as a member of the Outer Counties rather than the ruins that it laid in now.

'I was raised by a storyteller,' he said. 'A man who could tell great tales of fiction and recall events of history with such clarity that you would think he'd seen it all. As a child, I didn't know where the boundary between the two started and finished. But of all those stories, there were two he would repeat most: the destruction of Midhaven, where my family were murdered, and where he found me as an orphaned child, was one story; the other was the story of the Purge, which he described as the single greatest tragedy of Asturia's recent history. The common thread that linked these two stories together was the Elheim. The Elheim and their Arcana. As I grew older, the elements of those stories that seemed too horrific to be real, turned out to be true. Not just the crazed fictions of an old man. They were actual tragedies suffered by our people.'

The coinsmen all nodded along in agreement, or perhaps just in understanding. It was difficult to tell from their shadowed silhouettes.

'I was taught to never call any place home, to never get too involved, because the things I cared about could become the Elheim's next victims. After living that way for years, seeing everything from the outside and watching people lose everything time after time, a part of me decided that I couldn't watch it happen any longer.'

'If "some part" of you felt that way, what about the rest of you?' asked Keene. Her voice was soft and empathetic.

Tharian looked up, searching the shadow for the coinswoman's eyes, finding nothing but shadow. The question made him reflect. *What did that other part want him to do?*

He thought on it.

'I suppose the other part wanted to follow my guardian's instructions. Stay hidden, stay disconnected, and survive by keeping out of the Elheim's sight and reach.'

The Last of the Magi

'Those are very different stances to take. How did you end up here if you were so conflicted?'

Tharian smirked. His hand dropped to the hilt of his runeblade. His thoughts turned to his actions in Bryn. 'I suppose you could say one part of me has more power than the other.'

'I think we are all prone to the odd act of impulse from time to time, but this is something much bigger than that. Is it revenge for your lost family that drives you?'

'No,' he said. Quicker than he expected. 'It's not about revenge – the truth is I have no memories of my birth family or home. But that doesn't stop me from realising how much I've lost. When I see just how deeply others suffer from their losses, all because of the Elheim, I suppose I feel robbed of that. I lost the chance to have and appreciate those things in the way others did. And when I see their pain, it makes me realise just how devastating the Elheim's brutality has been, to so many good people who deserved better. Those people wouldn't dare strike back because they don't want to lose what they have left. I have nothing to lose; I don't have that fear. I have no other purpose, so I will make this my purpose.'

Faast then leaned forward in her seat and sighed. 'Your words carry much weight.' Her voice turned unusually soft. 'That you would lose your own home and family and see the oppressive regime of the Elheim with your own eyes, only to be inspired to take up the sword against them – that is to be commended in no small quantity.'

The others stayed silent, even Traykin.

'Whether what you propose is achievable or not, we have yet to see for certain. But go on your way knowing that the goal you seek to achieve is long overdue. Temper that storm brewing in you. Use that energy to support us in the way we ask, so we can support you.'

'Thank you, Coinswoman. I will.' He felt it was the right moment to bow slightly.

The coinsmen all nodded to Tharian and to each other in turn and then rose from their seats in unison. As they disappeared behind the lofty pillars of their elevated seating, the doors behind Tharian swung open and the guards entered the room with the blindfold in hand, ready to escort him back.

Chapter 26

Family, Beyond Blood

Traykin's Bazaar was warm and comfortable the next morning. The heat from the fireplace in the study wafted through to the shop floor where Tharian was strapping his runeblade back to his hip. Frigg approached from behind and helped him into his coat.

Tharian would leave soon. Back out on the open road, with nothing but Ombra, his coat, his blade, and his skills to keep him alive. There was no denying that the offer of warm lodgings and a freshly cooked hot breakfast each morning was a luxury he had long missed, but these were transient things. While others enjoyed locking themselves within their homes – their sanctuaries – with their mass of goods and personal possessions, Tharian's sanctuary was the outside world.

Tharian rubbed his eyes and laughed. *I'm starting to think like my old man.* Greycloak's rhetoric had a way of sneaking up on him. The lessons the old man had tried to instil in him had apparently sunk in – some of them, at least. Self-reliance and independence were qualities Greycloak promoted above all others.

'Thank you, Frigg,' Tharian said, as Frigg placed a pile of brown parcels on the shop counter, 'thank you for everything you've done since I arrived.'

Frigg smiled as he slotted the parcels into Tharian's satchel. He fastened it and then held the satchel out to Tharian. 'It's a p-pleasure as always, Master Tharian. Will you be gone long?'

Tharian took the satchel and sighed as he then had to remove his coat to put it over his shoulder and lay it flat against his back. He always preferred the satchel to be kept out of view. 'That depends entirely on how useful the old man feels like being.'

'Who are you calling old man?' Traykin sauntered down the stairs at the other end of the room. He glanced into the kitchen and sniffed approvingly, then looked over to Frigg and Tharian. Even in his early morning casualwear, he still donned his multi-coloured waistcoat.

'For once, not you.' Tharian laughed.

Traykin lifted a brow at him. 'Likely story, lad. Are you still griping?'

Tharian shook his head. 'I have not been griping! You should have told me you were a coinsman.'

'You should have known better! Did you think I'd just sit on my arse peddling gemstones until I choked it, lad?' Traykin laughed. 'It all worked out for the best, didn't it?'

'It did.'

'So,' Traykin lifted himself onto the high stool behind the shop counter. 'You're finally going to see him then?'

'My old man may be a babbling wreck, but he knows more people in Asturia than both of us combined, even if they don't always know him. I figure he's my best bet for finding a friendly face in one of the other cities.'

Traykin glanced at the ceiling and looked to be searching his thoughts. He then nodded. 'Aye. I know people all over, but not in the right circles for what we need. There's no harm in trying Greycloak. He will be pleased to see you, lad.'

'If he remembers me.'

'He will. He might not always show it, but you're the most important thing he has left.' Traykin's dark eyes were stern. But then they softened, and impish wrinkles appeared at their edges. 'Besides, you're too much of a nuisance to forget – even after a decade.'

'I guess that's why he still writes to you then?'

They laughed together, and even Frigg smirked.

'Speaking of – what was it that Greycloak said when he last wrote to you?' Tharian asked.

Traykin looked confused for a moment, and then he looked to Frigg. He snapped his fingers at his assistant and flung his hand towards the study, despite it being right beside where he sat.

Frigg dashed into the room and returned quickly with the letter in hand. Traykin read it aloud: 'The south-easterly wind did blow many things to Asturia. Some old, some new. Salvation is upon the horizon at long last – but upon the rubble of one empire, another shall always take root. Of all the songs sung in our lands, none tell tale of a lost Magi. That search will bring only sadness for the wayward son.'

'What do you suppose he means?'

Traykin grumbled. 'Hell if I know. At a guess, he thinks the Grand City's days are numbered. And he doesn't see much stock in your Magi survivor theory.'

'Funny that,' said Tharian. 'He has a lot of big ideas for an old man in a cave.'

Traykin chuckled and put a hand over his stomach. 'Nothing new there. Go ask him about it yourself.'

'I will. The sooner I see if he can help, the sooner I can move on to Lions' Rest or Ferenir.'

'Are you all set?'

Tharian nodded. 'As much as I can be. Frigg has helped a great deal with the preparations.'

'Good lad,' said Traykin, pointing his praise to Frigg. Frigg beamed and stood a little taller. 'You still know the way?'

'I'll never forget my way home,' Tharian said.

'Then you'd best be off.'

The three of them went to Traykin's yard, stepping out into the crisp, warm morning. At the end of the yard, Ombra was already waiting, saddled and laden with supply bags at her sides. She nodded as the three approached.

Tharian climbed into the saddle. Ombra didn't protest, she didn't even seem bothered by the saddle and bags. In fact, he could feel her eagerness to move. She had been here in this city far too long. They both had.

Frigg opened the gate at the end of the yard and latched it in place, he then dutifully returned to Traykin's side.

'Don't do anything stupid out there,' Traykin said.

'No promises.' Tharian smirked, and Traykin grinned. 'Thank you both. After so long away I thought I might have a battle on my hands to get this moving. But you pulled out all the stops to make this possible.'

'There's still a long way to go yet.'

Frigg then stepped forward. He scratched at Ombra's neck, and

The Last of the Magi

she leaned in to his hand.

Tharian reached down and squeezed Frigg's shoulder. 'And I need you to keep looking after Traykin for me, Frigg.' Tharian straightened and tugged at the reins to direct Ombra away, but he paused to turn back, whispering to Frigg. 'Maybe drop the meal sizes a bit, and go easy on his ale while you're at it.'

Frigg snorted at that. And he subtly nodded. 'May the light of the Divine protect you,' he said as he walked away.

Tharian's brows raised. He hadn't heard him say that before, nor was he sure what it meant, exactly. But it was familiar, and that nagged at him for a moment. Yet – coming from Frigg – it sounded like a kind gesture, so he took it as such.

Tugging lightly at Ombra's reigns, the two finally set off. They head through the back gate, onto the curving lanes that led to the outer wall. Tharian turned back once more to give a final nod and short wave of farewell.

From there, the lane took them to the Collectors Quarter gate and the gatekeeper cranked open the metal doors to let them back out beyond the city walls. They rode together for a few seconds to pierce through the smokescreen of smog cascading down the city walls. Beyond it, the rolling greens of the Outer Counties awaited them. It was still early enough in the day that the smog haze was quite thin and didn't reach far.

***

The first leg of the journey felt like dead time. The gate they used was on the north end of the city, and they needed to head south. So the first half-hour or so was spent simply riding aside the city perimeter. It took time, but Ombra was enjoying every moment. She preferred a longer ride out in the open over a quicker trot through the city centre any day. And Tharian knew that.

As soon as they reached the well-used dirt road that stretched from the Artisan Quarter's gates out into the depths of the southern reaches of the Outer Counties, Ombra picked up speed and peeled away from the hazy borders of the Trade Quarters, towards the natural haven that was western Asturia.

Tharian and Ombra were finally reunited as companions in nature, just as they had been for the last decade. Together they enjoyed the warmth of the morning sunlight. The air was clear, so clear in fact it took Tharian a few breaths to remember what normal breathing felt like. His lungs felt like they filled properly for the first time in weeks.

They passed horses and carts on the road, and even a few travellers on foot. The morning bustle of the trade routes. Tharian pulled up his hood and kept his face out of view as much as possible. He didn't want to stop and chat or linger long enough that someone might recognise or remember him. But that didn't stop the locals from offering their kind salutations as he passed them.

Eventually they slowed as they reached a fork in the road. A wooden sign marked the south-west road as leading into County Maris and County Haarb, but the other bearing east was marked as Ferenir. Before Tharian could even direct her, Ombra led them down the latter. He smirked and gently rubbed her neck as she raced on. She knew the way home too. She probably knew it better than him. No doubt she remembered exactly when they needed to break away from the road too, to find where Greycloak hid himself away from civilisation.

The journey would take some time, maybe more than a full day's ride. The road to Ferenir would eventually run alongside the forests of Arboreta. The forest stretched out to the foot of the Cartographer Mountains, and it was amongst those slopes that Greycloak had discovered a small, natural cavern to call his own.

Until they reached their destination, they both had time at least to enjoy their natural surroundings, away from the smog, dust, drama, and politics of a dense city.

This was a far cry from the Trade Quarters. Farmsteads on either side of the road gave way to fields of yellow, green, and red crops – and flowers of so much variety that Tharian almost found it hard to believe that the Trade Quarters sat within the same region of Asturia. The difference between what hid within the city walls and what reached beyond them was night and day.

Ombra was enjoying their journey just as much as he was. She jumped onto the bank alongside the road and raced between trees

The Last of the Magi

and hedgerows. She chased cliffhawks and kurigaw ravens that swooped across their path. Even a small family of wild lirrus emerged from the longer grass, seeming to challenge Ombra to a race. She accepted their challenge, even though it weaved them off their route occasionally.

Having fun are we? Tharian scratched at her neck. This peaceful travel was important to her, and it was important to him that she could enjoy it. Ten years in Feralland had given them many opportunities to travel together through the wilds, but whereas the Outer Counties of Asturia were safe, tranquil, and mostly populated by people and livestock, the wilds of Feralland were the stalking ground of many predators. So this peaceful travel was a rare treat for them both.

After a few hours of travel, Ombra veered away from the main road and took them onto a disused and overgrown patch of road that went further east. It was a familiar shortcut that would take them directly to Arboreta. The grass became darker and less nourished along this stretch of the journey, until they reached an enormous expanse of stone ruins and graveyards.

Ombra slowed.

They had reached the ruins of Oligar.

This place was a stark reminder of another tumultuous time in Asturia's difficult history. The once great city of Oligar was left to slowly crumble after the Oligari were defeated in a war that briefly united all Asturians, with the Magi carefully watching and standing proudly amongst the people. Greycloak had said the decaying remnants of the city should serve as a warning for what could happen if one nation or creed were allowed to amass too much power in this country.

That warning was either ineffective or it had already been forgotten. For the country was once again in the early throws of that cycle of oppression, this time under the white and blue banner of the Elheim. The manifestation of Elheim oppression did however take a different strategy compared to that of the Oligari, opting to seize power in the country through economics, cruel diplomacy, and fear tactics, rather than religious indoctrination. The Elheim approach was no less dangerous.

As Ombra led them on further, Tharian looked between the crumbled ruins of houses, mansions, paved roads, and the lavish courtyards of fallen Oligar. He and Greycloak had walked this road many times. Each time, Greycloak told him the story of the rise and fall of the Oligari. Yet another story that could well have been a blend of fact and fiction.

Tharian's memory of the first telling of that story always stuck with him most vividly. His imagination filled in any gaps in his recollection and kept the memory interesting each time he revisited it.

'What did the Oligar people do wrong?' the young Tharian had asked, as he span about to take in the sights around him.

'A great many things,' replied Greycloak, calmly in his deep and powerful voice.

'Like what?

Greycloak hummed with disapproval. He gave Tharian a familiar look, the look that adults gave children to tell them they were too young for the details. But his guardian continued, nonetheless.

'The Oligari behaved in a truly evil way. They used faith and promises of a peaceful life, and afterlife, to bring people together under a common banner—'

'That doesn't sound so bad,' Tharian interrupted.

'Patience, Tharian, there is more. You should know by now there is always more.'

Tharian sighed. He wasn't wrong, there was always more.

'Whilst they openly paraded through Asturia as bringers of peace, the truth was that the Oligari were using a form of magic to enthrall the people that supported them.'

'Enthrall?' Tharian remembered being confused by that word, because the description Greycloak then gave to its meaning was so stark to his inquisitive mind.

'It means they were prisoners. They lost their own will. They blindly followed the Oligari, even to the point of going to war for them against so-called enemies of Oligar who, in truth, had never once shown any aggression towards the Oligari.'

The Last of the Magi

Tharian hummed as he thought it through. *'Does that mean they lied?'*

'Lying was second nature to the Oligari. We cannot know for certain about some of the things they promised to their people. But what we do know is when the Oligari started to lose control over some parts of Asturia they somehow manufactured a plague which they spread in secret. They made people sick, Tharian. And just as the illness started to spread widely, they provided cures to the faithful who lived in Oligar.

'The people in the city got better, but those further away did not. The Oligari claimed that it was faith that cured the people of Oligar. That set the stage for them using that evil sickness as a weapon to convert more to their ways. It was then that the Magi appeared and helped to stop them.'

Tharian cheered and raised his hands in the air. *'Yeah! The Magi save the day again.'* Those stories were his favourite.

Greycloak chuckled, which was a rare thing, even then.

Tharian looked around again, taking in the sheer size of the ruins around them. He inhaled sharply as more questions formed in his curious mind. *'Oh, but how did the Magi know the Oligari were making people sick?'*

Greycloak smirked and wagged a finger in the air. *'A very good question, my boy. The illness deployed by the Oligari was also created by some form of magic, though nobody knows quite how it was done, or who made it. But the people of Asturia had no way of knowing this.'* Greycloak then tapped Tharian with the back of his hand. *'But to the Magi it was as clear as day. Not everyone believed the Magi when they tried to reveal the truth, but for those who ruled the other cities it finally gave them a reason to confront the Oligari and remove them for good.'*

'Were the Magi right about the Oligari?'

'Yes.'

'How do you know?'

Greycloak lowered his voice again. *'Tharian. Do we need to go over this again? The Magi devoted their lives to natural order. They were gifted with great powers, but that power'*—

'I know this part,' said Tharian eagerly. *'Their Magic made it so*

they could never lie or say anything bad. They always had to do the right thing.'

'That is putting it too simply, but yes you have the right of it. That is why the Magi were truly a blessing to Asturia. We must hope that they can now rest in peace, in a better place.'

How many stories had Greycloak told over the years? Tharian pondered that question for the entire time that he and Ombra made their way through the ruins of Oligar. There were just so many. Each one he recalled seemed to bring with it a reminder of another that was in some way linked to it. He could have spent the entire day reminiscing over those stories. Whether they were all true or not, he suspected he would never find out for certain, but so far most of them had turned out to at least bare a kernel of truth at their core.

By the time they reached the other end of the ruins it was settling into the early afternoon. As the ruined buildings became smaller and more disparate, the number of trees and wild plants grew in number, and off in the distance the dark green shape of Arboreta was coming into view.

They had travelled for so long already. Ombra needed to rest. Although she didn't protest or show signs of tiring, Tharian knew she would overwork her body if he didn't force her to stop. He directed her to a grove where the fields slopped down and short trees gathered along a river that pooled into a lake.

He dismounted and walked with Ombra down those slopes, and then Ombra cantered off to the glistening water. This would be a safe space for them to rest and camp down for the night.

***

Marla trudged her way into the kitchen for breakfast. It was a late start for her, but nobody had hurried to wake her. Marion and Brayne were already there. Brayne was scooping up the last scraps of food on his plate, pausing only to wash it down with the last of his coffee – always in a hurry to scurry off to the workshop.

He gave her a nod. Not the kind of nod that acknowledges an

The Last of the Magi

acquaintance in the street, but the kind that felt more like a 'good morning'. Their relationship was growing, and Marla welcomed every step forward.

She nodded back, but she avoided eye contact as he passed. She feared if she looked him in the eye, he would somehow know what she had discovered last night. The truth of his ailment. She had barely slept from thinking about the Violet Affliction, the horrors of the illness, and revisiting the trauma of watching her mother suffer and succumb to it.

Marion reached over the table and pulled Marla's breakfast plate over to the seat nearest to her, and then patted the table. 'It's getting cold, eat up.'

Marla smiled as warmly as she could, but her smile didn't reach her eyes. She could feel the insincerity of it. So she kept her eyes low. The twisting feelings from the night before were creeping out. That suffocating mix of gratitude, guilt, frustration and fear. If she let her emotions take over, she knew she'd say something out of turn, so she sat down and did her best to act as she normally would. Badly.

'Are you alright?' Marion asked. 'You look a bit pale – did you not sleep well?' Marion ducked her head low, trying to meet Marla's eyeline directly. Marla kept her eyes on her plate and tried to pick at the food.

No, I don't think I am alright. I'm confused. She thought. She moderated her thoughts before replying. 'I'm ok, thank you. It was a busy day yesterday; I think I might have just overdone it.'

Marion tutted. 'Is he working you too hard?'

Waving a hand dismissively, the side of Marla's lips curled into a wry smile. 'Not at all. I'm the one squeezing more work from him than he would like. But its ok, I had to work harder than this for my father sometimes.' *But never for several days and nights in a row,* she admitted to herself.

Marion furrowed her brow and brought her hands together on the table. She looked concerned. Marla then realised she had backed herself into a bit of a corner.

'If you're not working too hard then maybe you're a bit under the weather?'

'Yes, that must be it,' said Marla, grateful for the lifeline. 'But work must go on. I should go see if Brayne needs me.'

Marla scooped up the scraps of food and then rushed out of the room, following the hall round to the workshop at the other end of the house. A pang of guilt made her regret her quick departure. She would need to apologise later for that.

She ducked through the hanging plastic sheets that covered the opening to the workshop and then stopped against a cleared workbench, a short distance from Brayne's own. He had cleared this one for her to use.

Sucking in the heat and thick air, she felt more relaxed.

She approached Brayne's desk and glanced over the plans he had sprawled across it. He was working on a helmet today, in a decorative barbute style. She had never seen one made before. Guards in the Outer Counties only wore simple pot helms, or none at all. This was much more elaborate. This would be a good learning day for her, and a good distraction.

Or at least it could have been.

'If there's something on your mind, she'll get it out of you,' Brayne said.

Marla glanced over with wide eyes. 'What do you mean?'

'Going from bright-eyed and loud one day to quiet and reserved the next – you don't have to be too clever to notice that. You wear your mind on your face.'

Loud? The words stung a bit. She would have considered herself energetic, not loud. 'I just have a few things on my mind, it's nothing to worry about.'

Brayne put on his gloves and his headwear, ready to drop his visor over his face. 'I'm not prying. Your business is your business, and ours is ours. All I'm saying is that my wife is the type who likes to fix things. If she catches a scent, she doesn't let it go until the issue is dealt with.' He reached up for his visor again, but then paused, 'or she thinks it is.'

Those words stung even more, especially now that she knew about his illness. 'Noted,' she said, 'I'll take a leaf out of your book then and act like a rock.'

'It works.' Brayne snorted, but then he shook his head. 'You're

The Last of the Magi

far too young to be bitter. Keep those spirits up as long as you can.'

She turned back to the plans on the desk. Though his words didn't erase her frustration, what he said made sense. She had no right to be wound up by their private affairs. Maybe they *were* hiding something, or had some ulterior motives for letting her stay, but for the moment at least she was in a great place. She should stay thankful for that. Besides, she hadn't told them about the man in the alleyway, and the threat he made. She was hiding things too.

Marla put on her gloves and approached the anvil. 'So, helms today, is it?'

'It is.'

'That's a new one for me. Only really worked with the basics.'

Brayne brought out the metal he intended to work and then grabbed a mould shaped like a head from one of his high shelves. 'Pay enough attention and you might learn something new. Once we're done with this we can talk about your numbers.'

'My numbers?' she snapped back. Was this an industry term that she hadn't heard before?

'You came up short yesterday. You need to count what the War Quarter thugs pay you.'

Marla felt the blood drain from her cheeks as she paled again. She realised that she had just been handing over the goods to Brayne's customers and taking their coin without giving a second thought to their honesty and integrity. No customers in the Outer Counties would ever under-pay. 'I'm sorry, I had no idea. Father always handled the money.'

Brayne grunted and then dropped his visor. 'It was only slightly out. Probably unintentional,' he said, though his voice was barely audible through his visor and the crackling of the furnace.

Marla nodded and then watched Brayne get to work on his latest commission. She still had a lot to learn before she could be deemed a proper blacksmith by Trade Quarters standards, let alone Artisan standards. Being good with a hammer was only part of the game.

Chapter 27

Greycloak

The journey through the deepest part of the Arboreta Forest was a nostalgic one. Although it had been a decade since they last had to weave between the closely-knit, thick trees and tread over exposed roots, the route was as familiar as ever.

The forest was home to a bounty of wildlife. Litters of young lirrus scurried around the backs of trees in the distance, watching the intruders pass through with a fervent, but playful, curiosity. A variant of cliffhawks made the tree canopy their home. They swept below the roofline to investigate. They probably had nests to protect at this time of year.

This breed of the bird – folihawks to those concerned with such things – were small and sported a dark green-brown plumage in comparison to the tan and orange colours found amongst their mountain-dwelling kin.

The animals that called Arboreta home could be aggressive, if they needed to be, but they kept a respectful distance from Tharian and Ombra. Almost as if they knew them, recognised them.

Tharian and Ombra reached a part of the forest where the trees began to thin, and sunlight beamed down in magnificent swaying columns wherever the gentle breeze disrupted the canopy above. The ground slope upwards here, marking out the roots of the Cartographer Mountains.

Eventually the slope became much steeper, to the point of becoming a complete wall in their way. But this is where they were headed, as it was here that caves formed, diving deep into the mountain's base. They found the cave they wanted, the cave that Greycloak called home.

Tharian stood at the mouth of that cave for a while. It was pitch-black within, but he knew the way the cave tunnel curled, rose slightly, and then dipped back down until it reached Greycloak's basin. The old man could be nestled around a warm, roaring fire and

The Last of the Magi

the light wouldn't reach the cave opening. The cavern provided excellent shelter from the elements.

Tharian sighed heavily and glanced to Ombra. She flicked her nose towards the cave opening before walking away. *You're the boss*, he mused.

'Are you in there, old man?!' Tharian shouted. His voice echoed.

He paused and tapped his foot impatiently.

Don't keep me waiting.

The wind blew across Tharian and whistled around the cave entrance, initially tricking Tharian into thinking that he had received a response. After a few more seconds, a vibration from deep within the cave crept closer and closer until a voice finally emerged.

'The lost son returns.'

Tharian shook his head. The usual nonsense. Age and a lifetime of relative isolation had addled Greycloak's brain. His words were now as fanciful as some of the stories he told – as if fiction and reality truly had blended into one in his head.

Drawing his coat more tightly around his body, Tharian marched into the cave. He partly drew his runeblade out of its sheath just far enough that the one remaining rune revealed its glow, casting out a gentle blue light ahead. Not that he needed it, of course, as he knew this cave intimately – it had been his main home for most of his childhood. But after a decade of being overseas, Tharian had picked up plenty of defensive behaviours. Vicious predators liked to hide in the shadows.

A small flickering light eventually came into view from further down the curved path. Tharian pushed his sword back into its sheath with the palm of his hand and relaxed as he finally made it into the large, open chamber where Greycloak was sat, in a wooden chair of his own making, reading an old, crumbling tome against the firelight.

'The sapling weathered the elements and now is as the trees,' Greycloak said. His mind may have gone but the deep and powerful tones of his voice still came through between moments of cracking. His voice was surprising strong for someone who probably sat in silence most days, with nobody to talk to.

'You sound healthy as ever, have you been talking to yourself in here all these years.' Tharian smirked and crossed the space over to another seat covered in a sheet. The seat was laid just in front of a bay carved into the wall where Tharian had slept as a child. It still had blankets in it, as if it had been kept ready for his return.

Greycloak closed his book and placed it on the small stone slab beside his chair. He stared into the flames of his campfire. 'You seek a lost Magi?'

'Straight to the point,' replied Tharian. He sat back in the chair and looked around at the familiar bare stone walls. It seemed so much smaller than he remembered. 'Yes, I am looking for a Magi. Though I'm not here for that, not right now anyway. I need a favour.'

Greycloak plucked his gaze away from the fire and he looked directly to Tharian through the side of his hood. The light cast shadows over his wrinkled, sunken cheeks and reflected delicately off the remaining strands of his long grey hair and short beard.

'And what would an old recluse have to offer?'

Tharian leaned forward, resting his elbows on his thighs. 'I need to make some new friends. Powerful friends, in either Ferenir or Lions' Rest. Who do you still know?'

Greycloak's head shifted, causing his hood to pull slightly further from his face. 'I must disappoint you. There are none known to me with the gifts of influence.'

Tharian's stomach flipped. 'Nobody – not even an acquaintance or a former friend? Even just a name would be a start.'

Rising from his seat with great difficulty, Greycloak shuffled around to a pile of his possessions at the back of the chamber. 'None known to me,' he repeated.

'Alright then,' Tharian said, trying his best to mask his disappointment. 'It was worth a try.'

Tharian startled as something light landed in his lap. He looked down and scooped up the small metal trinket to hold it against the light.

It was a small, inconspicuous brooch. Its design was an odd, red shape which looked vaguely familiar to Tharian, but the shape was obscured by an embossed wrapping of green vines that wrapped around it. It was like one design had been laid over another.

The Last of the Magi

'What is this?' Tharian asked.

'It matters not what it is, nor how such a thing bequeathed itself to me. Know only that it is an artefact of great interest to Ferenir. Bring it before the eyes of those who serve that kingdom, and your way may open before you.' Greycloak slumped back into his seat and gazed blankly into the flames again.

Tharian examined the brooch. It was nothing more than a badge. Certainly not anything of any financial value. The metal was rusting on the back. Whatever it was, it had been long neglected.

But then he recalled his visit to Brynwell, where he spotted a simple piece of inexpensive jewellery which he immediately recognised as being of great ceremonial importance to the Awoken of Feralland. Sometimes the expense or the intricacy of something was not what mattered, it was the meaning or the sentimental value that gave it importance. *Another lesson*, Tharian coughed in amusement. Though on reflection he wasn't sure whether that was one of Greycloak's or Traykin's. Perhaps a bit of both.

'How long have you had this tucked away?'

Greycloak also coughed a short laugh which then turned into a deep, chesty cough instead. His exertions of breath caused the fire to twist and dance, as if pleased to receive the air from his lungs. 'Such a thing has been with me for a long time. A curious thing, never worn, but instantly recognisable to those who know it. Yet another artefact of antiquity, just like its current owner. It serves no purpose here.'

His riddles are getting worse, Tharian flustered. He then felt a pang of guilt for judging the old man's condition. He'd been gone for ten years. He didn't know how the man had been faring from day-to-day and, judging by the state of his reclusiveness, perhaps no one really did.

'Thank you,' Tharian said, solemnly, as he turned the brooch between his fingertips. 'I've always trusted your guidance, even if I don't always show it.'

Greycloak stared into the flames, not reacting to the words of his once-young ward – now fully grown.

'Although,' Tharian said with an impish grin, 'I do hope this wasn't misappropriated from somewhere... or someone. I don't want to be getting in trouble for having it.'

Greycloak's back arched as he huffed another laugh. 'Thievery and skulduggery are the tools of the damned. That item you hold symbolises the end of a shared history, and it found its way to this place in the same way most curious artefacts find their way to the Bazaar – through trade, the exchange of favours or the naivety of former owners.'

'Won it in a game, did you?' Tharian said flippantly, feeling some relief that his guardian's words were becoming slightly less tangled. He knew full well that Greycloak was no gambler, but he couldn't help but tease. The idea that it was gifted to him in exchange for a favour was much more likely. Greycloak had so many strange little tokens of seemingly no value beyond the sentimental.

Tharian sat with Greycloak for around an hour longer. They didn't exchange many more words, but Tharian thought to share some of his own stories. It was strange to be the one telling them for a change.

He talked about his travels through Feralland in vague terms, in much the same way that he did with Frigg. The people he met there were a private kind, and although that privacy had no risk of being disturbed by Greycloak, he felt it only proper that he spoke lightly of them.

He gave Greycloak a bit more detail. He talked about the beauty and ferocity of the land, and its creatures. He even hinted at the quiet conflict he discovered between two tribes of Awoken, and how they managed to live together despite their differences much more effectively than Asturians did. And that led him to bring up the Magi, and how those who understood magic overseas ubiquitously believed that an Asturian Magi still lived despite the Purge.

Greycloak barely stirred. The adventures Tharian had been on didn't evoke any reaction in his old guardian. The old man's expression was frozen, his eyes locked to the flames.

Tharian felt it only right to move on from Arboreta, in the hope that he could arrive on the border of Ferenir before nightfall.

He brushed the dust from his coat as he stood, and then dropped

The Last of the Magi

the brooch into one of his front pockets. Without moving any closer, Tharian gave Greycloak a final thank-you, and bowed his head in respect, and then made his way to the chamber's exit.

'How fares she who carries the night on her coat?' Greycloak said as Tharian was halfway to the tunnel.

Ombra? He assumed Greycloak was referring to her.

Before Tharian could muster a response, a sound of fluttering wings flooded down the tunnel. A stream of tiny cave bats rushed their way into the chamber and circled, screeching, above the fire.

They both watched the bats spin in the shadows above. Greycloak seemed dazed at first but after a few moments his eyes started to follow their motion with rapid proficiency, and a smile drew across his lips. The bats completed their laps and then rushed back through the tunnel. Tharian had to duck to avoid being barraged by their wings and tiny claws. One reflection of light caught his eye as the bats fled, a flash of amber.

When he straightened himself, Greycloak was watching him, with a peaceful, knowing expression on his face. 'A steadfast ally, to one another both. The synastry between man and beast is sacred.'

Ombra was indeed a true ally. The truest. The most reliable and the most helpful. Always there when he needed her. Always knowing what to do. Never protesting. Well, not much.

Tharian patted the ragged wall of the tunnel and then nodded one last time to his old guardian and mentor. 'I'll see you again, old man.'

Chapter 28

The Ferenir Magi
15 years before the Purge

King Reksar Thorius sighed heavily and pushed back against the solid oak spine of his throne. He had spent what felt like a lifetime listening to the desperate pleas of the outlying village-folk. This was no unusual task for the King of Ferenir to undertake. In fact, Ferenir Keep would regularly open its doors to welcome in representatives of the local village councils, the clergymen of the chapels, the shoremaster of the dockyards and captains of the city guard. The people of Ferenir came to voice concerns and on rare occasion convey their praise. This session was the same as any other in that regard.

The day was coming to an end. The red light of sunset was cascading through the tall windows of the King's Court. Reksar had lost count of just how many people he'd spoken to over the day. He leaned forward and glanced to the left of his throne. The court scribe had been busy noting the details of each visitor and recorded the decisions made by the king throughout the discussions. Any actions that needed to be taken were to be drawn up as Royal Commandments. The scribe now sat silently with his hands linked together on the desk. He nodded to the king and looked down to the gallery of the King's Court where a woman, flanked by two men, still waited to be addressed.

Reksar placed his hands on the arms of his throne and took in a deep breath. He paused for a moment. 'How many more times do we need to go through this?' he said.

He glared down at the three. They kneeled at the steps that led up to the throne. He could tell by their clenched fists that they despised the gesture of formality.

'Rise,' the king said through gritted teeth.

The woman was the first to stand. She brushed dust from her knee and adjusted her white uniform to ensure it still looked immaculate. She gestured to the men on either side of her and they

The Last of the Magi

too rose to their feet.

'So kind of you, your majesty. Might I say once again that it is an honour'—

'The answer remains the same,' growled Reksar, cutting the wealthily-clad woman off before she could finish her pompous and slithering address.

'My King?' she said.

'For years I have taken to the top of Ferenir Keep every morning to watch over my people from the southern ramparts. Lately, my gaze has turned to the north. For centuries the Eastern Expanse has been left verdant and untouched, but now I see that the Elheim family have begun work on a city befitting of their... image.'

'Lord Elheim's offer remains open to you, King Reksar. Many surrounding settlements have already decided to become part of the Grand City of Elheim. Our reach is expanding, your majesty. Lord Elheim only wants you to achieve the very best for your people.'

'The *best* for *my* people?' laughed King Reksar.

The king had been visited time and time again by messengers and consorts of the Elheim family for years. Each time, they offered an alliance of both land and resources. It was an attractive offer – at face value.

Ferenir was the largest city state in Asturia. It lacked the wealth of the Elheim family and the influence that came with that wealth, but it respected hard work, fostered equality and grew through the co-operation of all its people. The people and the monarchy of Ferenir knew what the Elheim family truly wished to achieve: control, of everything east of the Cartographer Mountains. Reksar had rejected their offer of unity in the early days of the Elheim's expansion and continued to reject it whilst their hold of the north grew. In truth, their expansion caused no immediate threat. But rumours spread amongst the people of Ferenir that oppressive takeovers and blackmail were behind their most recent 'acquisitions' of territory.

'As you leave this kingdom and begin your journey back to your palace in the north, I suggest you take a moment to see what *my people* have built for themselves. This kingdom is their home, and it stands as testament to their achievements. This crown does not give me ownership over them – I cannot sell what they have built. This crown represents a promise that for as long as Ferenir Keep remains atop this hill I shall protect and serve these people.'

Only the sound of frantic scratching could be heard as the scribe struggled to keep up with the king's passionate rebuke.

The woman in white laughed under her breath. She raised her hands to the king and approached the first step to his throne. Two guards stepped from the shadowy flanks of the gallery in response and pointed their spears at the woman. A third figure, dressed in a dark, hooded cloak approached the throne from behind and stood in their view.

'Let me make this clear, your majesty,' the woman said, her words leaving her lips like venom. 'Lord Elheim makes no threat to your people, but a time will come when these lands fall into the fold. Your people will either welcome this transition or wither away. You can be the one to lead Ferenir into a new era of prosperity or you can witness your monarchy come to an end.'

'You dare to threaten me, here?' the king pushed to his feet and wrapped his hand around the hilt of his sword, resting against his throne.

The cloaked figure reached his arm across the king's. He remained silent and watched the Elheim aggressors from the shadow of his hood.

'Your resistance is an unnecessary obstruction. You are holding Ferenir back.'

The king growled and wrapped his fingers around the sword tighter. He shoved the cloaked figure out of his way with his arm.

'A final peace offering then,' she continued. 'Lord Elheim extends an offer to you personally. If you support the Elheim family, your first-born son shall be invited to the Grand City to receive education and a life of wealth and opportunity far beyond what he could ever achieve here in Ferenir.' The woman reached inside her emblazoned white coat and teased out the corner of a rolled parchment. 'This offer is already committed to writing. Signed by Lord Elheim himself.'

The king paused. The cloaked figure stepped in closer and coaxed the sword out of his hand. He whispered something into the

The Last of the Magi

king's ear and then handed the sword to one of the court attendants who scurried off to return the weapon to the armoury.

King Reksar turned to the cloaked figure and spoke quietly to him. 'You are sure of this, counsel?'

His adviser took down his hood, revealing his long silver hair, light blue eyes and sunken facial features. He nodded and spoke softly. 'Stay true to your resolve, my King. Trust me to be your shield.'

The king put his hand on his adviser's shoulder and squeezed it firmly. He locked eyes with him for a few seconds and then took in a deep breath before addressing the guests in the gallery.

'Your words, like your intentions, are poison to Ferenir,' said the king. 'Leave these lands – immediately.'

The woman in white grunted. She tucked the parchment back into her coat and then her sly smile washed away. She scowled at the king and then at his adviser. She clicked her fingers and the two men on her flanks stepped forward to stand shoulder-to-shoulder with her.

'Then your choice is made. On behalf of the Grand City, I hereby declare you an enemy of Elheim. It is time for a change of leadership in Ferenir, your majesty.'

The two Elheim men turned outwards from the woman and reached their white-gloved hands up towards sconces that burned brightly from support pillars in the gallery. They flexed their fingers.

The flames waved erratically, as if being hit by a breeze. The fire curled unnaturally down from the great height of the pillar, descending towards the open palms of the Elheim men. They were manipulating the flames, somehow bending them to their command.

The king gasped. His very own Magi-adviser had performed such feats of strength many times before but never had any Elheim demonstrated such abilities. The adviser, too, was in awe. But this was no mere feat of strength or parlour trick, or tactic of intimidation.

It was an attack.

The Elheim men moved the amassed flames closer to their leader, and the strands of fire accumulated into two spheres in front of her. The sconces burnt out as the last strands of fire were ripped away.

The woman pulled up her sleeves and held out her hands below the position of the spheres. In one quick motion she pulled her hands together and then pushed her palms forward. The spheres slammed together and merged, forming a larger mass of fire and then it shot forward at the king.

With immaculate timing, the king's adviser jumped forward with his hands stretched out wide. He channelled his Magic and called upon the wind.

The windows on either side of the King's Court shattered inwards as a magnificent torrent of air rushed through. The wind flurried between the adviser and the fireball, causing the two to erupt into a wall of flames that split the room in half, but it kept him and the king out of reach from the emissaries of Elheim.

The adviser lowered his arms and turned to the king, his dark robe rippling against the force of the blustering flames.

'My King, we must move,' he said calmly.

The king was speechless, a wall of swirling flame stood before him in his own court, but he nodded. The adviser looked to each of the three guards positioned at the back wall with their weapons drawn, looking pale. 'Hold back the Elheim. I will get the king to safety.'

The adviser ushered the king to the back of the room, behind his throne, and urged him to run. Taking the advice, the king made a dash for the exit. He slipped through the open doorway while the adviser lingered at the threshold a moment to ensure the wall of magical fire was holding strong. Satisfied, he followed the king.

Ferenir Keep was a tactical stronghold, as such a structure should be. It had all the facilities needed to cater for the royal family and its staff but hidden within plain sight the great stone walls concealed a myriad of secret corridors and underground furrows that led to strategic positions across the kingdom; escape routes for royalty under threat, or entryways for city guard called to defend their king.

The doorway that the king and his adviser took ordinarily led to the royal quarters. However, as they reached the foot of the

The Last of the Magi

spiralling staircase, the king turned to a large regal cabinet lined with expensive silverware and other ceremonial trinkets. He planted his shoulder against the side of the cabinet and pushed it towards the staircase with a grunt, its movement revealing a dark, thin opening. This would serve as their escape.

A lit torch was mounted on the wall just beside the newly revealed opening. The adviser detached it and handed it to the king, pushing him into the passage.

The king marched a few steps into the darkness and waited for his adviser to follow.

The advisor was looking back towards the court. He could hear the clashing of metal and the sounds of fighting, but he couldn't clearly see what was happening. Though his view was obstructed, his ability to sense Magic was not – the wall of fire had dissipated. The guards had engaged the Elheim. He could hear their muffled screams.

Without wasting another second, the adviser dashed into the passage and reached out with his mind to the remnants of the blowing winds that still bounced around inside the King's Court. He willed the wind to follow them, and it obeyed. A flurry of air whistled down into the corridor and slammed against the cabinet, pushing it back into its original position. Most of the expensive silverware toppled from the shelving and shattered on the ground.

They were hidden from sight. Hidden from the Elheim.

The passage was narrow but still wide enough for them to move at pace. The king continued to lead the way, guided by torchlight. The adviser reached a hand towards the flame as he followed and manipulated its natural energies. He gently pulled some of the flame into his hand and the torch willingly gave some of itself to him. The torch remained fully lit without even a flicker of change in its intensity. Nurturing the small flame between his palms, it grew stronger and brighter without causing him any harm.

They continued through Ferenir Keep's hidden tunnels. Eventually the path beneath their feet changed from stone to dirt, and then the path ended with a one-foot drop to a low, wet trench which ran as far as they could see from left to right. The smell of damp was thick in the air.

The path to the right burrowed further underground and led towards the main city of Ferenir, and the left led to a point someway down the slopes of the hillside upon which the keep was built.

The king dropped into the trench and paused at the intersection to catch his breath. The adviser, still on the ledge above the trench seemed unstirred by the events. His brow was furrowed, but he was nonetheless calm and still held the naked flame in his palm.

'Tell me this,' the king stretched his back and sucked in the heavy, dank air, 'has this country become so twisted that even Magi can be bought by the Elheim?'

The adviser bowed his head. The flame in his palm waned and flickered slowly as if struck by sadness. 'Those were no Magi, my King.'

The adviser's mind raced with concerns, he couldn't help but relive the experience of watching the sconces in the King's Court being stripped of their life, their very energy torn from their cradles. It troubled him to see the elements perish under the manipulations of their magic. But one thing was clear to him: their magic was not the same as the Magic of *his* kind.

'If not Magi, what were they?' the king asked.

'Forgive me, but now is not the time. We must move on.'

'You are right, as always. Lead on – I will follow.'

The adviser dropped down into the trench to join the king. His modest boots sunk into the sodden mud tracks. He opted for the left path, the one that led away from the city proper. King Reksar followed closely behind, not concerned with muddying his regal attire.

They marched on a little further until the adviser stopped in his tracks. He looked over his shoulder, staring into the darkness behind the king. Reksar kept silent, not daring to look back.

The longer the adviser stared into the unpunctuated silence, the more troubled the king became. Eventually his anxiety took control, and he twisted his neck to try and look back. He froze as the distant sound of muffled steps echoed down the length of the tunnel. There were several prominent splashes and then, after a moment's pause, the sound of running.

The adviser grabbed the king by his arm and forced him

The Last of the Magi

forwards. The king ran ahead, guided by the torch that he gripped so desperately.

With a gesture of his hand, the adviser detached the conjured flame from his hand and let it float in the air in a ball. He enchanted the small fireball to head back down the tunnel. As soon as the adviser could make out the faint outline of the Elheim emissaries chasing them, he turned and sprinted after the king. They had already closed the gap between them, dramatically.

While the adviser ran, he felt his conjured flame be snuffed out abruptly as if it had been dropped into water. Darkness filled the tunnels once more, all around, except for where the king charged on ahead with the torch in hand. The adviser called upon Magic again. This time, he called upon the air immediately behind him and pulled it forward, to aid in his sprint. He did the same for the king up ahead. They moved further with each step than they ordinarily could.

The darkness didn't pervade their escape much longer, as the red-ish light of the sunset crept into the tunnel up ahead.

The king was the first to reach the mouth of the tunnel. The opening was guarded by widely spaced metal bars that stretched from floor to ceiling. King Reksar squeezed through the bars and waded through the overgrown bushes that had grown from the water that trickled out of the tunnel opening. The bushes served as an effective camouflage for this secret escape route.

Even though this escape route brought them quite far down the height of the hill, there was still a way yet to go.

King Reksar emerged from the foliage and sprinted over to the edge of the winding path that led further down the hill. He had a clear view of the Arboreta Forest and Cartographer Mountains to the north-west. The growing sprawl of the Grand City of Elheim could be seen in the distant north-east, though it stood as a monolithic shadow against the backdrop of the setting sun.

The king looked east to his kingdom, spread across the sloping land that stretched to the coast. He sighed. He had held the heavy title of king for no less than 25 years, and not once had he ever needed to escape his own stronghold on the hill. In generations past, such actions were needed during times of war and conflict, but

Ferenir was enjoying a time of prosperity and peace welcomed with open arms by his people. They would all be settling down to enjoy an evening with their families, safely within their homes, while the Elheim assaulted the keep and their king with their newfound magic.

The adviser eventually emerged from the tunnel too. The bushes and undergrowth at the opening bent and parted to allow him through. He spotted the king standing on the path's edge. He took a moment to check down the tunnel and then whispered something under his breath. A soft wind blew over the bushes and triggered a transformation in the plant-life. The twigs and branches of the plants contorted and twisted around each other, growing thorns as they moved. Under the influence of the Magi-adviser's Magic, the plants transformed into a twisted barricade twice its original size.

With his work done, he joined the king.

'We will not escape them. Not here. The Elheim have won.' the king said.

'You are wrong,' replied the adviser. 'There is time for you to escape. I will hold them here.'

'Don't be a fool. Even if you could hold them here alone, I will not get far by travelling across the Eastern Expanse for hours in plain sight. No horse. No carriage. Even the cover of darkness will not disguise me. The Elheim will find me. I will not lead them into the city, and *you* will not give your life for me or take a life in my name. Consider that my last Royal Commandment.'

'My King, I—'

King Reksar shot a fierce stare at his adviser. His lips curled the slightest smile, but his eyes were stern and sobering. 'Go.'

The adviser pulled up the sleeves of his dark robe. He hooked his thumbs inside his hood and lifted it up to cover his head, hiding away his silver hair. His piercing blue eyes stared at the woods in the distance.

'I serve a higher calling than that of the throne, King Reksar Thorius. My place is here.'

The king sighed a laugh at his adviser. 'You always were a stubborn old fool, Nehren, even during my father's reign.'

A loud bang punctuated the air from behind them, followed by cracking. The king and Nehren turned back to see the Elheim trio approaching. The barricade of branches and thorns had been destroyed, shattered into fragments on the ground.

The woman leading the Elheim shrugged as she approached. 'This could have been a lot easier. Clearly you didn't think this through.'

Neither of them responded.

'Nothing to say?'

Again, no response.

'We're wasting time here.'

The Elheim woman lifted her hands to the king and Nehren – stood at the hill's edge.

Nehren felt a scream cry out from the very elements of nature as flurries of air were commanded to obey the Elheim's incantations. Instinctively, he leapt in front of the king and threw his arms open to protect him from whatever magic was about to be cast forth.

A focused blade of air was indeed cast out from the Elheim's palm. Nehren's Magi senses could feel it. He didn't have time to react with any Magic of his own. He closed his eyes and looked away from the attack, hoping that his innate affinity with nature would serve as his shield.

Time crawled by as he awaited the impact.

He sensed a change in the attack, as if the attack had been strengthened by one or both other Elheim emissaries. He clamped his eyes tighter, expecting intense pain. But it didn't come.

He heard the impact, followed quickly by a sharp exhale.

Opening his eyes, the adviser realised he wasn't harmed. The three Elheim had not moved but each of them smirked at the adviser with detestable pride. He tried to turn back to the king but he stopped as a distant sound reverberated through the pit of his stomach. It was the sound of something hitting the ground. Something far away and down below, at the bottom of the hill's slope.

He slowly turned his head, hoping with all his being that his worst fear was not about to come true. He looked over his shoulder to where he last saw the king.

He was gone.

The magical attack had been redirected. It had curled around Nehren and buffeted into the king instead, knocking him off his feet and sending him plummeting to his end.

Nehren dropped to his knees and closed his eyes. For so many years he stood at the side of the incumbent kings of Ferenir. He had witnessed boys grow into men. He had guided princes on how to rule in a way that showed respect and honour for the natural world. Kings had died of age, poor health or on the battlefield, but never whilst under his direct protection.

He had failed the Kingdom of Ferenir, and all its people, perhaps the Magi too. He felt ashamed. He felt angry. But he held the last words of the king close in his mind:

'...and you will not give your life for me or take a life in my name. Consider that my last Royal Commandment.'

Nehren remained silent.

The woman in white paced to the edge of the hill, swinging her heels through the grass as she went. She peered over the edge.

'And there lies King Reksar Thorius, son of Kilian Thorius, ruler of Ferenir. He ruled fairly and with respect for all people within his lands. Such a pity.'

Nehren clenched his fists and let out a deep breath. Despite the emotion that tried to boil up within him, his respect for the king – and the innate stillness of mind and temperament that came with being a Magi – kept him from retaliating.

The woman crouched in front of him. She lifted his chin using her index finger, but he did not resist or protest. His face, as the evening light hit it, betrayed no emotion.

'You failed, old man,' she said. 'How pathetic you must feel now. A noble Magi brought so low. Look how far you've fallen.' She made a sound and brought a hand over her lips before laughing in Nehren's face. '*Fallen* – how insensitive of me.'

'You've done what you came to do,' said Nehren. 'Go tell your chancellor that the king has fallen and Ferenir stands undefended.'

The woman laughed again. She stood up straight and looked down at the defeated Magi. 'I think you misunderstand the situation.

The Last of the Magi

There will be a day that Ferenir joins the Grand City of Elheim, but today is not that day. For now, we take a better prize.'

The woman walked away to her two subordinates.

'Take him to the Grand City. Alive and unharmed.'

Chapter 29

Unexpected Arrivals

'Easy girl, focus on the path ahead.'

Tharian stroked Ombra's neck gently. She was restless as they travelled the road that crossed the border into Ferenir. His words were intended as a reassurance for her, but they served the same purpose for him too.

Their path led them closer to a towering hill, atop of which stood a fortress – Ferenir Keep. From there, the rest of the Kingdom of Ferenir rolled out from the shallows of the hill's slope, sprawling out to the coast.

But it wasn't Ferenir that filled them both with an ill feeling. In the distance, far beyond the left shoulder of Ferenir Keep, the horizon was marred by enormous structures of white. The Grand City of Elheim.

Though the Grand City was not even close to covering as much land as the Kingdom of Ferenir, it certainly stood much higher – thanks to the grandiose palace that nestled against the coastline. The entire city was also shielded behind a sanctimoniously obtuse wall of white stone – or perhaps it was marble, to add to the pomposity. It was hard to know for sure, but it would be built of finer materials than those used by the other city states.

Tharian didn't let his eyes linger in that direction. If he looked any longer, he knew his eyes would be drawn to the Dead Plains: the stretch of dead earth where the Magi had been massacred.

He had to keep focused. Ferenir was his priority.

Gently kicking, he encouraged Ombra to move at speed, to get away from that sight, and she willingly complied. It wasn't long before they were finally amongst the outskirt structures of the city.

Ferenir was bordered by wooden watchtowers, but the guards manning them didn't seem all that concerned by their presence, though they did glance at them side-on for brief moments. These men were not as fancifully armoured as Faast's elite guard, but they

The Last of the Magi

were certainly more efficiently dressed for battle than the Trade Quarter's regular guardsmen. Their red half-capes and brown gambesons made them look a force to be reckoned with.

Following one of the city's roads, marked by wide planks of wood across the dirt track, Tharian and Ombra reached the winding slope of Ferenir's iconic hill. The slope circled fully around the hill until it brought them to the gates of the keep.

As to be expected, the king's home was sealed and guarded. The guards standing in front of the giant ring handles of the gate had their hands grasped at their hilts.

'King Thorius is not taking any more guests today,' barked one of the soldiers. 'The next public surgery will be announced soon – come back then.'

Tharian didn't turn back. He remained still on Ombra's back and stared down at the soldiers from under his hood. 'I have urgent business with the king. He will be very interested in meeting with me.'

The first guard mocked Tharian with a childish laugh and turned to the other guard. 'D'you hear that? This one thinks himself important enough to call on the king whenever he fancies.'

The other guard drew his sword just enough to flash the blade at Tharian. 'Move along before we need to have you moved, sir.'

Tharian sighed and held the hilt of his own blade. 'I'm not here to fight. I've come a long way, and I won't be leaving until I'm allowed through.'

The second guard shrugged at the first, deferring the matter back his way. 'We hear this shit every day. Say it however you like, we are under strict orders. Final warning.'

Tharian sighed again. He reached into his coat pocket. *He better be right about this.* He drew out the brooch and held it high so the light glistened off its surface. 'As I've said, I believe the king will be *very* interested in speaking with me.' He was careful with his words. He still knew nothing about the brooch, and merely hoped the guards would recognise it, for good reasons rather than bad.

Both the guards squinted to look at the small trinket in Tharian's hand and then, in perfect unison, they blanched. They murmured to each other and then one withdrew into the keep.

Tharian wasn't made to wait long before the gates opened, and he was ushered inside. *So you weren't lying, old man.*

The remaining guard led him through a thick tunnel of stone with an arched roof. At the other end he was made to stop in a large open courtyard, decorated with small water features, decorative flowers, and benches. Some of the king's staff and other guardsmen moved about the space, going about their business in a hurry. They were too distracted by their tasks to pay him any mind.

A more heavily armoured guard now stood between Tharian and the next set of doors leading into the Keep's interior.

That guard stepped forward and eyed Tharian from within his elegant helm. He received a nod from his subordinate and then held out a gauntleted hand. 'Show me what you have there, traveller.'

Tharian calmed Ombra, who had stirred and stamped a hoof at the armoured man's approach. Hushing her, he then produced the brooch once more and showed it to the guard, though he didn't let the guard take it.

This guard did the same as those before. His head tilted, his eyes narrowed and then his face paled. 'Where did you get that?'

Tharian suddenly wished he had given this more thought over the long ride here. The truth would only sound ridiculous. Borrowing trinkets from old men in caves was hardly a common occurrence, nor was it a convincing explanation. His gaze drifted skyward for a few moments as ideas whirred. As soon as the right words came together in his mind, he stared back at the guard. 'That is no business of *yours*. I will only tell those details to the king.' Winging it never sounded so convincing.

'We shall see what the king has to say about that,' the guard replied, sounding angered. He swung an arm in a slack gesture to the junior guard and that prompted him to shuffle forwards and cup a hand below Tharian's to collect the brooch.

Tharian let it drop. The junior guard scurried off and disappeared into the keep.

As Tharian was made to wait again, he found himself on the receiving end of an interrogating stare from the armoured guard. The man barely even blinked.

What even is that thing? Tharian pondered.

The Last of the Magi

Looking around the courtyard again, Tharian noticed that most of the serving staff had now retreated away, but the duty guards had crept a little closer to surround him, taking up careful vantage points.

They seemed on edge. And now he, and Ombra, were on edge too. This brooch was more than just a mere accessory. Maybe it carried with it a darker significance that was known to the wider population of Ferenir, and the other guards looking in had seen it and recognised it too. Or maybe this behaviour was normal for Ferenir's guard. After all, the murder of the last king was within living memory, so there was certainly a precedent to justify a defensive approach to outsiders.

But Tharian was no Elheim; he was no enforcer. They would realise that soon enough after taking the time to hear him out, surely.

The inner gates swung open.

The king stepped out, surrounded by men and women in white uniforms.

King Thorius had enforcers at his side.

The enforcers left the king at the doorway and approached Tharian, forming a semi-circle around him and Ombra. Ombra stumbled back in fear and even Tharian felt his heart race and stomach sink. He clutched the reins tightly and pressed his feet against Ombra's sides to try and stop her rearing.

One of the enforcers held her gloved hand out, with the brooch pinched between thumb and finger.

'We have questions for you.'

Chapter 30

Horizons

Barely a word had left his father's lips since Brynport. That had suited both Darus and his father just fine. Every moment that Lanark remained silent was another moment where Darus could enjoy being free from his father's scolding and judgment.

But even in this silence, Darus felt no real peace or solitude. His emotions were at war. Like coloured dyes mixed into water, his grief, anger, and guilt swirled around and around in his stomach until they blended into something he had no words to describe.

His conscience was laden with the reality that he had killed four men. The pirate captain, his two sons... and Rik. Three men summarily executed for crimes they hadn't been tried for, and then the person he cared about most, killed in an accident of his own making. They all died by his hands, victims of his new *celebrated* power; an Arcane power that was winning him the admiration of the other enforcers in their party. As if that was supposed to be his consolation prize.

I don't want to be here, Darus told himself. *I should be running errands and taking notes for another enforcer. This is too much. Too soon. This shouldn't be happening.*

The anger within him died down, allowing the grief and guilt to take centre-stage. He felt a sickly warmth flood through his stomach and chest, and tears swelled in his eyes. He mustered all the strength he could to blink the tears away and push down the image of Rik being crushed in that rockfall. There was nothing he could do about the situation, and any expression of emotion would only alert his father and start a new discussion that he wasn't ready for.

The Elheim carriages stopped for a while not too far from Brynwell to give the feyren another chance to rest and recover. They had been restless since they felt the ground tremble at Brynport.

His father looked out the carriage windows, seeming to check whether any of the commonfolk from Bryn were anywhere nearby. Once his checks were completed, a malevolent smirk dressed his

The Last of the Magi

lips and he swung open the carriage door, ducking out to stand on the carriage steps. He called out for the attention of the other enforcers and then paused as they appeared at their carriage doors and windows. Darus apathetically watched through the window.

'Now that we are away from the Outer Counties' rabble, I must deliver an update I received from the Grand City: we are to return to the Trade Quarters. We are instructed to root out the criminal who attacked Lady Valivelle. He may be under the protection of the coinsmen, so we are authorised to take all *necessary* action to deal with this matter on behalf of our chancellor.'

The other enforcers smirked and cheered. You didn't have to be Lanark Valivelle's son to understand his intentions – his reputation preceded him, and he had demonstrated the brutality of his methods already. Darus was confident there were some enforcers among their party who would be more than eager to prove themselves to him, and the tone of his father's message suggested they might get their chance.

Swinging the carriage door shut again, his father propped his cane against the wall and took his seat. 'Did you hear that?'

'Yes, sir.'

'You should get some rest; your strengths may be called upon again in greater measure.'

Darus's eyes widened. He pictured the collapsing rock wall in the College Arcana, and then the dockhouse collapsing in Brynport. Surely he didn't expect him to... 'Raze an entire city?' His words took over his thoughts. 'I... don't think I can.'

His father looked at him flatly, dumbfounded. 'Do not be ridiculous, the Trade Quarters will not be razed. But a demonstration of such a possibility is not off the table.'

Darus felt slightly relieved. *Slightly*. But he also felt disturbed by the cruel plans his father spat out so easily.

'I suppose I should give you some credit,' he continued, 'the fact you considered the entire city being razed shows you are starting to give due weight to the severity of this issue.'

Darus resisted letting his bewilderment show on his face. His father was mocking him – he was sure of that. He didn't think like his father, nor could he – even if he tried to force it – and his father knew that. Or did he really think his son was starting to bend to his ways? Darus didn't try to figure it out. He was too tired; too drained.

'Although...' his father said, with some strain as he lifted one leg over the other, '...on the subject of credit, I should tell you that I sent a reply to the Grand City. I asked that the high imperator be made aware of the growing capability of your power. She will be pleased, and the scholars will be too.'

'Thank you, sir. It is an honour to serve the chancellor's will.' The words were lifeless as they left his lips. He was lying, of course. But at this point he had lost the will to show even the slightest resistance. To do so would bring him more pain – emotional and physical. 'Good. Now rest.'

Darus shuffled around in his cushioned seat until he found a comfortable spot. He closed his eyes and tried to rest. The cacophony of emotions warring within bubbled back up to the surface, making sleep an impossibility, but he kept his eyes closed and did his best to create the illusion of being asleep. Even if he couldn't sleep, he could avoid any further conversation.

Why do I have this power?

The question echoed from deep in his thoughts and surprised him. He hadn't even considered why he could do something no other enforcer had done before. Was he special, or had he just stumbled upon something by accident?

He remembered a lecture he attended at the College Arcana during the early part of his training, where a strict but passionate scholar had taken them into the very same indoor garden where Darus had discovered his new power. The lecture was an introduction into the use and mastery of the Arcane. The words, or a close approximation of them, repeated through his mind as if he was hearing it all over again:

'Achieving mastery over the Arcane is a truly difficult task. To master the Arcane is to assume the power to manipulate, shape and use the forces of the world that lie all around us. But In order to draw upon those forces, we must understand its source, its properties, and attune our mind to the sensitivity of exertion needed to assume control of it.'

The Last of the Magi

Darus remembered the lecture fondly. He later discovered that the scholar was simply quoting from a former principal of the College Arcana, having memorised a section of his written works which had become famous amongst enforcers.

Everyone knew the speech by the time they graduated. Yet, it was not the wording alone which made that part of the lecture so memorable, it was the performance of it. The scholar punctuated the delivery of his lesson by moving his arms about gracefully, evoking Arcana as he did to move the elements around him. Wind rushed through the bushes and disturbed the grass, and the water in the ponds lifted and thrashed about. All the apprentices were in awe at the demonstration. For most of the young men and women there, it was the first time they had seen Arcana used so theatrically.

'The study of Arcana is meditative and introspected. By learning to dive deep within your own mind, it is possible to extend one's own consciousness to interact with the forces of nature on a higher level.'

The scholar had then stopped his monologue and addressed the apprentices trailing after him directly. *'You have all achieved this Deep Thought state. You have felt the weightlessness of the air, and the speed at which it moves and interacts with and touches all around us. A smaller number of you will have also sensed the calming force of water, whether it be still and tranquil like the ponds in this garden or heavy and rhythmic like the sea. Those of you who attended classes in the evening may also have felt their senses overwhelmed by the crackling, scorching heat of the flames burning within our mantles. As we let our minds connect with these elements, we can feel them as an extension of ourselves.'*

Those classes had been thrilling. Darus remembered the first time he felt his mind connect with the breeze outside the walls of his classroom. What started as simply a deep trance of concentration was suddenly interrupted by a sensation that felt like a bluster of wind circling within his skull.

'As we become more familiar with these elements, we can start to control them, rather than simply feel them. You will know this process as Reaching and Grasping: the ability to focus the mind on a particular force of nature, to isolate it from the rest, and then

extend one's will to restrain it. From there, you will be taught to Command that which sits within your Grasp. But your development does not stop there. Once the ability to Command becomes second nature to you, you will be encouraged to dive deeper into your senses and Reach further. Some of our enforcers can Command the sky and clouds in small measures, even to the point of invoking lightning or thunder. Others have been able to solidify water and turn it into shapes and structures with full corporeality. The full limits are still unknown.'

Was it that simple? Had Darus just Reached somewhere new? He couldn't call forth lightning, nor could he hold water with such tension that he could walk upon it – not yet – but he could manipulate something as solid and as unyielding as the earth beneath his feet.

If it really was that simple, it would explain a lot of what Darus had experienced. As the scholar had once told him, the path to mastery started with concentration and meditation. Enforcers had to feel and understand an element before they could properly control it. Darus must have been Commanding the earth prematurely.

I need time. That much seemed clear now. *I need to concentrate in Deep Thought on the earth until I can safely build up to Commanding it. It's not safe to use this power again until I understand it better.*

But that didn't answer all his questions. His years of training had taught him that control of the elements required intense concentration. One needed to have an incredibly focused mind to be able to even detect and Reach out to certain elements through Arcana. And although Darus had been in a very deep state of concentration when he had caused the rock wall to crumble upon Rikkard, his two other experiences of moving the earth were not the same. The rumbling at the Cartographer Mountains, and the collapse of the dockhouse had both happened because he was emotional and distressed.

Was this a new process entirely, or did emotion have a way of triggering Deep Thought in the same way that concentration could?

There was a lot to consider.

Without realising, Darus's searches through his memories

The Last of the Magi

brought him some much-needed respite. Trying to rationalise the theory behind his new power took his attention away from the darker thoughts in his mind, to the point that he eventually drifted off to sleep mid-thought.

When Darus stirred some hours later, he looked out the carriage window with eyes blinked into narrow slits. The sight outside was confusing. It was still daytime, he assumed, as the carriage was bathed in a dim light, but the landscape outside was bathed in a thick, peachy-orange fog. It could have been sunlight filtering through just as easily as it could have been dusk-light or even the embers of a distant flame. He hoped not the latter.

The Feyren were snarling. That was what woke him. Darus dragged himself up from his slumped position and blinked hard until he could open his eyes properly. Looking outside again he caught passing glimpses of air-starved trees and the well-trodden road they followed. In the distance, the shape of a large structure was fading into view through the smog.

The Trade Quarters, Darus realised. That explained the smog. He swallowed hard and tried not to contemplate what his father had planned.

***

Marla reached the top of the staircase. She had ran up the last three or four flights much faster than she should have. Her chest was tight and she paused to catch her breath. She leaned back against a railing, oblivious to the sheer height of the wall she had climbed. The smog drifted about her in thick, heavy ropes as the heat carried it up from the city.

Once she felt comfortable enough to move again, she turned around and looked down at the path she had travelled. She had climbed twelve flights of stairs which brought her from the edge of the Market Quarter all the way to the top of the city wall.

She could see so much of the Trade Quarters from this height, despite the obscuring thickness of the smog. The four quarters were enormous from this view, clearly divided by their wide, main roads which all met at the central plaza. The buildings behind each main road were darker, more tightly knit together and less maintained the further behind the main roads they stretched. She had spent enough time weaving through those small roads and alleyways lately.

Down there, in those dark passages, she sometimes felt like a rat in a maze, but atop the wall she felt like a giant, towering over everything.

Marla crossed to the outside edge of the wall and looked out to the Outer Counties. But the Outer Counties might as well not have been there at all, for the smog was at its thickest where it gathered atop the wall and drooped out of the city. There was so little to see beyond vague silhouettes of withered trees.

That was enough sightseeing; she was on the clock.

Brayne had asked her to bring a consignment of arrows to the city guard watch post positioned in one of the turrets along this part of the wall. Making the arrowheads was job far beneath Brayne's skill, but he was still picking up extra jobs since the Crucible tourney, and no tender work had yet been posted by the coinswoman.

The turret was close by – she had spotted it as she reached the landing. She jogged over to its doorless archway.

'Hello there, I've got a delivery of arrows – I think they're for you?' She swung the quiver of arrows just inside the doorway.

The watchman, wearing the tan and green colours of the city guard, took his eyes off the horizon for a moment to regard her. He nodded. He flicked his head in the direction of a table to the side of Marla where a small bag of coins had been laid out ready.

'Perfect, thank you.' Marla scooped up the bag and stretched the drawstring open to count its contents. Brayne's lecture on the importance of properly counting coin was still fresh in her memory.

The watchman laughed at her. 'Suspicious of the city guard, are you?'

Marla flushed. 'No, not at all.'

Again, he laughed. He opened his arms out and looked over his own armour. 'You think Coinswoman Faast would allow one of us to cheat an artisan?'

Marla finished counting and tucked the bag of coins away. She shrugged. 'I don't really know. But still, it's not my money so I just

The Last of the Magi

do what I'm asked.'

'Fair. I meant nothing by it. We all have our jobs to do.' The watchman leaned against the open viewpoint of the turret and stared off into the fog again.

Something appeared to catch his eye immediately and he startled. He leaned out to get a closer look. He then quickly withdrew and grabbed a small cylindrical device with a strange red glass at one end and brought it over one eye.

He cursed. 'Not again!' He threw the device back over to the table and then went to sprint out of the turret. He paused as he realised that Marla was still standing there watching him. 'You need to go home.'

'Why, what is it?' she asked.

'Carriages from the Grand City.'

Marla felt a flutter in her heart. She moved out of his way as he sprinted off for the stairs. Marla followed behind. The thought of another *visit* from the Elheim enforcers filled her with dread. Especially after their last fiery spectacle.

She raced down the steps, hoping with all her heart that Marion was not out running errands of her own, or visiting friends elsewhere in the Quarters, as she often would be at this afternoon hour.

What do they want with us now? She wondered. Her experience in the Central Plaza, and then her more recent scare in the back alleys had quashed a lot of her usual curiosity. She wanted to get home.

Chapter 31

The Intervention at Ferenir

'Dismount,' said the enforcer.

Ombra had tried to retreat. She shuffled back, and Tharian knew that she wanted to rear up and kick at the enforcers surrounding them. She kept shuffling back nervously until suddenly she became unnaturally still and whinnied a harsh, high-pitched sound in fear.

Tharian kept hold of her reins as tightly as he could until she calmed, just a little. He looked at the woman staring back at him, her expression one of pure disgust. 'I do not take orders from Elheim,' he said.

The woman turned her head slightly and her eyes flashed with rage. 'If you value your life, and that of your beast, you will do as commanded. And don't think about trying to escape.' She clicked her fingers in the air to the other enforcers.

Two of them pointed their palms towards Tharian and Ombra, as if threatening an Arcane attack, and Tharian immediately felt Ombra seize up and panic again. But through her body he could feel something vibrating, causing her sudden seizing. He looked down Ombra's side and saw the air vibrating around her legs.

They were using Arcana. They were holding her in place. The enforcers had them blocked from the front and the Ferenir guard had the flanks. There could have been guards behind, or even peering down into the courtyard from the mezzanines above, but Tharian dared not look to check.

He had to decide his next move, fast. There was no way out, so what more danger could he put himself in by pushing the Elheims a bit further?

'Have I done something to trouble you, enforcer?' he asked calmly.

'I'm quite certain you know the issue. A stranger, riding an exotic animal, arrives in Ferenir and demands an audience with the king, presenting an old emblem of the Ferenir Magi counsel. Every

The Last of the Magi

syllable of this scenario offends me.'

Tharian went cold. Her fury made perfect sense now. The brooch was no throwaway trinket. Only a few Magi had been trusted enough by the late Kings of Ferenir to be granted the position of special adviser – of counsel – and those Magi were obliterated with the rest during the Purge. Although the brooch survived the Purge by some miracle, it nonetheless fell within the category of trinkets, artefacts and emblems that were criminalised by the Grand City. Their laws had no technical jurisdiction beyond their own walls, but that never stopped them from enforcing them as they saw fit. The enforcers were true to their titles.

'Oh. That old thing?' Tharian acted aloof, as convincingly as he could in the circumstances. 'It's been in the family for some time, I think.'

'Is that right?' said the enforcer. Her anger bled away and was replaced with something more sinister and scheming. She glanced back to the other enforcers. 'Test him.'

Test me? Tharian thought.

The two enforcers not preoccupied with restraining Ombra joined their leader and pointed their palms at Tharian. He cautiously moved his hand towards his sword in retaliation.

The air trembled. Not like the manipulations of wind that the enforcers so regularly displayed; this was something different, more like a pulsing. It surrounded Tharian's body, and he felt the pulsing go around him, and *through* him.

He was being... examined through their Arcana. That must have been it. Their powers touched him so invasively it couldn't possibly have meant anything else. He had never felt anything like this before.

'Unsettling, isn't it? I take it by your grimace this is your first time being scanned. It's a skill we seldom have need for now. Not since the Purge.'

Tharian tried to push back against the sensation, but it was useless. 'What... what are you doing to me?' he asked.

'Checking you for magic. Whether Magi Magic or otherwise. I will spare you an explanation. Suffice to say, if magic is present in or around you, we will feel it push back against our Arcana.'

The buzzing stopped and Tharian felt like he'd just been released from the grip of a giant hand. He looked down at the enforcers and found that the two scanning him gave each other confused looks.

'What is it?' their leader asked.

'We sensed something.'

The woman eyed Tharian and then she also raised her gloved hands at him, as if trying to strangle him from a distance. 'You are a Magi?' she hissed.

'What? No,' said Tharian.

'Dismount. Now.'

Tharian knew he had pushed this as far as he could. If they really could detect sources of magic, and they detected it on him, then he was in even more trouble than usual. He dismounted Ombra and kept his back pressed against her.

'Explain yourself.'

'I assure you, the magic you sense is not coming from within me.'

'Remove your coat – now!' she barked.

Tharian paused. Despite how serious the situation was, the demand to remove his coat felt too strong an order. But if it was that or his life, he would make a sensible choice for a change. He pulled at the edges of his coat. As he did, he worried that his sword would be revealed to them...

The runeblade... he realised. *Of course.*

The weapon still contained Arcana from the enforcer's attack at Brynwell. Perhaps that was what they could sense?

With great reluctance, he reached inside his coat and unhooked the clasp that attached the sheathe of his sword to a strap around his shoulder. He quickly calculated whether he could draw the blade and strike quickly, taking the chance to catch them by surprise before they could subdue him. It wouldn't end well, he concluded. There was only one of him against five enforcers. Even if the Ferenir guard joined him, he was hopelessly outnumbered.

The cautious part of him won the inner argument for a change. Deep down, he knew the right thing to do in the moment was comply. So, slowly, cautiously, he presented his beloved weapon to

The Last of the Magi

the enforcers.

'I believe this is what you're detecting,' he said.

The enforcer snatched the weapon out of his hands with Arcana, sucking it through the air into her own hand. She drew the sword until the light of the engorged rune cast a ghostly blue glow on her face. Her cheeks became red, her brow furrowed deep, and she glowered at Tharian.

'An enchanted weapon, too?' She tapped her fingers against the half-lit rune, and it flashed. Tharian flinched. Usually, the entire blade would then become a conduit for the magic contained within. But that didn't happen here. The glow disappeared from the rune and the light transferred to the enforcer's fingertips. The power was now within her control. Another skill he had not seen the enforcers use before.

'Such a crime is punishable by death.' She examined the crackling electricity. Curling her fingers, she manipulated it into a small ball of blue light that sparked erratically. She looked to be concentrating intensely to keep it contained. 'Execution by electrocution seems fitting, don't you think?'

Tharian's heart stopped. 'You don't need to do that. I'm sure we can come to some sort of arrangement.'

The enforcer glanced at Tharian over her hand. 'You think *you* have something to offer *us*?'

'Maybe I do,' he said. The rash part of him took over again, but he needed to think this through. He had already lost his runeblade because of his actions, so he needed to produce something of value for them if he wanted to get out of this alive.

He could tell them about why he had travelled to Ferenir, and why he sought an audience with the king. But could he really do that? That would unravel the plans he had finally set in motion after a decade away searching for hope. No, he'd rather they kill him than do that.

He could reveal himself as the one who attacked the enforcer at Brynwell. Yes – that could work. He would need to keep his reasons for travelling to Ferenir a secret for now, but that would give him some leverage, hopefully. The Valivelles who passed through the Trade Quarters made it clear they were looking for him.

The enforcer scoffed before he could continue. 'I'm not sure I'm in the mood for negotiating with the criminal who brought down Illian Valivelle'—that shot down his second idea—'so the rumours *are* true.' She looked again at the crackling electricity. 'Downed by her own Arcana. I'll be commended by the chancellor and Valivelle family both for dealing with you.'

She brought the orb of lightning closer to Tharian and made it flash and crackle. But then she paused. She lowered her hand slightly and had a look on her face as if she'd remembered something. 'Scan him again.'

The other enforcers looked between each other for a moment and then stepped in. Together they caused the buzzing, vibrating pulse to surge through his body again. The lead enforcer joined in this time, causing the pulse to radiate more strongly through him from three fronts, in three rhythms.

The waves of force penetrated through him. Then he felt another push back from behind him. It pushed where he leaned against Ombra's side.

He could feel her. And not just where his back touched against her body. He could sense her entire body in his mind as if an image was drawn in his thoughts, outlined in a warm glow.

Ombra was a special creature, one born in a far-away land where magic and nature blended into one. She had gifts. Gifts such as those that allowed her to understand him, and him to understand her. They could communicate without words. He had always thought her abilities were just unique to her kind, an evolutionary feature of their species. He never considered that this could have been a form of magic, but he recalled what the enforcer had said – the Arcana used in this scanning process would be pushed back by another form of magic. Without doubt he could feel that push coming from Ombra now.

That would explain so much: her intelligence; her ability to connect with Tharian; but also, of course, that *other ability* she had kept hidden since their return to Asturia.

Finally, the pulsing stopped. The enforcers nodded at each other to confirm the same verdict – there was indeed a source of magic present.

The Last of the Magi

Tharian raised his hands in the air. 'Please. It's *not* me'—

'I've heard enough.' The lead enforcer gestured to him again and caused the contained lightning in her hand to swell and crackle violently.

Tharian instinctively stood back, pushing further against Ombra. She felt his fear, and he felt hers too. An idea sprung into his mind, like a suggestion whispered from her to him and, out of desperation, he accepted it.

What happened next seemed to play out in slow motion, over the course of a single breath.

Tharian turned away from the enforcers and ducked under Ombra's stomach. As his body lowered to get under her, Ombra's body lifted. Tharian pressed a palm against Ombra's underside as he passed, and he could feel her coarse, short hair change. The hair became longer. Wider. *Feathered.*

As he emerged at the other side of her, he spun around to see her long legs retract out of their Arcane shackles and take new shape. Her front legs moved to the sides of her body while her back legs became skinnier and lost their hair.

Ombra was contorting unnaturally, and it was both horrific and stunning to watch. Parts of her body twisted and turned in ways that would break the bones and tear the muscles of any normal creature. But Ombra was no normal creature.

She was a Shifter.

What once was a beautiful, black steed, was now a large black bird with sprawling wings, sharp claws, and a long, dangerous beak. Ombra had completely transformed.

Tharian had seen this before, many, many times. But the enforcers had not, and it terrified them.

Free from her Arcane shackles, and no longer laden by the saddle and supply bags at her flanks, Ombra twisted through the air and buffeted the Enforcers with her wings before any could lay a hand on her. She then leapt up and latched on to the stone edge of the ramparts above and used them to propel herself into the open skies. A few of the guards on the upper level shrieked in horror as the enormous bird shot above them.

Tharian watched her in awe, smirking and praising her in his thoughts for her magnificent display.

'What was that?!' bellowed the enforcer as she marched into the centre of the courtyard and searched the sky above for Ombra. 'How did it do that?' She directed her question directly to Tharian.

'I told you,' he said as he caught his breath, still hunkered down from where he had ducked under Ombra. 'The magic you sensed didn't come from me. She is a Shifter.'

Amid the panic caused by Ombra's transformation, the enforcer had inadvertently released the orb of Arcane lightning from her hand.

'Enough of these games,' she growled.

A force slammed into Tharian's back. He was knocked prone. His face hit against the cold stone and his hands were locked in place at his sides. The sensation was blustering and cold. The air in the courtyard was being pressed down upon him.

His ribs ached as he was pushed flatter and flatter by the force of the wind. He had no way out. Not without his runeblade; not without Ombra.

The wind eased. Tharian gasped for breath and pushed back to his feet. The enforcers were staring at him with fire in their eyes.

The lead enforcer gave a nod to the others. Tharian bent his knees as he tried to spring sideways to escape. But tendrils of solid air whipped around his ankles and wrists before he could move. They pulled his limbs out, holding him still.

'Stop this!' Tharian cried out. 'I am not your plaything!'

The woman stepped forward. 'Are you not?' she laughed. She then waved the back of her hand towards him and Tharian was thrown across the courtyard and slammed into the wall, pinned under another torrent of air.

The woman stepped forward to her prisoner again. 'You're right. You're not. But these'—she curled her hands in the air, and a mote of flame coalesced over one hand from a mounted sconce, and then a sphere of water floated over the other from a nearby fountain— 'these *are*. And for as long as criminals like you insist on interfering with the Grand City's vision, we will make an example of you.'

'What vision?' he replied, though his voice struggled under the air forcing against his chest. 'All of Asturia in white and blue? The

The Last of the Magi

Grand City standing over the ashes of our people?'

The enforcer sighed heavily and shook her head. 'Your kind are so unrefined, so unsophisticated. You never listen and never learn. I will not waste my breath on the likes of you any further.'

Words were just another tool used by the Elheim to manipulate. He didn't want to hear their justification any more than she wanted to hear his protests.

His eyes widened as he watched the enforcer release the orbs of fire and water and then wave a hand upwards. The wind pressing him against the wall redirected and he closed his eyes tight as it blustered up across his face.

He heard a crack. He looked up, just as slabs of dislodged stone dropped upon him from the ceiling above. He felt the weight smash against his head. His body collapsed under the rubble.

***

'Your young prodigy has returned. He still has that fire within, and his drive to stand against the Grand City has not mellowed with time. Even after near-on a decade with the most placid people in Feralland.

'I suppose I should not be surprised. He is your ward, and I had a hand in raising him too. In my own way. Who are we to judge him for being stubborn? Things have only worsened in Asturia while he was away – he saw that in his first few days back on our shores – so I will not bother trying to turn him away from his big ideas. Perhaps it is finally time for action.

'What I did not expect (and you know a collector is rarely surprised) is how he wants to bring about the Grand City's end. Apparently the Awoken have put it in his head that there is a Magi still knocking around. And they hold the key to stopping Arcana. It's the first I'm hearing of it. You've got more years on me. What do you think?

'I'll send him your way when I can, he could do with your guidance.'

Greycloak tilted the crumpled paper against the light of his fire.

The words felt new. Like it was the first time he read them. But he was sure he had read and replied to this letter before – a part of him was sure, at least. The part of him that still clung to his memories and his ability to think freely. But *that* part of him was shrinking away and becoming weaker as time went on.

His mind was not much different to the fire he stoked every day and night. It could provide comfort, but it flickered and faded, struggling to fight back against the encompassing darkness around it. Sometimes the flame would engorge, and stay that way for a good while, but eventually it would wither and retreat again.

There was a time when his thoughts were still lucid, even though his body failed. That time was long gone. He was a creature of instinct now, so reliant on his base reactions to serve his physiological needs that those brief flashes of lucidity had become a sought-after luxury.

The wayward son, he mused. Tharian's return had reignited the flame for a time. The young curious boy had become a man. The young orphan he rescued from a grim fate was strong, bold and had a force to him that pushed him towards his cause.

Greycloak smiled. Despite everything the boy endured at a young age, and the dangers he must have encountered in Feralland, he persevered. He thrived.

This broken vessel has served its function.

He dropped the letter at his side and the gentle force of the flames pushed it away. His head dipped as he felt the emptiness take over his thoughts again. Hopefully this time for the last time. He no longer needed to struggle on with this daily fight to retain what little was left of himself.

He could enjoy peace now that he'd seen Tharian again.

Tharian.

He stirred. His head lifted back up abruptly, as if he had just taken a wrong step in the fledgling parts of a dream. The jolt brought him another wave of mental clarity.

A little longer, he thought. That distant part of his conscience, clinging on deep within, told him to hold on. But why? Sometimes he could feel the silhouette of a memory trying to remind him of something he had long forgotten. He couldn't even begin to comprehend what it was, but it was compelling enough for him to fight on.

The boy will return. He glanced over to Tharian's seat. A different memory clawed its way back to him. Tharian had wanted to talk about the Magi he searched for. If that was what his ward wanted, then he would hold on for that. He would wait for Tharian one more time.

'Then may I rest?' the words left his lips without him realising. Or did they? It was hard to tell. He gazed into the flames again, waiting for any kind of reaction within his mind.

Nothing.

That search will bring only sadness for the wayward son. Those were the words he wrote in reply to Traykin's letter. He remembered it now. The Magi of old had failed Asturia. What good would one serve now – surely they were better off staying lost?

The darkness crept in again. He closed his eyes and sat back, a gentle smile on his lips. It felt good to have this time, fleeting though it may have been.

***

All things considered, that could have gone worse.

Tharian sat with his head against the cool stone wall. The chill soothed the throbbing pain. Dried blood streaked down the side of his face. He tried rubbing it off, but he had been dazed since he woke. He just clutched his head against the wall in silence.

There was barely any light, the only lit sconces hung on the wall outside the doorway that led into this room of prison cells.

His first thought upon gaining consciousness was to wonder why he was still alive. People had died at the hands of enforcers for as little as stepping out of line, and he had done much, much more than that.

His second thought went to Ombra. She had played her hand – revealed her true nature as a Shifter, despite keeping it concealed since their return to Asturia – and then she took to the skies. Tharian didn't worry for her safety, but he did worry about where she might go. They hadn't been very far from each other over the last decade.

Why are the Elheim here? Why with the king? Tharian grimaced and clutched at his head again as pain throbbed through him with every thought.

Perhaps it was as Coinsman Velioth said? That the king was loosely under the thumb of the Elheim now, out of fear for what they might do if he refused to cooperate. The late King Reksar Thorius was one of those who opposed them, and his fate was enough to sober any opposition in the current young king.

Maybe that was it. Or maybe it was worse. Ferenir may have already fallen. What if it was a territory of the Grand City already, under the permanent occupation of Elheim enforcers?

Too many questions, and no answers could be gleamed from dark bricks, dust, and iron bars. The smell of old waste, probably poorly cleaned away years ago, didn't help him make sense of the situation either.

He had to push all those distractions to one side for now, he had more immediate issues to concern himself with: he had no Ombra; his runeblade was in enemy hands; he had no idea where he was or what would come next.

He should have done some reconnaissance work in the city before heading to Ferenir Keep. He got carried away, overconfident. His rash instincts took over his better judgement, as they often did.

Tharian looked over to the old mattress tucked in the corner of his cell. He crawled across to it and rolled on. It smelled dreadful, like the baked-in sweat of all those prisoners that came before him. Rarely cleaned. Or more likely never cleaned.

Grimacing, he rolled back onto the hard ground. He used the sleeve of his coat, much to his chagrin, to clear an area of the floor free of dust and debris. Turning onto his back, he laced his fingers behind his head and crossed one foot over the other to get as comfortable as he could.

Might as well rest while I have the chance. No use fretting over the unknown, he told himself. Yet, despite himself, he did feel a twinge of nerves – and frustration, too. The enforcers had stopped him so easily, effortlessly even. Had he just thrown away all his progress? Even if he did find a way out of this, Ferenir may be a lost cause. And the hunt for the Magi had still not even started.

Tharian bolted upright at a sound across the room. A cough. He

The Last of the Magi

hissed at the pain that seared from his head again from the quick movement.

'Is someone there?' he asked. His voice echoed.

Someone shushed him. Then a figure concealed in a full-length robe and upturned hood scurried over to his cell. 'Quiet,' said the whispering man. 'Voices carry down here.'

Tharian tried to catch a glimpse of the man's face, but the dim torchlight was behind him, casting a shadow over his face. However, he could see the robe in a bit more detail. It was very dark red in colour, perhaps brown, with some gold trimming here and there. A seal across the breast glinted out of the shadow. The seal was clear enough to Tharian, and unmistakable at that.

'If you're going to be sneaking around you might want to consider wearing something a bit less conspicuous, your majesty,' Tharian whispered back.

King Thorius pulled back his hood, revealing his immaculately well-groomed black hair, evenly trimmed stubble, and clear skin. He reeked of royalty, even his posture was courtly. 'How did you obtain that brooch?' he asked with an honest-sounding curiosity, rather than the simmering discontent of the enforcers.

Tharian had almost forgotten about it. It no longer seemed important in the circumstances he found himself in. 'I know some people who like to collect curious things.'

'So, you're not'—the king shook his head before he could finish his sentence—'why did you come here during an Elheim inspection?'

Tharian's heart lifted a little. The Elheim were not a permanent feature in Ferenir. Not yet. His timing was just terrible. 'Your majesty, I didn't know they were here. If I had, believe me I would not have come to your keep as boldly as I did. But I did come to seek an audience with you.'

King Thorius cocked his head. 'I'm aware. This is the best I can offer by way of granting an audience I'm afraid. Speak quickly, I do not have long.'

Tharian nodded. He sluggishly lifted himself off the ground and crept closer to the bars, though he was still a little dizzy from the head injury. The king watched him sheepishly, his eyes lingering upon what Tharian assumed was the dried blood on his face. 'I came to discuss the Grand City with you. I have a proposal to put to you, one that will see an end to their oppressive visits here and elsewhere.'

The king startled at the words. He scurried back to the door of the prison, peering out. He then gracefully returned. 'Those are bold words. As much as I agree with the sentiment, it's impossible. Arcana is stronger than any sword in our armoury and its brutality does not discriminate against its foes, regardless the size of their shield. You experienced its wrath for yourself.'

'My King, I agree with you completely. That is why I propose to seek the aid of someone with power that can match or maybe even surpass Arcana. Someone from a group long believed wiped out by the Grand City.'

King Thorius didn't blink. Again, the king's eyes searched him. If he was looking for any sign of connivance, insincerity, or mischief, he would find none. 'You seek to find a Magi?' he finally asked.

'I do.'

A deep breath left the king's lungs. He stepped away from the bars for a moment and rubbed his forehead with his thumb and finger, wrinkling his skin. 'So this *is* about the Magi after all. I thought when I saw that brooch'—the king interrupted himself again—'I would welcome their return, truly, but they are not soldiers. Surely you know that. Do I need to explain how I ended up on the throne?'

Tharian waved a hand. 'I know it sounds fanciful. But maybe a Magi could be more than we believed them to be, if persuaded. Or maybe they don't need to be soldiers at all. It's worth investigating, don't you think?'

'Even were that possible, there is a bigger hurdle to overcome here.'

Tharian nodded. 'The Grand City declared them all dead. I trust their words as much as I trust poison to relieve illness. I know that a Magi survived, and they have hidden themselves away. We only need to find them.'

The king laughed at him under his breath. 'I want to say you are

The Last of the Magi

mad. But you must truly believe your words if you were willing to ride into my keep in such a manner. Or maybe you are just a fool chasing a dream.'

'Most certainly a bit of both, and more, your majesty.'

King Thorius smiled, his teeth flashing against the low light. 'I did not expect to be having this conversation today. I get many visitors to my keep but not many who would speak so boldly against the Elheim and invoke the name of the Magi in the same breath. Who are you, sir?'

Tharian straightened. 'I'm someone who lost everything to the Elheim, so long ago that I no longer remember what I had. And despite all the years that have passed, their enforcers still destroy, and take all they can. I hate that nothing's changed. My name is Tharian, your majesty. But my name is not important. Yours, however, is. You have also lost so much to the Elheim, and your kingdom now looks to you for protection, so they don't suffer the same.'

The king paused. He flexed his jaw. 'You speak with passion, Tharian, I'll give you that.' He leaned closer to the bars, 'but do *not* bring my father's death into this. It is not the right of a king to put his kingdom at risk for personal revenge.'

'Forgive me, but the murder of King Reksar was a loss to the kingdom too. It goes beyond just your family.'

He nodded. 'Enough. You do not need to persuade me against the Grand City. Like my father before me, I have no desire to see Ferenir fall under the Elheim's shadow. Our people had to fight to win its independence from an oppressive force once before and I will not see it happen again during my rule. Be that as it may, my people equally do not deserve a war against a force whose weapons can devastate them from afar. Ferenir will *not* be the next civilisation to be purged.'

Tharian couldn't fault his words. In his reading about the history of the Trade Quarters, in preparation for the Coinsmeet, he read excerpts of Ferenir's history too. The two cities shared some common threads. Ferenir started its life as Olgorath, the second great city of the Oligari. It broke away from that campaign of religious oppression and fought for its independence like the king said. The conflict took its toll, on both sides. It was a wound that hadn't yet healed in full, a lesson learnt about the mutually destructive price of war.

'Your majesty,' Tharian said, 'taking a stand against the Grand City will be difficult, and will inevitably bring great risk, but there could be a day when this option is taken away from you. The Chancellor of the Grand City need only snap his fingers and decide to occupy your city and I'm sure you know more than I that it will be done.'

The king gave Tharian an understanding stare. 'I wish you would not speak of my kingdom being so easily conquered. Yet, I cannot argue with you. It is true. There is a lot to consider here.'

'That there is.'

The king glanced nervously back to the prison doorway 'I must take my leave before the enforcers notice my absence. We will continue this conversation.'

'I look forward to it. You know where to find me.' Tharian gestured sarcastically to his surroundings.

The king smirked and pulled his robe tighter around his body. He made for the door and paused to turn back to Tharian. 'I will try to send some fresh water and bedding, and alcohol for your wounds, if I can. I'm sorry, this is not how guests at Ferenir would normally be treated.' The king then ducked away.

Tharian rubbed his forehead with the back of his hand, feeling the flakes of dried blood finally start to chisel away. *All may not be lost after all.* He took a deep, slow breath and then returned to his cleared space on the ground to get some rest. He suddenly regretted not asking what the Elheim intended for him, but nevertheless he had made some progress with the king. That justified a rest to rebuild some of his strength.

Chapter 32

Elheim at the Door

As late afternoon rolled into night, storm clouds loomed over the Trade Quarters. Lanark watched the sky through the wide front window of his carriage. The clouds had turned grey and thick shortly after they left Brynport, apparently then developing into a full storm that was drenching the landscape by the time he woke at the border of the Trade Quarters.

Despite the tumultuous weather, the air was unusually fresh and light around the city. The wind accompanying the rainfall had cut through the industrial smog. Rainwater hit the top of the towering perimeter walls and poured down to the dry, withered land below.

The Elheim carriages were parked side by side at the closed west gate. The carriages, and the feyren pulling them, remained dry despite the storm.

Lanark rapped his hands around the head of his cane as he considered his next movements. One of the lower ranked enforcers had already approached the gates and demanded entry. He returned with word that the Trade Quarters would not open its doors to him again.

He ducked out onto the carriage steps to look at the Trade Quarters more clearly. He planted his cane onto one of the lower steps, taking care not to dip it into the moistened ground. He then looked overhead, checking that the Arcane barrier of air was still holding strong to keep the rain from touching their convoy. It was. The other enforcers were maintaining it as instructed. He could see the near-invisible swirl of movement overhead, where currents of air were forced to thread together to form a solid plane. The feyren were interested in it too; they peered up and growled woefully.

Cowardly creatures.

The other enforcers waited at their carriage windows, ready for instructions. He would keep them in suspense a little longer.

Lanark pulled his gloves tight and cracked his neck before

inhaling deeply to shout over the sound of the buffeting rainfall. He directed his voice to the top of the city wall. 'Summon your coinsmen – we have questions for them!'

There was a short pause. And then a very faint voice called back. 'You know the law, Enforcer Valivelle. The Trade Quarters is not a right of way, not even for the Grand City.'

He could just about see the guard atop the wall, despite the storm's haze. Disinterested, Lanark lowered his gaze to the gate. He lifted his left hand toward the door, palm facing out to the left. He Grasped at the blustering storm winds he could sense trapped behind the gate. Leaning his cane against the carriage, he did the same with his right hand, so the backs of his hands were then pressed together. The powerful draft behind the gate was now within his control.

'Run along and summon your coinsmen, otherwise we will upturn your city until we find them.'

There was a whistle in the distance. An enforcer from behind called out, warning him of movement along the top of the wall. Lanark found it, and he saw that archers had assembled with bows and arrows trained on him.

'Provocation then,' he whispered.

He swung his arms outwards and Commanded the air within his Grasp. the two heavy doors groaned, creaked, and then screeched as they bent against the force pulling against them from the other side. There was some resistance, as the locks and gears holding the gate closed held firm against his Arcana, but eventually they failed, much to the horror of the gate guards who immediately retreated in fear.

A second whistle sounded. Nocked arrows were loosed.

They didn't travel far.

The enforcers watching over Lanark had Commanded the water as it fell from the skies. the tiny droplets were plucked from their natural course, made to pool around the arrows in flight, sucked in as if pulled by magnetic attraction. The water slowed the arrows until they lost all momentum and fell to the ground.

His enforcers didn't stop there. Together, several of them then Reached for the thin wall of water pouring over the city wall's edge. They took it in their Grasp and Commanded the water to reverse its

The Last of the Magi

path, running back up the wall. The archers atop the wall had no way of seeing what came their way; the flood knocked them off their feet and washed them over the other side.

Lanark smirked at their shrieking. What use did their high walls and trained archers serve when Arcana could wash it all away with such ease? He breathed deeply through his nose, engorging himself on the fresh, cool air. His smirk faded at the dusty aroma that hit his senses. It repulsed him. It reminded him that these industry-driven people of Asturia, whether they be brought within the Grand City's purview or not, would always be *filthy*. Unworthy of the luxuries that came with the name Elheim.

He ducked back into the carriage, noting that Darus was gazing out the window. The horror on his face was clear, despite the efforts he clearly made to conceal it. *Another cowardly creature.* He thumped his cane against the roof and the carriage driver moved them on, driving them through the ripped-open gates. Lanark sat sideways in his seat, so that he could look through the front window – past the driver – at what lay ahead.

The carriages wheeled through the gates, single file, with the Valivelle carriage at the vanguard. They had to wind around curving pathways for a time, occasionally moving around the lifeless or groaning bodies of archers on the flooded cobbles.

As they finally rolled on to the main road of the Market Quarter, Lanark looked ahead to see the crowd of city guards amassing, forming a barricade of swords and shields in their path.

***

'They send the lapdogs to bar our path. I hadn't expected such bite from the Trade Quarters after our last visit,' his father said.

'I thought they might want to resolve things with words rather than... this,' Darus added. He felt a tug of fear in his stomach. Not so much for himself, but for the brave soldiers of the Trade Quarters that were doing their duty. They had surely seen what happened to their archers atop the wall. Surely, they knew the futility of bearing arms.

'Now is not the right time for full force,' his father said as he turned back from looking out the window. 'Our priority shall be to locate this fugitive and detain him. Then we will address the wider crimes of the Trade Quarters and its coinsmen.'

Darus looked his father in the eyes. He had expected a siege. Bloodshed. Brutality. Was diplomacy still on the cards? 'Yes, sir,' he said.

His father reached for the carriage door as they stopped a short distance from the blockade. 'Good. Then let's clear this obstruction and draw out the coinsmen. We will use a light touch for now, but we will defend our own with lethal force if attacked, is that understood?'

Darus nodded nervously. As much as he didn't want to cause harm to another, especially not intentionally, his conscience could accept those parameters.

His father left first, and Darus followed close behind, soon after joined by the full cohort of enforcers in their party. They marched forward, all under the cover of their moving ceiling of Arcana that protected them from the elements. Ahead of them, a line of shivering, nervous guards stood with bucklers and drawn shortswords. Their cuirasses and gambesons clung to their flesh, sodden to their skin.

Darus noticed movements in windows on either side of the road. So many faces pressed against glass, trying to get a glimpse of what was going on. Although the warm light from their homes cast shadows over the faces at the windows, he knew that some of them were just curious children. In one of the higher windows, he spotted a man holding his young child in his arms.

The enforcers came to a halt at his father's signal. To Darus's surprise, his father pushed him forward with the head of his cane. Darus turned back, confused.

'I wager that the art of mediation is more within your skillset. Put your *softness* to use. Make them move.'

Another test? This might be one he could handle. He felt pressure mounting as his peers watched him closely. But this time his body did not lock in fear, nor did a cold sweat assault his brow. He nodded to his father, acknowledging his orders, and stepped forward.

The Last of the Magi

He felt drops of rain hit against his head as he stepped out of the protection of the Arcane barrier. He had not been contributing to the barrier himself, so he quickly remedied that. Reaching overhead, he Grasped the barrier and Commanded more air to join it, extending the barrier over him.

He cleared his throat. 'S-soldiers of the Trade Quarters'—his voice cracked—'the Grand City has business with the coinsmen. There is no need for aggression. We have reason to believe that a fugitive lurks within your walls, and we seek to find him. Please assist us so we can resolve this quickly.'

The guards whispered between each other. It seemed that none held any rank over the other. *They must have assembled in a hurry,* Darus assumed. He surveyed the guards and noticed the inconsistencies in their armour and armaments.

'No need for aggression?' One of the guards called out in a mocking tone, waving his sword about brutishly. 'You can tell that to the families of those you dropped off the wall!'

Darus bowed his head for a moment. The man had a point. But that was an over-simplification of the situation. 'Your archers opened fire on us, unprovoked.'

More murmuring. More whispering. Then a few more voices shouted responses at Darus, but they blurred together into one susurrus of noise, especially against the sound of the rain.

Darus raised a hand to try and quiet them, and to his surprise it worked. He then returned his attention to the barrier overhead, Commanding more air to extend it over the guards too. They didn't notice at first, but when one realised the rain was hitting the ground everywhere except close to where they stood, the others quickly realised it too. A few of them hollered and threw up their bucklers as if expecting an attack from above.

'There is no need to panic,' said Darus. 'I just want to hear what you have to say. Please speak one at a time.'

The guards were stunned to silence. Some kept their eyes on him, others on the barrier overhead. Their wary reaction was not surprising, it was unlikely they had ever experienced such a gesture from an enforcer. They didn't trust the Arcane. But his idea had nonetheless borne some fruit, judging by the softening of their stances.

Another idea came to him. He dedicated a bit more of his concentration to invoke more Arcana. He Reached out to the gentle flames flickering in wall-mounted sconces and covered streetlamps on either side of the guards. He Grasped one at a time, Commanding each to burn with a bit more intensity. It was a difficult skill, but one he had managed to demonstrate with great success in one of the College exams. If he did it for too long, or stretched the heat of the flames too far, it would quickly die out.

'Warm yourselves,' Darus said as the guards noticed the heat blasting towards them. 'Let your clothes dry so we can discuss this more comfortably.'

Darus suddenly felt beyond himself, as if he was in the crowd watching his deeds from afar. He sounded convincing. Kindness and compassion may have been a tool in the armoury of great diplomats from history, but it had never been a tool used when exercising the will of the chancellor.

Another of the guards spoke out on their behalf. 'Is this a new game, enforcer? You think you can lower our guard with your nice words and then strike us down while our swords are low?'

Darus shuffled forwards, waving his hands in disagreement. His movements alerted the guards, so he slowed himself. 'Please. We can stand here and discuss the finer details for as long as you like, but all we ask is that you call for your coinsmen so we can discuss this fugitive with them.'

One of the guards whispered to another beside him and the latter turned away and ran off.

'Can I assume that means you will call them?'

'You can stay right there until we get our orders!' another guard bellowed.

'Very well, we shall wait.'

A few moments of awkward silence passed and then the line of guards became flustered and aggressive once more. Darus startled as his father appeared on his flank, staring forward with disgust at those in his way. 'I tire of waiting.'

'They have sent someone to get further instruction. I don't think we need to wait much longer, sir.'

The Last of the Magi

His father looked down his nose at Darus with a cocked brow. 'Fine. I hope for their sake they act quickly. My patience wears perilously thin.'

A few minutes passed, with only the dull sound of heavy rainfall striking the barrier overhead keeping them company.

Eventually the guard that retreated from the group returned and conferred with the others. He gestured back to the central plaza and both Darus and his father looked through the line to see what was going on.

A larger swathe of guards were gathering in the plaza, forming more barricades at the threshold to each of the other main roads. Much like what happened when they drove through the city in their carriages only a few days prior. Looking a little further, the golden glint of elite guard armour pierced through the evening dusklight. The elites were pacing to the plaza centre, escorting four figures.

'It seems your words struck their mark. Excellent work. I will take over from here,' his father said.

As his father walked off, the guards parted their barricade to allow him and the other enforcers to pass. The barrier overhead followed them as they went.

Darus kept just behind his father. He noticed as he looked around that many of the city residents had already assembled in the streets behind the guard barricades to watch what was happening, and all of them remained at the mercy of the rainfall, except the coinsmen at the other end who were under the cover of parasols being held over them from behind.

Darus released his Command over the flames behind him and instead he dedicated that concentration to extending the barrier of air across everyone gathered for this meeting. Fortunately, it didn't strain him as much as he anticipated, as so many enforcers had contributed their concentration to its maintenance already.

His father passed through the centre of the plaza, regarding the four towering statues as he did. He scoffed at them and then stopped just shy of the edge of the plaza closest to the coinsmen.

'Again we find ourselves in this position,' his father said.

'And again the Grand City takes no heed of our treaties,' said Coinswoman Faast, in her full plate armour, with her towering pike and shield in each hand. 'We take great issue with your conduct. Does your chancellor no longer respect the diplomatic arrangements that keep our country in balance?'

A smirk graced his father's lips. 'I extend my apologies for our earlier intrusion. However, on this occasion our reasons for being here *are* within the spirit of those treaties you cling to.'

Coinsman Velioth raised a pointed finger, 'You speak of this "fugitive", I assume?'

'I'm glad our message reached you. We have reason to believe that a criminal from the Outer Counties has taken refuge here. He assaulted an enforcer and must be made to answer for his crimes.'

Another of the coinsmen snorted.

'Does that amuse you?' his father hissed. He looked the large, scruffy coinsman up and down with pure spite in his eyes. 'I don't think we have been introduced – you must be the latest spokesperson for the collectors.'

Traykin feigned a small bow. 'Coinsman Jerard Traykin at your...' he looked pointedly at Lanark as he reconsidered his words '...actually, scratch that last part.'

Coinswoman Keene shot Traykin a scathing look of disapproval which stifled the man's laughter. Despite appearing at first glance to be a gentle and calm older woman of refinement, just her glare alone seemed to inspire deference in the other coinsmen. 'Lord Valivelle, if what you say is true then this is worthy of discussion, but this doesn't justify your forceful entry into the Quarters.'

'Far from it!' Faast interjected. 'Your actions have caused significant bodily harm to our guardsmen, and the damage to our western gates will cause us no small expense to repair, an expense to be indemnified from your deep coffers.'

Standing at the side of the discussion, Darus could see that his father was putting in considerable effort to bite his tongue. He could almost hear the gears churning in his father's head, contemplating the many ways that he could crush the four coinsmen for their words of wanton objection and resistance. Despite the futility of their posturing, the coinsmen postured nonetheless – Faast in particular.

'Let me make this plain,' his father said, 'actions on both sides have caused great offence to the other. I am not prepared to continue

The Last of the Magi

this discussion any further, nor shall I humour any discussion of indemnity, reparation or redress until this fugitive is delivered to us. Then, and *only* then, can we discuss other matters.'

'Lord Valivelle,' added Velioth, 'you cannot pronounce such things unilaterally. We should discuss this in private and decide together the correct approach.'

'Absolutely not!' bellowed Faast. She glared at Velioth and Lanark in turn. 'This is our jurisdiction. Any decision on action to be taken within our walls rests solely within our gift as coinsmen. There will be no discussion.'

Lanark threw his cane down to the ground and clasped his hands together in front of his face with a muted clapping sound. With that motion, he Commanded a shockwave of wind to blast out with a loud boom. The bickering coinsmen were instantly silenced as the wind blustered across them.

'I will only say this once more. I will not humour any further discussion. My enforcers will raid this entire city to draw out this criminal, with or without your assistance.'

The coinsmen froze. Even Coinswoman Faast held her tongue.

Keene looked at each of her fellow leaders in turn and they looked back at her expectantly. She was the most senior amongst them. she brushed her wavy, grey hair back out of her face. 'I am reluctant to invite another demonstration of your Arcana in our central plaza, Lord Valivelle. Please provide us with a description of the individual you seek, and we will carry out a search.'

'Gladly, Coinswoman.' Lanark stretched out his fingers and his cane levitated off the ground on a cushion of air and returned to his grasp. He then snapped his fingers at Darus.

Darus scurried over and approached the coinsmen cautiously to tell them what he knew of the fugitive's physical description from Alderman Navarya.

***

Even though the hour was already late, in the interest of dealing swiftly with the unwanted Elheim presence in the city, the coinsmen ordered the entire city guard to assist with the search. On the insistence of Enforcer Valivelle, every single resident was to be questioned. No exceptions.

The enforcers led small groups of city guard personally, to ensure the work was being done. The coinsmen, however, made their way to Velioth's home a short distance down the Market Quarter's main road. His was the closest estate to the plaza. From there they could coordinate the temporary lockdown of the Trade Quarters until the investigation concluded.

No sooner had Velioth clicked the door latch into place before Traykin cursed violently and at great volume, much to the distaste of the others.

'Calm yourself, please, there is no need for that language. You'll attract the attention of the entire quarter,' Velioth said, in a half-whisper.

Faast dropped her weapons by the mantle and awkwardly lowered herself into the largest armchair in Velioth's living room. She was still in her full armour. 'He is right to be perturbed,' she said.

'I understand the frustrations, but we need only let the enforcers carry out their investigations and they will be on their way!' said Velioth. He jolted as something rapped him across the back of the head. It wasn't painful but it caught him by surprise.

'C'mon kid, don't be dense,' said Traykin. He pressed the rolled newspaper into Velioth's palm. 'You heard the description, didn't you? Its Tharian they're looking for.'

Velioth then gazed into the fire as he connected the memory of Tharian's appearance with the description given by the enforcer. He let out a quiet 'oh'. Traykin was right.

'I thought you vouched for this young man, Jerard?' added Keene.

'I did. And I still do,' Traykin said. He paced up and down in front of Velioth's fireplace as Keene took to one of the other armchairs. 'That lad knows how to get himself into trouble, but it's almost always for good reasons. He was raised... *differently* to the rest of us. He doesn't always think through the consequences of his actions.'

Faast grunted. 'The particulars of one's upbringing does not

The Last of the Magi

vitiate the allegations. They say he struck down an enforcer with that runeblade?'

Traykin stopped his pacing and met Faast's stare. 'Wouldn't you do the same if you had the chance?'

The fire in Faast's eyes was clear to see. 'We are coinsmen. I, more than any of us, have a responsibility to strike against those that would move against us – when it is appropriate and strategic to do so – but I would do so out of duty and obligation, not out of sport.'

'But did you not hear *when* they said it happened?' Velioth added. He plucked a small black diary from the table beside Keene and swiftly rifled through its pages, stopping on the date referred to by the Elheim. 'Yes – I thought as much. The enforcer was struck down on the day that Brynfall was set ablaze.'

Faast folded her arms. 'It proves nothing, and it certainly serves as no defence to his actions. Brynfall may have been attacked *because* of him.'

Velioth made a sound of satisfaction as he raised a finger to Faast. He then turned back a few pages and planted his finger onto one of the pages. 'I highly doubt it. The Alderman of County Bryn had made it known to me that the Arcane Tax was becoming too onerous for Brynfall to manage. We know how the enforcers feel about defaulted payments. I'd guess that was the trigger. Besides, didn't that young enforcer say the attack happened in Brynwell?'

'That he did,' said Traykin with reluctant triumph. 'Regardless of the where's and when's, we've made our deal with Tharian. What's done is done. There is no use trying to backpedal now. We need to think about how we deal with this situation. If they discover anything that suggests Tharian had been here, they will demand an explanation – we need a consistent story.'

Traykin looked at each of them in turn, searching for any sign of ideas. Faast was stoic and unmoving. She kept her arms tightly folded and scowled unblinkingly at Traykin. When Traykin's gaze turned to Velioth, the youngest coinsman knew he was fidgeting awkwardly, so he glanced erratically around the room, as if the answer to their situation might be lying in one of the expensive art pieces hung on his walls. Keene, however, rest her chin in her hand, shaking her head slowly with a pensive expression.

'Nothing?' Traykin asked. 'Fine, then let's start at the beginning. Who might have come across Tharian?'

Velioth gave it some thought. His first encounter with Tharian was during one of the morning markets. He wasn't seen talking with the public but...

'Mors!' he shouted in realisation, intending for it to be heard in the next room.

The coinsman's trusted assistant emerged into the room with a pot of freshly brewed tea for them all. He set it down on the table and then nodded respectfully to Velioth.

'Stay with us, Mors. This concerns you as much as it does us.'

Traykin looked disappointed with the offering of refreshments. The collector was known to have a taste for stronger beverages. He sighed and rubbed his forehead. 'The same goes for Frigg back at mine. I doubt we have anything to worry about with him. He's a good lad, he knows what to say when people come asking about my business without invitation.'

Faast made a noise of frustration, and she threw her head against the back of her seat with a thud. 'The Crucible,' she said.

Velioth went cold. 'There were hundreds there. If I remember correctly, you said Tharian drew no small amount of attention to himself.'

Traykin hastened to interject, 'Yes, he was there. But he was just another combatant like all the others.'

Faast stared at Traykin blankly. 'He did indeed look plain that day, yet he brandished that runeblade for all to see. He even demonstrated its abilities. The witnesses did not miss that – I can say that with certainty, considering the volume of complaints alleging foul play.'

'Blast it all'.

'The matter worsens further. He acquired for himself the moniker of *Arcana Hunter* during the tourney. Though that title was redacted from all open records immediately after the tourney, I dare say the name still lingers in the minds of many. Given the allegations now levied against Tharian, people are likely to make the connection to what they saw in the Crucible and the man the enforcers are looking for.'

The Last of the Magi

Traykin's mouth fell open. He looked completely astounded. 'Tharian wouldn't be *that* foolish.'

'It happened, Traykin!'

Traykin edged backwards until he dropped into the large sofa. He put his head into his hands. 'What a complete mess.'

Velioth rhythmically tapped the notebook in his hand as he thought it all through. 'So, denying all knowledge of him is completely off the table. What else can we do other than carefully construct an alibi?'

Traykin looked up and pointed one of his thick fingers at Coinswoman Keene. 'You're staying awfully quiet. You've been doing this longer than all of us – share your wisdom,' he said.

Keene finally sat upright and sighed. She didn't hurry to speak, but her words eventually came. 'There is only one solution. We must accept that he was here but deny any direct association. The enforcers must be made to believe that we do not support him, that we do not endorse him, and certainly did not meet with him.'

Faast nodded solemnly, and Velioth found himself doing the same.

'But he stayed with me. I know the lad, and that might be hard to cover.'

Keene shook her head. 'He has been away, has he not? He is an old friend visiting after years away, Jerard – it need be no more complicated than that.'

'Maybe. And only Mors, Frigg, and a couple of Faast's elites know about the Coinsmeet. Mors and Frigg will be no trouble, and I highly doubt the enforcers are going to interrogate the guard.'

'Precisely,' said Keene. 'If his demonstration at the Crucible tourney is presented against us as evidence to suggest we knew of his misdeeds, I propose we put it down as something none of us witnessed for ourselves. A rumour of hearsay, one we believed spread by opportunistic gamblers to tilt the outcome of the tourney.'

Velioth still nodded along. 'That's good. That's very good.'

'That leaves me to figure out a convincing way of saying that Tharian was just a friend who needed lodgings,' said Traykin. He at least sounded more optimistic.

Faast collected her weapons from the mantle. 'An equitable

outcome from my perspective'—she turned to Traykin to loom over him—'you vouch for this man, but he is a risk *you* brought upon us. You shall bear this responsibility. I doubt the enforcers will just pack up and leave when this is done. There will be repercussions.'

Traykin huffed and pulled a mocking expression at Faast. 'Yes, yes, yes. I understood all of that, thank you very much. You needn't drive the knife any further.'

Making her way to the front door, Faast looked back to the others. 'If there is any positive to take from this catastrophe, I would at least take some comfort from knowing the enforcers are not completely infallible. It appears we have allied ourselves with the one man to have brought an enforcer to their knees – a Valivelle, no less.' Faast looked somewhat inspired. But that washed away quickly, and she regained her serious, stern composure. 'I shall instruct the city guard and my elites to be on high alert, but to continue cooperating with the Elheim until ordered otherwise. I suggest that each of you attend to your quarters and do what you can to reassure residents and prevent retaliations out of fear.'

Keene rose from the comfort of her armchair and joined Faast at the door, clasping for her velvet robe hung on the wall. She pulled it on and tied the cord at her waist. 'Much to be done. We must do what is necessary to ensure the safety of our city.'

They slipped out the door and Traykin gave it a couple of minutes before he sluggishly followed suit. He looked at the tray of tea and shook his head at Velioth before he left, chuckling all the way out.

Chapter 33

The Occupation of the Quarters

Darus walked down the road, half in a daze. He trailed behind a group of city guardsmen as they carried out the questioning at each property down the main road of this quarter. He let them do the talking – most of the time – to avoid his presence and his uniform causing any distress, but if the guards reported that the residents were not cooperating then he was under strict orders from his father to intervene.

Three hours of this already, he recounted. He glanced overhead. The clouds visible through the smog were dark and heavy, but he was grateful that at least the rain had given in for now. *All we have is some rumour about a fighter in the Crucible tourney. There's only so many times I can hear that story. Each time broadly the same, just with embellishments.*

He had already reported this rumour to his father, and that the fighter masqueraded under the moniker of '*Arcana Hunter*'. That had been enough to make his father's face turn violet. But there was little information to work with beyond that, so his father commanded him to get back to work to find out more. All enforcers were ordered to pursue this line of enquiry.

One of the guard captains approached Darus and pointed further down the main road. 'There's a few more business-owners we can question before we cut through to the tenements.'

With a yawn, Darus replied. 'Understood. I will accompany you with this one.' He hoped getting involved would keep him awake. He courteously gestured to the next store along their route, but he was too tired to take notice of its signage or any other specific features. They all looked so plain and unassuming compared to the commercial properties in the Grand City.

There were two doors entering this property. One was larger, chain-locked shut and looked more like a shopfront. The shopfront was an extension added on to a more modest home, with a separate smaller door set slightly further back from the road. The guard leading the way went up the steps to the smaller door and knocked. Darus followed closely at his side.

'Open up! This is official business of the coinsmen,' the guard shouted.

There was no answer. Darus felt his stomach twist. *Come on, open the door. We don't need another forced entry.* Too many homes had already been broken into. 'Could we survey the property for any other doors?' he asked.

The captain gave Darus a strange look, but he welcomed the suggestion. He pointed some commands at two of the other guards and they dashed down the thin alleys that flanked the building on either side.

***

'Marla! Marla! Wake up, quickly.'

At first, Marla thought she was dreaming. But as her body shook aggressively at the shoulders, she knew she was wrong. She had only gone upstairs for a brief rest.

'What's happening?' she muttered.

'It's the enforcers, they're in our quarter now.'

Suddenly she felt wide awake. She bolted upright. Without thinking, she reached for the clothes she wore the day before and threw them on over her nightclothes. 'What do we do?' she asked.

'Brayne will speak with them. We'll stay up here and listen. We have nothing to hide so hopefully they will move on.'

Marion was panicking. Although she wore her usual brave face and smile, her eyes betrayed her fear. Marla smiled as convincingly as she could in return and followed Marion to the landing, trying unsuccessfully to sweep a glance out of her bedroom window as she walked by.

Marion grabbed Marla's wrist and pulled her down to crouch by the stairs.

Brayne paced up a few steps until he saw the two of them crouched out of view. He nodded and then returned to the front door, finally opening to their unwanted visitors. 'It's late,' he said

The Last of the Magi

abruptly. 'We have a busy day ahead; do you need to do this now?'

A well-spoken, delicate voice responded. 'I apologise for disturbing you. We need to ask you a few questions about recent events in the Trade Quarters.'

Brayne stuttered for a moment. The good-manners of the visitor must have disarmed him – it lacked the acidic bile that usually came from an Elheim. 'Do I get a say in this?' he replied.

Another voice, this one more distant, said something mumbled. Even Brayne, standing directly at the door, had to lean out to catch the words. He must have heard them as he nodded and then gestured to his right, leading to their lounge.

A blonde-haired, pale-skinned man stepped in and swept through to the room. Marla just caught a flash of the man's white uniform. Her heart thumped. Marion hadn't exaggerated – he was an enforcer, there was no mistaking it. Her hand throbbed as Marion's grip on her wrist tightened.

A captain of the city guard came into the house and shut the door, and the three of them moved into the lounge. They hadn't gone far, so their conversation could just about be heard without too much difficulty.

'...looking for someone. A man bearing an illegal runeblade, responsible for assaulting an enforcer in the Outer Counties.'

Brayne snorted. The enforcer paused. He then continued.

'This fugitive is believed to have sought refuge in the Trade Quarters. We are told he was seen at the Crucible during the last tournament. He used the name *'Arcana Hunter.'* Do you have any information that might aid us in the swift resolution of our investigation?'

Marla shuddered. *Tharian,* she realised. They were looking for Tharian. The temptation to run downstairs and intervene, to tell them that he was simply defending the alderman and her guard from an Arcane attack, was overwhelming. But that would make the situation worse, disastrous maybe. She knew she had to stay out of sight, listen and wait this out.

Her attention was drawn back when she heard Brayne coughing. He coughed and coughed until he finally had the chance to catch his breath. He audibly inhaled and then responded to the enforcer. 'He caused a scene; I'll say that much. Ruined the tourney for the gamblers. A lot of hard-earned money was lost, and I hear the coinswoman hit the roof.'

'Yes, of course.' The enforcer sounded a bit deflated, though he remained polite. 'Is there anything else you can tell me about him?'

'Nothing at all. I saw him at the tourney, but that was the first and last I saw of him.'

'Very well.'

'We will need to question the others who live here,' added the captain.

'How many others?' the enforcer asked.

There was a sound of papers being rifled. 'Two.'

'Two?' said Brayne.

Marion paused mid-breath, with a muffled gasp that caught Marla's attention.

Marla frowned. There *were* two others in the house. Marion and her. Why was it surprising to hear the captain say it?

The captain continued speaking, in a monotone voice – clearly reading. 'Brayne Glanmore... Marion Glanmore... and Ayria Glanmore.'

The home became silent.

'Is that not correct, Mister Glanmore?' the enforcer asked.

'No. It is not,' Brayne said. 'Our daughter passed away late last year. The Affliction took her.'

The guard and the enforcer were quick to offer their condolences to Brayne.

Marla felt an urge to look back into her room.

The colours. The clothes in the wardrobe of all sizes. The welcoming, feminine features. Perfect for a child.

A daughter.

It all made sense now. The Violet Affliction that ran in Brayne's bloodline, it passed into their daughter. Against all the odds, the strain of the disease that manifested in their daughter must have been strong. They lost her.

The guilt and frustration Marla had buried away after reading the letter from the chirurgeons resurfaced like a punch to the gut. But it was just guilt now. She had intrusively read that letter and immediately resorted to suspicion against her generous hosts – as if there might have been some sinister motive behind welcoming her into their home. And the truth of it was now laid bare. They had good reason for their privacy; they mourned a devastating loss.

Marla couldn't bring herself to look at Marion. But she understood so much better now. They shared a common grief.

***

Darus felt floored. He was no doctor, nor chirurgeon or scholar of biological maladies, yet he knew enough about the effects of the Violet Affliction for the news of Ayria Glanmore's passing to unsettle him.

It was not becoming of an enforcer to care for the ill-fortune of those outside the Grand City, yet he felt for the man. The aggression of the disease was deeply unsettling. Even just reading about the symptoms in books was vivid enough.

The Violet Affliction took the breath of its victims. And it was so-named for the purplish hue that would emerge over parts of an infected person's skin over time – usually across the top of the chest, around the wrists and, less frequently, around the eyes.

The discolouration itself was harmless, but it marked its victims for death. Those afflicted would experience shortness of breath, or a progressively worsening cough long before the skin began to change. Once that change took hold, the chirurgeons from the time of Oligari rule averaged that it would be only three to six weeks until the illness took the victim. Depending on the age and constitution of the person.

The timescales may have varied, but the prognosis did not. No medical solution was discovered, and no natural resistance developed. Many of those faithful to the Oligari were said to have been cured somehow – supposedly a blessing bestowed by their deity for ongoing fealty – but the conflict that brought their civilisation to ruin destroyed any records of the truth. Curiously, the Violet Affliction no longer spread amongst Asturians after Oligar fell, however no cure was ever discovered to eradicate the strain of the disease that passed by blood from parent to child. Undetectable, dormant, until it decided to show its symptoms. Those carrying the strain would live each day wondering when the Affliction would take them in its grasp.

Darus had seen drawings of patients, starved of air at the end of their lives. The unusual pigmentation of their skin would almost cover their entire body as the lack of air shut them down from within.

Seeing an adult succumb to the illness would have been devastating. But for a parent watching their child? It didn't bear thinking about.

'I apologise again, Mister Glanmore.' Darus said. 'We will ask a few questions to your wife and then take our leave.'

Brayne was stood with his arms folded. He stared blankly out the lace covered window. 'She's upstairs. I'll call her down.'

'No need, please,' said Darus, trying to be courteous. He gave a gentle nod to the captain.

The captain took the hint and slipped out of the room.

Brayne made a startled noise and went to follow the captain, but the captain moved too quickly, and the stairs were just beyond the door. With a sigh, Brayne turned back to the window and shook his head.

A woman shrieked.

'Enforcer!' called the captain. 'Marion Glanmore is here with another – a young woman.'

Darus looked at Brayne expectantly. 'I thought you said…' He tried to be delicate.

'Marla,' Brayne said hesitantly. 'She is our lodger. My apprentice. She is new to the Quarters.'

Curious, but also a tiny bit suspicious, Darus lifted a brow. 'Even so, we must question everyone.' He then raised his voice for the captain's benefit. 'Bring them both down please!'

***

Marla had been brought downstairs to sit in the kitchen with Brayne while Marion was taken for questioning. She could hear parts of the conversation even more clearly across the hall. The enforcer asked

The Last of the Magi

questions about Marla, why she was there and where she had come from.

The questioning didn't last long, and Marion was shaking slightly as she finally stepped back into the kitchen – the captain hovering at her shoulder. Brayne jumped up to receive her and led her to his seat.

There wasn't enough time to exchange even a few words, for the captain beckoned Marla to follow him into the lounge. She shook her head as she complied. *This is their home. Our home. Not your office.*

Marla sat on the sofa. The enforcer was in Marion's usual spot. That was irritating enough, but his appearance irritated her more. His fair, pampered face, and the pristinely clean uniform of white and blue made him look so... *different*. It was like he was born to look better than *regular* Asturians. Elheim looked out of place in the Outer Counties – where people were humble and modest – and they looked even more out of place here. The Trade Quarters may have been more sophisticated than the Counties, but such pure colours and blemish-free features were alien in a city where smog and swirling steam coated everything on the daily.

The enforcer was smiling at her. A smile that seemed disturbingly kind and gentle, without an obvious hint of underlying acidity. Even his blue eyes were warm to look at. He was... attractive, perhaps? No, just well-kempt. And blonde hair was not so common amongst Asturian men. He looked like he spent more time each day on his appearance than she had in her entire lifetime. A luxury so many in the west could not afford.

'I'm told you came here recently from the Outer Counties,' the enforcer said, 'may I ask which part?'

'Bryn,' she replied. 'Brynfall, if you want to be precise about it.'

The enforcer shuffled in his seat uncomfortably. Not the reaction she expected. 'Did you witness the assault against Enforcer Valivelle in County Bryn?'

Marla paused. She didn't want to revisit that experience, nor did she want to assist an enforcer. Even so, if she cooperated quickly then, hopefully, he would leave. 'I did, yes.'

'And did you see who attacked the enforcer?'

'I saw him.'

The enforcer's eyes widened, and he leaned forward. 'Please, it's important that you tell me all you know about him.'

Marla looked to the guard captain, watching from the corner of the room. He nodded reassuringly. *Just get rid of him*, she told herself. But how much should she say? What would get this over with as quickly as possible? Before she could conclude her thoughts, the pressure of the enforcer's stare made her blurt out her response. 'His name is Tharian.' Marla opened her mouth again to carry on, but she paused as the enforcer's eyes locked onto her intensely. Suddenly she felt she had made a huge mistake.

'You know him?'

'Yes – well, no, not really – he visited my father's shop to have a sword sharpened. And then after the attack in Brynwell we both took the Quarters Road heading here.'

'That sword,' the enforcer said, 'did it have carvings in it that may have looked like'—

'I'm a blacksmith,' Marla interrupted, 'it was a runeblade.'

The enforcer nodded. He pressed his hands to his lips and then reached for his notepad laid along the arm of the chair. He focused on his writing for a few seconds, mouthing the words that he appeared to be writing. When he laid his pen back down upon the pad, he looked up. 'And what brought you both here?'

'It's hard to be a good town blacksmith when your town is just a pile of burnt wood and ash.' Marla's jaw tensed.

The enforcer looked away from her. 'I apologise. I did not mean to drag up that difficult experience. Can you tell me why Tharian came here?'

Difficult experience? She thought. *The Elheim are on a different world to the rest of us. Only they would describe a life-threatening attack as a 'difficult experience'.* She bit away the temptation to snap back at him. He at least attempted to offer a weak apology, not that she accepted it. 'I don't know why he wanted to come here. He wouldn't tell me.'

'And where did you see him last?'

The central plaza. At the end of her late-night deliveries, and straight after that black-cloaked man had done *something* to fight

The Last of the Magi

away that group of thugs. Something that resembled Arcana. Marla's throat closed. The man had told her not to speak of what she saw, and he threatened a visit to the Artisan Quarter if she did. So she had to push that memory, that fear, aside and focus on what happened after – when she saw Tharian blindfolded and being dragged through the plaza by the elite guard.

Something deep down screamed at her to say no more, but she had already said so much, would she be making things worse now by not sharing the full truth?

'I saw him in the central plaza,' she finally replied. 'It looked like he had been arrested by the elite guard,' she said.

The enforcer glanced to the captain with a frown, and the captain looked back the same way.

'I saw them stand between the statues of the founders. I looked away for a moment and then they were gone.'

'Gone?'

'I don't know where they took him.'

The enforcer gave the captain another concerned glare but quickly concealed it with another smile. 'Thank you very much for this information,' the enforcer said. 'You've been a great help. Are you sure that's all you saw?'

'I'm sure.'

The enforcer nodded and then stood. 'Captain, we must discuss this outside.' He then politely inclined his head to Marla and made for the front door.

'Yes, Enforcer Valivelle.' The captain sighed and followed.

Valivelle? Marla thought to herself. Another one. Every time she heard that name, destruction and terror followed soon after.

The name brought visions of fire to the front of her mind. Of burning homes, screaming children and destroyed livelihoods. She cursed herself for cooperating with an enforcer who carried *that name*. The enforcer in Brynwell had used lightning as her weapon. The one in the central plaza had used fire. But for this one, smiles and charm must have been his weapon. What game had he been playing with her?

The anger, the frustration and the rumbling hatred for the Elheim snapped away in a heartbeat as Brayne and Marion rushed back into the room. Marion wasted no time dropping into the seat next to her and clasped Marla's hands in her own. Brayne towered over the back of the sofa.

'Are you ok?' asked Marion.

'I'm fine. I just answered their questions and they left.'

Marion let out a bated breath. 'Thank the Divine.'

'Glad that's over,' said Brayne.

Marla hummed.

'No use sulking over this. It's done.' Brayne slapped the back of his hand against Marla's shoulder.

Marion tutted. 'Brayne, we've just had the city guard *and* an enforcer in our home. Have a bit of compassion.'

'No – it's ok, he's right,' said Marla. She took a deep breath and then looked at Marion and Brayne in turn. The adrenaline of the day, and the cocktail of emotion swirling within gave her the confidence to bring up the things she had learnt over the last few days. 'But I think we need to talk.'

'Oh?' said Brayne. He folded his arms.

'Yes. Look, your private business is your own, but if I'm going to stay here and help you out, I think we should be honest with each other. I heard you talk to them about your daughter, and what happened.' She paused as they both winced. Their expressions were pained. Marla softened her voice and continued. 'I'm so sorry that you lost your daughter – how old was she?'

'Six,' said Brayne.

Marion looked up at him and then down to the floor, avoiding Marla's eyes.

'I know what it's like to lose someone that close to you. It hurts every day. I really am sorry.' Again, Marla paused, then she braced herself for the question that was lingering in the back of her mind. 'I know I've no right to ask, but I feel like I need to – did you decide to let me stay here because of her?'

Brayne exhaled with all the force of a bull and then shook his head at Marion, deferring the subject to her. He then went to the window.

Marion gripped at the fabric of the sofa. She held still for a time. Then, with a slight whimper she cupped her face with her hand. Her

The Last of the Magi

eyes were glistening.

'Becoming a mother,' Marion said, 'it was the greatest thing to ever happen to me. Bringing my beautiful girl into this world gave my life more meaning than I ever thought possible.' She breathed slowly and brought the back of her hand over her mouth, a few gentle drops hit against the cushion in her lap. 'When we lost Ayria, it was like all of that meaning just slipped away. She fought so hard. She was so strong despite it all. I'll always be so proud of the brave little girl she was, even at the end.'

Brayne came back behind the sofa. He held Marion's shoulders. She clutched at his hands.

'When you appeared that day, I couldn't help myself. The way you stood up to Brayne, you were strong, ambitious, so full of life. Somehow, I knew that Ayria would have grown up to be just like you. It was like the Divine was sending us a sign.'

Marla's cheeks warmed. Marion was looking at her now, and she had a look on her face that Marla hadn't seen for so many years. Yet she recognised it instantly: a mother's pride.

'I'm sorry,' Marion said with a whimper. 'It was a selfish thing to do. I'm sorry to both of you. I just wanted to help you find your way and get some help for Brayne. I thought I was doing the right thing, I never really stopped to think about how selfish I was being.'

'You weren't being selfish. I understand,' Marla said, reaching to place her hand on Marion's, which still held Brayne's at her shoulder. 'I lost my mother when I was young. She was an apothecary in Bryn, a good one, but it wasn't enough to save her when she fell ill. She passed away so quickly.'

Marion laid her other hand atop Marla's, squeezing it tightly. 'I'm so sorry. No child should be without their mother.'

Marla nodded. 'It made me stronger though. Father taught me that whenever something bad happens in life, and I feel like I've hit a low I can't get out of, I should remember that I can only go up from there. Those sad days are a reminder of how happy I was before, and how good things can be again. So, there is always something positive to take from those hard days, something to learn.' Marla looked at the two of them fondly as she thought of her father. 'Most of that learning ended up revolving around smithing.'

Brayne coughed a laugh. 'Too right.'

Marla continued. 'I know the fear of losing someone again never really goes away. We just learn to get better at managing it, or hiding it. Right?' She then gave Brayne a sympathetic look. 'It's like that cough of yours.'

Marion bowed her head and covered both of Brayne's hands with hers again, stroking them with her fingers.

Brayne sighed. 'The Violet Affliction took my grandmother very late in her life. We thought that because it got her so late on, she might be the last in our family to get it. When Ayria's skin started to show the signs, we knew we were wrong.'

'And what about you?'

'Too soon to tell. This cough could be a sign of the Affliction coming for me next, or it could just be a weakness caused by it being in my blood. The cough comes and goes for now – I just need to check my skin each day now for the turn in colour.'

Marla curled her lips together. She nodded and then stood, pointing a finger defiantly at Brayne with an impish grin across her lips. 'It would take a horde of enforcers to beat you down. The Violet Affliction will have to try harder if it wants to get its grip on you.'

Brayne stood tall and gave her a muted smirk. He nodded. 'That's the idea.'

Marla smiled at them both. 'Thanks for opening up to me, both of you. I know it's not easy. Let's not linger in the past anymore today. With the enforcers lurking around, who knows what will happen next in the Quarters. How about we make some coin while we still can?'

Brayne clapped his hands together. 'Music to my ears.' He looked uncharacteristically inspired.

Rising to her feet slowly, Marion stared at Marla. She shook her head and took in a staggered breath, the emotion within her looking ready to burst out. 'Thank you. Thank you so much. The Divine was truly smiling on us the day it sent you our way.' She stepped forwards and threw her arms around Marla, grabbing her tightly.

Marla enjoyed the warmth of Marion's affection. 'Thank *you*, for everything you've done for me.'

Chapter 34

The New Coinsmen

His father paced for a good ten minutes.

Darus reported the new information about the fugitive and his actions in the Trade Quarters, and then his father barely said a word about it.

The quiet was uncomfortable. The three-beat rhythm of his father's pacing, cane in-hand, was much like a ticking clock, counting down to... whatever was going to happen next.

The quiet was made even more uncomfortable by the fact that Darus, his father, and the other enforcers were not alone. In the hour since Darus reported in, his father had ordered that the entire Trade Quarters' population be summoned to the plaza. The coinsmen too. While they waited for the coinsmen, the rest of the assembled crowds stood around the edge of the plaza and down its long roads, silent and still.

And then the coinsmen finally arrived, escorted by Coinswoman Faast's elite guard again. They emerged through the crowds at the threshold of their respective quarters and stepped onto the marbled forecourt in the plaza's centre.

'I am troubled by what I've heard thus far, coinsmen,' his father said. But he didn't look at any of them.

'You will need to be more forthcoming; we have not been regaled on the fruits of your efforts,' replied Faast. She was still wearing her amour, with her pike and tower shield drawn close to her chest.

'The fugitive was indeed here. He took part in *your* Crucible using a title that is an offence against the Grand City in its own right. I understand that you oversee that tournament.'

'What accusation are you—'

'I am *not* finished!' his father snapped.

Faast's face flushed red.

'Not only that, but witnesses saw him in the Collectors Quarter regularly. Not just anywhere in that Quarter, no – in the home of the coinsman!' He stared down Traykin, who stood in front of the statue of the wiry-haired and famously eccentric Fergus the Hoarder.

Coinsman Traykin didn't respond, but he maintained eye contact without hesitation. Darus guessed the man was biting his tongue. A wise move.

'And if that wasn't enough – the criminal was then brought here, to this very plaza, in the custody of publicly employed guards. Yet, miraculously, no guards questioned know anything about that event? It seems to me that the coinsmen know about this individual and have elected to keep quiet.'

'Now, now, let's not be too hasty here,' said Velioth, waving his hands. 'I'm sure there is a reasonable explanation for everything you have heard, Enforcer Valivelle.'

His father turned slowly to Velioth. His glare of vindictive judgment honing in. Before he spoke, he seemed to take a moment to compare the fair-faced young coinsman to the equally fair-faced depiction of Arikella the Importer towering over him. 'Is that so?' he said. 'The truth of the matter is this – I have no interest in your explanations or your excuses. I already know that you have been conspiring to keep information from me. Just as I already know that you all met with *Tharian the Arcana Hunter* and sent him on his way to Ferenir.'

Velioth's mouth dropped open and he looked to the other coinsmen. Their expressions were stern and unmoved. Velioth clenched his fists behind his back to steel himself, copying their stoic behaviour.

Darus listened to his father more intently at hearing this. Glancing around, he noted that many of his fellow enforcers had narrowed their eyes or cocked their heads at what his father just said. None of the enforcers reported on any movements towards Ferenir. *How can father know more than us?*

'You are foolish if you believe you can hide your misdeeds.'

Suddenly, and unexpectedly, his father turned to look back his way, and called to him by name. Darus felt a chill, a chill that only deepened as his father beckoned him with the curl of a finger. Despite the trepidation, Darus approached while his father

The Last of the Magi

continued speaking.

'Your non-compliance with our investigation is noted with prejudice, coinsmen. The number of offences committed in and by the Trade Quarters is growing rapidly. And these offences have consequences, penalties that I have the right to exact upon you. Perhaps a demonstration is required, to remind you of the seriousness of this situation?' – his father turned to him again and gave him an obviously fake smile – 'Darus, demonstrate a small fraction of your Arcane power.'

Darus flushed. Suddenly his uniform felt suffocating. The crowds were nervously shuffling around him. His father nodded towards the centre of the marbled plaza and Darus moved as directed. The crowds started to murmur now; some were pushing back to get away.

A small fraction. What does that even mean? The only comfort he could take from his father's order was that he only wanted something small.

'Darus,' his father repeated. It was a veiled command.

'Y-yes, sir.'

He had no choice. Better to act now than face his father's wrath and cause another disaster. Darus held his hands out close to his waist, with palms facing down. He let his mind sink. His consciousness waded beyond the smog-filled air, past the heat of nearby sconces, until his Reach stopped abruptly against the solid and coarse sensation of the earth beneath his feet.

Again, it was different this time. Not only could he feel the earth beneath his feet more lucidly than he had before, but he could feel the weight of the four towering stone statues surrounding him on all sides. Without adrenaline, fear, distress, or any other ill motivator – other than the low murmuring of anxiety in his gut – he could Reach for the earth with precision and caution. He was in control.

Exhaling slowly, he Grasped. And it worked. The earth tethered to his mind. He Commanded it to move gently. Not in the reckless, dangerous way that it had moved in the College Arcana or Brynport, but in a controlled way that felt more akin to the rippling of disturbed water.

The ground trembled, radiating out from Darus to reach the

crowds gathered at the edges of the wide plaza.

The coinsmen, the city guard, the Quartersfolk and even some of the enforcers stirred too. The trembling continued, and the stirring amongst the crowd grew into shrieking as they moved in panic.

Darus could feel his Arcane Command at work. He smiled with relief and embraced the sensation of it all. Though the ground rumbled heavily against his boots, he knew he held the reigns. Just as smoothly as he demonstrated his Arcana as ordered, he gently released his Command and loosened his Grasp of the earth.

Darus looked to his father and saw something rare. A nod of approval. He then noticed that his fellow enforcers were watching him, either with great interest – perhaps even awe – or with delight at the panic that his power was causing. Turning to the crowds, Darus felt his heart race. The controlled rumblings of the earth, though satisfying to him as evidence of his ability to control his power, had caused so much fear amongst the innocent people stood around him. To them, he realised, it felt like an earthquake, like the ground was about to swallow them up, or maybe raze their homes to the ground.

Feeling his brief spark of confidence crush to dust, Darus released his Grasp of the earth entirely. Guilt rushed at him like a flood.

The statues were the last to stop rocking. Fortunately, no damage was caused, but the amount of loose dust and rock that shook off their lofty figures made the air taste coarse and stale.

'An excellent demonstration – from my own son, no less. Do you understand now the *magnitude* of your wrongdoings, coinsmen?' his father stepped closer and planted a hand upon Darus's shoulder.

Darus flinched. Instinctively he expected a bruise from his father's touch, yet there was no force to his hand. It was... gentle.

His father quickly moved away, returning to his pacing. He was taking in the expressions – absorbing the palpable fear – of those watching him from the crowd.

'I find myself in a difficult position, good people of the Trade Quarters,' he said, raising his voice. 'On the one hand, by the treaties between our fair city states I am required to respect the

The Last of the Magi

independence of the Trade Quarters – *your* independence. But on the other'—his voice lowered—'I learn today that your coinsmen have conspired behind closed doors against the Grand City; have offered sanctuary to a terrible criminal; and have even willingly allowed us to interrogate you in your homes in the hopes that this would distract us from their foul play.

'Ordinarily I would see it fit to serve a stern rebuke upon your leaders and report this back to Chancellor Elheim for further instruction. However, I know the chancellor well. His fury would be unimaginable. I wish to spare you the risk of becoming victims of that fury, and so I believe it only proper that your coinsmen be removed from post with immediate effect.'

'You what?!' Traykin shouted.

With a sharp snap-look in Traykin's direction, suddenly the portly man was held still in place by a barrier of air that surrounded him on all sides – blowing at the other coinsmen who shuffled out of its reach.

Darus was in awe. The speed at which his father had Commanded such precise Arcana was astounding. Terrifying, even. The crowds shrieked as Coinsman Traykin was fettered by the Arcane bluster.

'Your government has failed you.' His father shook his head, levelling up the theatrics of his delivery. 'Decisions have been made without your knowledge that would have put you on the brink of war with the Grand City. Let's wipe that slate clean and start anew.'

Darus watched his father carefully. He had not chosen violence, nor summary execution for the coinsmen. What was he planning instead?

After a few more seconds of pacing, his father turned on his heels to face the coinsmen properly. He released the Arcana prison of air. 'Coinsman Traykin, Coinsman Velioth and Coinswoman Faast. Your positions and titles are herewith rescinded. I shall assume stewardship over the Trade Quarters in your place until such time as the damage caused by your actions can be undone.'

Faast stamped her shield against the ground. 'Your chancellor does not have jurisdiction to grant you authority over our government.' She marched over and squared up to Lanark, towering over him, much to the concern of her elite guards standing watch over the crowds, and the other enforcers scattered around the plaza. Darus, however, was only concerned with what might happen to Faast if she stoked his father's anger further. No amount of armour would protect her from him.

'You can debate the legalities all you like, but it is done. Your people will not challenge this decision.' He then addressed the crowd, turning away from Faast. 'Though this step may seem extreme to some of you, I propose a measure of balance to make it more palatable. Your existing tradition of maintaining a council of coinsmen shall be upheld.'

Darus raised his brows as his father's plans for the Trade Quarters unravelled before him.

His father stepped away from Faast as if she didn't exist and moved over to the crowd gathered before the Collector Quarter. 'For the collectors, in place of Jerard Traykin I appoint my son, Darus Valivelle, to be your new coinsman.'

Darus blinked. His father's arm was gestured towards him, presenting him to the crowd once again. He then swung his cane and moved over to the Market Quarter's crowd.

The gathered enforcers applauded in Darus's direction. He nervously smiled and felt his head begin to ache as he contemplated what such a role of governance and responsibility might entail. He was certainly not trained for this.

As the applause ended, his father reached the Market Quarter. 'In the place of Erilen Velioth, *I* shall preside as coinsman for the Market Quarter.' He continued his journey and the enforcers applauded again. The deposed Velioth looked to the others for reassurance, but none came. The ex-coinsmen just watched on, powerless to intervene.

Oddly, his father skipped over the next quarter and took the long walk around the plaza until he reached the last of the four.

'For the Quarter of War, I appoint someone who has been instrumental in uncovering the nefarious plotting of your previous coinsmen. In place of Kireyn Faast, I call upon Inquisitor Karagor Protelborn to serve.'

From the crowd assembled at that quarter, a man stepped

The Last of the Magi

forward wearing a hooded, billowing black robe. He pulled back his hood to reveal a well-kept, styled hairline and sharp, handsome features. Loosening the chord of his robe, he let it flow open as he stepped onto the plaza.

Darus immediately recognised the enforcer uniform concealed under the robe, unmistakable in design, except it was in completely different colours. It was black with threads and swirling patterns of red to decorate it. This *'Inquisitor'* – a title he'd never heard of before – was the shadow of the enforcers gathered in the plaza.

The man shook his father's hand and then stood at his side. His father then turned back to the Artisan Quarter, the one he had missed along his route.

'And then of course we must call upon one to represent the Artisan Quarter. I would invite Coinswoman Viviel Keene to retain her post.'

The crowd fell completely silent for a moment, and then broke out into quick whispers, punctuated by a few cheers of confused support for their long-serving coinswoman.

Darus watched intently as the coinswoman moved to join her new colleagues, without making eye contact with any of the ex-coinsmen. She did however look quite sternly to Inquisitor Protelborn. Darus looked to where she was heading and felt his father's piercing stare summon him forward too. He stepped across the plaza to join them.

Coinswoman Keene held her head high and smiled calmly. She nodded to Darus as he approached and then to his father as the four of them stood together.

'You may all now return to your homes,' his father said. 'Rest assured we will act immediately to unravel the mess caused by your former leaders.'

'What do you think you're playing at, Viv?!' Traykin shouted. 'You can't stand with *them*.'

'I do what I must for the ongoing safety of the Quarters, Jerard,' she said, though she didn't face him directly.

'Enough of that,' his father said. 'The former coinsmen shall be taken to the home of Erilen Velioth pending further investigation. You will be allowed to return to your own homes to collect any essential personal effects. Enforcers shall escort you. You are under house arrest from this moment.'

With that, the city guard gradually moved to disperse the crowd, albeit they looked awkwardly at each other and to the new and old coinsmen as they hesitantly carried out *Coinsman* Valivelle's will.

Enforcers flanked each of the deposed coinsmen to escort them away. Faast, however, shoved one of them hard, knocking the man to the ground, and she marched herself down the east road back to her keep, with elites quickly stepping in to follow. Velioth silently cooperated with his escort. Traykin cooperated too, though with a colourfully vocal protest.

***

Keene's manor was extravagant.

There were certainly some perks to being the representative of the most skilled craftsmen and labourers across the Trade Quarters. Her home was constructed with bricks dyed a brilliant white, that somehow retained their sheen despite the smog and smoke that washed the city each day. Not all that brickwork was on display however, as much of Keene's exterior walls were adorned with intricate sculptures depicting many of the artisanal crafts within her quarter – each design itself being crafted using a different art style to the others. It was a mosaic of masterpieces. But her home was not all carved stone and brick. The horticulturists had contributed to the façade also, nurturing a trellis of plant life creeping up the walls on either side of the front door that was beautiful to look at. Somehow, they escaped the toxicity of the smog too.

And the inside was no less opulent. Entering the reception, guests were greeted by fountains made of stone or marble placed seemingly in an erratic fashion around the room, yet on closer inspection it was clear their placements were careful and intentional, to ensure they caught enough natural light from the windows and to make the water glisten with iridescent beauty without detracting from the works of art that hung from the walls.

Coinswoman Keene took great care to introduce her new fellow coinsmen to every artistic choice that went into the design of her

The Last of the Magi

home as she graciously invited them in. She led them through a door at the other end of the reception that led to a generously sized meeting space that she called the 'Library.'

As Keene very enthusiastically explained, it was not the contents of the room that gave it its name. It was the decoration. All four of the walls had been painted so that if one were to stand in the room's centre, the paintwork would give the illusion of there being shelves of books on all sides, running into the distances. Shelves upon shelves had been painted, with pathways extending between each row. It was a curious design choice, as when stood from anywhere other than the room's centre, the illusion failed. So that was where the seating was placed.

Darus stared down those long, painted corridors in awe. Coinswoman Keene noticed that he, and the others, could not help but stare. It was then that she offered her reasoning for the strange decoration: 'make people feel like they are in a library,' she said, 'and invariably will act like they are.'

Refreshments were served to them by one of Keene's staff. Pots of freshly brewed Haarb-county tea were placed on small tables beside each of their armchairs. Just like with the façade of her home, each of these armchairs were created in a different style to the others.

'I trust you are satisfied with this new arrangement?' Lanark asked the coinswoman, while smirking insidiously into his tea.

Keene rapped her nails against the arm of her chair. 'Perhaps' she said softly, though she then made a questioning sound. 'Speaking freely, I did not expect such a dramatic and sudden takeover of the Trade Quarters so soon.'

'Nor did I,' added the inquisitor. His voice was considerably deeper than Darus expected. 'I am supposed to be appraised on all matters affecting the relationship between the Trade Quarters and the Grand City. Had I known you would be arriving, Lord Valivelle, this tiring investigation could have been ended sooner. I received no message of this plan from Enforcer Haraygar.'

'Please accept my humble apologies for any inconvenience,' his father said, bowing his head. 'I received a message directly from the chancellor on this matter. The recent events in the Outer Counties called for an elevated and rapid response.'

The inquisitor hummed with disapproval and then straightened himself. 'So be it. I must admit, the decision of the coinsmen to stand beside this rogue assailant had given me much cause for concern – I thought Enforcer Haraygar might not advise the next course of action in good time.'

'I echo the concerns of the inquisitor,' said Keene. She stirred her tea and then lightly tapped her spoon against the mug's edge, making it chime elegantly. 'Abrupt though it may be this change may have come at the right time.'

Darus watched and listened, trying to keep up. A thought in the back of his mind wondered whether he was missing something obvious, or perhaps he had drifted out of concentration and not caught an essential part of the conversation.

His father narrowed his eyes at him. 'An explanation is in order for our youngest coinsman, I think.'

All eyes fell upon him, and Darus awkwardly lowered his.

'Darus. It is important that you understand something about the Grand City that is not public knowledge. Though it is no secret that we maintain a suitable level of control over most of Asturia thanks to our Arcana, the chancellor and his senior advisers are no fools to think that force and aggression are the only ways to achieve that control.'

Darus nodded along.

'To that end, whilst our movements across Asturia have worked to slowly chip away at the independence of our neighbours, this has – in part – only been achievable by use of a more subtle means of influence within each location we inevitably takeover.'

His father then lifted his weaker leg over the other and leaned towards Inquisitor Protelborn.

Taking that as his cue, the inquisitor took over. 'Even before our people adopted the name Elheim, the member families of the Arcane Guild had their roots in economic manipulation, subterfuge, and the shadow-direction of politics. Our scale and focus may have changed since the founding of the Grand City, and the discovery of Arcana most notably, but we retain those roots. There are a few select enforcers who are trained in those ways. We inquisitors are

The Last of the Magi

taken out of the high imperator's rank and file and placed within the direct employ of the chancellor's senior advisers.'

Darus made a sound to confirm his understanding. 'So you are informants?'

Protelborn gave him a blunt look and then shook his head. 'Far too simplistic a summary. What we do is far greater than that. We are enforcers, and we act as such albeit with different methods. Where you interrogate, we inquire. Where you would intimidate, we would influence. And where you might raise a fist, we would flash a dagger. One hand at work in plain sight, whilst the other pulls strings. Always subtle, always precise.'

Darus nodded submissively to the inquisitor, hoping to repair any offence he may have caused.

'Eloquently put,' his father added, 'and the inquisitor found himself a steadfast ally in the Trade Quarters through Coinswoman Keene, no less.'

Darus looked to Keene as the grey-haired, elegant woman blissfully enjoyed her tea. He reflexively frowned. He had heard that Coinswoman Keene was the most senior of the coinsmen, and she had maintained that position for so long due to her fair and just leadership, kindness, and her devotion to her people. The woman sat before him now could not possibly be the same person, surely?

He wanted to ask why. But it wasn't his place to do so. Besides, motives were irrelevant now. His focus should be on the now, that the Trade Quarters had been brought under the control of the Grand City. But even with telling himself that, Darus couldn't look at the coinswoman without wondering what would cause someone supposedly so devoted to her people to work in the shadows to undermine them.

'What happens next, enforcers? I take it you will be announcing the Grand City's intent to retain control of the Quarters indefinitely?'

The inquisitor scoffed. 'Is that not plain already?'

Lanark raised a hand to stop the inquisitor. 'We should be strategic in our next movements. Coinswoman, you know your people – what would you say to their current state of mind?'

Keene shifted her weight to one side and let her chin rest

between her thumb and forefinger. She hummed. 'The unilateral appointment of three enforcers to the position of coinsman is no subtle thing, but with my position retained without full explanation and your words spoken about repairing the damage done by my deposed colleagues, it is possible that the Quartersfolk will see this as a temporary affair, rather than a paradigm shift in political relations.'

Lanark stared off, gazing down one of the painted corridors. 'I take your point. I may have been too generous in my phrasing. We shall make an announcement to rectify that.'

Keene sipped her tea and then mumbled to herself for a moment as she collected her thoughts. 'While I agree that such an announcement would leave none confused about the Grand City's position, perhaps we could leverage the current situation to our advantage?'

'Continue.' His father eyed the coinswoman with curiosity.

'You will forgive my bluntness, I'm sure. But announcing that the Trade Quarters is now wholly under the fist of the Grand City would not be received well. My people are not fond of the Elheim, nor do I feel they would ever truly become so during our lifetimes.' Keene eyed each of them and then paused as she looked Darus up and down. 'Or most of our lifetimes, at least. Though the city may indeed be under Grand City control, I propose that we delay any formal announcement of that fact until we have demonstrated to the people that this new situation is favourable to their interests.'

'An interesting proposition,' his father said as he nodded and rapped his fingers against the head of his cane propped beside his chair. 'The chancellor might need some persuading on that. If we delay an announcement, do you think your people would believe their independence remains un-tilted?'

'I do. If I tell them as such. I have been in my post long enough to know that the people of the Trade Quarters trust my words. If I were to lead on presenting our next announcement – with carefully tailored wording, agreed by all of course – I am confident the people would be persuaded. In time, the narrative can then be slowly adjusted.'

Inquisitor Protelborn made a derisive sound and leaned forward

The Last of the Magi

in his chair, shaking his head. 'I am unconvinced. These people are prone to gossip and rumourmongering. They trade in secrets and speculation just as much as they do commodities. We should be direct before the people become difficult to contain.'

'Your input is valuable, inquisitor, his father said, 'and to make my position clear on the matter I shall support whatever is the most prosperous option for the Grand City. The Trade Quarters is under Grand City jurisdiction now, whether the people of this city know that now or later.'

Darus felt the hairs on the back of his neck rise as his father then turned his attention to him.

'What say you? You are a coinsman now, make your voice heard.'

Darus stuttered. His first thought was to agree blindly with his father, but his father wanted *his* view, not a mere regurgitation. Equally he knew that an honest, passivist suggestion would lower him in the expectations of his father and Protelborn both. Yet another test. Would they ever end?

Taking in a deep breath, and releasing it slowly, he carefully considered a proposal of his own. 'Perhaps there is a solution that sits between the two approaches?'

'Go on,' his father said, curling a hand through the air.

'You told the people that the actions of the former coinsmen could have led the Trade Quarters into war with the Grand City. If we continue that narrative, maybe we could make our presence here look like an olive branch to avoid that worst-case scenario. We wouldn't be outright declaring our control, but neither would we be denying it.'

'Very good,' his father said. 'So how then would we describe our new relationship with the people of the Trade Quarters?'

'Perhaps a partnership, at first,' Darus continued, his father's praise fuelling him. 'One that ensures we can prevent any more plots against the Grand City, whilst allowing the Trade Quarters to continue trading with the rest of Asturia as normal. The people can have some time to acclimatise to us being in control, while the threat of war keeps them from interfering. Then, once some time has passed, we can publicly declare the Trade Quarters as Elheim territory.'

'I'm impressed, my son. I did not know you had such tact for strategy. Your appointment as a coinsman was not a foolish one on my part.'

Darus had surprised himself too. But the reality was he was just trying to find a medium point between Keene and Protelborn that would minimise unrest and aggression.

Inquisitor Protelborn shook his head again. 'Such a plan would need the chancellor's approval. But I accept that it avoids us denigrating ourselves to some lesser position in the Quarters. A partnership – though a fiction the term may be – does suggest an equal playing field, which is more tolerable. Then again'—he hummed as his thoughts developed—'I am still not convinced these people will believe that narrative when there are three Elheim in power.'

'Then perhaps you should be seen to offer something to the Quarters?' added Keene. 'Give these people reason to see candour in our message.' She smirked and glanced to the inquisitor.

'Protection?' his father asked.

'Let us be frank, Enforcer Valivelle. If the Outer Counties are anything to go by, the offer of protection will not be seen as a gift.'

'Then what do you propose?' His father looked disapproving of her bluntness.

'Nothing more than what has already been promised.'

'Ah,' said the inquisitor. 'Of course.'

His father looked between the two of them, with a look of frustration. For the first time in the conversation, he appeared as out of the loop as Darus had felt at the beginning of it. 'Explain yourselves,' he said.

The inquisitor rose from his seat and made his way to a drink's cabinet tucked in the corner of the room, behind where Keene was sat. He poured himself a glass of spirits with ice, chuckling to himself as he did so. 'As compensation for the coinswoman's contributions to my work, she has been promised the opportunity to learn the ways of the Arcane.'

Lanark bolted to his feet, snatching at his cane. 'What – is this true?!'

The Last of the Magi

'Indeed, it is,' Keene confirmed.

'Every word of it – I was as surprised as you to hear that Enforcer Haraygar was willing to accept the request.'

Darus had never known of anyone outside the Grand City being taught to use Arcana. That training came hand-in-hand with becoming an enforcer, and that was a profession most embarked upon in their youth. The full training at the College Arcana took years to complete.

Protelborn brought another drink over and placed it into his father's palm, whispering something into his ear before returning to his seat.

'An unexpected development,' his father said. 'Though I suppose if you are to eventually join the Grand City as one of us then it's plausible such training could be made available to you.' His father sighed and sipped at his drink. The ice rattled as it hit the edge of the glass. 'So that is how we shall package this. Coinswoman Keene will announce our *partnership*. We shall confirm, as a gesture of goodwill, that the secrets of Arcana will be extended to the coinswoman so that she can serve and protect her people to the best of her ability.'

Keene rose to meet his father and lifted her teacup into the air as a toast. 'To our partnership.'

He responded in kind.

An awkward silence then formed, which was swiftly broken by the inquisitor. 'I shall begin work on the appropriate form of wording for this announcement. I shall liaise with you all once I have a draft.'

'Excellent,' said Lanark, 'I shall prepare a missive for the chancellor – there is much to update him on.'

Inquisitor Protelborn collected his black robe from the back of his chair and bowed slightly to his fellow coinsmen before taking his leave.

As his father prepared to make his exit also, Darus hastened to follow at his side. His father paused and looked back at him over his shoulder.

'I would like you to remain here for now.'

'Of course, sir,' he replied. 'What would you have me do?'

'I need you to learn from Coinswoman Keene what duties will be expected of you as the coinsman for the Collectors Quarter. These titles are not superficial. There is a city to run. If this partnership charade is to succeed, you will need to fulfil your role diligently.'

Darus felt nervous. His mind filled with a myriad of questions – of known unknowns and unknown unknowns which swiftly brought him to the conclusion that he was not ready nor qualified for such a role of administrative leadership. He nodded nervously and looked sheepishly back to Coinswoman Keene, who smiled and raised her tea towards him.

'I will learn all that I can, sir.'

'That you will. In return for the coinswoman's wisdom, you shall teach her how to open her mind to the Arcane.'

Darus looked at his father with eyes wide. He had only recently graduated from the College Arcana himself – he was no teacher.

'Just repeat some of the rudimentary exercises with her. Only the simple ones, for now.'

'Y-yes, sir.'

His father bowed to Coinswoman Keene and regarded his son once more. 'I shall send for you if I need you.' He then marched out of the room.

Darus assumed she had been listening in to their conversation, as she now beamed from ear to ear. She gestured with a sweeping arm to the door behind her that led into the manor-house proper. Darus swallowed his nerves, as much as he could, and joined the coinswoman.

Chapter 35

Prisoner of Arcana

Tharian's eyes had adjusted to the dark. It had been days since he saw the king. Only the king's serving staff visited him since, bringing him food, water, and the bare minimum of sanitation facilities.

His confinement was suffocating. A few days without freedom felt like a lifetime of incarceration. His life up to this point had kept him constantly on the move. Whether he was travelling at Greycloak's side, roaming the open wilderness of Feralland or – more recently – scurrying around the streets of the Trade Quarters.

Although he felt deeply unsettled in his cell, Tharian hadn't spent the time sulking. He was thinking. Running through scenarios in his mind of how he might escape this cell and the enforcers. So far, none of the scenarios showed any promise. Had his sword still been at his hip, or Ombra at his side, he might have had a few options, but both were gone.

But he had to escape. Somehow. Not only for the sake of his own freedom, and not only so he could carry on furthering the plan he made with the Trade Quarters. He needed to prove that the enforcers couldn't stop him this easily. No ally would stand at his side if he could be subdued so effortlessly; words of revolution lost their bite when spoken through prison bars.

Tharian laid his head against the bars of his cell, and tightly grasped at the cold metal. He gritted his teeth and thrashed his arms about as if trying to pull the bars apart with his bare hands. They didn't move an inch, nor did they even rattle.

'It will *not* end here,' he snarled in the darkness. His throat cracked a little as he spoke. It had been a while since he last used his voice.

He marched to the opposite corner of his cell and sat against the stone wall, resting his arms outstretched on his knees. Shutting his eyes, he controlled his breathing and calmed himself. *Think, think,*

think. He had to prepare for the worst-case scenario. What would that be?

The enforcers might drag him to the Grand City. If that were the case, he could say goodbye to any chance of leaving there in one piece. But if they were to transport him somewhere, maybe he could break free on the way? The Arboreta Forest was not *too* far away. He could try and hide there, or even disappear into the Cartographer Mountains for a time. He could survive there easier than most.

No. The eastern half of Asturia was known as the 'Eastern Expanse' for good reason. Apart from the towering buildings in each of the three city states, and the cliffs along the north-east coast where Lions' Rest was neatly tucked away, the east was an open and unremarkable expanse of grassland, punctuated by small hamlets and farmsteads. Escape may well be possible, but he would be fleeing in plain sight. Recapture would be a guarantee, especially if Arcana was deployed against him.

Frustration boiled up within him. He tensed all over until he heard a coughing sound at the door to his cell which pull him from his feelings.

The figure at the door wore a different cloak to before, but his posture gave him away all the same.

'Your majesty?' said Tharian. He sluggishly lifted himself from the ground and shuffled over to greet the king through the bars.

'I have news for you.' The king sniffed the air for a few moments and scrunched up his face.

'It has been some time, your majesty. The facilities here are not generous for guests.'

The king sighed and scratched at his forehead with a bejewelled hand. 'I'm sorry. Time has escaped me while dealing with my guests. But that's why I'm here. The Elheim have concluded their inspection and extracted their tax from our coffers. They are satisfied that your arrival at the keep was unexpected and Ferenir has been absolved of any allegation of conspiracy against the Grand City.'

'They thought you'd invited me?'

The king nodded. 'It takes very little to agitate them. In this case, a man bearing the symbol of the long-dead Magi Adviser,

The Last of the Magi

wielding a runeblade at his hip and riding upon a Shifter was more than a slight suspicious.'

'I apologise,' Tharian said. He sobered as the king's words sank in. His actions – well intentioned though they may have been – had caused more difficulties for Ferenir than anticipated. He had spent days worrying about himself and the bigger picture of his plans, at the expense of the smaller, closer details. 'It was honestly not my intention to—'

The king waved his hand. 'It's quite alright. Something sets them off every time. It's a miracle that on this occasion, where conspiracy is your intent for my city, we remain innocent in their eyes. I cannot say the same for you, however. The Elheim will be leaving Ferenir this evening and they intend to take you to the Grand City with them.'

Tharian's heart sank even though the news was hardly surprising. 'When will it be evening?' he asked, gesturing to the featureless, windowless stone walls around him.

The king bowed his head apologetically. 'Of course – forgive me. They will leave in maybe three or four hours, after the evening banquet in my halls.'

'Then I better prepare myself.' Tharian turned away and started scratching at his scalp.

'I have considered what you said before'—Tharian paused and turned back slightly—'I still have a great many questions that I fear we have neither the time nor liberty to discuss.'

'I have the time, your majesty, but certainly not the liberty,'

Again, the king seemed disheartened. 'What you propose would bring an end to this invasive routine. My people would not have to suffer Elheim intrusion ever again. While I have thought it best to stand aside and not confront the Elheim for years now in hope of avoiding war and bloodshed, I have seen them trespass further on our sovereignty. I have let it go too far already – something needs to change.

'Seeing that brooch again after all these years reminded me… that there was a time when the mystic forces of Asturia were not used for oppression. The older generations lived alongside it, at peace with it. My people never before bowed to Magic, I will *not* see them bow to Arcana in its stead.'

Tharian stepped up to the bars, smiling at the king's passionate words. 'Then tell me what reassurances you need. If I can give them, I will.'

'I need to know why you think a Magi still lives.'

***

It took some time, but Tharian repeated much of his speech from the Coinsmeet. The words were still fresh in his mind. He spoke about the Awoken of Feralland to the distant west and their fine attunement to the presence of magic in the world. He told the king that they had not only sensed the presence of a Magi in Asturia, even from so far away, but they knew that the Magi had a power which could lock away magic altogether. A single Magi, if properly protected, may be able to stop the Elheim enforcers from using Arcana.

The king nodded along and hummed in agreement. At no point did he betray signs of scepticism or disbelief. Unlike the mixed reception Tharian received from the coinsmen, the king appeared eager to absorb every word.

When Tharian stopped, the king stepped back from the cell and checked for any sign of eavesdroppers. He then stood straight and confident, still nodding to himself.

'Though it has been generations since Asturians have met with the natives of Feralland – lawfully and openly, at least,' he added with a fleeting smirk, 'I have read about their... gifts. If they believe a Magi survived, then it must be true. If any were to know, it would be them. But that still leaves one critical concern that I must give consideration.'

'And what is that, my King?'

'The Grand City is a threat to us all, but perhaps more so to Ferenir than any other. We are their closest neighbour. If we stood against them and failed, we would fall quickly against the Grand City's retaliation. Our armies may be well honed against the lawless folk of the mountains, and the opportunistic mercenaries of the Outer Counties that dare to stray east in their aspirations, but we

The Last of the Magi

would not hold off enforcers alone. I don't think we would be able to protect a Magi against more than a handful of enforcers at most. Ferenir needs allies.'

Tharian smirked through the bars. 'You have an ally. Ferenir will not stand alone.'

King Thorius placed a hand on the bars. He met Tharian's eyes, and his brows were furrowed into a woeful shape. 'Tharian, your words are confident and compelling. But you are only one man. Ferenir needs allies of strength and number.'

'The Trade Quarters will be that ally.'

The king's eyes widened, and he pulled back from the bars. 'The coinsmen have pledged their support to this? I find that hard to believe. They are the most secure of all the city states, the least afflicted by the chancellor's influence.'

Tharian patted his chest, quickly remembering that his coat was curled up on the floor where he had used it as a blanket. He grimaced as he picked it up and saw the state it was in. With a sigh he reached in to one of its many inner pockets and pulled out a wax-sealed envelope which he handed through the bars.

'They have as much reason as you to be dissatisfied with current affairs. But do not believe my word alone – believe theirs.'

The king retreated with the letter to read it under the sconce-light trickling in through the doorway. As he finished reading, he read it again, letting out a sound of relief as he finished it the second time.

He returned and handed it back to Tharian. 'This changes things. If the Trade Quarters is prepared to take this chance, then the army of Ferenir must support them. There may only be one opportunity to try this, and we need to be united.'

Tharian felt a wash of relief, but he made a concerted effort to keep it hidden. This was another step in the right direction, another move forward. He pushed away that feeling of victory – he needed to keep sight of the finer details. He still needed to find that Magi, and he needed a way out of Ferenir to have any hope of doing it.

'Your majesty, I am very grateful to have your support in this. But the coinsmen are expecting me to return with your response – I need a way to get back to them,' said Tharian.

The king scratched at his short beard and then leaned forward.

'Yes, of course. I'm afraid there's not much I can do to help you on that front. All I can do is give you information.'

Tharian raised a brow and curled his lips. 'I'll take it.'

'The enforcers have called for their carriages. They will be drawn into the keep courtyard soon. They may be here already.' The king gestured with a ringed finger to the ceiling above. 'After much deliberation they decided that you will be a passenger in the first carriage along with the leader of their group, one Enforcer Quiryn.'

'Just the two of us?'

The king nodded. 'I believe so. The subject was discussed at length over the evening feast yesterday. By the way they excluded me from the conversation but spoke openly in my presence, I suspect they were trying to give me a warning of how I would be treated if I stepped out of line.'

'That sounds like their intimidation tactics alright. Please continue.'

'There is not much more to say. Enforcer Quiryn seems keen to return you to the Grand City without delay. The remaining enforcers will finish packing up their equipment to load onto the second carriage which will depart later.'

Tharian visualised the scene the king was describing for him. If he were to be escorted directly from this cell to the carriage, to be forced to sit opposite a powerful enforcer whilst unarmed, his options would be exceptionally limited. But knowing that it would be only he and that enforcer within the carriage gave him some comfort — one enforcer would always be less dangerous than more. That said, three insurmountable obstacles were not much different to one.

'Do you have any idea why they want to take me to the Grand City? I thought enforcers preferred executions with an audience.'

The king shook his head. 'They discussed that, but that part of the conversation was taken in private. Although, as they left my dining hall, they mentioned the Valivelle family several times – could that mean anything?'

With a sigh and a shake of his head, Tharian felt knocked back several paces. It was clear already that Enforcer Quiryn knew about his actions in County Bryn, but if their intent was to take him back and hand him over to the Valivelle family, an immediate public execution would be a mercy.

Tharian smiled nervously. 'Maybe so. What about my sword – do you know where they're keeping it?'

'That will be stored on the second carriage.'

Tharian's shoulders dropped. 'That is not helpful at all.'

'I apologise. If I could get it to you I would but the enforcers would know that either I or my staff intervened.'

'No, my King, you misunderstand me. That wasn't a complaint at you. Your information is valuable, you have already done so much just by speaking with me.'

'There is one other thing that might be of interest to you.'

Tharian glanced at him side-on. 'Oh?'

'Your Shifter has been sighted.'

'Ombra?' Tharian clutched at the bars and almost pushed his face all the way through the gap. 'Where is she?'

'My sentry guards inform me that the animal flew to the west after your arrest. It was not seen again until the early hours of this morning. She has been circling the keep for most of the day, keeping her distance.'

'Now *that* is *very* helpful,' said Tharian. He rubbed his hands together. 'If Ombra has made her way back then this might just tip things back in my favour.'

'How so?' asked the king, his head lifting and eyes glistening.

He didn't know for certain how Ombra's return would help him, but he knew it would. Tharian smirked. 'I'll spare you the details, my King. The less you know, the more genuinely you can deny any involvement.'

'I suppose that makes sense,' said King Thorius. He tilted his head to Tharian, and his tone lightened. 'That beast you travel with is remarkable. I have read about Shifters, but never seen one with my own eyes. Nor have I seen a cliffhawk of that size.'

'Her form is based on a Ferallian cliffhawk. There are bigger beasts than that overseas, I assure you.'

The king chuckled. 'Perhaps once this is over, I can see these great beasts for myself.'

The two smirked at each other. Tharian then hummed and turned serious. 'I believe that opportunity will come, your majesty. I think there is a way I can escape the enforcers, though I will need to ask two things from you. I appreciate its more than I have any right to ask.'

The king gestured with one hand and shrugged. 'With the way this is going, I think it worth the risk. Tell me what you need.'

'The first part is simple. Let the enforcers proceed with their plans to take me away. Do not try to interfere, even if you think it might help.'

Nodding, the king hummed two notes of approval.

'The second part may prove a little more challenging. Once I am in the first carriage and we are on our way to the Grand City, could you try to slow down the departure of the second carriage? I need as much time alone with Enforcer Quiryn as I can get.'

'I think that could be arranged. The Elheim command my staff to help with mounting supplies upon their carriages, I will oversee their work personally and try to slow things down.'

Tharian couldn't help but grin deeply. He would find a way out of this mess and get back to the Trade Quarters to deliver the good news. Ombra would help him, he was sure of it.

The king extended a hand to Tharian. 'If that is all, I will wish you good luck now. I must return, I've been gone too long.'

Shaking the king's warm hand, Tharian was surprised that such a delicate, pampered hand would offer a firm grip. But it did. The warmth, the grip and the gentle smile of the king filled Tharian with the confidence he needed to steel himself for the coming hours.

The king then went on his way.

Tharian's brows rose as another thought came to him and he called for the king in a whispered shout. 'One last thing, your majesty.'—the king looked back—'If you see them store my sword onto their carriage, that would be the perfect time to create a distraction. You may then see what a Shifter can do with your own eyes.'

The king looked confused at first, but then nodded. 'I'll do what I can.'

***

The Last of the Magi

The first of the carriages slowly wheeled into the courtyard backwards. Ferenir guards were hunkered down at its sides, pushing the vehicle into position while enforcers used lashings of Arcana to compel the feyren to awkwardly pace backward against their wishes. Enforcer Quiryn watched on, pleased to see the work carried out competently.

The silver-maned feyren roared and snarled while thrashing its head left and right, trying to see what was going on behind it. The wooden joists and leather straps connecting it to the carriage greatly restricted its movement.

Quiryn found the feyren amusing. *Even the wildest of beasts can be brought to heel with Arcana,* she mused. She looked over her shoulder to where the fugitive stood at a side door, surrounded by the king's armed guard. *How docile they become without their fangs.*

The king stepped out into the courtyard from the keep's main doors. Enforcer Quiryn noticed him and smothered a laugh. *Tamed creatures, all of them.*

With the courtyard gates propped wide open, the salty sea breeze from the Ferenir coast blew in and span around her, distracting her from her thoughts. The smell was offensive. It was nothing like the perfumed, fragranced aromas of the Grand City which disguised their own sea-drift.

Her eyes fixed upon the carriage door as the vehicle slowly reached its parking spot in the middle of the courtyard. Her fingers writhed at her side as she eagerly awaited the chance to return to the Grand City. Ferenir was not unpleasant, but it was simple and lacked the comforts and pristine finish she was used to.

The carriage stopped. The enforcers assisting came back into the keep to carry on packing their supplies.

'I shall take my leave, King Thorius,' Quiryn said without taking her eyes off the carriage. 'You can expect my next visit to be sooner than usual. The presence of the fugitive has distracted us from the full rigour of our usual inspection.'

The king stepped closer, coming into view on her right, with a member of his staff rushing forward at his instruction to open the carriage door. 'I trust your stay in Ferenir was nonetheless comfortable and productive?'

Quiryn drew her long, blonde hair behind her ears and then removed her gloves, tucking them into her pockets. She put a foot on the first step at the carriage door and then turned outwards, intentionally avoiding a direct glance to the king. 'It was what it was. I will be pleased to take this criminal out of your territory – that is, of course, one of the protections your payment of the Arcane Tax affords to you and your people. Speaking of which...' She looked over to the fugitive.

The armed guard of Ferenir Keep brought the prisoner closer to the carriage. Quiryn looked down at him. The black-haired man was draped in his dark green coat, covered in patches of dust and dirt. He met her gaze without so much as a flinch, though his eyes were narrowed slightly, and his head held slightly low, no doubt a symptom of being relegated to a dark dungeon for several days, starved of sunlight.

Disgusting, Quiryn thought. *I would be doing the world a favour if I put this one down, here and now.* Standard protocol was clear, as a senior enforcer she had the authority to execute this criminal – his possession of an illegal runeblade was enough to justify his death under Grand City decree – but this was a sensitive situation. By all accounts, this man met the description of the fugitive from County Bryn. The very same who brought down Illian Valivelle with her own Arcana. The event was unprecedented, and this man needed to be questioned properly...

...and the Valivelle family were the chancellor's left hand.

The enforcer responsible for bringing the fugitive into custody would earn the respect of not only the chancellor himself, but the Valivelles too. This man was a prize worth bending protocol for. Quiryn grinned at the thought of it. This prize might even secure her the role of high imperator or one of the coveted senior adviser positions in her later years.

'Bring him forward,' she said. She ducked into the carriage and took her seat at the front-end. Quiryn raised a hand, halting the guards as her prisoner appeared at the door. 'Hands forward.'

The prisoner looked overhead for a moment and then sighed. He

The Last of the Magi

brought his hands forward, palms open, and turned his hands over a few times.

Quiryn waved two fingers in the air, using the gesture to focus the aim of her concentrated Command of Arcana. The prisoner gasped as his wrists were forced together and bound by a rush of Arcane air, looping in a figure of eight.

Pleased with the results, and the reaction, she curled a finger and then the prisoner was pushed into the carriage. He took the seat opposite and sat in silence as the carriage door was slammed shut.

***

The warmth of the sunlight and the cushion of the carriage seat offered no real comfort. It was nice however to feel the cool sea breeze, which made a nice change from the stale dungeon air. Though Tharian was at last free of his cell, his new accommodation was far from an improvement. He rubbed at his tired, light-deprived eyelids with his bound hands, taking care not to sheer his face with the rushing Arcane air around his wrists.

He had seen her. Ombra. Just before he boarded the carriage. A quick glance skyward confirmed that Ombra was circling the keep. She would have seen him, just as he had seen her – she noticed everything. He called out to her in his mind, as he had in all times before when he needed her. She would hear him, somehow. She always did.

The carriage jerked forward and Tharian winced as the momentum made him jab at his own eyes. Blinking hard, he noticed the rattle of carriage wheels against cobbled stone, and then the overpowering scent of perfume which either came from the enforcer or the carriage itself. Enforcer Quiryn was staring at him with disapproval – and it seemed that in his sensory overload he had completely missed that she had been speaking to him.

She spoke again, harshly. 'Am I disturbing your daydreaming?'

Tharian lowered his hands and straightened his back against his seat. He had to awkwardly hover his arms over his lap as the bluster of the Arcana pushed his hands away from his legs. The Arcana felt cold and slightly abrasive as it rushed over his exposed wrists. If it stayed at this potency for long, he worried it would cause wind burns over time.

Trying not to think about that for now, he looked at the enforcer and waited for her to go on.

'Things are going to be very uncomfortable for you at the Grand City if you don't cooperate with me now. It will save everyone's time – perhaps even your life, for a time – if you tell me why you came here and where you obtained that beast and blade.'

Tharian didn't blink. He just shrugged and looked out of the window briefly.

'Nothing?' Quiryn asked. 'Well how about an easier one then. Where did you come from?'

'Midhaven,' Tharian said dryly in response, keeping his eye-line fixed on the vista of Ferenir, and the coast beyond, as the carriage started the slow descent down the winding hillside path. His eyes lingered for a moment on a small stone plinth at the edge of the path, laced with flowers. It was gone from his view before he could consider it properly.

Suddenly Tharian was lunged forward out of his seat, pulled by the Arcana that served as his shackles. He landed on his knees in the footwell, but he quickly gained a footing and went to push himself back.

But he couldn't move back, the strength of her Arcana was beyond anything his muscles could overcome. She had him locked by the wrists in this subdued position.

Quiryn leaned forward, looking him in the eyes. 'Do you think me simple? Midhaven is in ruins. Nobody has lived there in a generation.'

Tharian bared his teeth at the enforcer. The carriage wasn't even a third of the way down the hill. His fear told him to try and escape before the situation worsened, but with the carriage still being so close to the other enforcers, and still within Ferenir's border, his instincts said now was not the time to act.

'Perhaps your predecessors were not all that thorough in their destruction?'

Quiryn scoffed. 'You're pathetic. Why do people like you resist us so vehemently at every opportunity. Surely you see that things

The Last of the Magi

would be easier if you only learned to cooperate.'

Tharian shook his head in disbelief. 'Accepting Elheim oppression will never be *easier*. You have done nothing but crush those who stand up for their independence and disable those who don't fill your coffers with their hard-earned coin.'

Quiryn laughed in Tharian's face and then leaned back, resting an arm over the back of the seat. 'You see only what you choose to see. There is a reason that so many of the farmsteads, villages and hamlets of the Eastern Expanse have willingly joined with us. They are not so simple-minded. *They* see that our work is about much more than mere wealth and power.'

'Or maybe they only appeared to join willingly because the alternative was destitution and destruction?'

'You truly don't understand, do you?' Quiryn asked, with what sounded like genuine curiosity. 'It fascinates me that Asturians are so blinkered to things beyond their immediate, personal experiences.'

Tharian wanted to bite back. He was tired of the lies the Elheim weaved to justify their acts. But the enforcer's expression was peculiar, quizzical perhaps, so he held his tongue.

Quiryn continued. 'It is not my job to educate those who fail to pay attention to Asturian history, but maybe I can make you realise the gravity of your ignorance before your punishments are served upon you. I presume you know nothing of the Arcane Guild?'

She was right, but he didn't want to give her the satisfaction of knowing that. 'Just say what you have to say,' he replied.

'The Arcane Guild was formed nearly two centuries ago by the wealthiest families of Asturia. They came together with a common purpose – to ensure that our fair country could grow, prosper and develop free from the influence of foreign forces, or the tilted strength of their magics.'

With a flourish, Quiryn pushed Tharian back to his seat. He slammed with some force into the cushions, feeling the solid surface behind them hit against his spine. He winced, but he listened on as Quiryn continued.

'Asturia has been the victim of no insignificant number of tyrannical regimes in its history. Oligar was the most recent – the most significant by far, but by no means has it been the only one. Yet it's the only one Asturian historians care to remember. Through religious doctrine they turned people into mindless puppets, ever willing to follow their mystical faith to whatever ends were demanded of them. And then, of course, came the Wildcallers, those Magic-wielding Awoken from Feralland. Magi in all but name. They came here preaching that the Oligari were wrong and that we needed to be free of their grasp. And how did they go about pursuing that unsuccessful goal?' she paused like a teacher awaiting a response from her students, though her tone was clearly rhetorical. 'They infiltrated Lions' Rest. They would have used Magic to eradicate Oligar, and then – in the vacuum of power left in their wake – the Awoken would have assumed control. They would have claimed it was in our best interests, and maybe, just maybe, they may have achieved some good. But they would have simply filled the boots of the Oligari. One regime of magical tyranny in place of the other.

'Alas, they failed.' Quiryn sighed and spread her hands in the air. 'But the tale did not end there, did it? The Magi of Asturia then appeared. They *freed* us. Bravo – happy days for us all. No'—she snapped—'the Magi then became the next uncontrolled force at play. Yes, they may have had a certain gift for assisting the Outer Counties with their harvests and agriculture, and their ability to seemingly pacify conflict was without compare, but anyone observing with a critical eye would have asked this: what would the Magi have done if another force invaded this country?'

What would they have done? Tharian considered. As he considered the question, the words from one of Greycloak's old stories rang through his thoughts as if he was hearing it fresh in the moment:

The Magi devoted their lives to natural order. They were gifted with great power, but that power came at a cost. They served that power above all else, and were thus loathe to interfere in politics, trade or matters of law unless natural balance was at risk.

The Magi had indeed been instrumental in the downfall of Oligar, that much was irrefutable in Tharian's mind – but that intervention was only spurred by the sudden appearance of the

The Last of the Magi

Violet Affliction which threatened the lives of all Asturians. Aside from that bold interference, it was not the way of the Magi to take a stance for or against a cause. Some societies did seek advice from Magi who acted as neutral counsel, such as the Magi-advisers of Ferenir, but such advice was given under the caveat of that neutrality. Conflict was something they wantonly avoided.

They would have likely stood aside, Tharian surmised. It was a truth of their nature, that he knew might cause some hindrance to this movement against the Grand City, but that was why the armies of Ferenir and the Trade Quarters were instrumental in the plan.

'The Magi would not have fought for us,' Quiryn continued further. 'Not as an army, by any stretch of the imagination. Those few that might have stood against an invading force would have been cut down like wheat to the scythe. Yet, as the Magi in Asturia grew in number, it became increasingly apparent that if the Magi ever were to turn against us, they could so easily assume control over each of our weak, insular settlements clinging so desperately to independence. The Magi were not warriors, but even *their* Magic could overthrow our fragmented structures of governance with barely an exertion if that was their wish.

'The situation was untenable in Asturia, so the Arcane Guild sought to create a forum to ensure that the rich and powerful families of Asturia could maintain their earned positions in society and stand together as one, united against the Magi or any other new force that attempted dominion over our country. Yet one thing quickly became clear: wealth would never be enough on its own to protect Asturia. For as long as the myriad forms of thaumaturgy exist in our world, the Arcane Guild would never be able to achieve its goal of truly protecting Asturian sovereignty. So, when the Guild had finally amassed enough wealth to build their own city, those affluent families joined as one – becoming the Elheim – and they worked to find a way to add magic into their arsenal. Never again would Asturia fall under another's shadow.'

Tharian felt his heart race. This bombardment of information was mostly new to him. Neither Greycloak nor Traykin had ever talked about the Arcane Guild, the origin of the Elheim society or its motives. None he had met in his travels had mentioned it either.

But Quiryn had gone to some great lengths to paint the Elheim as a force designed to protect their country, with more detail and specificity than some of even Greycloak's tales could offer. Though even with this detail, and the confidence with which the enforcer delivered it, Tharian couldn't reconcile these lofty altruistic ideals with the present-day actions of the enforcers.

Tharian laughed at himself. He had actually considered the truth of her words for a moment. But these were just more Elheim lies. He needed to remember the *smaller* details for once. 'And I suppose you want me to believe me that the destruction of Midhaven and Brynfall were for the betterment of Asturia?' he asked calmly, flatly.

Quiryn leaned against the carriage wall, pressing two fingers to the bridge of her nose. 'So unsophisticated. You are not listening. The only way that Asturia can continue to grow, free from the threat of another invading force, is to unite. That unity must be absolute, and those who refuse to see that would be the first to fall during an invasion. We cannot risk offering our enemies a free quarter on our lands for the sake of some transient ideals of independence.'

Anger bubbled within Tharian's gut. He clenched his fists. 'And that is how you justify killing.' His determination to bring an end to the Grand City multiplied tenfold. Only an Elheim could justify the complete obliteration of entire settlements as being in the pursuance of some greater good. That 'good' being dictated and enforced by the Elheim themselves.

'I was right. You truly understand nothing. Use what few days you have left to consider what might happen if a force from overseas invaded us tomorrow. Would the factions of Asturia be able to loosen that steadfast grip over their independence to stand together against a common enemy as equals? Could that be achieved without some unifying banner flying overhead?'

His anger tempered slightly. Though questions formed in the back of his mind, about the Arcane Guild and the true intentions of the Grand City, the disgust and contempt he felt for Quiryn and her depiction of the Elheim was pushed aside as a smugness crept in. Because he knew there was a fatal error in the Elheim's position.

The people of Asturia would unite, he told himself. *It's already*

The Last of the Magi

happening.

Quiryn said nothing more, and Tharian had no words for her either. Frustrating though the conversation may have been, there was one redeeming quality to it in his mind: they had made progress on their journey during her diatribe.

Tharian spotted a sentry tower from the corner of his eye, passing by the carriage window. They were at the edge of the city. Soon they would be safely away from the other enforcers and beyond the reach of any Ferenir guard commanded to follow their orders.

Just a little further.

Enforcer Quiryn had apparently lost interest in their discussion. She stared off to the horizon where the faintest outline of the Grand City could be seen. There was little detail to make out from this distance, but the Elheim Palace stood out for miles, due to its sheer height and it's shining façade of marble and light stone.

As Tharian also looked that way, another flaw in Quiryn's account of Elheim history came to mind. If their objectives were truly so selfless, and beyond mere wealth and power, how did they explain the lavishness and luxury with which they lived – and the way they lorded that over all other Asturians.

Another sentry tower went by. Tharian shuffled over to the window and checked his surroundings. That was the last tower. The wood panels that marked out the road were gone, and the carriage rolled into the thicker grass of the Eastern Expanse. There was nothing but villages, farms, and fields from here to the Grand City.

It was now or never.

Tharian slowed his breathing and centred himself. He focused on the rustling of the carriage wheels through the grass and the rhythmic pounding of the feyren's mighty paws. That brought him a stillness of mind to concentrate on his next movements carefully.

Twisting in his seat, he looked out the back window. The sentry towers were shrinking away, and he couldn't see any sign of the next carriage making its way down the hill yet. The king must have managed to slow them.

'Time to get out of here,' Tharian whispered, and he repeated the words in his mind in the hope that Ombra would be listening from somewhere up above. He shuffled to the edge of his seat, reaching for the carriage door despite his shackles.

Quiryn bolted upright. She pushed Tharian back again. 'What do you think you're doing? You're not going anywhere.'

Tharian winced as he pried his hands forward again, pushing hard against the force of Quiryn's Arcana. She had shoved his wrists into his stomach with enough force to leave him feeling bruised. The Arcana around his wrists felt like sandpaper to his skin. Despite the pain, he reached out again. 'If it's all the same to you.'

'Stop!'

Another wave of Arcana lashed against him, this time much stronger than the last. The wind blustered from his wrists and spread to envelop his whole body, locking him against his seat, pressing hard against his chest.

Tharian gasped for air. This was not just a restraint; she was crushing him. It felt like the carriage had upturned and was now on top of him. He tried to draw breath through the force of her power, but it was too strong.

His heart rushed at first, and his pulse pounded in his ears. The more he struggled, the more he could feel his heartbeat become slower and more laboured. He tried desperately to find some calm before panic overcame him completely.

I need you... now, he called out in his mind.

Quiryn's voice was faint to him now, but he heard her speak. Just barely.

'I was content to make the rest of this journey in silence. If resistance is the path you choose, I will not allow you the luxury of consciousness.'

Tharian couldn't breathe at all. His eyes were heavy as the weight upon his chest became too much to bear. His body tried to convulse; his lungs screamed for relief.

His vision was just a blur, so he closed his eyes. His other senses failed quickly thereafter, with his hearing being the last to dim. He could just make out Quiryn's curses at him until the words no longer made sense. Only the distant echoes of his heartbeat remained.

A sensation, much like a breeze, brushed over him just as his arms dropped limply at his side.

Chapter 36

Steps in Opposite Directions

Looking out onto his courtyard, King Tyraean Thorius leaned on his hand against the stone doorway. His fingers probed the grooves of the stone as he stared at the back of the second carriage. Fortunately, without the guidance of their leader, the enforcers had not manoeuvred this carriage with the same expeditious discipline as the first.

The enforcers were now moving sluggishly through the keep, strolling between the guest rooms in the west wing to his right, and the reception hall behind him, where their travel cases were being filled by his staff. Tyraean looked over his shoulder, seeing the cushioned lockboxes laid open on every available surface – covering tables, filling armchairs, and strewn across the floor too.

Even the lockboxes, a simple container for carrying their essentials and travel supplies, were padded with quilted fabric to add luxury where none was needed. But the design matched the carriage, and Tyraean assumed that was the only purpose of its redundant decoration. He wondered woefully whether that was what the Arcane Tax money was being spent on. His people's money.

Tyraean snapped from his idle musings as one of his staff came dashing out to load a container onto the carriage. He winced a little at the man's speed. They were doing well to work slowly, though not *so* slowly as to attract the notice of the enforcers, but they were still making progress faster than he hoped.

He rubbed his hands together as he watched everyone at work. Whenever an enforcer emerged from one of the corridors to either peruse the reception hall or check on the carriage, Tyraean straightened himself and nodded respectfully to detract attention from his nervous behaviours. He was aware of those behaviours. His court attendants tried from an early age to teach those out of him, without success.

Or maybe it had been successful. As a child, one of the butlers

The Last of the Magi

assigned to look after him after his father's death would comment on how he wore his emotions heavily in his expression. But that was to be expected. He'd lost his father to the rage of the enforcers at such an early age, he had much emotion to display, and great reason to be nervous and unsteady in his kingship. Although that nervousness never left him, not many beyond his private advisers seemed to notice it. Maybe that had been the point all along; not to eliminate the emotion but to learn how to better manage that which lay beneath the surface.

Again, the king pulled himself from his thoughts. Yet another by-product of his nervous disposition: over-thinking.

Tyraean clutched at the side of his cape and marched into the reception hall. The warm, fireplace-lit room was laden with comfortable loungers and high-backed armchairs, and the smell of perfectly ripened fruit blended with the scented wood that stoked the flames. Some of his courtly advisers were gathered at the back of the hall, around a popular mantle laden with hunting trophies, trying to subtly watch what was going on with the enforcers. Failing in the subtlety part of that. He didn't blame them for enjoying the comforts of this hall, however. This was a room for all to enjoy when they had the time free from their other duties, the king included. The presence of Elheim, however, was a dampener to the sanctuary the hall offered its occupants.

It's almost over, he mused, *they are almost out the door. Then I can look at this room without dread.*

Tyraean looked at the heaps of clothes, travel equipment and personal effects that had been sorted, cleaned, and laid out across the loungers. He kept Tharian's request at the front of his mind: he needed to slow the second carriage down, for as long as possible. His head of staff had done all she reasonably could already. He needed to do something himself.

He brought a finger across his lips and placed his other hand at his hip. He paced around as his staff weaved in and out, each person startling him before he realised they weren't enforcers.

As he turned about the room, he spotted a pile of enforcer uniforms neatly folded into a pristine tower of white. They were balanced on a footrest. *Quite a precarious pile,* he lied to himself, though it sounded convincing enough in his head.

Looking about for any peering eyes, he noticed the group at the back of the hall looking back fleetingly. They all turned away when they noticed the king looking directly at them. With all witnesses otherwise preoccupied, he swept his arm through the pile and sent uniforms careening across the floor.

He clapped and called for a member of staff immediately. A young woman in a brown apron emerged, clutching a box at her hip. 'Yes, your majesty?'

'One of these piles has fallen, and these enforcer uniforms have all been on the ground. I'm afraid they will need checking over and refolding.' He spoke loudly in the hope that an enforcer might overhear him and be reassured that things were still in-hand.

An enforcer did then emerge at his side, startling him again as he didn't hear their approach. The enforcer groaned. 'Can your servants not handle such simple tasks?'

'I suspect the breeze took them, enforcer, I apologise. With all the keep gates open this area is prone to becoming a wind tunnel at times. Fret not, my staff will see to it. They will make sure your uniforms are in best condition.'

The enforcer nodded his approval. 'Good – no harm done then.'

Tyraean smiled at the young woman tending to the pile and she rushed around to pile the uniforms into her box. She did so quickly and diligently. The king bit the inside of his lip. He feared that had not bought much time at all.

He heard the footsteps of the enforcer leaving the hall, so he swept around and moved to pursue him.

'Excuse me, enforcer?' He called out. *I had best think of something worthwhile to say.*

The enforcer stopped and looked back over his shoulder. 'Yes?'

Tyraean smiled and met the enforcer at the corner, using the time to think. Fortunately, something did come to mind. 'Please forgive my curiosity, but I must ask. The weapon you confiscated from that strange man – Enforcer Quiryn seemed most concerned about it. What was it?'

Turning around fully, the enforcer arched a brow. 'An illegally enchanted weapon. A runeblade, to be precise. Why do you ask?'

The Last of the Magi

The king closed the gap between them and lowered his voice. 'I have never seen one for myself. May I see it before you depart?'

'No,' the enforcer said curtly. 'It is locked away. Artefacts of its kind are dangerous and are to be disposed of safely as soon as is practicable.'

The enforcer twisted as if to turn away but stepped back into his eyeline. 'Yes, of course. Although, I must confess I would not readily be able to recognise such a thing if another appeared in Ferenir. I would like to know how to identify one so I can ensure any others of its kind are confiscated if found.'

The enforcer glanced through the corridor window, to the carriage outside. His bottom lip tightened. He looked to be considering his options. 'Your cooperation is welcomed, your majesty. I will find out where it's being stored. A cursory glance should be all you need – runed weapons are very distinctive.'

Marching away, the enforcer went to the second door down the corridor, leaned through the threshold and called to another within. 'Angellia, where are we storing the runeblade?'

'I'm not sure,' she replied, though her voice was faint from the king's position. 'It's not in any of these boxes. It might have been placed on the carriage already.'

The enforcer pulled back into the corridor and squinted through the window to the carriage again. 'Perhaps. Thank you.' He then marched towards and then past the king. 'Follow me, your majesty.'

Tyraean followed diligently.

***

That breeze, where had it come from?

The carriage windows weren't open, and the enforcer's Arcana had been controlling the air within the confined space. So how could there be a breeze?

The question flashed through Tharian's mind. And that made him realise he was still conscious, only just, clinging to the edge of lucidity.

He sucked in a single, long breath. It was difficult, but he managed it. He then gasped for air and coughed violently as his lungs made the most of their restored freedom. His arms and legs felt heavy, but the weight of the Arcana was gone. He willed his body to move and gradually it did. He was no longer restrained. It took time for his strength to return.

Opening his eyes, Tharian saw a blur of green before him, and a moving white shape in the centre of his eyeline. Though his head hung low, he looked as far as he could to either side and could at least recognise the shape and colour of the carriage walls. Turning forward again he still saw the green horizon, broken only by the white shape.

He blinked hard, then did so again until his vision finally started to clear. The white blur was not the crisp suit of Enforcer Quiryn – it was the feyren. And the green backdrop was the Eastern Expanse. The front of the carriage was gone, as was the enforcer.

Scrambling to the ripped-open front of the carriage, stumbling over his half-numb legs, Tharian ran his hand along the jagged edges where the carriage now abruptly ended. The wooden framing had been torn to shreds by giant claws that left track marks through what was left of it.

Before Tharian could investigate further, he heard a distant scream. It became louder and closer with each moment. Looking beyond the feyren, and following its upward gaze, Tharian found the source of the sound. A blur of white dropped from above and slammed hard into the grass with a crunch. The screaming stopped instantly.

Tharian shuddered. Even the feyren startled. Enforcer Quiryn had dropped from the sky and now laid motionless.

There was no need to wonder what happened to the enforcer, as Ombra swept down in her cliffhawk form and landed near the carriage a moment later, staring with her piercing amber eyes between Tharian and the feyren.

A smile crept across Tharian's lips as he climbed cautiously out of the carriage opening, taking care to not disturb the feyren as he crept past. The beast sniffed and watched him, but it stayed calm.

He walked through the grass and approached Quiryn, crouching at her side. The once powerful enforcer was frail and broken. He could see movement at her chest. Somehow, she had survived the

The Last of the Magi

fall, but her breathing was shallow.

Tharian nodded to Ombra, smirking at her. He owed her for this, and she would not let him forget it, he was sure of that.

Once again, an enforcer had been beaten. Their over-confidence and illusion of indomitability made them ill-prepared for unexpected attacks. She must have been caught so off-guard that she couldn't prepare any Arcana to protect herself.

Ombra crept forward and curled her large beak towards Quiryn and chirped as the sharp point approached the enforcer's chest.

'No.' Tharian gently pushed her neck away. 'You've done more than enough.' Ombra's cliffhawk form was huge, she towered over him by at least half his height. She would have been able to kill the enforcer without much effort. That wasn't necessary. Though, as he stood over the pitiful body of the enforcer, he did wonder whether one day he would need to take the life of an enforcer to defend himself. He hoped it wouldn't come to that. He was more than willing to fight to defend but intentionally killing was a different matter.

Tharian pulled himself away from Quiryn's body. He waved for Ombra's attention and then gestured back to Ferenir, pointing to the keep atop the hill. 'There is something else you can do for me. They have something that belongs to us.' He pictured the runeblade in his mind.

Ombra chirped and clucked her beak, she understood what he was saying. As always. She stretched to her full height and unfurled her wide, black wings. She whipped the air and then sprung up to take flight.

She wouldn't need long. While she was away, Tharian was stuck in the Eastern Expanse with nowhere to go. He looked at Quiryn again and then to the feyren. While the former remained still in the grass, the latter eyed him and sniffed with its great, pulsing nostrils. The beast was calm.

Tharian shook his head at the feyren. 'How long have you had to serve the Elheim against your will?' he asked.

The beast shook a fly away from its ear and its silver mane waved back and forth against the gentle breeze. It made a rolling, rattling sound from deep in its throat. Unlike Ombra, there was no understanding in its eyes, his words didn't reach it the way they reached her but he had spent enough time around the beasts of Feralland to know it meant him no harm.

Tharian approached slowly, holding his hands open at his sides. He wanted to show the creature that he wasn't a threat. He maintained eye contact with the feyren as he inched closer and closer. The lions of the north coast were known for their ferocity and aggressive behaviour. The Elheim had apparently managed to breed a bit of that primal behaviour out of their white-haired feyren, but the beast's low snarl as he moved in made it clear that its defensive instincts weren't completely gone.

The feyren flashed its enormous fangs and upgraded its snarl to a full growl. Tharian stopped in his tracks and tried to coax the beast to stay calm. 'Easy, easy. I'm just trying to help.'

It narrowed its eyes at him and then slowly closed its mouth.

Tharian moved forward again, this time reaching out towards the feyren's mane, taking great care to avoid any sharp or sudden movements.

The feyren stretched its head forward and sniffed his open hand. Whatever it could smell must have put it at ease, as it relaxed and allowed Tharian to run his fingers through its mane. It was incredibly soft to the touch. Comforting, even. And the feyren enjoyed it too, as it pushed its head against his hand. Gentle though it may have felt, Tharian knew the creature had been groomed for the sake of its presentability rather than the feyren's comfort. Pampered, as all things from the Grand City were. The beast relaxed more as he roughed up its mane and scratched at its head. It looked a bit more dishevelled as a result, but the feyren purred with satisfaction.

'You don't belong in these restraints,' he said. The feyren deserved freedom from Elheim oppression just the same as anyone else. Setting it free now would be another small victory, and all victories were welcomed in this fight. Before he set about loosening the beast's restraints he wondered where it might go from here. Arboreta was the nearest natural haven that wasn't just open fields. Scenic though it was, that wouldn't be a suitable environment for a feyren. But the Cartographer Mountains that stretched north all the

The Last of the Magi

way to Lions' Rest might be. The black-haired lions made the northern cliffs and surrounding grasslands their home. He had no idea whether a feyren would do well amongst the feral lions with which it shared a heritage, but it was better than serving the whims of the Elheim.

'Let's get you out of this.' Tharian moved down the beast's side as it watched him eagerly. He traced the straps of leather which attached it by a harness to the carriage, and he found where those straps fastened to the wooden joists extending forward from the vehicle's flanks. Luckily, they were fastened only by a meddle of knots rather than anything that would need tools to extract. Tharian got to work unravelling it.

The first binds came free. The feyren shuffled, reacting instantly to the range of movement it had just gained. It didn't even hesitate as Tharian moved around its front to the other side. In fact, it thrust its head at him as if to nudge him along.

As soon as the other bindings dropped to the ground, the feyren lunged forward and embraced its new-found freedom. It cleared a distance from the carriage in seconds and stretched its legs, back and neck before craning back to look expectantly at Tharian.

Tharian laced his arm around the wooden joist and shooed the feyren. 'You're free. Off you go.' He pointed north. Instead, it approached him, head held low, presenting its mane for him again. Tharian chuckled and scratched at its head with both hands. 'Oh, it's like that, is it? Just a bit more then.'

The feyren purred with such volume and force that Tharian could feel it rattling through his arms. As he worked his way around the animal, giving it more affection than he suspected it had ever experienced in its life, the feyren dropped onto its side and lifted a paw onto his arm.

'Yeah, yeah, ok. I get it, you like it. But you are very heavy!' He had to wrap both arms around the paw to lift it back down onto the floor.

Eventually he stepped back and flicked a hand through the air.

'That's enough. Off you go.'

The feyren got up and nuzzled against Tharian affectionately. It then turned away and sprinted off across the field, heading to the rocky cliffs to the north as directed.

Tharian watched on, smiling. The beast ran through the fields like an infant animal enjoying its first taste of autonomy. Perhaps this was the first time it could properly run free. After it bounded about for a time, it veered west and looked to be choosing to travel along the roots of the mountain. Its instincts clearly recognised some sense of home there. Hopefully it would find everything it needed to survive out in the wilderness. If it found its way back to its native kin in the north, it would surely learn to adapt in time.

Tharian turned back towards Ferenir, where Ombra was swooping in wide motions around the keep.

***

The runeblade was magnificent. Far more intricate than even the ceremonial sword he had to wear during official functions. The metal of the blade itself was dark blue, almost purplish, assumedly coloured that way by some artificial means as no metal used in Ferenir held that shade naturally. Even its shape was unique. The blade was mostly straight, like a regular longsword, but it had small, jagged spikes in symmetrical points near the hilt.

And yet, even that was not its most interesting feature. The flat of the blade had three small shapes etched into it that looked like lettering.

Those markings, according to the enforcer, were the 'runes' which gave the blade its name.

'It is not the blade itself that is outlawed by Grand City decree – we are concerned with these markings,' the enforcer continued. 'These runes can contain and redeploy magic at will. I would be surprised if you found anything like this in your kingdom. Runecrafting is an outlawed profession and we have already carried out several raids to gather and destroy artefacts of its kind.'

Tyraean only listened with half an ear. He wasn't truly concerned about the backstory to runed weaponry this was just a stalling tactic. While he indulged the enforcer, and took genuine interest in the weapon's unique appearance, his focus was on what to do next. He located Tharian's weapon, as asked, but what was he

The Last of the Magi

supposed to do with that information?

In his idle musings, he hadn't noticed that the enforcer had stopped talking. Their eyes met and the king nodded and made sounds to suggest he had been listening intently.

'Now I understand,' he said. 'This is a distinctive thing to behold. Hopefully we will see no more of its kind, but I will instruct the guard to keep an eye out nonetheless.'

Slamming the lockbox shut and refastening the buckles holding it onto the carriage, the enforcer nodded. 'Good. We will be leaving shortly, so I hope all preparations are nearly concluded.' The enforcer then left him at the carriage.

Tyraean stared at the lockbox. He then remembered the other part of Tharian's request, to cause a distraction once the runeblade was located.

But what kind of distraction? The king considered. He couldn't go rushing back into the reception hall to tip over more uniforms or disrupt his staff's work – that would be far too obvious. Besides, the remaining enforcers and a group of his staff were gathered in the hall now as the preparations were drawing to a finish.

A sound caught his attention from above. He looked skyward just in time to catch a fleeting glimpse of giant wings lapping overhead. The Shifter. Whatever it was he needed to do, now must have been the time to do it.

The king patted himself down and turned about on the spot, searching for something that might keep the enforcers' attentions away from the carriage for a time. They would surely recognise the giant beast overhead if they stepped into the courtyard now.

His blood chilled as the enforcer from moments earlier came strolling back towards him, escorting one of his staff carrying a lockbox. Once again, Tyraean acted before his ideas had fully taken form – it worked for him last time – and he stumbled into the enforcer's path.

'I've just had a thought,' he started, smiling nervously as his eyes darted around for inspiration. Over the enforcer's shoulder he spotted some bottles set about on one of the tables. 'The last time you visited, your chancellor ordered a crate of Ferynshore Ale. Now, that was some time ago, so he must have gone through that by now. Perhaps he would like another?'

The enforcer rolled his shoulders. 'Perhaps he would. What has inspired this gratuity, your majesty?'

'Here, here, let me take this,' the king said as he coerced the lockbox from the young man beside the enforcer, balancing it onto his own arms, much to the man's horror. He winced as he realised that his pampered, unused muscles struggled to manage its weight. 'I just thought that considering the *misunderstanding* over this criminal being found entering my courtyard, a gesture of goodwill might not go amiss.'

The enforcer smirked and he shifted his weight to one side. 'Enforcer Quiryn would have loved to hear you speak those words.'

'I imagine so. Please excuse any coldness or lack of hospitality I have directed your way during your stay here. The burdens of leadership can be taxing, and everything that has happened of late has thrown me into disarray.'

'I understand.'

'What do you say then, enforcer?' Tyraean asked. But before he gave the enforcer a chance to attempt a response, he leaned in with a grin. 'Perhaps you could even say it was *your* suggestion?'

The enforcer folded his arms and stared blankly into the courtyard. 'Now *that* is an idea I like.'

Tyraean shuffled sideways to step back into his eyeline, blocking his view of the courtyard. 'I thought you might. Let's discuss it with one of my runners, they can get you a crate purchased and brought up here before you know it. You'll hardly notice the delay.'

The enforcer hummed an approving note and then placed a hand under the lockbox across the king's arms.

To his surprise, the burden on his arms suddenly lifted, as did the lockbox, as it levitated on a pocket of air above the enforcer's palm. With only the tiniest sign of exertion from the enforcer, he made the box move, floating through the air over to one of the empty slots on the carriage. The enforcer then gestured for the king to lead on, back to the reception hall.

'No, please, after you,' he said, with a courteous half-bow.

The enforcer obliged. Together, they made their way back into

The Last of the Magi

the reception hall and the enforcer marched straight to one of the king's runners. Tyraean held back and slumped against the stone wall at the doorway. He let out a bated breath and looked back outside.

And he chose the perfect moment to do so, just as the Shifter descended into the courtyard. She landed quietly on the roof of the carriage. With her wings spread, she looked so much larger than the carriage, yet, somehow, she moved with a stealth that even rodents would envy. The king could faintly hear a few gasps and murmurs from his archers positioned on the ramparts above. Bearing his gritted teeth, the king watched on with trepidation as Ombra perched and leaned her long neck over the sides of the carriage to sniff at the boxes mounted below.

It only took seconds for her to find her mark, the boxes at the rear. She sniffed it out like prey. Her head twisted as she eyed the lockboxes in their buckled restraints, and then with one snip of her beak she severed the straps holding them in place. She turned sideways and reached a scrawny, three-clawed foot down to grasp the box that piqued her senses, sinking her talons into the quilted padding.

She looked up, and around, before pausing her gaze on the king for a few moments.

Instinctively, he also looked around, checking for the prying eyes of any enforcers. To his relief, they were still in the reception hall discussing the final preparations, and the Ferynshore Ale. They were oblivious to the Shifter raiding their supplies.

Tyraean turned to Ombra and tried to give a reassuring nod, not knowing whether the gesture would mean anything to her. Ombra shifted her weight onto her other foot and then launched herself back up into the air, using the full strength of her wings to propel upwards, disappearing out of view with the lockbox in her grasp.

The king laughed under his breath with relief. He turned back into the room, suddenly realising that the tension of watching the Shifter at work had caused him to breathe heavily. He wiped his face with his hand and composed himself. He spotted the enforcer he was just talking to in conversation with one of his staff. He scurried to join them.

'Let me handle that ale order for you, enforcer!'

***

Ombra landed with such grace and precision, casting the lockbox aside with a flick of her talons. Her body contorted and twisted as soon as both feet were planted in the grass. She lurched forward, her wings bending unnaturally to support the weight of her chest as her shape changed and her limbs took on new purpose. It took only seconds for her cliffhawk form to melt away, transforming back into her horse form.

Tharian watched on in awe. The transformation was not new to him, not at all – she took on so many varied forms while in Feralland – but the process was nonetheless spectacular, if a little disturbing when witnessed for the first time. The way in which the creature's bones and muscle mass somehow liquified to welcome in a new shape that reset as bone and flesh mere moments later, it made Tharian's own bones itch with a gruesome curiosity.

He rushed to the lockbox and snapped it open. Retrieving his runeblade and returning it to his hip, he swung onto Ombra's back and wasted no time in setting her into a rapid charge back towards Arboreta. They had to move quickly to avoid being noticed by the second carriage, but her saddle and saddlebags were back in Ferenir after her last transformation, so she was unburdened by their weight.

The Elheim would find their first carriage shortly after leaving Ferenir, and the body of Enforcer Quiryn with it. He needed to get as far away as he could. It was only as he looked back at the remains of the carriage that Tharian realised the carriage had a driver, who must have tumbled onto the roof after Ombra's initial attack and passed out. The other enforcers could deal with him.

Ombra galloped around the edge of the city, giving the sentry towers a wide berth. Tharian kept his eyes on the hilltop while Ombra maintained their course. The second carriage did eventually emerge onto the first curl of the hill, but it disappeared as it passed around the back of the hill while Tharian and Ombra raced further west. Even if they had been seen, they would have appeared as nothing more than distant travellers. The hill served as the perfect

The Last of the Magi

cover to get them safely to the cover of the treeline of Arboreta.

They reached it safely. From there, Tharian dismounted and walked at speed with Ombra at his shoulder. Again, she shifted. This time she took lirrus form, giving her the mobility to bounce around the trees and lope over the thick roots that would have unsteadied her hooves. The transformation was less spectacular this time, only shrinking from one short-haired, hooved animal to one that was smoother-bodied and pad-footed.

No words were needed between them. No thoughts to communicate their intentions. They simply tread on, against the backdrop of a setting sun that barely reached the canopies above. In their haste, they quickly reached the slopes of the mountains, and the mouth to Greycloak's cave. They marched in together.

Despite how cold, dark, and dank it was, the cave never failed to make Tharian feel calm and safe. Perhaps it was something about the shape of the dome ceiling, or the way the sound gently echoed about as conversations were held within. Or maybe it was the complete lack of contact with the noise and nuisance of the outside world and the machinations of modern society.

Or perhaps it was even simpler than that. It was, after all, Tharian's childhood home. As unusual a place as it was for the upbringing of a child, that didn't change what it was. He suspected it was a feeling much like a child being in its mother's arms, though he had no direct memories to draw upon to confirm it.

Greycloak had his small fire burning. As usual. This time a wooden contraption was hoisting a selection of mushrooms and flower bulbs on wooden spits over the lapping flames. They were already toasted on their undersides, so Tharian rotated the spits while Greycloak was at the back of the cave using a wooden bowl to cup some water from a natural recess that he filled each day from a nearby stream.

The old man knew he was there. Though he didn't look back when Tharian entered the cave, Ombra had brushed up against his feet and he made a sound of pleasant surprise. When he eventually turned around, he nodded at Tharian and made his way back to his seat by the fire, balancing the bowl of water carefully in his palms. Even that small weight laboured him greatly.

'You've been in the belly of the beast,' Greycloak muttered. He poured some of the water into a cup beside his chair and placed the bowl next to it.

'I have,' Tharian said, 'but I got out.'

'And how fares the young ward-king?'

Tharian furled his sleeve over one hand and swiped a mushroom from the spit, tossing it into his mouth. The dense, meaty flavour was powerful. Another familiar reminder of his childhood. Though, back then they were not so unevenly cooked.

'Not a ward any longer,' Tharian said as he sucked in air to cool the mushroom he rolled around in his mouth. 'He is capable, if a little unconventional. I wouldn't be here without him.'

'Such is the gift of kingship.'

Tharian finally swallowed. 'Thanks for the brooch by the way, that really did the trick for drawing attention.'

Greycloak sniffed heavily and shook his head while gazing into the flames. 'But like opposite spokes upon the wheel, as one side turns in pursuit of its goal so does the other. Each oblivious to its opposite. The movements unseen.'

Tharian tilted his head. 'What do you me—'

His blood chilled. For once the metaphor of the old man's language just seemed to click. Something had gone wrong. 'What's happened?'

Greycloak sighed and shrugged. 'Not one kurigaw from the bazaar.'

He suddenly felt removed from his body. He had only been gone a few days. Did the Elheim return to the Quarters? Or maybe they'd done more damage to the Outer Counties and the coinsmen had seen it necessary to intervene. He had no way of knowing. He felt a foreboding sensation in the pit of his stomach.

Tharian paced around the cave, rubbing his forehead as he considered the possibilities. His head suddenly told him to just stop, to sit down and return to his old life of living on the outside of these troubles between the peoples of Asturia. Just as Greycloak taught him. It would be an easier life, for certain.

But then there was the other part of his conscience, that smaller but more powerful part deeper within that fought back. He had to

The Last of the Magi

find out what had happened and do something about it. 'I'll go back to the Quarters. Traykin may need me.'

Clearing his throat to attract attention, Greycloak pointed a bony finger towards Tharian's chair. Tharian sat down. Greycloak seemed more lucid today.

'With Ferenir and the Trade Quarters at your side, what next?' he asked.

'You know what comes next. We'll search high and low for the lost Magi and make sure they are protected.'

Greycloak looked at Tharian through his hood. His blue eyes almost appeared orange against the flames. 'There are no lost Magi.'

The certainty of his words left Tharian a bit stunned. 'What makes you so sure?'

'No Magi is ever lost. For as long as Magic remains within them, the forces of our world will always guide them on their proper path.'

'And that's what led them to the Purge, was it?' Tharian said, more crudely than he intended. Greycloak's narrowed eyes confirmed his disapproval. 'If what you say is true, I find it hard to believe that their Magic would lead them to their doom so readily. Maybe you don't know how they work as well as you think.'

Greycloak only grunted, staring into the flames.

Tharian sighed. 'Look, I trust what you say. If you're right, then maybe the Magi will find their way back to us when the time is right.' What he said was naive, he knew, yet he truly did value the fractured wisdom of his guardian. The Magi were all killed when Tharian was too young to understand what they were, so Greycloak was the closest thing he had to an authority on them.

Greycloak also sighed, and then he stood with some difficulty. He trundled over to Tharian and planted his hand on his shoulder. 'This pursuit will only lead you to despair. Turn away. Do not put your faith in the defeated Magi.'

'What else is there?' His words echoed about the cavern. 'We have lived on the fringes for so long. We can't just let them carry on like this. Asturia is our home too. The Elheim will claim it all, even Arboreta. Even this place.'

Greycloak said nothing further. He just smiled sadly, clutching at Tharian's shoulder for at least a minute before he went back to his seat.

When Greycloak returned to his seat, his expression was blank, and his eyes looked empty. The time they had together was slipping away again.

'I'm proud of you, my boy' Greycloak said, his eyes locked to the flames.

Chapter 37

Out of Sight

Though the ground floor of the Arcana Infirmary was sterile and clinical, that was not the case for the first floor. The first floor was reserved for the most important patients, who were on the road to good health. The lavish 'recovery suites' were large and decorated with flowers, statues, and paintings. Every room had its own balcony with flowing light curtains to filter the daylight. No expense was spared in ensuring these rooms were comfortable.

Lorenna Elheim had come to the Arcana Infirmary after hearing a rumour that she simply couldn't ignore. She told nobody she was coming. As the sister of Chancellor Vasilarius, it was hard enough moving freely throughout the Grand City without the College Arcana demanding she have an escort. She stood on the balcony of recovery suite one, looking out over the lower levels of her city as she ran her fingers through the flowers weaved around the balcony railing.

The city was beautiful. Everything about it was perfect. The houses were built in wonderful curving patterns that created small hamlets around public gardens and parks. The white, pale blue and yellow stones used to construct the spacious homes made the entire city glisten during the day and glow during the night. And then there was the Elheim Palace too. The sheer marvel of its construction couldn't be understated. The same could be said for all the buildings on the palace vicinage, of which the Arcana Infirmary was one of them.

Despite all that elegance and beauty, Lorenna felt a twisting in her stomach. She so often felt unwell like this, yet she suffered from no illness or affliction. It was a dark, unsettling feeling, like everything about her life was wrong. The sensation came whenever she looked at the city for too long or when she stopped to reflect upon her life or the state of affairs in Asturia.

She had tried to live her life with some degree of ignorance, turning a blind eye to those things that troubled her, to avoid the harsh truths she might encounter. But she tried in vain. She was no fool. She was the sister of the chancellor. She was privy to details on most things going on in Asturia, and she heard or overheard even more beyond that. And once she had some information, she needed to know the rest. Not the rhetoric, the spinning or the gloss that came through the reports of her brother's advisers – she needed the objective truth.

The twisting in her stomach was more intense than usual today, because of what was in the room behind her.

'Lady Elheim, I didn't realise you were here.'

The voice startled her. She turned slightly to catch a glimpse of who entered the suite. It was High Imperator Ulyria Mantleshawn.

'Don't mind me, Ulyria,' Lorenna said. 'I'm sure you have much to investigate here, I will not get in your way.'

Ulyria stepped cautiously into the middle of the room. She looked around hesitantly. Her brows were furrowed. Her reaction was the same as Lorenna's own when she first walked in. Something felt wrong. Yet the suite and all its furnishings were in good condition – immaculate even – except for the strewn-about state of the bedsheets.

'Where is Lady Valivelle?' Ulyria asked.

'Gone. Apparently she woke suddenly, found her uniform, and then stormed out. She left quite the trail of fury behind her as she went. Did you see the attendant at the door?'

Ulyria hummed a disappointed note. 'Unfortunately,' she said. 'She will recover, the doctor said some bed rest is all she needs. Thankfully the force from being pushed to the wall left no lasting damage.'

'I'm glad. I never expected one of our own to behave this like – though a combustible temper is a hallmark of the Valivelle,' Lorenna said mutely, still gliding her hands through the flowers of the balcony rail. 'But you feel it, don't you, Ulyria?'

Ulyria and Lorenna were of a similar age. Though Ulyria was slightly her senior, their time at the College Arcana overlapped and they had become fast friends over that time.

Lorenna had always felt slightly guilty about their friendship.

The Last of the Magi

Many senior enforcers gossiped, though only in hushed whispers, about whether Ulyria Mantleshawn had acquired her position as the leader of all enforcers due to their friendship. Although Lorenna had recommended Ulyria to the position, it was not their connection that had won her the role, it was her level-headedness and keen intellect, as well as her proficiency in the Arcane. She was objectively the most suitable for the role. She had proven herself time and time again since her appointment, but Lorenna would never forget the earlier years where Ulyria had to assert herself to dismiss those rumours.

'I feel... something,' Ulyria said as she joined Lorenna on the balcony, 'Though I'm not sure what that something is.'

Lorenna curled a hand to point where the balcony joined the wall.

The blooming, beautiful flowers, in all their white and yellow majesty, lost some of that majesty where they were closer to the suite. Those ones had become grey, brown, and withered.

'Oh.' Ulyria ducked back into the suite and huffed through her nose as she paced over to the bedside tables and then across to the corners of the room, before re-joining Lorenna. 'We won't hear the end of this from the scholars if they get in here.'

Lorenna faked a smile. Ulyria had now noticed what caught Lorenna's attention: the plants in the suite were withered. 'You're probably right,' Lorenna said. 'I wonder whether it would even make a difference.'

'My Lady? What do you mean?'

Lorenna turned and gently planted her hand on Ulyria's arm, and she guided her friend forward to stand at her side. 'The scholars will write their reports. They will advise my brother of what sense they can make of it all, and then...' she let the words trail off.

Ulyria hummed. She seemed to be considering the words carefully. 'I'm sure the chancellor would take the time to consider those reports, or at least listen to the counsel of his advisers, my Lady.'

Lorenna laughed, leaning forward over the railing. 'Ulyria,' she said sternly, 'I know you are on duty, but you know I prefer it when you speak plainly around me. Sometimes I forget what my name sounds like.'

The high imperator relaxed her rigid stance and leaned her hip against the railing. 'Whatever you say, Lorenna.'

'That's more like it.'

'I can't say whether your brother will see this as a serious issue. In all honesty, I'm not sure whether it is one. The scholars have dabbled in this subject before, but no concrete findings were ever reached.'

Lorenna straightened. She curled her blonde hair behind her ear and then put a hand against Ulyria's back, pointing with the other hand to the city wall in the distance. 'Is that not evidence enough?'

It was to the south-west, beyond the city wall, that she pointed. To the Dead Plains outside the city, the stretch of dead land where the Purge was enacted. That mile-or-so stretch of grey, lifeless earth.

Ulyria's lips tightened, and she moved her back to dislodge Lorenna's hand. 'That was very different. The sheer amount of Arcana used on the day of the Purge was beyond measure – I'm not surprised an assault of that intensity would cause a lasting scar.'

That response irked her, though she did her best to conceal her irritation. 'Whether it is a mile-long stretch of grass, or the petals of a blooming flower, you cannot deny the connection before your own eyes. Arcana was used in each instance, and this was the result.'

'I'm not denying the similarity,' Ulyria said, 'I'm only saying that this may be different. The scale of Arcana used here was miniscule by comparison. There could be another explanation.'

'Arcana did this. We cannot look away and ignore it. My brother cannot look away.'

'I understand you feel strongly about this, but we cannot distract the scholars. Ever since the incident with the Valivelle apprentice, the chancellor demanded they renew their efforts to search for more uses for Arcana.'

'Of course,' Lorenna sighed. 'Discovering more ways to weaponise Arcana will make it all better.'

'Lorenna.'

She felt the high imperator tug at her arm. She turned to meet her friend's stern eyes.

The Last of the Magi

'The chancellor has made our priorities clear. Even if I had the scholars to spare, I don't think *this* would be enough to warrant a second study into the effects of Arcana.'

Lorenna frowned and then darted into the suite. She took her shawl from a coat stand and pulled it around her shoulders, letting the near-transparent sheet of pink fabric fall neatly over her arms. In her sleeveless, slightly off-white dress, she was always dressed more for ceremony as the Lady Elheim than for function as an enforcer.

If this is not enough to make you take this seriously...

She marched back to the open balcony doors. 'Have you ever been to the Elheim private gardens?' She beckoned Ulyria with a finger and then marched out of the suite, pausing only briefly at the door to make sure Ulyria was following.

Ulyria looked stunned by the question. 'Of course not,' she said. 'They are the Elheim *private* gardens – for your family alone. To my knowledge, no enforcer has ever been permitted access.'

'What do you know of it?' Lorenna asked as she led her friend back to the infirmary's entrance.

'Of the gardens?'

'Yes.'

'Only what is common knowledge, and a little extra from what I suppose is just rumour.'

'Tell me.'

'The Arcane Guild would meet in private where the gardens are now situated, to discuss the economic and political welfare of Asturia. The area is significant to our history, and so they are given pride of place as the Elheim family's own private estuary.'

Lorenna shrugged and waved her hand. 'Is that all?'

'Is this a test?' Ulyria sounded frustrated.

'Humour me, please.'

Ulyria continued as they crossed the road outside the infirmary and walked together towards the palace. 'People say it's a marvel to behold. A huge cut of land home to trees, flowers and exotic fruit-bearing foliage that cannot be found anywhere else in Asturia. It is said to feature a range of horticulture so exotic that even the collectors of the Trade Quarters would be drawn to envy.'

'Good, thank you.' Lorenna said.

'Why do you ask?'

Lorenna ignored that question and pressed on ahead. She was however glad that Ulyria's depiction of the private gardens was in line with what she expected to hear.

She had to ignore the conversation for a time anyway. As her attention was drawn to the many men and women going about their days, and the families who strolled about. They all greeted her warmly as they passed. Men tipped their hats, or pretended to in this heat, and women curtsied and gave respectful salutations to her as the Lady Elheim.

Lorenna made sure to give each of them a response, whether it be a warm look or a short wave. They were her people. Like it or not, the people of the Grand City treated her like royalty, as if she had built all this splendour with her own two hands. It was flattering, but uncomfortable.

Sometimes it felt a duplicitous life. Like every time she opened her arms to embrace her people approaching from the front, she was really shielding them from the harsh truths she concealed at her back. But that was the burden of her status, of bearing the name Elheim. Her burdens came hand-in-hand with a lifestyle of luxury and comfort beyond compare. Those luxuries were meant to make it easier to bear. It wasn't working.

They crossed a neatly paved road and reached the palace steps. Lorenna pulled at the side of her dress as she cantered up the steps, rising between the two flanking structures that joined together at the upper levels. They wouldn't need to climb to the top, they weren't heading to the private residences for her family and their staff. She instead stopped them at a landing about halfway up.

'Care to explain?' Ulyria said as she reached the landing, without any shortness of breath. 'People might become concerned if they see the two of us hurrying around in broad daylight.'

'Don't be paranoid, Ulyria. This way.'

Lorenna led Ulyria to the left tower, into a plain corridor, decorated only with a royal-blue strip of carpet that ran down the middle of the floor and portraits of founding members of the Elheim family on the walls. They passed many doors, and corridors that

The Last of the Magi

branched off at their sides, but Lorenna carried on following the corridor as it curved, until they reached a single enforcer on guard duty at a doorway.

He dutifully opened the door for Lorenna, but he looked noticeably concerned as the high imperator approached at her side. He stuttered and looked to Lorenna for guidance.

'The high imperator will be accompanying me. This is a private matter, I'm sure you understand.'

The enforcer relaxed and stepped aside for them both to pass.

They continued into the next section of corridor, which was much the same as the last except for the lack of off-shooting pathways. Ulyria brought herself to Lorenna's side.

'That was novel,' Ulyria said.

'What was?'

'I don't think any of my enforcers have ever had to consider barring my way like that.'

Lorenna laughed softly. 'Don't you worry, Ulyria, I'm sure your authority has not been demeaned by the experience.'

Ulyria barked a laugh back. 'That wasn't my concern. I know the rules, the private areas of the palace are for you and your family only. I'm pleased my enforcers are carrying out their duties correctly. It was still an odd experience.'

They reached a large metal door at the end of the corridor. The corner tables and the empty bookshelves, covered in dust as they were, confirmed something that Lorenna had suspected: nobody had visited the private gardens in a long time.

Lorenna pulled at the silver necklace around her neck to reveal a small, ornate key and a ring that hung from the chain.

She looked at the ring for a moment, it was her mother's, and she smiled solemnly as she then slid it away within her palm so she could get the key into the lock of the metal door. As she turned the key, there was a sound of sliding metal, then another, and then another. With the door finally unlocked, she pushed it ajar just a fraction and gestured for Ulyria to go through.

'After you, High Imperator.'

Ulyria gave her a look. Lorenna knew her voice had lost its usual energy. She was usually good at hiding her emotions, but a visit to the private gardens pushed her into a place where completely masking her feelings became too difficult. She didn't want to do this. But it was necessary.

***

The Elheim private gardens truly did live up to their rumoured size. From the height of the veranda at the back of the palace, Ulyria could see perhaps a mile or so off into the distance where the stretch of land finally reached the sea all around them. And it was an unusual shape. The land closest to the middle of the palace was incredibly shallow, being only thirty or forty paces deep until it hit a still pool of water. The land stretched left and right and curled out like two crescent moons towards the sea, almost touching at their apex, creating a large basin to contain a lake.

The garden was a sight to behold – for all the wrong reasons.

The two stretches of land looked more like the horns of a great beast. And upon those horns there was nothing more than grey grass, grey leafless trees and the festering remains of hedgerows and plantbeds. Even the lake seemed... sick. It was still – far too still for a body of water linked to the constantly moving sea. Its stillness was not calming, nor was it beautiful. It was lifeless.

To those not trained in the Arcane, the garden would look like it was experiencing a private winter, with nature having retreated into a slumber until warmer days rolled back around. But these were warmer days. And for someone as gifted in the Arcane as Ulyria, she couldn't ignore what her senses were telling her. Whatever happened here, or was still happening here, it was not natural, and it was not good.

'I don't understand. How is this possible? Is the land fouled, the water poisoned?' Ulyria turned to Lorenna who stood a distance from the veranda's edge.

Lorenna raised her shoulders and then took the stairs that led down to the garden itself. Ulyria followed.

'You know that's not it,' Lorenna replied. 'You can feel it as well as I can, as can my brother. I can see it in your eyes.'

Ulyria surveyed her surroundings. Her eyes shifted about as she

The Last of the Magi

searched desperately for some redeeming quality amongst the dead landscape. There wasn't one. She instead focused on the steps as they descended. 'How long has it been like this?'

'Since the Purge. The change took hold suddenly,' Lorenna said, in a matter-of-fact tone. 'I only show you this because it's necessary. I need to make you see that this issue is more serious than a few dead flowers in the infirmary. *This,* Ulyria—'

'Is the price we pay for Arcana.'

Lorenna hummed. 'I see no other explanation. I'm afraid there's more to show you.'

'I'm not sure I want to see it.'

'If it helps, it's not something to see with your eyes.'

They reached the ground and stepped onto the lawn. The grey grass crunched under Ulyria's boots, as if each blade were coated in a frost. The air was stale and motionless, but Ulyria felt grateful for that. She feared the scent of rotting vegetation might carry upon the air, especially in the warmth of summer.

'Focus on the lake,' Lorenna continued. 'Reach out to it with Arcana. Grasp and Command it if you want.'

Ulyria hesitated, wondering what Lorenna was expecting her to feel. She looked down her nose at the water, just a few paces away. She pushed away the distractions in her mind and quickly cycled through to her Deep Thought state, Reaching out in same the way she would with any other body of water.

But there was nothing.

She couldn't feel *anything*. Not the water in the lake, the stagnated air, or any other elements that she could pull upon to Command. It was as if they were not there... or were truly lifeless.

Ulyria's breathing quickened. This was the first time her Arcana had failed her. It was disarming.

She didn't hide the confusion and fear in her face as she turned back to Lorenna. Lorenna frowned, though her eyes were sympathetic and soothing. She could use Arcana too, so she must have experienced this unsettling feeling for herself.

'So, there is a link.' Ulyria said. She felt defeated.

Lorenna moved over to one of the benches not far from the foot of the stairs and adjusted her dress around her feet as she perched on its edge. 'The power to move and Command the elements... and destroy them too.'

Ulyria rubbed her forehead. The scholars of the College Arcana had hypothesised that there was *some* link between the use of Arcane and the withering or depletion of natural life – and that maybe there was some link between the natural life force of the world and the source of Arcane energy – such that their relationship to each other might be either symbiotic or parasitic in nature. The theory had been based on evidence gathered long ago of small instances of change in the natural world where Arcana had been used. None of the evidence was compelling enough to justify any action. The theories were put to bed, said to be nothing more than the idle conjecture of over-enthusiastic academics. But this was different, this was on a scale too large to be ignored, much like the Purge itself.

But it *was* being ignored.

The Purge had been written off as a unique incident, with the dead land outside the city gates being attributed to the sheer destructive force used to slaughter the Magi. But this painted a different picture. The Arcana used that day was directed in the opposite direction, away from these gardens, but when the Arcane blast was being conjured atop the palace this place would have been the closest source of abundant nature to its epicentre. This complicated things. It gave the theories more credence. At the very least, it justified exploring those theories further.

Ulyria's eyes widened, and she marched over to Lorenna, standing over her with a fierce determination. 'The chancellor knows about this?'

Lorenna nodded.

'How long has he known?'

Lorenna made a sweeping gesture, directed at the enormous gardens before them. 'A long time, and I think my father might have known too. When I was a child, we were regularly brought here to practice Arcana together, before we were old enough to join the college. Even back then there were spaces that started to show signs of decay. Father would make us use a different space each time. I thought nothing of it back then.' She clutched at the small ring

The Last of the Magi

attached to her necklace. 'This transformation happened in the space of weeks after the Purge. I was only nine – I came here a week or so after the funeral – and as I sat on this very bench, I noticed that the colours were starting to fade.

'I thought it was just one of those fallacies, like the kind you read about in stories. Maybe the gardens just looked a bit less bright without my parents around. Maybe it was just grief that greyed my view of the world. I was wrong. The life in this place was draining away, and that carried on until it became like this. It's like a reminder of how much suffering Arcana has caused.' Lorenna shifted uncomfortably. She laced her little finger through the ring on her necklace.

Despite knowing each other for a very long time, since their teenage years, Ulyria had never seen Lorenna look so solemn. She was a bright, positive person, yet this issue with Arcana and its effects on the environment troubled her very deeply.

Ulyria felt awkward. Comforting others was not a skill within her repertoire. Arcana, she understood – at least, she thought she did before today – but emotions were like a form of magic she couldn't master. Instead of offering words of comfort, she straightened, put her hands behind her back and drew upon the formality she so often defaulted to in the presence of the Elheim family. 'I'll report this to the scholars.'

She hoped that would offer her friend some reassurance, yet Lorenna just sniffed and wiped her eyes against the back of her hand before rising from her seat. As her hand dropped from her face, her expression had become cold and serious. 'No. I agree that this issue needs investigating, but you must not mention the gardens to anyone. If my brother found out, he would do everything he could to silence us. You know as well as I that bonds of family offer no protection against his vision of progress for Asturia.'

'Lorenna, I hold the position of high imperator. It is my duty to watch over the use and development of Arcana. I must have this investigated.'

'I know.' Lorenna smiled. 'Then gather those scholars you trust. Ask them to investigate Lady Valivelle's recovery suite. Maybe the Dead Plains again too. There's more than enough there to justify an investigation. Tell them it's a private research project for me, and so their findings should be sent to my chambers. That should keep things away from the prying eyes of Vasilarius and the registrar.'

Folding her arms, Ulyria smirked. 'That sounded rehearsed.'

'I've known about this for so long, and I've been waiting for the right catalyst to justify doing something about it.'

'You don't need to explain yourself. I'm with you on this. But the scholars might think it odd that I'm asking them to carry out covert investigations, especially when the chancellor has directed resources away from this in the past.'

'I agree. That's why you should entrust this only to the scholars you believe are reliable. If there are any who were denied the chance to work on this before then they would be best placed to be given the opportunity now.'

Ulyria's smirk widened. Lorenna may have been docile in comparison to many who went through the full rigour of the College Arcana training, but her mind was sharp. Incredibly so. 'Very well, I will see that a suitable cohort of scholars are put to work.' Ulyria bowed slightly and then turned towards the steps to make her way back the way they came.

Lorenna caught Ulyria's shoulder before she escaped her reach. 'Thank you, Ulyria. I knew I could trust you with this.'

'As your high imperator, it is my duty, and as your friend, my pleasure.'

'And I hope that you can locate Lady Valivelle soon, too.'

'As do I, Lorenna, as do I.'

Ulyria then marched up the stairs, back to the lofty veranda where she could see the gardens in their entirety. On the way up, she noticed that the back walls of the palace had no windows or balconies from which the gardens could be viewed. But, judging by the discolouration of some areas of the walls, there once had been many. She gave the gardens one last look before she went back inside, letting the image of this dying place print into her mind.

There was much to think about. When the chancellor last called a meeting of his senior advisers, she saw a new side to him. He presented one face to his advisers in open meeting, the same charming, subtle, and charismatic persona they were all used to –

that the people of the Grand City were used to – and then, when away from prying eyes, he became calculating and vindictive. The accommodating, welcoming leader on one front, and the sinister tactician on the other. If this covert investigation was uncovered, she was in no doubt as to which of those personas she would have to answer to. She shuddered at that thought.

Chapter 38

Buried Deep

Darus rubbed at his temples and blinked hard as he tried to shake the dull ache that pulsed from behind his forehead. The work of a coinsman was demanding. Since Coinswoman Keene had addressed the Quartersfolk on the new arrangements for their city – the so-called partnership to restore 'balance and peace' to the Trade Quarters – things had been incredibly busy.

Keene and Protelborn had taken to dealing with the swathe of enquiries coming in from the people; they knew the city best amongst the four of them. Keene's reports suggested that her involvement in this new paradigm of governance had done much to ease concerns, and had certainly prevented riots or protests, but that didn't stop the letters from being written. They were coming in thick and fast. The people wanted personalised explanations setting out what this new arrangement meant for *them* and *their* livelihoods. Were they citizens of the Grand City now? Were their homes and families at risk? Would taxation rates change? Would new contracts be made available to tender for the Grand City?

The letters covered the full spectrum of issues. Some were accusing, others were opportunistic, but all had questions that demanded answers.

Darus didn't have as much to do as Keene and Protelborn, but there were many collectors who had submitted applications to open new shops, or to extend the type of wares that they could offer from their existing stores. A lot of those requests came in during Jerard Traykin's tenure, and they remained outstanding. They were his problem now.

For Darus, whose knowledge in matters of economics, law and governance were limited to only cursory lessons at the College Arcana, each molehill felt like a mountain. For even the simplest applications he had to check records upon records to see exactly what the Trade Quarters bylaws said about each facet of the

The Last of the Magi

collectors' requests, and then he needed to sort those requests into categories so he could consult the existing roster of licenses before making any decisions.

Thanks to Keene's instructions, he learnt one thing very quickly – the Collectors Quarter only thrived because of the diversity and tight competition of its stores. If he made too many approvals in one area and rejected too many in others, the economic balance of the Quarter could be thrown into disarray. Before Coinswoman Keene had left him to his work, she chuckled to herself as she recounted a tale about how rash decisions in that quarter once wreaked havoc on the social trends of the city. A series of constraints on the right to sell gemstones resulted in a relatively common blue gem becoming an exclusive item for one vendor in the Collectors Quarter. That gemstone quickly became the height of opulence in the trends of fashion at the time. But with that vendor having such an abundant stock, it didn't take long for everyone to have several of the gems in their possession. Just as quickly as the gemstone rose into popularity, it then became so ubiquitous that nobody would buy it for a full year thereafter. The story made it clear how important the coinsman's role was to the quarter, and to the city as a whole.

The whole process was part-science and part-art. The former was more familiar to Darus than the latter.

'Could I assist you with any refreshments, Coinsman Valivelle?'

Darus dropped his hands from his face and bolted upright in his chair. His father said he would be busy for a few days – he didn't expect him to return so soon.

As Darus peered beyond the dim light of his table lamp, to the door leading out of his new office, he could see a tall, older man looking in. It was the assistant that had been assigned to him. The man shuffled awkwardly and then repeated the question.

The assistant was addressing *him,* he realised. He was not used to his new title. Much like the titles of 'Enforcer Valivelle', or 'Lord Valivelle', Darus associated such monikers with his father's rank and station, rather than his own.

'Please forgive me, I thought—' Darus said, shrugging away his thoughts before continuing. 'Do you have anything that can help with head pains or weariness?'

The assistant nodded enthusiastically. 'I will check for you. Lady Keene has asked that you meet her in the tearoom as soon as convenient. Should I prepare the tonic in there for you?'

Keene is back already? Darus turned in his chair to glance out the window. The evening was settling in. He looked over the piles and piles of paper strewn across his desk and the scrawls of his inky handwriting. *How many hours have I been doing this?*

Not wanting to be rude, he dragged his attention away from the papers and smiled to the assistant. 'Yes, please do. Could you let the coinswoman know I will be with her shortly?'

'Certainly. I will see to the completed license applications while you're away.'

'Thank you, that would be very helpful.'

The assistant bowed and left.

Darus dropped his head back into his hands and groaned. He had been working on these documents all day and he'd hardly made a dent. But he had reached a decision on *some* of the applications today, and the pile of completed work was larger than it was the day before. He tried to take some comfort in that, but then the aching at his forehead washed away that small victory.

He wanted desperately to rest, to lay down somewhere with a cold towel across his face and sleep. He would get to that eventually, though for now he had to meet with Keene. They met each night to share their knowledge and skills with each other, just as his father wanted. They took turns teaching each other. One evening Keene would lecture him on the inner workings and history of the Trade Quarters, then the next night Darus would explain Arcana and take Keene through the basic exercises that enabled one to access and use it.

Tonight, it was his turn to be the teacher again.

Taking a deep breath through his nose, he blew out slowly through pursed lips. He did this a few times before eventually reaching over the desk to straighten the pile of completed applications before he left.

As he reached, his elbow caught against a pile of journals at the corner of the desk. They slid off the table and slammed against the dark-wood floor.

The Last of the Magi

His heart skipped. The sound of the books hitting the ground echoed, then amplified, then echoed and amplified even more in his head. He breathed heavily as he hunched over the table and clutched at his head. The sound got louder and louder and sounded less like books and more like a landslide of stone. Each syllable of sound bringing with it a deep pain in his skull.

It was like he was back there again. In the training hall. Watching Rikkard disappear within that tomb of stone.

How can I, of all people, be trusted to train another to use Arcana safely.

Whenever that memory haunted him before, it was coloured with guilt and sadness, but now – knowing that Rikkard didn't recover from his injuries – the memory was unbearable. He would never be able to enjoy an evening walk around the outskirts of the city with his closest companion. The only one he had ever been *that* close to.

Darus pushed those painful thoughts away, back to that place where he pushed all the things that hurt him. He picked up the journals and piled them back at the edge of the table, making sure to push them slightly further inward this time.

He took a moment to collect himself, and then finally left the office. He crossed the hall and made his way through the lavishly furnished corridors and lounges until he found Keene's tearoom. She was already there, perched at the edge of her favourite armchair with a tray of tea already laid out over the low table. She perused the notebook she used for their sessions.

She looked up as he took a seat across from her. She wasted no time in closing her book and pouring him some tea, as she always did during their evenings together.

'Are your duties challenging you?' Keene asked, as she finished pouring with a flourish. She pushed the mug closer to Darus, beside a glass of water with a swirling green mist mixing into it from being recently stirred.

Darus reached eagerly for the tonic first. He took a generous mouthful. 'Challenging is an apt description. The work isn't all that difficult, there's just so many variables to consider. And then, even when all that's sorted, there's trying to figure out what the right decision is.' He glanced over to Keene, and she was grinning at him. 'It is slowly getting easier.'

Keene smirked. 'That's the spirit. Every coinsmen feels this way in the beginning. In time you will be able to deal with most requests without giving them more than a cursory glance – if you choose to be so lax with things, that is.'

'I don't think I could ever be so lax.'

'Then you have the makings of a conscientious coinsman. The Collectors Quarter is in dire need of one. Jerard is a good man, but he operates on whim rather than structure.'

'I hope I perform the role well.' Darus necked the rest of the tonic. He then checked the temperature of the steaming mug of tea before cupping it between his palms. 'But enough about business, you will teach me more tomorrow night, I'm sure.'

'Ah – of course!' said Keene as she took a quick sip of her tea and hastily returned it to the table, 'It's my turn to be the student.'

'It is. How did you find the Deep Thought exercises?'

'Challenging,' she said, and they both laughed. 'In a different way to what I'm used to. I'm so busy with handling all these enquiries that finding a time to clear my head and meditate is almost impossible.'

'Almost?' That qualification didn't escape his notice.

Keene shifted her weight and leaned against the arm closest to Darus. 'Well, I tried it just before bed straight after we first talked about the exercises, and I've tried it each night since. I did exactly as you described but I had no luck with it – until last night, that is.'

'What happened?'

'I managed to clear my head, and as I sat there and just concentrated on what was around me, I felt myself slipping somewhere deeper. I have to say, it was a frightfully odd experience. At first, I thought I might be dozing off, but it was more like my mind was pushing into a space it hadn't been before.'

'Let me guess,' Darus said, 'instinctively you pulled away?'

'Yes!' Her eyes widened and she looked excited to hear that her experience was a recognised one.

'That's normal. Deep Thought is pretty much what you just described – a feeling of your mind moving beyond its normal confines and becoming aware of things beyond yourself. It's... uncomfortable at first.'

'So, what should I do next?'

'You just need to let go and take the plunge. You need to push through that discomfort until you start to *feel* your environment. It takes practice, there's no rush. You're already on the right track. With practice you'll be able to trigger the Deep Thought state in the blink of an eye.'

Keene scoffed and curled one leg over the other. 'That's kind of you. But at my age picking up new skills takes a lot of work.'

Darus shrugged and then used his weight to shift his chair round to face the coinswoman more directly. She watched with a cocked brow as the chair scraped its way across her floor. 'I disagree that your age is any issue here,' Darus said. 'In fact, I'd argue you have an advantage.'

With an amused hum, Keene tilted her head in a way that told him to continue.

'Apprentices join the College Arcana at an age where they have so many distractions, of both body and mind. So much is expected of us at a time when focus is so difficult to achieve. You have distractions too – different distractions, sure enough – yet they are distractions all the same. And even with those distractions, you have managed to make progress with Deep Thought in a matter of days, whereas it takes first year apprentices a few weeks.'

Keene smiled. 'You flatter me. So, teacher, what would you suggest for today?'

The question sent a surge of doubt through him. She was ready to move forward with her exercises already, yet the voice of reason in his head screamed at him to stop. He would only be adding one more Arcane weapon into the world. That reality loomed over him like a dark cloud. But he had orders from his father, so he had to continue. That somehow made it easier and harder at the same time.

Darus rubbed his hands together and leaned forward. 'We should see if you can sense Arcana. Try and enter Deep Thought now.'

'Very well,' she replied. She uncurled her leg and rest her hands on the arms of her chair. She sat just the way he'd suggested in their first lesson. By removing areas where limbs overlapped and ensuring no muscles were strained abnormally by one's posture, the mind could more easily drift into relaxation, unlaboured by tension in the body.

Darus moved behind her chair and looked around the room for something he could use to demonstrate the sensation of Arcana at work. Frustratingly, this room was deep enough inside Keene's estate to eliminate drafts, and no flames lapped in the fireplace.

His eyes danced over the teapot, then went back to it. The liquid within would serve his purposes perfectly.

'How are you getting on?' he whispered gently.

She started to nod, but Darus could see that she resisted the urge to move. Instead, she whispered back. 'I'm trying.'

Darus remembered how hard it was to reach Deep Thought the first time. 'Think of it like walking into the Library, a place that you know well. A safe space. Walk through that door in your mind and tell me what you can feel around you.'

Keene's eyes stopped moving behind their lids. Her brows furrowed. 'Nothing,' she said. 'Only your voice. Not even the chair at my back.'

Darus felt a small rush. She was doing well. Though she sounded uncertain, perhaps even a little frustrated, her response told him that she was doing it right. She was no longer focusing on herself, instead she was starting to sense beyond her body. She only needed something to catch her attention now.

'Stay exactly as you are, but if you feel anything unusual, please say.'

She hummed, then her breathing became deep and controlled.

Darus focused on the teapot again. It was in Keene's reach, so any Arcana used that close should be impossible to miss. He Reached out with his mind, passing into the Deep Thought state without even thinking about it. his senses detected and enveloped the tea, ready to Grasp and Command it at will.

The liquid was an extension of him now. That half-globe of tea sat snug within the pot, with a small flat edge on the bottom. Through Arcana, he could feel more than just the presence of the tea; he could feel its heat. Not literally, like when touching a finger

The Last of the Magi

against a hot surface, instead it was as if the characteristics of the liquid in his Grasp were being translated into his brain as information, like reading a label. Arcana always gave its user the ability to understand intuitively a lot about the thing within its Grasp. Over time it was easy to forget that skill, as the elements quickly became familiar and repetitive, or the user had little need to make use of that knowledge. When feeling something different, such as water that had been boiled and altered by tea leaves, that sense suddenly became acute once more.

As if plucking the string of an instrument, Darus used Arcana to Command the tea to ripple within the teapot. Just enough to disturb the tea without rattling the pot.

Darus noticed the coinswoman's brow twitching. Her mouth opened slightly.

He manipulated the tea again, with a little more strength this time.

'There!' she said. 'I felt something.'

'Describe it.'

'I'm not sure I can,' her brow furrowed. 'It was a buzzing. A bit like when you hear someone's voice through a wall. Did you whisper something?'

Darus stifled a laugh. 'No, no I didn't. What else can you feel?'

'I think,' she paused, tilting her head. 'There is a sensation, of something heavy. But... it also feels light. Or maybe it's just small? I can't quite put my finger on it.'

Darus Commanded the tea a third time, this time letting the vibration in the teapot continue. 'How about now?'

'What is that?'

That, Lady Coinswoman, is your tea.'

She gawped and then a broad smile crept across her lips. 'It is! I can feel it more clearly now. It's so close. On the table.'

'Focus on that now, and that alone.' Darus moved to the side of her chair and dropped to one knee so he could more easily examine Keene's expression as he continued with his demonstration.

Flexing his will with a bit more concentration, he Commanded a tendril of the tea to creep out through the spout of the teapot and lift into the air. With precise manipulations of Arcana, he kept the tea in a thin ribbon-stream as it moved unnaturally through the open air.

Keene's mouth dropped open. 'What? That can't be... are you doing what I think you're doing? It's like I can see what's happening in my head. No – I can *feel* it.'

The tea moved and danced through the air at his Command. He made it swirl and spin up and down, then left and right, and then in irregular and unpredictable directions, weaving through the air as if the stream of tea was trying to tie itself into knots. Looking at Keene, he could see through the lids of her eyes that she was watching it in her mind, following every movement. *She really is ahead of the curve.*

Satisfied with his demonstration, he carefully directed the tea to retract back down the spout – a task much more complicated than he had expected. With the tea fully contained, he placed his hand on Keene's wrist, and she opened her eyes.

'That was spectacular,' she said. 'Really it was.'

Darus went back to his seat and reached forward for the teapot, refilling her cup. 'That's nothing, I assure you. Arcane training covers much more advanced techniques than that, more aggressive techniques which give you the skills to Command a wider range of elements and in much larger quantities. It's an impressive thing, but I've always preferred the techniques that require precision. Here, your tea.'

Taking the tea, she looked deep into the cup and then to Darus with a look of concern.

Darus chuckled. He used Arcana to lift his own neglected tea from his mug and decanted it into his used glass. Then he refilled his mug with fresh tea and swiftly brought it to his lips. 'It won't harm you.' He drank it in front of her as proof.

Smiling, she toasted her cup in the air to him and then took a sip herself. As she placed the cup back onto its saucer, she licked her lips and looked at the dark drink piercingly. 'Must be the bottom of the pot,' she said as she grimaced.

Darus took another sip, paying more attention to its taste this time. The tea did taste a bit more bitter than he expected.

They both lowered their drinks to the table and laughed.

'What you just did, we refer to as Reaching. Deep Thought gives

The Last of the Magi

you access to Arcana, and the ability to notice the elements around you. Reaching is the process of extending that concentration to a specific substance, so you can examine it, track its motions, or prepare to Grasp it. Grasping takes you beyond mere observation, allowing you to seize whatever was in your Reach. As you get better at Grasping, you can then finally start to control those elements freely. This, the pinnacle of Arcane skill, we call Commanding.'

'Yes,' Keene replied, softly. I have been re-reading my notes on that process. Deep Thought, Reach, Grasp and then Command. To think that I am already wading into the second step.'

Darus smiled. She really was doing well. She sounded like she might now be believing it. 'As you master each step, the ones before start to become muscle memory. In time you will innately feel the elements around you, ready to be controlled through Arcana. The texture and temperament of each element will be recognisable to your senses even if your eyes cannot see them.'

That piqued Keene's attention. She pulled her notebook back onto her lap and leafed through to a blank page, drawing a pen between her fingers. 'Recognisable how?'

'Each element is different, both in terms of what it can do when Commanded and how it feels when we Reach for it. For example, the air moves gracefully around us in ever-changing streams and colliding currents. You can feel the passion and fury that flickers in an open fire, or the slow, calm strength that ebbs and flows in water. Even the—' Darus stopped himself as he tapped the ground with his foot. His energy suddenly sapped away. He cleared his throat before speaking again. 'You'll experience it all for yourself soon enough.'

She eyed him, she must have noticed his abrupt change. Thankfully she didn't pry. She finished the sentence in her notebook and then snapped it closed with a smile. 'I can't wait. Thank you for this.'

***

She had been knocking on his door for five minutes. She knew he was there; he couldn't possibly be anywhere else at this hour. The carriages were all parked outside the palace, and no staff were missing from their posts to serve as his escort. Nothing was out of place – and her brother was not one to take late night strolls on his own.

So she carried on knocking. Eventually Vasilarius opened the door and said nothing as he met his sister's fierce and narrowed gaze.

'Vas,' she said, bitterly.

'It is late.'

'Yes, it is.' She pushed the door open and forced her way into the room, closing it quickly as she entered.

Despite it being so late, Vasilarius had not yet removed his royal uniform. Even with its extra flourishes of navy-blue thread, and the draping fabric at his back, to her it was just another enforcer uniform.

His room was lit by a few mounted lanterns and a single fireplace in the centre of the suite that cast a menacing shadow against his sharp cheekbones.

Lorenna stepped back from him, feeling a little of her strength and courage waiver at seeing him this way. He was not an evil looking man, but the lighting made him look sinister.

'For what purpose do I have the honour of this late invasion, Lorenna?' his words were polite, but his tone was not.

'The Trade Quarters, Vas. I was invited for dinner with Percivor and his family this evening, and he mentioned receiving an unexpected letter from his inquisitor in the Quarters.'

Vasilarius moved to a desk in the corner and pulled out a chair that he then placed in the middle of the room. He gestured to it. 'Take a seat, calm yourself, and tell me more.'

Lorenna swept her arm towards the chair and a gust of air lashed from her, spinning the chair across the room and back under the desk. 'I will not *calm myself.* You told us that we would take a diplomatic approach to handling this issue in the Trade Quarters. What kind of diplomacy is this?'

Vasilarius smirked as he glowered between the desk and where he had placed the chair. He looked as though he was admiring the use of Arcana. She may not wear the uniform of an enforcer – nor did she perform their duties – but she was nonetheless incredibly

The Last of the Magi

capable in the Arcane all the same. Even so, he wasn't talking her words seriously. And that frustrated her immensely.

'You barge into my room with talk of the Trade Quarters and a letter received this evening from an inquisitor. If you are to speak with such accusation, at least do me the courtesy of explaining what crimes you believe I have committed.'

She grimaced, *so he is going to play this game.* 'The Trade Quarters were forcefully entered by Lord Valivelle's expedition party, and now three enforcers sit as coinsmen. No enforcer would act so rashly unless under your order.'

'Lord Valivelle has assumed control of the Trade Quarters? This is the first I am hearing of it, I assure you.'

Lorenna shook her head. She folded her arms. 'I am not a fool; your words do not charm me like they do your advisers.'

Her brother gestured to the chair Lorenna had batted across the room and he used Arcana to draw it back to his side so that he could take a seat instead.

'Sister, you assume the worst in me. What cause have I given you to believe that I would lie or mislead my own advisers?'

The muscles in Lorenna's face tightened, as did her fists. 'That's a dangerous line to take, Vas. Are you sure you want to go down that road?'

He didn't even blink. He only nodded slightly, egging her on.

'Our parents,' she said bluntly, 'How did they die?'

Vasilarius held his hands out and sighed derisively. 'We have been over this time and time again. You know as much as I. They enacted the Purge against the Magi; they went up to the spire of this palace and they did not return. They were at the epicentre of the Arcana they conjured. Sadly they underestimated the gravity of their own strength.'

'The same story as always. How about the gardens then?' she said through gritted teeth. Her eyes narrowed intensely upon her brother's sharp features. 'You know there's a risk to using Arcana and yet you hide away what you know from those who could study that risk and do something about it.'

'I *know* nothing of the sort. I will not upturn the resources of our people to investigate the idle hypotheses of a few eccentric scholars.'

Lorenna went to lurch forward, to launch her counterargument, but Vasilarius raised a hand to pause her. It worked, much to her chagrin.

'This theory, that there is a link between Arcana and the forces of natural life, is no more than that – theory. Even if there was substance to it, which was not proven in preliminary investigations, the point is an academic one. It was the Purge that gave rise to the theory that has you so concerned, and I will not allow a Purge-like event to happen again. Arcana shall not be used at that volume. It is better that our enforcers continue believing they are indomitable rather than have them fret over hypothetical drawbacks that none of them will ever cause to manifest. Their resolve to serve our vision must remain unshaken.'

Lorenna felt stunned. Her first thought was that his argument sounded... reasonable. Logical, even. Though that feeling didn't last, because she knew her brother and his ability to misdirect and persuade with his words. She was no fool and wouldn't be so easily led. 'You know more about this. What have you learnt?'

He coughed a short, chesty laugh as he lifted an arm over the back of his chair. 'I have read the reports. I have spoken with the scholars myself and I have made sure that I know as much as I need to know. Nothing has been definitively proven, but there is enough research available for me to form an educated opinion on the matter. And my opinion is this: we are more than safe to continue with our way of life.'

Lorenna swallowed down her anger. On this front, at least, she felt she would be fighting a losing battle to push the point further. He was stubborn. Besides, if all went to plan with Ulyria and the scholars, she would be able to discover the truth for herself.

'Is that all, Lorenna? I have answered your accusations, can you not spare me this latest suspicion? The implications of the Trade Quarters being occupied by the Valivelle enforcers are far-reaching and will demand much of my time to deal with, if things truly are as you and Enforcer Haraygar say.'

She didn't have enough evidence to publicly accuse him of a cover-up, and he had more resources and influence at his back than

The Last of the Magi

she did. The scales were weighted too heavily against her.

'Fine. Deflect me as you always do – one day your arm will tire.'

Vasilarius stood and twirled his chair back to its proper place. He held out one arm towards her and another towards the door. 'Or perhaps there might one day be nothing more to deflect, hm?'

Lorenna chose not to bite back. She frowned at him and went to the door. She just managed to slip her shoulder through the doorway when she turned back to meet his thin smile bearing down on her. 'Not all problems can be pushed away. Unless you want me to end up like Kel?' She immediately regretted bringing their younger brother's name into it, but it brought her a degree of catharsis – his name always got a reaction.

His smile vanished. Folds appeared around his eyes and lips as he stared unblinkingly into her eyes. 'That is *not* what I was suggesting.' his voice was much deeper now. His façade was gone. 'You know that's not what I meant.'

'I know well enough, brother. One way or another the obstacles to your vision all fall away.'

Lorenna jumped as a hand wrapped around her arm. Vasilarius gripped her tightly and she felt her bravado bleed away.

'Kel—' he paused. He looked at the opened door and then lowered his voice. 'The requirements of the Purge were plain for all to understand. There were to be no exceptions.'

'Not even for a child. An innocent boy?'

Vasilarius shook his head. 'Not even. Our father's order was clear. Why do you hold me accountable for doing as our chancellor demanded?'

'Because'—her voice quivered—'*you* told them about him.'

With all the strength she had, she swung her arm free of her brother's grip and escaped through the door, slamming it shut as quickly as she could. She ran down the corridor, rushing back to her private chambers. She clutched at the ring around her neck with one hand, whilst brushing away tears from her cheek with the other.

As she ran, she felt a renewed drive to uncover the truth of all this. For her people, for Asturia, and for her baby brother who died standing amongst the Magi on that blighted day.

PART III

Chapter 39

Quarters Return

The towering metal walls of the Trade Quarters looked menacing. Like they stood so tall to hide a dark secret behind them. Tharian couldn't shake the foreboding feeling. Even Ombra shuffled nervously in her equine form as she tiptoed closer to the gate.

If Greycloak's instincts were right, which they often were, Tharian needed to prepare for danger.

Together they reached the southern gate. Much like when Tharian last returned to the Quarters, he managed to talk his way past the gatekeeper quite easily. He presented himself as a merchant from County Marris, attending the Trade Quarters for a pre-arranged appointment with a fishmonger in the Market Quarter. He spoke confidently enough that the gatekeeper bought it, but he did mumble something about 'letting all kinds through these days.' As Tharian passed through the gate threshold, the gatekeeper gave him a strange look, examining him.

Once inside, Tharian dismounted and whispered for Ombra to take flight. She trotted away to find a private place to shift, and then moments later she flew over his shoulder as a small kurigaw raven. She shot up and over the tenements, disappearing into the smog.

It was comforting to know she would be watching from above. A sorely needed comfort at that, as Tharian took no more than twenty paces into the city proper before his worst suspicions were confirmed.

Marching just a short distance ahead of him, following the curving street that led to the Market Quarter main road, he spotted two city guardsmen flanking a man dressed in a white uniform. An enforcer.

Tharian cursed. He quickly tried to calculate what this meant for the Trade Quarters, and for his plan. Had he secured the allyship of King Thorius of Ferenir just to lose his foundation in the Quarters whilst his back was turned?

Ducking into a side alley, he took to the back roads to find his way to the Collectors Quarter. He checked every corner before any moves. The unsavoury characters that frequented the back roads gave him strange looks, but they didn't fixate on him for long – there were much stranger things to be seen in the shadows than an armed man skulking around. He still looked dishevelled from his time in the Ferenir prison cell, so he didn't look out of place in these alleyways. It took the better part of an hour, but he made it safely to an opening that led onto the main road of the Collectors Quarter.

He looked left and right. No enforcers in sight. In fact, nothing looked out of the ordinary. The collectors were conducting their normal business without change. Almost as if the Elheim presence was of no concern to them at all.

Tharian ducked back as he spotted a door across the road swing open. Loud, abrupt sounds bled out into the street. Instinctively, Tharian's hand dropped to the hilt of his sword. But as his senses caught up to his instincts, he realised the sound that startled him was laughter. A large man appeared out of the doorway first, balancing a carefully wrapped parcel in his palm and clutching at his stomach as he gave way to his customer. That customer was an enforcer. The enforcer wiped at his eyes as he controlled his laughter and carefully took the parcel from the collector.

'This will do nicely. If this perfume is as effective as you say, collector, I will need to save my strength for when I return home!'

The collector chortled and then tucked himself back into the doorway of his shop. 'There is no finer scent in Asturia, I assure you. Use it with moderation, mind you, or else you'll be laboured with more children than you can handle. I can promise you it's not as enjoyable caring for them as it is making them!'

The enforcer waved a hand at the collector as he stepped onto the road to leave. 'You'll be seeing me again if it works!'

Tharian watched on. He shuddered at the exchange. The enforcer had been a customer like any other, and the collector seemed to welcome him as such. Tharian hoped the collector was just playing the part of the accommodating businessowner – perhaps because there was no realistic alternative – but the interaction seemed genuine. After all, it was not completely unheard of for Elheim to

The Last of the Magi

visit the Trade Quarters on shopping excursions. Politics and trade were – at least partly – divorced from one another. And collectors were perhaps the most opportunistic of all traders.

He would learn nothing more from lurking in the shadows. So Tharian pulled up his hood, stepped out onto the road, and headed to Traykin's Bazaar.

He ignored the solicitations bellowed at him from either side of the road, from those same opportunistic collectors wanting to secure a sale from their next customer. Though he kept his head down for most of them, he occasionally locked eyes with one or two along the way and felt compelled to wave them away and confirm he wasn't interested in their wares. Only that would silence them.

As he crept closer to the Bazaar, he noticed that the voices began to dim. They no longer called out, instead they exchanged hushed words with each other.

'Is that—' one said.

'A green coat, I'm sure that's what they said. You don't think…' said another to his neighbour.

'I'm not sure. Maybe we should contact the city guard,' said the neighbour.

Tharian's ears were burning. He quickened his pace, though tried not to make it obvious. With his haste, it wasn't long until he could just see Traykin's Bazaar through the thin smog hanging in the air.

The Bazaar was under surveillance.

An elite guard was standing close to an enforcer near the front door, luckily with their backs turned to him as he approached. They looked to be discussing the peculiar shape and features of the building itself.

Tharian retreated a few steps. He hoped the smog was thick enough that if he backtracked fast enough, he would vanish from their view if they turned. But he was stood in the middle of a wide road. Terrible cover.

His feet itched for him to make a dash for the nearest alley, yet he paused as he spotted a familiar face emerge from the side of the house. It was Frigg. He was looking at the floor as he walked, as he often did, but just as he reached the corner he looked up and met

Tharian's eyes. Frigg peered around the corner, noting that the guard and enforcer were still there, and he backed away, shaking his head as he waved his hand erratically at his side.

A warning, Tharian surmised. This was no longer a safe place for him, even if he could sneak past the enforcer at the front. Was Traykin trapped inside?

No. Frigg wouldn't have shooed him away so readily if Traykin was in there with him.

Tharian turned on his heels and dashed back into the nearest alleyway.

This time, instead of hiding himself within the twists and turns of the dark back roads, he found a building with a low roof and searched for a drainpipe. Using the pipe's metal fixtures as footholds, he climbed to the roof. He hopped the short distance from that roof to its neighbour, a building that joined on to a taller structure. He searched the walls until he found bricks that were uneven enough for him to scale up to the next roof above. These were not artisan constructs, so imperfections were easier to find.

From his vantage point, Tharian sent a thought out to Ombra, calling for her help, though he couldn't see where she was through the smog.

He thought of Traykin's Bazaar, as it had been the last time they visited without the armed guard. He also thought of Greycloak's cave. It was a simple series of thoughts, relating to safety and security. He then described what he could see in his head, hoping that Ombra would somehow find him.

***

'I still don't get it,' Marla said as she marched down the artisan's road with Marion at her side.

Brayne was a few steps ahead, in a hurry to get home as always. He had precisely zero interest in Marion's faith meetings and had spent the whole time shuffling irritably. He didn't want to be there, but Marion had insisted and insisted until she wore him down.

'Which part didn't you understand?' Marion asked. She seemed eager to talk about the meeting. No doubt Brayne had never shown

The Last of the Magi

any interest before.

'I get the words; I just don't understand what you get from it.' Marla said as she adjusted her satchel strap at her shoulder. 'We just sat there, listening to people talk about impossible things.'

'What makes you so sure it's impossible?' Marion probed.

'It just is, Marion,' said Brayne, with only a cursory look over his shoulder. 'Listen to the girl, she has some sense.'

Marla tried to hide her smile. 'I guess I can't be sure,' she said, 'but I've never heard of anyone suddenly being cured of their illnesses like *that* before. If the chirurgeons can't do it, what good will praying do?'

Marion tutted but her expression confirmed that she still enjoyed the chance to talk through her faith. 'Just because you haven't heard of it, seen it, or experienced it yourself, does that mean it has to be impossible?'

'No,' Marla mumbled, 'but it makes it harder for me to understand how it works.'

'Ah – how about magic then?'

Marla looked at Marion questioningly. 'What about it?'

'Do you understand how magic works?'

Marla laughed. 'No. Not in the slightest.'

'But you know it exists.'

'Unfortunately,' Marla said grimly.

Marion winced, probably realising that she was bringing up the memory of her hometown ablaze with Arcane fire. 'Well maybe there are other kinds of magic out there that can make our lives better.'

'That would make a nice change from everything we *do* see magic used for.'

The sermon delivered in the meeting hall by the man robed in gold had contained much the same message. He told tales of the 'Divine', as if it were some higher being that worked its own magic in, around and through everyone and everything. Though he hadn't described it as magic, the analogy Marion presented was helpful.

He talked about illness and disease cured in those who remained devout to the Divine faith. In his view, those who put absolute trust in the will of the Divine would never be made to suffer for long, and any such suffering would only ever be a test of faith. Those who kept true to their faith would ride through those dark times and be rewarded with the blessing of 'the Divine's radiance'.

Marla wanted to ask what the Divine's radiance was, but she knew she would only approach the subject with curious scepticism. That might offend Marion, who had sat through the entire session gripping at their hands tightly as she hung upon every word of the sermon, miming, or muttering the words back to herself. Marion had lost her daughter to illness, and she might even lose her husband to it too one day, so perhaps all this talk of miraculous recoveries and tests of faith were just a way for Marion to process and find peace in that pain.

Who am I to question that? Marla considered. She looked to Marion and smiled warmly at her. 'It sounds fascinating, really. I'll come with you next week as well if you like.'

Marion made a chirping sound and hooked her arm through Marla's for the rest of their walk home together.

Back at the Glanmore home, as they took off their bags and coats in the hallway, Marla looked around the home and then looked warmly at the Glanmores, as if this was the first time she had seen them in some time. Marla felt lucky to be with them. If Marion believed they had found each other because of the Divine's intervention, then so be it. Whether luck or the Divine, Marla was just grateful to be where she was.

Brayne approached Marla with his hand held out. She picked up the satchel she just dropped against the wall and passed it to him. It was filled with sheets of exotic metals collected from the Collectors Quarter earlier that morning.

He coughed into the back of his hand and nodded with thanks, then went to the workshop to carry on his work.

Marion shrugged and went into the lounge.

Marla went to the kitchen. She hadn't yet had the chance to wash her hands since handling the metal Brayne had ordered, and she had sat through the entire faith meeting straight after.

While there, Marla took a little time to just enjoy looking out the window into the back yard as she slowly scrubbed her hands clean.

The yard of the Glanmore's home was small and not all that

The Last of the Magi

inviting due to the tall fences that boxed it in from the neighbours' homes and the alleyway that ran down the right side of the house, to Marla's left from her current perspective. The fence panels were each taller than her and she was certain that if they all fell in one day they would completely eclipse the small garden space.

It wasn't much to look at. Most of that small space was paved with slabs of stone with only a couple of small pots laid against the back wall of the house for Marion to grow some herbs. Or try to, at least. The city air was hardly ideal for growing fresh plants.

Marla then realised that she had never once gone out there. Yet she would spend so much time staring at it from the window, whenever she was doing chores in the kitchen. It almost felt as if the yard was some far-off place.

She considered finally stepping out the back door and seeing it for herself, to see whether the small, paved yard had more charm when not viewed from behind glass. But before that idea could take shape, she was distracted by a sudden rattling sound and then something rolling over the top of the fence and landing in a slump on the floor.

She gasped as the green lump on the ground immediately moved, springing to its feet. It was a man. And as the man straightened and threw back his hood, she knew instantly who it was.

Tharian!?

She unlocked the back door, as quietly as she could to not alert Marion in the other room. She stepped out.

'Tharian?' she said in her best loud whisper.

Tharian startled, reacting defensively to her voice, but his brows rose as he recognised her.

'You?' he exclaimed in a similarly hushed tone. He glanced up for a second and then back to her. 'What are you doing here?'

'*I* live here.'

The two stared at each other, both mouthing their bewilderment at this unexpected reunion.

A black bird landed on Tharian's shoulder, a kurigaw raven if Marla wasn't mistaken. She hadn't seen many of those since she left home.

Tharian didn't flinch. 'Of course,' he muttered under his breath as he looked at the bird. 'You really did keep an eye on her.'

'What?' She asked with an ear turned towards him.

'It doesn't matter. I'm glad to see you're ok.'

Marla shook her head and then looked over the fences. There were enough neighbouring buildings taller than the Glanmore's home with windows that looked over the yard. 'I'm not sure if I can say the same for you just yet. You better come inside.'

Without another word, the bird hopped from Tharian's shoulder. By the time it touched the ground it had changed. It longer had feathers or talons, instead it had changed before her eyes into a small lirrus. It bounded between Marla's legs and disappeared inside the house.

Marla looked up from her feet and stared open-mouthed at Tharian. 'A Shifter?' she said. He nodded. She had never seen one of the transforming creatures in the flesh. Before either could say anything else, Marion shrieked from the living room.

Marla closed her eyes and sighed. She then waved into the house. 'In, quickly.'

Tharian swept inside and Marla took a quick look at the neighbours' windows for any spectators before heading in. Fortunately, there were none.

***

After chasing Ombra through the living room for a few minutes, Marla eventually grabbed her and thrust the snarling feline into Tharian's arms.

Tharian just stood awkwardly in the doorway, cradling Ombra – much to their mutual disapproval – as Marla comforted the startled woman. He overheard Marla call her Marion.

Marla pointed Tharian's way, and Marion noticed him for the first time. Marla opened her mouth to say something – to introduce him, he assumed – but then she paused. Tharian heard heavy footsteps as someone approached behind him.

'Brayne!' Marla said, and she dashed away from Marion and stood in front of the burly blacksmith, pushing Tharian a bit further

The Last of the Magi

into the room. 'Sorry, things got a little excitable in here.'

The blacksmith, Brayne, looked him up and down. His eyes held over Tharian's coat and then his brows furrowed, and his cheeks flushed red. 'It's him,' he said.

Marla shuffled sideways and blocked Brayne's path into the room. 'I can explain. He isn't here to cause us any trouble.' She turned back and looked directly at Tharian. 'Right?'

Tharian nodded. He thought it best to just go along with whatever Marla was doing.

Brayne grunted. He looked to the window that faced the Artisan Quarter main road. 'Workshop. Now.' He turned on his heels and walked away.

With a sigh, Marla ushered Tharian to follow, and so he did. The corridor wound to the left and took them through a plastic sheet, leading to a hot, steaming blacksmithing workshop. The forge was lit, and the heat washed over Tharian as soon as he entered the room. He felt instantly dehydrated.

Brayne leaned against his anvil and stared squarely at him. 'Give me one good reason why I shouldn't throw you out on the street?'

Tharian shrugged and put Ombra down, she was writhing to escape from the heat. 'I can't. If you want me to go, I will go.'

Brayne looked stumped. He cocked his head slightly.

'I was looking for somewhere safe to lay low while I figured out what was going on here,' Tharian continued. 'I didn't intend to disturb you but when I saw Marla, I was happy to see a friendly face.'

Brayne huffed and turned away for a moment before directing his scowl at Marla this time, as if asking her for an explanation.

'I told you at the tourney that I'd met him before,' she said. He helped me get here after I left Bryn. He was a bit reluctant to help me, I should add'—she smirked at Tharian—'but he did it nonetheless. I trust him.'

The blacksmith looked irate. 'I remember what he did at the tourney. We've been working double-shift since he pulled that stunt with the runeblade, in case you'd forgotten, and the Elheim are looking for him.'

'For me?' Tharian said, he tried to keep his voice low and hide his concern. The enforcers were here for him. 'Tell me what's going on, please.'

'The enforcers forced their way into the city and summoned the coinsmen,' Marla said calmly, 'they said there was a fugitive here, with an illegal runeblade, wanted for crimes against the Grand City. They knocked on every door to question people.'

Tharian cursed under his breath. 'I didn't mean for this to happen. I'm sorry for what you've all had to endure because of me, especially when I wasn't even here.'

Brayne stepped closer to Tharian and folded his arms. He was tall and loomed over him slightly. Tharian held his stance and didn't allow himself to be cowed. He slipped his hand under his coat to the hilt of his blade, as a precaution.

The blacksmith noticed. He looked down. 'So, it *was* a runeblade?'

Tharian paused. It wasn't the question he was expecting. He smirked and flicked the drape of his coat from his waist and then drew out his sword. He tilted the dark blue metal so the light from Brayne's furnace reflected into the blacksmith's face.

Even though Brayne's eyes widened and almost glistened at the sight of the weapon, Tharian noticed something that he'd forgotten: there was no Arcana left in the blade. Enforcer Quiryn had bled the runes dry.

Yet, the lack of glow in the blade's engraved runes didn't disappoint Brayne. He ran his fingers over them.

'The runes absorb and hold magic—'

Brayne snorted. 'You don't need to explain Artificer Blacksmithing to *me*, mate.'

Tharian raised a brow. He hadn't heard that term before.

'Runecrafting,' Brayne clarified. 'The way I see it, if you used this to give the enforcers a taste of their own medicine, it serves them right. It's about time they got knocked on their asses.'

'I couldn't agree more, but looking at what's happened to the Quarters as a result... I'm not sure it was worth it.'

Marion stepped forward, fanning herself with her hand to combat the dry heat of the workshop. 'You said you were out of the city – why did you come back?'

The Last of the Magi

Tharian dropped his head slightly and sheathed his sword. 'I have an important message to deliver to the coinsmen, from Ferenir. I was on my way to Traykin's Bazaar until I saw his home was under watch.'

'He isn't there,' added Brayne. 'The former coinsmen are under house arrest at Velioth's place.'

'Former coinsmen?' Tharian asked. But no sooner had his question left his lips when his intuition answered it for him. The enforcers would not occupy the Trade Quarters without also taking control of the city. Control was their hallmark. 'Who are the coinsmen now?'

Brayne nodded to Marion, deferring to her.

'Enforcer Valivelle represents the Market Quarter while his son represents the Collectors Quarter. They had some kind of informant already in the city – they called him Inquisitor Protelborn – he now leads the Quarter of War. The only saving grace for us in this mess, thank the Divine, is that Coinswoman Keene has been allowed to remain in her post.'

Valivelle. More enforcers from the Valivelle family were in the Trade Quarters. Now he could see why they were taking such bold steps to track him down. They were hungry for a taste of revenge.

As for the inquisitor, he hadn't heard that title before. If Inquisitor Protelborn was truly a spy for the Grand City, Tharian felt sick to his stomach. How much did he know about their plan. The situation was now so tangled. Maybe he would be better off leaving the city, returning home to Greycloak and abandoning this pointless mission altogether?

No.

There was no use fretting, he wouldn't find out more by hiding away. He needed to reach Traykin and the other coinsmen. He needed to tell them the good news from Ferenir, and maybe that would inspire the deposed leaders to take action, or at the least they could advise him on what he should do next to push the Elheim out of the Quarters. This wasn't over. Not yet. His gut told him there was more to be done.

'I had no idea things were this bad,' Tharian said. 'I'm sorry. You risk a lot just by me being here. I won't trouble you anymore –

I'll find a way to reach the former coinsmen.'

'You assume I'm not planning on handing you over,' said Brayne. His brows almost covered his eyes.

Marla bolted forward. 'You can't do that, they'll kill him. We're all on the same side here!'

'No, girl, we're not!' shouted Brayne. 'Our side is the side of the Trade Quarters. We may not like the Grand City but we're not about to fight them – just like we aren't going to throw our lot in with any of the other city states or the Outer Counties. You heard Coinswoman Keene's announcement, once the Elheim have cleaned up this mess, things will go back to normal.'

'You didn't really believe that did you?' said Marla, 'I get why you trust Keene, but she made that announcement with enforcers at her side. They might have been making her say that!'

'Maybe. It doesn't change what the Elheim will do to us if they hear we had *him* in our house.' Brayne flicked a hand towards Tharian without looking at him. 'We're better handing him over while we can still explain ourselves.'

Marla opened her mouth to speak and then looked desperately to Brayne, then Marion and then finally Tharian. Marion looked deep in thought. Brayne's stance was stoic.

'He's right,' said Tharian. 'Every moment I stay here puts you all at risk. Whether report me to the guard is your prerogative – and I'd respect your reasons for doing so – but'—Tharian turned and shifted his weight on to one leg as if ready to spring away on a moment's notice—'I will not sit here quietly and wait for them to come and detain me.'

Brayne's shoulders raised as he stretched to his full height. 'Is that right? And if you evade arrest, what will you do then?'

The man's blunt expression and harsh tone lit a fire within Tharian's gut. He answered him confidently, 'I will do everything in my power to remove the Elheim from this city, and then from Asturia.'

Brayne's was serious and stern. Then his lips curled into a half smile, which then grew into a full one. He relaxed and laughed. A laugh cut short by a harsh cough. He took in a deep breath. 'I like this one.'

The Last of the Magi

Tharian looked to Marla for reassurance, and she was just smiling at Brayne with an impish look.

'The enemy of our enemy is our friend, isn't that what they say?' Brayne continued.

Tharian shrugged. 'They do. I suppose this means you aren't handing me over?'

Brayne turned to Marla. 'You're sure he can be trusted?'

Marla shrugged. 'I can't guarantee anything,' she redirected her impish look Tharian's way, 'but I think he may have saved a lot of lives back in Bryn. I owe him something for that.'

'You better not pull another fast one, like you did at the Crucible.'

'That was different,' Tharian replied, 'It was a means to an end, to bring me close to the coinsmen. But it paid off.' He reached inside his coat and pulled out the letter that the coinsmen had given him to present to the King of Ferenir. He held it out to Brayne.

Brayne pushed his hand in Marion's direction, and she took the letter. She scanned it, her eyes darting over the lettering at rapid speed. 'I don't believe it,' she said, 'this is from the coinsmen – our coinsmen, I mean. It confirms that he has authority to speak with the King of Ferenir on behalf of the coinsmen.'

'If the coinsmen support you, they must have had bloody good reason to,' said Brayne. 'That'll do it for me. What's your plan; what do you need?'

Tharian felt a rush. This burly blacksmith who, not a moment ago, threatened to hand him over to the enforcer had seemingly backtracked. He wouldn't question it; all allies were welcomed at this stage. 'I *had* a plan, but things have changed now the Elheim are here. I need to speak with the former coinsmen. Any ideas on how I can get into Velioth's home?'

Marion clicked her fingers and pulled open one of the drawers under Brayne's desk. She licked her finger and rifled through a tightly packed file of papers. 'This might do the trick!'

She brandished the papers in the air in front of them all, and then handed a sheet of paper covered in drawings to Brayne.

'Good idea,' Brayne said, and then he tapped the paper with his finger and looked to Tharian. 'It's an old order from Coinsman

Velioth himself for a bracer, from back when he was trying his hand at archery. If we hide the date stamp and remake the order, we might be able to get a delivery to him. The house is under guard, but deliveries are still being allowed through.' He held the design out for Marla. 'Think you can handle that?'

She took it eagerly. She frowned and turned the paper about, examining it from various angles. 'It's simple enough, a bit flashy but not complicated. I can do this.'

'No use standing around then.' Brayne turned and stoked the fire of the furnace while Marla grabbed tools and metal from the back of the workshop.

Tharian watched on with amusement as the young blacksmithing apprentice from the peaceful town of Brynfall now moved confidently around an artisan's workshop. She had clearly upped her game since arriving in the Quarters. Or maybe she had always been that way, and he had made a poor assumption about the work ethic and skill of those in the Outer Counties. Either way, he took the time to notice the confidence she displayed now, with Brayne supervising and only making small corrective comments along the way.

He was stirred from watching the two get to work by Marion gently pushing him back towards the door.

'Let them have their fun,' she said. 'We had better get you out of that filthy coat, you stand out a mile in that thing.'

He looked at his sleeves. She was right, of course. His coat may have served his stealthy lifestyle well when he spent a decade travelling through forests and expansive fields, but here, in a city of grey, brown, and red, he was garishly visible. And it hadn't been cleaned in weeks.

Chapter 40

Art of the Artisan

Marion was tugging at Tharian's shoulders, trying to wiggle him out of his coat in the middle of her living room.

He struggled in protest. 'I'd rather not be without this coat,' he said. 'I know it stands out, but I wear it for good reason.' He peeled open one side and pointed to a couple of the concealed pockets hidden within the stitching. They could hold all sorts of emergency supplies: dried ration supplies, a bag of coins, bandages. Most of those supplies had been depleted long ago, but the point still stood. Moreover, the coat was thick, it gave him shelter from the elements and a little extra padding if he found himself in a fight.

Marion pursed her lips as she acknowledged the handiwork. Feeling uncomfortable, Tharian pulled his coat tightly about himself and folded his arms.

'The Elheim have given everyone your description. If you go out there wearing that, someone will call for the enforcers. But if you're adamant you need to keep it on, maybe we can hide it instead. I have an idea. Wait here.'

She darted away before he could say anything. Her footsteps thumped up the stairs. A few seconds later, back down she came. She strode back into the living room with a long brown trench coat in hand, that she urged him to wear. It was obviously one of Brayne's coats as the sleeves and hemline dropped too low on him, and his shoulders were barely broad enough to fill it. Tharian sighed and rolled his eyes. He caught a glimpse of himself in the wall-mounted mirror over the fireplace. He looked ridiculous, like a boy in his father's clothes – but also looking oddly bulky at the same time from wearing one coat over another.

'This is a terrible idea,' he said.

Marion tutted and then turned him away from the mirror. She held a packet of pins, and at her waist was a small belt of tailoring tools. 'Just wait and see,' she said.

At a remarkable pace, Marion worked on the garments. She tucked the sleeves and the hems around the inside of his own coat and locked the two garments together with the pins. She held more pins between her lips as she worked her way around him.

She raised his arms up. If he lowered them even slightly, she slapped them back into place. 'Keep still,' she mumbled while still holding the pins between her lips.

She pulled a threaded needle from her belt. Without a word, she whizzed around Tharian with her hand moving in a figure-eight motion. It only took her a few minutes to finish working her way back through all the areas of the two coats that were pinned together. As she reappeared back at Tharian's front, she had all the pins pinched between her fingers again, and the needle no longer had thread running through it.

Stepping back, she eyed him. She scratched at her head and leaned in to examine her work more closely.

Eventually she straightened and smiled. 'That will do the trick,' she said.

Tharian's arms were aching from where he held them out for too long. They soothed as he finally lowered them.

She turned him around, back to the mirror. Tharian let out a short laugh as he noticed his new appearance. His green coat had been entirely concealed. But not only that, Marion had made Brayne's trench coat fit firm to his own, as if there was nothing underneath at all. It was incredibly convincing. Even the hood was covered, though he was sure Brayne's coat didn't have a hood on it when she started. But it did now. The combined garment was heavy, but that was no trouble. That was the least of his concerns.

The colour wasn't attractive, but that was for the better. Brown was a much more common colour amongst the merchants, couriers and tradespeople that regularly roamed the streets of the Market Quarter.

Tharian smiled at Marion. 'This is amazing.'

Marion shrugged. 'Blacksmithing isn't the only skill in this house. I'm a bit out of practice, but the old tailoring muscles are still there.'

The living room door swung open, and Marla stepped in. She,

The Last of the Magi

too, had donned a long leather overcoat, in a darker brown shade like wet mud, and she wore an old cap that, again, must have been Brayne's by its size. It suited her though.

She took in Tharian's new colours with a pout. 'Nice look. Nearly didn't recognise you.' She then held out a package for Tharian, it was a rectangular shape wrapped in brown paper and tied with a silver thread.

Assuming it to be the bracer, he took it under his arm and then looked over her change of clothing. 'Are you going somewhere?'

'I'm coming with you.'

Both Tharian and Marion balked at her.

'No, you're not,' said Marion sternly. 'It's far too dangerous.'

Marla waved her hand through the air. 'They destroyed my home. Literally set it on fire while I was still there. I can handle this. I'm not going to sit on the side-line and wait for them to do the same here.

'Brayne won't let you, he—'

'I've already had this argument with him,' Marla interrupted. 'I told him he can't stop me.' She then looked to Tharian just as he was about to add to the objections. 'And the same goes to you. I'll follow you like I did from Brynwell if I have to.'

Tharian sighed and rubbed his forehead with the back of his hand while he found the words to contain his thoughts. 'If we get caught, the enforcers will probably do to you whatever they plan to do to me.'

Marla rolled her eyes and then pointed at Tharian's reflection in the mirror. 'Nobody will recognise you. They're looking for a green coat and a runeblade, the enforcers will have no reason to challenge you now, looking like that. Besides, if you're going to pretend to be an artisan, you'll need someone with experience to make it sound convincing.'

Tharian frowned for a moment and then half-smiled. 'You have a point,' he said. He curled the side of his coat behind his waist and gestured to the hilt of his sword. 'I better make sure they don't see this.'

'Leave it here,' said Marion. 'We can take care of it. Brayne can even give it a once over with a whetstone.'

'No. I'm not letting this sword out of my sight again. It's my only defence against them if things go wrong.'

'All the more reasons to have me with you then. I'll do the talking, and hopefully you will go mostly unnoticed,' Marla said triumphantly. Neither he nor Marion had any quick response. 'Then it's decided, then. We're going together.'

Marla put her hands on her hips and the sides of her coat parted outwards slightly. Tharian caught a glimpse of the handles of her handaxes affixed to her legs. Judging by the determined look on her face, there was no way she would be talked out of this.

'I suppose we are.'

With a chirping purr, Ombra sauntered into the room and brushed up against Marla's ankles. His team were assembled.

Marla moved around Tharian to reach Marion. She hugged her tightly, then she held Marion out at a forearms distance. 'I'll be back before you know it. Don't worry about me. Brayne is upstairs, I think he could do with some air and maybe a fresh drink. All this excitement isn't good for him.'

Marion glanced to the ceiling and then nodded. She hurried towards the door and then held herself at the frame for a moment. 'Take care of her, Tharian.'

'I will,' he said. Marion then slipped away. Tharian turned back to Marla. 'You're sure about this?'

'Without a doubt – let's go.'

***

As soon as the pair left the house, Tharian quickly steered off the artisan's main road in the hope they could get to the Market Quarter through the roads less travelled by the guard. But Marla pulled at his arm and dragged him back away from the alley opening before he could disappear into the shadows.

'Don't be stupid, Tharian,' she said. 'We're artisans. It will look more suspicious if we take the back roads rather than going direct like other couriers to the coinsmen would.'

He looked down the alley, his feet wanting to pull him into the darkness. She had a point. Taking her advice, they walked openly

The Last of the Magi

down the main road instead.

Tharian followed at Marla's side and watched the artisans as they went about their business at their shopfronts. They passed a dressmaker and Marla called out a greeting to the woman who stepped out to hang up an immaculately bejewelled dress as a display piece. The woman waved back and returned the greeting.

Despite the pleasantries, Tharian felt the first shot of adrenaline enter his system. This was not his way of doing things. Marla was actively attracting attention and he felt like eyes in all directions were now staring at him, even though from a cursory glance he knew that wasn't the case. He walked on autonomously, focusing on keeping a lookout for any white and blue uniforms turning a corner up ahead or emerging from a shop.

Whether he liked it or not, this was a smart plan. Marla was behaving naturally, just playing the role of an artisan, because – he guessed – she was one of them now. He would put his confidence in her. If he needed any more comfort, he only needed to glance overhead, where Ombra looped over buildings in her raven form to act as their scout.

They passed another business, this time a brewer of alcohol and spirits. This younger artisan, with a wide, wiry moustache leaned in his doorway with a pipe to his lips. He called out to them. 'Has he got you playing messenger again, Marla?' His voice was smooth and confident.

Marla spread her hands in the air. 'As always. Nothing new!'

'And who's this with you?'

Tharian met the man's eyes nervously then quickly looked to Marla. A second shot of adrenaline surged.

She rolled her eyes. 'The apprentice's apprentice,' she replied with a laugh.

'Ha! Business must be good for the Glanmores. Good luck to you.'

Tharian shook his head in disbelief and glanced at Marla side-on. 'You're far too good at this.'

She tilted her head and looked confused. 'Good at what?'

'Blending in.'

'This isn't blending in, Tharian. I live here now. These are my colleagues.'

Tharian considered her words. Stealth and subtlety had for too long been his way of getting to where he needed to be and finding out what he needed to know. Admittedly his time back in Asturia had called for a more direct and abrasive approach to achieving his goals, but those were just flashes of necessity against his otherwise quiet and reclusive tendencies. Sometimes he forgot that other people lived *normal* lives. The kind of lives where the exchange of passing pleasantries between familiar faces was not a risk to anyone's liberty. Not every prying eye had a malicious agenda.

You've made me paranoid, old man. He groaned internally. *Could I live like this?*

What would he even do with himself if he had the chance to live a normal life? He was a survivalist. He could survive anywhere because of his years growing up as Greycloak's ward, but his skills were hardly marketable as a business venture.

Tharian wondered as they walked. *Maybe a mercenary?* He concluded.

That didn't feel right. He remembered when he and Marla had arrived in the Trade Quarters together. Within minutes they were approached by villainous thugs looking for easy prey. That was not the kind of work Tharian would want to do. He was good at stopping fights, or avoiding them, but starting them was not really his way. He had never seriously injured or killed another person with his own hands. His attack on the Valivelle enforcer was the most harm he had ever done to someone – and that was just reflecting an Arcane assault. Even Enforcer Quiryn's brutal injuries were inflicted by Ombra instead of him.

No, not a mercenary then, he wondered further. *What then?*

They reached the central plaza, and Tharian let the feeling of wanderlust in his stomach fade away. He had enough distractions to keep him occupied as they circled left around the marbled plaza towards the Market Quarter's main road.

'These lot are brilliant,' Marla said, pointing to a couple of dancers who performed within a half-circle of bards. Their movements were slow and graceful, and the melody was complex and powerful.

The Last of the Magi

Though Marla enjoyed the performance, the music unsettled Tharian. A lifetime of travelling had exposed him to many styles of music. This was no sea shanty or tavern ditty put together to amuse the masses. No, this music didn't have the familiar bounce or softness that came with the melodies crafted from the major city states of their country.

This could only be music from the Grand City. It was pleasant enough to the ear, like the kind of symphonic piece that might be played in a ballroom, Tharian assumed. But it was *their* music, nonetheless.

To make it worse, there was a gathering of Quartersfolk clapping along and throwing coins into the small cradles dotted around the performance area. They unwittingly – or maybe wittingly – celebrated this covert injection of Grand City culture into their city. He hoped most of them had just never heard the music before.

He then spotted enforcers in the crowd, enjoying the music just like the others. Marla must have noticed them a few seconds after he did, as she suddenly dragged her gaze away and hastened for the Market Quarter. 'Idiots,' he heard Marla mutter under her breath. She had a guilty look on her face.

Tharian again wanted to dash away out of sight and would have done so if Marla wasn't bolting on ahead around the outside edge of the plaza. He caught up to her. 'Don't let it get to you,' Tharian reassured her. 'If there's one thing the Elheim are good at, its branding their culture to be something worthy of applause and celebration. They know how to conceal poison barbs beneath carefully placed roses.'

Marla sighed and shrugged, then she pressed on ahead. Tharian held back slightly, to examine the crowd a little more while he still could. He noted the crowds were slightly thinner where the enforcers stood, yet there were still many gathered around. Possibly collectors and artisans judging by their richer or more quirky wardrobe choices. None seemed to shirk away from those enforcers though. A few people even engaged in conversation with them.

Quartersfolk and Elheim stood together in the same crowd. Why were people not rioting in the street? Seeing them stand shoulder-to-shoulder made the words of Enforcer Quiryn replay in his head vividly:

"The Arcane Guild was formed... with a common purpose — to ensure that our fair continent could grow, prosper, and develop free from the influence of foreign forces or the tilted strength of their magics...

"...The only way that Asturia can continue to grow, free from the threat of another invading force, is to unite. That unity must be absolute, and those who refuse to see that would be the first to fall in an invasion. We cannot risk offering our enemies a free quarter on our lands for the sake of some transient ideals of independence."

Tharian looked away from the crowd and followed Marla as she turned the corner into the Market Quarter. In the back of his mind, thoughts were beginning to bubble into questions. Seeing the Quartersfolk and the Elheim standing together – was this the unity the Arcane Guild, now the Grand City of Elheim, strived for? Or were these people just prisoners playing nice in front of their jailors?

He assumed the latter. He hoped the latter. That this was an illusion of peace.

A dusty, warm breeze flurried through his weighty coat. The heat against his face pulled him from his thoughts. Marla was waiting for him at the corner to the Market Quarter main road. When he caught up, they walked together again.

'Velioth's manor is just ahead. It will come up on our left, you really can't miss it,' Marla said.

Walking through the Market Quarter with Marla was very different to the Artisan Quarter. People didn't call friendly greetings to them as they passed. And there was a lot more footfall. Where the artisan's road was open and neatly laid out with tidy, constrained displays of goods for sale and adverts for specialist services, the market's road was more like... a controlled chaos. Market stalls, rikshaws and bounty-laden carts turned the straight road into a weaving series of thinner footpaths bustling with trade.

It would be easy to get side-tracked, distracted by the gradual transition from crates of fresh fruits through to sliced meats mounted in trays of ice to fend off the heat. And then there was the cacophony of voices, people trading and bartering in every

The Last of the Magi

direction, fighting to be heard.

Instead of giving the market his attention, Tharian looked through, around and above the stalls until he saw Velioth's elaborately decorated manor-house appearing on their left, just as Marla said it would. The pair slowed their approach as they spotted the guards at the door – an enforcer stood with two elite guards.

Marla scrunched her face, not making the slightest effort to conceal her frustration. Tharian quickly stepped in front of her and turned his back on the manor, blocking her view of the guards – and their view of her. He grabbed her shoulder and twisted her towards the market stall near to them.

'Don't let this throw you,' Tharian said. 'We carry on as planned.'

Marla looked at the wrapped bundle still nestled under Tharian's arm and she swallowed before nodding in agreement. 'Shall I do the talking?'

Tharian smirked. 'I think that might be wise, don't you?'

'Agreed,' she chuckled. She tugged the parcel out from his arm.

Stepping aside, Tharian gestured courteously for Marla to take the lead. He followed closely behind. He pulled his coat tight, making sure his runeblade was hidden.

'Stop there,' said the nearest elite guard. He squared up to Marla in his black and gold armour and tilted his spear to block her path. The guard twisted and called to the enforcer who was whispering something to the other guard.

The enforcer exhaled hard through her nostrils and swaggered over lethargically. 'What is your business here? Speak quickly.'

Marla stuttered at first. The words she tried to say became a jumble of awkward sounds as she stood only a foot or so from the white and blue uniform. The enforcer leaned in, pulling an expression of disgust until Marla finally found her words. 'We have a delivery for Mister Erilen Velioth,' she said.

'What is it?' the enforcer asked.

'A bracer, an artisan commission. I believe Mister Velioth wants it for his archery practice.'

The enforcer glanced behind to the other elite guard who had a bow and quiver fastened to her back. Her eyeline drifted to the guard's wrists.

Following the glance, Tharian was relieved to notice that the guard's armour featured bracers that looked sturdier and of a higher quality than those worn by the other guard. That part of their story was plausible, even to one not experienced in martial combat and weaponry.

But when the enforcer turned back to Marla, her eyes lingered on the parcel for a time. She slowly scanned Marla up and down, and then did the same to Tharian – making his stomach churn – before she spoke again. 'I fail to see what use he would have for such a thing within the confines of his private home.'

The guard closest to Marla and Tharian lifted his spear and leaned into the conversation. 'I believe there is a small archery range at the back of the manor, we've rented it for target practice in the past,' he said to the enforcer. He then looked at Marla. 'Do you have a proof of order?'

Marla smiled confidently and brandished the old order letter from her jacket pocket. She unfolded the document and held it in such a way that the signature and the specifications were clear to see, with her thumb delicately placed to obscure the date line which had been crudely scrubbed away and written over.

The guard's eyes hovered over that part of the page, and he peered at Marla through his helm. He squinted one eye at her, and his lowered brow came into view under his helm.

Tharian's blood chilled. He suspected Marla felt the same, even if her face didn't show it. She waved the document forward again, as if the guard hadn't looked at the document at all.

Then the guard's eyes softened. 'The paperwork is in order, enforcer.' The guard winked at Marla before returning to his post.

'Very well,' she said as she stepped closer to Marla. 'And who is this?' she pointed to Tharian.

'I'm an apprentice, ma'am.' Tharian said, calmly, as he tried to copy the drawl that the common folk of the Trade Quarters spoke in.

The enforcer looked surprised. 'Is an apprentice really needed to help deliver a small parcel?'

Tharian's pulse quickened. But Marla interjected before he had to scramble for a response. 'The owner insists. Being a good artisan

The Last of the Magi

is just as much about courtesy and customer care as it is craft. No better way to learn than by seeing it done first-hand.'

'If you say so,' replied the enforcer. Her tone was dismissive. She eyed the package, holding out a hand. 'I'll take this in myself. You can go.'

Marla clutched at the parcel more tightly and swung her body away from the enforcer's outstretched hand. 'No, you can't.'

'Excuse me?'

'Our instructions are to negotiate the price with Mister Velioth directly.'

That was some quick thinking, Tharian thought with a smirk. He hid it quickly as the enforcer looked him over.

The enforcer looked around to the two guards and they both shrugged. The one in the background just muttered the word 'artisans' derisively. Her gloved hands balled into fists and the tension in her jaw was visible through her gaunt cheeks. She stared at Marla for a while and then looked once more at the parcel.

Tharian lowered his hand closer to his runeblade. He didn't like the look on the enforcer's face at all. He'd seen that look on Enforcer Valivelle back in Bryn, and Enforcer Quiryn in the carriage from Ferenir. He braced himself for an attack.

The enforcer then spoke. 'Go ahead,' she said, much to Tharian's surprise. 'But do not linger.' She then turned away and returned to her conversation with the guard down the far end of the manor-front.

Marla turned back to Tharian, her cheeks were flushed, and she had a look of bewilderment and disbelief. Tharian moved his hand quickly away from his coat and pushed her forward.

Together they made for the lavish, black-dyed wood of the manor's front door and slipped through as quickly as they could.

They pushed the door closed and both released their held breaths. They only had a few seconds of respite in Velioth's manor before they were greeted by an older man with a white beard. He seemed to almost glide from the grace of his walk as he turned the corner into the room. He had dark circles under his eyes and his butler uniform looked dishevelled.

Tharian recognised this man as Mors, the attendant who was

never far from Velioth's heel. He was there when Tharian met with Velioth at the morning market, and he was at the Coinsmeet too.

Mors addressed them hesitantly, but courteously, and was in the middle of asking what business they had at the manor when he met Tharian's eyes and realised who was stood before him.

'Master Tharian? Please, follow me,' Mors said.

He turned on his heels and made for a door at the far end of the reception room. They followed without hesitation. The door took them into a courtyard, with a covered walkway that ran around its perimeter. Mors led them along that walkway. They passed many doors, revealing that Velioth's manor was huge despite its frontage not taking up too much space on the main road.

Velioth's manor was more lavish on the inside than its façade suggested too. Down the opposite end of the courtyard, the property rose an extra level higher, and a plinth of stone rose from the roof with a hollowed-out circle near its apex. The circle had two lines of brick crossing its diameter, one horizontal and another vertical. Judging by its positioning, Tharian guessed that at the height of the afternoon, on a clearer day like today, the sunlight passing through the plinth would cast a shadow on the courtyard in the shape of the Trade Quarters itself. It must have been by design, if the intricacy of the flower arrangements in the courtyard and the décor on the walls were anything to go by.

Instead of being led into one of the many side doors, Mors took a sharp right and passed through an opening that took them into the courtyard itself. He weaved them towards a shaded area around a small pond filled with shimmering fish.

There, concealed behind a small mound of grass, sat three individuals. The deposed coinsmen.

Velioth himself was laid against the mound with his hands laced behind his head. Faast was sat rigidly upright in a wooden chair by a hedge, modestly dressed for once without her full armoured regalia. And then Traykin was sat sideways on a stone bench, leaning over the pond. None of them looked up as Tharian and Marla approached.

'My Lords and my Lady, I have Mister Tharian here, with a companion, to meet with you.'

The Last of the Magi

Velioth, Faast and Traykin all shot glances their way at breakneck speed. Traykin instantly grinned.

'Now *this* is an unexpected pleasure!' said Traykin. 'You've missed all the fun, lad.'

'So I've heard. You're looking a little worse for wear.'

Traykin scoffed and looked to his colleagues. Velioth looked down at himself and then fastened the buttons on the black, floral shirt he wore and pulled his tailored clothes more tightly to his body. Faast, however, just stared at Tharian with an unambiguously disapproving look.

'We don't just look it, we feel it. We should bring you up to speed – a lot has changed.'

Tharian waved his hand, 'no need,' he said, 'I know the Elheim have taken control, that much is obvious just from walking the streets. But I don't understand why only you three are here. What's happening with Coinswoman Keene?'

Faast grunted and exchanged a tense glare with Velioth, who shrugged and looked away from her.

Traykin breathed between tightly pursed lips. 'We're still trying to figure that one out. To say we've had disagreements on the subject is putting it lightly.'

Faast rose to her feet and stood at her full lofty height, towering over the other deposed coinsmen with her arms folded. Even in just a plain white shirt and dark grey trousers, she looked no less formidable. 'Apparently, she stands with the Elheim willingly. She betrayed the trust of our people, and us.'

'You don't know that, Faast,' sighed Velioth. Evidently this was the disagreement Traykin was talking about. He lifted onto his elbows, using the hill as a support. 'You heard her public address. As the most senior amongst us, she has been retained to facilitate a smooth transition and to help restore trust between the Grand City and the Trade Quarters.'

'Open your eyes, you child,' barked Faast. 'She is to receive Arcane training as a "gesture of good will" from the Grand City? When have the Elheim ever offered such a thing to any not of their creed. What other conclusion is there to draw than our city's *beloved* coinswoman is unravelling some machination of ulterior motives for personal gain?'

Velioth shook his head, but he didn't raise his voice to match her volume. He spoke softly. 'I cannot say anything for certain. My guess is as good as yours. All I know is Coinswoman Keene has served the best interests of the Quarters for decades. I cannot see why she would feel the need to throw her lot in with the Grand City now. Maybe she had no choice in the matter, maybe she is being forced, or maybe she truly is trying to soften the harshness of this sudden change.'

Faast sat down and growled through gritted teeth. Between the heat of Faast's fiery words, and the placid optimism of Velioth's, Traykin remained quiet and contemplative.

'What's your view, Traykin?' asked Tharian. He knew that Traykin and Keene had history together – though he wasn't sure what that history was. It was Traykin who rallied Keene to agree to the Coinsmeet off the back of being owed a few 'favours.' Perhaps he knew more.

Traykin blinked at Tharian as the question sunk in. It looked as if he had been pulled out of a deep, private thought. He shrugged and glanced blankly around the courtyard. Taking a moment longer, he eventually answered. 'I don't know, lad. I know Keene well enough to agree that she always served the best interests of the Quarters. Even when we disagreed on matters of law or policy, her views always ended up being the right one for the people.

'But then again,' he slowed and lowered his voice to a more serious tone – perhaps a defeated tone, which was odd for Traykin. 'The four coinsmen, you and Mors were the only ones who knew exactly what happened at the Coinsmeet, and yet Enforcer Valivelle and that Inquisitor Protelborn character knew everything. And now we're here and she is there. I can't overlook the evidence that says she sold us out.'

'I'm pleased to hear that none of you suspected me, then,' replied Tharian. He glanced sideways to Faast in particular, who caught the glance and smothered the slightest smirk in response. Velioth narrowed his eyes, staring somewhere beside Tharian, as if he was considering that possibility for the first time.

Faast responded. 'Suspicious though your activities have been, it

The Last of the Magi

would take a certain degree of insanity to tread the line of public disorder as finely as you did, all to secure a Coinsmeet, just to then throw away everything you sought to gain from it. That, I dare say, goes quite a leap beyond even *your* recklessness.'

Tharian laughed. 'It sounds like you really gave that some thought.'

'Yes, it does,' added Velioth. He pinched at the bridge of his nose and grimaced. 'We've had plenty of time to think about things while we've been stuck here.'

Faast continued. 'And the fact that it is *you* who now appears before us, with no enforcers at your shoulder, at least offers some solace that your cause is still a genuine one.'

Tharian felt a warmth in his chest. Despite how badly things had changed in the Trade Quarters, the coinsmen still had some trust and confidence in him.

'Wipe that smirk from your face, lad. Your cause may be genuine, but you're still an ass,' Traykin chuckled.

Tharian hadn't realised he was smirking, but he nodded and forced his expression to a more neutral state. 'Fair.'

'Now enough about all that,' Traykin continued. 'I'd like to know how you managed to get in here past those charming doormen we've been assigned, and I'd like even more to know why you haven't introduced us to your friend here. I'd wager this is the young lady you travelled to the Quarters with?'

Tharian felt his cheeks blush. He had completely forgotten about Marla, who was still stood just behind his shoulder. He looked back and smiled to her, gesturing for her to step forward and join the discussion. 'This is Marla, a blacksmith from Brynfall, and now a resident of the Artisan Quarter. Its thanks to her that we managed to slip past your guards under the pretence of making a delivery.'

'That's actually an intelligent plan,' said Traykin, 'I guess you had nothing to do with it, lad?' he laughed at himself.

Tharian eyed Traykin, smirking again. 'Very good. But you're not wrong. I wouldn't have been able to do this without her and the artisan family she lives with.'

'Who would that be?' asked Velioth.

'Brayne and Marion Glanmore,' Marla said, awkwardly. She

inclined her head to the coinsmen as she addressed them, which made Traykin laugh again.

'The Glanmores?' chirped Velioth. 'I'm familiar with their work, Brayne Glanmore is one of the most capable and reliable blacksmiths in his quarter.'

'He is certainly putting me through my paces, I'm learning a lot from him.'

'It's thanks to them, and Marla, that we managed to convince the enforcer at the door that this was genuine artisan business. It can't be easy having an Elheim and the elite guard holding you hostage here.'

Velioth rolled his eyes. 'Why the enforcers think that armed guard are needed to contain *us* is beyond me.' he pointed at his own slender frame and elegant garb and then shrugged his head towards the rotund Traykin. 'Now, armed guards to keep Faast under arrest, that I can understand, but two elites and an enforcer is excessive. We're traders and politicians, not criminals.'

Traykin then cleared his throat and cut into the conversation. He pointed to Marla. 'Did he say you were from Brynfall, lass?'

Marla nodded solemnly.

'I'm sorry for what the Elheim did to your home. It was a beautiful place.'

Marla nodded and then shrugged. But then she smiled confidently. 'Seeing my father's workshop set ablaze was tough, but he knew the alderman was walking us into that fate sooner or later. We were as ready as we could be for what happened. If nothing else, it gave me the opportunity to move on and start building my own future.'

Traykin smiled back, though it didn't reach his eyes. 'You've got grit, lass'

'Thanks,' she said. 'We knew the Elheim would do something drastic one day. But that doesn't mean we accept what happened. I certainly don't accept it. The people of County Bryn have wanted to oppose the Grand City for ages, we just didn't know how we could do it. But that's in the past now. I'm here, safe, and happy, and don't want to see the Quarters burn next. If there is any way I can help stop this, I'm ready to do what I can.'

The Last of the Magi

Faast stood again and she approached Marla, towering over her by at least a foot. She gave her an assessing look from head to toe. Despite the intimidating stature of the coinswoman, Marla didn't flinch. If anything, she looked intrigued and took the opportunity to assess the strong physique and powerful stance of the woman that stood before her in return.

'Impressive,' Faast said. 'A young woman with your spirit would do well in my guard.'

Marla met Faast's gaze. 'I think I'll stick with being an artisan if that's alright with you. But if you need a new spear or shield, you know where to go.'

Faast's thin lips curled, and she nodded before stepping back. She didn't look disappointed by that response.

Tharian finally took a seat on one of the free benches and gestured for Marla to sit too. 'So, what do we do now – to undo all of this and push the Elheim back out?'

Faast scoffed. Velioth shook his head and lowered his gaze.

'Look at us, lad,' said Traykin, gesturing to his colleagues. 'We're prisoners here. Even Mors gets an escort when running errands in the city for us, the poor old goat. Enforcers roam our streets freely now Tharian, we're powerless.'

'Then call upon Ferenir. The king is willing to make a stand.'

Velioth balked, with an open mouth. 'He is? You met with him?'

'King Thorius is dealing with increasing pressure from the Grand City. They practically pull his strings when they do their inspections. He's had enough. He's ready to stand up for the independence of his people before it's completely eroded away. If the Trade Quarters makes a stand, Ferenir will join.'

'That is exceptional news,' said Velioth. He folded his legs and sat completely upright, some colour returning to his demeanour.

'Agreed, but its value is hypothetical,' Faast paced around. 'We cannot call upon our ally to pull us from this suppressed state. The king was asked if he would stand shoulder-to-shoulder with us when we are ready to take the offensive against the Grand City. We cannot call upon our ally so quickly for our defence.'

Tharian cocked his head and glowered at Faast. 'Then what is the alternative – surrender? We can't give in now, I did exactly what you asked.'

'Your determination is without fault,' Faast said. 'But the arena has shifted. We are no longer able to plot an uprising against the Grand City when the Elheim have us pinned, their enforcers scurrying through our roadways like vermin. Now is not the time to talk of Asturia coming together to push back a common enemy. That goal has become a distant ideal. We have made progress towards that goal – *you* have made that progress – but we yet have no leads on finding a Magi, and we have lost our own city. Our priority now must be to drive the Elheim out, so that we might then call upon our allies in earnest and give them reason to believe that our aim is an achievable one. And if we cannot drive them out, then the remainder of the plan collapses at its base.'

The others all fell silent. Only the distant sound of the Market Quarter rabble carried into the courtyard as they each exchanged looks with each other.

Tharian curled his fists so tight that he felt his nails dig into his palms. Just the suggestion that this plan was falling apart felt insulting. It felt like a crashing wave washing away his efforts in Ferenir. He wanted to lash out. Everything he had done since leaving Asturia ten years ago had been done to help his countrymen, and now his progress felt reset to zero.

Yet, something kept him calm. Faast wasn't a pessimist; she was a realist. Though her words dampened his spirits, she had been fair and reasoned in saying them. And there was still hope in those words. *If* they could drive out the Elheim together, the plan would be back on track, and their people and their allies would see that a stand against the Grand City was not hopeless. Not by far.

Then we will push them out, Tharian resolutely told himself. He then looked up to Velioth. 'Do you have an office we can use?'

'Of course I do. Why?'

Tharian stood. 'If we have time on our hands, we're going to put it to use and figure this out. We'll need a map of the city.'

Chapter 41

Cunning of the Coinsmen

Velioth's study was immaculate... when they entered. That didn't last long.

They all gathered around a large table and Tharian grabbed a roll of paper and a pen to bring together thoughts and ideas. He scribbled questions about the enforcers that needed answering: where were they staying; did they have set patrol routes; what resources did they have with them; and did they have any weakness in their formations? He added to those questions some more general ones about the city, the elite guard, and the city guard. He then bombarded the coinsmen with these questions, with Marla contributing answers too from the perspective of someone looking up from the grassroots rather than down from the lofty seats of governance.

Together they gathered intel fast. The Elheim who now held the positions of coinsmen hadn't been in post long enough to make any substantial changes to the systems and processes that kept the Trade Quarters running. So Tharian was fortunate to find himself amongst those who knew the city better than any others.

By the time they had made a dent in their planning, the room was filled with a chaotic spread of their notes and thoughts. But the chaos was needed, it was like an injection of knowledge about the Trade Quarters straight into Tharian's brain.

Even with all that information, Tharian quickly realised he didn't have the experience to know what should come next. Fortunately, he was surrounded by coinsmen, and they *did* know. Tharian's fervent questioning was making them think deeply and creatively about their situation.

Velioth laid out another large roll of paper across the middle of the table, so everyone could see. He plucked at various pages that Tharian had already scribbled on, and from these he started to draw out a grid. Across the top he wrote headings: issue; risk; strategy;

solution.

He compiled a long list under the first heading. "Enforcers", "Arcana", "Guards" and "Reinforcements" were just the first few. Those were already difficult issues to deal with.

Velioth then led the next phase of the planning, laying out a city map at one corner of the table to serve as a point of reference. He didn't come up with many ideas himself, relying on Faast to provide much of the analysis as to what risks they faced in relation to each identified issue, and how they might be mitigated.

Tharian commented along the way, with input from the others. He would be the one executing most of this plan, again, so he needed to think through each step carefully before agreeing to what was suggested.

Together, they were a well-oiled machine. Tharian admired how well the coinsmen worked together under pressure. Faast assessed risk and proffered options. Traykin added details either related to the city or who and what was in it, much to the surprise of the other coinsmen. Velioth considered the logistics. And Marla's contributions were equally as essential. She added some reality to the planning, pointing out areas where the coinsmen's top-down beliefs didn't reflect reality – such as the strictness of guard patrols, or the laxness of their watch – and she gave them all the street-level detail that the others couldn't provide.

Tharian did his best to visualise how he might eliminate or avoid each threat, vaulting over or breaking through each obstacle as the others suggested.

Eventually, once the first sheet had been fully fleshed out with all issues addressed or eliminated, Velioth drew another large sheet over the first, one which was thin enough to still see the words faintly underneath. He then pulled together the points that they agreed.

Tharian moved to Velioth's side and watched his writing closely.

'So...' Tharian said, rubbing his chin, 'we create a distraction. Something big enough to draw the attention of all the enforcers.'

'Yes,' added Faast, 'the mercenary factions in my quarter can be hired to orchestrate those distractions. It will be expensive, and they may well oppose the suggestion at first, but if they are clearly instructed to distract and disengage, they will co-operate. It will be an easy profit for their light work, and many will be eager to frustrate the Elheim.'

'And if we give the city guard advance notice of the distractions, they can step aside and leave the enforcers short-handed.'

Faast nodded.

Tharian traced his fingers around the thin alleyways marked on the city map. 'Assuming we can trust the mercenaries to lead the enforcers in circles through the back alleys, that should leave Keene's manor mostly unguarded. If the elite guard are willing to rally with us, we can charge down the three Elheim leaders camped there. Three enforcers will still be tough to handle, but I think with enough back-up I might be able to put this runeblade to work. Catching them off-guard will be key.'

'You can do it,' said Marla. 'I saw you do it in Bryn, you can do it again.'

Tharian shook his head and smiled. 'Thanks for the vote of confidence. There was only one enforcer marching on me that day. Three will be very different, and no doubt they won't fall for the same simple tricks.'

'My elite guard may not have the gifts to counter Arcana directly, but they know how to protect their charge. They will give you all the protection they can offer.'

'I'll be counting on it. If we can take down those three, the rest would be easy to pick off. They will be exhausted from the mercenaries running riot.' Tharian stepped back from the table and looked over the completeness of Velioth's notes. 'That's it, that's how we stop them.'

Velioth nodded. 'It's dangerous, but I think you're right.'

'Except for one thing,' Tharian added. The biggest practical concern he had about this plan was still to be addressed. 'This relies on me getting a lot done. I will only have a couple of days to get around the Quarters very quickly and pull all these strings together before the Elheim find out what's going on. It's going to be exhausting, and I need to be ready to fight at Keene's manor.'

'Then let me do some of the legwork.'

All heads turned to Marla. She stood at the corner of the table.

'Don't give me that look. I can handle myself. Besides, it makes sense. I've been delivering orders to the mercenaries, the city guard, the elite guard, the lot. The enforcers will barely know my face. The people we need to trust, however, many of them know me.'

'No,' said Tharian, and heads shook with him. 'You've already done enough.'

'I hate to say it,' Traykin said, 'but the lass is right. Tharian, you're good at what you do. Hell, you're good at everything you do – annoyingly – but there are those who might recognise you from the Crucible. Not everyone will want to throw their lot in with you, you need to limit where you go'—he then pointed at Marla—'but Marla here is an artisan. Everyone trusts the artisans.'

'Traykin…'

'She's volunteering to deliver messages and payments to contractors. You can still do the parts that are likely to get you killed.'

'Thanks for that,' Tharian said with a tired smile. He couldn't fault either of them on their logic. 'Thank you, Marla. Your help will be invaluable. Again.'

Marla nodded and wrote her name besides parts of the plan. 'That works for me. If I died to an enforcer out there, Marion would kill you anyway, so I'm happy taking the safer jobs.'

Tharian looked to the coinsmen. 'What about you three, is there anything you can do to help from here?'

'Through Mors we can relay some coded messages,' said Velioth, 'to those who can be reached safely.'

'Beyond that, our wrists are shackled.' Faast added, defeatedly. 'If the guards at our door are also drawn away by the mercenary infractions, I might be able to convene with you at Keene's manor to command the elites.'

Tharian nodded. Having Faast at his back in a fight would be comforting.

'Our hands might be tied, but our heads aren't.' Traykin grabbed a sheet of Velioth's green-dyed letterhead from a desk against the wall and started scribbling away in his tilted, sharp handwriting. 'While you try to reclaim our city, *we* can start looking for leads on

The Last of the Magi

this Magi.'

Tharian turned sharply to Traykin. 'Seriously?'

'You rallied Ferenir for us, lad. You did something we weren't sure could be done. I think it's only right that we pull our weight and try to do the same.'

'And how are we going to achieve this while confined?' asked Faast.

With a flourish, Traykin finished his letter and folded it, sliding it into one of the pockets of his vest. 'I know a historian who might have some ideas. A collector, mind, so she is a bit more interested with curating secrets rather than straight history. I reckon we could get her here and pick her brains. She might have some ideas.'

Faast grunted. Yet, she didn't protest.

Velioth hummed a sound of curiosity. 'I had thought curating knowledge of such things was outlawed?'

'Well,' Traykin said with a snort, 'It's not her day-job. She's a herbalist by trade, but I suppose you could say she moonlights as a magic-enthusiast.'

'You've been holding out on me, Traykin,' Tharian said, folding his arms. Why hadn't he mentioned this colleague sooner?

Traykin laughed. 'In truth lad, I hadn't thought of it. I haven't spoken to the old girl in years, and if you recall I was helping you arrange a Coinsmeet. It's funny what you remember when you've got nothing to do but sit in a garden for a few days.'

A fair excuse, Tharian decided. 'It's worth a shot. Hopefully your contact can give us some hope.'

A knock sounded at the door. Mors slipped into the room, looking immediately aghast at the state of Velioth's office. He cleared his croaky throat and addressed his coinsman.

'Lord Velioth, Enforcer Baralyne is expressing concerns that your guests have yet to leave.'

Velioth cursed as his eyes looked to the clock above the door. Tharian noticed it too. They had been in Velioth's manor for hours.

'Our time is up,' said Tharian. He had been too distracted to give the enforcer and the guards at the door any thought. 'We've figured out as much as we can. I'll get started tomorrow.'

As Tharian folded the sheet of paper with the final set of notes and tucked it into his pocket, he noticed Faast staring at him with narrowed eyes.

'You understand the repercussions of this going wrong, don't you?'

'I'll be imprisoned, maybe beaten around with Arcana for a bit. And then either I'll be executed here or taken back to the Grand City so they can make a show of it.'

Faast nodded. 'You can say such a thing so nonchalantly?'

'Yes,' he said, without hesitation. 'I know the stakes. I don't want to live the rest of my life in Asturia if it means being under Elheim rule. If I fail, die, and they take over this country, I think I'd have got the better deal.'

'That's bloody grim, Tharian,' said Traykin. He was shaking his head while scratching out another note, though not on Velioth's letterhead this time.

Tharian laughed. 'I don't see it that way. I don't see death as some horrible end. Greycloak spent enough time teaching me about the balance and harmony of the natural world for it to give me a kind of fearlessness towards it. I prefer being alive, of course. And I'd prefer that even more if the Elheim weren't sapping the life out of us all. I choose to live a full life as a free Asturian, not a half-life as an Elheim slave.'

Tharian nodded and thumped the table. 'Crack on then, lad. But be careful.'

'I will.'

'You better be,' added Marla. 'You're not getting me killed.'

'Noted,' he said with a smirk. 'Let's get going.'

Tharian and Marla joined Mors at the door. Traykin approached Mors too, holding two folded notes – one on green and one on white – and he slipped them into the assistant's hand. 'Get these to Frigg, please. Subtle as you can.'

Mors nodded, he then looked over to the others, still sat at the table. 'Will that be all, coinsmen?'

'Yes, thank you. Sorry again to keep you running around,' said Velioth. 'And thank *you*, Tharian, and you Marla. You are taking a great risk for us, yet again.'

Chapter 42

Vengeance of Valivelle

Darus pressed his fingers against the lower lids of his eyes as he woke. He could feel the dark rings that had settled in. He blinked hard and opened his eyes as wide as he could, as if stretching his eyelids would wake him up more.

After three solid days of dawn-to-dusk hard work, the backlog of requisitions and license applications had been cleared. More were still arriving each morning, but Coinswoman Keene reassured him he'd tackled the fire well enough to start taking things a bit easier. He treated himself to an earlier night. He felt no more rested for it this morning.

The last few days had been unusual. He had been left to his devices working alongside Keene without interruption from his father or Inquisitor Protelborn. Their interruptions had only been very brief before, seemingly more of a courtesy visit, or an obligatory "checking-in", but the awkwardness of the light conversation made each visit exhausting. It was a welcome reprieve to not see either of them. No doubt they had more important matters to deal with that went beyond the administration of the Trade Quarters.

Darus rolled from his bed and threw a dressing robe over his bedclothes. He moved sluggishly to the balcony door in his suite and drew back the drapes. He groaned as bright sunlight assailed him. Opening one of the balcony doors, he held out a hand while turning away from the light. Gentle warmth pricked at his skin.

Keene had been very accommodating. She had given the three of them suites large enough to serve as offices, with private washroom facilities. They were not of the calibre found within the mansions of the Grand City, but they were not far off. For a city renowned for its dusty, smoggy roads and shady back-alleyways, this was an impressive standard of hospitality.

Removing the dressing robe, he braved the warmth of the

balcony in only his bedclothes.

He shielded his eyes from the sunlight as he looked out over the vista of the Trade Quarters. The city was a lot more handsome than he expected from this height. The smog, noxious though it was, caught the sunlight and painted the city in a peachy haze. It was as if staring at a watercolour rather than seeing it with his own eyes.

Nothing here could even begin to compare to the bright, shining splendour of the Grand City, the sparkling waters of the River Arne that cut through its middle, or the abundance of parks and flora that were regimentally maintained just to ensure every turn of the city was beautiful. Yet, even without those features – instead replaced by tightly packed buildings of dark wood and brick, all sealed within towering border walls of patchwork metal – the Trade Quarters still had a charm of its own.

It was different. Perhaps that's all it was. The Trade Quarters was raw in form and made no attempt to disguise its identity or the variety of people that called it home.

From the balcony, he could clearly see much of the artisan's main road, running from the outer wall to the central plaza. The stores fronting it were all large and well maintained, each seeming to tell something about the Artisans living within by its design and decoration. And then the buildings behind those gradually diminished in quality until the fog obscured the furthest ones from view entirely.

So, this is what life outside the Grand City looks like? Darus breathed deeply. The sooty air filled his nostrils together with a sharp smell of paint that was strong enough for him to taste. *And this is what life outside the Grand City smells like?* He chuckled to himself. Though he had been away from the Grand City for some time now, this was the first time their caravan had remained in one place long enough for him to experience his surroundings properly. It was exciting and exhilarating, even if that experience was dampened by the circumstances and nature of their aggressive arrival.

He contemplated what he might do with his slither of freedom for the morning. Coinswoman Keene had recommended several shops in the Market Quarter he could visit, and then she had written

The Last of the Magi

him a list of a few reputable collectors he could bargain with to buy exotic gifts to take home.

At first, he had considered that idea with eagerness, but now that eagerness sobered as he remembered who he would be buying those gifts for.

Mother doesn't care for anything crafted outside the Grand City. If you cut her open, she would bleed white and blue. And there's little point buying for Marken. He's never home.

Darus rapped his fingers against the balcony as he tried to recall the last time he had even seen his older brother. Being a few years his senior, Marken had been assigned a senior enforcer to work with a while back. He would only make the most fleeting of home visits, and only when there was no alternative.

There's certainly no reason to consider a gift for father. He'd probably find it offensive somehow. Beyond that, there's only one—

Darus stopped himself. He was getting better at pulling himself away from the dark thoughts that plagued him. His stomach flipped all the same. Rik was the only one he would have cared to buy a gift for. And he would have been so grateful to receive it too, no matter what it was.

He leaned on the railing of the balcony and rest his head against his folded arms. Sometimes he wished he could be as cold and unshakable as his father. Then his emotions wouldn't have such a hold over him. But even as he stood there on the balcony, drained of all enthusiasm by the churning in his stomach, he knew that deep down... he never wanted to be anything like his father.

There was a knock at the door to his suite. The visitor didn't wait for his response, inviting themselves in immediately. It was the kindly older man who had been assisting him in his duties.

'Please excuse the sudden intrusion, Coinsman. I have been ordered to bring you to Coinsman Valivelle's suite immediately.'

Darus groaned but did his best to conceal it. 'Give me two minutes while I get dressed, please.'

The older man nodded and slipped back out the door.

Darus scurried around his room and pulled together a freshly pressed uniform. He dragged on the white trousers, securing them in place with a belt, which he then hid from view under the tailored white and blue trimmed jacket that covered him to his neck. His jacket felt a little loose, he had been neglecting meals while focusing so heavily on his work. He was grateful for the lighter fit, as his uniform had always felt rather suffocating.

He pulled his boots on loosely and then dashed for the door, stamping his feet into them properly as he went. As he felt the cold metal of the door handle bite against his skin, he turned back to find his gloves.

Shuffling out from his suite with unconvincing composure, he gestured for the man to lead on. The kindly man hastily led Darus down another corridor to his father's suite and knocked twice on the door before opening it for Darus to enter.

Darus straightened his uniform and pulled his gloves further up his wrists before marching into the centre of the room.

His father's suite was identical to his own but mirrored. The balcony door was at the opposite side of the room, slightly to the right of where Darus had stopped, with an obscenely large, four-poster bed over to the left side of the room. Under a window, next to the balcony doors, his father sat sideways in a seat at an ornate escritoire, an opened letter between his fingers. The stationary of the Grand City was unmistakable.

His father didn't turn to address him. He only raised a finger in the air as he continued reading the last line of the letter that had his attention.

'I am told you are handling your duties expeditiously,' he finally said.

'Yes, sir. The arrangement with Coinswoman Keene has proven to be very effective. She has taught me a lot about the administration of the Quarters.'

'I'm glad,' Lanark said, though his tone suggested disinterest. 'And how goes the coinswoman's induction into the Arcane?'

'Very well. Her senses are developing quickly, and I believe she will be ready to—'

'Good,' Lanark interrupted. His lips curled into a wicked smile as he re-read the final line of his letter. 'Inquisitor Protelborn and I have been discussing what should be done about the former coinsmen and this fugitive who eludes us.'

The Last of the Magi

Darus shuffled where he stood and waited for his father to continue.

'Suffice to say we could not reach an accord on the subject. Fortunately, the chancellor has resolved the matter for us.' Lanark waved the letter over the back of his chair to Darus.

Darus stepped forward, took the letter, and then moved back to the centre of the room to read it.

The letter was indeed from the chancellor. It went on for some length praising his father for his efforts, and that of Inquisitor Protelborn too. But then, in the final paragraph, Darus found the message his father referred to:

'That the Coinsmen of the Trade Quarters share liability for harbouring this criminal is not a matter for questioning. They cannot be trusted, and evidently present a live threat to the Grand City's vision, which the people of the Trade Quarters and Elheim both should not be prepared to tolerate. Their actions harm us all.

'I authorise an execution, preferably of a public nature to discourage any further criminal detractions.'

His heart thumped in his ears as he read the final line several times. Darus looked to his father. He wore a gleeful smirk. He looked invigorated. He stood from his seat and stepped forward to take the letter back without even reaching for his cane first. He returned the letter to its envelope and tucked it inside his coat.

'Our instructions are clear,' he said.

'Y-yes, sir.' The thought of more deaths made Darus feel nauseated.

'The only matter which our wise chancellor has left ambiguous is the question of Coinswoman Keene.'

Darus swallowed. He dared not ask what his father meant, though he wanted to know. 'Am I to stop her training?'

Lanark coughed a laugh and looked down his nose at his son. 'Don't be naïve. You can continue to train her as agreed, we would not want to make the coinswoman suspicious. But do not get attached, Darus. Viviel Keene was one of the four in office at the time the coinsmen met with this criminal behind closed doors. She is as guilty as the rest for not arresting him and handing him over to us as soon as that man appeared within these walls.'

Darus held his breath. He couldn't deny that he still had his suspicions about Coinswoman Keene – about her motivations for working against her own people – but she seemed a good ally to the Elheim now. Her execution would be excessive, unnecessary. She would surely have a defence to the crimes levied against her.

He then remembered the sailors back in the dockhouse. His father had no interest in defences or arguments of mitigation. But that was a very different situation, wasn't it?

'Was it not Coinswoman Keene who kept the inquisitor informed about their meetings with the fugitive?'

'Yes, it was. And she performed her function perfectly as an informant. But even if the Grand City were to accept allies from the likes of these people, should we be prepared to trust someone who would betray those she stood to represent? Should we trust *her* with the power of the Arcane? What if her allegiances shifted again?'

He hated to admit it, but his father had a point. If someone betrayed one cause to join another, that did not absolve them of being a betrayer. That was the lesson his father was trying to instil in him, and it was one he couldn't confidently challenge. 'I understand,' he said.

'I hope that you do. These are the types of decisions that people with power must be prepared to make. The path to achieving the chancellor's vision for Asturia is not one already paved. We must make the difficult decisions so that our people can thrive.'

Darus nodded. A question then appeared in his mind. He felt cold for thinking of it, but he at least felt it was a question he could raise without fear of reprisal. 'If Coinswoman Keene is to be executed,' he said, as calmly as he could, 'who would replace her as Coinsman for the Artisan Quarter?'

'One of our own, of course.'

The reply didn't come from his father.

Darus turned to his right. There, sat on one of the sofas against the wall, was another enforcer. Not just any enforcer. Darus knew

The Last of the Magi

this one well. It was his aunt: Illian Eyris Valivelle.

Darus straightened himself even more than usual and bowed his head respectfully to his aunt. 'Aunt Illian, it's good to see you recovered from your injuries.'

She grunted and stood. Holding her hands behind her back, she flicked her head to move a strand of hair from her face. As she did, Darus was able to catch a glimpse of the slightly greyed areas around her temples and across one cheek where her skin had not yet fully recovered from the electrical burns she suffered in County Bryn.

'We Valivelles are never out of the picture for long, nephew.'

Lanark leaned against the wall and laughed. 'I think you're the first in living memory to ever be put out of the picture, Illian.'

She snarled. 'Tread lightly down that path, my brother.'

Lanark raised his hands in the air. 'I apologise.' He then turned to Darus. 'You see, now we have adequate resources to maintain control over the Trade Quarters until the chancellor decides to publicly declare the city within our territory. We will make the arrangements to have the coinsmen dealt with in an appropriate manner, and when we find the criminal we will hand him over to Illian.'

'I shall make an example of him, I assure you both.'

The feeling of dread in the pit of Darus's stomach intensified and twisted as his father and aunt relished in the thought of killing. It was just another victory in their eyes. Another way of furthering the vision. Darus had naively hoped that his aunt's injuries might have done *something* to satisfy the tempestuous bloodlust she was famous for. Quite the opposite.

His father then gestured for Darus to leave. 'I shall send you details of how we intend to carry out our chancellor's wishes. You must be ready to act upon them on a moment's notice, do you understand?'

'Yes, I understand.'

'Good. And do not under any circumstances discuss any of this with the coinswoman. Continue dealing with her as usual and do not give her reason to suspect anything.'

'Yes, sir.'

'Excellent.' Lanark then led Darus through the door and closed it firmly.

Darus shuddered. He stood there a few seconds, processing what he had just seen and heard. He looked left to where the corridor led back towards his room and then right to where it reached a staircase that went back down to the offices he and Keene were working from.

Taking a deep breath, he went downstairs. He no longer had any appetite for venturing out into the city. He needed the distraction of his work.

***

Lanark poured himself and his sister a drink from the decanter on the chest of drawers beside the sofa. He filled his with ice and left hers without, knowing how she preferred it.

He handed her a glass, taking the opportunity to again notice those subtle changes in his sister. Her skin was lightly scarred in some places, and even her grey hair was looking darker and wiry at the ends. Singed, no doubt, by her own Arcane lightning.

'You're sure you're ready to get involved in this?'

'Stop asking that,' she snapped. 'Do not coddle me. I am not addled by my injuries. Do I look any less able to you?'

'Of course not. But your arrival was unexpected, you will forgive your younger brother for showing some familial concern.'

'No. I won't.'

Lanark sat at his desk. His leg was starting to ache, and he preferred to be seated than let his sister see his limp take hold. 'Do you think this fugitive poses any risk to us?'

Illian scoffed and sat back on the sofa. 'Absolutely not'—she raised a finger just as he pursed his lips in response—'Bryn was an anomaly. Had I known someone in the shadows was lurking with a runeblade, things would have played out very differently. It's been so long since any enchanted weaponry has been seen in Asturia, I had no reason to suspect it.'

'There could be more out there. There are plenty in this city who collect oddities. I wouldn't be surprised if more illegal artifacts were

The Last of the Magi

hidden away in private collections.'

Illian downed her drink in one gulp and planted the glass on the table with her fingers branched over the rim. 'Then the first recommendation to the chancellor after the official takeover would be to purge the Collectors Quarter.'

'That may be a tad excessive.'

Illian leaned forward and gave him a piercing glower. 'Is it? If there is anything we can take from my time in the infirmary, it's that we can no longer leave the city states of Asturia unchecked. We know so little of what they hide away from us. Any one of us could fall foul of their trickery. You included.'

With a confident smirk, Lanark brought his glass to his lips. He halted as he noticed the glass felt lighter, and there was no clinking of ice. As he looked in his sister's piercing eyes, he felt the presence of Arcana at work.

Glancing down, he saw that the ice cubes were now floating in the air a few inches from his neck, reshaped into spikes. Cold water dropped into his lap.

'The time for giving others the benefit of the doubt is over. We cannot rely on our presence alone to keep these barbarians in line. They are becoming too bold. We need force.'

'You've made your point, Illian.' He Grasped the spikes of ice and Commanded them to drift further from his neck, turning their sharp points away.

Illian raised a gloved hand towards the ice and Commanded them again. The ice spikes drifted together, liquified into one mass and then became ice once more. 'Resistance. That is what the fugitive represents. If left unchecked, others will believe they can push back at us without punishment.' The ice then became one larger spike that hovered between them like a small spear.

'We must blunt their resolve,' she continued. As she said the words, the points of the spear melted away and dripped onto the floor. 'We cannot let them believe they can surprise us. And we cannot let them believe there is weakness in our ranks.'

The ice completely liquified and dropped onto the carpet, soaking into its fibres.

'You don't need to preach to me.'

Illian stood abruptly. 'Then do not question if I am ready for this. Because from where I'm stood it looks like you're just playing house until the chancellor gives you orders. We are the chancellor's favoured enforcers for a reason. Our judgment is trusted. We must take this city.'

Lanark raised his hand to his sister. 'We will, Illian. We will. The plans are clicking into place with each passing moment. But you must remember that this is the Trade Quarters, not some backwater hamlet in the Counties.'

Lanark felt the hairs at the back of his neck raise up as his sister folded her arms and stared at him. 'Do not forget who you are talking to. I was once the enforcer emissary to the Kingdom of Ferenir. I was the one to bring their monarchy to heel while you were barely out of the college. I know how to subdue a rebellious city state.'

The temptation to bring up her fall in Bryn again was there, even if just to dampen her ego for a moment. But he knew his sister, and he would almost certainly come out of it more bruised than her ego ever would be. Besides, she was right. County Bryn had not stepped out of line since she set Brynfall to the flame. The Arcane Tax was being paid and there were no signs of significant deviance from the new alderman.

Thinking better of the opportunity to score a cheap point, Lanark leaned back in his chair and sipped his drink. He then nodded and raised his glass to her. 'Then I welcome your input on how we might plan this execution. If you are so keen to act, I'm prepared to hear your suggestions.'

'That's more like it.' Illian said with a grimacing smirk.

Chapter 43

Conflicts of Conscience

Footsteps entered the office. Darus startled. He groaned at the ugly line he'd just scratched across the signature line of his document. He had worked on that for the last half-hour. It would need re-drafting.

The powerful scent of bitter tea filled his senses as he glanced up to see that it was Coinswoman Keene who startled him. She paced through the beams of dusty sunlight cast across the middle of the room. She had a bowl cupped between her palms. She laid it down on the edge of his desk.

'Now look at this,' she said.

Darus put his pen down and rest his hand on his other arm, giving her a wave to proceed.

She held the edge of the bowl until the black fluid within stilled. She carefully lifted her hand away and then closed her eyes. The lines across her forehead deepened and her lips twitched as she concentrated.

Such studious determination, Darus thought. *She is trying so hard to learn, to develop her skills in the Arcane. Its cruel to let her go on, she might not ever go much further than Grasping.*

Keene opened her eyes, and she cheered as she pointed a finger to the bowl. The tea was rippling. It was gentle, but still a ripple. Small enough that it could have been caused by a knock at the table's edge, or a heavy-footed gait in the hall.

'There it is! At first, I thought I was seeing things, but you see it too, don't you?'

He did see it. To anyone else it would have been unremarkable, but to one already skilled in the Arcane it was unmistakably the touch of Arcana. His own Deep Thought confirmed it. Darus made an approving sound and then held his hand over the bowl. In that gesture, he Commanded the tea to become still. 'Do it again,' he said, gesturing to the stilled tea, 'but try and maintain the rippling.'

She pouted slightly and then repeated the same process as

before. Her face scrunched up less this time, and it didn't take long for the tea to start rippling softly, rhythmically. Like it was mirroring her own heartbeat.

'Impressive,' Darus said, flatly. 'You're getting the hang of it.'

Keene scoffed. 'You say that, but it took me all last night and then two hours this morning to make that happen.'

'It's to be expected.'

Keene narrowed her eyes at Darus. She stared at him bluntly and looked to be examining him where he sat. 'You seem disturbed, young man. You are usually sprtielier than this.'

'Am I?' He made a concerted effort to speak with more energy to dispel her suspicions. He gestured to the bowl again. 'You know you don't have to use tea?'

'There's more tea in this house than water.' She laughed, only for a moment. She pulled a chair to his desk and took a seat. 'Something is troubling you. Out with it. Little of value gets done with a laboured mind.'

Her words were disarming. He looked into Keene's eyes, her expression was gentle and genuine. 'It's nothing. I think I'm just a bit deflated.'

Keene nodded knowingly. 'Velioth was the same when he started. Always dashing around trying to solve every problem before it started. It can burn out even the youngest and fittest among us. Mind you,' she trailed off as she gazed over her shoulder for a moment. 'He *still* dashes about all over the place, just not doing as much work as he should.'

Despite the good humour of her words, the humour didn't reach him. He frowned. Velioth was one of the coinsmen she had worked with for years. One of those she wilfully helped depose in support of the Grand City's occupation. Why?

This may be my only chance to ask. He felt guilty just looking at Keene, knowing she was blissfully ignorant of what was being planned by her own houseguests. The futility of it all compelled him to finally brooch the subject. 'Can I ask you something?' he said.

Keene's brows lifted. 'Of course, ask away.'

'Why do you support the Grand City?' He didn't expect the question to come out so directly. Yet it did.'

The Last of the Magi

Keene, looked surprised, uncomfortable maybe. She gazed into the tea as if trying to divine her answer from it. 'That's…' she paused and then started again '…It's a very difficult thing to explain in brief.'

'I'm sorry, I shouldn't have asked.'

'No, no, it is not a problem. If I am to work alongside Elheim, it's only natural that you would question my motivations.' She hummed for a moment. 'Walk with me.'

Darus stood and reached to pick up the bowl from his desk.

'Leave that,' Keene insisted.

The coinswoman silently led Darus out the room and down the corridor. They passed through the Library and then through her opulent reception room with the fountains and flower displays that drew a snaking path to the front door. One of her attendants bowed and opened the door for them. She stepped out, and Darus followed.

The sunlight and breeze were welcome, even if the soot and dust were not.

Artisans, messengers, and passers-by offered warm greetings to the coinswoman as they strolled together. It seemed odd that being side-by-side with an enforcer didn't startle or concern them, not obviously anyway. However, after they walked for a short while, Darus spotted the first group to avert their eyes away from him.

Keene returned their greetings with kind words, referring to many by name. She did that until the novelty of the coinswoman walking openly through the street apparently died off. Then Keene continued where they left off, lowering her voice to just above a whisper. 'My family had contacts in the Arcane Guild. I bet you're too young to even know what that is.'

Darus frowned. 'At the College Arcana we're expected to learn our history in detail. The idea being that everyone will one day celebrate the day that the powerful families of Asturia had the foresight to band together for the betterment of Asturia.'

'Sounds a bit pompous, even by Grand City standards.'

Darus agreed. It was pompous.

'Well, believe it or not, my grandparents almost joined the guild. I could have been an Elheim by right.'

Was there a spark of irritation in her voice? Darus watched her from the side as she continued.

'Many artisan families had the connections and affluence to qualify for membership. My family were offered the chance to join the guild and move east, or they could stay here and maintain their firm foothold here. They decided to stay with the Trade Quarters, where their wealth and influence was already strong – that's the risk-sensitive way of the artisans for you. By the time I was born, the guild had already taken the name Elheim, and their city was taking shape.'

Keene released a haughty sigh. 'It wasn't so bad, for the most part. It was only after the Purge that I began to realise what my family had really done. They had chosen the easy option, placing us firmly on the wrong side of the divide between Asturian and Elheim people. The power that my family accumulated is now fading.'

'I wouldn't have put you down as power-hungry, Coinswoman Keene.'

She gave him a smile. 'It's not that superficial. I am not motivated by power or wealth. My point here is that there was a time when the principles and aspirations that my family stood for aligned so neatly with the Arcane Guild. They were intelligent enough to read the fine-print and understand the vision, and what you truly aim to achieve, but were not bold enough to take the risk of joining something new. That, I believe, was a mistake.'

'But look at the position you now hold because of that choice. Your people admire you,' Darus said as they turned onto the central plaza and started a slow walk towards the statues. 'The Grand City is a wonderful place to live, I wouldn't dare say otherwise, but it loses some of that wonder when everyone else in the country despises us.'

'They just don't understand. Not yet.'

Not yet? Darus followed Keene to the space between the statues and she pointed up to the nearest of them. It was the figure of a tall man with broad shoulders, a chiselled jaw and wraps of cloth around his head, waist and draped down the sides of his legs.

'When Baalt founded this quarter, he had great ambitions that stretched far beyond just our own shores. He wanted to sculpt a perfect, unified Asturia with his bare hands, creating an example

The Last of the Magi

that could then be taken forward and replicated across all Aetheria. An optimist, without doubt, but one whose head remained in the realms of fancy. His personal aspirations were ultimately suffocated by the wishes of the majority. Although he never achieved his dream, I believe it had merit.'

Darus folded his arms as the coinswoman continued to glance longingly at the towering statue of stone. His eyes widened as her words connected in the back of his mind. 'You think our chancellor will make that dream a reality?'

Keene pulled in a deep breath and then nodded. 'I do. Don't get me wrong, dear boy, were it within my power to change the way the Elheim went about pursuing their vision, I would change it in a heartbeat. There has been so much destruction, fear-mongering and political game-playing. As difficult as it is to push that all aside, we must do so to see the greater good. The alternative is to stay static and accept a future without progress.'

Her words were not new to him. The instructors at the College Arcana often referred to the chancellor's vision for a unified Asturia in similar terms. It was the vision of the Elheim family that started their society. This was the first time he heard a non-Elheim speak knowingly of it.

But then, as he watched Keene visualising the dream she shared with her forbearer, he felt sick with guilt again. Even if the Elheim could achieve the vision for a unified Asturia, she, like Baalt, would never get to see that future.

'Asturia is fragmented,' she continued. 'Things rumble along well enough, but we are all just tugging at the purse-strings of our neighbours, fighting to improve only our own life experience, or that of those connected to us. All this time and energy wasted just going around and around in circles, never moving forward. The Elheim share the vision that Baalt had then, that I have now. United, with our resources pooled and powers like Arcana at our fingertips, we can look beyond our shores again and improve our position in the world, whilst protecting ourselves from those that see us as weak.'

'I suppose so.'

Keene locked eyes with him. 'You are Elheim, yet you sound

unconvinced?'

'It's not that I'm unconvinced. I've heard the vision time and time again. I just can't see how my people could ever drop their pride low enough to live as equals with everyone in Asturia. They see everyone else as beneath them.'

'Maybe they can't. But would they need to? For this vision to work, Asturia will need those with fierce wills and unquestioning loyalty – they will be the ones who ultimately protect the rest of us in times of danger.'

Darus squinted one eye slightly and scratched the back of his neck. 'I hadn't thought of it that way.' His brother, Marken, would fit into that role easily, so would his father and aunt for that matter. In senior roles of power and authority, of course. As Asturian enforcers rather than just Elheim enforcers. But Darus couldn't see himself fitting that mould.

'It's difficult to keep sight of the end goal when the enforcers do what they do,' Keene said. Darus winced at her words, and she noticed. 'What *some* enforcers do.' She stepped away from the statue and moved closer to him. 'I honestly believe that in the end, the Elheim's vision for our country is the right one. It is right for the independent city states, right for the Outer Counties and right for my own people. I only need look at the situation as it is today to see that my people will not suffer under the colours of the Grand City.'

He felt numb. Her words were genuine and sincere. Little did she know she had been branded an enemy of the Elheim. The thought made him sweat. The look in Keene's face told him she was looking forward to a bright future for Asturia, and her place in it.

Keene turned to him, and her brows quickly furrowed. 'You look deathly pale, are you falling ill?' she asked.

Darus turned away. Breathing suddenly felt hard, as if his conscience was literally bearing down on his chest. 'I'm fine, I just need some air.'

Keene swept around to his front and pushed him to rest against the statue of Baalt. 'What's wrong – should I call for a chirurgeon?'

His legs went weak, so he slid down the statue until he hit the ground. Emotion erupted from within. A cacophony of anger, grief, guilt, and crippling anxiety. The crushing totality of it was all too

The Last of the Magi

familiar, but that made it no easier to bear. 'I can't live like this anymore,' he mumbled.

Keene dropped to his side and drew a cloth from her coat pocket to dab at his temples. 'What do you mean?'

'I want to believe like you do. Really, I do. But how can I see a good future for Asturia after what happened to Midhaven, Brynfall, Brynport and now here? At my father's order I've had to—'

He paused to catch his breath and blink away the welling of tears in his eyes.

'People have suffered. People have died. And the justification for it is always the same, that it's necessary to further the vision.'

He took a few deep breaths, wiping his face with his hands as tears streaked. 'How can our vision for Asturia be right when we execute people who should have been put on trial. How can it be right when I was *celebrated* for killing someone by accident, as if his life didn't even matter. He was—'

Keene hushed him and wiped at his eyes with the same cloth. It was a gentle touch, reassuring. He paused and took shivering breaths until he calmed a little.

'It's never easy being on the front lines of change. You must make difficult choices and there will always be sacrifices along the way.'

Sacrifices.

The word stung. Sacrifices were sometimes needed for the greater good, he knew that much, but those sacrifices were to be made by noble heroes and altruists who were ready to throw down their lives to benefit others. Not by the innocent who only wanted to protect their own, or by those who didn't chose to make that sacrifice. That wasn't sacrifice. That was murder.

Would she speak so easily of sacrifice if she knew she was next? Darus pulled his knees to his chest and curled up.

'Come now,' Keene said, in a hushed voice. 'Though the road ahead is difficult, the people you seek to protect will one day celebrate you for the role you played in this. The things that feel like atrocities now will eventually be accepted as brave necessities. Hold on to that.'

Darus raised his head and met Keene's eyes. He was convinced she still meant her words, though he knew deep down that if anyone were to be credited by name for the work of the enforcers it wouldn't be him. Not that he wanted any credit for the horrible things they did. But there was something in the way she spoke so assuredly that made Darus feel pity for the naivety hidden beneath her wisdom.

'Is that the future you see for yourself?' he asked.

She leaned back from him. 'I suppose it is. There will be those that accuse me of pursuing personal motivations of greed. And I accept that. In the short term, I suppose I have pursued my own ideals for our country over and above what my people would choose for themselves. But once the dust settles, I believe people will see the stronger Asturia that rises through, and then people will understand.'

'Do you believe the people of Elheim will accept you as a figurehead in *their* Asturia?' His jaw tensed as his sadness shifted into frustration.

Keene turned her head to the side just a slight. 'I have had many assurances that my skills will be needed in the difficult transition that lies ahead. Figurehead might be too strong a label for my role, but the Grand City needs familiar faces within the settlements under their control, and people who know the inner workings of each system of governance.'

Darus nodded along, though he fixed his gaze on a wall in the distance rather than look at her. 'But what then? What happens after all Asturia is brought under the banner, and what happens once you have trained a younger Elheim to understand those systems like you say?'

'I imagine I can then finally retire. Enjoy the luxuries of my position in the Quarters,' she laughed.

Darus slid his gaze towards her, not sharing in her amusement. Her smile shrunk away.

She searched his eyes for a short time, until hers widened dramatically in sudden realisation. She darted to her feet and covered her mouth with the back of her hand.

Darus stood too; his strength returned. 'Sacrifices for the greater good,' he said.

The Last of the Magi

'No. The Grand City wouldn't be so duplicitous. We have an arrangement.' Keene's voice rose, but she hastened to lower it.

'The Elheim vision is to unite Asturia and make it strong by ridding our country of rebels, defectors, and conspirators. Even though you are helping to make that vision a reality, the way you have gone about it makes you a risk in the chancellor's eyes.'

Keene looked offended. 'I'm to be branded a conspirator?'

Her expression was twisted and uncomfortable, she was struggling to understand the truth of his words. But that changed quite quickly. Darus could see the dots joining in her mind, as she paled and became sombre.

'I've been a fool. How did I miss it? My well-meaning intentions betray me, just as I have betrayed my people's trust.' She stared at the floor for a while, shaking her head slowly. But she remained composed. She looked up to Darus again. 'How long do I have?'

'I don't know.'

'I see.' She turned away and faced her quarter.

Despite the dark news he delivered, Darus found strength in what he had just done. He had defied the direct command of his father, but he did what he thought was right. He was grateful for that strength, as he steeled himself now for the myriad of questions Keene would no doubt have to throw his way about her impending fate.

The coinswoman straightened and her shoulders lifted. Then she turned back to him. She was smiling 'If this is my penance for trying to do the best by my people, then so be it. Perhaps I was wrong.'

Her words punched away his newfound strength.

She stepped forward and put a hand on his shoulder. Her composure was already restored. She held herself proudly. 'Thank you for warning me. But I must ask why you would tell me this?'

Why? It felt obvious now, after hearing all she had to say. She was in this mess because she did what she thought was right, rather than what others told her was right. Her words had given him some inspiration to do what *he* felt was right, despite the consequences that might follow. 'You deserve to know,' he said. 'I think you've earned that much. You don't deserve to be branded an enemy by both sides for doing what you thought was right for everyone.'

Keene laughed shortly and she looked at Darus with sympathetic eyes. 'Thank you, I will use what time I have left to prepare myself.' She sighed and then smiled again. 'But I will say this. Though my actions might put a stain on my long time as a coinsman – maybe even going as far as demonising my memory once I'm gone – I am warmed to have met you, Darus Valivelle. You have proven to me that there is heart behind the uniform of Elheim. There may be hope for our Asturia's future, so long as people like you are part of it.'

Darus couldn't muster any words. He was stunned, not only by what she said but by her unnerved composure as she said it. He didn't believe her words, not fully, but he appreciated them.

'You are too kind,' he said, after a pause. A thought then entered his mind, and he spoke it before giving himself chance to think it through. 'Will you let me continue our lessons?'

Keene hummed and seemed torn by the question. He understood why. It was a futile exercise now, a distraction from what was coming.

'Please,' he continued, 'you've come a long way in such a short amount of time. And I know you're enjoying it. At least let me show you how to properly Grasp.'

She shrugged. 'If you insist. Though it may ruin my tea, I would quite like to see it do more than just ripple.'

A sad but genuine smile crept onto Darus's face. 'I will show you how.'

She had already proven that she could engage Deep Thought and start Reaching. In developmental terms, she had learnt to stand – teaching her to Grasp would be like breaking into a gentle walk. She might never hone the mental muscle with enough acuity to truly Command, but at the very least she would get to experience the wonder of reshaping and redirecting the elements within her Grasp.

'Come on then. Let's head back before we are missed.'

He straightened his uniform and stepped at Keene's side as she put on her smile and led them back to her manor.

Chapter 44

Pride and Power

'Are the rumours about him true?'.

Lanark startled, grasping at the rung of the ladder to regain balance. He was examining a shelf in Keene's library. Her actual library, not *the* Library. He saw Illian now stood at the door, her arms firmly crossed.

'They are,' Lanark said, rolling his eyes derisively. He wondered how long it would take her to bring this up.

'What have you done about it?'

Lanark dropped down to the bottom rung. He was satisfied the coinswoman's library held a healthy backlog of ledgers that chronicled the activities of the Trade Quarters. *More than enough to learn from,* he concluded. He sighed at his sister, knowing that she didn't take kindly to being ignored. 'What have I done about it?' he said harshly. It wasn't unusual for his sister, or any of the senior Valivelle family members to pry openly into each other's affairs. 'I have done all that is necessary to stamp out any distractions, so he can focus his attentions to his duties and enhancing his abilities.'

He stepped off the ladder, swiping for his cane, and then walked past Illian, avoiding her eyes.

A gust of Arcane air wrapped around his arm like a cold hand and pulled him back to face her. With a quick Command of his own, he took control of the air and immediately pushed it back her way. She shuddered as the blades of air hit against her shoulder.

'You have a duty to do more, Lanark.'

'A *duty*?' he spat. 'He is my son, and he will be dealt with as I see fit!'

Illian looked at him with fury in her eyes, but he shot the same fury back at her in return. 'This is a family concern. We should all be consulted, especially when Valivelle reputation hangs in the balance.'

Lanark curled his fists and turned to walk away again. This time he Commanded the air to form a blustering barrier between them, so he could move unhindered. The books on either side of them rattled. He looked back her way as he reached the doorway. 'My son's inclinations are no concern of yours, Illian. I encourage you to accept what I have said – I have done all that is necessary.'

Illian swiped a hand downwards in front of her and the barrier of wind erupted outwards and slammed into the shelves on either side, causing journals and dusty old tomes to fall. The dust that came with them span and lifted through the air as it caught on the Arcane draft.

'I have no interest in his inclinations! I need assurance that when the opportunity presents itself, he will share his gift with the rest of the family, preferably before the College Arcana.'

Lanark froze.

'I am quite eager to experience the earth move at my Command,' she said insidiously, 'Perhaps you could arrange a demonstration?'

Lanark stuttered, and then stifled a laugh of relief. He marched back in towards his sister, who now gazed at him curiously with her head lifted high. 'Apologies, Illian, I misunderstood you.' This was not the rumour he thought she was referring to. He forgot his sister had been unconscious for some time. 'You will get your demonstration. I intend for Darus to put his power to good use – at the execution.'

Illian's eyes flashed, and her teeth pierced through the thinnest of smiles. 'What an excellent idea. Are you sure he is up for it?' she paused as her eyes briefly searched over his shoulder. 'He is not as… *confident* as most enforcers.'

'He has done it before. He just needs encouragement. And once that matter is dealt with, and our duties in this city are lightened, we can set about learning how he accesses this strength.'

'I would enjoy nothing more than to bury that criminal from the Outer Counties beneath the earth.'

They laughed together and then Lanark invited his sister to accompany him to his meeting with Inquisitor Protelborn to discuss the execution arrangements. 'Trust in my plans, Illian, and you will get your chance.'

Chapter 45

Musings of the Magi

'I read your letter, Jerard. This is a curious time to take interest in thaumaturgic studies, don't you think?'

'These are strange times, Madam Trulayne. We're grateful that you agreed to come,' Traykin raised his glass to her. It amused him that he always saw her wearing the same thing: a fur-lined coat with sleeves that ruffled at the cuffs with exotic feathers.

Mors approached the head of the table and pulled out a seat for her and she gracefully took it. She dropped a heavy bag beside herself. Food was then quickly served to her and the former coinsmen.

Madam Trulayne flourished her bejewelled hands and immediately started examining her meal. She pouted with her thick raspberry lips.

Exchanging glances with the others, Traykin gave them nervous smiles. He gave Madam Trulayne a little longer before clearing his throat to get her attention.

'Yes... I think this will suffice as part-payment, Jerard.' She picked up her fork and began tousling at the vegetables neatly laid around half of the plate. 'I brought the texts most relevant to your enquiries. Though I've more or less memorised them.'

Sat opposite Traykin, Velioth twirled his fork over his plate and leaned forward. 'If I may, Madam Trulayne – apologies for my directness, especially as I don't believe we've met before today – but we are likely to be limited for time this afternoon.'

Trulayne nodded. 'I respect that. House arrest must be very demanding of your time.'

Traykin shirked.

'Where would you like to begin?' she asked.

'The Purge,' Faast said, bluntly, 'is it possible that any Magi survived?'

Trulayne paused with a fork of food in front of her mouth.

'A curious place to begin a discussion of the Magi. I'm afraid there is no direct answer to that. The Magi were not a creed to hold a census. But for years we assumed that if so many of the Magi decided to assemble at the Grand City's gates, then surely they *all* must have been there.'

'Sounds like you don't believe that,' said Traykin.

'No. I suppose you could say it doesn't quite add up. Magi had exceptional gifts, some of my colleagues believe they had a kind of foresight or clairvoyance – like an additional sense unique to them – and if that were true, it seems preposterous that their vassal bond would allow them to walk so boldly to their deaths. There are known events of Magi sacrificing themselves for good causes, certainly, but not on that scale.'

'Vassal bond?' asked Velioth.

'I did say the Purge was a curious place to begin this discussion,' she said with a sigh.

'We can get to that,' Traykin added. He then rolled his hand through the air. 'So, what you're saying is…'

'I suspect some Magi survived. There were a few notable Magi who, despite their bond, acted with more autonomy than the others. Ismelde Marks and Nehren Conseil, to name a couple. If any were to turn away from what was happening that day, it would have been the ones who acted as they did.'

Velioth had started scratching notes upon a napkin, 'Have there been any sightings of Magi since the Purge?'

'Sadly not,' she said, chewing on her food obnoxiously. 'Not confirmed at least.'

Traykin frowned. 'What does that mean?'

She rolled her eyes and reached down for one of the books from her bag. Licking one finger, she leafed through its pages until she found a page towards the back where the printed text became handwritten notes. 'Every now and again a Magi-enthusiast tries to label some eccentric character as being a Magi.' She flicked back and forth between a few pages. 'A cloaked figure herding away groups of feral lirrus here. A stranger lurking around the ruins of Midhaven there. Strange behaviours in County Dellow. County Haarb. Arboreta. It goes on.'

The Last of the Magi

'So, nothing more than rumour?' asked Faast.

'That's a matter of personal interpretation. I prefer to believe the Magi are still out there, albeit living a quieter life to avoid the attention of the Elheim. When your people have experienced genocide, it might persuade one to keep away from the executors, don't you think?'

'That offers some semblance of optimism,' added Faast.

Trulayne smiled and pointed her loaded fork towards Faast. 'I like to think so.'

Faast poured herself some wine from a decanter served by Velioth's staff. 'The other matter of concern relates to the capability of the Magi. The potential of their Magic, to be plain.'

Madam Trulayne slapped her book shut and swapped it for a smaller tome with a tree-bark cover. She pulled the book open by the string slid in its middle and hummed with satisfaction at the page that opened before her. 'A much more interesting subject. Yes, I have plenty on that.'

'We have heard a theory,' said Velioth, 'that the Magi could stop other magic from being used somehow. Is this true?'

Trulayne hummed again and looked to the ceiling, resting her neck into the fur-lining at the back of her coat. She mumbled for a bit and then gave a small nod. 'It's certainly possible. It sounds like an extreme interpretation of their abilities, in my opinion.'

'Please go on, we are grateful for anything you might know.'

She leaned over her books. 'Look – we barely understand the thaumaturgy that exists in our world. All we have is observation and theory to work with. I have read everything I can get my hands on when it comes to the Magic of the Magi, and there are certainly some trends to the way they used their powers. For instance, their Magic was only ever used to interact with the natural environment. They would either enhance, pacify or transform the things around them.

'Depending on what their vassal bond required of them, they might cause the wind to blow a bit harder, or maybe become still and calm. On other occasions they might make rain fall on a clear day or banish the rain altogether. You ask me about an ability to stop other forms of thaumaturgy – what you are describing is different to the acts we have documented, and those examples I just gave you, but it's still in line with the trend, if you follow.'

Traykin raised a brow. 'How is stopping magic in any way like making it rain?' he chuckled, though the other former coinsmen were hanging on for Trulayne's answer.

'Think it through. As far as we know, thaumaturgy is not a gift obtained artificially. It is a natural product of our world. If the Magi can pacify the elements, its plausible they can pacify thaumaturgy too, in the sense that it too is *natural*.'

'Another hypothetical,' grunted Faast.

Trulayne then made a disgruntled squeak and she furrowed her way through the pages of her book in a stupor, muttering as if trying to convince the book to take her where she wanted to go.

Her fingertip planted into the page. 'It might be better than hypothetical. Yes, there was a story passed amongst thaumaturgy historians which might fit this description. Incapable of being proven, of course. The story tells of a wealthy family becoming very irate when one of their sons displayed signs of being a Magi in his early years. They apparently called upon a visiting Magi for help, asking him to change the boy's fate.'

'And the Magi took away his magic?' asked Velioth.

'Possibly. Some tellings of the tale say that's what he did. Others, the majority, say that the Magi examined the boy and claimed there was no potential for Magic in him at all.'

'Where was this?' asked Faast.

Trulayne shrugged. 'The flavoursome details change each time the story was told. When I first heard the story, it involved a family in Ferenir, but nothing more specific than that. The peculiar aspect of this story was that it first circulated only around twenty-or-so years ago.'

Velioth tilted his head and looked around to everyone. 'I don't understand, why is that peculiar?'

'Because this was *after* the Purge. A strange time for a Magi story to surface, don't you think?'

It was strange. Traykin knew instinctively that there was something in this. Not only because it added some credence to what Tharian had heard from the Awoken of Feralland, but because the

The Last of the Magi

story Trulayne told was familiar to him. He had heard it too, just once or twice. Greycloak had told it to him. The finer details were again different, tainted with the old man's creative embellishments, yet the core story was the same.

Greycloak told the story for the young Frigg and Tharian's benefit – a fairytale of sorts to keep them amused – so it was easy enough for him to have forgotten it. The old man always had stories to tell. He had as many stories in him as colours in Traykin's vests.

The lad might just be right about this. All of it.

'So what does this all mean for us?' asked Velioth, swilling his wine glass beneath his nose, taking in the scent even as he concentrated on the discussion.

Faast grunted. 'It means little. There is no certainty to take from any of this conjecture.'

'No. Can't you see it, Faast?' Traykin said, lowering his voice and succumbing to the urge to be uncharacteristically serious. 'It means there is hope in this. Tharian travelled here from *Feralland* with rumours of a living Magi and a power that might help us. Now, here with a historian who collects information on the Magi, we are hearing rumours that marry up with what we're looking for. It's not a simple coincidence.'

'Don't think me base, Traykin. I made the connections. But this takes us not one pace closer to finding this reclusive Magi or enlisting this strength into our arsenal.'

Traykin made a dismissive sound at Faast and then turned back to Trulayne, giving her his winning smile. 'One more question?'

She nodded; one brow cocked with curiosity as she put down her cutlery.

'If a Magi is out there, what can we do to seek them out?'

Madam Trulayne laughed. 'Now *that* would be where the vassal bond comes into the picture.' She took a deep swig of wine. 'The Magi truly were – *are* – gifted with great abilities. But those gifts came with a cost. In a stark opposite to the Elheim and their Arcana, all accounts suggest that the Magi were servants to their Magic. To put it another way, they did not swan around Asturia doing as they please and showboating their incredible powers. Not at all. They appeared where they were needed, and they used Magic where it was required. The Magi fulfilled a function in Asturia, carrying out duties that only they knew and understood. We called this phenomenon the vassal bond, a term which they adopted for our benefit.

'They only ever did things for one of two reasons: because it had to be done, or because they were asked to do it. Mind you, they didn't always do what was asked of them, not if it went against their vassal bond. With that said, I can offer you a plain answer to this one: you cannot seek out a Magi in hiding. They will appear only where their vassal bond requires them to be.'

Traykin slumped in his seat. He looked over and saw that Velioth had done the same.

Faast, however, did not look so defeated. 'I can follow the logic in much of what you have said, Madam Trulayne. But if the vassal bond is truly as you say it to be, I cannot understand why the entire order of Magi would assemble at the gates of the Grand City to be annihilated. You suggest also they had some degree of precognition, yet their actions on that day fly in the face of both of those qualities.'

Trulayne nodded. 'A subject that has garnered much debate. Away from prying Elheim ears, of course. The Purge was a strange anomaly indeed. Some Magi were dragged by enforcers to the Eastern Expanse that day, but equally many more assembled voluntarily with their kin. Men, women, and children alike. My theory is this: either the Magi felt that they *had* to be there by virtue of their vassal bond, or they simply went there by choice for some reason known only to them.'

Faast had no response.

Traykin digested everything he heard, as fully as he could. There was something positive to take from all this, that Tharian's theories about the Magi may well be true. Some may have survived, and they may truly have the power they needed to counter Arcana. But then there was the vassal bond. If Trulayne was right, they had no way of summoning the Magi or compelling them to act. They were an order with a reputation for non-intervention and pacifism, so the likelihood of them voluntarily joining an uprising seemed slim.

Raising a glass to Trulayne, Traykin forced a smile. 'Thank you,

The Last of the Magi

Madam Trulayne. You've given us a lot to think about.'

'I could go on. I could even delight you with tales of other forms of thaumaturgy rumoured to exist elsewhere,' she said, 'but judging by your pensive expressions I have given you a lot to think about.'

Velioth nodded. 'You have. It's a private matter, one that we—'

'The affairs of the coinsmen are the affairs of the coinsmen,' she interrupted, 'you may not hold your titles anymore, but I respect that you still have your private matters. Traykin has offered both feast and coin for my information, and that is payment enough for my services.'

Traykin raised his glass again. 'I'll drink to that!'

The others joined in the toast, but the air in the room was dampened by all the talk of genocide, lost Magi, and the inhibiting nature of the vassal bond. But as Traykin looked at the uncomfortable faces around the table with him, as usual he couldn't resist chuckling at the awkwardness of it all. Velioth smirked and laughed under his breath too, and Madam Trulayne couldn't resist joining them.

Faast, however, just shook her head and took to her drink.

Chapter 46

Rallying for Reclamation

Leaning against the wall in one of the back alleys of the Quarter of War, Tharian waited at the agreed meeting point. He arrived early just in case Marla managed to finish her errands sooner than expected. She was delivering routine orders to mercenary bands across the Quarter of War and using the opportunity to offer them the work they discussed with the coinsmen.

If all went to plan, the mercenaries would cause enough mayhem in the city to pull the enforcers and some of the guards away from the main streets. They would be dealing with the nuisance in the alleys for hours, getting led in circles by those who knew those dark pathways better than any other.

Then, Tharian and the elite guard could make their stand at Keene's manor, cornering the Elheim and driving them out of the Quarters.

Marla came jogging out of the shadows of another alley. She paused to catch her breath. She caught glimpse of Tharian lurking and gave him a thumbs-up as she approached.

'It went well?'

She stretched, planting her hands at the small of her back. 'I think so. Not the most reliable bunch, but Mors gave me enough money to get their eyes sparkling.'

'Great work. Next, we need to get to the city guard and elite guard. Any suggestions?'

Marla smiled. 'I deliver to a few of the turrets on the wall, I can talk to the archers I know. But I don't have any sway with the elites.'

'That works for me, I'll talk to the elites.'

'You're sure?'

Tharian pushed off the wall and checked down all the alleyways in sight, in case anyone might be approaching or listening in. He already knew they were clear, as Ombra was keeping watch from above, but old habits made him cautious. 'I'm sure. I imagine at least one of them will have a score they want to settle with me. I am a *Champion of the Crucible,* after all.'

Marla chuckled. 'I bet they will absolutely love seeing you again.'

'It wasn't my finest moment, but it got the job done.' He tucked a hand into his coat pocket, just to feel for the handle of his blade underneath his layers. 'Let's get moving before someone notices us here. I assume the elites guard are based at the coinswoman's barracks?'

'Yeah, and as far as I can tell the enforcers don't spend much time there. All that extra dust and soot isn't to their liking apparently.'

Tharian smothered a laugh. He then turned away in the direction of the barracks, but Marla tugged at his coat and pulled him back. She suddenly looked concerned.

'Before we go, I need to tell you something. I probably should have mentioned it earlier, but with so much going on I didn't have a chance to think.'

'What is it?' he raised a brow.

'I think I've done something bad.'

'Marla – out with it.'

She was suddenly quite red-faced, and she looked down. 'When the Elheim broke into the city, they started doing a city-wide sweep looking for you.'

'Yes, I know. We've been over that already.'

'Yes, but they came to the house. They asked us questions about the Crucible tourney and if we knew who you were.'

Tharian groaned. He didn't like where this was heading. And Marla's shrinking as he groaned confirmed he wasn't going to like what he heard.

'I panicked. One of the enforcers was literally sat there in our home asking me what I knew. At the time, all I could think about was getting rid of the enforcer as quickly as I could.'

He stepped closer to Marla and placed his hands on her shoulders. She met his eyes. 'Don't worry. Just tell me what you said. It's better that I know.'

She grimaced and pulled back as far as his arm length would let her go. 'I told them your name, and that we travelled together from Bryn.'

Tharian flushed. Suddenly his disguise felt redundant. That wasn't really the case, of course. Someone knowing his name and where he had travelled from was hardly enough to identify him in the street. Those hallmarks were hidden away still. But they knew his name now and that was unsettling. He softened his face, realising that he was scowling, and squeezed her shoulders lightly. 'You did what you had to. I can't fault you for that. I don't think it will change anything.'

Her posture lifted. 'Really? You're sure?'

He dropped his hands from her shoulders. 'As sure as I can be. I think they know enough now about what I look like for my name to be of little consequence. It's a common enough name, anyway.'

'I'm sorry, I shouldn't have told them anything.'

'It's fine, apology accepted. Now come on.' He smiled, tapped her arm with the back of his hand and then walked off. She followed close behind.

Keeping a shoulder close to the wall, Tharian dashed down the alley beside him, racing along the damp, uneven cobbles. The path twisted and turned many times. He glanced back only fleetingly to ensure Marla was keeping pace. She was, with a certain bounce in her step now she had lifted her conscience with that confession.

There were a lot of obstacles on those dark roads. Crates and sacks littered some of the paths, some torn open by rodents, spilling their contents across the ground. On other paths, people were crowded together, either drinking, smoking, or having hushed conversations away from prying eyes and ears. Some of those people called out for their attention but they dashed on through without paying them any mind.

Tharian instinctively became defensive, just in case one of them decided to reach for them or step in their way. But when he next looked over his shoulder to check on Marla again, he noticed she was completely unfazed by the vagrants and drunkards.

Truly one of the Quartersfolk, he mused.

She ran around him and pulled him to a different branching path,

The Last of the Magi

'This way is quicker,' she huffed.

The change took him off the route he recognised. Even so, he trusted her. And she was right. After a few more roads, they stopped together at the end of the path. They were a step away from a curving street that bordered the enormity of Faast's keep, which meant they must have run all the way to the edge of the Quarter of War.

'We good to go?' she asked.

Tharian looked up. As he did, Ombra landed on a rooftop above and gave Tharian a calm blink. She hadn't seen anything they needed to worry about. He gave Marla the nod to go ahead.

She walked out calmly and crossed the road to walk alongside the keep's outer wall. Tharian followed until they stopped at a point where the wall dropped a bit lower – about half his height taller than him – and he could hear voices coming from somewhere on the other side.

Judging by the sound, and the shape of the wall bordering the area, there was a courtyard or basilica on the other side of the wall, rather than another structure extending from the keep itself. And there must have been quite a few people gathered there, as there were pockets of conversation, punctuated by laughter, then occasionally sounds of clashing wood and metal.

Marla stopped at a part where the wall was topped by grey tiles that tilted down towards them. There was a door a little further along, but she didn't take him that far. She looked to him and gestured with a thumb towards the wall.

'The elite guards gather in this courtyard when they're off-duty.'

'You've been here before, then?'

'Only the once,' she rolled her eyes. 'I didn't like it. It was just meant to be a quick delivery, but they made me wait at the door behind me for ages. The other elites milling around just stared at me like I was a threat they needed to be wary of.'

'I suppose that's to be expected in their line of work.' Tharian walked over to the metal door and looked it over. There were locks at the top, bottom, and middle of the door. They were made of a thick metal, and the doorframe was substantial enough that it jutted out inches from the stonework around it. He rolled up his sleeves.

'They've locked the door from this side, I'll have to go over the top.'

Marla laughed. 'I thought you might say that.'

Instead of stepping back, she moved in front of him. She crouched and cupped her hands together beside one knee. 'While you're in there, I'll head up the wall and have a word with some of the city guard. Meet back here?'

Tharian smiled. *Resourceful. Efficient. Faast was right – she probably would make a good elite.* He pointed over to the alley they emerged from. 'We'll meet back there. If you get in any trouble, Ombra will let me know.'

'And if you get in trouble?'

His smile widened. 'Ombra will let you know, I'm sure.

There was a squawk overhead, and Ombra swept over them, disappearing back over the tenements a moment later.

They both laughed. Then Tharian planted his foot in Marla's hands and waited for a nod from her before using the locks on the door as a support for his other foot. He then vaulted himself up the wall. He rolled over the tiles at the top and dropped off the other side, twisting his body to secure a safe landing on his feet.

He straightened slowly.

Suddenly the courtyard became a rush of movement. Swords, spears, knives, and other weapons were drawn and pointed his way. The platoon of black and gold armoured warriors advanced and cornered him at the wall.

He slowly raised his open hands into the air. Hoping they would notice he was not bearing arms of his own. 'Please,' he said, and they all halted. 'I'm here on behalf of Faast.'

A broad-shouldered guard pulled off his helm, revealing his bald head and scarred scalp. He pushed away a spear pointed across his path and stepped forward. He squinted and then spat on the ground.

'You? From the coinswoman? Is this a new Elheim game or is this somethin' else.'

Tharian kept still as the tower-of-a-man closed in. 'Something else. I think you can tell from my clothing that I'm not Elheim.'

The man grunted. 'Pale like 'em, though. Or maybe you just don't get out much. Who are you?'

The Last of the Magi

Tharian cursed in his head. How many times would he leap first and think later. He had to make a quick decision about whether to be honest or not. He realised he was too deep into this now to lie or mislead those who he sorely needed as allies.

'You don't know me. Well, not all of you. I entered your last Crucible tourney, and I was given the name Arcana Hunter.'

The bald man just squinted even more tightly at him and planted a fist at his waist. He exchanged glances with his cohort. They then all stared at Tharian together, weapons still drawn forward like the jagged teeth of a giant beast.

Then they laughed. The elite guard lowered their weapons, with each leaning over to a neighbour to laugh more and make jokes between themselves about Tharian and his bold claim. 'Nice try,' the elite said.

Tharian balked. Why was that so hard to believe? 'It's true,' he said, 'and I can prove it.'

The laughter stopped. The elite looked back and searched amongst his peers, stopping when he found one at the edge of the crowd, to Tharian's right.

'Goreson, do you recognise him?'

The elite in question had a double-bladed sword in his hands. He pulled off his helm and dropped it, revealing grey hair shaved short underneath. Tharian felt a rush of adrenaline. Goreson was his opponent in the Crucible.

Goreson shuffled forward, huffing loudly and shaking his head. He peered at Tharian and then looked back to the other elite. 'I don't recognise him.'

'There you have it, then.'

Frustrated, Tharian went to move his coat and show them the weapon at his hip, but he paused as the elites all pointed their weapons at him again. 'Wait!' he shouted. 'You might not recognise me, but you'll recognise my blade.'

Goreson and the elite looked to each other. Goreson shrugged and then the other elite gave Tharian a nod.

Tharian peeled back his coat and slowly drew part of his runeblade from it sheath. Just enough to show the first rune. They didn't laugh this time. Goreson growled and nodded to the other elite, confirming to all of them the truth of what they were seeing.

'Alright then, Arcana Hunter, what do you want? We're not enlisting you if that's why you're here.'

Tharian pushed his sword back with his palm. 'I doubt I'd fit in. I only won my match thanks to a cheap trick – sorry about that, Goreson.'

Goreson pouted and nodded.

'I'm working with Coinswoman Faast to undo what the Elheim have done here. And I need your help.'

'You think we'd help you? You're a criminal. You should be locked up. You're the reason they're here. We should be handing you over.'

'You could do that,' Tharian replied candidly. 'I've caused trouble, I know that, but there's a reason the Elheim are trying so hard to find me, and it's not just because I carry an illegal weapon. It's because I've taken a few of their enforcers out, and they don't like being made to look weak.'

'That's what people are saying, but what's the truth? Weapons can't beat Arcana.'

'That *is* the truth. Arcana is powerful but it doesn't make the Elheim invulnerable. They can't stop what they don't see coming.'

In a dramatic flourish, he drew out his runeblade and laid it across his palms so the elites could see it. 'I was able to take down an enforcer because she didn't think she could be stopped – especially not in the Outer Counties during a routine inspection. She didn't watch her flanks, she had no defences, and she didn't see my attack coming.'

'And you think your cheap tricks will be enough to drive them all out?'

'No,' he replied, truthfully. 'Not alone. But with the greatest fighters in the Trade Quarters at my side, fighting intelligently, creatively and cautiously, I think *we* could do it.'

'You're just trying to save your own skin,' the elite said, suddenly turning sour again.

Another tall elite stepped forward, this one armed with only a plain longsword. 'Hear him out, Varks.'

Varks gave the smaller one a questioning look.

The Last of the Magi

'I was there after the tourney. I overhead his conversation with Faast in the keep. She agreed to hear him out, and he even got her to sign a missive for a Coinsmeet.'

Varks turned sharply to the other and then back to Tharian. 'What?'

'It's true,' Tharian confirmed, trying not to smirk as he felt his status with the elites improving. 'And that Coinsmeet happened. Everything I have done in the Quarters has been geared towards making a stand against the Grand City. And your coinsmen agreed to stand with me.'

'If he works with Faast, I say we help,' said Goreson, attracting a few startled looks from the others. 'Look, its either that or we sit here and become the useless muscle of the Elheim. We trained to stop invaders, didn't we? Not roll over and accept them the moment they arrived. Whether we trust this guy or not, we swore to protect the Quarters and I reckon we've done a bad job of it lately.'

'Thank you,' said Tharian.

Varks groaned and twisted his head, seeming to be on the edge of forming a decision. He eventually sighed. 'This isn't for any one of us to decide. But there's enough of us here to decide together. You wait there, *Arcana Hunter*.' Varks then led the other elites across the courtyard to the far end where stuffed mannequins were laid out in a row for their training. They huddled together and immediately broke out into fiery conversations, but none of it was clear enough through their drawl for Tharian to make out more than a few words. Some pointed his way, however, and their gestures looked far from complimentary.

***

No matter how many times she had to scale the colossal height of the border walls, it never got easier. Despite the burning sensation in her thigh muscles, she had enough adrenaline to push on through, getting her to the top.

Marla jogged over to the nearest sentry post. The city guard within, with her red-tinted binoculars, heard her coming.

'Is it my birthday?' the woman shouted.

'Huh?'

'I didn't order anything this time, yet here you are.'

Marla chuckled. 'Ah. No, no deliveries this time.' She ducked into the small stone structure and perched on the bench beside the open window that looked out into the smoggy beyond. 'I actually need something from you this time.'

'Really?' the guard replied. 'I'm on duty.'

'I know, don't worry. It's not anything you need to do right now.'

'Alright, let's hear it.'

Marla gave herself a few seconds to catch her breath and pull together her words. She had been having similar conversations with the mercenary guilds all day, so she felt well-rehearsed by this point.

'The coinsmen – *our* coinsmen – are planning something big for tomorrow. There's going to be chaos in the Quarters, and the coinsmen need you and as many of the guard as possible to be on the right side of it.'

The woman gave Marla a stunned look. 'What kind of chaos?'

'A few of the mercenary factions are coming together to riot against the Elheim. They're going to distract the enforcers, drawing them away from the main roads.'

'What? Have they gone mad. What would drive them to do that?'

Marla gave her a stern look. 'It will keep the enforcers away from the new coinsmen at Keene's manor. The fugitive the enforcers are looking for is back in the Quarters, and he's going to rally the elites to drive the Elheim out of our city.'

The woman's mouth dropped open. She paled. 'You're joking.'

'I'm not. Faast, Velioth and Traykin are working with him. They're doing all they can to make this work.'

'They'll all be killed. Its suicide.' The guard started to look about, panicked by what Marla was saying.

Marla reached for the woman and grabbed her wrist firmly, which kept her still. 'Listen. It's happening. There's no way to stop it. You don't need to join the fight, but there's a way you can help.'

The guardswoman paused, meeting Marla's eyes directly.

The Last of the Magi

'Tell all those you trust in the guard to carry on as normal tomorrow. But if any of them are called upon by the enforcers to help deal with the mercenaries, they need to do what they can to keep the enforcers distracted. If they can help the mercenaries without putting themselves at risk, they should do it. The longer the enforcers are kept busy, the more time Tharian and the elites will have at Keene's manor.'

'Is that it?'

'Yes, that's it. You could even convince people to stay at home tomorrow, abandon their posts for a day. The mercenaries will be doing the heavy lifting around the city. The rest of you just need to do what you can to help us or hinder them.'

'Marla, I'm not sure about—'

Marla squeezed her wrist again. 'It's happening, ok? Tomorrow. Whether you like it or not. You can either side with the Elheim or side with your coinsmen. This might be the last time you get that choice.'

The guardswoman swallowed. 'I'll spread the word at drinks this evening. I can't guarantee I'll get to many, or that they will even believe me. But I'll do it.'

'Thank you.'

The guard gave her a dumbfounded look. 'How did you get involved in this, aren't you an artisan?'

'It's a long story,' Marla said with a smile. 'Wrong place at the wrong time. Or the right place, maybe.'

'Don't put yourself in danger. You and the Glanmores need to keep yourselves safe.'

'I know, and we will. The same goes for you too.'

Marla then turned to leave, but the woman softly said her name. 'Do you think the coinsmen are making a mistake?'

The question was not what she was expecting. She frowned and just made a questioning noise, inviting her to expand.

'Coinswoman Keene said this was just a transition. A time to put things right, back to how they should be. What if this makes things worse? The Elheim will have to stay even longer.'

Marla's first thought was to snap back at the guard, calling her out for sympathising with the Elheim. But it was more complicated than that. This was someone who had most likely lived a calm and easy life under the tenure of Coinswoman Keene and the other coinsmen. Marla had to remember that she was still new to this city, and there were others living here who had trusted in the words of Coinswoman Keene for many years.

'I can tell you from experience that things will get worse if we do nothing,' she said. 'I get that you trust the coinswoman, but you cannot trust the Elheim. They outnumber her three-to-one. If they decide one day to burn down homes to make a point, or to remove Keene from office and replace her with another Elheim, they will do it in a heartbeat. The enforcers won't hold back on using Arcana on us just because Keene objects. I'm from Bryn, I have seen for myself what they're capable of.'

The guard still looked a little unsure, but she sighed and nodded. 'You're probably right.'

'Then let's hope everything goes to plan tomorrow.' As the guardswoman gave her another nod in agreement, Marla scratched at her neck and left the sentry post. It was unsettling to think there might be some, even amongst the city guard, that would consider laying down and accepting this new regime in the hope of avoiding conflict. It wasn't hard to believe, because the thought of standing against skilled enforcers and their Arcana was truly terrifying, but it was still unsettling.

Regardless, she had done what she came to do. That gave her some inspiration. She needed that energy to help her rally a few more friendly faces to their cause before she went back to meet Tharian.

As she walked further along the city wall, she looked around for any sign of Ombra. She made sure to check along the wall as well as above and over the vista of the city in case she had taken a different form, now she knew the animal was a Shifter.

Nothing. Ombra was nowhere to be seen. Marla took that to mean Tharian was still safe.

Chapter 47

Securing the Strategy

It was an awkwardly long wait. Tharian felt uncomfortable just standing there. He had tried pacing, jostling around a little to fight off the apprehension while the elites had their hushed meeting. It didn't help.

So he just kept still, until Goreson – the one he had bested unfairly in the Crucible – splintered away from the group and came back to him.

'It's looking like you have our support. There's a few who aren't interested, Vark is working on them. If you're working with Faast, what's her plan?'

Tharian almost sighed with relief. This was a big win. 'There's going to be a lot going on tomorrow. Enforcers will be driven off the streets, and you may be called upon to aid them. If that happens, you need to understand that the conflict in the city will be happening by design. It's all just a distraction. Keep the enforcers occupied, or better yet don't go to their aid at all.'

'Conflict? What kind of distraction have you planned?'

'I'm not sure for certain what will be happening, but we have hired mercenaries to do whatever they can to keep the enforcers busy.'

Goreson laughed. 'That will be interesting. They can be quite creative. What about those of us not called to the enforcers?'

'Assemble in the alleyways around Keene's manor. When you see me or Coinswoman Faast step out onto the road, that will be your cue to join.'

Goreson's brows lifted. He looked amused. 'The coinswoman will be joining us?'

'If she can make it out of Velioth's unscathed, yes.'

'We'll see if we can get her out and suited up.'

'Good. She'll be glad to get back in her armour, I'm sure. You'll need to be careful though, don't do anything rash or aggressive against the enforcers unless it's necessary. We need them to think it's just another day, and that the mercenary activity is just a low-level disruption that isn't part of a bigger scheme – otherwise they will probably rally together in the Artisan Quarter.'

'Makes sense. We'll send a few elites to the Market Quarter to aid the coinsmen if the opportunity comes. We'll keep the area as clear as possible without attracting attention.'

Tharian nodded, 'that sounds like a plan.'

'It does.'

Tharian looked over Goreson's shoulder, though he had to bounce onto his toes to do so. 'Do you need me to stick around?'

Goreson looked behind and then turned back with a sharp shake of his head. 'Nah, I've got the instructions. We'll sort our logistics out. Even if some of this lot back out, they won't go ratting us out to the Elheim.'

'Glad to hear it. Faast trained you well.'

Goreson cocked a brow. 'We're loyal to our city and our coinsmen by choice. We're not dogs.'

Tharian shirked. 'Sorry, I didn't mean any offence.'

'Good. Now go before an enforcer turns up with orders.'

Tharian stepped away and went back to the wall he had vaulted over. It looked twice as high from this side as it did from the other. The doorway was also sunken into the brick-face on this side, so he had less footing to work with.

Goreson stepped into view and squatted against the wall in a similar way to how Marla did. 'Out the way you came in then?'

'If you don't mind.'

He laughed. 'You're a dramatic one.'

Tharian stepped onto Goreson's cupped hands and then bent his knees ready to jump. But just as he was ready to spring himself and reach for the top of the wall, Goreson sprung up first, catapulting him upwards.

Tharian gasped as he lost balance in the air. He twisted and righted himself just in time to land crouched on top of the tiles, having to flurry his hands over the edge to secure his position.

Goreson cackled, and the other elites looked over and took pleasure in his panicked flight too.

The Last of the Magi

'Next time we fight, Arcana Hunter, I expect a fair match,' Goreson said, with a flourish of his blades. 'When it comes to the enforcers though, fight as dirty as you like.'

'You can count on it.'

Tharian dropped, landing back out in the Quarter of War.

Catching his breath from that unexpected flight, he straightened himself and checked over his coat just in case any of the stitching had come loose to reveal his green coat underneath the sewn-on overlay. Fortunately, the stitching held strong.

He then went to cross the road and slowed as his eyes met Marla's. She was leaning against the wall where they agreed to meet.

'I'm hoping you launching over the wall like that was a good sign. It didn't look like it.'

'It went very well actually,' he said. 'How did you get on?'

'I've got a few friends spreading the word. I'm not sure how far that word will spread before tomorrow, though. We'll have to see.'

'Don't worry about it. We don't need everyone to be involved. Just enough to give us the space we need in the Artisan Quarter. It will rouse less suspicion if more guards are carrying on as normal.'

'Yeah, I just hope it'll be enough.'

Marla looked pained. She stared off to the side and the middle of her forehead was creased with deep lines between her brows.

'Marla, don't worry about it. You've already done a lot to help with this. Without your help, we would be worse off.'

She snapped from her stare. 'I know. I understand that.'

'Then why do you look so troubled?'

She fidgeted, much like someone who didn't want to speak their mind. But she had not been one to hold back her thoughts this far.

'One of the guards I spoke to, she seemed sort of reluctant to do anything. Like letting the Elheim carry on would be the easier option. I think a lot of people here put all their trust in Coinswoman Keene, and they will follow her for as long as she is still a coinswoman, even if that means standing with the Elheim.'

Tharian now had the same expression she did. That was a troubling idea, one that could become dangerous if left to grow out of control. Although he had never been attached to any city long enough to become familiar with any political to that extent, he could understand the complacency and sense of routine that came with a lack of change. Those instincts that would drive some of the Quartersfolk to want consistency and calm in their home city, were the same as those that made Tharian want to pull himself away from such attachments, and towards change. The thought process made sense even though, in this case, he opposed it.

He sighed. 'That's the risk of letting this carry on for any longer than it already has. There are those that will sympathise with the Elheim, those that will grin and bear it and then those that will look the other way. Every day we wait makes those group grow larger, so we need to stop this before it's too late.'

Marla nodded, unconvincingly. But then she blinked hard and looked at Tharian directly, nodding a second time with more vigour. 'You're right. They're just hoping the Elheim won't turn on them. But they will, sooner or later.'

'Exactly,' said Tharian. He looked around and noticed some civilians walking their way. He pushed Marla gently towards the alley. 'Let's head back.'

Together they ducked back into the shadows.

As they walked through the winding paths, Tharian still kept a wary eye on all the branching pathways they passed. A white and blue uniform could emerge from any one of them without warning. Ombra still looped overhead, appearing in the peachy haze above for seconds at a time as she swept one way and the next. She would spot them; he kept telling himself. The white and blue uniforms would be unmistakable against the dark hues of the Trade Quarters backstreets.

They continued, walking at speed but not moving so fast this time as to attract the unwanted commentary from those who made these pathways their home.

And then Tharian's blood ran cold as Marla let out a shriek behind him.

He spun on his heels, tucking a hand inside his coat and bending his knees in readiness to spring into action.

Marla had a hand over her mouth and held her other hand out towards Tharian, patting the air in a downwards motion that he took

The Last of the Magi

to mean "stand down". She pointed down to the ground as she stepped over a pair of legs that stretched across part of the path.

He must have stepped over them without noticing. The legs were stretching out of a large box opened on its side.

'Sorry,' she said. 'He gave me a fright.'

'Are they dead?' he asked.

The body in the box grunted and then rolled onto its side. Bottles could be heard rolling into each other.

'Not yet,' Marla said, rolling her eyes as she stepped back to his side. She rubbed at her heart. 'Let's keep going, I can smell him now.'

Tharian laughed and continued forward. He relaxed and lowered his hand from his hilt. They took the next few steps slowly, checking the ground more carefully until they reached their next turn in the road.

Tharian led the way. He turned and immediately grunted as he walked into someone that turned the corner at the same time. Someone draped in black.

Chapter 48

Antithesis of Assumption

Tharian was pushed back. He hit hard against the alley wall. It happened so fast, Marla almost blinked and missed it. The figure in black only lifted his arm slightly and Tharian was pushed as if a carriage had just driven into him at speed.

Tharian looked pained and stunned, but he got up. He looked pale and horrified.

The black-clad man stepped into view. 'You miscreants might want to tread more carefully. You could have caused an injury,' he said.

Marla knew the voice instantly. Suddenly she was reliving that haunting experience from a few weeks ago, when this same man threw mercenaries around like playthings with Arcana. He had threatened her into silence that night, and she hoped dearly he wouldn't recognise her today.

'Inquisitor Protelborn?' she said, trying to sound courteous. She gave him a forced, nervous smile. 'We're sorry about that. We've been out all morning running deliveries – eager to get back home for the afternoon shift. We'll be more careful.'

The inquisitor turned to her slowly. 'Inquisitor is a title for the Grand City. I am your coinsman, am I not?'

She flushed. 'Yes, of course. Sorry. Coinsman Protelborn.'

His attention lingered on her a little longer. The small amount of light casting from a sconce a little way behind them made his eyes look like molten glass. 'I know your face,' he said. 'You did as you were told.'

Her heart fluttered. He did remember her. 'I didn't tell a soul what I saw.'

'You're a good girl,' he said. 'I believe you. Your face might show confidence, but I can see your hands trembling, and you turn yourself away from me just enough to expose your fear. You didn't take my warning lightly, did you? Wise.'

The Last of the Magi

She smiled awkwardly, glancing down to notice the subtle changes in her physicality that he had somehow spotted despite the darkness.

'And you travel with a companion this time, young artisan? I do hope that's not because of our last encounter.'

'He is an artisan apprentice. I'm showing him the ropes.'

Protelborn turned to look at Tharian. 'The runt will be shown the rope if he obstructs my path again. What promise do you offer to the artisans?'

Tharian stopped hunching against the wall. He stood to his full height and gave Marla a concerned look, one that made her feel uncomfortable. But he ignored the inquisitor's question, and that made her heart race even more.

Protelborn swivelled back to her. 'Where are his manners? Perhaps you need to teach your apprentice to fear me, as you do.'

Something in those words triggered a change in Tharian. He looked at Protelborn now with a very different look in his eyes. Anger.

'What did you do?' he said.

Protelborn laughed and turned to Tharian again. 'So, he *does* speak?'

'What did you do to make her fear you?'

The air in the tight alleyway suddenly felt hot. Tharian sounded different. Not calm and nonchalant as he usually did. But stoked like the furnace in Brayne's workshop. Despite Tharian's aggression, Protelborn seemed unmoved. In fact, he looked like he was enjoying the rebellion. His perfectly white teeth flashed in the darkness.

'You do not ask me questions. Consider that your only warning.'

'Don't threaten me, enforcer. You're a long way from home and right now the odds aren't in your favour.'

Protelborn's smile vanished. Then it returned as a thin, wide grin. Marla froze as he turned her way once more. 'Tell your master he will be needing a new apprentice. Perhaps someone more obedient.'

The inquisitor reached out towards a sconce in the distance. The flame ripped from its cradle and flew towards Tharian. Marla dived out of the way and hunkered down against the wall to avoid it.

Tharian drew his runeblade and swung it quickly enough to catch the ball of fire against the flat of the blade. The fire coated the dark metal and then twisted into a small vortex that sucked into one of the runes, which then glowed blue with the absorbed magic. He tapped two fingers on the same rune, it flashed, and he swept the blade at Protelborn. The fire reappeared, bathing the blade, and then surged at the inquisitor in an arc that mirrored the swing.

Protelborn jumped back with unnatural force, causing a surge of air to pop beneath his feet. He disappeared into the darkness as the sconce died out.

'Run!' shouted Tharian.

Marla's wrist was suddenly in his grip, and they sprinted away from the scene. She reached to her thigh and drew out a handaxe, though she hoped she wouldn't need to use it. She had never used them for anything other than fending off aggressive wildlife while travelling the Outer Counties.

Tharian just kept pulling and pulling and pulling. He dragged her left and right, seemingly choosing his route at random, trying to get as much distance as possible from the inquisitor.

He suddenly stopped and turned to her. He spoke quickly. 'Did he hurt you?'

'I'm fine,' she said, fighting to catch her breath. 'I got out of the way.'

'No. Whatever he did to make you fear him – did he hurt you?'

She felt a wash of embarrassment, then a warmth of affection. Did he stand up to Protelborn just because he was worried about her? 'No, he didn't hurt me. I saw him meeting someone in the alleys while I was running deliveries. Long before all this. He was attacked by thieves, and he stopped them with Arcana. He told me not to say anything. Somehow, he knew where I lived, so I had to protect Marion and Brayne.'

Tharian looked incensed, but only for a moment. His eyes became gentle, and he softened his voice. 'These Elheim deserve what's coming to them – he definitely didn't hurt you?'

'He didn't lay a finger on me.'

Tharian nodded but she could tell there was still a fire burning in him, though he tried to hide it. As he turned to carry on running,

The Last of the Magi

Marla instinctively grabbed his wrist, making him look back. 'Thank you.'

He put his hand on her wrist. 'Don't thank me yet, we need to get out of here.'

A sound bellowed in the distance. It was like a rumble of thunder. The air around them started to shake.

Tharian stared off in the direction of the sound, and then he looked up as if something had just called to him.

It was Ombra. She was following them overhead. But that wasn't all. Higher than Ombra, terrifyingly high above them all, another figure was rocketing through the air. Even without being able to see clearly, Marla knew it had to be Protelborn.

The smog and mist wrapped around his body as he soared through the air, just a small black blur in the distance. And then he descended. Hurtling down to them at speed.

Tharian pulled her forward again, veering down the first path they reached. Protelborn disappeared behind the towering buildings, but only for a few seconds. There was another surge in the air, and then a thud as Protelborn landed on the rooftop above, chasing them.

Where they ran, he followed. When they turned, he jumped from one building to the next. His Arcana was carrying his motions. Judging by Tharian's wide-eyed looks, he hadn't seen this before either.

'This way!' Tharian shouted. He veered and twisted them down another path. People loitering in the alleys had heard the commotion and were dashing away also, either slipping down other paths or tucking back into their tenements. That cleared their path as they ran, but also made it easier for Protelborn to follow. They couldn't escape him. All they could do was keep him moving so he couldn't pause to attack.

They skidded out onto a long road. Tharian cursed. There was no cover against him here. And to make matters worse, the clouds had suddenly darkened overhead, and rain came with it.

They couldn't go back. They ran as fast as they could, even as the sound of footsteps on rooftiles above closed in.

They didn't get much further before Marla was thrown off her feet. She hadn't tripped, her foot was grabbed and pulled back from under her. Her body was flipped upside down and she screamed as she was lifted off the ground.

She looked at her foot. A rope was looped around her ankle, connected to guttering above her. Beside it, Protelborn was leering over the edge of a roof with a knife glittering in his palm.

The sensation on her ankle was strange. She looked at the rope again. Except it wasn't a rope at all. It was water. Water that had somehow become solid, but not like ice. The water was still fluid and moving yet held in shape as if it flowed through invisible tubes.

Protelborn stepped off the roof. His black and red uniform fluttered as he controlled his descent with Arcana, slowly floating down to Marla with his knife glinting.

'Brace yourself!' Tharian shouted.

Before she could figure out where Tharian was, he came hurtling over her and brought his runeblade through the water stream. She fell, reacting quickly enough to throw her hands up and cushion her head from hitting the cobbles.

It still hurt, and she cried out as her body slammed heavily across the uneven ground, but it could have been much worse.

'The fugitive,' Protelborn said. He landed a short distance away.

Marla rolled onto her back, and Tharian appeared at her side to help her up. 'Are you alright?' he whispered.

'I'm ok.'

'Keep going down this road, I'll get rid of him.'

'Don't be stupid, you can't—'

'Go.' Tharian's eyes were serious and stern. But not afraid.

She nodded and shuffled back.

Tharian stood his ground against Protelborn.

***

'You're resourceful, I'll give you that,' Protelborn said, holding his knife in a stance that suggested he knew how to use it.

Tharian held his runeblade close. This *inquisitor* was very different to an enforcer. No less sinister and sadistic, but his use of Arcana was surgical and purposeful rather than boastful and dramatic.

'I will make this much less painful for you both if you come quietly for questioning.'

'Only an Elheim makes an offer like that while holding a knife.'

'You disregard my charity? Very well. Do not make the mistake of thinking your runeblade can save you from me.'

Tharian flourished his blade into a two-handed stance. He kept the runes facing the wall, trying to hide the fact that one was glowing from the Arcane water he sliced it through. 'We'll see about that, won't we?'

'The arrogance. I will be well rewarded for bringing you to the Valivelles.'

'You're not the first to say that. Yet here I stand.'

'Not for much longer.' Protelborn waved a hand overhead, and a draft surged up along the walls and slammed into the guttering on either side of the alley. The shunting of the metal sent a torrent of water spilling over, dropping together with the dislodged rain from the Arcane updraft. Protelborn directed the deluge at Tharian.

Tharian side-stepped, but the force and volume of the water caught him. He was slammed to the ground, soaked, and bruised instantly. He rolled and bounced back up to his feet, just in time to jump away from that same water stream being redirected at his feet like a tripwire.

Protelborn closed in at speed. His knife flashing in the sconce-light. Tharian only just raised his blade in time to defend himself.

But that didn't discourage the inquisitor. He stabbed and swiped again and again. Tharian had to pull his runeblade close and twist its position as fast as he could to deflect the light and fast strikes. Despite the disadvantage of his blade's weight, Tharian could just about handle the knife strikes, as Protelborn was lunging back and forth to avoid any counterstrike, which slowed him down. But while Tharian strained his arms to keep up, he could hear the water under Protelborn's control rushing around.

Somehow Protelborn attacked on both fronts at once. Knife jabs from the front, lashings of water from the sides and behind. Tharian moved as much as he could to dodge attacks from the water, while keeping his focus on the jabbing knife. Many of the water strikes hit him, the heavier hits almost knocking him down, but he kept going.

After a few near misses, Tharian got into his stride. Protelborn was clearly capable, attacking in two different ways, yet Tharian eventually noticed that he couldn't jab with the knife while also moving the water at the same time. That gave him a chance to figure out where the next attack was coming from.

And Protelborn adapted too. As soon as Tharian made an advance, the inquisitor hopped back and focused on his Arcana. The lashings of water were light, but incredibly fast. Tharian dodged and shifted as fast as he could, but it was like he was in a tight crowd being pushed and elbowed from all sides.

'Watch out!' shouted Marla from behind.

Tharian wasn't sure what it meant, but he reflexively slid to one side. He was briefly blinded as a flash of light reflected off Protelborn's knife as it flew past his face, missing him by a few inches. And then it flew back again as Protelborn pulled the air around the knife and brought it back to his hand.

Tharian's heart pounded in his chest. This man was a monster. Ruthless and brutal.

Fire licked at his back next. He felt the heat first, but he had no way to know it was coming as it hit against him so fast while he was still reeling from the knife throw. As the heat bore down on his spine, Tharian was more afraid of the exposed elements around him than he was of the knife in the man's palm.

Protelborn charged forward again. Thinking quickly, Tharian made a wide sweep at him, forcing him to abandon his charge and propel himself backwards several bounds with Arcana. That gave Tharian the time he needed to sweep his blade around to his back and press the flat against the fire burning through his layers.

He felt the searing heat taper off and brought the blade back to his front. Two runes now thrummed with trapped magic. He could assess himself for burns later, adrenaline kept any pain at bay.

Protelborn put his knife away and lowered his arms. Without gesturing, he doubled his efforts with Arcana. Darts of air, whips of water and sparks of flame were ripped from the environment around them and flung at Tharian.

The Last of the Magi

The blade was too cumbersome to be swung defensively on so many fronts. The elements were too fast. For every strike he dodged, another two would hit against him before he could recover. The strikes had enough momentum to push him around, pummel him and completely break his balance.

Tharian was under too much strain. He had to escape or strike back. If he waited much longer, he would slow too much and become an easy target, or the assault on his body would beat him to the ground. But as he held his ground, steeling himself as much as he physically could, he noticed something unexpected. The elements Protelborn controlled were weakening: the fire only lasted a few more strikes before it burnt out entirely; the water splashed against him more than it thumped at his sides; and the air only pushed at him where before it lashed.

It was a contest of constitution; one he couldn't win. Even if the Arcane strikes became too weak to harm him, Tharian would be too worn down to defend himself. Protelborn, however, wasn't moving a muscle. He was biding his time, his knife arm ready.

A flurry of air hit Tharian in the shoulder from the front, and a whip of water hit the other from behind. Tharian was spun around, and he tripped over his feet, dropping to his knees on the damp cobbles.

Marla was still there. She was supposed to have carried on running. Instead, she was running back to him.

Tharian threw up a hand to try and make her stop, but her attention wasn't on him. She had both of her handaxes drawn, and she had Protelborn in her sights. She roared as she threw one, and it whirled like a disk through the air.

It didn't get far. Protelborn saw the attack coming and took hold of the air around the axe, freezing it in place instantly and then dropping it to the ground.

Her attack gave Tharian a moment to think. He caught Marla's attention, nodded to her other axe, and then waved his head in an arcing motion towards Protelborn. She cocked a brow, but a moment later she understood. She reeled her arm back ready for the next throw.

Tharian got on one knee. He held his runeblade close and then tapped the second lit rune. The blade filled with heat, and then erupted in flames. Drawing on what strength he had left, Tharian spun on his knees to face Protelborn and swung his blade overhead. The swing sent a storm of fire surging forward, and Marla threw her second axe to follow behind it.

Protelborn was fast. He ripped the flames apart effortlessly and they wilted into black smoke. But he didn't see the axe quickly enough. It flew straight for his head.

He gasped and ducked, only just escaping a fatal blow. The attack didn't hit him, but it was enough to throw him off-balance.

Tharian stood. He tapped the second rune and felt the chill flow of water enrich his weapon. With a stabbing motion, he cast Arcane water at Protelborn in a rushing torrent.

Protelborn was too stunned to react. The water enveloped him and dragged him down the cobbles, his body rolling in the flood.

As soon as the last of the water drained from the rune, Tharian ran back to Marla, ignoring the pain of his bruised body. He pulled her back down the path until they finally reached a turn onto another alley. They made their escape while the window of opportunity was there.

The next alley was another long one. And it was thinner, again with no intersecting pathways to turn down. They just had to keep moving forward and hope that they had enough time to—

Another burst of air.

Tharian looked up.

Nothing.

He looked back.

Protelborn was there. His knife was drawn again, and he started to run after them. He moved inhumanly fast. Each step took him further than it should, with the air around him pushing him forward with each bound.

Tharian winced. His blade had no more magic stored. His body was tired. Marla's axes had been thrown. They were out of tricks. He considered stopping, making one last attempt to hold off Protelborn for Marla to finally flee. He looked back to see how close Protelborn was to sinking his knife into his back.

And then he saw Protelborn fall, knocked to the ground with a

The Last of the Magi

great thump. A black mass had tackled him from behind, and it skidded in the tight gap between the inquisitor behind it, and Tharian and Marla in front.

It was a lirrus. A feral sized one this time. With hulking great fangs and a slim body that showed off all the sharp points of its bone structure. The beast flashed an amber eye at Tharian.

'What's happening?!' shouted Marla.

Tharian smirked. 'It's Ombra, keep running.'

Protelborn's grunt of frustration echoed down the length of the path as he dragged himself to his feet and presented his knife to Ombra's lirrus form. She held her ground, blocking his way.

The air in the alley sucked back, tugging at Tharian's coat as it coalesced at Protelborn's position.

Protelborn was about to jump above them again. Ombra, however, was quicker. Her smooth body grew feathers, her muzzle became long and sharp, and her front paws lifted to become wings.

Just as Protelborn started his launch upwards, Ombra took off and planted her talons at his shoulders, pinning him down. The Arcana tried to propel them both to the smog above, but Ombra pushed hard and sent him back down. Protelborn hit the ground and rolled back down the alley in a heap.

Tharian and Marla reached the path's end, and it branched several ways. Ombra raced over to them at the junction and spread her wings to block any view of which way they would go next. Tharian led them down the path to their right. 'Thank you!' he shouted as they sprinted away.

Protelborn didn't propel himself above the tenements again, nor did they hear him accelerate himself down the alleyways. Tharian assumed they had finally escaped him, leaving the inquisitor in the darkness of the alleys.

Chapter 49

The Night Before

'Are you still making progress in your training with the coinswoman?' his father asked.

'Yes,' said Darus. 'Actually, she's been progressing through the stages of Arcane control much quicker than—'

'No.' His father cut him off abruptly, snatching at his wine glass on the balcony ledge. 'I'm interested in *your* progress.'

'Sorry, sir.' Darus felt embarrassed by the enthusiasm with which he went to speak about their Arcane lessons. He sobered that enthusiasm. 'It's going well. I understand most of the core functions of a coinsman now. There's still a lot of variables to manage, but I know where to find the information I need.'

'Very good.' His father turned to Illian. 'Perfect timing, wouldn't you agree?'

'It's convenient, brother, don't get carried away,' Illian said, sipping her wine and staring off into the smoggy distance. 'His progress is irrelevant.'

This was supposed to be a celebration of their achievements in the Trade Quarters, by his father's own words, but the atmosphere was far from jovial. While his father and aunt were quietly enjoying their wine, Darus felt awkward beside them.

Coinswoman Keene had recommended this restaurant to them in the Quarter of War, tucked away on the top floor of one of the inns in the circle around the Crucible arena. Their hosts had immediately shown them to a private dining balcony at the backside of the restaurant which looked out over the tenements between the Quarter of War and the Collectors Quarter. It wasn't a particularly pretty view, yet it was nice by Trade Quarters' standards.

His father and aunt were already midway through their second glasses of red wine. Darus was still nursing his first glass of white. Thankfully they didn't comment on his pace. They had plenty to get through between them, and he suspected that if there was more left

The Last of the Magi

for them, they wouldn't complain.

'We are making history here,' Illian said. 'It's only a matter of time before the rest fall in line. We've waited long enough for this.'

'Agreed,' his father said, swilling his glass in the air. 'Father would have given anything to see this unfold.'

Illian scoffed. 'I'll give you credit, Lan. I doubt he'd have had the gall to move through the Quarters with such a small force at his side. Father was capable but he was more cautious than either of us. I think your son inherited his hesitancy and studiousness.'

'I hadn't thought of it like that,' Lanark laughed. He then eyed Darus side-on. 'A thought exercise for you, Darus. After the Trade Quarters formally falls under Grand City control tomorrow, how do you think the rest of Asturia will react?'

Tomorrow? Darus repeated in his head. Was *that* what they were celebrating – the eve of the execution? It had only been a couple of days. Darus wrongly assumed it would be weeks away.

He had already paused too long. And eyes were on him. He took a deep drag of his wine and swallowed it slowly to buy himself time. He put his glass down before any shaking in his wrist became obvious.

'I-I guess,' he struggled to fight with his own thoughts. That very evening he had been showing Keene how to use Grasping techniques to catch and move Arcane air as he Commanded it. They parted in such high spirits after that. He swallowed again. 'I guess the Outer Counties would join us soon after. Many of the villages rely on the Trade Quarters. If we control the supply lines, we have economic control of the west.'

'Excellent. Go on.' Lanark said.

'Ferenir would hold its ground for a time, I think. That won't last though. We would be able to strain their economy. They will have to accept the reality of their position eventually.'

'And Lions' Rest?' added Illian. 'What about those who isolate themselves from all else?'

Darus blinked and took another sip of the wine. He finished it without even realising.

'I don't know. They still rely on trade from here like everyone else. But I think they would maybe need a presence at their door before they would consider a transition to Elheim rule. I don't really know enough about their ways.'

'Like I said,' Illian replied. 'Hesitancy and studiousness.'

'But he is right,' his father said. He then waved his glass in Darus's direction. 'You took your studies at the College seriously. More seriously than Marken did, that much is certain.'

'Thank you, sir,' Darus said hesitantly. Praise from this conversation didn't feel rewarding at all.

The other two went back to their quiet drinking. They exchanged a few more words here and there, though his aunt spent most of it in subtle chastisement of his father. She was always one for a pecking order of seniority that kept her near or at the top of the tree. Even though Valivelle custom for generations dictated that the oldest son would stand as family patriarch – which gave his father the superior position. The custom was showing its age, however, as even Darus could see that his father respected his aunt's position as the elder of them.

A waiter shuffled out and laid out another carafe of red wine. He bowed to the senior enforcers, and Illian waved him away without even a word of thanks or a cursory glance to acknowledge his existence.

That added to Darus's guilt. The citizens of this city were worthless in their eyes, only fit to serve the Elheim and play a subservient role in the wider vision for Asturia. Those without wealth or resources to offer were just nameless labour, pawns to move and dispose of as needed. Those deemed criminals or unsavoury characters were locked up or executed. Only those with *value* to offer would have any status in the Elheim's future for the country.

Keene and the other coinsmen fell into that middle category. Just another nuisance to eradicate. A problem to be removed.

Darus took his glass again and turned slightly away from the others. Though the glass was empty, he tried to distract himself by just taking in the remnants of the wine's fruity notes. There was nothing he could say or do to change what was to come now, so his only choice was to try and brace himself for the dark day he was dreading.

The Last of the Magi

The sun was getting low. It was difficult to see through the peachy haze, but he could just make out the point where the light in the sky was more forceful over the city wall. He stared off that way blankly, in the hope that watching the obscured sun would slow its descent into nightfall.

More footsteps entered the balcony. Darus didn't turn. He just carried on gazing forward.

'I've been searching for you for hours.'

It was Inquisitor Protelborn. The low, dark rumble of his voice was unmistakable, but it was lower, darker, and angrier now.

'Ah, Protelborn, come take a seat and enjoy some wine. We are celebrating our success,' his father said, reaching over to pour wine into a spare glass.'

'There's a problem.'

His father looked back to Protelborn properly, and then he made a sound of surprise. That made Darus reflexively look back too. The inquisitor was stood tall in his black and red uniform, but it had tears around the shoulders and scuffs of dirt all over the front. He also looked damp.

'What have you been doing?' asked Illian.

Protelborn shut the balcony doors behind him. 'I found your fugitive.'

'Where?!'

'Skulking around in the back alleys between this quarter and the next.'

'You're sure?' Illian replied.

'I would not mistake a runeblade, Enforcer Valivelle. I fought him but he got away.'

Illian jumped to her feet and slammed her glass down, almost shattering it. 'What do you mean he got away?'

'Don't raise your voice at me. You, more than any, should understand the difficulty of fighting a skilled swordsman who has a runeblade. Arcana loses its bite. He still has allies in this city beyond the deposed coinsmen, and a Shifter too.'

'A Shifter?' his father asked. 'Where did he find that?'.

'Did you not tell us he arrived at Brynport from Feralland?'

Lanark hummed. 'Yes, I did.' He gave Illian a look, and her face was beet red.

'Where has he gone?' she barked. 'Why aren't you pursuing him?'

'I was outnumbered. The beast kept me grounded, and they used the winding pathways to their advantage. Even if I had every enforcer mobilised to search for him, we could barely cover the inroads of one Quarter.'

'That's not good enough.'

His father stayed seated, but he pressed a hand onto his sister's arm. 'Relax, Illian. You are in no place to judge on this.'

Illian's eyes widened.

He waved his hand and grabbed his cane. 'This is not worth fighting over. Protelborn, we have the execution tomorrow – do you suggest we postpone?'

That suggestion perked Darus up. He turned more towards Protelborn and stared fiercely while the inquisitor chewed over his thoughts.

Protelborn folded his arms and rapped his fingers against his sleeves. 'Postponement isn't necessary. Continue as planned. With your agreement, I would excuse myself from the execution tomorrow to search the Artisan Quarter with a group of enforcers. I believe he may be hiding there.'

'No objection from me,' said Lanark. 'Illian brought a few extra enforcers from the Grand City, so we have plenty able hands at the ready.'

Illian still looked furious. 'We will *not* be stalled. How is it possible that one Asturian can cause this much disruption – who is he?'

Lanark looked skyward, 'We know very little about who he is. Our inquiries uncovered a name, but it escapes me.'

'Tharian,' Darus said, in a deflated tone.

Lanark nodded to him. 'Yes, that's it.'

'Tharian?' said Illian. 'I'll carve that name into his grave myself. He's a fool to have returned here. I will break him myself.'

They talked so bluntly of killing, yet again, it made Darus feel sick. He shrunk down, hoping to somehow disappear from this balcony and be away from this dark discussion.

The Last of the Magi

His father stood and joined the others. 'Good. Then we proceed as planned tomorrow. The coinsmen will be executed, the Trade Quarters will fall under Elheim rule, and we shall draw out and deal with the fugitive properly before we finish our work here and report to the chancellor.'

'Agreed,' said Protelborn.

'Agreed, and no more mistakes,' said Illian. She looked to Protelborn as she said it. He gave her a flat stare in return.

'I think that concludes our celebrations. Let's retire and ensure we are fully prepared for the morning. Much to be done.'

The three peeled off and left the balcony, leaving Darus behind. He took a shivered breath and squeezed his eyes closed. He then straightened his sleeves, wiped his face, and regained his composure before following the others.

Chapter 50

Giving No Quarter

Tharian stared into the slow, crackling flames of the fireplace, his hands templed over his lips. Ombra was on his lap, back in her domestic lirrus form, peacefully purring away with only the smallest scratches on her skin from her tussle with the inquisitor.

Neither he nor Marla had managed to get much sleep that night. Marla had camped in the living room when they got in, and she was still there when Tharian woke on the sofa early in the morning. She was clearly unsettled, taking to a sentry-like vigil at the window. Only sitting still for a few minutes at a time.

Before Tharian slept, she had been mumbling to herself. 'He knows. He definitely knows,' she'd said, maybe fifty times. 'He knew I was here. He must have seen me.'

After she'd explained the full story of stumbling upon the inquisitor in the dark alleys a few weeks ago, Tharian understood why she was distressed. Apparently Protelborn had been living in the Quarters in secret for some time. It was possible he had been keeping watch on her in case she spoke about what she saw.

Tharian tried to reassure her. Knowing that someone was a regular in the Artisan Quarter was very different to knowing where that person lived. But he knew his words were of little comfort. She was entitled to be distressed. He just didn't expect to find her still awake.

'Sit down,' he said, patting the sofa seat. He stood, putting Ombra into his space, and moved to the window where she stood. He gently moved her away and took her place sitting on the sill. 'I'll take over.'

She was reluctant, but she moved away. She put a hand on Ombra and sat at the edge of the seat. Her eyes were drooping, eclipsed with dark circles. Exhaustion was taking its toll. 'What time is it?' she said with eyes half-closed.

'Not important. Just get some rest.'

The Last of the Magi

'I'm sorry,' she said. She buried her face in her hands.

Tharian sighed. 'It's alright. You've every reason to be worried. But it's morning now, and nobody has come. Any minute now the mercenaries will start making their moves. When that happens, the inquisitor will have lost his window to come for us.'

'I know, I know. I just need everything to start so I can stop worrying.'

Tharian laughed. 'You'll stop worrying *after* our attack on the Elheim begins?'

She trilled air through her lips. 'You know what I mean.'

'I do.'

Marla stayed still for a few minutes, then she startled just as she was drifting off. She looked around the room in a panic, then she groaned and hunched over her knees. 'I can't do this!'

'You can,' Tharian said sternly. 'The Glanmores are safe. They've left the quarter. You only need to keep yourself out of trouble for the next few hours and then it'll all be over.'

'I know,' she said. She threw herself back against the chair, waking Ombra, and she grabbed a cushion to press over her face.

Tharian stepped away from the window and approached her. He pulled the cushion away. 'Look, this is going to be dangerous for everyone. Even for those not involved. You need to keep it together as best you can. After its done, you can scream into a cushion for as long as you like.'

'If I survive,' she said bluntly.

Tharian gave her a disapproving look.

'Sorry. I'll pull it together. You're right.'

'Lay down. I'll wake you before I go.'

She nodded and grabbed the cushion back. She pushed it into the corner of the sofa and curled up against it.

Tharian returned to the window. Though his words seemed to calm Marla enough for her to settle down, they didn't offer him the same comfort. Very soon he would be back out on the streets, ready to lead an attack against the Elheim. The first of its kind. He would face off against some of the most capable enforcers known to Asturia, and an inquisitor too.

It was not quite the charge against the Grand City he'd hoped for

– and he still had no Magi in his corner – but this was nonetheless an important move forward. If they pulled this off – if *he* pulled this off – he would have proven to the Quartersfolk, the coinsmen and the King of Ferenir that the Elheim truly were fallible. That they could fall just as any other.

But if he failed, the Elheim would have proven themselves indomitable. That outcome wasn't worth considering. If it came to that, he wouldn't be around to see what happened next. That, at least, was at least a mercy.

He shook himself from that creeping doubt. He had to keep his mind focused on succeeding. This was going to be the most dangerous day of his life, but also the most important. This day could generate the momentum that all Asturians needed to push back the tide of white and blue.

White and blue. Those unmistakable colours; those unmistakable uniforms. Like the ones coming down the artisan main road, led by Inquisitor Protelborn.

Tharian bolted to his feet and pulled the curtains to a narrow slit. He called to Marla. 'Get up. They're coming!'

Marla cursed, and she and Ombra both got up. 'What do we do?' she said in a daze.

'Out the back, hurry.'

They rushed to the back door. Marla opened it with a fumble, and they stepped out into the small garden courtyard.

'We need to draw them away or make them move along. We can't afford another fight. There's too many of them this time.'

'How many?'

'Three or four enforcers, I think, and the inquisitor is leading them.'

She cursed again. 'We're trapped out here unless we climb the fence.'

Tharian looked up. The Glanmore's home was two storeys tall, but there was no second storey above the kitchen. It had a small flat ledge beside the guttering before the roof tiles then slanted upwards. The fence was slightly lower than the wall. 'We'll get on the roof,' he said.

Tharian found a barrow next to some dried potted plants. He

The Last of the Magi

wheeled it over to the fence. Stepping in, he then put a foot on the horizontal support beam of the fence. It felt sturdy enough to hold his weight. Artisan quality, of course. He jumped up from the beam and hoisted himself atop the fence. There was barely a flat edge to balance on, so he shuffled quickly over to the roof and stepped onto it. He shuffled a couple of feet along, so he was away from the fence. He then pointed to the ground beneath him, just in front of Marla.

'Bring the barrow here and I can pull you up.'

She did so. She stepped into the barrow and reached up.

Tharian groaned as he used his entire weight as an anchor to lift Marla up, digging his heels against the metal guttering, bending it slightly. It wasn't easy. Marla had a strong build that made her weightier than he expected, as much as her baggy clothes disguised it. And Tharian wasn't built for strength.

Ombra shifted into a larger lirrus form and used her nose to help lift Marla. She then shifted again, back into a small avian form and joined them on the roof.

They shuffled onto the sloping tiles of the roof. They took it slowly. Tharian wasn't feeling confident that the creaking roof could hold their weight. The tiles clinked as they moved too, and the last thing they needed was for the enforcers to hear them. They shuffled along to the corner of the house and then hopped across to the adjoining building. They climbed up its sloping roof until they could hunker down behind its chimneys. From there, they had a partial view of the artisan main road.

The inquisitor and the enforcers were huddled in the middle of the road just a short distance from the house. The inquisitor pointed around to different buildings, appearing to assign each one to a different enforcer.

They then split up and approached their targets.

'They don't know where we were,' Marla whispered.

'I told you. Now keep still.'

Protelborn took the building opposite whilst a different enforcer approached the Glanmore's main door, rather than the larger one that led into the blacksmithing shop.

The enforcers all knocked on their respective doors. Several of them opened and there was a low buzz of conversation. Some of the enforcers were let in, others were kept outside.

Tharian ducked down and sat his back against the chimney. Marla copied him. 'This is really unhelpful.'

Marla pointed away from the main road, towards the next quarter nearest to them. 'We could try and get over to the Quarter of War from here.'

'That's not where I need to be.'

'I know, but unless you can jump the full width of the artisan road, you're not getting over to Keene's manor without being spotted. I'm going to take a guess and say that's not in your skillset.'

Ombra pranced across the tiles, back in her nimble feline form and looked over the roof's peak.

Marla pointed to her. 'Can Ombra fly you across? She can turn into one of those huge cliffhawks, right?'

Tharian smiled. He peered round the chimney to see Ombra looking back their way with a very wide-eyed expression. 'I'm not sure about that. It would draw too much attention. The inquisitor will have thought of some tricks to deal with Ombra, I'm sure.'

Ombra turned back to the road, seemingly satisfied with Tharian's dismissal of the idea.

Crawling up to Ombra's position, Tharian cautiously assessed the situation a bit more closely. His brows knitted together as he noticed more enforcers joining the search. As he laid there, the first few enforcers came back out onto the street to move on to the next houses. He tapped his fingers against the tiles, trying to think of another plan.

He then noticed Ombra's ears pull back. She craned her neck to investigate whatever she could hear behind them.

'Tharian,' Marla said in a hissed whisper. 'Look.'

He looked back. Marla was pointing across the city. Following her finger, Tharian saw what caught her attention. Small plumes of red and brown smoke had appeared across the landscape. A couple down the length of the Quarter of War's main road and then several smaller ones between the tenements in the back alleys. And more were appearing, slowly fanning out across the city towards them.

The Last of the Magi

It's started, Tharian realised. He turned away from the artisan main road and waved for Marla to follow him. He quickly surveyed the nearby rooftops to find a route that would get them onto the rooftops deeper into the quarter. The buildings were higher there so they would need to work their way up more slanted roofs and climb drainpipes. As he plotted the path, a few smoke plumes appeared in the artisan quarter too. He needed to take a closer look.

Leading the way, Tharian took them from rooftop to rooftop. They stepped and jumped from one roof to the next where it was safest to do so. Once they were at the height of the back-alley tenements, things got easier. These roofs were flatter.

Tharian dashed over to the roof's edge, peering down into the alleys. He went from one edge to the next to check as many areas as he could.

Eventually he found what he wanted. He crouched and waved for Ombra and Marla to join him. 'There,' he said, pointing below.

A group of armed mercenaries scurried along the cobbles. There were even a few city guards amongst their numbers. One guard and one mercenary huddled together below a sconce, but Tharian was too far to see or hear what they were doing.

A spark flashed between the two of them and then they shouted and ran in opposite directions.

A rush of smoke plumed up. Tharian grabbed Marla and Ombra and pulled them back from the edge just as the tower of billowing smoke would have blasted over their faces.

Marla was looking up at the smoke plume with a glassy-eyed look of fear. Tharian planted his hand on her shoulder, pulling her attention away from the smoke. 'You did it,' he said.

'What?' she gave him a bewildered look.

'It's the mercenaries and city guard, they're working together to draw the attention of the enforcers.'

Her eyes widened and she rushed over to peer down at another section of the alleyway. She then turned back to him looking excited. 'It's really happening!'

'Come on,' said Tharian. He rushed back towards the Glanmore's home. Those scurrying through the alleys below were advancing towards the Artisan Quarter. Tharian needed to see with his own eyes whether the enforcers would take the bait.

There was a spring in his step as he bounded his way back across the rooftops. To add to his boost of morale, he noticed that some mercenary archers were taking to the rooftops as well. They started shooting arrows down into the alleys that made loud cracking sounds as they hit the floor. Tharian assumed they were some kind of novelty ballistic arrowheads.

Everything was going to plan. The city was awash with noise, movement, and smoke.

Tharian bounded across to the Glanmore's roof and scaled the tiles, peering over the top to the road beyond. The artisan main road was a very different sight now. Arrows and stones were flying at the enforcers, now huddled together. Voices shouted and hurled abuse at the Elheim from all sides. Their words, much like their weapons, bounced off invisible manipulations of the air that kept the enforcers safe from harm. But the mercenaries were not so safe. As the enforcers deflected the attacks, they pushed out, with Protelborn once again pointing and barking orders. They shuffled together a few steps, then suddenly they broke ranks and charged in all directions, rushing the alleyways.

'They did it,' Tharian said triumphantly. The enforcers were scattered in the alleys. Even the inquisitor.

Tharian led Marla and Ombra back down the Glanmore's roof, they reached the ledge and Tharian cautiously stepped out onto the fence. He waved Marla forward again and then dropped down the outside of the fence, into the thin alley between the Glanmore's house and the next.

He hoped the elite guard would play their part too and would be moving into position to surround Keene's manor.

Tharian helped Marla down from the fence, and Ombra bounded to the ground gracefully by using his shoulder as a ledge.

'So far so good,' he said.

'Do you think it's going to work?' she asked.

'It has to. We're too far in to fail now.'

Marla nodded and smiled. Her nerves before were gone. They were both fuelled on adrenaline at this point.

Tharian looked down the alley to the main road. No enforcers

The Last of the Magi

passed by their view, so he assumed the road was still clear. He then opened his mouth to speak but another voice cut him off.

'There you are.'

The speaker emerged from the shadows deeper down the alley. Their silhouette was dark and much of what they wore was black. As the figure stepped forward, glints of gold on their body caught the light, and then finally their face became visible.

It was Goreson, the elite guard. He was in full battle armour and had his unmistakable weapon in hand.

Tharian pressed a hand to his chest and sighed with relief. Marla was just as surprised by the elite's sudden appearance. 'Don't ever do that again,' Tharian said with a nervous laugh. 'I'm glad to see you've joined us.'

'The city is a mess,' he said. But he said it with a wry smirk.

Tharian shrugged. 'I guess more people had an appetite to get involved than we expected. Are the elites ready to join the fight at Keene's?'

'Yes, but we need to move quickly.' Goreson's face looked taut with concern.

'Is there a problem?'

'Not sure.' he squeezed past them and peered out onto the road. 'The Elheim are acting strangely. Not many of the enforcers turned up for their patrols this morning. I see a few of them were deployed here, but another group were spotted heading to the Market Quarter. A few of that group splintered off to deal with the mercs, but unlike here the others carried on.'

Tharian cocked his head. The Market Quarter. Velioth's manor was the only thing they would be interested in down there. Where Traykin, Velioth and Faast were being held.

'I don't like the sound of that,' Tharian said. 'I guess that means Faast won't be joining us.'

'Unlikely. We decided not to send any elites that way. We need to focus our numbers where we need them most.'

'Makes sense. Let's get this done quickly so we can get the coinsmen out.'

Goreson nodded. 'Agreed.'

'I'll go see what's going on,' said Marla.

Tharian turned back to her. 'No, you won't. Your part is done now. Get in the house, or over to where the Glanmores are staying if you can get there safely. Leave the rest to us.'

She looked determined, rebelliously so. 'I'm not going in the house. Brayne and Marion are staying at the Market Quarter, it's on the way. I'll go to them after I've checked what's going on. If there's a problem I will come and find you.'

Goreson looked over his shoulder. 'Don't argue with an artisan, mate. They always think they know best.'

'Because we do,' she said.

Tharian rubbed his forehead and snarled. 'Fine.' He whistled and Ombra flew up onto his shoulder, back in kurigaw raven form. 'She's coming with you. First sign of trouble and you get to safety – got it?'

'Yes sir,' Marla laughed. She then turned down the alley and dashed away, leaving Tharian with Goreson.

The two men nodded to each other and then crept onto the artisan main road. The road was calm and empty. The only noise being the commotion going on in the back alleys.

With the enforcers gone, doors and windows started to open, and people watched Tharian and Goreson walk calmly towards their goal. As they passed alleyways on either side, other elites emerged from their hiding places, filing in to join the two of them, until a full contingent of elites swarmed at Tharian's back.

The Quartersfolk of the artisan main road gathered in their doors. They kept quiet, huddling together with their families, watching respectfully. Nobody cried out to summon the enforcers back or to protest. It was like they were showing their silent support for what was about to happen. At last, Tharian felt like the people were truly with him. His and Marla's concerns about their allegiances were misguided.

The group gathered around Keene's manor. Nobody arrived to stop them. No enforcers lurched out from the dark to repel their advance. No Arcana lashed at them from places unseen.

Was this too easy? Tharian shook away the thought. There was nothing to gain from doubting, especially when he had seen with his own eyes how the pieces were falling together.

The Last of the Magi

Tharian drew his runeblade as he and the others reached the immaculate façade of Keene's manor and its beautiful white doors. He reached for the door handle.

Unlocked. Tharian tucked himself against the door as cover as he gently pushed it open. He heard a trickling sound within. He pushed the door further. The room beyond was a reception, with artwork, vases and water features strewn about in a maze-like arrangement he couldn't make sense of.

But there were still no guards. No enforcers.

Tharian waved for the elites to follow. They all had their varied weapons drawn, clanking up to the door to join him. He underestimated how noisy they would be. But it couldn't be helped.

He led them across the room. He kept his blade forward, ready to swing in defence of any Arcana loosed in his direction. He managed to navigate the coinswoman's reception to reach the other end without anything stopping him. There were a few doors across the wall, and he went for the one in the middle. It was bigger and looked more important than the others, so it had to lead to somewhere more meaningful.

Again, he cautiously opened the door. There was a shuffling sound in the room. Tharian gave the elites a signal to suggest they should be prepared.

He pushed the door fully open with force and lunged in.

Tharian heard the shuffling again, but he didn't see what caused it. He angled his runeblade defensively across his chest. 'I can hear you!' He called out.

A woman shrieked. Her head suddenly appeared from the other side of a sofa halfway across the room. She saw Tharian and the elites surrounding him. She ducked down and started sobbing. 'Wh-who a-are y-you?' she cried.

'Where are the enforcers?' he shouted back. As he waited for a response, standing closer to where the woman was cowering, he only then realised the strange decoration choice in this room. The walls were painted to give the illusion of there being bookshelves stretching into the distance in every direction.

One of the elites pushed to the front and marched fearlessly to the woman's hiding place.

She cried as his looming figure approached. 'Please, I haven't done anything. There are no enforcers here, I swear,' she begged.

The guard lifted her by the arm. She was a young woman wearing a simple black and white uniform.

'She's with Keene's staff,' he said. 'Not an Elheim.' He then released her, and she dropped to the ground, whimpering.

They had to be here. That was the plan. The whole point of this was to catch them by surprise — no back-up, no reinforcements. Why wouldn't they be here?

Tharian moved to the sofa and kneeled beside the woman, keeping his weapon away from her eyeline. 'I'm sorry we frightened you. Where are the enforcers now?' he asked.

She rubbed her arm, squeezing at the area where the guard had grabbed her with a gauntleted hand. 'The enforcers left early this morning with Coinswoman Keene. They didn't say where they were going.'

Tharian frowned. The woman and the guards stared at him, awaiting his next words. But he was stuck.

He looked around frantically, as if an answer to the situation might be painted on the curious walls. He looked to the other elites who were still spread out in the reception room, and he did a double take as he spotted Goreson.

He remembered what Goreson had told him. The enforcers were up to something. They were behaving strangely.

In the Market Quarter.

***

Marla ducked behind the steps leading to the front door of the quaint house where Brayne and Marion were staying. The house and adjoined shop belonged to a well-known merchant; one Marion had worked for briefly. It was a modest clothier, selling plain shirts and trousers for general use.

She kept as low as she could, hoping not to be spotted by the figures she could faintly see further down the market main road, around Velioth's home. It was difficult to see for certain – the haze of the smog was starting to mix with the red and brown smoke

The Last of the Magi

clouds still pluming overhead and out of the alleyway junctions — but she could make out the look of white figures surrounding the doors. Three shapes were distinct, there could have been more. Enforcers, without doubt, just as the elite guard had said.

Now that Marla was here, her exhaustion was really taking hold. She wanted to run to Brayne and Marion, hide away from everything and rest. But she had already come this far, she had to investigate further, just in case it was important. Seeing enforcers gathered at Velioth's home was already strange enough, what was stranger was their apparent lack of concern at the commotion happening elsewhere in the city.

Marla moved closer while she could. Tharian's recklessness was rubbing off on her. She used every bollard, fence, wooden post and set of steps along the way to keep out of sight. The enforcers in the distance were becoming clearer through the haze. She could make out their features now.

Two men. One woman. One man with darker hair, peppered with grey, leaning on a cane. The other with short blonde hair. And the woman, with greyed shoulder-length hair, stood beside them with fists curled. The woman she didn't recognise. The other two, however, they were the new coinsmen for the Market Quarter and Collectors Quarter: Lanark and Darus Valivelle.

Marla's blood chilled as she realised, they were supposed to be at Keene's manor. Tharian and the elites were raiding the building looking for them. Yet they were here. Why?

Velioth's front doors fanned open, and Coinswoman Keene marched out. She was dressed very formally, in a brown and grey suit with her black, velvet coat draped over it. She nodded to the three enforcers and then they turned to head in Marla's direction.

Instinctively Marla's feet moved, and she almost bolted away, but then she saw Traykin, Velioth and Faast follow out of the building and step in line behind the enforcers. She shuffled back to the corner of the building at her left. There were a few crates piled together haphazardly and Marla slipped in the gaps between them and hunkered down. From there she could cautiously watch as the group walked past.

They all wore stern expressions, and not one of them spoke. Not even Jerard Traykin.

People were starting to emerge from their homes, either to investigate what was going on across the city or in reaction to their former coinsmen being led through the street by the current ones. The Quartersfolk started to follow the enforcers from a safe distance, all heading to the central plaza.

Marla decided to follow as well, feeling glad that she could blend in with the crowds. As she stepped in line with the others, she spotted Ombra circling the air above the coinsmen. She must have been curious too.

Her heart thumped heavily. Every time the enforcers had gathered in the plaza, something bad happened. The demonstration of fire. The deposing of the former coinsmen. What were they going to do this time?

Chapter 51

The Execution

Erilen Velioth. Kireyn Faast. Jerard Traykin.

Lanark Valivelle named each of them in turn, leaving a generous pause between each for dramatic effect. The three were left to stand together just beside the statute of Arikella the Importer – the founder of Velioth's quarter – while the three enforcer-coinsmen stood in the plaza's centre with Coinswoman Keene.

Marla joined the crowd at the mouth to the Market Quarter. People were pouring in from the other quarters as well. All while the commotion across the city continued. The crowds were quite small, with only the strong, fit, and able gathering. The rest no doubt hid in their homes.

The deposed coinsmen had their backs to her, so she couldn't see their faces, but she could see the enforcers and Coinswoman Keene clearly. Lanark Valivelle and the female enforcer looked boastful and confident, but Darus Valivelle and Coinswoman Keene looked nervous, perhaps even fearful.

'Residents of the Trade Quarters!' Lanark called out to the gathered crowds, 'we apologise for yet another disruption. I would like to personally thank all of you for the calm cooperation you have offered to us during this difficult period of transition. Today is a day of frustration and unrest for so many. Your city is in pain, we know that. We see it, and we hear it. But I promise you that we will end that pain here today, drawing a line under what came before, and renewing our focus on the prosperity to come. While you bravely stand here, our enforcers are acting quickly to subdue those that would seek to throw this city into turmoil for their own gain.'

He paced about the marble plaza, assisted by his cane.

'You have already had to endure so much. Our presence here has been difficult for you, let us be frank about that, but this has all been necessary to uncover the depths of the conspiracy orchestrated by your former leaders. They plotted against the Grand City, without consulting with you, threatening to throw your people into war with ours in a conflict which would have resulted in the deaths of so many of your friends and loved ones. Despite all this disruption and change, despite this veiled betrayal from those who had your trust, you have carried on living your lives, doing your important work, allowing your city to thrive.'

He raised a hand to the crowd and turned full circle to regard them all. 'One could never fault the resilience and dedication of the Trade Quarters – that I say without reservation.'

'What's going on?!' called a voice from somewhere deep in the crowd.

Lanark grimaced for a moment but caught himself before most could notice. Marla was staring at him the whole time, so she did notice.

'For those who wish to stand here and bear witness, I am ready to confirm the result of our investigation.' He gestured to where Faast, Velioth and Traykin were stood. 'We are in no doubt that the steps taken against the Grand City by your former coinsmen – into whom you poured your trust and confidence – were carried out with malice and aforethought. They would have brought war upon you all. You would have had only two choices in that war: to become soldiers of the Trade Quarters, to be thrown at the might of our Arcana; or to flee your homes, seeking refuge elsewhere. And, to make matters worse, your former coinsmen allied themselves with a criminal, a vagabond who openly flaunted Grand City decree, and they would have dragged others into this fruitless, pointless conflict. Think of the casualties that would have ensued.'

Voices filled the air as the crowd murmured in hushed tones. The cacophony of sound built until the hushed whispers sounded more like crashing waves of noise.

Lanark was bathing in it, letting the murmuring run its course. He looked over to the female enforcer, and she nodded back at him. This was all a game to them. A performance. If Marla could see it, she hoped others could too.

As the crowd settled, Lanark waved a hand through the air to bring the focus back and then he continued. 'I'm sure you will all join me when I say that either of those outcomes would have been deeply unsatisfactory. Certainly not a fate you would have chosen for yourselves. But as the new Coinsmen of the Trade Quarters, it falls to us to decide how to deal with these crimes. The punishment for this level of conspiracy is without ambiguity under Grand City decree, and I see no good reason to depart from that prescription in these circumstances.' Lanark let out an affected sigh, as if his own words weighed upon him. It wasn't even remotely convincing. But it brought the crowd to silence.

Lanark straightened again, and cleared his throat, 'The sentence for these crimes is summary execution. To be carried out with immediate effect.'

The central plaza boomed with gasps, shrieks and not an insignificant number of enraged roars, with Marla's involuntary gasp being amongst them. On all sides, Marla heard conflicts of position. Some cursed the Elheim for their interference, while others scolded their former leaders. The loudest voice rising above the crowd, however, was Faast's.

'You unscrupulous, despicable coward of a man! How dare you seize control of our city only to flaunt the integrity of our laws and treaties. You have no jurisdiction to damn us to death; present your evidence, call a trial!'

Marla couldn't see Faast's face, but she imagined it was red with rage. The former coinswoman broke away from the group and stomped towards the enforcers. She may have been strong, she may have been tall, and she may have been intimidating, but without her armour and weaponry she had nothing to defend her against their Arcana. Yet she stomped on, fearless.

The female enforcer raised her hand at Faast, and with that gesture her Arcana held Faast back. Invisible restraints locked her in place, and Faast snarled and cursed Lanark Valivelle's name, trying desperately to force her way through the magic that pushed against her. All the while as she screamed in anger, Traykin remained still and calm. He had wrapped his hand around Velioth's shoulder, to try and soothe the younger man who looked to be shaking.

As soon as a break appeared between the crowd's murmuring and Faast's colourful cursing, Lanark stepped closer to the deposed coinsmen and pointed at each of them in turn.

'Erilen Velioth, former Coinsman of the Market Quarter, I sentence you to death.'

Velioth's knees buckled. He would have dropped to the ground were it not for Traykin reeling him in. Traykin whispered something to him. Velioth then forced himself upright and looked back with glazed eyes to his own quarter. His face was as pale as freshly laid snow.

Lanark moved his hand to the next in his view. 'Kireyn Faast, former Coinswoman of the Quarter of War, I sentence you to death.'

She didn't react this time, she had stopped trying to charge at them. She stayed still in her prison.

'Jerard Traykin, former Coinsman of the Collectors Quarter, I sentence you to death.'

'Didn't see that coming,' Traykin shouted back. He quietly laughed and then turned his attention back to Velioth.

'The crime is conspiracy against the Grand City, with the intent to cause war, terror, or serious harm. For your role as an aider, abettor, co-conspirator, or instigator,'—Lanark lowered his hand and slowly twisted to his side—'I sentence *you* to death, Coinswoman Viviel Keene.'

Gasps again. From everywhere except the centre of the plaza.

Marla's ears were ringing. This was all going wrong. While smoke flooded overhead, and the mercenaries and guardsmen worked bravely to keep the other enforcers distracted, the main targets were here, united and together, and they were about to kill the coinsmen. Without them, all of Tharian's plans would unravel. Ferenir would withdraw its support too.

Coinswoman Keene looked so composed, despite the sudden declaration of her imminent execution. She made sure her suit looked neat and tidy and then she smiled to Lanark Valivelle and bowed her head, as if accepting the wisdom of his decision. Without being instructed, she started on her way to join the others in the execution line-up.

But she did something strange on the way. She paused beside Darus Valivelle. Just long enough to pat his arm and share a few words. Even in this dire moment, it was still unclear whose side she was on.

The Last of the Magi

Keene's face was dark once she was away from the enforcers. Her eyes seemed barely open, with shadows looming over them. Marla could tell Keene was making an effort to pull herself together before she turned back to face the enforcers, yet she avoided looking at the crowds. She stood together with her former colleagues, to face their shared fate.

'From this day forth,' Lanark said, tapping his cane on the marble, 'I promise to you all a stronger and greater Trade Quarters – one that is free of corruption. You will be safe, protected, nurtured, and given a new lease to prosper, side-by-side with the Grand City. To get to that point we must rid this place of the foul infestation of yesterday, and usher in the renewed purity of tomorrow.'

Lanark turned away from the crowd and then gestured to his son.

***

'To close this chapter, I call upon the Coinsman of the Collectors Quarter, Enforcer Darus Valivelle, to deliver unto these criminals their final sentence.'

Darus looked sharply to his father. His throat closed. His heart raced and heat swelled within his palms whilst a cold sweat flooded his brow.

Surely, he doesn't mean…

His father gestured to the deposed coinsmen, gathered on the dirt track ground that surrounded the marbled plaza. His aunt then appeared behind his shoulder.

'Show me that new strength of yours, nephew. Make your family proud.' Her words were like ice at his neck, making him shiver. She pushed him forward with force.

…He did mean it.

His vision became hazy as he stepped heavily between two of the founder statues. He was met by the piercing stares of narrowed eyes from the deposed coinsmen. He stopped where the momentum of his aunt's shove ran out. The faces looking at him were pale. And he knew his was too.

I cannot do this. Not again.

He tried to turn back, to object, but his body wouldn't let him.

L. G. Harman

He couldn't move at all. His aunt stepped in close and spoke in his ear again, making the hairs at his neck raise. 'They are defenceless, this is your moment. Bury them.'

Darus shuddered. He would never understand how anyone could speak so laxly of killing. He looked at his hands and considered his options. He couldn't escape, he had no real choice, he had to do this. But maybe he could do it in a way that was as painless as possible.

He could create an implosion of air, with them at the centre – but that might not be fatal. Pulling the air away from them would be just as bad, if not worse, as the resulting asphyxiation would be slow and seen by everyone. Burying them as his aunt suggested would at least remove their suffering from view, but just the thought of it kicked up memories that made him pull back in fear of himself.

He pushed those ideas away. What else was there? There were enough lit sconces keeping the central plaza bright through the smog to enshroud them in fire. That thought made his skin tingle. Could he put them to the flame? No. So that left only one other idea that came to mind, electrocution.

Darus looked overhead. The smog was thick, but there would probably be some clouds overhead. If not, enough focus would make them coalesce. Would he be able to feel the static that moved through the clouds and pull it down upon them with pinpoint accuracy? He had never tried – that was his aunt's technique. She might even be impressed if he pulled that off.

What was he thinking? Had he become so numb that he could think through this execution so academically? There was no winning in this situation. He would never win. He was doomed to a life of failure the moment he was born with a softer heart than everyone else in his family.

Darus looked into Keene's eyes. She nodded slowly, as she had done to Lanark. But this was different. He knew, deep down, that she was trying to reassure him that it was ok. She understood, and she was prepared to accept her fate.

This is wrong, he told himself. *This isn't the right way. They don't deserve this. Keene doesn't deserve this.*

His eyes became heavy with tears, but he blinked hard to push them away. He kept eye contact with Keene for as long he could,

The Last of the Magi

trying to offer the same kind of comfort that she had offered him.

A smile almost made it to his lips as he remembered how well Keene had been adapting to the Grasping lessons that he had given her just the night before. She had come so far in so little time. As he revelled in that memory, his hands instinctively moved. His fingers curled as if massaging an invisible ball held between them, much like he had done when demonstrating the sensation of Grasping in his last lesson with Keene.

Darus snapped out of his stupor, suddenly conscious of how long he'd been stood there, still, doing nothing. He had to act, soon. It would be better if he took charge of this moment rather than letting his father or aunt take over with their brutal ways.

He noticed that Keene's expression had changed. She looked thoughtful, in concentration, and she looked at her own open palms.

Darus straightened his arms. He had made up his mind. He would try summoning down the bolt from above. It was the quickest and most humane way he could do this. He reached one hand up high.

But he didn't get the chance to act.

There was a deep growl of frustration behind him. Then the plaza was suddenly consumed by a wicked, blustering wind that circled around the entire space – with small embers of flame carried in its draft.

Trails of fire painted the air as the flames from every sconce and brazier pulled unnaturally from their sources to join the twisting winds. Those trails then coalesced around the coinsmen into an enormous sphere of raging fire. It swelled, engorged, and grew around them while the citizens watching on screamed.

Darus looked back. It was his father. He had taken matters into his own hands, weaving Arcana with a complexity and scale he had never sensed before. Through his mastery of Command, he was siphoning the flames from around the plaza, carrying them upon manipulations of wind and then holding the accumulated fire in place as a scorching prison around the coinsmen.

Darus stared at that twisting maelstrom. Not for its beauty, nor for the finesse of the craft involved. He watched because he felt duty-bound to do so, to etch this moment in his memory. To watch what *he* – albeit vicariously – had played a part in: the execution of four city leaders. Sweat was already starting to coat his neck and run down his temples, despite standing at a distance. He could only imagine how hot it must have been within the sphere.

Darus had to step back, guilt-ridden though he felt for doing so. The heat was too much. It was stinging at him, burning the back of his eyes and suffocating him in the tight wrap of his uniform.

His shoulder hit against something behind him and then felt the tight grip of a hand at the back of his neck, keeping him fixed with his face forward to the flames. From the corner of his eye, he could see a shoulder in black with red lining.

'Your son appears to be shirking from his duties, Lanark,' said Inquisitor Protelborn. At some point in the commotion, he must have joined their gathering.

Protelborn was then pulled away as his father stepped into the space. 'Take your hands off my son, he is my burden to handle. You shouldn't even be here. Maintain the flames.'

'I will not waste any more time on the games being played across this city.' Protelborn moved away to do as he was ordered. 'I leave the boy to you.'

Darus turned and was met by his father's cold, disapproving stare. He heard the creak in his father's gloves, and then saw his cane rising high.

Chapter 52

The Last

For the first time in his life, Tharian was grateful the Elheim spoke in such long, drawn out and dramatic speeches. That gave him time to push his way through the tightly packed crowd. He paused only for a moment when he heard screaming and then the crowds ahead of him started to thin as people moved in panic.

Tharian almost called out in horror as he reached the front of the crowd and saw the cocoon of flames, held together unnaturally by Arcana. The coinsmen were nowhere to be seen. They must have been inside it. His stomach flipped.

'Traykin...'

Tharian drew his blade and charged to the flames. He didn't know how to stop it, but he had empty runes that could siphon away some of the Arcana and he needed to try.

As he closed in, he had to turn his face away from the flames. The heat became stronger with each foot passing in front of the other. He was only a few seconds away; he could suffer the heat if it saved them.

He pointed the runeblade forward at the wall of fire as it came within reach.

And then something buffeted into his chest. A blast of cold and force that held him still in place and wrapped around his body. His arm was stuck reaching forward, his blade teasingly close to the flames. The heat of it scolded his face, but he couldn't pull himself away.

Tharian looked to his right. He saw a face he didn't expect to see. It was the enforcer from County Bryn. There she was, clear as day, with her hand convulsed in a taut shape that mirrored the hold she now had over his body. She bared her teeth and tightened her grip.

The prison of air around Tharian's body clamped down and crushed against his chest. The gusts rippling over his coat sent the loose parts flapping erratically. His coat was being pulled and twisted in many directions. Then he felt something tear. Brayne's trench-coat was ripped free and blew away, revealing the green hidden underneath.

The grip over his body loosened a moment as the Valivelle enforcer looked him over. 'So... it *is* you.'

She slowly crossed towards him, lowering her hand but keeping her Arcane manifestations at work.

'You,' she said. That word alone was enough to make Tharian's skin crawl. 'I have thought of nothing but crushing you since my recovery.'

Now that she was closer, Tharian could see the patches over her skin where she had been burned by the Arcane lightning. He felt like he was back in Bryn again. Except the roles were reversed this time, as she was the one to surprise him.

But he remembered what he said to her that day in Bryn. And those words came back to him as vividly as when he first said them. Though he struggled to speak against the forces pressing against him, he made sure he could be heard. 'I told you,' he said, 'the Elheim's days are numbered. You should have taken the warning.'

Illian Valivelle tugged at the rim of her gloves. 'Your end shall be a gruelling one. I shall deliver the sentence myself, make an example of you for all to see.'

She brought her hand up again, and a vein in her forehead pulsed as she exerted her will. The air tightened on him, slowly, deliberately so.

The pressure on his chest became a great weight. He could feel his ribs bending inwards, close to snapping, and his muscles were squeezed against his bones. Even his throat was being crushed.

He pushed back with all his might. He did so even though he knew it was pointless. He couldn't muscle his way out of Enforcer Quiryn's prison of Arcana, he wouldn't be able to do it against a Valivelle.

Tharian called out in pain as his body started to fail under the pressure. His vision became hazy.

But then the Arcana was suddenly gone. Tharian saw something big and black swarming around Enforcer Valivelle. It was Ombra.

The Last of the Magi

Of course it was. She had rescued him again.

Tharian dropped hard to his knees, panting and trying to recover his strength.

Ombra was viciously clawing and whipping her wings at Illian like she had gone feral. But she was changing too, shifting her talons into claws, and then back again, changing a wing into a paw, and then a hoof and then around again in a cycle. She was attacking the enforcer with all the weapons she knew how to shift her body into.

Yet, Illian seemed prepared. She switched so quickly into defensive uses of her Arcana that Ombra couldn't even touch the enforcer.

Tharian used the time she had bought for him to drag himself back to his feet. He balanced and readied himself. He would not let this opportunity go to waste.

Illian siphoned some of the fire from the sphere and lashed it at Ombra like a blazing whip. Ombra took flight and left the two of them to their stand-off.

Tharian jumped forward and swung at the enforcer with all his strength. She dodged to the side and smirked. 'You're an idiot to think you can do this a second time.'

'We'll see,' he said, taking another leap and another swing, this time trying to feint at first to throw the enforcer off her guard.

She was faster. Arcane bursts of air helped her to move, though not as dramatically as when the inquisitor did the same thing. But it made her unnaturally agile, nonetheless. She dodged each strike almost playfully and yet let him continue. He swung the blade through the air faster and faster, varying his techniques, switching from high strikes to low at random. And she stepped, jumped, ducked, and pushed herself around the marbled ground like she was skating on ice.

Eventually she attacked. Tharian didn't see it coming. She went for his legs first, lashing air against his calves from behind. She knew what she was doing. He almost fell but he managed to reposition his feet quickly.

Tharian went in for an overhead swing, but she took advantage of his exposed position. A thump of air slammed into his stomach and lifted him off the ground. He flew back and slammed against the ground, prone and aching.

'That was too easy. Again,' she said. She was aiming her attacks so they had no chance of touching the runeblade. His strongest defence was pointless now.

There was a rushing cold sensation under Tharian's body and then he was propelled upwards, forced to struggle in the air to land safely on his feet. He had no choice; she was forcing him to fight on. Sword in hand, he charged in again. He swung and swung and swung, and even tried to throw in a punch or kick to see if that might throw her off. It didn't. She laughed, cackled even.

'The Hero of Bryn, the Champion of the Trade Quarters, the *Arcana Hunter,* no less. Is this all you can do? How will you bring about our end if this is all you can offer?'

Tharian roared and lashed out. Her words exposed the futility of everything he worked so hard for. Brynfall was in ruins. The coinsmen were burning. He was weak.

'Then kill me,' Tharian said. 'I don't want to live in *your* Asturia. You will crush the life from everyone and everything. And it will all be for your own glory.'

Her brows climbed and she shook her head dismissively. She sent a shot of Arcane air at his wrist, pushing his sword-arm away from his body, and then with a mimed punch she sent another blast that pushed Tharian off the marble tiles. He hit the ground again and rolled across the dirt track until he crashed into a water trough laid against the wall.

The water splashed over him, and then it abruptly stopped. It became solid like ice and restrained his hands and waist that were fully submerged.

Illian walked over to him, swinging her boots through the dirt. She stood at his side but looked to the flames. 'The future of Asturia will be glorious. A united, indomitable country. Free of detractors and rebels. You think this all about our *glory*?' She then looked down to him. 'There is no *glory* in stepping on roaches as they squirm in their warrens, scrabbling to protect the defiled land they call home. The glory is yet to come, for all Asturia. And we will not apologise for wanting to secure our place in the upper echelons of

The Last of the Magi

that glorious future. Such ambition is what drives progress.'

Tharian couldn't do anything but listen. His body was locked still again, and he had nothing more to say to the pious justifications for Elheim oppression.

He spotted movement overhead. Ombra was circling. Once again, she came to his aid. She swept down with talons primed to strike at the enforcer. But Illian saw it coming this time. Illian's eyes flitted to the side and then she trapped Ombra in the air, in the same prison of air she had used on Tharian.

Tharian watched on helplessly as Ombra tried to shift form to wriggle free, but Illian adapted the prison of wind to clamp down on her, shrinking smaller and smaller with each transformation. Eventually Ombra was nothing but a malformed black mass of feathers and fur, writhing with no recognisable shape at all.

The enforcer was crushing Ombra. Tharian tried to pull himself free, wanting to reach his companion and set her free somehow. He felt her suffering as if it was his own.

Illian Valivelle turned back to Tharian. 'Is this truly all you have? A pity – I'm not finished with you yet' she said, grinning.

***

Darus clutched at his cheek. His father's cane hit him so hard that he was almost floored. He thought his jaw might have fractured. The next strike hit his thigh from behind and that brought him to one knee. The third and final strike was at the middle of his spine. The handle at the head of the cane punched a dent into his back that made him scream.

Darus threw his arms up over his head and prayed there wouldn't be a fourth hit.

'You were making progress,' his father said. 'You showed promise in your work, and efficiency in your role as coinsman. We master these skills so that we can lead others to do those lesser duties in our stead. To be an enforcer is an infinitely higher calling. To be an Elheim is to be greater than a mere Asturian. And to be a Valivelle bears with it the highest demands of duty in our society, and in the society to come.' He then sighed. 'And yet, whenever you are proffered the opportunity to serve your people and prove yourself capable of standing among us, you wilt and become *this*.'

Darus snivelled in his curled-up state. He still clutched at his head, but slowly turned to look at his father while cowering. 'Father, please.'

Lanark kicked him, hard. It knocked him onto his side. 'Don't you dare ask for mercy. Don't ask for forgiveness or reprieve. These things are *beneath* you.'

The pain was just too much. His body, and his heart and mind were racked with it. But there was something final about this moment, something resolute. Darus could hear it in his father's voice. He was ready to discard his son, disown him or worse. He had failed just too many times.

'Stand, Darus.'

'No.' The reply came without thought.

'Stop mumbling and stand!'

'No.' He lowered his hands to the ground. 'No matter what I say or do, I will always be a failure in your eyes. I will never be worthy of your name because I am different to you.'

His father straightened and tightened his grip around his cane. 'Do not pretend to speak my mind. Get up and go. Get back to the manor and I will deal with you later. Now is not the time for this.' His father then looked around, to Protelborn weaving the flames that held the coinsmen captive, and then to his aunt who had the fugitive Tharian apprehended. His interest in his son was dissolving rapidly.

'You're not listening,' Darus said, dragging himself to his feet. He glared at his father through tear-fogged eyes. 'I don't want to be trapped like this anymore. I won't go and sit in that house and wait for you to punish me and then drag me around until you can find another way to make me fail one of your tests. I am worthless to you.'

'Darus,' his father said, softening his voice slightly, but noticeably. 'You are not worthless.'

Darus turned his head and waited for the condition to that veiled compliment.

'You have power. And there is potential in that power for greatness.'

The Last of the Magi

Darus shook his head. 'Power is all you want from me. You don't see me as a son, just a tool to improve your status with the chancellor.'

His father's voice became harsh again. 'If you want to be more. Bury this weakness.'

'I can't just bury who I am! That's what you don't understand.'

'You managed it well enough with the Nostrum boy!'

Those words were like the tip of his father's rapier jabbing straight through his heart and twisting. Before he would have backed down, surrendered. Not this time. His eyes dried and he filled with anger.

'Go, Darus. Now.'

'No.'

'Fine.' His father raised his cane once more and swept it sidelong towards Darus's face.

Darus stopped it. He Commanded the air to hold it back.

'You would use Arcana to impede me? This is insubordination.'

Darus felt his father's Arcana Grasp at his, and he dispersed it with a Command of his own. His father then stepped back and Commanded flames from the sphere to siphon over to where they stood. He shook his head as he propelled the tendril of flame to strike at Darus.

Commanding the air, Darus defended himself again.

Their clash of Arcana was powerful. Darus could feel a strain in his mind as the strength of his will battled against his father's. The air was rippling on both sides of their struggle. Waves of heat radiated from the flames on his father's side of the clash, while the invisible rushing and pulling of air shook everything in front of Darus.

Though his father's mastery of Arcana was clearly superior, Darus had an advantage. Fire was more limited than air. While the flames gorged on the air feeding into the clash, it would still wither over time.

Lanark drew in more fire from the sphere, whipping tendrils out of Protelborn's control and adding it to his attack against Darus.

Darus did the same, sucking more and more air inwards to create a mighty barricade.

'There is no place for you in the Elheim vision for Asturia,' his father said. The words only just reached him over the noise of their clash.

The heat was unbearable, yet his father added more and more lashings of fire to the assault. The wall of fire was starting to bend around Darus's Arcane barrier, eating away what little safe space he had left.

He only had one choice left. He would give his father what he wanted.

'I won't bury who I am for you,' he said.

Darus put everything he had into holding his father's Arcana at bay, but he found the willpower to splinter just a small part of his mental energy away to dive deep into his consciousness and through the elements. He Reached for the ground beneath them, Grasped at its raw force and then Commanded it to obey him.

Darus screamed as he pushed his Arcana harder than ever before. It was a pained sound, one of anguish, but one that became something monstrous as the sound of trembling earth rose to meet it.

The marble between them cracked and parted, and then the splits in the earth stretched out in all directions across the plaza, encompassing the entire marbled area and a bit further beyond.

'What are you doing?' his father shouted.

'What is this?' screeched Protelborn.

The split in the ground went right between Protelborn's feet. The inquisitor released the sphere of flame and went to conjure up air to propel himself away, but the ground split apart too quickly. He fell, collapsing into the darkness below, with large chunks of stone, dirt and marble tumbling in after him.

Lanark looked panicked. 'Darus! Stop this at once!'

His words fell on deaf ears. Darus screamed out again and pushed his Arcana even further.

This is the power you wanted, father. He told himself, resolutely.

His father released the flames and focused on maintaining his balance. But in releasing his Arcana, the remnants of Darus's air barrier erupted forward. His father was caught in it, and it threw him back into the statue of Baalt the Sculptor.

Lanark looked up just as the statue cracked in half at the waist

The Last of the Magi

and the top segment of the famous artisan collapsed down onto him. He threw his hands up and conjured just enough Arcana to slow its descent and hold it.

And then the floor gave way. Lanark fell, the statue tumbling down with him. The rest of the plaza started caving in too, with each of the founder statues crumbling to pieces and falling into the dark cavern below.

Darus finally stopped. Exhausted and broken. He released his Command of the earth and went numb. His consciousness faded as the ground fell beneath his feet as well. He didn't fight it. He closed his eyes and fell with the others.

***

Tharian heard the trembling, but he couldn't see what was happening because of the way Illian had him held in place. He had to close his mouth and eyes as dust suddenly flushed through the air like a sandstorm.

And then he was free again. His heart was racing too fast to feel any relief from it. Ombra, too, cowered beside him. She had shifted into a rodent form, but she cowered beside the trough breathing heavily.

Tharian pulled himself up. He stepped forward through the swirling dust to find out what had happened.

The central plaza was gone. Illian was looking too. She'd seen more than he had, and she looked beyond horrified. The entire marbled ground had caved in, taking the founder statues with it. And the other Elheim were gone too.

Illian's fists were clenched. She looked away, to where the coinsmen had been trapped in their prison of flames. It was hard to see it, but the harsh glow through the dust confirmed it was still there, but it was waning quickly.

Tharian tried not to think about the flames for now. He was too late. The coinsmen were dead, burned alive in the most horrible execution. The crowds were gone too. He wasn't sure when they fled the scene, but it was no surprise that they had. The flames, the fighting, the collapse of the plaza, it was catastrophic.

But Illian Valivelle was not done with him. She had made that clear, and by the look in her eyes as she slowly turned his way, he knew that hadn't changed.

'They were all weak... I will finish this.'

Tharian sighed. He walked closer to the enforcer, stopping at the edge of the dirt track where the marbled plaza had once been. He brought his blade up with what little energy he had left, holding it steady with both hands. He opened his mouth to speak.

Illian reacted too quickly. She raised her hand skyward. The clouds flashed, and a deafening crack rang out as she pulled a bolt of lightning from the heavens. She directed it at Tharian.

He had no hope of dodging the attack. The lightning hit his leg and his whole body convulsed. The heat of it burnt through his clothes and scorched his skin. When the electricity finally released him, he was left with a red and bloody strip from his thigh to his ankle, and he gasped in relief. He was still standing, but only just.

He lifted his blade again. To his surprise, the rune nearest his hand was glistening a light blue, ever so slightly. The Arcana surging through him must have charged it. He tapped the rune with shaking hands and a crackling energy surged in the metal.

Groaning, he swung the blade and flung a bolt of Arcane lightning back at the enforcer, and it danced in a zig-zagging motion in her direction.

She caught it. It froze in the air in front of her, assaulting the city with blinding, flashing light. Its energy then ran out and it faded away.

Tharian's arms drooped. He could barely keep the runeblade above the ground now. What more could he do? Even through the pain, with blood running down his leg and into his boot, he dragged himself forward. He still lived. He still breathed. His part was not yet over.

Three steps forward. Then four. Then five. The enforcer just laughed at him.

Do you worst, enforcer, he told himself.

And she did. He wasn't even halfway towards her before she swept her arm through the air like she was slamming a door closed. There was the briefest of delays, and then it hit him. He heard a

The Last of the Magi

crack against his side, and then he was off the ground. His body was spinning, hurtling across what remained of the plaza. He saw sky, then caved-in floor, then sky again, then floor. He twisted and turned, completely out of control, until he hit the ground and rolled for several feet. He came to a stop face down in the dirt.

He didn't dare breathe as he laid there. When he finally gasped for air, the pain in his shoulders, face and chest erupted. His mouth wrenched open in pain, but no sound came out other than a croak.

Everything faded in and out of focus. He tried to reach his arm out – too pained to tell if it was even moving – and he went to use his sword as a crutch to get himself up. But his hand was empty. The runeblade had flown from his hand as he hit the ground.

Gritting his teeth through the pain, he lifted onto an elbow. He saw his runeblade just out of reach, with no energy left in its runes.

The pain started to numb. All of him started to numb. And that brought him some clarity and peace. In that moment, as he laid back down in the dirt and became still, he tried to comfort himself by thinking to the future.

He had lost. Despite his failure, he could say with honesty that his efforts had proven the enforcers to be beatable. They were powerful but not invulnerable. He had stopped Illian Valivelle once. He stopped Enforcer Quiryn. In his attempt to liberate the Trade Quarters, at least three more of them had fallen.

Maybe his death would inspire others? Maybe someone else would take up his charge and seek out the Magi to finish what he started. His death could have purpose.

It wasn't the end he wanted, but it was enough.

***

The dust cloud was too thick to see more than a few feet ahead. It was thinning slowly, but with all the wind the enforcers had whipped up, and the storm clouds that had suddenly swarmed the skies, everything was difficult to see. Marla pushed forward anyway. She knew she wasn't imagining things; she saw the prison of fire weaken. Not only that, as she moved ever closer to where she saw the fierce light of the flames, it had faded away. Something had changed. She had to check, just in case.

It was right here, where are they? she wondered.

She looked around to check as much space as she could, holding a hand over her eyes against the dust.

And eventually she found four shapes. Two bodies on the ground, and two others over them. She dashed over and waved at the air in front of her to clear her vision, fruitless though it was.

She found Traykin and Faast. They were alive.

Their clothes were drenched with sweat and parts of their faces were red raw with traces of dried blood.

'You're alive!' she shouted as she reached them. They were kneeling over the bodies of Velioth and Keene.

Traykin's eyes were haunting, but he forced a smile and reached for her as she closed in. 'Apparently,' he said. 'I think we have Keene to thank for that.'

'What do you mean?' Marla asked.

Faast abruptly looked up at her. 'Not now. We can discuss it later. We're not safe. Help us get these two to safety – to the Market Quarter. Velioth's manor will suffice.'

'No,' Marla said quickly. 'We should take them to Keene's. Tharian led your elites there, they might still be nearby.'

Faast thought on it for a few seconds. 'Very well, to the Artisan Quarter then.'

Traykin nodded. 'Velioth passed out early on. I don't blame him. But Keene, well she took the brunt of it. Help me lift the lad.'

Marla looked down at them. Velioth looked no worse off than the other two, but he was a limp mess on the floor. Keene, however, had considerably more burns on her skin. Even her hair was singed.

With little visible effort, Faast looped her hands under Keene's back and knees and lifted her. She started walking in the direction of the Artisan Quarter, knowing her way despite the thickness of the dust and smoke in the air. Marla took one of Velioth's arms while Traykin took the other, and together they hoisted him off the ground and dragged him with his arms around their shoulders. They followed on, quietly but quickly.

Traykin's breathing was unsteady. She could feel his trembling through Velioth's arm. This wasn't the time to ask how they

The Last of the Magi

survived. They were afraid and shaken, even if Faast didn't show it.

The air was much clearer as they passed into the Artisan Quarter. A few of Faast's elites saw them and raced over to help, taking Velioth and Keene so their coinsmen could walk freely and proudly the rest of the way. They looked surprised to see them, but they focused on getting them to safety rather than asking the questions Marla also wanted to ask.

Traykin grabbed one of the elite guards by the shoulder and pulled him close. 'Tharian is still in the plaza. Illian Valivelle has him. Help the lad if you can, please.'

'We'll do what we can, Coinsman.'

Somebody else interjected before one of the elites could dash away to the plaza.

'Focus on aiding your people. Leave the boy to me.'

They all looked forward. A wizened old man, draped in a ragged, dark grey robe stepped forward.

Traykin made an exasperated sound. 'You? Why are you here, today of all days? You old fool.'

The robed man pulled a piece of paper from his sleeve. It was a letter, and it looked to have Traykin's handwriting on it. Was this the other letter Traykin had written when they were planning all of this?

'I came because I was asked.'

'I didn't ask you to come! It's too dangerous for you here, Greycloak.'

He waved a hand through the air slowly. 'By your words, perhaps not. But by its implications, I am needed. Where is Tharian?'

Marla looked at Traykin. This meant nothing to her, same for Faast. Even though she had no idea who this man was, he spoke in a strong, croaking voice that somehow made her feel calm. For some reason she immediately trusted him.

Traykin just pointed his thumb over his shoulder. 'The plaza. Be careful, an enforcer has him.'

The old man bowed his head to all of them. He stepped around their group and continued down the road to the plaza.

Despite her curiosity, Marla resisted the urge to ask who he was.

She wanted to get them to Keene's manor first and make sure their injuries could be tended to. Her curiosities could be dealt with later. Whatever was going on, it clearly troubled Traykin.

***

The sounds of boots crunching in the dirt stopped a short distance from where Tharian was laying. He didn't bother to look up.

'You are resilient. You would have made a good enforcer if you were born into a different life.'

Illian crouched in front of Tharian's face. She pushed at his back, causing him to shriek. She laughed, then she did it again and again.

'I tire of you now. I will put you down.'

Tharian closed his eyes and waited for his death. There was some relief to think that the pain might soon end. He heard the crackling of flames overhead and felt heat bearing down upon him.

It didn't lash at him like he expected.

'The elements cry out for mercy; would you not grant them their well-deserved reprieve?'

The voice emerged from somewhere nearby, but Tharian couldn't see who was speaking.

The flames snuffed out. Illian rose from her squatted position. 'Return to your home. This is none of your concern.'

Slow shuffling footsteps came closer and an old voice replied to the enforcer. 'My home is wherever I am needed. Right now, that is here, where I stand.'

'Leave, now. Or you will share his fate.'

The old man stepped even closer and then Tharian felt hands touch gently against him, carefully turning him over onto his back. Somehow it didn't hurt as much as he expected.

He knew the man looking down at him, with long silvery hair draped around his aged face. It was Greycloak. He didn't recognise his voice at first, it had been years since he spoke with such strength and clarity. He even looked healthier, more present. Greycloak even managed to get Tharian back on his feet.

Then there was another surge of heat washing over them from

The Last of the Magi

Illian's direction. She had taken a few paces back and ripped a tendril of flame from a nearby brazier. She whipped it at them. Tharian would have shouted a warning to his guardian, but he was too exhausted. Greycloak, however, had seen it and was unfazed.

Greycloak stepped between Tharian and the attack and let it lash at him. But the flames didn't touch him. It transformed into sizzling steam where it came close to his body. Drops of hissing water hit the dusty ground.

'What's going on?' Tharian whispered.

'The steps you take here,' Greycloak said, looking back at Tharian, 'are the beginnings of a change in the tide. The scales of balance can indeed be righted. Stay true to your convictions and stand close with your allies, you will need stability and assistance now more than ever. The wayward son will never again have to stand alone during the challenges to come.'

Tharian winced and sighed. 'It's not the time for riddles. Are you saying you will help find the lost Magi?'

Greycloak shook his head. 'No, my boy. Remember what I taught you. No Magi is ever lost.' He pushed Tharian back a few paces and then turned to face the enforcer.

She was looking at her hands and the trail of damp dirt left behind from her attempt at attacking them. 'How is this possible?' She drew out the very last of the flame from the brazier, snuffing the life from its coals. She brought it to bear against the old man stood before her.

Greycloak raised a palm and the flame stopped before it reached him. He traced his hand along the tendril, starting at its tip, and it began to change. Where once it was blustering and crimson, it became smooth and lost its colour. This change spread further down the length of the flame until the entire tendril became a thick rope of harmless water. The transformation stopped just before the end of the flames, and with a flick of Greycloak's wrist that last spark shot back into the brazier and reignited the coals, as if the enforcer had never disturbed it.

Greycloak lowered his hand and the water dropped out of the enforcer's control and soaked into the ground.

'What is this?' she hissed.

She lashed out again, this time sending blades of air at him.

Again, Greycloak didn't retaliate. He merely lifted the same hand and the air diffused into the gentlest, most nourishing of breezes that washed over him and Tharian. It was pure and soothing. Not just air free of Arcana, but air free of smog and dust. No air in the Trade Quarters ever felt so refreshing.

A third attack. This time she thrust her palm up to pull down another bolt of lightning. Greycloak copied her, and the bolt didn't reach her palm. It froze, suspended in the air in a jagged line of flashing blue and yellow. The crack of thunder rumbled continuously as the bolt tried to push down towards her, sounding like it threatened to tear the skies asunder.

Tharian watched. Was this Greycloak's doing? He couldn't look away. He watched the sky as the dust and soot parted around the lightning and revealed the dark, heavy rainclouds that frowned down at them.

What is he doing? Is this…Magic? He couldn't believe what he was seeing. This was not Arcana.

Greycloak hummed a disapproving sound that Tharian remembered from his childhood. Everything then became lighter and brighter. The sky relaxed and the rainclouds twisted out as if unravelling a painful knot. That cut off the source of the lightning bolt. It disappeared into static and the rumbling and flashing finally calmed.

The central plaza was clearer and brighter than it had been all day. Even the dust and smog were parting, with Greycloak standing at the centre of the clearing.

The sphere of flame was gone too, and Tharian could now see the totality of the cave-in. The marbled area was gone, as were the statues and a sizeable portion of the dirt path that ran around it all. He was lucky he hadn't fallen in it when the enforcer threw him across the plaza.

'You cannot be,' Illian said. 'None of your kind survived the Purge.'

Greycloak muttered. 'Those that perished, did so because it was their time. They had fulfilled their purposes. Those that survived, survived because they yet had more to do. The line of Magi cannot

The Last of the Magi

ever end, for as long as there are those that would tilt the tender forces of this world out of shape.'

The words stunned Tharian just as much as they stunned Illian. He felt some blend of amazement, confusion, and deep-rooted frustration. His guardian – the man who took him in as an orphan – was now playing his hidden hand. But why now? Why raise him on stories that stressed the permanence of the Magi's defeat? He even tried to push Tharian off this path, going as far as writing to Traykin to warn about the futility of seeking out the Magi.

Greycloak had stood aside as Tharian spent ten long years searching Feralland for a solution to oppose the Elheim. Why? Why did he let Tharian walk such a dangerous and long path, knowing full well that what he sought had been beside him all along. He had more questions than his tired, broken body could muster to speak.

Greycloak pulled at his ill-fitting cloak and stretched his neck and back. He yet had more to say to this enforcer. 'For many years I have hidden myself away. My purpose as a Magi was to wait, conceal myself and keep this lost son safe. I knew there would be a day where I needed to reveal myself. And it is for that reason my mind is clear today: my reserved strength unleashed; my life, lasted out to this moment. It is my purpose to cross your path a second time, and I do so without hesitation.'

Illian's eyes became wide and large. She shook her head slowly in disbelief as a cruel and sinister grin pulled at her lips. She barked in laughter. 'Tell me it is not so. Nehren Conseil? Of all the Magi to survive, it is you that stands here now?'

Slowly, Greycloak nodded.

Conseil? Tharian knew the name. He had heard it many times in his childhood. But where? The realisation slowly sunk in. On the day the late King Thorius of Ferenir was killed in cold blood, he had been accompanied by his Magi-adviser. Nehren Conseil was his name. Tharian's guardian was the Magi who failed to protect that king.

The brooch, Tharian figured. It was the insignia of the Ferenir Magi-adviser. Tharian felt stupid. Had the writing been on the wall the whole time – had he just been too close to ever question it?

Illian took pleasure from knowing who he really was. 'I thought you were dragged out to the Purge with the rest of them.'

Greycloak smiled sympathetically. 'So easily blinded you are by your confidence and ambition. Your people assumed my death was an inevitability. Yet, an intervention within your own walls spared my life. Much like the true nature of the Arcana you wield, you and your people fail to see the truth of things.'

'Enough lecturing!' she bellowed. 'If you choose to be a thorn in the Grand City's side, I shall not afford you the luxury of living a moment longer. Let this be the final act of the Purge.'

Greycloak nodded again. Tharian's heart raced as the old man held his hands out as if welcoming her next attacks.

She immediately conjured two large flurries of air from her flanks that slammed into a larger blustering mass at her front. The air rippled ferociously between them. Then she pushed the attack at Greycloak.

Greycloak stayed still again. The mass of air was bigger than his whole body, yet he didn't try to move aside or push it back. And then – just as it should have hit him – the air split back into two streams again, redirecting to curl around Greycloak's sides and slip behind him.

The attack was coming for Tharian. He braced himself for it.

Greycloak's fingers flexed, and his hands shot out at his sides, as if he were about to catch the gales in their path. But that wasn't what he did. Instead, the pulses of air still curled around the old man and collided again behind his back, erupting into a wall of blustering wind that formed a barrier which kept Tharian away from them.

Tharian heard Illian's banshee-like scream as she lunged forward. She didn't use Arcana this time. She just thrust her hands around Greycloak's throat and bore down upon him.

Greycloak didn't fight back, he didn't even raise his hands to try and push her back. Tharian panicked. He wanted to help, but the wall of air was too powerful and too wide for him to manoeuvre around in time, even if his legs could muster more than a few steps. He just had to stand there, clutching at his ribs, leaning to one side to relieve the pain he felt... everywhere. But he shouted, calling for Greycloak to resist or fight back. He felt helpless as the old man's knees buckled, his body collapsing under the enforcer's weight.

The Last of the Magi

There was nothing he could do except watch the eccentric, enigmatic old man – the man that had been a father to him – perish before his eyes. The last living Magi had been found and lost all within the same hour.

Something off to his side caught his eye. A movement. A thin, long strip of metal came coursing through the air. His runeblade. It was levitating, floating on a bed of air that carried it gracefully through the wall of air that parted to let it through.

Tharian could see the fury in Illian's eyes now. 'This is how the Magi end. Weak and alone. Your fallen king would be ashamed of the faith he placed in you.'

Somehow, Greycloak mustered a few words in response with the last of his breath. 'As I told him… I serve… a higher calling.'

Tharian's runeblade lunged forward, cutting straight through Greycloak's spine, piercing through his chest and then through Illian's.

She gasped and released him. She stumbled back, pulling free of the blade.

Greycloak dropped into a slump on the ground. The enforcer's white and blue uniform filled with red as blood soaked through the fabric. Her hands were shaking over the wound. Her mouth trembled and she met Tharian's eyes, finally looking pale and afraid. Her eyes rolled and she stumbled back. She kept stumbling until there was no more floor beneath her feet, and she joined the other fallen enforcers below.

Tharian threw himself forward, biting through the pain to get closer to his guardian. His legs couldn't hold his weight and he collapsed beside him. They were laid in opposite directions, upside down at each other's eyeline.

They both fought for every breath. Tharian's breathing became more stable with time, as the stillness helped to avoid the pain, but Greycloak's became shallow. 'Why didn't you tell me?' Tharian asked, reaching out and pressing a hand against his guardian's cheek. It was so cold.

Greycloak's eyes struggled to find him. He searched for Tharian until their eyes locked together. He smiled. 'The time was not right.'

'What do you mean?'

Greycloak brought his hand up and cupped it over Tharian's. He twisted, as much as the blade through his chest would let him, and he stared up to the sky, a sky that was much clearer and brighter now because of him. 'I was broken long ago by the Grand City. They took me and made me their prisoner... all to try and discover the secrets of Magic and the agenda they believed we had for Asturia. When I finally got away, on that dark day... when my brothers and sisters gave their lives, my purpose became protecting you, Tharian. I was no longer strong enough to walk the path of bringing balance to Asturia... but I could protect and steer you, until it was *your* time to walk it.'

Tharian was too panicked and flustered by Greycloak's fading condition to really appreciate the clarity of his last words. But he listened, squeezing Greycloak's hand. 'I'm already walking it. You didn't need to do this. We still need you, with your help we can stop their Arcana.'

'My purpose is done, my boy.' His eyes rolled to Tharian. 'But *yours* is only now beginning.'

'Don't talk like that. We still need you.' Tharian felt tears in his eyes which he fought to hide. But he knew Greycloak had noticed. 'This didn't have to happen.'

'This was meant to happen. It had to, to help you on your way.' He squeezed Tharian's hand again, though it was a much weaker squeeze. 'The power you seek. I used it once before... it took every part of my mind to keep it going for so long. But I had to do it... to fulfil my purpose. Your purpose... will require something more.' Greycloak's words became slower and more hushed.

Tharian lowered his head. 'I don't understand. What do I do now?'

'Carry on...'

Tharian pulled himself closer to Greycloak, just as the old man's eyes glazed over. Though he laid in a pool of his own blood, Greycloak looked truly calm and at peace as he breathed his last.

He was gone. Tharian rolled onto his back, ready for grief to consume him, as tears silently streamed down his face. But even his grief escaped him. Something else consumed him instead. He gasped as a peculiar sensation washed through him and made his

The Last of the Magi

head spin.

Tharian clutched at his chest. His breathing became fast. His heart pounded. Whatever was happening felt uncomfortable and surreal, but it wasn't painful. He stared at the sky. Were the clouds getting closer? Was the air softer than before? Even the hard earth at his back felt... comforting.

Everything felt different. He laid there, listening to the racing of his heart until everything he could feel and see faded into a blinding white and then a senseless black.

Chapter 53

The First

Marla sat patiently. She had been waiting two hours for one of the chirurgeons to come out and let them in to the ramshackle infirmary tent.

Guardsmen flooded in and out with supplies, helping to pull together the emergency medical stations that had popped up in the safe parts of the plaza after the dust of the conflict settled. Visitors had been limited due to the condition of many the patients – this was not the time to spread even the most mundane of illness to those who were injured.

Marla jumped to her feet as the masked and fully covered chirurgeon tilted back the sheet door that gave the patients some privacy, even though it did very little to block out the sound of their pained groans. They ushered her in with a tilt of the head.

She looked back to Marion and Brayne who waited there with her. They also ushered her to go ahead, and she gave a thankful nod to them, and to the nervous man who sat a couple of seats beside them. He'd been waiting for almost as long as she had. He said he was there to see Traykin, but he knew Tharian too apparently. She doubted him at first, until she noticed the tiny black-skinned lirrus curled up in his lap, flashing its amber eyes her way from time-to-time. Ombra looked safe in his care, so he must have been a friend.

She felt guilty going on alone, but she needed to see Tharian's condition with her own eyes.

The chirurgeon led Marla through the tent. Men and women in identical overalls rushed about all over the place, weaving through and across their path and bringing salves, vials of fluid and bandages to people left and right. Marla did her best to avert her gaze from the other patients in their beds. She felt it disrespectful to look, and she was not sure her stomach could take the sight of any gruesome injuries while she already feared what she was being led to.

The Last of the Magi

And yet, despite the grim state of the guards, elites and mercenaries laid up in those beds, they had done it. The other enforcers had fled the city as soon as they realised their leaders had fallen. They gathered in a defensive formation around their carriages and then drove east as soon as they could. They had been beaten, but during the city-wide commotion they had used their Arcana to subdue and injure as many as they could.

Together, they had freed the Trade Quarters.

The chirurgeon stopped for a moment and pointed to his right before rushing off to assist one of his colleagues at the end of the tent.

And there he was, laid in a collapsible medical bed with a light sheet pulled up to his bruise-covered stomach. Tharian looked terrible. His arms were laid over the sheet, covered haphazardly with bandages. Without his coat and his leather cuirass, he looked like any other man. His skin was paler than she expected. And he no longer looked like the mysterious man who had stepped into the path of a bolt of Arcane lightning in Brynwell, nor the 'Arcana Hunter' that fought in the Crucible. In this moment, Tharian was just an injured man in need of care.

Marla sighed with relief. Apart from the burns and bruising, and the cuts and scratches already treated and wrapped in bandages with only faint traces of blood soaking through, he looked much better than she expected. He had fought against a Valivelle. Few could say they had crossed a Valivelle enforcer and survived. And now he had done it twice.

She laid her hands on the end of his bed frame and sighed. 'Thank the Divine you're alive,' she said. His face was scrunched in a pained expression – as if he was stuck in a nightmare he couldn't wake from.

'Good to see you again, lass,' said a voice from beside the bed.

She looked over to see Traykin. She had been too distracted by Tharian's injuries to notice the coinsman sat there smirking. 'And you too,' she said, 'how are you doing?'

Traykin chuckled, ending it with a hearty cough. 'Pretty well, all things considered. No injuries other than a few burns.' He then nodded to a bed opposite Tharian's. Marla turned and saw that

Viviel Keene was in it. 'I think the Elheim actually told the truth for once when they said they would train her to use Arcana.'

Marla turned back to him, confused.

He continued. 'Whatever she did in that'—he paled and suddenly looked fearful—'in that hell… it kept us out of harm's way. It took a lot out of her. She had nothing left to give when the fire finally faded.'

Marla looked across the room again. Coinswoman Keene. *She used Arcana?* She considered the surrealness of it, an Asturian woman using the weapon of the Elheim. That would explain how they survived so long in a prison of roaring flames.

'She'll have a lot to answer for, that one. For now, I think she has earned her rest.'

Humming in agreement, Marla looked back over Tharian. 'What about Coinsman Velioth?'

Traykin coughed again and laughed. 'Oh, he's fine. We took him back home when he woke. Mors is looking after him. He's just shaken.'

Marla then nodded to Tharian. 'And how is *he* doing?'

Traykin breathed heavily through his nose, shook his head, and shrugged. 'By all accounts, he's alright. But he's not responding.'

'What does that mean?'

Traykin thumped the edge of Tharian's bed lightly. 'Hell if I know. I'm a collector, this is not my area. But them lot keep murmuring to each other about him being in a very deep sleep, unlikely to wake until whatever is wrong with him rights itself.'

'I see.' Marla pulled the seat on the opposite side of the bed towards Tharian and sat. She patted Tharian's hand. 'He'll pull through it,' she said, smiling to Traykin.

Traykin smirked. 'Oh, I know that. And he knows that too, because he knows that I'll have some colourful words for him if he doesn't. Look,' he pointed to a small vase on the table beside the bed on Marla's side which contained a single, slightly wilted, hand-picked flower with round yellow petals. 'I even watered that sodding thing. I'm getting soft.'

Marla looked at the flower and laughed. Though she quickly sobered again. 'What happened to him?'

The Last of the Magi

'Not sure. By the time he was found he was already down, though he was laid beside his old man.'

'His father?'

Traykin shook his head and then shrugged. 'The closest thing he had to one. The old fool that we passed on the road. He must have tried to protect the lad from the enforcer. Something went wrong though because he had Tharian's blade through his back. Can't understand why. But one of the guards who went to find the enforcers in the wreckage said that one of them had a similar wound. The old man didn't make it, but I'm thankful that they were at least together at the end. He deserved that much for raising him.'

Marla looked at Tharian sympathetically. She patted his hand again, offering her condolences to him in the only way she could in his current state. 'I guess we're lucky the other enforcers turned on each other.'

Traykin frowned and he leaned to look at the bed behind Marla. 'Maybe not lucky enough. That one made it out – people think he was the one to turn on the others.'

Marla turned around to see the blonde-haired enforcer, Darus Valivelle, asleep in the next bed along from Tharian's. His condition was similar. She shuddered and hurried to move her chair as far from him as she could.

'Relax. He is under careful watch,' Traykin added. Marla then realised that three of Faast's elite guards, fully armed and armoured stood watch over his bed. 'We'll have plenty of questions for him, too. He will be run through the mill just as hard as Keene, but if what people are saying about him is true, we might have just found our first Elheim defector.'

Instinctively she rejected that idea. The Elheim were too proud and one-minded to fight against their own cause. Yet she then remembered what she saw in the plaza before the crowds scattered and the dust cloud blew up from the cave-in, Darus Valivelle was fighting *against* his father. They were arguing, and then he started screaming – and the ground started shaking in tandem.

'So what happens now?' she asked.

'How do you mean, lass?'

'What do we do next? You said you were going to investigate

L. G. Harman

Tharian's lost Magi theory.'

Traykin frowned and then stood. 'We can think about that later. For now, I've got to meet with the others to think about what we do when the Chancellor of the Grand City decides he wants a word about his missing enforcers. That's assuming he doesn't just send the rest of his enforcers down to take control again. We've done well here, but we're not out of the woods yet.'

He was right, of course, but Marla hadn't thought that far ahead. Her stomach flipped. The Elheim had burnt her village down just for refusing to pay the Arcane Tax – this was an infinitely more serious situation. There were dead enforcers in the city.

Traykin patted her on the shoulder with a heavy hand. 'Try not to worry. If Ferenir really are prepared to throw their lot in with us, then what happened here might just prove to them that we can do this bloody thing.' He smiled, a genuine smile that met his eyes. He then sauntered down the length of the tent, exchanging haughty exchanges with the few who were awake and able to speak as he went.

Marla sat back in her chair and tried to clear her mind. There was no use lingering on the danger of the future. That was a reality to face another day. For now, she dedicated her thoughts to wishing Tharian a speedy recovery. There were reasons to be positive, to celebrate. The city was free, the enforcers had been defeated, and the Trade Quarters and its people were still standing despite it all. That was a win – a win many would have thought impossible.

Tharian stirred. His hands twitched and he took in a deep, slow breath. She perked up, hoping he might be rousing from his sleep. He exhaled heavily and then became still again. No such luck.

Marla noticed a movement in the corner of her eye. She looked over to the flower on the side table, the side of it closest to Tharian looked like it was changing. The yellow of the petals looked more vibrant, and the few wilts in its leaves faded away. She blinked at it, assuming it was just her own exhaustion playing tricks on her. But it wasn't. The side closer to the unconscious enforcer definitely looked worse than the side closer to Tharian. Something had changed.

She was tired. She had barely slept over the last two days,

worrying about whether this would all go to plan, and then worrying about whether Tharian had survived.

She had the answers now. Tharian was alive. Unconscious, but very much alive. So, with that, she patted Tharian on the hand once more and decided she could go home and rest.

'Don't make us wait too long,' she said as she lifted her hand from his and left the infirmary.

***

With no-one beside his bed any longer, Tharian stirred in his deep slumber again. This time, as he breathed deeply through his nose, a breeze blew across him. It made the sheets on his bed ripple, and even the small vase beside his bed was caught in it and span a quarter of the way around, rattling until it stopped. A few seconds later, the petals now closest to him, and those closest to the enforcer, reacted to their new positions and started to change.

One side blooming, the other wilting.

Chapter 54

Epilogue

Lorenna sat at her desk, looking out the window of the office in her private chambers. The window pointed north, giving her a coastal view that stretched for miles. She watched the waves lapping on the shoreline. It was peaceful.

The sun was waning. But there was still plenty to do.

One of the scholars had come to her rooms just as the working day was done. He had in his arms a bundle of neatly assembled pages, sealed together into a thick journal of sorts. The front page was lacking the markings of official College Arcana research.

She rapped her fingers over the papers. The sun hadn't even started to set when the papers were delivered, and now evening was closing in.

Arcana: A Compilatory Treatise on its Observed and Hypothesised Effects and Impacts.

She had read its title every hour. Each time it made her look away. She feared what she might find in this lengthy, extensive document, even though it was her idea to have it commissioned. She feared it would prove that which was already certain in her mind – that Arcana came at a cost; a cost which they could ill afford to ignore. One which her brother *chose* to ignore.

She finally flicked open the cover and reviewed the contents page. The first few chapters were introductory content, dealing with the basis of the research and the methodology involved, together with a chronology of activity. The bulk of the chapters dealt with specific incidents that had been observed or reported in the past. The penultimate section of chapters dealt with hypothetical situations based on those observations. And then, at the end, there was a summary of the scholarly conclusions.

Lorenna was not ready for the bluntness of the conclusion pages. Instead, her eyes were drawn to two chapters on the contents page. One dealt with the Purge, the other discussed the death of her

The Last of the Magi

parents.

She turned to the Purge chapter first. She took a deep breath, building her strength by staring out at the waves once more. And then she finally started to scan the page. She immediately found words she expected to see in those blocky paragraphs:

Symbiotic; Parasitic; Perishing environments; Decaying effects; Arcane toll; *Irreparable harm.*

She slapped the document shut and turned away from it. That was only one chapter. One amongst so many more. Lorenna bowed her head into her hands. She would need to discuss this with Ulyria. The high imperator needed to know. This had serious implications on the work of their enforcers, and the foundations of their very culture.

Against her better judgment, she turned back and looked at the contents page again. She was not ready to look at the chapter about her parents just yet, she knew that much. The last thing she wanted to read right now was that her parents' use of Arcana to enact the Purge was the cause of their own deaths. She lost both parents and a brother that day. It was traumatic enough already.

In time, she would review those pages in full. She had to. For her own sanity and out of a sense of duty as the Lady Elheim.

She picked another chapter for now. She chose the one that dealt with the aftermath of Midhaven's destruction. She didn't know for certain why that entire town was burnt to the ground. Perhaps the chapter would offer some insight. Even if it didn't, the observations about Arcana were still important.

She took a few more deep breaths, reminding herself over and over that this was for the betterment of her people. For the betterment of all Asturians. She then turned to the Midhaven chapter and started reading.

Printed in Great Britain
by Amazon